HIJACK ACCORDING TO PLAN

On the bridge of th[...]life. A Borthudian offi[...]dead black to a cat-lith[...]though hairless and ti[...]dered under a narrow forehead. Behind him could be seen his own bridge, a companion who sat before a fire-control terminal, and the usual six-armed basalt idol.

"Terrestrial ship ahoy!" He ripped out fluent Anglic, harshly accented by the shapes of larynx and mouth. "This is Captain Rentharik of the Kossalu's frigate *Gantok*. By the law, most sacred, of the Kossaluth of Borthu, you are guilty of trespass on the domains of His Mightiness. Stand by to be boarded."

"Why, you out-from-under-wet-log-crawling cockypop!" Van Rijn made himself flush turkey red. "Not bad enough you hijack my men and transports, with their good expensive cargoes, but you have the copperbound nerve to call it legal!"

Rentharik fingered a small ceremonial dagger hung about his neck. "Old man, the writ of the Kossalu runs through this entire volume of space. You can save yourself added punishment—nerve-pulsing—by submitting peacefully to judgment."

"It is understood by *civilized* races that interstellar space is free for every innocent passage."

Rentharik smiled, revealing bright-green teeth of non-human shape. "We enforce our own laws here, Captain."

"*Ja*, but by damn, this time you are trying to use force on *van Rijn*. They are going to be surprised back on the dingleberry you call your home planet."

Everything was going exactly as van Rijn had planned . . .

BAEN BOOKS by POUL ANDERSON

The Technic Civilization Saga

The Van Rijn Method

POUL ANDERSON

Compiled by
Hank Davis

BAEN

THE VAN RIJN METHOD

"Planets and Profits" copyright ©, 2008 by Hank Davis; "A Chronology of Technic Civilization" by Sandra Miesel, copyright © 2008 by Sandra Miesel.

A Baen Book

Baen Publishing Enterprises
P.O. Box 1403
Riverdale, NY 10471
www.baen.com

ISBN: 978-1-4391-3326-2

Cover art by David Seeley

First Baen paperback printing, December 2009

Distributed by Simon & Schuster
1230 Avenue of the Americas
New York, NY 10020

Library of Congress Cataloging-in-Publication Data:
2008020726

Printed in the United States of America

10 9 8 7 6 5 4 3 2

CONTENTS

Acknowledgements

"The Saturn Game," first published in *Analog*, February, 1981. Copyright © 1981 by Davis Publications, Inc.

Introduction to "Wings of Victory," first published in *The Earth Book of Stormgate*, Berkley Putnam, 1978, copyright 1978 by Poul Anderson.

"Wings of Victory," first published in *Analog*, April 1972. Copyright 1972 by Condé Nast Publications, Inc.

Introduction to "The Problem of Pain," first published in *The Earth Book of Stormgate*, Berkley Putnam, 1978, copyright 1978 by Poul Anderson.

"The Problem of Pain," first published in *The Magazine of Fantasy and Science Fiction*, February, 1973; copyright 1973 by Mercury Press, Inc.

Introduction to "Margin of Profit," in *The Earth Book of Stormgate*, Berkley Putnam, 1978, copyright 1978 by Poul Anderson.

"Margin of Profit," first published in a different form in *Astounding Science Fiction*, September 1956. Copyright 1956 by Street & Smith Publications, Inc. Revised version copyright 1978 by Poul Anderson.

Introduction to "How to be Ethnic in One Easy Lesson," first published in *The Earth Book of Stormgate*, Berkley Putnam, 1978, copyright 1978 by Poul Anderson.

"How to be Ethnic in One Easy Lesson," first published as "How to be Ethnic" in *Future Quest*, ed. Roger Elwood, Avon, 1974. Copyright 1974 by Roger Elwood.

Introduction to "The Three-Cornered Wheel," first published in *The Trouble Twisters*, Doubleday, 1966. Copyright 1966 by Poul Anderson.

"The Three-Cornered Wheel," first published in *Analog*, October 1963. Copyright 1963 by Condé Nast Publications, Inc.

PLANETS AND PROFITS:

❂ INTRODUCING NICHOLAS VAN RIJN ❂
AND THE POLESOTECHNIC LEAGUE . . .

. . . and also introducing one of the grandest sagas in science fiction: the Technic Civilization series. It begins in the not-distant future, with humans still locked in the Solar System and recovering from a hinted-at time of chaos (which might be our own present day), voyaging outward to explore the moons of Saturn. It ends over five thousand years later, with human civilization, now sprawling across a vast span of the galaxy, recovering from another, much longer time of chaos—the Long Night which followed the fall of the Terran Empire.

The writing of the saga and its appearances in print spanned a time far shorter, but still unusually long in the field, beginning with the novelet "Tiger by the Tail," published in the January 1951 issue of that grand old pulp *Planet Stories*, and ending with the novel *The Game of Empire*, published in 1985. However, those two yarns do not mark the end points of the series, the stories comprising which were written very much out of sequence. Both fall late in the timeline, being episodes in the flamboyant career of Captain Sir Dominic Flandry, who'll make his swashbuckling appearance in volume four of the Technic Civilization series. (Be patient, please—after all, Flandry won't be born until about 570 years after the last story in this first volume.)

If this book's title doesn't make it obvious, the main player in the book you're holding in your hands is the blustering, vulgar and bigger than life (both literally and figuratively) human volcano named Nicholas van Rijn (rhymes with "fine"), a merchant prince in the star-spanning Poulsotechnic, pardon me, Polesotechnic League, a loose-knit organization of interstellar traders. That authoritative expert on Poul Anderson's writings, Sandra Miesel, writes that the word "Polesotechnic" was coined by Poul's wife Karen Anderson from the Greek for "selling skills." By that meaning, van Rijn is beyond doubt the most polesotechnical of the polesotechnicians.

On van Rijn, Poul Anderson wrote, "While some readers couldn't stand this burly, beery, uninhibited merchant prince, on the whole he was probably the most popular character I ever hit upon, and the stories about him enjoyed a long and lusty run." Van Rijn's first appearance in the saga (and in this book) was the novelette "Margin of Profit," published in the September 1956 issue of *Astounding Science Fiction*, though the version of "Margin of Profit" in these pages is the one which Anderson rewrote for the 1978 collection, *The Earth Book of Stormgate*, to give Nick more of his inimitable

mannerisms than he had displayed in his debut appearance, and also to eliminate a few discrepancies with the Technic Civilization universe as it later developed. (More about that later.)

"Two meters in height and more than broad enough to match," van Rijn is described on his first appearance, and he may remind the reader of Falstaff, but Nick's no mere braggart, no empty suit—he makes good on his brags and delivers the goods. Poul Anderson once mentioned Long John Silver as another influence on his creation of van Rijn, and *that* charismatic scoundrel was certainly no empty suit (ahrrrr!). Van Rijn unravels mysteries and solves problems as well as any sf hero of old, without benefit of the heretofore obligatory square jaw, steely gaze and laconic dialogue of the classic pulp hero. Still there's muscle under the fat, augmented by quick reflexes, as enemies (and occasionally, his employees) have been chagrined to learn. He's a capitalist hero, too, always thinking of making a buck (or a credit), even in desperate situations, who'd rather sell things to his enemies than fight them. He started out dirt poor and built his Solar Spice & Liquors Company up from a shoestring. Move over, John Galt.

He's no ascetic either, and never misses a chance to enjoy good food, good booze, and a good smoke, usually with Mozart playing in the background. He appreciates the ladies, too, and while financial considerations are often involved, this is not always the case. He also appreciates art and classic literature, though the latter doesn't seem to have helped his malaprop-prone speech, full of twisted turns of phrase. Someday, somebody might imitate Heinlein's *The Notebooks of Lazarus Long* and do a short book of classic van Rijnisms, such as:

"I have no fine university degrees,
I learned in the school of hard knockers."

"I make no skeletons about it . . . "

"Put that in your pipe and stick it!"

"This is the times that fry men's souls."

And there's more where *those* came from . . .

Van Rijn's ongoing war with the King's Anglic notwithstanding, he did play the silver-tongued orator on one memorable occasion, in the full-length novel included in this volume, *The Man Who Counts*, when he had to convince squabbling factions of the winged Diomedeans to unite against the common enemy. A lesser writer than Poul Anderson would have attempted to compose a stirring speech for his hero and brought forth a clunker that's dead both on the page and on arrival. A good, but less ingenious writer would have composed a stirring speech that was actually *stirring*. Poul Anderson, being both very good and very ingenious, did something entirely different. And I won't spoil anyone's first encounter with that part of the novel by giving it away here.

Also on stage is one of van Rijn's employees, David Falkayn, first seen as an ambitious young man trying to make his mark, and not sure he'll succeed, or even survive. You may think that I'm not giving him his due in this introduction, but the scales will be balanced in the next volume, where he plays a larger role (as indicated by the title of the second Technic Civilization book, *David Falkayn: Star Trader*; reserve your copy now). Further,

Falkayn is going to become part of a trader team, one member of which, Adzel the dragonlike Buddhist, you'll encounter briefly in one of the stories herein, but you'll have to wait for volume two to meet Chee Lan, the third member of the team. And this team is very much more than the sum of its parts.

I'll also mention that Falkayn's influence on the course of human history arguably is even greater than that of van Rijn (more on that in future volumes). In any case, it's obvious that Falkayn, like his creator, is a fan of Leslie Charteris, and how could I slight a fellow acolyte of the Saintly chronicles?

And now, the master chef . . . Poul Anderson was one of the most prolific writers in science fiction and fantasy, and possibly the *most* prolific. His bibliography has something like seventy sf or fantasy novels and over forty story collections published, drawn from his hundreds of sf and fantasy short stories. While he wrote in many fields—historical fiction, mysteries, horror fiction, non-fiction books and essays, and poetry—the realms of science fiction and fantasy were his true home, and there he was one of the best. I doubt that any sf writer who might come close to matching him for quantity could show such a consistently high quality of work.

He was also a writer who got the science right, which was no surprise since he had a degree in physics, and had a lifelong passion for all the hard sciences. Before he set a story on a planet, he would do research and calculations to come up with a world that wasn't just a cardboard backdrop—Diomedes in *The Man Who Counts* is a prime example, and he gave a solid scientific explanation how the winged natives can fly there, when they would be too heavy to fly on Earth. He got more than science right, too. The brief introduction to "The Three-Cornered Wheel" quotes Sturgeon's Revelation ("ninety percent of *everything* is crud"). It happens that Sturgeon's Revelation is usually and wrongly named as Sturgeon's *Law*, but when Sturgeon formulated it in his book review column for *Venture* in the late 1950s, he called it Sturgeon's *Revelation*. And Anderson gets the name right, to my appreciative applause. (If you'll pardon a digression, Sturgeon himself complained about people miscalling his Revelation as his Law, and noted that he already had a Sturgeon's Law, first stated in the story "The Claustrophile" in a 1956 *Galaxy*, usually rendered as "nothing is always absolutely so.")

But Anderson's getting the science right didn't preclude having prose that is always fluent and often sings, perhaps emulating the Scandinavian sagas which he knew by heart. For example, in "Esau":

> . . . a range of ice mountains flashed blindingly;
> Suleiman's twelve-hour day was drawing to a close
> and Osman's rays struck level through a break in
> roiling ruddy cloud cover. Elsewhere a storm lifted
> like a dark wall on which lightning scribbled. The
> dense air brought its thunder-noise to Dalmady as
> a high drumroll.

Larry Niven once described Anderson as "a poet who happens to write science fiction." Just so, though critics have rarely included Anderson with other notable stylists such as Sturgeon or Bradbury.

It's not surprising that Anderson won seven Hugo Awards and three Nebula Awards ("The Saturn Game," the first story in this book, took home one of each), as well as a Gandalf Grand Master award, a John W. Campbell Memorial Award, and four Prometheus Awards (including the Lifetime Achievement Prometheus Award). Speaking of lifetime achievement, he also received the Grand Master Award for that very thing from the Science Fiction and Fantasy Writers of America. Nor was it remarkable that when *Locus* in the 1970s did a poll of its readers for Best All-Time SF Writer, he nailed the fifth spot from the top. If anything, it's surprising that he didn't have a much longer shelf full of honors and rank even higher in that poll. Likely, Anderson wrote too much, too well, and made it look far too easy to stand out among the flashier scribes.

Eric Flint, comparing Anderson to Joe DiMaggio, "who," as he put it, "never did anything in baseball better than anyone else, but always did everything superbly well," thought that Anderson was less appreciated than, for example, Robert A. Heinlein for that reason. Still, master storytellers are not easy to come by, and now that, for the first time, his monumental Technic Civilization series will be published in internal chronological order in these volumes, the arbiters of science fiction as literature may give him his due. His grateful readers gave him his rightful due long ago, of course, and still do.

※ ※ ※

A word about the introductions to the stories and novel: all were written by Poul Anderson and accompanied the stories when they appeared in such collections as *Trader to the Stars*, *The Trouble Twisters*, and *The Earth Book of Stormgate*. The *Stormgate* introductions were written as if by a Ythrian historian. (You'll meet the Ythrians in the second and third stories in this book.) In the case of *The Man Who Counts*, there was an embarrassment of riches: an introduction "by" Hloch the Ythrian plus a second introduction which Poul Anderson wrote for another publication of the novel. I've placed the latter as an afterword. The only introduction to "The Saturn Game" of which I'm aware didn't give much information about the story, so I haven't included it here. (It appeared in his collection *Going for Infinity*, Tor, 2002, a book I highly recommend.)

And many, many thanks to Sandra Miesel, Poul Anderson expert extraordinaire, both for compiling her definitive Chronology of the Technic Civilization stories (without which, publishing the stories in the right order would have been a *lot* more difficult) and for permitting its inclusion in this book; and also for her essays on Poul Anderson, which have greatly influenced and improved this introduction (but please to call it research), though she should be held blameless for any of my usual stupidities which are doubtless lurking like demented gremlins behind the exclamation marks and semicolons.

Finally, I mentioned earlier that Poul Anderson rewrote van Rijn's debut story, "Margin of Profit," and that the rewritten version is the one between these covers. I would have liked to include the earlier version as well, but space wouldn't permit. However, cyberspace permits much more than Euclidean space, and the earlier version has been included as an appendix to the online version of *The Van Rijn Method*. As another bonus, Sandra Miesel's lucid and informative essay on *The Man Who Counts* is also included. Coming soon to a computer terminal near you. And there are lots more online goodies at www.baen.com.

—Hank Davis, 2008

THE SATURN GAME

If we are to understand what happened, which is vital if we would avoid repeated and worse tragedies in the future, we must begin by dismissing all accusations. Nobody was negligent; no action was foolish. For who could have predicted the eventuality, or recognized its nature, until too late? Rather should we appreciate the spirit with which those people struggled against disaster, inward and outward, after they knew. The fact is that thresholds exist throughout reality, and that things on their far sides are altogether different from things on their hither sides. The *Chronos* crossed more than an abyss, it crossed a threshold of human experience.

—Francis L. Minamoto, *Death Under Saturn: A Dissenting View* (Apollo University Communications, Leyburg, Luna, 2057)

"The City of Ice is now on my horizon," *Kendrick says. Its towers gleam blue.* "My griffin spreads his wings to glide." *Wind whistles among those great, rainbow-shimmering pinions. His cloak blows back from his shoulders; the air strikes through his ring-mail and sheathes him in cold.* "I lean over and peer after you." *The spear in his left hand counterbalances him. Its head flickers palely with the moonlight that Wayland Smith hammered into the steel.*

"Yes, I see the griffin," *Ricia tells him,* "high and far, like a comet above the courtyard walls. I run out from under the portico for a better look. A guard tries to stop me, grabs my sleeve, but I tear the spider-silk apart and dash forth into the open." *The elven castle wavers as if its sculptured ice were turning to smoke. Passionately, she cries,* "Is it in truth you, my darling?"

"Hold, there!" *warns Alvarlan from his cave of arcana ten thousand leagues away.* "I send your mind the message that if the King suspects this is Sir Kendrick of the Isles, he will raise a dragon against him, or spirit you off beyond any chance of rescue. Go back, Princess of Maranoa. Pretend you decide that it is only an eagle. I will cast a belief-spell on your words."

"I stay far aloft," *Kendrick says.* "Save he use a scrying stone, the Elf King will not be aware this beast has a rider. From here I'll spy out city and castle." *And then—? He knows not. He knows simply that he must set her free or die in the quest. How long will it take him, how many more nights will she lie in the King's embrace?*

"I thought you were supposed to spy out Iapetus," Mark Danzig interrupted.

His dry tone startled the three others into alertness. Jean Broberg flushed with embarrassment, Colin Scobie with irritation; Luis Garcilaso shrugged, grinned, and turned his gaze to the pilot console before which he sat harnessed. For a moment silence filled the cabin, and shadows, and radiance from the universe.

To help observation, all lights were out except a few dim glows at instruments. The sunward ports were lidded. Elsewhere thronged stars, so many and so brilliant that they well-nigh drowned the blackness which held them. The Milky Way was a torrent of silver. One port framed Saturn at half phase, dayside pale gold and rich bands amidst the jewelry of its rings, nightside wanly ashimmer with starlight and moonlight upon clouds, as big to the sight as Earth over Luna.

Forward was Iapetus. The spacecraft rotated while orbiting the moon, to maintain a steady optical field. It had crossed the dawn line, presently at the middle of the inward-facing hemisphere. Thus it had left bare, crater-pocked land behind it in the dark, and was passing above sunlit glacier country. Whiteness dazzled, glittered in sparks and shards of color, reached fantastic shapes heavenward; cirques, crevasses, caverns brimmed with blue.

"I'm sorry," Jean Broberg whispered. "It's too beautiful, unbelievably beautiful, and . . . almost like the place where our game had brought us—Took us by surprise—"

"Huh!" Mark Danzig said. "You had a pretty good idea of what to expect, therefore you made your play go in the direction of something that resembled it. Don't tell me any different. I've watched these acts for eight years."

Colin Scobie made a savage gesture. Spin and gravity were too slight to give noticeable weight. His movement sent him through the air, across the crowded cabin, until he checked himself by a handhold just short of the chemist. "Are you calling Jean a liar?" he growled.

Most times he was cheerful, in a bluff fashion. Perhaps because of that, he suddenly appeared menacing. He was a big, sandy-haired man in his mid-thirties; a coverall did not disguise the muscles beneath, and the scowl on his face brought forth its ruggedness.

"Please!" Broberg exclaimed. "Not a quarrel, Colin."

The geologist glanced back at her. She was slender and fine-featured. At her age of forty-two, despite longevity treatment, the reddish-brown hair that fell to her shoulders was becoming streaked with white, and lines were engraved around large gray eyes. "Mark is right," she sighed. "We're here to do science, not daydream." She reached forth to touch Scobie's arm, smiled shyly. "You're still full of your Kendrick persona, aren't you? Gallant, protective—" She stopped. Her voice had quickened with more than a hint of Ricia. She covered her lips and flushed again. A tear broke free and sparkled off on air currents. She forced a laugh. "But I'm just physicist Broberg, wife of astronomer Tom, mother of Johnnie and Billy."

Her glance went Saturnward, as if seeking the ship where her family waited. She might have spied it, too, as a star that moved among stars, by the solar sail. However, that was now furled, and naked vision could not find even such huge hulls as *Chronos* possessed, across millions of kilometers.

Luis Garcilaso asked from his pilot's chair: "What harm if we carry on our little *commedia dell' arte?*" His Arizona drawl soothed the ear. "We won't be landin' for a while yet, and everything's on automatic till then." He was small, swart, deft, still in his twenties.

Danzig twisted the leather of his countenance into a frown. At sixty, thanks to his habits as well as to longevity, he kept springiness in a lank frame; he could joke about wrinkles and encroaching baldness. In this hour, he set humor aside.

"Do you mean you don't know what's the matter?" His beak of a nose pecked at a scanner screen which magnified the moonscope. "Almighty God! That's a new world we're about to touch down on—tiny, but a world, and strange in ways we can't guess. Nothing's been here before us except one unmanned flyby and one unmanned lander that soon quit sending. We can't rely on meters and cameras alone. We've got to use our eyes and brains." He addressed Scobie. "You should realize that in your bones, Colin, if nobody else aboard does. You've worked on Luna as well as Earth. In spite of all the settlements, in spite of all the study that's been done, did you never hit any nasty surprises?"

The burly man had recovered his temper. Into his own voice came a softness that recalled the serenity of the Idaho mountains whence he hailed. "True," he admitted. "There's no such thing as having too much information when you're off Earth, or enough information, for that matter." He paused. "Nevertheless, timidity can be as dangerous as rashness—not that you're timid, Mark," he added in haste. "Why, you and Rachel could've been in a nice O'Neill on a nice pension—"

Danzig relaxed and smiled. "This was a challenge, if I may sound pompous. Just the same, we want to get home when we're finished here. We should be in time for the Bar Mitzvah of a great-grandson or two. Which requires staying alive."

"My point is, if you let yourself get buffaloed, you may end up in a worse bind than—Oh, never mind. You're probably right, and we should not have begun fantasizing. The spectacle sort of grabbed us. It won't happen again."

Yet when Scobie's eyes looked anew on the glacier, they had not quite the dispassion of a scientist in them.

Nor did Broberg's or Garcilaso's. Danzig slammed fist
into palm. "The game, the damned childish game," he
muttered, too low for his companions to hear. "Was nothing saner possible for them?"

❀ II ❀

Was nothing saner possible for them? Perhaps not.

If we are to answer the question, we should first review
some history. When early industrial operations in space
offered the hope of rescuing civilization, and Earth, from
ruin, then greater knowledge of sister planets, prior to
their development, became a clear necessity. The effort
must start with Mars, the least hostile. No natural law
forbade sending small manned spacecraft yonder. What
did was the absurdity of as much fuel, time, and effort
as were required, in order that three or four persons
might spend a few days in a single locality.

Construction of the *J. Peter Vajk* took longer and cost
more, but paid off when it, virtually a colony, spread its
immense solar sail and took a thousand people to their
goal in half a year and in comparative comfort. The payoff grew overwhelming when they, from orbit, launched
Earthward the beneficiated minerals of Phobos that they
did not need for their own purposes. Those purposes, of
course, turned on the truly thorough, long-term study of
Mars, and included landings of auxiliary craft, for ever
lengthier stays, all over the surface.

Sufficient to remind you of this much; no need to
detail the triumphs of the same basic concept throughout
the inner Solar System, as far as Jupiter. The tragedy of
the *Vladimir* became a reason to try again for Mercury,
and, in a left-handed, political way, pushed the Britannic-
American consortium into its *Chronos* project.

They named the ship better than they knew. Sailing time to Saturn was eight years.

Not only the scientists must be healthy, lively-minded people. Crewfolk, technicians, medics, constables, teachers, clergy, entertainers, every element of an entire community must be. Each must command more than a single skill, for emergency backup, and keep those skills alive by regular, tedious rehearsal. The environment was limited and austere; communication with home was soon a matter of beamcasts; cosmopolitans found themselves in what amounted to an isolated village. What were they to *do*?

Assigned tasks. Civic projects, especially work on improving the interior of the vessel. Research, or writing a book, or the study of a subject, or sports, or hobby clubs, or service and handicraft enterprises, or more private interactions, or—There was a wide choice of television tapes, but Central Control made sets usable for only three hours in twenty-four. You dared not get into the habit of passivity.

Individuals grumbled, squabbled, formed and dissolved cliques, formed and dissolved marriages or less explicit relationships, begot and raised occasional children, worshipped, mocked, learned, yearned, and for the most part found reasonable satisfaction in life. But for some, including a large proportion of the gifted, what made the difference between this and misery was their psychodramas.

—Minamoto

Dawn crept past the ice, out onto the rock. It was a light both dim and harsh, yet sufficient to give Garcilaso the last data he wanted for descent.

The hiss of the motor died away, a thump shivered through the hull, landing jacks leveled it, stillness fell. The crew did not speak for a while. They were staring out at Iapetus.

Immediately around them was desolation like that which reigns in much of the Solar System. A darkling plain curved visibly away to a horizon that, at man-height, was a bare three kilometers distant; higher up in the cabin, you saw farther, but that only sharpened the sense of being on a minute ball awhirl among the stars. The ground was thinly covered with cosmic dust and gravel; here and there a minor crater or an upthrust mass lifted out of the regolith to cast long, knife-edged, utterly black shadows. Light reflections lessened the number of visible stars, turning heaven into a bowlful of night. Halfway between the zenith and the south, half-Saturn and its rings made the vista beautiful.

Likewise did the glacier—or the glaciers? Nobody was sure. The sole knowledge was that, seen from afar, Iapetus gleamed bright at the western end of its orbit and grew dull at the eastern end, because one side was covered with whitish material while the other side was not; the dividing line passed nearly beneath the planet which it eternally faced. The probes from *Chronos* had reported the layer was thick, with puzzling spectra that varied from place to place, and little more about it.

In this hour, four humans gazed across pitted emptiness and saw wonder rear over the world-rim. From north to south went ramparts, battlements, spires, depths, peaks, cliffs, their shapes and shadings an infinity of fantasies. On the right Saturn cast soft amber, but that was nearly lost in the glare from the east, where a sun dwarfed almost to stellar size nonetheless blazed too fierce to look at, just above the summit. There the silvery sheen exploded in brilliance, diamond-glitter of shattered light, chill blues and greens; dazzled to tears, eyes saw the vision glimmer and waver, as if it bordered on dreamland, or on Faerie. But despite all delicate intricacies, underneath was a sense of chill and of brutal mass: here dwelt also the Frost Giants.

Broberg was the first to breathe forth a word. "The City of Ice."

"Magic," said Garcilaso as low. "My spirit could lose itself forever, wanderin' yonder. I'm not sure I'd mind. My cave is nothin' like this, nothin'—"

"Wait a minute!" snapped Danzig in alarm.

"Oh, yes. Curb the imagination, please." Though Scobie was quick to utter sobrieties, they sounded drier than needful. "We know from probe transmissions the scarp is, well, Grand Canyon-like. Sure, it's more spectacular than we realized, which I suppose makes it still more of a mystery." He turned to Broberg. "I've never seen ice or snow as sculptured as this. Have you, Jean? You've mentioned visiting a lot of mountain and winter scenery when you were a girl in Canada."

The physicist shook her head. "No. Never. It doesn't seem possible. What could have done it? There's no weather here . . . is there?"

"Perhaps the same phenomenon is responsible that laid a hemisphere bare," Danzig suggested.

"Or that covered a hemisphere," Scobie said. "An object seventeen hundred kilometers across shouldn't have gases, frozen or otherwise. Unless it's a ball of such stuff clear through, like a comet. Which we know it's not." As if to demonstrate, he unclipped a pair of pliers from a nearby tool rack, tossed it, and caught it on its slow way down. His own ninety kilos of mass weighed about seven. For that, the satellite must be essentially rocky.

Garcilaso registered impatience. "Let's stop tradin' facts and theories we already know about, and start findin' answers."

Rapture welled in Broberg. "Yes, let's get out. Over *there.*"

"Hold on," protested Danzig as Garcilaso and Scobie nodded eagerly. "You can't be serious. Caution, step-by-step advance—"

"No, it's too wonderful for that." Broberg's tone shivered.

"Yeah, to hell with fiddlin' around," Garcilaso said. "We need at least a preliminary scout right away."

The furrows deepened in Danzig's visage. "You mean you too, Luis? But you're our pilot!"

"On the ground I'm general assistant, chief cook, and bottle washer to you scientists. Do you imagine I want to sit idle, with somethin' like that to explore?" Garcilaso calmed his voice. "Besides, if I should come to grief, any of you can fly back, given a bit of radio talk from *Chronos* and a final approach under remote control."

"It's quite reasonable, Mark," Scobie argued. "Contrary to doctrine, true; but doctrine was made for us, not vice versa. A short distance, low gravity, and we'll be on the lookout for hazards. The point is, until we have some notion of what that ice is like, we don't know what the devil to pay attention to in this vicinity, either. No, we'll take a quick jaunt. When we return, then we'll plan."

Danzig stiffened. "May I remind you, if anything goes wrong, help is at least a hundred hours away? An auxiliary like this can't boost any higher if it's to get back, and it'd take longer than that to disengage the big boats from Saturn and Titan."

Scobie reddened at the implied insult. "And may I remind you, on the ground I am the captain? I say an immediate reconnaissance is safe and desirable. Stay behind if you want—In fact, yes, you must. Doctrine is right in saying the vessel mustn't be deserted."

Danzig studied him for several seconds before murmuring, "Luis goes, however, is that it?"

"Yes!" cried Garcilaso so that the cabin rang.

Broberg patted Danzig's limp hand. "It's okay, Mark," she said gently. "We'll bring back samples for you to study. After that, I wouldn't be surprised but what the best ideas about procedure will be yours."

He shook his head. Suddenly he looked very tired. "No," he replied in a monotone, "that won't happen. You see, I'm only a hardnosed industrial chemist who saw this expedition as a chance to do interesting research. The whole way through space, I kept myself busy with ordinary affairs, including, you remember, a couple of inventions I'd wanted leisure to develop. You three, you're younger, you're romantics—"

"Aw, come off it, Mark." Scobie tried to laugh. "Maybe Jean and Luis are, a little, but me, I'm about as otherworldly as a plate of haggis."

"You played the game, year after year, until at last the game started playing you. That's what's going on this minute, no matter how you rationalize your motives." Danzig's gaze on the geologist, who was his friend, lost the defiance that had been in it and turned wistful. "You might try recalling Delia Ames."

Scobie bristled. "What about her? The business was hers and mine, nobody else's."

"Except afterward she cried on Rachel's shoulder, and Rachel doesn't keep secrets from me. Don't worry, I'm not about to blab. Anyhow, Delia got over it. But if you'd recollect objectively, you'd see what had happened to you, already three years ago."

Scobie set his jaw. Danzig smiled in the left corner of his mouth. "No, I suppose you can't," he went on. "I admit I'd no idea either, till now, how far the process had gone. At least keep your fantasies in the background while you're outside, will you? Can you?"

In half a decade of travel, Scobie's apartment had become idiosyncratically his—perhaps more so than was usual, since he remained a bachelor who seldom had women visitors for longer than a few nightwatches at a time. Much of the furniture he had made himself; the agrosections of *Chronos* produced wood, hide, fiber as well as food and fresh air. His handiwork ran to massiveness and archaic carved decorations. Most of what he wanted to read he screened from the data banks, of course, but a shelf held a few old books, Childe's border ballads, an eighteenth-century family Bible (despite his agnosticism), a copy of *The Machinery of Freedom* which had nearly disintegrated but displayed the signature of the author, and other valued miscellany. Above them stood a model of a sailboat in which he had cruised Northern European waters, and a trophy he had won in handball aboard this ship. On the bulkheads hung his fencing sabers and numerous pictures—of parents and siblings, of wilderness areas he had tramped on Earth, of castles and mountains and heaths in Scotland where he had often been too, of his geological team on Luna, of Thomas Jefferson and, imagined, Robert the Bruce.

On a certain evenwatch he had, though, been seated before his telescreen. Lights were turned low in order that he might fully savor the image. Auxiliary craft were out in a joint exercise, and a couple of their personnel used the opportunity to beam back views of what they saw.

That was splendor. Starful space made a chalice for *Chronos*. The two huge, majestically counter-rotating cylinders, the entire complex of linkages, ports, locks, shields, collectors, transmitters, docks, all became Japanesely exquisite at a distance of several hundred kilometers. It was the solar sail which filled most of the screen, like a turning golden sun-wheel; yet remote vision could also appreciate its spiderweb intricacy, soaring and subtle curvatures, even the less-than-gossamer thinness. A mightier work than the Pyramids, a finer work than a refashioned chromosome, the ship moved on toward a Saturn which had become the second brightest beacon in the firmament.

The doorchime hauled Scobie out of his exaltation. As he started across the deck, he stubbed his toe on a table leg. Coriolis force caused that. It was slight, when a hull this size spun to give a full gee of weight, and a thing to which he had long since adapted; but now and then he got so interested in something that Terrestrial habits returned. He swore at his absent-mindedness, good-naturedly, since he anticipated a pleasurable time.

When he opened the door, Delia Ames entered in a single stride. At once she closed it behind her and stood braced against it. She was a tall blonde woman who did electronics maintenance and kept up a number of outside activities. "Hey!" Scobie said. "What's wrong? You look like—" he tried for levity—"something my cat wouldn't've dragged in, if we had any mice or beached fish aboard."

She drew a ragged breath. Her Australian accent thickened till he had trouble understanding: "I . . . today . . . I happened to be at the same cafeteria table as George Harding—"

Unease tingled through Scobie. Harding worked in Ames' department but had much more in common with him. In the same group to which they both belonged, Harding likewise took a vaguely ancestral role, N'Kuma the Lionslayer.

"What happened?" Scobie asked.

Woe stared back at him. "He mentioned . . . you and he and the rest . . . you'd be taking your next holiday together . . . to carry on your, your bloody act uninterrupted."

"Well, yes. Work at the new park over in Starboard Hull will be suspended till enough metal's been recycled for the water pipes. The area will be vacant, and my gang has arranged to spend a week's worth of days—"

"But you and I were going to Lake Armstrong!"

"Uh, wait, that was just a notion we talked about, no definite plan yet, and this is such an unusual chance—Later, sweetheart. I'm sorry." He took her hands. They felt cold. He essayed a smile. "Now, c'mon, we were going to cook a festive dinner together and afterward spend a, shall we say, quiet evening at home. But for a start, this absolutely gorgeous presentation on the screen—"

She jerked free of him. The gesture seemed to calm her. "No, thanks," she said, flat-voiced. "Not when you'd rather be with that Broberg woman. I only came by to tell you in person I'm getting out of the way of you two."

"*Huh?*" He stepped back. "What the flaming hell do you mean?"

"You know jolly well."

"I don't! She, I, she's happily married, got two kids, she's older than me, we're friends, sure, but there's never been a thing between us that wasn't in the open and on the level—" Scobie swallowed. "You suppose maybe I'm in love with her?"

Ames looked away. Her fingers writhed together. "I'm not about to go on being a mere convenience to you, Colin. You have plenty of those. Myself, I'd hoped—But I was wrong, and I'm going to cut my losses before they get worse."

"But . . . Dee, I swear I haven't fallen for anybody else, and I, I swear you're more than a body to me, you're a fine person—" She stood mute and withdrawn. Scobie gnawed his lip before he could tell her: "Okay, I admit it, a main reason I volunteered for this trip was I'd lost out in a love affair on Earth. Not that the project doesn't interest me, but I've come to realize what a big chunk out of my life it is. You, more than any other woman, Dee, you've gotten me to feel better about the situation."

She grimaced. "But not as much as your psycho-drama has, right?"

"Hey, you must think I'm obsessed with the game. I'm not. It's fun and—oh, maybe 'fun' is too weak a word—but anyhow, it's just little bunches of people getting together fairly regularly to play. Like my fencing, or a chess club, or, or anything."

She squared her shoulders. "Well, then," she asked, "will you cancel the date you've made and spend your holiday with me?"

"I, uh, I can't do that. Not at this stage. Kendrick isn't off on the periphery of current events, he's closely involved with everybody else. If I didn't show, it'd spoil things for the rest."

Her glance steadied upon them. "Very well. A promise is a promise, or so I imagined. But afterward—Don't be afraid. I'm not trying to trap you. That would be no good, would it? However, if I maintain this liaison of ours, will you phase out of your game?"

"I can't—" Anger seized him. "No, God damn it!" he roared.

"Then goodbye, Colin," she said, and departed. He stared for minutes at the door she had shut behind her.

Unlike the large Titan and Saturn-vicinity explorers, landers on the airless moons were simply modified Luna-to-space shuttles, reliable but with limited capabilities. When the blocky shape had dropped below the horizon, Garcilaso said into his radio: "We've lost sight of the boat, Mark. I must say it improves the view." One of the relay micro-satellites which had been sown in orbit passed his words on.

"Better start blazing your trail, then," Danzig reminded.

"My, my, you *are* a fussbudget, aren't you?" Nevertheless Garcilaso unholstered the squirt gun at his hip and splashed a vividly fluorescent circle of paint on the ground. He would do it at eyeball intervals until his party reached the glacier. Except where dust lay thick over the regolith, footprints were faint, under the feeble gravity, and absent when a walker crossed continuous rock.

Walker? No, leaper. The three bounded exultant, little hindered by spacesuits, life support units, tool and ration packs. The naked land fled from their haste, and even higher, ever more clear and glorious to see, loomed the ice ahead of them.

There was no describing it, not really. You could speak of lower slopes and palisades above, to a mean height of perhaps a hundred meters, with spires towering farther still. You could speak of gracefully curved tiers going up those braes, of lacy parapets and fluted crags and arched openings to caves filled with wonders, of mysterious blues in the depths and greens where light streamed through translucencies, of gem-sparkle across whiteness where radiance and shadow wove mandalas—and none of it would convey anything more than Scobie's earlier, altogether inadequate comparison to the Grand Canyon.

"Stop," he said for the dozenth time. "I want to take a few pictures."

"Will anybody understand them who hasn't been here?" whispered Broberg.

"Probably not," said Garcilaso in the same hushed tone. "Maybe no one but us ever will."

"What do you mean by that?" demanded Danzig's voice.

"Never mind," snapped Scobie.

"I think I know," the chemist said. "Yes, it is a great piece of scenery, but you're letting it hypnotize you."

"If you don't cut out that drivel," Scobie warned, "we'll cut you out of the circuit. Damn it, we've got work to do. Get off our backs."

Danzig gusted a sigh. "Sorry. Uh, are you finding any clues to the nature of that—that thing?"

Scobie focused his camera. "Well," he said, partly mollified, "the different shades and textures, and no doubt the different shapes, seem to confirm what the reflection spectra from the flyby suggested. The composition is a mixture, or a jumble, or both, of several materials, and varies from place to place. Water ice is obvious, but I feel sure of carbon dioxide too, and I'd bet on ammonia, methane, and presumably lesser amounts of other stuff."

"Methane? Could they stay solid at ambient temperature, in a vacuum?"

"We'll have to find out for sure. However, I'd guess that most of the time it's cold enough, at least for methane strata that occur down inside where there's pressure on them."

Within the vitryl globe of her helmet, Broberg's features showed delight. "Wait!" she cried. "I have an idea—about what happened to the probe that landed." She drew breath. "It came down almost at the foot of the glacier, you recall. Our view of the site from space seemed to indicate that an avalanche buried it, but we couldn't understand how that might have been triggered. Well, suppose a methane layer at exactly the wrong location melted. Heat radiation from the jets may have warmed it, and later the radar beam used to map contours added the last few degrees necessary. The stratum flowed, and down came everything that had rested on top of it."

"Plausible," Scobie said. "Congratulations, Jean."

"Nobody thought of the possibility in advance?" Garcilaso scoffed. "What kind of scientists have we got along?"

"The kind who were being overwhelmed by work after we reached Saturn, and still more by data input," Scobie answered. "The universe is bigger than you or anybody can realize, hotshot."

"Oh. Sure. No offense." Garcilaso's glance returned to the ice. "Yes, we'll never run out of mysteries, will we?"

"Never." Broberg's eyes glowed enormous. "At the heart of things will always be magic. The Elf King rules—"

Scobie returned his camera to its pouch. "Stow the gab and move on," he ordered curtly.

His gaze locked for an instant with Broberg's. In the weird, mingled light, it could be seen that she went pale, then red, before she sprang off beside him.

Ricia had gone alone into Moonwood on Midsummer Eve. The King found her there and took her unto him as she had hoped. Ecstasy became terror when he afterward bore her off; yet her captivity in the City of Ice brought her many more such hours, and beauties and marvels unknown among mortals. Alvarlan, her mentor, sent his spirit in quest of her, and was himself beguiled by what he found. It was an effort of will for him to tell Sir Kendrick of the Isles where she was, albeit he pledged his help in freeing her.

N'Kuma the Lionslayer, Bela of Eastmarch, Karina of the Far West, Lady Aurelia, Olav Harpmaster had none of them been present when this happened.

The glacier (a wrong name for something that might have no counterpart in the Solar System) lifted off the plain abruptly as a wall. Standing there, the three could no longer see the heights. They could, though, see that the slope which curved steeply upward to a filigree-topped edge was not smooth. Shadows lay blue in countless small craters. The sun had climbed just sufficiently high to beget them; a Iapetan day is more than seventy-nine of Earth's.

Danzig's question crackled in earphones: "Now are you satisfied? Will you come back before a fresh landslide catches you?"

"It won't," Scobie replied. "We aren't a vehicle, and the local configuration has clearly been stable for centuries or better. Besides, what's the point of a manned expedition if nobody investigates anything?"

"I'll see if I can climb," Garcilaso offered.

"No, wait," Scobie commanded. "I've had experience with mountains and snowpacks, for whatever that may be worth. Let me study out a route for us first."

"You're going onto that stuff, the whole gaggle of you?" exploded Danzig. "Have you completely lost your minds?"

Scobie's brow and lips tightened. "Mark, I warn you again, if you don't get your emotions under control we'll cut you off. We'll hike on a ways if I decide it's safe."

He paced, in floating low-weight fashion, back and forth while he surveyed the jökull. Layers and blocks of distinct substances were plain to see, like separate ashlars laid by an elvish mason—where they were not so huge that a giant must have been at work. The craterlets might be sentry posts on this lowest embankment of the City's defenses. . . .

Garcilaso, most vivacious of men, stood motionless and let his vision lose itself in the sight. Broberg knelt down to examine the ground, but her own gaze kept wandering aloft.

Finally she beckoned. "Colin, come over here, please," she said. "I believe I've made a discovery."

Scobie joined her. As she rose, she scooped a handful of fine black particles off the shards on which she stood and let it trickle from her glove. "I suspect this is the reason the boundary of the ice is sharp," she told him.

"What is?" Danzig inquired from afar. He got no answer.

"I noticed more and more dust as we went along," Broberg continued. "If it fell on patches and lumps of frozen stuff, isolated from the main mass, and covered them, it would absorb solar heat till they melted or, like-lier, sublimed. Even water molecules would escape to

space, in this weak gravity. The main mass was too big
for that; square-cube law. Dust grains there would simply
melt their way down a short distance, then be covered as
surrounding material collapsed on them, and the process
would stop."

"H'm." Broberg raised a hand to stroke his chin,
encountered his helmet, and sketched a grin at himself.
"Sounds reasonable. But where did so much dust come
from—and the ice, for that matter?"

"I think—" Her voice dropped until he could barely
hear, and her look went the way of Garcilaso's. His
remained upon her face, profiled against stars. "I think
this bears out your comet hypothesis, Colin. A comet
struck Iapetus. It came from the direction it did because
of getting so near Saturn that it was forced to swing in
a hairpin bend around the planet. It was enormous; the
ice of it covered almost a hemisphere, in spite of much
more being vaporized and lost. The dust is partly from
it, partly generated by the impact."

He clasped her armored shoulder. "*Your* theory, Jean.
I was not the first to propose a comet, but you're the
first to corroborate with details."

She didn't appear to notice, except that she murmured
further: "Dust can account for the erosion that made
those lovely formations, too. It caused differential melting and sublimation on the surface, according to the patterns it happened to fall in and the mixes of ices it clung
to, until it was washed away or encysted. The craters,
these small ones and the major ones we've observed from
above, they have a separate but similar origin.
Meteorites—"

"Whoa, there," he objected. "Any sizeable meteorite
would release enough energy to steam off most of the
entire field."

"I know. Which shows the comet collision was recent, less than a thousand years ago, or we wouldn't be seeing this miracle today. Nothing big has since happened to strike, yet. I'm thinking of little stones, cosmic sand, in prograde orbits around Saturn so that they hit with low relative speed. Most simply make dimples in the ice. Lying there, however, they collect solar heat because of being dark, and re-radiate it to melt away their surroundings, till they sink beneath. The concavities they leave reflect incident radiation from side to side, and thus continue to grow. The pothole effect. And again, because the different ices have different properties, you don't get perfectly smooth craters, but those fantastic bowls we saw before we landed."

"By God!" Scobie hugged her. "You're a genius."

Helmet against helmet, she smiled and said, "No. It's obvious, once you've seen for yourself." She was quiet for a bit while still they held each other. "Scientific intuition is a funny thing, I admit," she went on at last. "Considering the problem, I was hardly aware of my logical mind. What I thought was—the City of Ice, made with starstones out of that which a god called down from heaven—"

"Jesus Maria!" Garcilaso spun about to stare at them.

Scobie released the woman. "We'll go after confirmation," he said unsteadily. "To the large crater you'll remember we spotted a few klicks inward. The surface appears quite safe to walk on."

"I called that crater the Elf King's Dance Hall," Broberg mused, as if a dream were coming back to her.

"Have a care." Garcilaso's laugh rattled. "Heap big medicine yonder. The King is only an inheritor; it was giants who built these walls, for the gods."

"Well, I've got to find a way in, don't I?" Scobie responded.

"Indeed," *Alvarlan says.* "I cannot guide you from this point. My spirit can only see through mortal eyes. I can but lend you my counsel, until we have neared the gates."

"Are you sleepwalking in that fairytale of yours?" Danzig yelled. "Come back before you get yourselves killed!"

"Will you dry up?" Scobie snarled. "It's nothing but a style of talk we've got between us. If you can't understand that, you've got less use of your brain than we do."

"Listen, won't you? I didn't say you're crazy. You don't have delusions or anything like that. I do say you've steered your fantasies toward this kind of place, and now the reality has reinforced them till you're under a compulsion you don't recognize. Would you go ahead so recklessly anywhere else in the universe? Think!"

"That does it. We'll resume contact after you've had time to improve your manners." Scobie snapped off his main radio switch. The circuits that stayed active served for close-by communication but had no power to reach an orbital relay. His companions did likewise.

The three faced the awesomeness before them. "You can help me find the Princess when we are inside, Alvarlan," *Kendrick says.*

"That I can and will," *the sorcerer vows.*

"I wait for you, most steadfast of my lovers," *Ricia croons.*

Alone in the spacecraft, Danzig well-nigh sobbed, "Oh, damn that game forever!" The sound fell away into emptiness.

❀ III ❀

To condemn psychodrama, even in its enhanced form, would be to condemn human nature.

It begins in childhood. Play is necessary to an immature mammal, a means of learning to handle the body, the perceptions, and the outside world. The young human plays, must play, with its brain too. The more intelligent the child, the more its imagination needs exercise. There are degrees of activity, from the passive watching of a show on a screen, onward through reading, daydreaming, storytelling, and psychodrama . . . for which the child has no such fancy name.

We cannot give this behavior any single description, for the shape and course it takes depend on endlessly many variables. Sex, age, culture, and companions are only the most obvious. For example, in pre-electronic North America little girls would often play "house" while little boys played "cowboys and Indians" or "cops and robbers," whereas nowadays a mixed group of their descendants might play "dolphins" or "astronauts and aliens." In essence, a small band forms; and each individual makes up a character to portray, or borrows one from fiction. Simple props may be employed, such as toy weapons, or any chance object—a stick, for instance—may be declared something else such as a metal detector, or a thing may be quite imaginary, as the scenery almost always is. The children then act out a drama which they compose as they go along. When they cannot physically perform a certain action, they describe it. ("I jump real high, like you can do on Mars, an' come out over the edge o' that ol' Valles Marineris, an' take that bandit by surprise.") A large cast of characters, especially villains, frequently comes into existence by fiat.

The most imaginative member of the troupe dominates the game and the evolution of the story line, though in a rather subtle fashion, through offering the most vivid possibilities. The rest, however, are brighter than average; psychodrama in this highly developed form does not appeal to everybody.

For those to whom it does, the effects are beneficial and lifelong. Besides increasing their creativity through use, it lets them try out a play version of different adult roles and experiences. Thereby they begin to acquire insight into adulthood.

Such playacting ends when adolescence commences, if not earlier—but only in that form, and not necessarily forever in it. Grown-ups have many dream-games. This is plain to see in lodges, for example, with their titles, costumes, and ceremonies; but does it not likewise animate all pageantry, every ritual? To what extent are our heroisms, sacrifices, and self-aggrandizements the acting out of personae that we maintain? Some thinkers have attempted to trace this element through every aspect of society.

Here, though, we are concerned with overt psychodrama among adults. In Western civilization it first appeared on a noticeable scale during the middle twentieth century. Psychiatrists found it a powerful diagnostic and therapeutic technique. Among ordinary folk, war and fantasy games, many of which involved identification with imaginary or historical characters, became increasingly popular. In part this was doubtless a retreat from the restrictions and menaces of that unhappy period, but likely in larger part it was a revolt of the mind against the inactive entertainment, notably television, which had come to dominate recreation.

The Chaos ended those activities. Everybody knows about their revival in recent times—for healthier reasons, one hopes. By projecting three-dimensional scenes and appropriate sounds from a data bank—or, better yet, by having a computer produce them to order—players gained a sense of reality that intensified their mental and emotional commitment. Yet in those games that went on for episode after episode, year after real-time year, whenever two or more members of a group could get together to play, they found themselves less and less dependent on such appurtenances. It seemed that, through practice, they had regained the vivid imaginations of their childhoods, and could make anything, or airy nothing itself, into the objects and the worlds they desired.

I have deemed it necessary thus to repeat the obvious in order that we may see it in perspective. The news beamed from Saturn has brought widespread revulsion. (Why? What buried fears have been touched? This is subject matter for potentially important research.) Overnight, adult psychodrama has become unpopular; it may become extinct. That would, in many ways, be a worse tragedy than what has occurred yonder. There is no reason to suppose that the game ever harmed any mentally sound person on Earth; on the contrary. Beyond doubt, it has helped astronauts stay sane and alert on long, difficult missions. If it has no more medical use, that is because psychotherapy has become a branch of applied biochemistry.

And this last fact, the modern world's dearth of experience with madness, is at the root of what happened. Although he could not have foreseen the exact outcome, a twentieth-century psychiatrist might have warned against spending eight years, an unprecedented stretch of time, in as strange an environment as the *Chronos*. Strange it certainly has been, despite all efforts—limited, totally man-controlled, devoid of countless cues for which our evolution on Earth has fashioned us. Extraterrestrial colonists have, thus far, had available to them any number of simulations and compensations, of which close, full contact with home and frequent opportunities to visit there are probably the most significant. Sailing time to Jupiter was long, but half of that to Saturn. Moreover, because they were earlier, scientists in the *Zeus* had much research to occupy them en route, which it would be pointless for later travelers to duplicate; by then, the interplanetary medium between the two giants held few surprises.

Contemporary psychologists were aware of this. They understood that the persons most adversely affected would be the most intelligent, imaginative, and dynamic—those who were supposed to make the very discoveries at Saturn which were the purpose of the undertaking. Being less familiar than their predecessors with the labyrinth that lies, Minotaur-haunted, beneath every human consciousness, the psychologists expected purely benign consequences of whatever psychodramas the crew engendered.

—Minamoto

Assignments to teams had not been made in advance of departure. It was sensible to let professional capabilities reveal themselves and grow on the voyage, while personal relationships did the same. Eventually such factors would help in deciding what individuals should train for what tasks. Long-term participation in a group of

players normally forged bonds of friendship that were
desirable, if the members were otherwise qualified.

In real life, Scobie always observed strict propriety
toward Broberg. She was attractive, but she was monoga-
mous, and he had no wish to alienate her. Besides, he
liked her husband. (Tom did not partake of the game.
As an astronomer, he had plenty to keep his attention
happily engaged.) They had played for a couple of years,
their bunch had acquired as many as it could accommodate in a narrative whose milieu and people were becoming complex, before Scobie and Broberg spoke of
anything intimate.

By then, the story they enacted was doing so, and
maybe it was not altogether by chance that they met
when both had several idle hours. This was in the weightless recreation area at the spin axis. They tumbled
through aerobatics, shouting and laughing, until they
were pleasantly tired, went to the clubhouse, turned in
their wingsuits, and showered. They had not seen each
other nude before; neither commented, but he did not
hide his enjoyment of the sight, while she colored and
averted her glance as tactfully as she was able. Afterward,
their clothes resumed, they decided on a drink before
they went home, and sought the lounge.

Since evenwatch was approaching nightwatch, they
had the place to themselves. At the bar, he thumbed a
chit for Scotch, she for pinot Chardonnay. The machine
obliged them and they carried their refreshments out
onto the balcony. Seated at a table, they looked across
immensity. The clubhouse was built into the support
frame on a Lunar gravity level. Above them they saw the
sky wherein they had been as birds; its reach did not
seem any more hemmed in by far-spaced, spidery girders

than it was by a few drifting clouds. Beyond, and straight
ahead, decks opposite were a commingling of masses and
shapes which the scant illumination at this hour turned
into mystery. Among those shadows the humans made
out woods, brooks, pools, turned hoar or agleam by the
light of stars which filled the skyview strips. Right and
left, the hull stretched off beyond sight, a dark in which
such lamps as there were appeared lost.

The air was cool, slightly jasmine-scented, drenched
with silence. Underneath and throughout, subliminal,
throbbed the myriad pulses of the ship.

"Magnificent," Broberg said low, gazing outward.
"What a surprise."

"Eh?" asked Scobie.

"I've only been here before in daywatch. I didn't antic-
ipate a simple rotation of the reflectors would make it
wonderful."

"Oh, I wouldn't sneer at the daytime view. Mighty
impressive."

"Yes, but—but then you see too plainly that everything
is manmade, nothing is wild or unknown or free. The
sun blots out the stars; it's as though no universe existed
beyond this shell we're in. Tonight is like being in Maranoa," *the kingdom of which Ricia is Princess, a kingdom
of ancient things and ways, wildernesses, enchantments.*

"H'm, yeah, sometimes I feel trapped myself," Scobie
admitted. "I believed I had a journey's worth of geological data to study, but my project isn't going anywhere
very interesting."

"Same for me." Broberg straightened where she sat,
turned to him, and smiled a trifle. The dusk softened her
features, made them look young. "Not that we're entitled
to self-pity. Here we are, safe and comfortable till we

reach Saturn. After that we should never lack for excitement, or for material to work with on the way home."

"True." Scobie raised his glass. "Well, skoal. Hope I'm not mispronouncing that."

"How should I know?" she laughed. "My maiden name was Almyer."

"That's right, you've adopted Tom's surname. I wasn't thinking. Though that is rather unusual these days, hey?"

She spread her hands. "My family was well-to-do, but they were—are—Jerusalem Catholics. Strict about certain things; archaistic, you might say." She lifted her wine and sipped. "Oh, yes, I've left the Church, but in several ways the Church will never leave me."

"I see. Not to pry, but, uh, this does account for some traits of yours I couldn't help wondering about."

She regarded him over the rim of her glass. "Like what?"

"Well, you've got a lot of life in you, vigor, sense of fun, but you're also—what's the word?—uncommonly domestic. You've told me you were a quiet faculty member of Yukon University till you married Tom." Scobie grinned. "Since you two kindly invited me to your last anniversary party, and I know your present age, I deduced that you were thirty then." Unmentioned was the likelihood that she had still been a virgin. "Nevertheless —oh, forget it. I said I don't want to pry."

"Go ahead, Colin," she urged. "That line from Burns sticks in my mind, since you introduced me to his poetry. 'To see oursels as others see us!' Since it looks as if we may visit the same moon—"

Scobie took a hefty dollop of Scotch. "Aw, nothing much," he said, unwontedly diffident. "If you must know, well, I have the impression that being in love wasn't the single good reason you had for marrying Tom. He'd already been accepted for this expedition, and given your personal qualifications, that would get you in too. In short, you'd grown tired of routine respectability and here was how you could kick over the traces. Am I right?"

"Yes." Her gaze dwelt on him. "You're more perceptive than I supposed."

"No, not really. A roughneck rockhound. But Ricia's made it plain to see, you're more than a demure wife, mother, and scientist—" She parted her lips. He raised a palm. "No, please, let me finish. I know it's bad manners to claim somebody's persona is a wish fulfillment, and I'm not doing that. Of course you don't want to be a free-roving, free-loving female scamp, any more than I want to ride around cutting down assorted enemies. Still, if you'd been born and raised in the world of our game, I feel sure you'd be a lot like Ricia. And that potential is part of you, Jean." He tossed off his drink. "If I've said too much, please excuse me. Want a refill?"

"I'd better not, but don't let me stop you."

"You won't." He rose and bounded off.

When he returned, he saw that she had been observing him through the vitryl door. As he sat down, she smiled, leaned a bit across the table, and told him softly: "I'm glad you said what you did. Now I can declare what a complicated man Kendrick reveals you to be."

"What?" Scobie asked in honest surprise. "Come on! He's a sword-and-shield tramp, a fellow who likes to travel, same as me; and in my teens I was a brawler, same as him."

"He may lack polish, but he's a chivalrous knight, a compassionate overlord, a knower of sagas and traditions, an appreciator of poetry and music, a bit of a bard . . .

Ricia misses him. When will he get back from his latest quest?"

"I'm bound home this minute. N'Kuma and I gave those pirates the slip and landed at Haverness two days ago. After we buried the swag, he wanted to visit Bela and Karina and join them in whatever they've been up to, so we bade goodbye for the time being." Scobie and Harding had lately taken a few hours to conclude that adventure of theirs. The rest of the group had been mundanely occupied for some while.

Broberg's eyes widened. "From Haverness to the Isles? But I'm in Castle Devaranda, right in between."

"I hoped you'd be."

"I can't wait to hear your story."

"I'm pushing on after dark. The moon is bright and I've got a pair of remounts I bought with a few gold pieces from the loot." *The dust rolls white beneath drumming hoofs. Where a horseshoe strikes a flint pebble, sparks fly ardent. Kendrick scowls.* "You aren't with . . . what's his name? . . . Joran the Red? I don't like him."

"I sent him packing a month ago. He got the idea that sharing my bed gave him authority over me. It was never anything but a romp. I stand alone on the Gerfalcon Tower, looking south over moonlit fields, and wonder how you fare. The road flows toward me like a gray river. Do I see a rider come at a gallop, far and far away?"

After many months of play, no image on a screen was necessary. *Pennons on the night wind stream athwart the stars.* "I arrive. I sound my horn to rouse the gatekeepers."

"How I do remember those merry notes—"

That same night, Kendrick and Ricia become lovers. Experienced in the game and careful of its etiquette,

Scobie and Broberg uttered no details about the union; they did not touch each other and maintained only fleeting eye contact; the ultimate goodnights were very decorous. After all, this was a story they composed about two fictitious characters in a world that never was.

The lower slopes of the jökull rose in tiers which were themselves deeply concave; the humans walked around their rims and admired the extravagant formations beneath. Names sprang onto lips, the Frost Garden, the Ghost Bridge, the Snow Queen's Throne, *while Kendrick advances into the City, and Ricia awaits him at the Dance Hall, and the spirit of Alvarlan carries word between them so that it is as if already she too travels beside her knight.* Nevertheless they proceeded warily, vigilant for signs of danger, especially whenever a change of texture or hue or anything else in the surface underfoot betokened a change in its nature.

Above the highest ledge reared a cliff too sheer to scale, Iapetan gravity or no, *the fortress wall.* However, from orbit the crew had spied a gouge in the vicinity, forming a pass, doubtless plowed by a small meteorite *in the war between the gods and the magicians, when stones chanted down from the sky wrought havoc so accursed that none dared afterward rebuild.* That was an eerie climb, hemmed in by heights which glimmered in the blue twilight they cast, heaven narrowed to a belt between them where stars seemed to blaze doubly brilliant.

"There must be guards at the opening," *Kendrick says.*

"A single guard," *answers the mind-whisper of Alvarlan,* "but he is a dragon. If you did battle with him, the noise and flame would bring every warrior here upon you. Fear not. I'll slip into his burnin' brain and weave him such a dream that he'll never see you."

"The King might sense the spell," *says Ricia through him.* "Since you'll be parted from us anyway while you ride the soul of that beast, Alvarlan, I'll seek him out and distract him."

Kendrick grimaces, knowing full well what means are hers to do that. She has told him how she longs for freedom and her knight; she has also hinted that elven lovemaking transcends the human. Does she wish for a final time before her rescue? . . . Well, Ricia and Kendrick have neither plighted nor practiced single troth. Assuredly Colin Scobie had not. He jerked forth a grin and continued through the silence that had fallen on all three.

They came out on top of the glacial mass and looked around them. Scobie whistled. Garcilaso stammered, "I-I-Jesus Christ!" Broberg smote her hands together.

Below them the precipice fell to the ledges, whose sculpturing took on a wholly new, eldritch aspect, gleam and shadow, until it ended at the plain. Seen from here aloft, the curvature of the moon made toes strain downward in boots, as if to cling fast and not be spun off among the stars which surrounded, rather than shone above, its ball. The spacecraft stood minute on dark, pocked stone, like a cenotaph raised to loneliness.

Eastward the ice reached beyond an edge of sight which was much closer. ("Yonder could be the rim of the world," Garcilaso said, and *Ricia replies,* "Yes, the City is nigh to there.") Bowls of different sizes, hillocks, crags, no two of them eroded the same way, turned its otherwise level stretch into a surreal maze. An arabesque openwork ridge which stood at the explorers' goal overtopped the horizon. Everything that was illuminated lay gently aglow. Radiant though the sun was, it cast the light of only, perhaps, five thousand full Lunas upon Earth. Southward, Saturn's great semidisc gave about one-half more Lunar shining; but in that direction, the wilderness sheened pale amber.

Scobie shook himself. "Well, shall we go?" His prosaic question jarred the others; Garcilaso frowned and Broberg winced.

She recovered. "Yes, hasten," *Ricia says*. "I am by myself once more. Are you out of the dragon, Alvarlan?"

"Aye," *the wizard informs her*. "Kendrick is safely behind a ruined palace. Tell us how best to reach you."

"You are at the time-gnawed Crown House. Before you lies the Street of the Shieldsmiths—"

Scobie's brows knitted. "It is noonday, when elves do not fare abroad," *Kendrick says* remindingly, commandingly. "I do not wish to encounter any of them. No fights, no complications. We are going to fetch you and escape, without further trouble."

Broberg and Garcilaso showed disappointment, but understood him. A game broke down when a person refused to accept something that a fellow player tried to put in. Often the narrative threads were not mended and picked up for many days. Broberg sighed.

"Follow the street to its end at a forum where a snow fountain springs," *Ricia directs*. "Cross, and continue on Aleph Zain Boulevard. You will know it by a gateway in the form of a skull with open jaws. If anywhere you see a rainbow flicker in the air, stand motionless until it has gone by, for it will be an auroral wolf. . . ."

At a low-gravity lope, the distance took some thirty minutes to cover. In the later part, the three were forced to detour by great banks of an ice so fine-grained that it slid about under their bootsoles and tried to swallow them. Several of these lay at irregular intervals around their destination.

There the travelers stood again for a time in the grip of awe.

The bowl at their feet must reach down almost to bedrock, a hundred meters, and was twice as wide. On this rim lifted the wall they had seen from the cliff, an arc fifty meters long and high, nowhere thicker than five meters, pierced by intricate scrollwork, greenly agleam where it was not translucent. It was the uppermost edge of a stratum which made serrations down the crater. Other outcrops and ravines were more dreamlike yet . . . was that a unicorn's head, was that a colonnade of caryatids, was that an icicle bower . . . ? The depths were a lake of cold blue shadow.

"You have come, Kendrick, beloved!" *cries Ricia, and casts herself into his arms.*

"Quiet," *warns the sending of Alvarlan the wise.* "Rouse not our immortal enemies."

"Yes, we must get back." Scobie blinked. "Judas priest, what possessed us? Fun is fun, but we sure have come a lot farther and faster than was smart, haven't we?"

"Let us stay for a little while," Broberg pleaded. "This is such a miracle—the Elf King's Dance Hall, which the Lord of the Dance built for him—"

"Remember, if we stay we'll be caught, and your captivity may be forever." Scobie thumbed his main radio switch. "Hello, Mark? Do you read me?"

Neither Broberg nor Garcilaso made that move. They did not hear Danzig's voice: "Oh, yes! I've been hunkered over the set gnawing my knuckles. How are you?"

"All right. We're at the big hole and will be heading back as soon as I've gotten a few pictures."

"They haven't made words to tell how relieved I am. From a scientific standpoint, was it worth the risk?"

Scobie gasped. He stared before him.

"Colin?" Danzig called. "You still there?"

"Yes. Yes."

"I asked what observations of any importance you made."

"I don't know," Scobie mumbled. "I can't remember. None of it after we started climbing seems real."

"Better you return right away," Danzig said grimly. "Forget about photographs."

"Correct." Scobie addressed his companions: "Forward march."

"I can't," *Alvarlan answers*. "A wanderin' spell has caught my spirit in tendrils of smoke."

"I know where a fire dagger is kept," *Ricia says*. "I'll try to steal it."

Broberg moved ahead, as though to descend into the crater. Tiny ice grains trickled over the verge from beneath her boots. She could easily lose her footing and slide down.

"No, wait," *Kendrick shouts to her*. "No need. My spearhead is of moon alloy. It can cut—"

The glacier shuddered. The ridge cracked asunder and fell in shards. The area on which the humans stood split free and toppled into the bowl. An avalanche poured after. High-flung crystals caught sunlight, glittered prismatic in challenge to the stars, descended slowly and lay quiet.

Except for shock waves through solids, everything had happened in the absolute silence of space.

Heartbeat by heartbeat, Scobie crawled back to his senses. He found himself held down, immobilized, in darkness and pain. His armor had saved, was still saving his life; he had been stunned but escaped a real concussion. Yet every breath hurt abominably. A rib or two on the left side seemed broken; a monstrous impact must have dented metal. And he was buried under more weight than he could move.

"Hello," he coughed. "Does anybody read me?" The single reply was the throb of his blood. If his radio still worked—which it should, being built into the suit—the mass around him screened him off.

It also sucked heat at an unknown but appalling rate. He felt no cold because the electrical system drew energy from his fuel cell as fast as needed to keep him warm and to recycle his air chemically. As a normal thing, when he lost heat through the slow process of radiation—and, a trifle, through kerofoam-lined bootsoles—the latter demand was much the greater. Now conduction was at work on every square centimeter. He had a spare unit in the equipment on his back, but no means of getting at it.

Unless—He barked forth a chuckle. Straining, he felt the stuff that entombed him yield the least bit under the pressure of arms and legs. And his helmet rang slightly with noise, a rustle, a gurgle. This wasn't water ice that imprisoned him, but stuff with a much lower freezing point. He was melting it, subliming it, making room for himself.

If he lay passive, he would sink, while frozenness above slid down to keep him in his grave. He might evoke superb new formations, but he would not see them. Instead, he must use the small capability given him to work his way upward, scrabble, get a purchase on matter that was not yet aflow, burrow to the stars.

He began.

Agony soon racked him, breath rasped in and out of lungs aflame, strength drained away and trembling took its place, he could not tell whether he ascended or slipped back. Blind, half suffocated, Scobie made mole-claws of his hands and dug.

It was too much to endure. He fled from it—

His strong enchantments failing, the Elf King brought down his towers of fear in wreck. If the spirit of Alvarlan returned to its body, the wizard would brood upon things he had seen, and understand what they meant, and such knowledge would give mortals a terrible power against Faerie. Waking from sleep, the King scryed Kendrick about to release that fetch. There was no time to do more than break the spell which upheld the Dance Hall. It was largely built of mist and starshine, but enough blocks quarried from the cold side of Ginnungagap were in it that when they crashed they should kill the knight. Ricia would perish too, and in his quicksilver intellect the King regretted that. Nevertheless he spoke the necessary word.

He did not comprehend how much abuse flesh and bone can bear. Sir Kendrick fights his way clear of the ruins, to seek and save his lady. While he does, he heartens himself with thoughts of adventures past and future—

—and suddenly the blindness broke apart and Saturn stood lambent within rings.

Scobie belly-flopped onto the surface and lay shuddering.

He must rise, no matter how his injuries screamed, lest he melt himself a new burial place. He lurched to his feet and glared around.

Little but outcroppings and scars was left of the sculpture. For the most part, the crater had become a smooth-sided whiteness under heaven. Scarcity of shadows made distances hard to gauge, but Scobie guessed the new depth as about seventy-five meters. And empty, empty.

"Mark, do you hear?" he cried.

"That you, Colin?" rang in his earpieces. "Name of mercy, what's happened? I heard you call out, and saw a cloud rise and sink . . . then nothing for more than an hour. Are you okay?"

"I am, sort of. I don't see Jean or Luis. A landslide took us by surprise and buried us. Hold on while I search."

When he stood upright, Scobie's ribs hurt less. He could move about rather handily if he took care. The two types of standard analgesic in his kit were alike useless, one too weak to give noticeable relief, one so strong that it would turn him sluggish. Casting to and fro, he soon found what he expected, a concavity in the tumbled snowlike material, slightly aboil.

Also a standard part of his gear was a trenching tool. Scobie set pain aside and dug. A helmet appeared. Broberg's head was within it. She too had been tunneling out.

"Jean!"

"Kendrick!" She crept free and they embraced, suit to suit. "Oh, Colin."

"How are you?" rattled from him.

"Alive," she answered. "No serious harm done, I think. A lot to be said for low gravity. . . . You? Luis?" Blood was clotted in a streak beneath her nose, and a bruise on her forehead was turning purple, but she stood firmly and spoke clearly.

"I'm functional. Haven't found Luis yet. Help me look. First, though, we'd better check out our equipment."

She hugged arms around chest, as if that would do any good here. "I'm chilled," she admitted.

Scobie pointed at a telltale. "No wonder. Your fuel cell's down to its last couple of ergs. Mine isn't in a lot better shape. Let's change."

They didn't waste time removing their backpacks, but reached into each other's. Tossing the spent units to the ground, where vapors and holes immediately appeared and then froze, they plugged the fresh ones into their suits. "Turn your thermostat down," Scobie advised. "We won't find shelter soon. Physical activity will help us keep warm."

"And require faster air recycling," Broberg reminded.

"Yeah. But for the moment, at least, we can conserve the energy in the cells. Okay, next let's check for strains, potential leaks, any kind of damage or loss. Hurry. Luis is still down underneath."

Inspection was a routine made automatic by years of drill. While her fingers searched across the man's spacesuit, Broberg let her eyes wander. "The Dance Hall is gone," *Ricia murmurs.* "I think the King smashed it to prevent our escape."

"Me too. If he finds out we're alive, and seeking for Alvarlan's soul—Hey, wait! None of that!"

Danzig's voice quavered. "How're you doing?"

"We're in fair shape, seems like," Scobie replied. "My corselet took a beating but didn't split or anything. Now to find Luis . . . Jean, suppose you spiral right, I left, across the crater floor."

It took a while, for the seething which marked Garcilaso's burial was minuscule. Scobie started to dig. Broberg watched how he moved, heard how he breathed, and said, "Give me that tool. Just where are you bunged up, anyway?"

He admitted his condition and stepped back. Crusty chunks flew from her toil. She progressed fast, since whatever kind of ice lay at this point was, luckily, friable, and under Iapetan gravity she could cut a hole with almost vertical sides.

"I'll make myself useful," Scobie said, "namely, find us a way out."

When he started up the nearest slope, it shivered. All at once he was borne back in a tide that made rustly noises through his armor, while a fog of dry white motes blinded him. Painfully, he scratched himself free at the bottom and tried elsewhere. In the end he could report to Danzig: "I'm afraid there is no easy route. When the rim collapsed where we stood, it did more than produce a shock which wrecked the delicate formations throughout the crater. It let tons of stuff pour down from the surface—a particular sort of ice that, under local conditions, is like fine sand. The walls are covered by it. Most places, it lies meters deep over more stable material. We'd slide faster than we could climb, where the layer is thin; where it's thick, we'd sink."

Danzig sighed. "I guess I get to take a nice, healthy hike."

"I assume you've called for help."

"Of course. They'll have two boats here in about a hundred hours. The best they can manage. You knew that already."

"Uh-huh. And our fuel cells are good for perhaps fifty hours."

"Oh, well, not to worry about that. I'll bring extras and toss them to you, if you're stuck till the rescue party arrives. M-m-m . . . maybe I'd better rig a slingshot or something first."

"You might have a problem locating us. This isn't a true crater, it's a glorified pothole, the lip of it flush with the top of the glacier. The landmark we guided ourselves by, that fancy ridge, is gone."

"No big deal. I've got a bearing on you from the directional antenna, remember. A magnetic compass may be no use here, but I can keep myself oriented by the heavens. Saturn scarcely moves in this sky, and the sun and the stars don't move fast."

"Damn! You're right. I wasn't thinking. Got Luis on my mind, if nothing else." Scobie looked across bleakness toward Broberg. Perforce she was taking a short rest, stoop-shouldered above her excavation. His earpieces brought him the harsh sound in her windpipe.

He must maintain what strength was left him, against later need. He sipped from his water nipple, pushed a bite of food through his chow-lock, pretended an appetite. "I may as well try reconstructing what happened," he said. "Okay, Mark, you were right, we got crazy reckless. The game—Eight years was too long to play the game, in an environment that gave us too few reminders of reality. But who could have foreseen it? My God, warn *Chronos!* I happen to know that one of the Titan teams started playing an expedition to the merfolk under the Crimson Ocean—on account of the red mists—deliberately, like us, before they set off. . . ."

Scobie gulped. "Well," he slogged on, "I don't suppose we'll ever know exactly what went wrong here. But plain to see, the configuration was only metastable. On Earth, too, avalanches can be fatally easy to touch off. I'd guess at a methane layer underneath the surface. It turned a little slushy when temperatures rose after dawn, but that didn't matter in low gravity and vacuum . . . till we came along. Heat, vibration—Anyhow, the stratum slid out from under us, which triggered a general collapse. Does that guess seem reasonable?"

"Yes, to an amateur like me," Danzig said. "I admire how you can stay academic under these circumstances."

"I'm being practical," Scobie retorted. "Luis may need medical attention earlier than those boats can come for him. If so, how do we get him to ours?"

Danzig's voice turned stark. "Any ideas?"

"I'm fumbling my way toward that. Look, the bowl still has the same basic form. The whole shebang didn't cave in. That implies hard material, water ice and actual rock. In fact, I see a few remaining promontories, jutting out above the sandlike stuff. As for what *it* is—maybe an ammonia-carbon dioxide combination, maybe more exotic—that'll be for you to discover later. Right now . . . my geological instruments should help me trace where the solid masses are least deeply covered. We all carry trenching tools, of course. We can try to shovel a path clear, along a zigzag of least effort. Sure, that may well often bring more garbage slipping down on us from above, but that in turn may expedite our progress. Where the uncovered shelves are too steep or slippery to climb, we can chip footholds. Slow and tough work; and we may run into a bluff higher than we can jump, or something like that."

"I can help," Danzig proposed. "While I waited to hear from you, I inventoried our stock of spare cable, cord, equipment I can cannibalize for wire, clothes and bedding I can cut into strips, whatever might be knotted together to make a rope. We won't need much tensile strength. Well, I estimate I can get about forty meters. According to your description, that's about half the slope length of that trap you're in. If you can climb halfway up while I trek there, I can haul you the rest of the way."

"Thanks," Scobie said, "although—"

"Luis!" shrieked in his helmet. "Colin, come fast, help me, this is dreadful!"

Regardless of pain, except for a curse or two, Scobie sped to Broberg's aid.

Garcilaso was not quite unconscious. In that lay much of the horror. They heard him mumble, "—Hell, the King threw my soul into Hell, I can't find my way out, I'm lost, if only Hell weren't so cold—" They could not see his face; the inside of his helmet was crusted with frost. Deeper and longer buried than the others, badly hurt in addition, he would have died shortly after his fuel cell was exhausted. Broberg had uncovered him barely in time, if that.

Crouched in the shaft she had dug, she rolled him over onto his belly. His limbs flopped about and he babbled, "A demon attacks me, I'm blind here but I feel the wind of its wings," in a blurred monotone. She unplugged the energy unit and tossed it aloft, saying, "We should return this to the ship if we can." Not uncommonly do trivial details serve as crutches.

Above, Scobie gave the object a morbid stare. It didn't even retain the warmth to make a little vapor, like his and hers, but lay quite inert. Its case was a metal box, thirty centimeters by fifteen by six, featureless except for two plug-in prongs on one of the broad sides. Controls built into the spacesuit circuits allowed you to start and stop the chemical reactions within and regulate their rate manually; but as a rule you left that chore to your thermostat and aerostat. Now those reactions had run their course. Until it was recharged, the cell was merely a lump.

Scobie leaned over to watch Broberg, some ten meters below him. She had extracted the reserve unit from Garcilaso's gear, inserted it properly at the small of his back, and secured it by clips on the bottom of his packframe. "Let's have your contribution, Colin," she said. Scobie dropped the meter of heavy-gauge insulated wire which was standard issue on extravehicular missions, in case you needed to make a special electrical connection or a repair. She joined it by Western Union splices to the two she already had, made a loop at the end and, awkwardly reaching over her left shoulder, secured the opposite end by a hitch to the top of her packframe. The triple strand bobbled above her like an antenna.

Stooping, she gathered Garcilaso in her arms. The Iapetan weight of him and his apparatus was under ten kilos, of her and hers about the same. Theoretically she could jump straight out of the hole with her burden. In practice, her spacesuit was too hampering; constant-volume joints allowed considerable freedom of movement, but not as much as bare skin, especially when circum-Saturnian temperatures required extra insulation. Besides, if she could have reached the top, she could not have stayed. Soft ice would have crumbled beneath her fingers and she would have tumbled back down.

"Here goes," she said. "This had better be right the first time, Colin. I don't think Luis can take much jouncing."

"Kendrick, Ricia, where are you?" Garcilaso moaned. "Are you in Hell too?"

Scobie dug heels into the ground near the edge and crouched ready. The loop in the wire rose to view. His right hand grabbed hold. He threw himself backward, lest he slide forward, and felt the mass he had captured slam to a halt. Anguish exploded in his rib cage. Somehow he dragged his burden to safety before he fainted.

He came out of that in a minute. "I'm okay," he rasped at the anxious voices of Broberg and Danzig. "Only lemme rest a while."

The physicist nodded and knelt to minister to the pilot. She stripped his packframe in order that he might lie flat on it, head and legs supported by the packs themselves. That would prevent significant heat loss by convection and cut loss by conduction. Still, his fuel cell would be drained faster than if he were on his feet, and first it had a terrible energy deficit to make up.

"The ice is clearing away inside his helmet," she reported. "Merciful Mary, the blood! Seems to be from the scalp, though; it isn't running any more. His occiput must have been slammed against the vitryl. We ought to wear padded caps in these rigs. Yes, I know accidents like this haven't happened before, but—" She unclipped the flashlight at her waist, stooped, and shone it downward. "His eyes are open. The pupils—yes, a severe concussion, and likely a skull fracture, which may be hemorrhaging into the brain. I'm surprised he isn't vomiting. Did the cold prevent that? Will he start soon? He could choke on his own vomit, in there where nobody can lay a hand on him."

Scobie's pain had subsided to a bearable intensity. He rose, went over to look, whistled, and said, "I judge he's doomed unless we get him to the boat and give him proper care almighty soon. Which isn't possible."

"Oh, Luis." Tears ran silently down Broberg's cheeks.

"You think he can't last till I bring my rope and we carry him back?" Danzig asked.

" 'Fraid not," Scobie replied. "I've taken paramedical courses, and in fact I've seen a case like this before. How come you know the symptoms, Jean?"

"I read a lot," she said dully.

"They weep, the dead children weep," Garcilaso muttered.

Danzig sighed. "Okay, then. I'll fly over to you."

"*Huh?*" burst from Scobie, and from Broberg: "Have you also gone insane?"

"No, listen," Danzig said fast. "I'm no skilled pilot, but I have the same basic training in this type of craft that everybody does who might ride in one. It's expendable; the rescue vessels can bring us back. There'd be no significant gain if I landed close to the glacier—I'd still have to make that rope and so forth—and we know from what happened to the probe that there would be a real hazard. Better I make straight for your crater."

"Coming down on a surface that the jets will vaporize out from under you?" Scobie snorted. "I bet Luis would consider that a hairy stunt. You, my friend, would crack up."

"Nu?" They could almost see the shrug. "A crash from low altitude, in this gravity, shouldn't do more than rattle my teeth. The blast will cut a hole clear to bedrock. True, then surrounding ice will collapse in around the hull and trap it. You may need to dig to reach the airlock, though I suspect thermal radiation from the cabin will keep the upper parts of the structure free. Even if the craft topples and strikes sidewise—in which case, it'll sink down into a deflating cushion—even if it did that on bare rock, it shouldn't be seriously damaged. It's designed to withstand heavier impacts." Danzig hesitated. "Of course, could be this would endanger you. I'm confident I won't

THE SATURN GAME 49

fry you with the jets, assuming I descend near the middle
and you're as far offside as you can get. Maybe, though,
maybe I'd cause a . . . an ice quake that'll kill you. No
sense in losing two more lives."

"Or three, Mark," Broberg said low. "In spite of your
brave words, you could come to grief yourself."

"Oh, well, I'm an oldish man. I'm fond of living, yes,
but you guys have a whole lot more years due you. Look,
suppose the worst, suppose I don't just make a messy
landing but wreck the boat utterly. Then Luis dies, but
he would anyway. You two, however, you should have
access to the stores aboard, including those extra fuel
cells. I'm willing to run what I consider to be a small
risk of my own neck, for the sake of giving Luis a chance
at survival."

"Um-m-m," went Scobie, deep in his throat. A hand
strayed in search of his chin, while his gaze roved around
the glimmer of the bowl.

"I repeat," Danzig proceeded, "if you think this might
jeopardize you in any way, we scrub it. No heroics,
please. Luis would surely agree, better three people safe
and one dead than four stuck with a high probability
of death."

"Let me think." Scobie was mute for minutes before
he said: "No, I don't believe we'd get in too much trouble
here. As I remarked earlier, the vicinity has had its avalanche and must be in a reasonably stable configuration.
True, ice will volatilize. In the case of deposits with low
boiling points, that could happen explosively and cause
tremors. But the vapor will carry heat away so fast that
only material in your immediate area should change
state. I daresay that the finegrained stuff will get shaken
down the slopes, but it's got too low a density to do

serious harm; for the most part, it should simply act like
a brief snowstorm. The floor will make adjustments, of
course, which may be rather violent. However, we can
be above it—do you see that shelf of rock over yonder,
Jean, at jumping height? It has to be part of a buried
hill; solid. That's our place to wait. . . . Okay, Mark, it's
go as far as we're concerned. I can't be absolutely certain,
but who ever is about anything? It seems like a good bet."

"What are we overlooking?" Broberg wondered. She
glanced down to him who lay at her feet. "While we
considered all the possibilities, Luis would die. Yes, fly
if you want to, Mark, and God bless you."

But when she and Scobie had brought Garcilaso to
the ledge, she gestured from Saturn to Polaris and: "I
will sing a spell, I will cast what small magic is mine, in
aid of the Dragon Lord, that he may deliver Alvarlan's
soul from Hell," *says Ricia.*

◈ IV ◈

No reasonable person will blame any interplanetary
explorer for miscalculations about the actual environment, especially when *some* decision has to be made, in
haste and under stress. Occasional errors are inevitable.
If we knew exactly what to expect throughout the Solar
System, we would have no reason to explore it.

—Minamoto

The boat lifted. Cosmic dust smoked away from its
jets. A hundred and fifty meters aloft, thrust lessened
and it stood still on a pillar of fire.

Within the cabin was little noise, a low hiss and a
bone-deep but nearly inaudible rumble. Sweat studded

Danzig's features, clung glistening to his beard stubble, soaked his coverall and made it reek. He was about to undertake a maneuver as difficult as rendezvous, and without guidance.

Gingerly, he advanced a vernier. A side jet woke. The boat lurched toward a nosedive. Danzig's hands jerked across the console. He must adjust the forces that held his vessel on high and those that pushed it horizontally, to get a resultant that would carry him eastward at a slow, steady pace. The vectors would change instant by instant, as they do when a human walks. The control computer, linked to the sensors, handled much of the balancing act, but not the crucial part. He must tell it what he wanted it to do.

His handling was inexpert. He had realized it would be. More altitude would have given him more margin for error, but deprived him of cues that his eyes found on the terrain beneath and the horizon ahead. Besides, when he reached the glacier he would perforce fly low, to find his goal. He would be too busy for the precise celestial navigation he could have practiced afoot.

Seeking to correct his error, he overcompensated, and the boat pitched in a different direction. He punched for "hold steady" and the computer took over. Motionless again, he took a minute to catch his breath, regain his nerve, rehearse in his mind. Biting his lip, he tried afresh. This time he did not quite approach disaster. Jets aflicker, the boat staggered drunkenly over the moonscape.

The ice cliff loomed nearer and nearer. He saw its fragile loveliness and regretted that he must cut a swathe of ruin. Yet what did any natural wonder mean unless a conscious mind was there to know it? He passed the lowest slope. It vanished in billows of steam.

Onward. Beyond the boiling, right and left and ahead, the Faerie architecture crumbled. He crossed the palisade. Now he was a bare fifty meters above surface, and the clouds reached vengefully close before they disappeared into vacuum. He squinted through the port and made the scanner sweep a magnified overview across its screen, a search for his destination.

A white volcano erupted. The outburst engulfed him. Suddenly he was flying blind. Shocks belled through the hull when upflung stones hit. Frost sheathed the craft; the scanner screen went as blank as the ports. Danzig should have ordered ascent, but he was inexperienced. A human in danger has less of an instinct to jump than to run. He tried to scuttle sideways. Without exterior vision to aid him, he sent the vessel tumbling end over end. By the time he saw his mistake, less than a second, it was too late. He was out of control. The computer might have retrieved the situation after a while, but the glacier was too close. The boat crashed.

"Hello, Mark?" Scobie cried. "Mark, do you read me? Where are you, for Christ's sake?"

Silence replied. He gave Broberg a look which lingered. "Everything seemed to be in order," he said, "till we heard a shout, and a lot of racket. and nothing. He should've reached us by now. Instead, he's run into trouble. I hope it wasn't lethal."

"What can we do?" she asked redundantly. They needed talk, any talk, for Garcilaso lay beside them and his delirious voice was dwindling fast.

"If we don't get fresh fuel cells within the next forty or fifty hours, we'll be at the end of our particular trail. The boat should be someplace near. We'll have to get out of this hole under our own power, seems like. Wait here with Luis and I'll scratch around for a possible route."

Scobie started downward. Broberg crouched by the pilot.

"—alone forever in the dark—" she heard.

"No, Alvarlan." She embraced him. Most likely he could not feel that, but she could. "Alvarlan, hearken to me. This is Ricia. I hear in my mind how your spirit calls. Let me help, let me lead you back to the light."

"Have a care," advised Scobie. "We're too damn close to rehypnotizing ourselves as is."

"But I might, I just might get through to Luis and . . . comfort him . . . Alvarlan, Kendrick and I escaped. He's seeking a way home for us. I'm seeking you. Alvarlan, here is my hand, come take it."

On the crater floor, Scobie shook his head, clicked his tongue, and unlimbered his equipment. Binoculars would help him locate the most promising areas. Devices that ranged from a metal rod to a portable geosonar would give him a more exact idea of what sort of footing lay buried under what depth of unclimbable sand-ice. Admittedly the scope of such probes was very limited. He did not have time to shovel tons of material aside in order that he could mount higher and test further. He would simply have to get some preliminary results, make an educated guess at which path up the side of the bowl would prove negotiable, and trust he was right.

He shut Broberg and Garcilaso out of his consciousness as much as he was able, and commenced work.

An hour later, he was ignoring pain while clearing a strip across a layer of rock. He thought a berg of good, hard frozen water lay ahead, but wanted to make sure.

"Jean! Colin! Do you read?"

Scobie straightened and stood rigid. Dimly he heard Broberg: "If I can't do anything else, Alvarlan, let me pray for your soul's repose."

"Mark!" ripped from Scobie. "You okay? What the hell happened?"

"Yeah, I wasn't too badly knocked around," Danzig said, "and the boat's habitable, though I'm afraid it'll never fly again. How are you? Luis?"

"Sinking fast. All right, let's hear the news."

Danzig described his misfortune. "I wobbled off in an unknown direction for an unknown distance. It can't have been extremely far, since the time was short before I hit. Evidently I plowed into a large, um, snowbank, which softened the impact but blocked radio transmission. It's evaporated from the cabin area now. I see tumbled whiteness around, and formations in the offing. . . . I'm not sure what damage the jacks and the stern jets suffered. The boat's on its side at about a forty-five degree angle, presumably with rock beneath. But the after part is still buried in less whiffable stuff—water and CO_2 ices, I think—that's reached temperature equilibrium. The jets must be clogged with it. If I tried to blast, I'd destroy the whole works."

Scobie nodded. "You would, for sure."

Danzig's voice broke. "Oh, God, Colin! What have I done? I wanted to help Luis, but I may have killed you and Jean."

Scobie's lips tightened. "Let's not start crying before we're hurt. True, this has been quite a run of bad luck. But neither you nor I nor anybody could have known that you'd touch off a bomb underneath yourself."

"What was it? Have you any notion? Nothing of the sort ever occurred at rendezvous with a comet. And you believe the glacier is a wrecked comet, don't you?"

"Uh-huh, except that conditions have obviously modified it. The impact produced heat, shock, turbulence. Molecules got scrambled. Plasmas must have been momentarily present. Mixtures, compounds, clathrates, alloys—stuff formed that never existed in free space. We can learn a lot of chemistry here."

"That's why I came along. . . . Well, then, I crossed a deposit of some substance or substances that the jets caused to sublime with tremendous force. A certain kind of vapor refroze when it encountered the hull. I had to defrost the ports from inside after the snow had cooked off them."

"Where are you in relation to us?"

"I told you, I don't know. And I'm not sure I can determine it. The crash crumpled the direction-finding antenna. Let me go outside for a better look."

"Do that," Scobie said. "I'll keep busy meanwhile."

He did, until a ghastly rattling noise and Broberg's wail brought him at full speed back to the rock.

Scobie switched off Garcilaso's fuel cell. "This may make the difference that carries us through," he said low. "Think of it as a gift. Thanks, Luis."

Broberg let go of the pilot and rose from her knees. She straightened the limbs that had threshed about in the death struggle and crossed his hands on his breast. There was nothing she could do about the fallen jaw or the eyes that glared at heaven. Taking him out of his suit, here, would have worsened his appearance. Nor could she wipe tears off her own face. She could merely try to stop their flow. "Goodbye, Luis," she whispered.

Turning to Scobie, she asked, "Can you give me a new job? Please."

"Come along," he directed. "I'll explain what I have in mind about making our way to the surface."

They were midway across the bowl when Danzig called. He had not let his comrade's dying slow his efforts, nor said much while it happened. Once, most softly, he had offered Kaddish.

"No luck," he reported like a machine. "I've traversed the largest circle I could while keeping the boat in sight, and found only weird, frozen shapes. I can't be a huge distance from you, or I'd see an identifiably different sky, on this miserable little ball. You're probably within a twenty or thirty kilometer radius of me. But that covers a bunch of territory."

"Right," Scobie said. "Chances are you can't find us in the time we've got. Return to the boat."

"Hey, wait," Danzig protested. "I can spiral onward, marking my trail. I might come across you."

"It'll be more useful if you return," Scobie told him. "Assuming we climb out, we should be able to hike to you, but we'll need a beacon. What occurs to me is the ice itself. A small energy release, if it's concentrated, should release a large plume of methane or something similarly volatile. The gas will cool as it expands, recondense around dust particles that have been carried along—it'll steam—and the cloud ought to get high enough, before it evaporates again, to be visible from here."

"Gotcha!" A tinge of excitement livened Danzig's words. "I'll go straight to it. Make tests, find a spot where I can get the showiest result, and . . . how about I rig a thermite bomb? No, that might be too hot. Well, I'll develop a gadget."

"Keep us posted."

"But I, I don't think we'll care to chatter idly," Broberg ventured.

"No, we'll be working our tails off, you and I," Scobie agreed.

"Uh, wait," said Danzig. "What if you find you can't get clear to the top? You implied that's a distinct possibility."

"Well, then it'll be time for more radical procedures, whatever they turn out to be," Scobie responded. "Frankly, at this moment my head is too full of . . . of Luis, and of choosing an optimum escape route, for much thought about anything else."

"M-m, yeah, I guess we've got an ample supply of trouble without borrowing more. Tell you what, though. After my beacon's ready to fire off, I'll make that rope we talked of. You might find you prefer having it to clean clothes and sheets when you arrive." Danzig was silent for seconds before he ended: "God damn it, you *will* arrive."

Scobie chose a point on the north side for his and Broberg's attempt. Two rock shelves jutted forth, near the floor and several meters higher, indicating that stone reached at least that far. Beyond, in a staggered pattern, were similar outcrops of hard ices. Between them, and onward from the uppermost, which was scarcely more than halfway to the rim, was nothing but the featureless, footingless slope of powder crystals. Its angle of repose gave a steepness that made the surface doubly treacherous. The question, unanswerable save by experience, was how deeply it covered layers on which humans could climb, and whether such layers extended the entire distance aloft.

At the spot, Scobie signalled a halt. "Take it easy, Jean," he said. "I'll go ahead and commence digging."

"Why don't we together? I have my own tool, you know."

"Because I can't tell how so large a bank of that pseudo-quicksand will behave. It might react to the disturbance by a gigantic slide."

She bridled. Her haggard countenance registered mutiny. "Why not me first, then? Do you suppose I always wait passive for Kendrick to save me?"

"As a matter of fact," he rapped, "I'll bargain because my rib is giving me billy hell, which is eating away what strength I've got left. If we run into trouble, you can better come to my help than I to yours."

Broberg bent her neck. "Oh. I'm sorry. I must be in a fairly bad state myself, if I let false pride interfere with our business." Her look went toward Saturn, around which *Chronos* orbited, bearing her husband and children.

"You're forgiven." Scobie bunched his legs and sprang the five meters to the lower ledge. The next one was slightly too far for such a jump, when he had no room for a running start.

Stooping, he scraped his trenching tool against the bottom of the declivity that sparkled before him, and shoveled. Grains poured from above, a billionfold, to cover what he cleared. He worked like a robot possessed. Each spadeful was nearly weightless, but the number of spadefuls was nearly endless. He did not bring the entire bowlside down on himself as he had half feared, half hoped. (If that didn't kill him, it would save a lot of toil.) A dry torrent went right and left over his ankles. Yet at last somewhat more of the underlying rock began to show.

From beneath, Broberg listened to him breathe. It sounded rough, often broken by a gasp or a curse. In his spacesuit, in the raw, wan sunshine, he resembled a knight who, in despite of wounds, did battle against a monster.

"All right," he called at last. "I think I've learned what to expect and how we should operate. It'll take the two of us."

"Yes . . . oh, yes, my Kendrick."

The hours passed. Ever so slowly, the sun climbed and the stars wheeled and Saturn waned.

Most places, the humans labored side by side. They did not require more than the narrowest of lanes—but unless they cut it wide to begin with, the banks to right and left would promptly slip down and bury it. Sometimes the conformation underneath allowed a single person at a time to work. Then the other could rest. Soon it was Scobie who must oftenest take advantage of that. Sometimes they both stopped briefly, for food and drink and reclining on their packs.

Rock yielded to water ice. Where this rose very sharply, the couple knew it, because the sand-ice that they undercut would come down in a mass. After the first such incident, when they were nearly swept away, Scobie always drove his geologist's hammer into each new stratum. At any sign of danger, he would seize its handle and Broberg would cast an arm around his waist. Their other hands clutched their trenching tools. Anchored, but forced to strain every muscle, they would stand while the flood poured around them, knee-high, once even chest-high, seeking to bury them irretrievably deep in its quasi-fluid substance. Afterward they would confront a bare stretch. It was generally too steep to climb unaided, and they chipped footholds.

Weariness was another tide to which they dared not yield. At best, their progress was dismayingly slow. They needed little heat input to keep warm, except when they took a rest, but their lungs put a furious demand on air recyclers. Garcilaso's fuel cell, which they had brought along, could give a single person extra hours of life, though, depleted as it was after coping with his hypothermia, the time would be insufficient for rescue by the teams from *Chronos*. Unspoken was the idea of taking turns with it. That would put them in wretched shape, chilled and stifling, but at least they would leave the universe together.

Thus it was hardly a surprise that their minds fled from pain, soreness, exhaustion, stench, despair. Without that respite, they could not have gone on as long as they did.

At ease for a few minutes, their backs against a blue-shimmering parapet which they must scale, they gazed across the bowl, where Garcilaso's suited body gleamed like a remote pyre, and up the curve opposite to Saturn. The planet shone lambent amber, softly banded, the rings a coronet which a shadow band across their arc seemed to make all the brighter. That radiance overcame sight of most nearby stars, but elsewhere they arrayed themselves multitudinous, in splendor, around the silver road which the galaxy clove between them.

"How right a tomb for Alvarlan," *Ricia says in a dreamer's murmur.*

"Has he died, then?" *Kendrick asks.*

"You do not know?"

"I have been too busied. After we won free of the ruins and I left you to recover while I went scouting, I encountered a troop of warriors. I escaped, but must needs return to you by devious, hidden ways." *Kendrick strokes Ricia's sunny hair.* "Besides, dearest dear, it has ever been you, not I, who had the gift of hearing spirits."

"Brave darling. . . . Yes, it is a glory to me that I was able to call his soul out of Hell. It sought his body, but that was old and frail and could not survive the knowledge it now had. Yet Alvarlan passed peacefully, and before he did, for his last magic he made himself a tomb from whose ceiling starlight will eternally shine."

"May he sleep well. But for us there is no sleep. Not yet. We have far to travel."

"Aye. But already we have left the wreckage behind. Look! Everywhere around in this meadow, anemones peep through the grass. A lark sings above."

"These lands are not always calm. We may well have more adventures ahead of us. But we shall meet them with high hearts."

Kendrick and Ricia rise to continue their journey.

Cramped on a meager ledge, Scobie and Broberg shoveled for an hour without broadening it much. The sand-ice slid from above as fast as they could cast to down. "We'd better quit this as a bad job," the man finally decided. "The best we've done is flatten the slope ahead of us a tiny bit. No telling how far inward the shelf goes before there's a solid layer on top. Maybe there isn't any."

"What shall we do instead?" Broberg asked in the same worn tone.

He jerked a thumb. "Scramble back to the level beneath and try a different direction. But first we absolutely require a break."

They spread kerofoam pads and sat. After a while during which they merely stared, stunned by fatigue, Broberg spoke.

"I go to the brook," *Ricia relates.* "It chimes under arches of green boughs. Light falls between them to sparkle on it. I kneel and drink. The water is cold, pure, sweet. When I raise my eyes, I see the figure of a young woman, naked, her tresses the color of leaves. A wood nymph. She smiles."

"Yes, I see her too," *Kendrick joins in.* "I approach carefully, not to frighten her off. She asks our names and errands. We explain that we are lost. She tells us how to find an oracle which may give us counsel."

They depart to find it.

Flesh could no longer stave off sleep. "Give us a yell in an hour, will you, Mark?" Scobie requested.

"Sure," Danzig said, "but will that be enough?"

"It's the most we can afford, after the setbacks we've had. We've come less than a third of the way."

"If I haven't talked to you," Danzig said slowly, "it's not because I've been hard at work, though I have been. It's that I figured you two were having a plenty bad time without me nagging you. However—Do you think it's wise to fantasize the way you have been?"

A flush crept across Broberg's cheeks and down toward her bosom. "You listened, Mark?"

"Well, yes, of course. You might have an urgent word for me at any minute—"

"Why? What could you do? A game is a personal affair."

"Uh, yes, yes—"

Ricia and Kendrick have made love whenever they can. The accounts were never explicit, but the words were often passionate.

"We'll keep you tuned in when we need you, like for an alarm clock," Broberg clipped. "Otherwise we'll cut the circuit."

"But—Look, I never meant to—"

"I know," Scobie sighed. "You're a nice guy and I daresay we're overreacting. Still, that's the way it's got to be. Call us when I told you."

Deep within the grotto, the Pythoness sways on her throne, in the ebb and flow of her oracular dream. As nearly as Ricia and Kendrick can understand what she chants, she tells them to fare westward on the Stag Path until they met a one-eyed graybeard who will give them further guidance; but they must be wary in his presence, for he is easily angered. They make obeisance and depart. On their way out, they pass the offering they brought. Since they have little with them other than garments and his weapons, the Princess gave the shrine her golden hair. The knight insists that, close-cropped, she remains beautiful.

"Hey, whoops, we've cleared us an easy twenty meters," Scobie said, albeit in a voice which weariness had hammered flat. *At first the journey, through the land of Narce, is a delight.*

His oath afterward had no more life in it. "Another blind alley, seems like." *The old man in the blue cloak and wide-brimmed hat was indeed wrathful when Ricia refused him her favors and Kendrick's spear struck his own aside. Cunningly, he has pretended to make peace and told them what road they should take next. But at the end of it are trolls. The wayfarers elude them and double back.*

❁ ❁ ❁

"My brain's stumbling around in a swamp, a fog." Scobie groaned. "My busted rib isn't exactly helping, either. If I don't get another nap I'll keep on making misjudgments till we run out of time."

"By all means, Colin," Broberg said. "I'll stand watch and rouse you in an hour."

"What?" he asked in dim surprise. "Why not join me and have Mark call us as he did before?"

She grimaced. "No need to bother him. I'm tired, yes, but not sleepy."

He lacked wit or strength to argue. "Okay," he said, stretched his insulating pad on the ice, and toppled out of awareness.

Broberg settled herself next to him. They were halfway to the heights, but they had been struggling, with occasional breaks, for worse than twenty hours, and progress grew more hard and tricky even as they themselves grew more weak and stupefied. If ever they reached the top and spied Danzig's signal, they would have something like a couple of hours' stiff travel to shelter.

Saturn, sun, stars shone through vitryl. Broberg smiled down at Scobie's face. He was no Greek god, and sweat, grime, unshavenness, the manifold marks of exhaustion were upon him, but—For that matter, she was scarcely an image of glamour herself.

Princess Ricia sits by her knight, where he slumbers in the dwarf's cottage, and strums a harp the dwarf lent her before he went off to his mine, and sings a lullaby to sweeten the dreams of Kendrick. When it is done, she passes her lips lightly across his, and drifts into the same gentle sleep.

❀ ❀ ❀

Scobie woke a piece at a time. "Ricia, beloved," *Kendrick whispers, and feels after her. He will summon her up with kisses—*

He scrambled to his feet. "Judas priest!" She lay unmoving. He heard her breath in his earplugs, before the roaring of his pulse drowned it. The sun glared farther aloft, he could see it had moved, and Saturn's crescent had thinned more, forming sharp horns at its ends. He forced his eyes toward the watch on his left wrist.

"Ten hours," he choked.

He knelt and shook his companion. "Come, for Christ's sake!" Her lashes fluttered. When she saw the horror on his visage, drowsiness fled from her.

"Oh, no," she said. "Please, no."

Scobie climbed stiffly erect and flicked his main radio switch. "Mark, do you receive?"

"Colin!" Danzig chattered. "Thank God! I was going out of my head from worry."

"You're not off that hook, my friend. We just finished a ten hour snooze."

"What? How far did you get first?"

"To about forty meters' elevation. The going looks tougher ahead than in back. I'm afraid we won't make it."

"Don't *say* that, Colin," Danzig begged.

"My fault," Broberg declared. She stood rigid, fists doubled, features a mask. Her tone was steady. "He was worn out, had to have a nap. I offered to wake him, but fell asleep myself."

"Not your fault, Jean," Scobie began.

She interrupted: "Yes. Mine. Perhaps I can make it good. Take my fuel cell. I'll still have deprived you of my help, of course, but you might survive and reach the boat anyway."

He seized her hands. They did not unclench. "If you imagine, I could do that—"

"If you don't, we're both finished," she said unbendingly. "I'd rather go out with a clear conscience."

"And what about my conscience?" he shouted. Checking himself, he wet his lips and said fast: "Besides, you're not to blame. Sleep slugged you. If I'd been thinking, I'd have realized it was bound to do so, and contacted Mark. The fact that you didn't either shows how far gone you were yourself. And . . . you've got Tom and the kids waiting for you. Take my cell." He paused. "And my blessing."

"Shall Ricia forsake her true knight?"

"Wait, hold on, listen," Danzig called. "Look, this is terrible, but—oh, hell, excuse me, but I've got to remind you that dramatics only clutter the action. From what descriptions you've sent, I don't see how either of you can possibly proceed solo. Together, you might yet. At least you're rested—sore in the muscles, no doubt, but clearer in the head. The climb before you may prove easier than you think. Try!"

Scobie and Broberg regarded each other for a whole minute. A thawing went through her, and warmed him. Finally they smiled and embraced. "Yeah, right," he growled. "We're off. But first a bite to eat. I'm plain, old-fashioned hungry. Aren't you?" she nodded.

"That's the spirit," Danzig encouraged them. "Uh, may I make another suggestion? I am just a spectator, which is pretty hellish but does give me an overall view. Drop that game of yours."

Scobie and Broberg tautened.

"It's the real culprit," Danzig pleaded. "Weariness alone wouldn't have clouded your judgment. You'd never have cut me off, and—But weariness and shock and grief did lower your defenses to the point where the damned game took you over. You weren't yourselves when you fell asleep. You were those dream-world characters. They had no reason not to cork off!"

Broberg shook her head violently. "Mark," said Scobie, "you are correct about being a spectator. That means there are some things you don't understand. Why subject you to the torture of listening in, hour after hour? We'll call you back from time to time, naturally. Take care." He broke the circuit.

"He's wrong," Broberg insisted.

Scobie shrugged. "Right or wrong, what difference? We won't pass out again in the time we have left. The game didn't handicap us as we traveled. In fact, it helped, by making the situation feel less gruesome."

"Aye. Let us break our fast and set forth anew on our pilgrimage."

The struggle grew stiffer. "Belike the White Witch has cast a spell on this road," *says Ricia*.

"She shall not daunt us," *vows Kendrick*.

"No, never while we fare side by side, you and I, noblest of men."

A slide overcame them and swept them back a dozen meters. They lodged against a crag. After the flow had passed by, they lifted their bruised bodies and limped in search of a different approach. The place where the geologist's hammer remained was no longer accessible.

"What shattered the bridge?" *asks Ricia*.

"A giant," *answers Kendrick.* "I saw him as I fell into the river. He lunged at me, and we fought in the shallows until he fled. He bore away my sword in his thigh."

"You have your spear that Wayland forged," *Ricia says,* "and always you have my heart."

They stopped on the last small outcrop they uncovered. It proved to be not a shelf but a pinnacle of water ice. Around it glittered sand-ice, again quiescent. Ahead was a slope thirty meters in length, and then the rim, and stars. The distance might as well have been thirty light-years. Whoever tried to cross would immediately sink to an unknown depth.

There was no point in crawling back down the bared side of the pinnacle. Broberg had clung to it for an hour while she chipped niches to climb by with her knife. Scobie's condition had not allowed him to help. If they sought to return, they could easily slip, fall, and be engulfed. If they avoided that, they would never find a new path. Less than two hours' worth of energy abode in their fuel cells. Attempting to push onward while swapping Garcilaso's back and forth would be an exercise in futility.

They settled themselves, legs dangling over the abyss, and held hands and looked at Saturn and at one another.

"I do not think the orcs can burst the iron door of this tower," *Kendrick says,* "but they will besiege us until we starve to death."

"You never yielded up your hope ere now, my knight," *replies Ricia, and kisses his temple.* "Shall we search about? These walls are unutterably ancient. Who knows what relics of wizardry lie forgotten within? A pair of phoenix-feather cloaks, that will bear us laughing through the sky to our home—?"

"I fear not, my darling. Our weird is upon us." *Kendrick touches the spear that leans agleam against the battlement.* "Sad and gray will the world be without you. We can but meet our doom bravely."

"Happily, since we are together." *Ricia's gamin(e) smile breaks forth.* "I did notice that a certain room holds a bed. Shall we try it?"

Kendrick frowns. "Rather should we seek to set our minds and souls in order."

She tugs his elbow. "Later, yes. Besides—who knows?—when we dust off the blanket, we may find it is a Tarnkappe that will take us invisible through the enemy."

"You dream."

Fear stirs behind her eyes. "What if I do?" *Her words tremble.* "I can dream us free if you will help."

Scobie's fist smote the ice. "No!" he croaked. "I'll die in the world that is."

Ricia shrinks from him. He sees terror invade her. "You, you rave, beloved," *she stammers.*

He twisted about and caught her by the arms. "Don't you want to remember Tom and your boys?"

"Who—?"

Kendrick slumps. "I don't know. I have forgotten too."

She leans against him, there on the windy height. A hawk circles above. "The residuum of an evil enchantment, surely. Oh, my heart, my life, cast it from you! Help me find the means to save us." *Yet her entreaty is uneven, and through it speaks dread.*

Kendrick straightens. He lays hand on Wayland's spear, and it is though strength flows thence, into him. "A spell in truth," *he says. His tone gathers force.* "I will not abide in its darkness, nor suffer it to blind and deafen

you, my lady in domnei." *His gaze takes hold of hers,
which cannot break away.* "There is but a single road to
our freedom. It goes through the gates of death."

She waits, mute and shuddering.

"Whatever we do, we must die, Ricia. Let us fare
hence as our own folk."

"I—no—I won't—I will—".

"You see before you the means of your deliverance.
It is sharp, I am strong, you will feel no pain."

She bares her bosom. "Then quickly, Kendrick, before
I am lost!"

He drives the weapon home. "I love you," he says. *She
sinks at his feet.* "I follow you, my darling," *he says,
withdraws the steel, braces shaft against stone, lunges
forward, falls beside her.* "Now we are free."

"That was . . . a nightmare." Broberg sounded barely
awake.

Scobie's voice shook. "Necessary, I think, for both of
us." He gazed straight before him, letting Saturn fill his
eyes with dazzle. "Else we'd have stayed . . . insane?
Maybe not, by definition. But we'd not have been in
reality either."

"It would have been easier," she mumbled. "We'd
never have known we were dying."

"Would you have preferred that?"

Broberg shivered. The slackness in her countenance
gave place to the same tension that was in his. "Oh, no,"
she said, quite softly but in the manner of full consciousness. "No, you were right, of course. Thank you for
your courage."

"You've always had as much guts as anybody, Jean.
You just have more imagination than me." Scobie's hand

chopped empty space, a gesture of dismissal. "Okay, we should call poor Mark and let him know. But first—" His words lost the cadence he had laid on them. "First—"

Her glove clasped his. "What, Colin?"

"Let's decide about that third unit—Luis'," he said with difficulty, still confronting the great ringed planet. "Your decision, actually, though we can discuss the matter if you want. I will not hog it for the sake of a few more hours. Nor will I share it; that would be a nasty way for us both to go out. However, I suggest you use it."

"To sit beside your frozen corpse?" she replied. "No. I wouldn't even feel the warmth, not in my bones—"

She turned toward him so fast that she nearly fell off the pinnacle. He caught her. "*Warmth!*" she screamed, shrill as the cry of a hawk on the wing. "Colin, we'll take our bones home!"

"In point of fact," said Danzig, "I've climbed onto the hull. That's high enough for me to see over those ridges and needles. I've got a view of the entire horizon."

"Good," grunted Scobie. "Be prepared to survey a complete circle quick. This depends on a lot of factors we can't predict. The beacon will certainly not be anything like as big as what you had arranged. It may be thin and short-lived. And, of course, it may rise too low for sighting at your distance." He cleared his throat. "In that case, we two have bought the farm. But we'll have made a hell of a try, which feels great by itself."

He hefted the fuel cell, Garcilaso's gift. A piece of heavy wire, insulation stripped off, joined the prongs. Without a regulator, the unit poured its maximum power through the short circuit. Already the strand glowed.

"Are you sure you don't want me to do it, Colin?" Broberg asked. "Your rib—"

He made a lopsided grin. "I'm nonetheless better designed by nature for throwing things," he said. "Allow me that much male arrogance. The bright idea was yours."

"It should have been obvious from the first," she said. "I think it would have been, if we weren't bewildered in our dream."

"M-m, often the simple answers are the hardest to find. Besides, we had to get this far or it wouldn't have worked, and the game helped mightily. . . . Are you set, Mark? Heave ho!"

Scobie cast the cell as if it were a baseball, hard and far through the Iapetan gravity field. Spinning, its incandescent wire wove a sorcerous web across vision. It landed somewhere beyond the rim, on the glacier's back.

Frozen gases vaporized, whirled aloft, briefly recondensed before they were lost. A geyser stood white against the stars.

"I see you! Danzig yelped. "I see your beacon, I've got my bearing, I'll be on my way! With rope and extra energy units and everything!"

Scobie sagged to the ground and clutched at his left side. Broberg knelt and held him, as if either of them could lay hand on his pain. No large matter. He would not hurt much longer.

"How high would you guess the plume goes?" Danzig inquired, calmer.

"About a hundred meters," Broberg replied after study.

"Uh, damn, these gloves do make it awkward punching the calculator. . . . Well, to judge by what I observe of it, I'm between ten and fifteen klicks off. Give me an hour or a tadge more to get there and find your exact location. Okay?"

Broberg checked gauges. "Yes, by a hair. We'll turn our thermostats down and sit very quiet to reduce oxygen demand. We'll get cold, but we'll survive."

"I may be quicker," Danzig said. "That was a worst case estimate. All right, I'm off. No more conversation till we meet. I won't take any foolish chances, but I will need my wind for making speed."

Faintly, those who waited heard him breathe, heard his hastening footfalls. The geyser died.

They sat, arms around waists, and regarded the glory which encompassed them. After a silence, the man said: "Well, I suppose this means the end of the game. For everybody."

"It must certainly be brought under strict control," the woman answered. "I wonder, though, if they will abandon it altogether—out here."

"If they must, they can."

"Yes. We did, you and I, didn't we?"

They turned face to face, beneath that star-beswarmed, Saturn-ruled sky. Nothing tempered the sunlight that revealed them to each other, she a middle-aged wife, he a man ordinary except for his aloneness. They would never play again. They could not.

A puzzled compassion was in her smile. "Dear Friend—" she began.

His uplifted palm warded her from further speech. "Best we don't talk unless it's essential," he said. "That'll save a little oxygen, and we can stay a little warmer. Shall we try to sleep?"

Her eyes widened and darkened. "I dare not," she confessed. "Not till enough time has gone past. Now, I might dream."

INTRODUCTION

❂ WINGS OF VICTORY ❂

To those who read, good flight.

It is Hloch of the Stormgate Choth who writes, on the peak of Mount Anrovil in the Weathermother. His Wyvan, Tariat son of Lythran and Blawsa, has asked this. Weak though his grip upon the matter be, bloodpride requires he undertake the task.

Judge, O people. The father of Hloch was Ferannian and the mother was Rennhi. They held the country around Spearhead Lake. He was an engineer who was often in Gray, Centauri, and other towns, dealing with humans. They in their turn came often thither, for travel routes crisscrossed above and there was, too, a copper mine not far off. Hloch's parents were guest-free and would house whoever pleased them for days in line, giving these leave to roam and hunt. Moreover, as you well know, because of its nearness to populous Gray, our

choth receives more humans into membership than
most. Hence we younglings grew up friendly with many
of this race and familiar with no few of the winds that
blow on their souls.

Rennhi was a quester into the centuries, remembered
for her scholarship and for the flame she kindled in those
whom she saw fit to teach. High above all, she is remembered for writing *The Sky Book of Stormgate*. In this, as
you well know, she traced and described the whole history of our choth. Of the ancestors upon Ythri; of the
founders here upon Avalon; of the descendants and their
doings unto her own years; of how past and present and
future have forever been intermingled and, in living
minds, ever begetting each other—of this does her work
pursue the truth, and will as long as thought flies over
our world.

God stooped upon her before she could begin the next
chronicle. Already she had gathered in much that was
needful, aided in small compass by her son Hloch. Then
came the Terran War, and when it had passed by, ruined
landscapes lay underneath skies gone strange. We are
still raising our lives anew from the wreckage left by that
hurricane. Hloch, who had served in space, afterward
found himself upon Imperial planets, member of a merchant crew, as trade was reborn. Thus maychance he
gained some further sight across the human species.

So did the Wyvan Tariat think of late, when Hloch
had wearied of the void and returned to the winds. His
word: "We have need to grasp the realness of those folk,
both those who dwell among us and those who are of
the Empire. For this, your mother knew, it is best to fly
their ways and see through their eyes—ancestral still
more than incarnate, that we may sense what is rising

ahead of us in time. Hloch, write the book she did not
live to write."

Therefore, behold these annals, from the Discovery
and on through the World-Taking. They are garnered
from different trees, and few of them will seem at once
to grow toward the same sun. Yet they do, they all do.
This is the tale, told afresh, of how Avalon came to settlement and thus our choth to being. This is the tale as
told, not by Rennhi and those on whom she drew for the
Sky Book, but by Terrans, who walk the earth. Hloch
will seek to explain what is alien: though only by swinging
your mind into that same alienness may you hope to
seize the knowledge behind.

Then read.

—Hloch of the Stormgate Choth
The Earth Book of Stormgate

WINGS OF VICTORY

Our part in the Grand Survey had taken us out beyond the great suns Alpha and Beta Crucis. From Earth we would have been in the constellation Lupus. But Earth was 278 light-years remote, Sol itself long dwindled to invisibility, and stars drew strange pictures across the dark.

After three years we were weary and had suffered losses. Oh, the wonder wasn't gone. How could it ever go—from world after world after world? But we had seen so many, and of those we had walked on, some were beautiful and some were terrible and most were both (even as Earth is) and none were alike and all were mysterious. They blurred together in our minds.

It was still a heart-speeding thing to find another sentient race, actually more than to find another planet colonizable by man. Now Ali Hamid had perished of a poisonous bite a year back, and Manuel Gonsalves had not yet recovered from the skull fracture inflicted by the club of an excited being at our last stop. This made Vaughn Webner our chief xenologist, from whom was to issue trouble.

Not that he, or any of us, wanted it. You learn to gang warily, in a universe not especially designed for you, or you die; there is no third choice. We approached this latest star because every G-type dwarf beckoned us. But we did not establish orbit around its most terrestroid attendant until neutrino analysis had verified that nobody in the system had developed atomic energy. And we exhausted every potentiality of our instruments before we sent down our first robot probe.

The sun was a G9, golden in hue, luminosity half of Sol's. The world which interested us was close enough in to get about the same irradiation as Earth. It was smaller, surface gravity 0.75, with a thinner and drier atmosphere. However, that air was perfectly breathable by humans, and bodies of water existed which could be called modest oceans. The globe was very lovely where it turned against star-crowded night, blue, tawny, rusty-brown, white-clouded. Two little moons skipped in escort.

Biological samples proved that its life was chemically similar to ours. None of the microorganisms we cultured posed any threat that normal precautions and medications could not handle. Pictures taken at low altitude and on the ground showed woods, lakes, wide plains rolling toward mountains. We were afire to set foot there.

But the natives—

You must remember how new the hyperdrive is, and how immense the cosmos. The organizers of the Grand Survey were too wise to believe that the few neighbor systems we'd learned something about gave knowledge adequate for devising doctrine. Our service had one law, which was its proud motto: "We come as friends." Otherwise each crew was free to work out its own procedures. After five years the survivors would meet and compare experiences.

For us aboard the *Olga,* Captain Gray had decided that, whenever possible, sophonts should not be disturbed by preliminary sightings of our machines. We would try to set the probes in uninhabited regions. When we ourselves landed, we would come openly. After all, the shape of a body counts for much less than the shape of the mind within. Thus went our belief.

Naturally, we took in every datum we could from orbit and upper-atmospheric overflights. While not extremely informative under such conditions, our pictures did reveal a few small towns on two continents—clusters of buildings, at least, lacking defensive walls or regular streets—hard by primitive mines. They seemed insignificant against immense and almost unpopulated landscapes. We guessed we could identify a variety of cultures, from Stone Age through Iron. Yet invariably, aside from those petty communities, settlements consisted of one or a few houses standing alone. We found none less than ten kilometers apart; most were more isolated.

"Carnivores, I expect," Webner said. "The primitive economies are hunting-fishing-gathering, the advanced economies pastoral. Large areas which look cultivated are probably just to provide fodder; they don't have the layout of proper farms." He tugged his chin. "I confess to being puzzled as to how the civilized—well, let's say the 'metallurgic' people, at this stage—how they manage it. You need trade, communication, quick exchange of ideas, for that level of technology. And if I read the pictures aright, roads are virtually nonexistent, a few dirt tracks between towns and mines, or to the occasional dock for barges or ships—Confound it, water transportation is insufficient."

"Pack animals, maybe?" I suggested.

"Too slow," he said. "You don't get progressive cultures when months must pass before the few individuals capable of originality can hear from each other. The chances are they never will."

For a moment the pedantry dropped from his manner. "Well," he said, "we'll see," which is the grandest sentence that any language can own.

We always made initial contact with three, the minimum who could do the job, lest we lose them. This time they were Webner, xenologist; Aram Turekian, pilot; and Yukiko Sachansky, gunner. It was Gray's idea to give women that last assignment. He felt they were better than men at watching and waiting, less likely to open fire in doubtful situations.

The site chosen was in the metallurgic domain, though not a town. Why complicate matters unnecessarily? It was on a rugged upland, thick forest for many kilometers around. Northward the mountainside rose steeply until, above timberline, its crags were crowned by a glacier. Southward it toppled to a great plateau, open country where herds grazed on a reddish analogue of grass or shrubs. Maybe they were domesticated, maybe not. In either case, probably the dwellers did a lot of hunting.

"Would that account for their being so scattered?" Yukiko wondered. "A big range needed to support each individual?"

"Then they must have a strong territoriality," Webner said. "Stand sharp by the guns."

We were not forbidden to defend ourselves from attack, whether or not blunders of ours had provoked it. Nevertheless the girl winced. Turekian glanced over his shoulder and saw. That, and Webner's tone, made him flush. "Blow down, Vaughn," he growled.

Webner's long, gaunt frame stiffened in his seat. Light gleamed off the scalp under his thin hair as he thrust his head toward the pilot. "What did you say?"

"Stay in your own shop and run it, if you can."

"Mind your manners. This may be my first time in charge, but I *am*—"

"On the ground. We're aloft yet."

"Please." Yukiko reached from her turret and laid a hand on either man's shoulder. "Please don't quarrel . . . when we're about to meet a whole new history."

They couldn't refuse her wish. Tool-burdened coverall or no, she remained in her Eurasian petiteness the most desired woman aboard the *Olga*; and still the rest of the girls liked her. Gonsalves' word for her was *simpático*.

The men only quieted on the surface. They were an ill-assorted pair, not enemies—you don't sign on a person who'll allow himself hatred—but unfriends. Webner was the academic type, professor of Xenology at the University of Oceania. In youth he'd done excellent field work, especially in the trade-route cultures of Cynthia, and he'd been satisfactory under his superiors. At heart, though, he was a theorist, whom middle age had made dogmatic.

Turekian was the opposite: young, burly, black-bearded, boisterous and roisterous, born in a sealtent on

Mars to a life of banging around the available universe. If half his brags were true, he was mankind's boldest adventurer, toughest fighter, and mightiest lover; but I'd found to my profit that he wasn't the poker player he claimed. Withal he was able, affable, helpful, popular—which may have kindled envy in poor self-chilled Webner.

"Okay, sure," Turekian laughed. "For you, Yu." He tossed a kiss in her direction.

Webner unbent less easily. "What did you mean by running my own shop if I can?" he demanded.

"Nothing, nothing," the girl almost begged.

"Ah, a bit more than nothing," Turekian said. "A tiny bit. I just wish you were less convinced your science has the last word on all the possibilities. Things I've seen—"

"I've heard your song before," Webner scoffed. "In a jungle on some exotic world you met animals with wheels."

"Never said that. Hm-m-m . . . make a good yarn, wouldn't it?"

"No. Because it's an absurdity. Simply ask yourself how nourishment would pass from the axle bone to the cells of the disc. In like manner—"

"Yeh, yeh. Quiet, now, please. I've got to conn us down."

The target waxed fast in the bow screen. A booming of air came faint through the hull plates and vibration shivered flesh. Turekian hated dawdling. Besides, a slow descent might give the autochthons time to become hysterical, with perhaps tragic consequences.

Peering, the humans saw a house on the rim of a canyon at whose bottom a river rushed gray-green. The structure was stone, massive and tile-roofed. Three more buildings joined to define a flagged courtyard. Those were of timber, long and low, topped by blossoming sod. A corral outside the quadrangle held four-footed beasts, and nearby stood a row of what Turekian, pointing, called overgrown birdhouses. A meadow surrounded the ensemble. Elsewhere the woods crowded close.

There was abundant bird or, rather, ornithoid life, flocks strewn across the sky. A pair of especially large creatures hovered above the steading. They veered as the boat descended.

Abruptly, wings exploded from the house. Out of its windows flyers came, a score or better, all sizes from tiny ones which clung to adult backs, up to those which dwarfed the huge extinct condors of Earth. In a gleam of bronze feathers, a storm of wingbeats which pounded through the hull, they rose, and fled, and were lost among the treetops.

The humans landed in a place gone empty.

Hands near sidearms, Webner and Turekian trod forth, looked about, let the planet enter them.

You always undergo that shock of first encounter. Not only does space separate the newfound world from yours; time does, five billion years at least. Often you need minutes before you can truly see the shapes around, they are that alien. Before, the eye has registered them but not the brain.

This was more like home. Yet the strangenesses were uncountable.

Weight: three-fourths of what the ship maintained. An ease, a bounciness in the stride . . . and a subtle kines-thetic adjustment required, sensory more than muscular.

Air: like Earth's at about two kilometers' altitude. (Gravity gradient being less, the density dropoff above sea level went slower.) Crystalline vision, cool flow and murmur of breezes, soughing in the branches and river clangorous down in the canyon. Every odor different, no hint of sun-baked resin or duff, instead a medley of smokinesses and pungencies.

Light: warm gold, making colors richer and shadows deeper than you were really evolved for; a midmorning sun which displayed almost half again the apparent diameter of Earth's, in a sky which was deep blue and had only thin streaks of cloud.

Life: wild flocks, wheeling and crying high overhead; lowings and cacklings from the corral; rufous carpet underfoot, springy, suggestive more of moss than grass though not very much of either, starred with exquisite flowers; trees whose leaves were green (from silvery to murky), whose bark (if it was bark) might be black or gray or brown or white, whose forms were little more odd to you than were pine or gingko if you came from oak and beech country, but which were no trees of anywhere on Earth. A swarm of midgelike entomoids went by, and a big coppery-winged "moth" leisurely feeding on them.

Scenery: superb. Above the forest, peaks shouldered into heaven, the glacier shimmered blue. To the right, canyon walls plunged roseate, ocher-banded, and cragged. But your attention was directed ahead.

The house was of astonishing size. "A flinking castle," Turekian exclaimed. An approximate twenty-meter cube, it rose sheer to the peaked roof, built from well-dressed blocks of granite. Windows indicated six stories. They were large openings, equipped with wooden shutters and wrought-iron balconies. The sole door, on ground level, was ponderous. Horns, skulls, and sculptured weapons of the chase—knife, spear, shortsword, blowgun, bow and arrow—ornamented the façade.

The attendant buildings were doubtless barns or sheds. Trophies hung on them too. The beasts in the corral looked, and probably weren't, mammalian. Two species were vaguely reminiscent of horses and oxen, a third of sheep. They were not many, could not be the whole support of the dwellers here. The "dovecotes" held ornithoids as big as turkeys, which were not penned but were prevented from leaving the area by three hawk-like guardians. "Watchdogs," Turekian said of those. "No, watchfalcons." They swooped about, perturbed at the invasion.

Yukiko's voice came wistful from a receiver behind his ear: "Can I join you?"

"Stand by the guns," Webner answered. "We have yet to meet the owners of this place."

"Huh?" Turekian said. "Why, they're gone. Skedaddled when they saw us coming."

"Timid?" Yukiko asked. "That doesn't fit with their being eager hunters."

"On the contrary, I imagine they're pretty scrappy," Turekian said. "They jumped to the conclusion we must be hostile, because they wouldn't enter somebody else's land uninvited unless they felt that way. Our powers being unknown, and they having wives and kiddies to worry about, they prudently took off. I expect the fighting males—or whatever they've got—will be back soon."

"What are you talking about?" Webner inquired.

"Why, . . . the locals." Turekian blinked at him. "You saw them."

"Those giant ornithoids? Nonsense."

"Hoy? They came right out of the house there!"

"Domestic animals." Webner's hatchet features drew tight. "I don't deny we confront a puzzle here."

"We always do," Yukiko put in softly.

Webner nodded. "True. However, facts and logic solve puzzles. Let's not complicate our task with pseudoproblems. Whatever they are, the flyers we saw leave cannot be the sophonts. On a planet as Earthlike as this, aviform intelligence is impossible."

He straightened. "I suspect the inhabitants have barricaded themselves," he finished. "Well go closer and make pacific gestures."

"Which could be misunderstood," Turekian said dubiously. "An arrow or javelin can kill you just as dead as a blaster."

"Cover us, Yukiko," Webner ordered. "Follow me, Aram. If you have the nerve."

He stalked forward, under the eyes of the girl. Turekian cursed and joined him in haste.

They were near the door when a shadow fell over them. They whirled and stared upward. Yukiko's indrawn breath hissed from their receivers.

Aloft hovered one of the great ornithoids. Sunlight struck through its outermost pinions, turning them golden. Otherwise it showed stormcloud-dark. Down the wind stooped a second.

The sight was terrifying. Only later did the humans realize it was magnificent. Those wings spanned six meters. A muzzle full of sharp white fangs gaped before them. Two legs the length and well-nigh the thickness of a man's arms reached crooked talons between them. At their angles grew claws. In thrust after thrust, they hurled the creature at torpedo speed. Air whistled and thundered.

Their guns leaped into the men's hands. "Don't shoot!" Yukiko's cry came as if from very far away.

The splendid monster was almost upon them. Fire speared from Webner's weapon. At the same instant, the animal braked—a turning of quills, a crack and gust in their faces—and rushed back upward, two meters short of impact.

Turekian's gaze stamped a picture on his brain which he would study over and over and over. The unknown was feathered, surely warm-blooded, but no bird. A keel-bone like a ship's prow jutted beneath a strong neck. The head was blunt-nosed, lacked external ears; fantastically, Turekian saw that the predator mouth had lips. Tongue and palate were purple. Two big golden eyes stabbed at him, burned at him. A crest of black-tipped white plumage rose stiffly above, a control surface and protection for the backward-bulging skull. The fan-shaped tail bore the same colors. The body was mahogany, the naked legs and claws yellow.

Webner's shot hit amidst the left-side quills. Smoke streamed after the flameburst. The creature uttered a high-pitched yell, lurched, and threshed in retreat. The damage wasn't permanent, had likely caused no pain, but now that wing was only half-useful.

Turekian thus had time to see three slits in parallel on the body. He had time to think there must be three more on the other side. They weirdly resembled gills. As the wings lifted, he saw them drawn wide, a triple yawn; as the downstroke began, he glimpsed them being forced shut.

Then he had cast himself against Webner. "Drop that, you clot-brain!" he yelled. He seized the xenologist's gun wrist. They wrestled. He forced the fingers apart. Meanwhile the wounded ornithoid struggled back to its companion. They flapped off.

"What're you doing?" Webner grabbed at Turekian.

The pilot pushed him away, brutally hard. He fell. Turekian snatched forth his magnifier.

Treetops cut off his view. He let the instrument drop. "Too late," he groaned. "Thanks to you."

Webner climbed erect, pale and shaken by rage. "Have you gone heisenberg?" he gasped. "I'm your commander!"

"You're maybe fit to command plastic ducks in a bathtub," Turekian said. "Firing on a native!"

Webner was too taken aback to reply.

"And you capped it by spoiling my chance for a good look at Number Two. I think I spotted a harness on him, holding what might be a weapon, but I'm not sure." Turekian spat.

"Aram, Vaughn," Yukiko pleaded from the boat.

An instant longer, the men bristled and glared. Then Webner drew breath, shrugged, and said in a crackly voice: "I suppose it's incumbent on me to put things on a reasonable basis, if you're incapable of that." He paused. "Behave yourself and I'll excuse your conduct as being due to excitement. Else I'll have to recommend you be relieved from further initial-contact duty."

"*I* be relieved—?" Turekian barely checked his fist, and kept it balled. His breath rasped.

"Hadn't you better check the house?" Yukiko asked.

The knowledge that something, anything, might lurk behind yonder walls restored them to a measure of coolness.

Save for livestock, the steading was deserted.

Rather than offend the dwellers by blasting down their barred door, the searchers went through a window on grav units. They found just one or two rooms on each story. Evidently the people valued ample floor space and high ceilings above privacy. Connection up and down was by circular staircases whose short steps seemed at variance with this. Decoration was austere and nonrepresentational. Furniture consisted mainly of benches and tables. Nothing like a bed or an *o-futon*, was found. Did the indigenes sleep, if they did, sitting or standing? Quite possibly. Many species can lock the joints of their limbs at will.

Stored food bore out the idea of carnivorousness. Tools, weapons, utensils, fabrics were abundant, well made, neatly put away. They confirmed an Iron Age technology, more or less equivalent to that of Earth's Classical civilization. Exceptions occurred: for example, a few books, seemingly printed from hand-set type. How avidly those pages were ransacked! But the only illustrations were diagrams suitable to a geometry text in one case and a stonemason's manual in another. Did this culture taboo pictures of its members, or had the boat merely chanced on a home which possessed none?

The layout and contents of the house, and of the sheds when these were examined, gave scant clues. Nobody had expected better. Imagine yourself a nonhuman xenologist, visiting Earth before man went into space. What could you deduce from the residences and a few household items belonging to, say, a European, an Eskimo, a Congo pygmy, and a Japanese peasant? You might have wondered if the owners were of the same genus.

In time you could learn more. Turekian doubted that time would be given. He set Webner in a cold fury by his nagging to finish the survey and get back to the boat At length the chief gave in. "Not that I don't plan a detailed study, mind you," he said. Scornfully: "Still, I suppose we can hold a conference, and I'll try to calm your fears."

After you had been out, the air in the craft smelled dead and the view in the screens looked dull. Turekian took a pipe from his pocket. "No," Webner told him.

"What?" The pilot was bemused.

"I won't have that foul thing in this crowded cabin."

"I don't mind," Yukiko said.

"I do," Webner replied, "and while we're down, I'm your captain."

Turekian reddened and obeyed. Discipline in space is steel hard, a matter of survival. A good leader gives it a soft sheath. Yukiko's eyes reproached Webner; her fingers dropped to rest on the pilot's arm. The xenologist saw. His mouth twitched sideways before he pinched it together.

"We're in trouble," Turekian said. "The sooner we haul mass out of here, the happier our insurance carriers will be."

"Nonsense," Webner snapped. "If anything, our problem is that we've terrified the dwellers. They may take days to send even a scout."

"They've already sent two. You had to shoot at them."

"I shot at a dangerous animal. Didn't you see those talons, those fangs? And a buffet from a wing that big—ignoring the claws on it—could break your neck."

Webner's gaze sought Yukiko's. He mainly addressed her: "Granted, they must be domesticated. I suspect they're used in the hunt, flown at game like hawks though working in packs like hounds. Conceivably the pair we encountered were, ah, sicced onto us from afar. But that they themselves are sophonts—out of the question."

Her murmur was uneven. "How can you be sure?"

Webner leaned back, bridged his fingers, and grew calmer while he lectured: "You realize the basic principle. All organisms make biological sense in their particular environments, or they become extinct. Reasoners are no exception—and are, furthermore, descended from nonreasoners which adapted to environments that had never been artificially modified.

"On nonterrestroid worlds, they can be quite outré by our standards, since they developed under unearthly conditions. On an essentially terrestroid planet, evolution basically parallels our own because it must. True, you get considerable variation. Like, say, hexapodal vertebrates liberating the forelimbs to grow hands and becoming centauroids, as on Woden. That's because the ancestral chordates were hexapods. On this world, you can see for yourself the higher animals are four-limbed.

"A brain capable of designing artifacts such as we observe here is useless without some equivalent of hands. Nature would never produce it. Therefore the inhabitants are bound to be bipeds, however different from us in detail. A foot which must double as a hand, and vice versa, would be too grossly inefficient in either function. Natural selection would weed out any mutants of that tendency, fast, long before intelligence could evolve.

"What do those ornithoids have in the way of hands?" He smiled his tight little smile.

"The claws on their wings?" Yukiko asked shyly.

" 'Fraid not," Turekian said. "I got a fair look. They can grasp, sort of, but aren't built for manipulation."

"You saw how the fledgling uses them to cling to the parent," Webner stated. "Perhaps it climbs trees also. Earth has a bird with similar structures, the hoactzin. It

loses them in adulthood. Here they may become extra
weapons for the mature animal."

"The feet." Turekian scowled. "Two opposable digits
flanking three straight ones. Could serve as hands."

"Then how does the creature get about on the
ground?" Webner retorted. "Can't forge a tool in midair,
you know, let alone dig ore and erect stone houses."

He wagged a finger. "Another, more fundamental
point," he went on. "Flyers are too limited in mass. True,
the gravity's weaker than on Earth, but air pressure's
lower. Thus admissible wing loadings are about the same.
The biggest birds that ever lumbered into Terrestrial
skies weighed some fifteen kilos. Nothing larger could
get aloft. Metabolism simply can't supply the power
required. We established aboard ship, from specimens,
that local biochemistry is close kin to our type. Hence it
is not possible for those ornithoids to outweigh a maximal
vulture. They're big, yes, and formidable. Nevertheless,
that size has to be mostly feathers, hollow
bones—spidery, kitelike skeletons anchoring thin flesh.

"Aram, you hefted several items today, such as a stone
pot. Or consider one of the buckets, presumably used to
bring water up from the river. What would you say the
greatest weight is?"

Turekian scratched in his beard. "Maybe twenty
kilos," he answered reluctantly.

"There! No flyer could lift that. It was always superstition about eagles stealing lambs or babies. They weren't
able to. The ornithoids are similarly handicapped. Who'd
make utensils he can't carry?"

"M-m-m," Turekian growled rather than hummed.
Webner pressed the attack:

"The mass of any flyer on a terrestroid planet is insufficient to include a big enough brain for true intelligence.

The purely animal functions require virtually all those cells. Birds have at least lightened their burden, permitting a little more brain, by changing jaws to beaks. So have those ornithoids you called 'watchfalcons.' The big fellows have not."

He hesitated. "In fact," he said slowly, "I doubt if they can even be considered bright animals. They're likely stupid . . . and vicious. If we're set on again, we need have no compunctions about destroying them."

"Were you going to?" Yukiko whispered. "Couldn't he, she, it simply have been coming down for a quick, close look at you—unarmed as a peace gesture?"

"If intelligent, yes," Webner said. "If not, as I've proven to be the case, positively no. I saved us some nasty wounds. Perhaps I saved a life."

"The dwellers might object if we shoot at their property," Turekian said.

"They need only call off their, ah, dogs. In fact, the attack on us may not have been commanded, may have been brute reaction after panic broke the order of the pack." Webner rose. "Are you satisfied? We'll make thorough studies till nightfall, then leave gifts, withdraw, hope for a better reception when we see the indigenes have returned." A television pickup was customary among diplomatic presents of that kind.

Turekian shook his head. "Your logic's all right, I suppose. But it don't smell right somehow."

Webner started for the airlock.

"Me too?" Yukiko requested. "Please?"

"No," Turekian said. "I'd hate for you to be harmed."

"We're in no danger," she argued. "Our sidearms can handle any flyers that may arrive feeling mean. If we plant sensors around, no walking native can come within bowshot before we know. I feel caged." She aimed her smile at Webner.

The xenologist thawed. "Why not?" he said. "I can use a levelheaded assistant." To Turekian: "Man the boat guns yourself if you wish."

"Like blazes," the pilot grumbled, and followed them.

He had to admit the leader knew his business. The former cursory search became a shrewd, efficient examination of object after object, measuring, photographing, commenting continuously into a mini-recorder. Yukiko helped. On Survey, everybody must have some knowledge of everybody else's specialty. But Webner needed just one extra person.

"What can I do?" Turekian asked.

"Move an occasional heavy load," the other man said. "Keep watch on the forest. Stay out of my way."

Yukiko was too fascinated by the work to chide him. Turekian rumbled in his throat, stuffed his pipe, and slouched around the grounds alone, blowing furious clouds.

At the corral he gripped a rail and glowered. "You want feeding," he decided, went into a barn—unlike the house, its door was not secured—and found a haymow and pitchforks which, despite every strangeness of detail, reminded him of a backwoods colony on Hermes that he'd visited once, temporarily primitive because shipping space was taken by items more urgent than modern agromachines. The farmer had had a daughter. . . . He consoled himself with memories while he took out a mess of cinnamon-scented red herbage.

"You!"

Webner leaned from an upstairs window. "What're you about?" he called.

"Those critters are hungry," Turekian replied. "Listen to 'em."

"How do you know what their requirements are? Or the owners'? We're not here to play God, for your information. We're here to learn and, maybe, help. Take that stuff back where you got it."

Turekian swallowed rage—that Yukiko should have heard his humiliation—and complied. Webner was his captain till he regained the blessed sky.

Sky . . . birds. . . . He observed the "cotes." The pseudohawks fluttered about, indignant but too small to tackle him. Were the giant ornithoids kept partly as protection against large ground predators? Turekian studied the flock. Its members dozed, waddled, scratched the dirt, fat and placid, obviously long bred to tameness. Both types lacked the gill-like slits he had noticed. . . .

A shadow. Turekian glanced aloft, snatched for his magnifier. Half a dozen giants were back. The noon sun flamed on their feathers. They were too high for him to see details.

He flipped the controls on his grav unit and made for the house. Webner and Yukiko were on the fifth floor. Turekian arced through a window. He had no eye, now, for the Spartan grace of the room. "They've arrived," he panted. "We better get in the boat quick."

Webner stepped onto the balcony. "No need," he said. "I hardly think they'll attack. If they do, we're safer here than crossing the yard."

"Might be smart to close the shutters," the girl said.

"And the door to this chamber," Webner agreed. "That'll stop them. They'll soon lose patience and wander off—if they attempt anything. Or if they do besiege us, we can shoot our way through them, or at worst relay a call for help via the boat, once *Olga*'s again over our horizon."

He had re-entered. Turekian took his place on the balcony and squinted upward. More winged shapes had joined the first several; and more came into view each second. They dipped, soared, circled through the wind, which made surf noises in the forest.

Unease crawled along the pilot's spine. "I don't like this half a bit," he said. "They don't act like plain beasts."

"Conceivably the dwellers plan to use them in an assault," Webner said. "If so, we may have to teach the dwellers about the cost of unreasoning hostility." His tone was less cool than the words, and sweat beaded his countenance.

Sparks in the magnifier field hurt Turekian's eyes. "I swear they're carrying metal," he said. "Listen, if they are intelligent—and out to get us, after you nearly killed one of 'em—the house is no place for us. Let's scramble. We may not have many more minutes."

"Yes, I believe we'd better, Vaughn," Yukiko urged. "We can't risk . . . being forced to burn down conscious beings . . . on their own land."

Maybe his irritation with the pilot spoke for Webner: "How often must I explain there is no such risk, yet? Instead, here's a chance to learn. What happens next could give us invaluable clues to understanding the whole ethos. We stay." To Turekian: "Forget about that alleged metal. Could be protective collars, I suppose. But take the supercharger off your imagination."

The other man froze where he stood.

"Aram." Yukiko seized his arm. He stared beyond her. "What's wrong?"

He shook himself. "Supercharger," he mumbled. "By God, yes."

Abruptly, in a bellow: "We're leaving! This second! They *are* the dwellers, and they've gathered the whole countryside against us!"

"Hold your tongue," Webner said, "or I'll charge insubordination."

Laughter rattled in Turekian's breast. "Uh-uh. Mutiny."

He crouched and lunged. His fist rocketed before him. Yukiko's cry joined the thick smack as knuckles hit—not the chin, which is too hazardous, the solar plexus. Air whoofed from Webner. His eyes glazed. He folded over, partly conscious but unable to stand while his diaphragm spasmed. Turekian gathered him in his arms. "To the boat!" the pilot shouted. "Hurry, girl!"

His grav unit wouldn't carry two, simply gentled his fall when he leaped from the balcony. He dared not stop to adjust the controls on Webner's. Bearing his chief, he pounded across the flagstones. Yukiko came above. "Go ahead!" Turekian bawled. "Get into shelter, for God's sake!"

"Not till you can," she answered. "I'll cover you." He was helpless to prevent her.

The scores above had formed themselves into a vast revolving wheel. It tilted. The first flyers peeled off and roared downward. The rest came after.

Arrows whistled ahead of them. A trumpet sounded. Turekian dodged, zigzag over the meadow. Yukiko's gun clapped. She shot to miss, but belike the flashes put those archers—and, now, spearthrowers—off their aim. Shafts sang wickedly around. One edge grazed Webner's neck. He screamed.

Yukiko darted to open the boat's airlock. While she did, Turekian dropped Webner and straddled him, blaster drawn. The leading flyer hurtled close. Talons of the right foot, which was not a foot at all but a hand, gripped a sword curved like a scimitar. For an instant, Turekian looked squarely into the golden eyes, knew a brave male defending his home, and also shot to miss.

In a brawl of air, the native sheered off. The valve swung wide. Yukiko flitted through. Turekian dragged Webner, then stood in the lock chamber till the entry was shut.

Missiles clanged on the hull. None would pierce. Turekian let himself join Webner for a moment of shuddering before he went forward to Yukiko and the raising of his vessel.

When you know what to expect, a little, you can lay plans. We next sought the folk of Ythri, as the planet is called by its most advanced culture, a thousand kilometers from the triumph which surely prevailed in the mountains. Approached with patience, caution, and symbolisms appropriate to their psyches, they welcomed us rapturously. Before we left, they'd thought of sufficient inducements to trade that I'm sure they'll have spacecraft of their own in a few generations.

Still, they are as fundamentally territorial as man is fundamentally sexual, and we'd better bear that in mind.

The reason lies in their evolution. It does for every drive in every animal everywhere. The Ythrian is carnivorous, aside from various sweet fruits. Carnivores require larger regions per individual than herbivores or omnivores do, in spite of the fact that meat has more calories per kilo than most vegetable matter. Consider how each antelope needs a certain amount of space, and how many antelope are needed to maintain a pride of lions. Xenologists have written thousands of papers on the correlations between diet and genotypical personality in sophonts.

I have my doubts about the value of those papers. At least, they missed the possibility of a race like the Ythrians, whose extreme territoriality and individualism—with the consequences to governments, mores, arts, faiths, and souls—come from the extreme appetite of the body.

They mass as high as thirty kilos; yet they can lift an equal weight into the air or, unhampered, fly like demons. Hence they maintain civilization without the need to crowd together in cities. Their townspeople are mostly wing-clipped criminals and slaves. Today their wiser heads hope robots will end the need for that.

Hands? The original talons, modified for manipulating. Feet? Those claws on the wings, a juvenile feature which persisted and developed, just as man's large head and sparse hair derive from the juvenile or fetal ape. The forepart of the wing skeleton consists of humerus, radius, and ulnar, much as in true birds. These lock together in flight. Aground, when the wing is folded downward, they produce a "knee" joint. Bones grow from their base to make the claw-foot. Three fused digits, immensely lengthened, sweep backward to be the alatan which braces the rest of that tremendous wing and can, when desired, give additional support on the surface. To rise, the Ythrians usually do a handstand during the initial upstroke. It takes less than a second.

Oh, yes, they are slow and awkward afoot. They manage, though. Big and beweaponed, instantly ready to mount the wind, they need fear no beast of prey.

You ask where the power comes from to swing this hugeness through the sky. The oxidation of food, what else? Hence the demand of each household for a great hunting or ranching demesne. The limiting factor is the oxygen supply. A molecule in the blood can carry more than hemoglobin does, but the gas must be furnished. Turekian first realized how that happens. The Ythrian has lungs, a passive system resembling ours. In addition he has his supercharger, evolved from the gills of an amphibianlike ancestor. Worked in bellows fashion by the flight muscles, connecting directly with the bloodstream, those air-intake organs let him burn his fuel as fast as necessary.

I wonder how it feels to be so alive.

I remember how Yukiko Sachansky stood in the curve of Aram Turekian's arm, under a dawn heaven, and watched the farewell dance the Ythrians gave for us, and cried through tears: "To fly like that! To fly like that!"

INTRODUCTION

❈ THE PROBLEM OF PAIN ❈

This happened early in the course of starflight. The tale is in *Far Adventure* by Maeve Downey, the autobiography of a planetologist. Aside from scientific reports which the same expedition rendered, it appears to be the first outside account of us.

You well know how the Discovery gale-seized those peoples who had the learning to see what it meant, so that erelong all Ythri could never again speak in full understanding, through books and songs and art, with the ancestors. The dealings with Terrans as these returned, first for study and later for trade; the quest and strife which slowly won for us our own modern technics; the passion of history through life after life: these are in many writings. What is less known than it should be is how the Terrans themselves were faring meanwhile.

Their Commonwealth had been formed out of numerous nations. A few more came into being and membership afterward. To explain the concept "nation" is stiffly upwind. As a snatching at the task—Within a sharply defined territory dwell a large number of humans who, in a subtle sense which goes beyond private property or shared range, identify their souls with this land and with each other. Law and mutual obligation are maintained less by usage and pride than by physical violence or the threat thereof on the part of that institution called the government. It is as if a single group could permanently cry Oherran against the entire rest of society, bring death and devastation wherever it chose, and claimed this as an exclusive right. Compliance and assistance are said to be honorable, resistance dishonorable, especially when one nation is at war with another—for each of these entities has powers which are limited not by justice, decency, or prudence, but only by its own strength.

You well know how most humans on Avalon still maintain a modified form of government. However, this is of sharply limited force, both in practice and in law. It is merely their way. You cannot mind-grasp the modern Terran Empire without knowing what a nation truly is.

To curb these inordinate prerogatives of a few, whose quarrels and mismanagement threatened to lay waste their native planet, the Commonwealth was finally established, as a nation of nations. This did not happen quickly, easily, or rationally. The story of it is long and terrible. Nevertheless, it happened: and, for a time, the Commonwealth was on the whole a benign influence. Under its protection, both prosperity and freedom from demands flourished ever more greatly.

Meanwhile exploration exploded throughout this part of the galaxy. Human-habitable worlds which had no intelligent life of their own began to be settled. Our species, in slow youngling wise, began to venture from its nest, at first usually in a flock with Terrans.

The same expedition which made the Discovery of Ythri had chanced upon Avalon. Though rich prey for colonists, at the time it lay too far from Sol and remained nameless. The season came at last for taking real knowledge of it. Because Ythrians were also a-wing in this, there happened an incident which is worth the telling here. Rennhi found the account, transcribed from a recording made on Terra, in the archives of the University of Fleurville upon the planet Esperance. It was originally part of a private correspondence between two humans, preserved by the heirs of the recipient after his death; a visiting historian obtained a copy but never published it. God hunted down all persons concerned so long ago that no pride will be touched by planting the story here.

The value of it lies in the human look upon us, a look which tried to reach down into the spirit and thereby, maychance, now opens for us a glimpse into theirs.

—Hloch of the Stormgate Choth
The Earth Book of Stormgate

THE PROBLEM OF PAIN

Maybe only a Christian can understand this story. In that case I don't qualify. But I do take an interest in religion, as part of being an amateur psychologist, and—for the grandeur of its language if nothing else—a Bible is among the reels that accompany me wherever I go. This was one reason Peter Berg told me what had happened in his past. He desperately needed to make sense of it, and no priest he'd talked to had quite laid his questions to rest. There was an outside chance that an outside viewpoint like mine would see what a man within the faith couldn't.

His other reason was simple loneliness. We were on Lucifer, as part of a study corporation. That world is well named. It will never be a real colony for any beings whose ancestors evolved amidst clean greenery. But it might be marginally habitable, and if so, its mineral wealth would be worth exploiting. Our job was to determine whether that was true. The gentlest-looking environment holds a thousand death traps until you have learned what the difficulties are and how to grip them. (Earth is no exception.) Sometimes you find problems which can't be solved economically, or can't be solved at all. Then you write off the area or the entire planet, and look for another.

We'd contracted to work three standard years on Lucifer. The pay was munificent, but presently we realized that no bank account could buy back one day we might have spent beneath a kindlier sun. It was a knowledge we carefully avoided discussing with teammates.

About midway through, Peter Berg and I were assigned to do an in-depth investigation of a unique cycle in the ecology of the northern middle latitudes. This meant that we settled down for weeks—which ran into months—in a sample region, well away from everybody else to minimize human disturbances. An occasional supply flitter gave us our only real contact; electronics were no proper substitute, especially when that hell-violent star was forever disrupting them.

Under such circumstances, you come to know your partner maybe better than you know yourself. Pete and I got along well. He's a big, sandy-haired, freckle-faced young man, altogether dependable, with enough kindliness, courtesy, and dignity that he need not make a show of them. Soft-spoken, he's a bit short in the humor department. Otherwise I recommend him as a companion. He has a lot to tell from his own wanderings, yet he'll listen with genuine interest to your memories and brags; he's well read too, and a good cook when his turn comes; he plays chess at just about my level of skill.

I already knew he wasn't from Earth, had in fact never been there, but from Aeneas, nearly 200 light-years distant, more than 300 from Lucifer. And, while he'd gotten an education at the new little university in Nova Roma, he was raised in the outback. Besides, that town is only a faroff colonial capital. It helped explain his utter commitment to belief in a God who became flesh and died for love of man. Not that I scoff. When he said his prayers, night and morning in our one-room shelterdome, trustingly as a child, I didn't rag him nor he reproach me. Of course, over the weeks, we came more and more to talk about such matters.

At last he told me of that which haunted him.

We'd been out through the whole of one of Lucifer's long, long days; we'd toiled, we'd sweated, we'd itched and stunk and gotten grimy and staggered from weariness, we'd come near death once: and we'd found the uranium-concentrating root which was the key to the whole weirdness around us. We came back to base as day's fury was dying in the usual twilight gale; we washed, ate something, went to sleep with the hiss of storm-blown dust for a lullaby. Ten or twelve hours later we awoke and saw, through the vitryl panels, stars cold and crystalline beyond this thin air, auroras aflame, landscape hoar, and the twisted things we called trees all sheathed in glittering ice.

"Nothing we can do now till dawn," I said, "and we've earned a celebration." So we prepared a large meal, elaborate as possible—breakfast or supper, what relevance had that here? We drank wine in the course of it, and afterward much brandy while we sat, side by side in our loungers, watching the march of constellations which Earth or Aeneas never saw. And we talked. Finally we talked of God.

"—maybe you can give me an idea," Pete said. In the dim light, his face bore a struggle. He stared before him and knotted his fingers.

"M-m, I dunno," I said carefully. "To be honest, no offense meant, theological conundrums strike me as silly."

He gave me a direct blue look. His tone was soft: "That is, you feel the paradoxes don't arise if we don't insist on believing?"

"Yes. I respect your faith, Pete, but it's not mine. And if I did suppose a, well, a spiritual principle or something is behind the universe—" I gestured at the high and terrible sky—"in the name of reason, can we confine, can we understand whatever made *that*, in the bounds of one little dogma?"

"No. Agreed. How could finite minds grasp the infinite? We can see parts of it, though, that've been revealed to us." He drew breath. " 'Way back before space travel, the Church decided Jesus had come only to Earth, to man. If other intelligent races need salvation—and obviously a lot of them do!—God will have made His suitable arrangements for them. Sure. However, this does not mean Christianity is not true, or that certain different beliefs are not false."

"Like, say, polytheism, wherever you find it?"

"I think so. Besides, religions evolve. The primitive faiths see God, or the gods, as power; the higher ones see Him as justice; the highest see Him as love." Abruptly he fell silent. I saw his fist clench, until he grabbed up his glass and drained it and refilled it in nearly a single savage motion.

"I must believe that," he whispered.

I waited a few seconds, in Lucifer's crackling night stillness, before saying: "An experience made you wonder?"

"Made me . . . disturbed. Mind if I tell you?"

"Certainly not." I saw he was about to open himself; and I may be an unbeliever, but I know what is sacred.

"Happened about five years ago. I was on my first real job. So was the—" his voice stumbled the least bit—"the wife I had then. We were fresh out of school and apprenticeship, fresh into marriage." In an effort at detachment: "Our employers weren't human. They were Ythrians. Ever heard of them?"

I sought through my head. The worlds, races, beings are unknowably many, in this tiny corner of this one dust-mote galaxy which we have begun to explore a little. "Ythrians, Ythrians . . . wait. Do they fly?"

"Yes. Surely one of the most glorious sights in creation. Your Ythrian isn't as heavy as a man, of course; adults mass around twenty-five or thirty kilos—but his wingspan goes up to six meters, and when he soars with those feathers shining gold-brown in the light, or stoops in a crack of thunder and whistle of wind—"

"Hold on," I said. "I take it Ythri's a terrestroid planet?"

"Pretty much. Somewhat smaller and drier than Earth, somewhat thinner atmosphere—about like Aeneas, in fact, which it's not too far from as interstellar spaces go. You can live there without special protection. The biochemistry's quite similar to ours."

"Then how the devil can those creatures be that size? The wing loading's impossible, when you have only cell tissue to oxidize for power. They'd never get off the ground."

"Ah, but they have antlibranchs as well." Pete smiled, though it didn't go deep. "Those look like three gills, sort of, on either side, below the wings. They're actually more like bellows, pumped by the wing muscles. Extra oxygen is forced directly into the bloodstream during flight. A biological supercharger system."

"Well, I'll be a . . . never mind what." I considered, in delight, this new facet of nature's inventiveness. "Um-m-m . . . if they spend energy at that rate, they've got to have appetites to match."

"Right. They're carnivores. A number of them are still hunters. The advanced societies are based on ranching. In either case, obviously, it takes a lot of meat animals, a lot of square kilometers, to support one Ythrian. So they're fiercely territorial. They live in small groups—single families or extended households—which attack, with intent to kill, any uninvited outsider who doesn't obey an order to leave."

"And still they're civilized enough to hire humans for space exploration?"

"Uh-huh. Remember, being flyers, they've never needed to huddle in cities in order to have ready communication. They do keep a few towns, mining or manufacturing centers, but those are inhabited mostly by wing-clipped slaves. I'm glad to say that institution's dying out as they get modern machinery."

"By trade?" I guessed.

"Yes," Pete replied. "When the first Grand Survey discovered them, their most advanced culture was at an Iron Age level of technology; no industrial revolution, but plenty of sophisticated minds around, and subtle philosophies." He paused. "That's important to my question —that the Ythrians, at least of the Planha-speaking *choths*, are not barbarians and have not been for many centuries. They've had their equivalents of Socrates, Aristotle, Confucius, Galileo, yes, and their prophets and seers."

After another mute moment: "They realized early what the visitors from Earth implied, and set about attracting traders and teachers. Once they had some funds, they sent their promising young folk off-planet to study. I met several at my own university, which is why I got my job offer. By now they have a few spacecraft and native crews. But you'll understand, their technical people are spread thin, and in several branches of knowledge they have no experts. So they employ humans."

He went on to describe the typical Ythrian: warm-blooded, feathered like a golden eagle (though more intricately) save for a crest on the head, and yet not a bird. Instead of a beak, a blunt muzzle full of fangs juts before two great eyes. The female bears her young alive. While she does not nurse them, they have lips to suck the juices of meat and fruits, wherefore their speech is not hopelessly unlike man's. What were formerly the legs have evolved into arms bearing three taloned fingers, flanked by two thumbs, on each hand. Aground, the huge wings fold downward and, with the help of claws at the angles, give locomotion. That is slow and awkward—but aloft, ah!

"They become more alive, flying, than we ever do," Pete murmured. His gaze had lost itself in the shuddering auroras overhead. "They must: the metabolic rate they have then, and the space around them, speed, sky, a hundred winds to ride on and be kissed by. . . . That's what made me think Enherrian, in particular, believed more keenly than I could hope to. I saw him and others dancing, high, high in the air, swoops, glides, hoverings, sunshine molten on their plumes; I asked what they did, and was told they were honoring God."

He sighed. "Or that's how I translated the Planha phrase, rightly or wrongly," he went on. "Olga and I had taken a cram course, and our Ythrian teammates all knew Anglic; but nobody's command of the foreign tongue was perfect. It couldn't be. Multiple billion years of separate existence, evolution, history—what a miracle that we could think as alike as we did!

"However, you could call Enherrian religious, same as you could call me that, and not be too grotesquely off the mark. The rest varied, just like humans. Some were also devout, some less, some agnostics or atheists; two were pagans, following the bloody rites of what was called the Old Faith. For that matter, my Olga—" the knuckles stood forth where he grasped his tumbler of brandy—"had tried, for my sake, to believe as I did, and couldn't.

"Well. The New Faith interested me more. It was new only by comparison—at least half as ancient as mine. I hoped for a chance to study it, to ask questions and compare ideas. I really knew nothing except that it was monotheistic, had sacraments and a theology though no official priesthood, upheld a high ethical and moral standard—for Ythrians, I mean. You can't expect a race which can only live by killing animals, and has an oestrous cycle, and is incapable by instinct of maintaining what we'd recognize as a true nation or government, and on and on—you can't expect them to resemble Christians much. God has given them a different message. I wished to know what. Surely we could learn from it." Again he paused. "After all . . . being a faith with a long tradition . . . and not static but a seeking, a history of prophets and saints and believers . . . I thought it must know God is love. Now what form would God's love take to an Ythrian?"

He drank. I did too, before asking cautiously: "Uh, where was this expedition?"

Pete stirred in his lounger. "To a system about eighty light-years from Ythri's," he answered. "The original Survey crew had discovered a terrestroid planet there. They didn't bother to name it. Prospective colonists would choose their own name anyway. Those could be human or Ythrian, conceivably both—if the environment proved out.

"Offhand, the world—our group called it, unofficially, Gray, after that old captain—the world looked brilliantly promising. It's intermediate in size between Earth and Ythri, surface gravity 0.8 terrestrial; slightly more irradiation, from a somewhat yellower sun, than Earth gets, which simply makes it a little warmer; axial tilt, therefore seasonal variations, a bit less than terrestrial; length of year about three-quarters of ours, length of day a bit under half; one small, close-in, bright moon; biochemistry similar to ours—we could eat most native things, though we'd require imported crops and livestock to supplement the diet. All in all, seemingly well-nigh perfect."

"Rather remote to attract Earthlings at this early date," I remarked. "And from your description, the Ythrians won't be able to settle it for quite a while either."

"They think ahead," Pete responded. "Besides, they have scientific curiosity and, yes, in them perhaps even more than in the humans who went along, a spirit of adventure. Oh, it was a wonderful thing to be young in that band!"

He had not yet reached thirty, but somehow his cry was not funny.

He shook himself. "Well, we had to make sure," he said. "Besides planetology, ecology, chemistry, oceanography, meteorology, a million and a million mysteries to unravel for their own sakes—we must scout out the death traps, whatever those might be.

"At first everything went like Mary's smile on Christmas morning. The spaceship set us off—it couldn't be spared to linger in orbit—and we established base on the largest continent. Soon our hundred-odd dispersed across the globe, investigating this or that. Olga and I made part of a group on the southern shore, where a great gulf swarmed with life. A strong current ran eastward from there, eventually striking an archipelago which deflected it north. Flying over those waters, we spied immense, I mean immense, patches—no, floating islands—of vegetation, densely interwoven, grazed on by monstrous marine creatures, no doubt supporting any number of lesser plant and animal species.

"We wanted a close look. Our camp's sole aircraft wasn't good for that. Anyhow, it was already in demand for a dozen jobs. We had boats, though, and launched one. Our crew was Enherrian, his wife Whell, their grown children Rusa and Arrach, my beautiful new bride Olga, and me. We'd take three or four Gray days to reach the nearest atlantis weed, as Olga dubbed it. Then we'd be at least a week exploring before we turned back—a vacation, a lark, a joy."

He tossed off his drink and reached for the bottle. "You ran into grief," I prompted.

"No." He bent his lips upward, stiffly. "It ran into us. A hurricane. Unpredicted; we knew very little about that planet. Given the higher solar energy input and, especially, the rapid rotation, the storm was more violent than would've been possible on Earth. We could only run before it and pray.

"At least, I prayed, and imagined that Enherrian did."

Wind shrieked, hooted, yammered, hit flesh with fists and cold knives. Waves rumbled in that driven air, black and green and fang-white, fading from view as the sun sank behind the cloud-roil which hid it. Often a monster among them loomed castlelike over the gunwale. The boat slipped by, spilled into the troughs, rocked onto the crests and down again. Spindrift, icy, stinging, bitter on lips and tongue, made a fog across her length.

"We'll live if we can keep sea room," Enherrian had said when the fury first broke. "She's well-found. The engine capacitors have ample kilowatt-hours in them. Keep her bow on and we'll live."

But the currents had them now, where the mighty gulfstream met the outermost islands and its waters churned, recoiled, spun about and fought. Minute by minute, the riptides grew wilder. They made her yaw till she was broadside on and surges roared over her deck; they shocked her onto her beam ends, and the hull became a toning bell.

Pete, Olga, and Whell were in the cabin, trying to rest before their next watch. That was no longer possible. The Ythrian female locked hands and wing-claws around the net-covered framework wherein she had slept, hung on, and uttered nothing. In the wan glow of a single overhead fluoro, among thick restless shadows, her eyes gleamed topaz. They did not seem to look at the cramped-ness around—at what, then?

The humans had secured themselves by a line onto a lower bunk. They embraced, helping each other fight the leaps and swings which tried to smash them against the sides. Her fair hair on his shoulder was the last brightness in his cosmos. "I love you," she said, over and over, through hammerblows and groans. "Whatever happens, I love you. Pete, I thank you for what you've given me."

"And you," he would answer. *And You,* he would think. *Though You won't take her, not yet, will You? Me, yes, if that's Your will. But not Olga. It'd leave Your creation too dark.*

A wing smote the cabin door. Barely to be heard through the storm, an Ythrian voice—high, whistly, but resonant out of full lungs—shouted: "Come topside!"

Whell obeyed at once, the Bergs as fast as they could slip on life jackets. Having taken no personal grav units along, they couldn't fly free if they went overboard. Dusk raved around them. Pete could just see Rusa and Arrach in the stern, fighting the tiller. Enherrian stood before him and pointed forward. "Look," the captain said. Pete, who had no nictitating membranes, must shield eyes with fingers to peer athwart the hurricane. He saw a deeper darkness hump up from a wall of white; he heard surf crash.

"We can't pull free," Enherrian told him. "Between wind and current—too little power. We'll likely be wrecked. Make ready."

Olga's hand went briefly to her mouth. She huddled against Pete and might have whispered, "Oh, no." Then she straightened, swung back down into the cabin, braced herself as best she could and started assembling the most vital things stored there. He saw that he loved her still more than he had known.

The same calm descended on him. Nobody had time to be afraid. He got busy too. The Ythrians could carry a limited weight of equipment and supplies, but sharply limited under these conditions. The humans, buoyed by their jackets, must carry most. They strapped it to their bodies.

When they re-emerged, the boat was in the shoals. Enherrian ordered them to take the rudder. His wife, son, and daughter stood around—on hands which clutched the rails with prey-snatching strength—and spread their wings to give a bit of shelter. The captain clung to the cabin top as lookout. His yelled commands reached the Bergs dim, tattered.

"Hard right!" Upward cataracts burst on a skerry to port. It glided past, was lost in murk. "Two points starboard—steady!" The hull slipped between a pair of rocks. Ahead was a narrow opening in the island's sheer black face. To a lagoon, to safety? Surf raged on either side of that gate, and everywhere else.

The passage was impossible. The boat struck, threw Olga off her feet and Arrach off his perch. Full reverse engine could not break loose. The deck canted. A billow and a billow smashed across.

Pete was in the water. It grabbed him, pulled him under, dragged him over a sharp bottom. He thought: *Into Your hands, God. Spare Olga, please, please*—and the sea spewed him back up for one gulp of air.

Wallowing in blindness, he tried to gauge how the breakers were acting, what he should do. If he could somehow belly-surf in, he might make it, he barely might. . . . He was on the neck of a rushing giant, it climbed and climbed, it shoved him forward at what he knew was lunatic speed. He saw the reef on which it was about to smash him and knew he was dead.

Talons closed on his jacket. Air brawled beneath wings. The Ythrian could not raise him, but could draw him aside . . . the bare distance needed, and Pete went past the rock whereon his bones were to have been crushed, down into the smother and chaos beyond. The Ythrian didn't get free in time. He glimpsed the plumes go under, as he himself did. They never rose.

He beat on, and on, without end.

He floated in water merely choppy, swart palisades to right and left, a slope of beach ahead. He peered into the clamorous dark and found nothing. "Olga," he croaked. "Olga. Olga."

Wings shadowed him among the shadows. "Get ashore before an undertow eats you!" Enherrian whooped, and beat his way off in search.

Pete crawled to gritty sand, fell, ánd let annihilation have him. He wasn't unconscious long. When he revived, Rusa and Whell were beside him. Enherrian was further inland. The captain hauled on a line he had snubbed around a tree. Olga floated at the other end. She had no strength left, but he had passed a bight beneath her arms and she was alive.

At wolf-gray dawn the wind had fallen to gale force or maybe less, and the cliffs shielded lagoon and strand from it. Overhead it shrilled, and outside the breakers cannonaded, their rage aquiver through the island. Pete and Olga huddled together, a shared cloak across their shoulders. Enherrian busied himself checking the salvaged material. Whell sat on the hindbones of her wings and stared seaward. Moisture gleamed on her grizzled feathers like tears.

Rusa flew in from the reefs and landed. "No trace," he said. His voice was emptied by exhaustion. "Neither the boat nor Arrach." Through the rust in his own brain, Pete noticed the order of those words.

Nevertheless—He leaned toward the parents and brother of Arrach, who had been beautiful and merry and had sung to them by moonlight. "How can we say—?" he began, realized he didn't have Planha words, and tried in Anglic: "How can we say how sorry we both are?"

"No necessity," Rusa answered.

"She died saving me!"

"And what you were carrying, which we needed badly." Some energy returned to Rusa. He lifted his head and its crest. "She had deathpride, our lass."

Afterward Pete, in his search for meaning, would learn about that Ythrian concept. "Courage" is too simple and weak a translation. Certain Old Japanese words come closer, though they don't really bear the same value either.

Whell turned her hawk gaze full upon him. "Did you see anything of what happened in the water?" she asked. He was too unfamiliar with her folk to interpret the tone: today he thinks it was loving. He did know that, being creatures of seasonal rut, Ythrians are less sexually motivated than man is, but probably treasure their young even more. The strongest bond between male and female is children, who are what life is all about.

"No, I . . . I fear not," he stammered.

Enherrian reached out to lay claws, very gently and briefly, on his wife's back. "Be sure she fought well," he said. "She gave God honor." (Glory? Praise? Adoration? His due?)

Does he mean she prayed, made her confession, while she drowned? The question dragged itself through Pete's weariness and caused him to murmur: "She's in heaven now." Again he was forced to use Anglic words.

Enherrian gave him a look which he could have sworn was startled. "What do you say? Arrach is dead."

"Why, her . . . her spirit—"

"Will be remembered in pride." Enherrian resumed his work.

Olga said it for Pete: "So you don't believe the spirit outlives the body?"

"How could it?" Enherrian snapped. "Why should it?" His motions, his posture, the set of his plumage added: Leave me alone.

Pete thought: *Well, many faiths, including high ones, including some sects which call themselves Christian, deny immortality. How sorry I feel for these my friends, who don't know they will meet their beloved afresh!*

They will, regardless. It makes no sense that God, Who created what is because in His goodness he wished to share existence, would shape a soul only to break it and throw it away.

Never mind. The job on hand is to keep Olga alive, in her dear body. "Can I help?"

"Yes, check our medical kit," Enherrian said.

It had come through undamaged in its box. The items for human use—stimulants, sedatives, anesthetics, antitoxins, antibiotics, coagulants, healing promoters, et standard cetera—naturally outnumbered those for Ythrians. There hasn't been time to develop a large scientific pharmacopoeia for the latter species. True, certain materials work on both, as does the surgical and monitoring equipment. Pete distributed pills which took the pain out of bruises and scrapes, the heaviness out of muscles. Meanwhile Rusa collected wood, Whell started and tended a fire, Olga made breakfast. They had considerable food, mostly freeze-dried, gear to cook it, tools like knives and a hatchet, cord, cloth, flashbeams, two blasters and abundant recharges: what they required for survival.

"It may be insufficient," Enherrian said. "The portable radio transceiver went down with Arrach. The boat's transmitter couldn't punch a call through that storm, and now the boat's on the bottom—nothing to see from the air, scant metal to register on a detector."

"Oh, they'll check on us when the weather slacks off," Olga said. She caught Pete's hand in hers. He felt the warmth.

"If their flitter survived the hurricane, which I doubt," Enherrian stated. "I'm convinced the camp was also struck. We had built no shelter for the flitter, our people will have been too busy saving themselves to secure it, and I think that thin shell was tumbled about and broken. If I'm right, they'll have to call for an aircraft from elsewhere, which may not be available at once. In either case, we could be anywhere in a huge territory; and the expedition has no time or personnel for an indefinite search. They will seek us, aye; however, if we are not found before an arbitrary date—" A ripple passed over the feathers of face and neck; a human would have shrugged.

"What . . . can we do?" the girl asked.

"Clear a sizeable area in a plainly artificial pattern, or heap fuel for beacon fires should a flitter pass within sight—whichever is practicable. If nothing comes of that, we should consider building a raft or the like."

"Or modify a life jacket for me," Rusa suggested, "and I can try to fly to the mainland."

Enherrian nodded. "We must investigate the possibilities. First let's get a real rest."

The Ythrians were quickly asleep, squatted on their locked wing joints like idols of a forgotten people. Pete and Olga felt more excited and wandered a distance off, hand in hand.

Above the crag-enclosed beach, the island rose toward a crest which he estimated as three kilometers away. If it was in the middle, this was no large piece of real estate. Nor did he see adequate shelter. A mat of mossy, intensely green plants squeezed out any possibility of forest. A few trees stood isolated. Their branches tossed in the wind. He noticed particularly one atop a great outcrop nearby, gaunt brown trunk and thin leaf-fringed boughs that whipped insanely about. Blossoms, torn from vines, blew past, and they were gorgeous; but there would be naught to live on here, and he wasn't hopeful about learning, in time, how to catch Gray's equivalent of fish.

"Strange about them, isn't it?" Olga murmured.

"Eh?" He came, startled, out of his preoccupations.

She gestured at the Ythrians. "Them. The way they took poor Arrach's death."

"Well, you can't judge them by our standards. Maybe they feel grief less than we would, or maybe their culture demands stoicism." He looked at her and did not look away again. "To be frank, darling, I can't really mourn either. I'm too happy to have you back."

"And I you—oh, Pete, Pete, my only—"

They found a secret spot and made love. He saw nothing wrong in that. Do you ever in this life come closer to the wonder which is God?

Afterward they returned to their companions. Thus the clash of wings awoke them, hours later. They scrambled from their bedrolls and saw the Ythrians swing aloft

The wind was strong and loud as yet, though easing off in fickleness, flaws, downdrafts, whirls, and eddies. Clouds were mostly gone. Those which remained raced gold and hot orange before a sun low in the west, across blue serenity. The lagoon glittered purple, the greensward lay aglow. It had warmed up till rich odors of growth, of flowers, blent with the sea-salt.

And splendid in the sky danced Enherrian, Whell, and Rusa. They wheeled, soared, pounced, and rushed back into light which ran molten off their pinions. They chanted, and fragments blew down to the humans: "*High flew your spirit on many winds. . . . be always remembered. . . .*"

"What *is* that?" Olga breathed.

"Why, they—they—" The knowledge broke upon Pete. "They're holding a service for Arrach."

He knelt and said a prayer for her soul's repose. But he wondered if she, who had belonged to the air, would truly want rest. And his eyes could not leave her kindred.

Enherrian screamed a hunter's challenge and rushed down at the earth. He flung himself meteoric past the stone outcrop Pete had seen; for an instant the man gasped, believing he would be shattered; then he rose, triumphant.

He passed by the lean tree of thin branches. Gusts flailed them about. A nearly razor edge took off his left wing. Blood spurted; Ythrian blood is royal purple. Somehow Enherrian slewed around and made a crash landing on the bluff top, just beyond range of what has since been named the surgeon tree.

Pete yanked the medikit to him and ran. Olga wailed, briefly, and followed. When they reached the scene, they found that Whell and Rusa had pulled feathers from their breasts to try staunching the wound.

Evening, night, day, evening, night.

Enherrian sat before a campfire. Its light wavered, picked him red out of shadow and let him half-vanish again, save for the unblinking yellow eyes. His wife and son supported him. Stim, cell-freeze, and plasma surrogate had done their work, and he could speak in a weak roughness. The bandages on his stump were a nearly glaring white.

Around crowded shrubs which, by day, showed low and russet-leaved. They filled a hollow on the far side of the island, to which Enherrian had been carried on an improvised litter. Their odor was rank, in an atmosphere once more subtropically hot, and they clutched at feet with raking twigs. But this was the most sheltered spot his companions could find, and he might die in a new storm on the open beach.

He looked through smoke, at the Bergs, who sat as close together as they were able. He said—the surf growled faintly beneath his words, while never a leaf rustled in the breathless dark—"I have read that your people can make a lost part grow forth afresh."

Pete couldn't answer. He tried but couldn't. It was Olga who had the courage to say, "We can do it for ourselves. None except ourselves." She laid her head on her man's breast and wept.

Well, you need a lot of research to unravel a genetic code, a lot of development to make the molecules of heredity repeat what they did in the womb. Science hasn't had time yet for other races. It never will for all. They are too many."

"As I thought," Enherrian said. "Nor can a proper prosthesis be engineered in my lifetime. I have few years left; an Ythrian who cannot fly soon becomes sickly."

"Grav units—" Pete faltered.

The scorn in those eyes was like a blow. Dead metal to raise you, who have had wings?

Fierce and haughty though the Ythrian is, his quill-clipped slaves have never rebelled: for they are only half-alive. Imagine yourself, human male, castrated. Enherrian might flap his remaining wing and the stump to fill his blood with air; but he would have nothing he could do with that extra energy, it would turn inward and corrode his body, perhaps at last his mind.

For a second, Whell laid an arm around him.

"You will devise a signal tomorrow," Enherrian said, "and start work on it. Too much time has already been wasted."

Before they slept, Pete managed to draw Whell aside. "He needs constant care, you know," he whispered to her in the acrid booming gloom. "The drugs got him over the shock, but he can't tolerate more and he'll be very weak."

True, she said with feathers rather than voice. Aloud: "Olga shall nurse him. She cannot get around as easily as Rusa or me, and lacks your physical strength. Besides, she can prepare meals and the like for us."

Pete nodded absently. He had a dread to explain. "Uh . . . uh . . . do you think—well, I mean in your ethic, in the New Faith—might Enherrian put an end to him-self?" And he wondered if God would really blame the captain.

Her wings and tail spread, her crest erected, she glared. "You say that of him?" she shrilled. Seeing his concern, she eased, even made a *krr* noise which might answer to a chuckle. "No, no, he has his deathpride. He would never rob God of honor."

After survey and experiment, the decision was to hack a giant cross in the island turf. That growth couldn't be ignited, and what wood was burnable—deadfall—was too scant and stingy of smoke for a beacon.

The party had no spades; the vegetable mat was thick and tough; the toil became brutal. Pete, like Whell and Rusa, would return to camp and topple into sleep. He wouldn't rouse till morning, to gulp his food and plod off to labor. He grew gaunt, bearded, filthy, numb-brained, sore in every cell.

Thus he did not notice how Olga was waning. Enherrian was mending, somewhat, under her care. She did her jobs, which were comparatively light, and would have been ashamed to complain of headaches, giddiness, diarrhea, and nausea. Doubtless she imagined she suffered merely from reaction to disaster, plus a sketchy and ill-balanced diet, plus heat and brilliant sun and—She'd cope.

The days were too short for work, the nights too short for sleep. Pete's terror was that he would see a flitter pass and vanish over the horizon before the Ythrians could hail it. Then they might try sending Rusa for help. But that was a long, tricky flight; and the gulf coast camp was due to be struck rather soon anyway.

Sometimes he wondered dimly how he and Olga might do if marooned on Gray. He kept enough wits to dismiss his fantasy for what it was. Take the simple fact that native life appeared to lack certain vitamins—

Then one darkness, perhaps a terrestrial week after the shipwreck, he was roused by her crying his name. He straggled to wakefulness. She lay beside him. Gray's moon was up, nearly full, swifter and brighter than Luna. Its glow drowned most of the stars, frosted the encroaching bushes, fell without pity to show him her fallen cheeks and rolling eyes. She shuddered in his arms; he heard her teeth clapping. "I'm cold, darling, I'm cold," she said in the subtropical summer night. She vomited over him, and presently she was delirious.

The Ythrians gave what help they could, he what medicines he could. By sunrise (an outrageousness of rose and gold and silver-blue, crossed by the jubilant wings of waterfowl) he knew she was dying.

He examined his own physical state, using a robot he discovered he had in his skull: yes, his wretchedness was due to more than overwork, he saw that now; he too had had the upset stomach and the occasional shivers, nothing like the disintegration which possessed Olga, nevertheless the same kind of thing. Yet the Ythrians stayed healthy. Did a local germ attack humans while finding the other race undevourable?

The rescuers, who came on the island two Gray days later, already had the answer. That genus of bushes is widespread on the planet. A party elsewhere, after getting sick and getting into safety suits, analyzed its vapors. They are a cumulative poison to man; they scarcely harm an Ythrian. The analysts named it the hell shrub.

Unfortunately, their report wasn't broadcast until after the boat left. Meanwhile Pete had been out in the field every day, while Olga spent her whole time in the hollow, over which the sun regularly created an inversion layer.

Whell and Rusa went grimly back to work. Pete had to get away. He wasn't sure of the reason, but he had to be alone when he screamed at heaven, "Why did You do this to her, why did You do it?" Enherrian could look after Olga, who had brought him back to a life he no longer wanted. Pete had stopped her babblings, writhings, and sawtoothed sounds of pain with a shot. She ought to sleep peacefully into that death which the monitor instruments said was, in the absence of hospital facilities, ineluctable.

He stumbled off to the heights. The sea reached calm, in a thousand hues of azure and green, around the living island, beneath the gentle sky. He knelt in all that emptiness and put his question.

After an hour he could say, "Your will be done" and return to camp.

Olga lay awake. "Pete, Pete!" she cried. Anguish distorted her voice till he couldn't recognize it; nor could he really see her in the yellowed sweating skin and lank hair drawn over a skeleton, or find her in the stench and the nails which flayed him as they clutched. "Where were you, hold me close, it hurts, how it hurts—"

He gave her a second injection, to small effect.

He knelt again, beside her. He has not told me what he said, or how. At last she grew quiet, gripped him hard and waited for the pain to end.

When she died, he says, it was like seeing a light blown out.

He laid her down, closed eyes and jaw, folded her hands. On mechanical feet he went to the pup tent which had been rigged for Enherrian. The cripple calmly awaited him. "She is fallen?" he asked.

Pete nodded.

"That is well," Enherrian said.

"It is not," Pete heard himself reply, harsh and remote. "She shouldn't have aroused. The drug should've—Did you give her a stim shot? Did you bring her back to suffer?"

"What else?" said Enherrian, though he was unarmed and a blaster lay nearby for Pete to seize. *Not that I'll ease* him *out of his fate!* went through the man in a spasm. "I saw that you, distraught, had misgauged. You were gone and I unable to follow you. She might well die before your return."

Out of his void, Pete gaped into those eyes. "You mean," rattled from him, "you mean . . . she . . . mustn't?"

Enherrian crawled forth—he could only crawl, on his single wing—to take Pete's hands. "My friend," he said, his tone immeasurably compassionate, "I honored you both too much to deny her her deathpride."

Pete's chief awareness was of the cool sharp talons.

"Have I misunderstood?" asked Enherrian anxiously. "Did you not wish her to give God a battle?"

Even on Lucifer, the nights finally end. Dawn blazed on the tors when Pete finished his story.

I emptied the last few ccs. into our glasses. We'd get no work done today. "Yeh," I said. "Cross-cultural semantics. Given the best will in the universe, two beings from different planets—or just different countries, often—take for granted they think alike; and the outcome can be tragic."

"I assumed that at first," Pete said. "I didn't need to forgive Enherrian—how could he know? For his part, he was puzzled when I buried my darling. On Ythri they cast them from a great height into wilderness. But neither race wants to watch the rotting of what was loved, so he did his lame best to help me."

He drank, looked as near the cruel bluish sun as he was able, and mumbled: "What I couldn't do was forgive God."

"The problem of evil," I said.

"Oh, no. I've studied these matters, these past years: read theology, argued with priests, the whole route. Why does God, if He is a loving and personal God, allow evil? Well, there's a perfectly good Christian answer to that. Man—intelligence everywhere—must have free will. Otherwise we're puppets and have no reason to exist. Free will necessarily includes the capability of doing wrong. We're here, in this cosmos during our lives, to learn how to be good of our unforced choice."

"I spoke illiterately," I apologized. "All that brandy. No, sure, your logic is right, regardless of whether I accept your premises or not. What I meant was: the problem of pain. Why does a merciful God permit undeserved agony? If He's omnipotent, He isn't compelled to.

"I'm not talking about the sensation which warns you to take your hand from the fire, anything useful like that. No, the random accident which wipes out a life . . . or a mind—" I drank. "What happened to Arrach, yes, and to Enherrian, and Olga, and you, and Whell. What happens when a disease hits, or those catastrophes we label acts of God. Or the slow decay of us if we grow very old. Every such horror. Never mind if science has licked some of them; we have enough left, and then there were our ancestors who endured them all.

"Why? What possible end is served? It's not adequate to declare we'll receive an unbounded reward after we die and therefore it makes no difference whether a life was gusty or grisly. That's no explanation.

"Is this the problem you're grappling with, Pete?"

"In a way." He nodded, cautiously, as if he were already his father's age. "At least, it's the start of the problem.

"You see, there I was, isolated among Ythrians. My fellow humans sympathized, but they had nothing to say that I didn't know already. The New Faith, however. . . . Mind you, I wasn't about to convert. What I did hope for was an insight, a freshness, that'd help me make Christian sense of our losses. Enherrian was so sure, so learned, in his beliefs—

"We talked, and talked, and talked, while I was regaining my strength. He was as caught as me. Not that he couldn't fit our troubles into his scheme of things. That was easy. But it turned out that the New Faith has no satisfactory answer to the problem of *evil*. It says God allows wickedness so we may win honor by fighting for the right. Really, when you stop to think, that's weak, especially in carnivore Ythrian terms. Don't you agree?"

"You know them, I don't," I sighed. "You imply they have a better answer to the riddle of pain than your own religion does."

"It seems better." Desperation edged his slightly blurred tone:

"They're hunters, or were until lately. They see God like that, as the Hunter. Not the Torturer—you absolutely must understand this point—no, He rejoices in our happiness the way we might rejoice to see a game animal gamboling. Yet at last He comes after us. Our noblest moment is when we, knowing He is irresistible, give Him a good chase, a good fight.

"Then He wins honor. And some infinite end is furthered. (The same one as when my God is given praise? How can I tell?) We're dead, struck down, lingering at

most a few years in the memories of those who escaped
this time. And that's what we're here for. That's why
God created the universe."

"And this belief is old," I said. "It doesn't belong just
to a few cranks. No, it's been held for centuries by millions of sensitive, intelligent, educated beings. You can
live by it, you can die by it. If it doesn't solve every
paradox, it solves some that your faith won't, quite. This
is your dilemma, true?"

He nodded again. "The priests have told me to deny
a false creed and to acknowledge a mystery. Neither
instruction feels right. Or am I asking too much?"

"I'm sorry, Pete," I said, altogether honestly. It hurt.
"But how should I know? I looked into the abyss once,
and saw nothing, and haven't looked since. You keep
looking. Which of us is the braver?

"Maybe you can find a text in Job. I don't know, I tell
you, I don't know."

The sun lifted higher above the burning horizon.

INTRODUCTION

❁MARGIN OF PROFIT❁

Too many of us unthinkingly think of David Falkayn as
if he flashed into being upon Avalon like a lightning
bolt. The Polesotechnic League we know of only in its
decadence and downfall. Yet for long and long it was
wing and talon of that Technic civilization which humans
begot and from which many other races—Ythrians too,
Ythrians too—drew fresh blood that still flows within
them.

Remote from the centers of Technic might, unaccus-
tomed to the idea that alien sophonts are alien in more
than body, our ancestors in the first lifetimes after the
Discovery were little aware of anything behind the occasional merchant vessels, scientists, hired teachers and
consultants, that came to their planet. The complexity of
roots, trunks, boughs, which upbore the leaf-crown they

saw, lay beyond their ken. Even the visits of a few to Terra brought scant enlightenment.

Later ancestors, moving vigorously into space on their own, were better informed. Paradoxically, though, they had less to do with the League. By then they required no imports to continue development. Furthermore, being close to the stars in this sector, they competed so successfully for trade that League members largely withdrew from a region which had never been highly profitable for them. The main point of contact was the planet Esperance and it, being as yet thinly settled, was not a market which drew great flocks from either side.

Thus the ordinary Ythrian, up to this very year, has had only a footgrip upon reality where the League is concerned. He/she/youngling must strengthen this if the origins of the Avalonian colony are to be made clear. What winds did Falkayn ride, what storms blew him hitherward at last?

His biographies tell how he became a protégé of Nicholas van Rijn, but say little about that merchant lord. You may well be surprised to learn that on numerous other worlds, it is the latter who lives in folk memory, whether as hero or rogue. He did truthfully fly in the front echelon of events when several things happened whose thunders would echo through centuries. With him as our archetype, we can approach knowledge.

Though hardly ever read or played anymore upon this globe, a good many accounts of him exist in Library Central, straightforward, semifictional, or romantic. Maychance the best introduction is the story which follows, from *Tales of the Great Frontier* by A. A. Craig.

—Hloch of the Stormgate Choth
The Earth Book of Stormgate

MARGIN OF PROFIT

It was an anachronism to have a human receptionist in this hall of lucent plastic, among machines that winked and talked between jade columns soaring up into vaulted dimness—but a remarkably pleasant one when she was as long-legged and redheaded a stunblast as the girl behind the desk. Captain Torres drew to a crisp halt and identified himself. Traveling down sumptuous curves, his glance was jarred by the needle gun at her waist.

"Good day, sir," she smiled. "I'll see if Freeman van Rijn is ready for you." She switched on an intercom. A three-megavolt oath bounced out. "No, he's still in conference on the audivid. Won't you be seated?"

Before she turned the intercom off, Torres caught a few words: "—he'll give us the exclusive franchise or we embargo, *ja*, and maybe arrange a little blockade too. Who in Satan's squatpot do these emperors on a single planet think they are? Hokay, he has a million soldiers under arms. You go tell him to take those soldiers, with hobnailed boots and rifles at port, and stuff them—" *Click.*

Torres wrapped cape around tunic and sat down, laying one polished boot across the other knee of his white culottes. He felt awkward, simultaneously overdressed and naked. The formal garb of a Lodgemaster in the Federated Brotherhood of Spacefarers was a far remove from the coverall he wore in his ship or the loungers of groundside leave. And the guards in the lobby, a kilometer below, had not only checked his credentials and retinal patterns, they had made him deposit his sidearm.

Damn Nicholas van Rijn and the whole Polesotechnic League! Good saints, drop him on Pluto with no underwear!

Of course, a merchant prince did have to be wary of kidnappers and assassins, though van Rijn himself was said to be murderously fast with a handgun. Nevertheless, arming your receptionist was not a polite thing to do.

Torres wondered, a trifle wistfully, if she was among the old devil's mistresses. Perhaps not. However, given the present friction between the Company—by extension, the entire League—and the Brotherhood, she'd have no time for him; her contract doubtless had a personal fealty clause. His gaze went to the League emblem on the wall behind her, a golden sunburst afire with jewels, surrounding an ancient rocketship, and the motto: *All the traffic will bear.* That could be taken two ways, he reflected sourly. Beneath it was the trademark of this outfit, the Solar Spice & Liquors Company.

The girl turned the intercom back on and heard only a steady rumble of obscenities. "You may go in now, please," she said, and to the speaker: "Lodgemaster Captain Torres, sir, here for his appointment."

The spaceman rose and passed through the inner door. His lean dark features were taut. This would be a new experience, meeting his ultimate boss. It was ten years since he had had to call anybody "sir" or "madam."

The office was big, an entire side transparent, overlooking a precipitous vista of Djakarta's towers, green landscape hot with tropical gardens, and the molten glitter of the Java Sea. The other walls were lined with the biggest datacom Torres had ever seen, with shelves of extraterrestrial curios, and, astonishingly, a thousand or more codex-type books whose fine leather bindings showed signs of wear. Despite its expanse, the desktop was littered, close to maximum entropy. The most noticeable object on it was a small image of St. Dismas, carved from Martian sandroot. Ventilators could not quite dismiss a haze and reek of tobacco smoke.

The newcomer snapped a salute. "Lodgemaster Captain Rafael Torres speaking for the Brotherhood. Good day, sir."

Van Rijn grunted. He was a huge man, two meters in height and more than broad enough to match. A triple chin and swag belly did not make him appear soft. Rings glittered on hairy fingers and bracelets on brawny wrists, under snuff-soiled lace. Small black eyes, set close to a great hook nose under a sloping forehead, peered with laser intensity. He continued filling his pipe and said nothing until he had a good head of steam up.

"So," he growled then, basso profundo, in an accent as thick as himself. "You speak for the whole unspeakable union, I hope. Women members too? I have never understood why they want to say they belong to a brotherhood." Waxed mustaches and long goatee waggled above a gorgeously embroidered waistcoat. Beneath it was only a sarong, which gave way to columnar ankles and bare splay feet.

Torres checked his temper. "Yes, sir. Privately, informally, of course . . . thus far. I have the honor to represent all locals in the Commonwealth, and lodges outside the Solar System have expressed solidarity. We assume you will be a spokesman for the master merchants of the League."

"In a subliminary way. I will shovel your demands along at my associates, what of them as don't hide too good in their offices and harems. Sit."

Torres gave the chair no opportunity to mold itself to him. Perched on the edge, he proceeded harshly: "The issue is very simple. The votes are now in, and the result can't surprise you. We are not calling a strike, you realize. But contracts or no, we will not take any more ships through the Kossaluth of Borthu until that menace has been ended. Any owner who tries to hold us to the articles and send us there will be struck. The idea of our meeting today, Freeman van Rijn, is to make that clear and get the League's agreement, without a lot of public noise that might bring on a real fight."

"By damn, you cut your own throats like with a butterknife, slow and outscruciating." The merchant's tone was surprisingly mild. "Not alone the loss of pay and commissions. No, but if Sector Antares is not kept steady supplied, it loses taste maybe for cinnamon and London dry gin. Nor can other companies be phlegmatic about what they hawk. Like if Jo-Boy Technical Services bring in no more engineers and scientists, the colonies will train up their own. Hell's poxy belles! In a few years, no more market on any planet in those parts. You lose, I lose, we all lose."

"The answer is obvious, sir. We detour around the Kossaluth. I know that'll take us through more hazardous regions, astronomically speaking, unless we go very far aside indeed. However, the brothers and sisters will accept either choice."

"What?" Somehow van Rijn managed a bass scream. "Is you developed feedback of the bowels? Double or quadruple the length of the voyage! Boost heaven-high the salaries, capital goods losses, survivors' compensation, insurance! Halve or quarter the deliveries per year! We are ruined! Better we give up Antares at once!"

The route was already expensive, Torres knew. He wasn't sure whether or not the companies could afford the extra cost; their books were their own secret. Having waited out the dramatics, he said patiently:

"The Borthudian press gangs have been operating for two years now, you know. Nothing that's been tried has stopped them. We have not panicked. If it had been up to the siblings at large, we'd have voted right at the start to bypass that horrorhole. But the Lodgemasters held back, hoping something could be worked out. Apparently that isn't possible."

"See here," van Rijn urged. "I don't like this no better than you. Worse, maybe. The losses my company alone has took could make me weep snot. We can afford it, though. Naked-barely, but we can. Figure it. About fifteen percent of our ships altogether gets captured. We would lose more, traveling through the Gamma Mist or the Stonefields. And those crews would not be prisoners that we are still working to have released. No, they would be kind of dead. As for making a still bigger roundabout through nice clear vacuum, well, that would be safe, but means an absolute loss on each run. Even if your brotherhood will take a big cut in the exorbital wages you draw, still, consider the tieup of bottom on voyages so long. We do have trade elsewheres to carry on."

Torres' temper snapped across. "Go flush your dirty financial calculations! Try thinking about human beings for once. We'll face meteoroid swarms, infrasuns, rogue planets, black holes, radiation bursts, hostile natives—but have you *met* one of those impressed men? I have. That's what decided me, and made me take a lead in getting the Brotherhood to act. I'm not going to risk it happening to me, nor to any lodge sibling of mine. Why don't you and your fellow moneymen conn the ships personally?"

"Ho-o-o," murmured van Rijn. He showed no offense, but leaned across the desk on his forearms. "You tell me, ha?"

Torres must force the story out. "Met him on Arkan III—on the fringe of the Kossaluth, autonomous planet, you recall. We'd put in with a consignment of tea. A ship of theirs was in too, and you can bet your brain we went around in armed parties, ready to shoot any Borthudian who might look like a crimp. Or any Borthudian at all; but they kept to themselves. Instead, I saw him, this man they'd snatched, going on some errand. I spoke to him. My friends and I even tried to capture him, so we could bring him back to Earth and get reversed what that electronic hell-machine had done to him—He fought us and got away. God! He'd've been more free if he were in chains. And still I could feel how he wanted out, he was screaming inside, but he couldn't break the conditioning *and he couldn't go crazy either—*"

Torres grew aware that van Rijn had come around the desk and was thrusting a bottle into his hand. "Here, you drink some from this," the merchant said. The liquor burned the whole way down. "I have seen a conditioned man myself once, long ago when I was a rough-and-tumbler. A petty native prince had got it done to him, to keep him for a technical expert when he wanted to go home. We did catch him that time, and took him back for treatment." He returned to his chair and rekindled his pipe. "First, though, we got together with the ship's engineer and made us a little firecracker what we blew off at the royal palace." He chuckled. "The yield was about five kilotons."

"If you want to outfit a punitive expedition, sir," Torres rasped, "I guarantee you can get full crews."

"No." Curled, shoulder-length black locks swished greasily as van Rijn shook his head. "You know the League does not have much of a combat fleet. The trouble with capital ships is, they tie up capital. It is one thing to use a tiny bit of force on a planetbound lordling what has got unreasonable. It is another thing to take on somebody what can take you right on back. Simple tooling up for a war with Borthu, let alone fighting one, would bring many member companies close to bankrupture."

"But what about the precedent, if you tamely let these outrages go on? Who'll be next to make prey of you?"

"Ja, there is that. But there is also the Commonwealth government. We try any big-size action, we traders, even though it is far outside the Solar System, and right away we get gibberings about our 'imperialism.' We could get lots of trouble made for us, right here in the heart of civilization. Maybe we get called pirates, because we is not a government ourselves with politicians and bureaucrats telling people what to do. Maybe Sol would actual-like intervene against us on behalf of the Kossaluth, what is 'only exercising sovereignty within its legitimate sphere.' You know how diplomats from Earth has not made any hard effort for getting Borthu to stop. In fact, I tell you, a lot of politicians feel quite chortlesome when they see us wicked profiteers receiving some shaftcraft."

Torres stirred in his seat. "Yes, of course, I'm as disgusted as you with the official reaction, or lack of reaction. But what about the League? I mean, its leaders must have been trying measures short of war. I take it those have come to naught."

"You take that, boy, and keep it for yourself, because I for sure don't want it. *Ja.* Correct. Threats the Borthudians grin at, knowing how hard pinched we is and where. Not good trade offers nor economic sanctions has worked; they is not interested in trade with us. Rathermore, they do expect we will soon shun their territory, like you now want us to. That suits their masters well, not having foreign influentials. . . . Bribes? How do you bribe a being what ranks big in his own civilization and species, both those alien to you? Assassins? *Ach,* I am afraid we squandered several good assassins for no philanthropic result." Van Rijn cursed for two straight minutes without repeating himself. "And there they sit, fat and greedy-gut, across the route to Antares and all stars beyond! It is not to be stood for! No, it is to be jumped on!"

Presently he finished in a calmer tone: "This ultimatum of yours brings matters to a head. Speaking of heads, it is getting time for a tall cold beer. I will soon throw a little brainbooting session with a few fellows and see what oozes out. Maybe we can invent something. You go tell the crewmen they should sit bottom-tight for a while yet, *nie?* Now, would you like to join me in the bar?—No? Then good day to you, Captain, if possible."

◎ ◎ ◎

It is a truism that the structure of a society is basically determined by its technology. Not in an absolute sense—there may be totally different cultures using identical tools—but the tools settle the possibilities; you can't have interstellar trade without spaceships. A race limited to a single planet, possessing a high knowledge of mechanics but with its basic machines of industry and war requiring a large capital investment, will inevitably tend toward collectivism under one name or another. Free enterprise needs elbow room.

Automation and the mineral wealth of the Solar System made the manufacture of most goods cheap. The cost of energy nosedived when small, clean, simple fusion units became available. Gravitics led to the hyperdrive, which opened a galaxy to exploitation. This also provided a safety valve. A citizen who found his government oppressive could often emigrate elsewhere, an exodus—the Breakup, as it came to be called—that planted liberty on a number of worlds. Their influence in turn loosened bonds upon the mother planet.

Interstellar distances being what they are, and intelligent races having their separate ideas of culture, there was no political union of them. Nor was there much armed conflict; besides the risk of destruction, few had anything to fight about. A race rarely gets to be intelligent without an undue share of built-in ruthlessness, so all was not sweetness and fraternity. However, the various balances of power remained fairly stable. Meanwhile the demand for cargoes grew huge. Not only did colonies want the luxuries of home, and home want colonial products, but the older civilizations had much to swap. It was usually cheaper to import such things than to create the industry needed to make synthetics and substitutes.

Under such conditions, an exuberant capitalism was bound to arise. It was also bound to find mutual interests, form alliances, and negotiate spheres of influence. The powerful companies might be in competition, but their magnates had the wit to see that, overriding this, they shared a need to cooperate in many activities, arbitrate disputes among themselves, and present a united front to the demands of the·state—any state.

Governments were limited to a few planetary systems at most; they could do little to control their cosmopolitan merchants. One by one, through bribery, coercion, or sheer despair, they gave up the struggle.

Selfishness is a potent force. Governments, officially dedicated to altruism, remained divided. The Polesotechnic League became a loose kind of supergovernment, sprawling from Canopus to Deneb, drawing its membership and employees from perhaps a thousand species. It was a horizontal society, cutting across political and cultural boundaries. It set its own policies, made its own treaties, established its own bases, fought its own battles . . . and for a time, in the course of milking the Milky Way, did more to spread a truly universal civilization and enforce a solid *Pax* than all the diplomats in known history.

Nevertheless, it had its troubles.

A mansion among those belonging to Nicholas van Rijn lay on the peak of Kilimanjaro, up among the undying snows. It was an easy spot to defend, just in case, and a favorite for conferences.

His car slanted down through a night of needle-sharp stars, toward high turrets and glowing lights. Looking through the canopy, he picked out Scorpio. Antares flashed a red promise. He shook his fist at the fainter, unseen suns between him and it. "So!" he muttered. "Monkey business with van Rijn. The whole Sagittarius direction waiting to be opened, and you in the way. By damn, this will cost you money, gut and kipper me if it don't."

He thought back to days when he had ridden ships through yonder spaces, bargaining in strange cities or stranger wildernesses, or beneath unblue skies and in poisonous winds, for treasures Earth had not yet imagined. For a moment, wistfulness tugged at him. A long time now since he had been any further than the Moon . . . poor, aging fat man, chained to a single planet and cursed whenever he turned an honest credit. The Antares route was more important than he cared to admit aloud. If he lost it, he lost his chance at the pioneering that went on beyond, to corporations with offices on the other side of the Kossaluth. You went on expanding or you went under, and being a conspicuous member of the League wouldn't save you. Of course, he could retire, but then what would there be to engage his energies?

The car landed itself. Household staff, liveried and beweaponed, sprang to flank him as he emerged. He wheezed thin chill air into sooty lungs, drew his cloak of phosphorescent onthar skin tightly around him, and scrunched up a graveled garden path to the house. A new maid stood at the door, pert and pretty. He tossed his plumed cap at her and considered making a proposition, but the butler said that the invited persons were already here. Seating himself, more for show than because of weariness, he told the chair, "Conference room" and rolled along corridors paneled in the woods of a dozen planets. A sweet smell of attar of janie and a softly played Mozart quintet enlivened the air.

Four colleagues were poised around a table when he entered, a datacom terminal before each. Kraaknach of the Martian Transport Company was glowing his yellow eyes at a Frans Hals on the wall. Firmage of North American Engineering registered impatience with a puffed cigar. Mjambo, who owned Jo-Boy Technical Services, was talking into his wristphone, but stopped when his host entered. Gornas-Kiew happened to be on Earth and was authorized to speak for the Centaurian conglomerate; "he" sat hunched into "his" shell, naught moving save the delicate antennae.

Van Rijn plumped his mass into an armchair at the head of the table. Waiters appeared with trays of drinks, snacks, and smokes catered for the individuals present. He took a large bite from a limburger-and-onion sandwich and looked inquiringly at the rest.

Kraaknach's face, owlish within the air helmet, turned to him. "Well, Freeman who receives us," he trilled and croaked, "I understand we are met on account of this Borthudian *hrokna*. Did the spacemen make their expected demand?"

"*Ja*." Van Rijn chose a cigar and rolled it between his fingers. "The situation is changed from desperate to serious. They will not take ships through the Kossaluth, except to fight, while this shanghai business goes on."

"I suppose it is quite unfeasible to deliver a few gigatons' worth of warhead at the Borthudian home planet?" asked Mjambo.

Van Rijn tugged his goatee. "Death and damnation!" He checked his temper. After all, he had invited these specific sophonts here precisely because they had not yet been much concerned with the problem. It had affected their enterprises in varying degrees, of course, but interests elsewhere had been tying up their direct attention. This tiny, outlying corner of the galaxy which Technic civilization has slightly explored is that big and various. Van Rijn was hoping for a fresh viewpoint.

Having repeated the objections he had given Torres, he added: "I must got to admit, also, supposing we could, slaughtering several billion sentients because their leaders make trouble for us is not nice. I do not think the League would long survive being so guilty. Besides, it is wasteful. They should better be made customers of ours."

"Limited action, whittling down their naval strength till they see reason?" wondered Firmage.

"I have had more such programs run through the computers than there is politicians in hell," van Rijn answered. "They every one give the same grismal answer. Allowing for minimal losses, compensations, salaries, risk bonuses, construction, maintenance, replacement, ammunition, depreciation, loss of business due to lack of supervision elsewhere, legal action brought by the Solar Commonwealth and maybe other governments, bribes, loss of profit if the money was invested where it ought to be, et bloody-bestonkered cetera . . . in a nutshell, we cannot afford it." Reminded, he told the butler, "Simmons, you gluefoot, a bowl of mixed-up nuts, chop-chop, only you don't chop them, understand?"

"You will pardon my ignorance, good sirs," clicked Gornas-Kiew's vocalizer. "I have been quite marginally aware of this unpleasantness. Why are the Borthudians impressing human crews?"

Firmage and Mjambo stared. They had known Centaurians are apt to be single-minded—but this much?

Van Rijn simply cracked a Brazil nut between his teeth, awing everybody present except for Gornas-Kiew, and reached for a snifter of brandy. "The gruntbrains have not enough of their own," he said.

"Perhaps I can make it clear," said Kraaknach. Like many Martians of the Sirruch Horde—the latest wave of immigrants to Earth's once desolate neighbor—he was a natural-hatched lecturer. He ran a clawed hand across gray feathers, stuck a rinn tube through the intake sphincter on his helmet, and lit it.

"Borthu is a backward planet, terrestroid to eight points, with autochthons describable as humanoid," he began. "They were at an early industrial, nuclear-power stage when explorers visited them, and their reaction to the presence of a superior culture was paranoid. At least, it was in the largest nation, which shortly proceeded to conquer the rest. It had modernized technologically with extreme rapidity, aided by certain irresponsible elements of this civilization who helped it for high pay. United, the Borthudians set out to acquire an interstellar empire. Today they dominate a space about forty light-years across, though they actually occupy just a few Solar-type systems within it. By and large, they want nothing to do with the outside universe: doubtless because the rulers fear that such contact will be dangerous to the stability of their regime. Certainly they are quite able to supply their needs within the boundaries of their dominion—with the sole exception of efficient space-men. If we ourselves, with all our capabilities in the field of robotics, have not yet been able to produce totally automated spacecraft which are reliable, how much worse must the Borthudians feel the lack of enough crews."

"Hm," said Firmage. "I've already thought about sub-version. I can't believe their whole populace is happy. If we could get only a few regularly scheduled freighters in there . . . double agents . . . the Kossalu and his whole filthy government overthrown from within—"

"Of course we will follow that course in due course, if we can," van Rijn interrupted. "But at best it takes much time. Meanwhile, competitors sew up the Sagittarius frontier. We need a *quick* way to get back our routes through that space."

Kraaknach puffed oily smoke. "To continue," he said, "the Borthudians can build as many ships as they wish, which is a great many since their economy is expanding. In fact, that economy requires constant expansion if the whole empire is not to collapse, inasmuch as the race-mystique of its masters has promoted a population explosion. But they cannot produce trained spacehands at the needful rate. Pride, and a not unjustified fear of ideological contamination, prevents them from sending students to Technic planets, or hiring from among us; and they have only one understaffed astronautical academy of their own."

"I know," said Mjambo. "It'd be a whopping good market for me if we could change their minds for them."

"Accordingly," Kraaknach proceeded, "they have in the past two years taken to waylaying our vessels. Doubtless they expect to be shunned eventually, as the Brotherhood has now voted to do. But then they can afford to let much of their population die back, while using what manned ships they have to maintain the rest. Without fear of direct or indirect interference from outside, the masters can 'remold' Borthudian society at leisure. It is a pattern not unknown to Terrestrial history, I believe.

"At present, their actions are obviously in defiance of what has been considered interstellar law. However, only the Commonwealth, among governments, has the potential of doing anything about it—and there is such popular revulsion on Earth at the thought of war that the Commonwealth has confined itself to a few feeble protests. Indeed, a strong faction in it is not displeased to see the arrogant Polesotechnic League discomfited. Certain spokesmen are even arguing that territorial sovereignty should be formally recognized as extending through interstellar space. A vicious principle if ever there was one, *hru*?"

He extracted the rinn tube and dropped it down an ashtaker. "In any event," he finished, "they capture the men, brain-channel them, and assign them to their own transport fleet. It takes years to train an astronaut. We are losing a major asset in this alone."

"Can't we improve our evasive action?" inquired Firmage. "Any astronomical distance is so *damn* big. Why can't we avoid their patrols altogether?"

"Eighty-five percent of our ships do precisely that," van Rijn reminded him. "It is not enough. The unlucky minority—"

—who were detected by sensitive instruments within the maximum range of about a light-year, by the instantaneous pseudogravitational pulses of hyperdrive; on whom the Borthudians then closed in, using naval vessels which were faster and more maneuverable than merchantmen—

"—they is gotten to be too many by now. The Brotherhood will accept no more. Confidential amongst the we of us, I would not either. And, *ja*, plenty different escape tactics is been tried, as well as cutting engines and lying low. None of them work very good."

"Well, then, how about convoying our ships through?" Firmage persisted.

"At what cost? I have been with the figures. It also would mean operating the Antares run at a loss—quite apart from those extra warcraft we would have to build. It would make Sagittarian trade out of the damned question."

"Why can't we arm the merchantmen themselves?"

"Bah! Wasn't you listening to Freeman Kraaknach? Robotics is never yet got to where live brains can be altogether replaced, except in bureaucrats." Deliberately irritating, which might pique forth ideas, van Rijn added what was everybody's knowledge:

"A frigate-class ship needs twenty men for the weapons and instruments. An unarmed freighter needs only four. Consider the wages paid to spacefolk; we would really get folked. Also, sixteen extra on every ship would mean cutting down operations elsewhere, for lack of crews. Not to mention the cost of the outfitting. We cannot afford all this; we would lose money in big fat globs. What is worse, the Kossalu knows we would. He need only wait, holding back his fig-plucking patrols, till we is too broke to continue. Then he would maybe be tempted to start conquering some more, around Antares."

Firmage tapped the table with a restless finger. "Everything we've thought of seems to be ruled out," he said. "Suggestions, anybody?"

Silence grew, under the radiant ceiling.

Gornas-Kiew broke it: "Precisely how are captures made? It is impossible to exchange shots while in hyperdrive."

"Statistically impossible," amended Kraaknach. "Energy beams are out of the question. Material missiles have to be hypered themselves, or they would revert to true, sublight velocity and be left behind as soon as they emerged from the drive field. Furthermore, to make a hit, they must be precisely in phase with the target. A good pilot can phase in on another ship, but the operation involves too many variables for any cybernet of useful size."

"I tell you how," snarled van Rijn. "The pest-bedamned Borthudians detect the vibration-wake from afar. They compute an intercept course. Coming close, they phase in and slap on a tractor beam. Then they haul themselves up alongside, burn through the hull or an airlock, and board."

"Why, the answer looks simple enough," said Mjambo. "Equip our craft with pressor beams. Keep the enemy ships at arm's length."

"You forget, esteemed colleague, that beams of either positive or negative sign are powered from the engine," said Kraaknach. "A naval vessel has much stronger engines than a merchantman."

"Give our crews small arms. Let them blast down the boarding parties."

"The illegitimate-offspring-of-interspecies-crosses Borthudians already have arms, also hands what hold weapons," snorted van Rijn. "Phosphor and farts! Do you think four men can stand off twenty?"

"M-m-m . . . yes, I see your point." Firmage nodded. "But look here, we can't do anything about this without laying out *some* cash. I'm not sure what the mean profit is—"

"On the average, for everybody's combined Antarean voyages, about thirty percent on each run," said van Rijn promptly.

Mjambo started. "How the devil do you get the figures for my company?" he exclaimed.

Van Rijn grinned and drew on his cigar.

"That gives us a margin to use," said Gornas-Kiew. "We can invest in military equipment to such an extent that our profit is less—though I agree there must still be a final result in the black—for the duration of this emergency."

"It'd be worth it," said Mjambo. "In fact, I'd take a fair-sized loss just to teach those bastards a lesson."

"No, no." Van Rijn lifted a hand which, after years in offices, was still the broad muscular paw of a working spaceman. "Revenge and destruction are un-Christian thoughts. Also, I have told you, they do not pay very well, since it is hard to sell anything to a corpse. The problem is to find some means inside our resources what will make it unprofitable for Borthu to raid us. Not being stupid heads, they will then stop raiding and we can maybe later do business."

"You're a cold-blooded one," said Mjambo.

"Not always," replied van Rijn blandly. "Like a sensible man, I set my thermostat according to what is called for. In this case, what we need is a scientifical approach with elegant mathematics—"

Abruptly he dropped his glance and covered a shiver by pouring himself another glassful. He had gotten an idea.

When the others had argued for a fruitless hour, he said: "Freemen, this gets us nowhere, *nie*? Perhaps we are not stimulated enough to think clear."

"What do you propose?" sighed Mjambo.

"Oh . . . an agreement. A pool, or prize, or reward for whoever solves this problem. For example, ten percent of everybody else's Antarean profits for the next ten years."

"Hoy, there!" burst from Firmage. "If I know you, you robber, you've come up with an answer."

"No, no, no. By my honor I swear it. I have some beginning thoughts, maybe, but I am only a poor rough old space walloper without the fine education you beings have had. I could too easy be wrong."

"What is your notion?"

"Best I not say yet, until it is more fermented. But please to note, he who tries something active will take on the risk and expense. If he succeeds, he saves profits for all. Does not a tiny return on his investment sound fair and proper?"

There was more argument. Van Rijn smiled with infinite benevolence. He settled at last for a compact, recorded on ciphertape, whose details would be computed later.

Beaming, he clapped his hands. "Freemen," he said, "we have worked hard tonight and soon comes much harder work. By damn, I think we deserve a little celebration. Simmons, prepare an orgy."

Rafael Torres had considered himself unshockable by any mere words. He was wrong. "Are you serious?" he gasped.

"In confidentials, of course," van Rijn answered. "The crew must be good men like you. Can you recommend more?"

"No—"

"We will not be stingy with the bonuses."

Torres shook his head violently. "Out of the question, sir. The Brotherhood's refusal to enter the Kossaluth on anything except a punitive expedition is absolute. This one you propose is not, as you describe it. We can't lift the ban without another vote, which would necessarily be a public matter."

"You can publicly vote again after we see if the idea works," van Rijn pressed him. "The first trip will have to be secret."

"Then the first trip will have to do without a crew."

"Bile on a boomerang!" Van Rijn's fist crashed against his desk. He surged to his feet. "What sort of putzing cowards do I deal with? In my day we were men! And we had ideals, I can tell you. We would have boosted through hell's open gates if you paid us enough."

Torres sucked hard on his cigarette. "The ban must stand. None but a Lodgemaster can—Well, all right, I'll say it." Anger was a cold flaring in him. "You want men to take an untried ship into enemy sky and invite attack. If they lose, they're condemned to a lifetime of praying, with what's left of their free wills, for death. If they succeed, they win a few measly kilocredits. In either case, you sit back here plump and safe. God damn it, no!"

Van Rijn stood quiet for a while. This was something he had not quite foreseen.

His gaze wandered forth, out the transparency, to the narrow sea. A yacht was passing by, lovely in white sails and slender hull. Really, he ought to spend more time on his own. Money wasn't that important. Was it? This was not such a bad world, this Earth, even when one was being invaded by age and fat. It was full of blossoms and burgundy, clean winds and lovely women, Mozart melodies and fine books. Doubtless his memories of earlier days in space were colored by nostalgia. . . .

He reached a decision and turned around to face his visitor. "A Lodgemaster can come on such a trip without telling peoples," he said. "The union rules give you discretion. You think you can raise two more like yourself, hah?"

"I told you, Freeman, I won't so much as consider it."

"Even if I myself am the skipper?"

The *Mercury* did not, outwardly, look different after the engineers were finished with her. Her cargo was the same as usual, too: cinnamon, ginger, pepper, cloves, tea, whisky, gin. If he was going to Antares, van Rijn did not intend to waste the voyage. He did omit wines, doubting their quality could stand as rough a trip as this one would be.

The alterations were internal, extra hull bracing and a new and monstrously powerful engine. The actuarial computers estimated the cost of such an outfitting as three times the total profit from all her journeys during an average service life. Van Rijn had winced, but put a shipyard to work.

In truth, his margin was slim, and he was gambling more on it than he could afford to lose. However, if the Kossalu of Borthu had statisticians of his own—always assuming that the idea proved out—

Well, if it didn't, Nicholas van Rijn would die in battle, or be liquidated as too old for usefulness, or become a brain-channeled slave, or be held for a ruinous ransom. The possibilities looked about equally bad.

He installed himself, dark-haired and multiply curved Dorcas Gherardini, and a stout supply of brandy, tobacco, and ripe cheese, in the captain's cabin. One might as well be comfortable. Torres was his mate, Captains Petrovich and Seiichi his engineers. The *Mercury* lifted from Quito Spaceport without fanfare, waited unpretentiously in orbit for clearance, then accelerated on negagrav away from Sol. At the required distance, she went on hyperdrive and outpaced light.

Van Rijn sat back on the bridge and lit his churchwarden pipe. "Now is a month's going to Antares," he said piously. "Good St. Dismas, watch over us."

"I'll stick by St. Nicholas, patron of travelers," replied Torres. "In spite of his being your namesake."

Van Rijn looked hurt. "By damn, do you not respect my morals?"

Torres shrugged. "Well, I admire your courage—nobody can say you lack guts—" van Rijn gave him a hard look—"and if anybody can pull this off, you can. Set a pirate to catch a pirate."

"You younger generations got a loud mouth and no manners." The merchant blew malodorous clouds. "In my day, we said 'sir' to the captain even when we mutinied."

"I'm still worried about a particular detail," admitted Torres. He had had much more to occupy mind and body than the working out of strategies, mainly the accumulation of as many enjoyable memories as possible. "I suppose it's a fairly safe bet that the enemy hasn't yet heard about our travel ban. Still, the recent absence of ships must have made him think. Besides, our course brings us so near a known Borthudian base that we're certain to be detected. Suppose he gets suspicious and dispatches half a dozen vessels to jump us?"

"The likelihood of that is quite low, because he keeps his bloody-be-damned patrol craft cruising far apart, to maximize their chances of spotting a catch. If he feels wary of us, he will simply not attack; but this also I doubt, for a prize is valuable." Van Rijn heaved his bulk onto his feet. One good thing about spacefaring, you could set the gravity-field generator low and feel almost lissome again. "What you at your cockamamie age do not quite understand, my friend, is that there are hardly any certainties in life. Always we must go on probabilities. The secret of success is to make the odds favor you. Then in the long run you are sure to come out ahead. It is your watch now, and I recommend you project a book on statistical theory to pass the time. The data bank has an excellent library. As for me, I will be in conference with Freelady Gherardini."

"I wish to blazes I could run commands of mine the way you run this of yours," said Torres mournfully.

Van Rijn waved an expansive hand. "Why not, my boy, why not? So long as you make money and no trouble for the Company, the Company does not peek over your shoulder. The trouble with you young snapperwhippers is you lack initiative. When you are a poor old feeble fat man like me, you will look back and regret your lost opportunities."

Low-gee or no, the deck thumped beneath his feet as he departed.

Heaven was darkness filled with a glory of suns. Viewscreens framed the spilling silver of the Milky Way, ruby spark of Antares, curling edge of a nebula limned by the glare of an enmeshed star. Brightest in vision stood Borthu's, yellow as minted gold.

The ship drove on as she had done for a pair of weeks, pulsing in and out of four-space at thousands of times per second, loaded with a tension that neared the detonation point.

On a wardroom bench, Dorcas posed slim legs and high prow with a care so practiced as to be unconscious.

She could not pull her eyes from the screen. "It's beautiful," she said in a small voice. "Somehow that doubles the horror."

Van Rijn sprawled beside her, his majestic nose aimed aloft. "What is horrible, my little sinusoid?" he asked.

"Them . . . waiting to pounce on us and—In God's name, why did I come along?"

"I believe there was mention of a tygron coat and flamedrop earrings."

"But suppose they do capture us." Cold, her fingers clutched at his arm. "What will happen to me?"

"I told you I have set up a ransom fund for you. I told you also, maybe they will not bother to collect it, or maybe we get broken to bits in the fight. Satan's horns and the devil who gave them to him! Be still, will you?"

The audio intercom came to life with Torres' urgent words: "Wake of high-powered ship detected, approaching to intercept."

"All hands to stations!" roared van Rijn.

Dorcas screamed. He tucked her under one arm, carried her down the passageway—collecting a few scratches en route—to his cabin, where he tossed her on the bed and told her she'd better strap in. Puffing, he arrived on the bridge. The visuals showed Petrovich and Seiichi in the engine room, armored, their faces a-glisten with sweat. Torres sat gnawing his lip, fingers unsteady as he tuned instruments.

"Hokay," said van Rijn, "here is the thing we have come for. I hope you each remember what you have to do, because this is not another rehearsal where I can gently correct your thumb-brained mistakes." He whacked his great bottom into the main control chair and secured the safety harness. When his fingers tickled the console, giving computers and efferent circuits their orders, he felt the sensitive response of that entire organism which was the ship. Thus far *Mercury* had been under normal power, the energy generator half-idle. It was good to know how many wild horses he could call up.

The strange vessel drew in communication range, where the two drive fields measurably impinged on each other. As customary, both pilots felt their way toward the same phase and frequency of oscillation, until a radio wave could pass between them and be received. On the bridge of the human craft, the outercom chimed. Torres pressed the accept button and the screen came to life.

A Borthudian officer looked out. His garments clung dead black to a cat-lithe frame. The face was semihuman, though hairless and tinged with blue; yellow eyes smoldered under a narrow forehead. Behind him could be seen his own bridge, a companion who sat before a fire-control terminal, and the usual six-armed basalt idol.

"Terrestrial ship ahoy!" He ripped out fluent Anglic, harshly accented by the shapes of larynx and mouth. "This is Captain Rentharik of the Kossalu's frigate *Gantok*. By the law, most sacred, of the Kossaluth of Borthu, you are guilty of trespass on the domains of His Mightiness. Stand by to be boarded."

"Why, you out-from-under-wet-logs-crawling cocky-pop!" Van Rijn made himself flush turkey red. "Not bad enough you hijack my men and transports, with their good expensive cargoes, but you have the copperbound nerve to call it legal!"

Rentharik fingered a small ceremonial dagger hung about his neck. "Old man, the writ of the Kossalu runs through this entire volume of space. You can save yourself added punishment—nerve-pulsing—by submitting peacefully to judgment."

"It is understood by *civilized* races that interstellar space is free for every innocent passage."

Rentharik smiled, revealing bright-green teeth of non-human shape. "We enforce our own laws here, Captain."

"*Ja,* but by damn, this time you are trying to use force on van Rijn. They are going to be surprised back on that dingleberry you call your home planet."

Rentharik spoke at a recorder in his native language. "I have just made a note recommending you be assigned to the Ilyan run after conditioning. Organic compounds in the atmosphere there produce painful allergic reactions in your species, yet not so disabling that we consider it worthwhile to issue airsuits. Let the rest of your crew pay heed."

Van Rijn's face lit up. "Listen, if you would hire space-men honest instead of enslaving them, we got plenty of antiallergenic treatments and medicines. I would be glad to supply you them, at quite a reasonable commission."

"No more chatter. You are to be grappled and boarded. Captured personnel receive nerve-pulsing in proportion to the degree of their resistance."

Rentharik's image blanked.

Torres licked sandy lips. Turning up the magnification in a viewscreen, he picked out the Borthudian frigate. She was a darkling shark-form, only half the tonnage of the dumpy merchantman but with gun turrets etched against remote star-clouds. She came riding in along a smooth curve, matched hypervelocities with practiced grace, and flew parallel to her prey, a few kilometers off.

The intercom gave forth a scream. Van Rijn swore as the visual showed him Dorcas, out of her harness and raving around his cabin in utter hysterics. Why, she might spill all his remaining liquor, and Antares still eleven days off!

A small, pulsing jar went through hull and bones. *Gantok* had reached forth a tractor beam and laid hold of *Mercury*.

"Torres," said van Rijn. "You stand by, boy, and take over if somewhat happens to me. I maybe want your help anyway, if the game gets too gamy. Petrovich, Seiichi, you got to maintain our own beams and hold them tight, no matter what. Hokay? We go!"

Gantok was pulling herself closer. Petrovich kicked in full power. For a moment, safety arcs blazed blue, ozone spat forth a smell of thunder, a roar filled the air. Then equilibrium was reached, with only a low droning to bespeak unthinkable energies at work.

A pressor beam lashed out, an invisible hammerblow of repulsion, five times the strength of the enemy tractor. Van Rijn heard *Mercury*'s ribs groan with the stress. *Gantok* shot away, turning end over end, until she was lost to vision among the stars.

"Ha, ha!" bellowed van Rijn. "We spill their apples, eh? By damn! Next we show them real fun!"

The Borthudian hove back in sight. She clamped on again, full-strength attraction. Despite the pressor, *Mercury* was yanked toward her. Seiichi cursed and gave back his full thrust.

For a moment van Rijn thought his ship would burst open. He saw a deckplate buckle under his feet and heard metal elsewhere shear. But *Gantok* was batted away as if by a troll's fist

"Not so hard! Not so hard, you dumbhead! Let me control the beams." Van Rijn's hands danced over the console. "We want to keep him for a souvenir, remember?"

He used a spurt of drive to overhaul the foe. His right hand steered *Mercury* while his left wielded the tractor

and the pressor, seeking a balance. The engine noise
rose to a sound like heavy surf. The interior gee-field
could not compensate for all the violence of accelerations
now going on; harness creaked as his weight was hurled
against it. Torres, Petrovich, and Seiichi made themselves part of the machinery, additions to the computer
systems which implemented the commands his fingers
gave.

The Borthudian's image vanished out of viewscreens
as he slipped *Mercury* into a different phase. Ordinarily
this would have sundered every contact between the vessels. However, the gravitic forces which he had locked
onto his opponent paid no heed to how she was oscillat-
ing between relativistic and nonrelativistic quantum
states; her mass remained the same. He had simply made
her weapons useless against him, unless her pilot
matched his travel pattern again. To prevent that, he
ordered a program of random variations, within feasible
limits. Given time to collect data, perform stochastic
analysis, and exercise the intuition of a skilled living
brain, the enemy pilot could still have matched; such a
program could not be random in an absolute sense. Van
Rijn did not propose to give him time.

Now thoroughly scared, the Borthudian opened full
drive and tried to break away. Van Rijn equalized positive
and negative forces in a heterodyning interplay which,
in effect, welded him fast. Laughing, he threw his own
superpowered engine into reverse. *Gantok* shuddered to
a halt and went backwards with him. The fury of that
made *Mercury* cry out in every member. He could not
keep the linkage rigid without danger of being broken
apart; he must vary it, flexibly, yet always shortening the
gap between hulls.

"Ha, like a fish we play him! Good St. Peter the Fisherman, help us not let him get away!"

Through the racket around him, van Rijn heard something snap, and felt a rushing of air. Petrovich cried it for him: "Burst plate—section four. If it isn't welded back soon, we'll take worse damage."

The merchant leaned toward Torres. "Can you take this rod and reel?" he asked. "I need a break from it, I feel my judgment getting less quick, and as for the repair, we must often make such in my primitive old days."

Torres nodded, grim-faced. "You ought to enjoy this, you know," van Rijn reproved him, and undid his harness.

Rising, he crossed a deck which pitched beneath his feet almost as if he were in a watercraft. *Gantok* was still making full-powered spurts of drive, trying to stress *Mercury* into ruin. She might succeed yet. The hole in the side had sealed itself, but remained a point of weakness from which further destruction could spread.

At the lockers, van Rijn clambered into his outsize spacesuit. Hadn't worn armor in a long time . . . forgotten how quickly sweat made it stink. . . . The equipment he would need was racked nearby. He loaded it onto his back and cycled through the airlock. Emerging on the hull, he was surrounded by a darkness-whitening starblaze.

Any of those shocks that rolled and yawed the ship underfoot could prove too much for the grip of his bootsoles upon her. Pitched out beyond the hyperdrive fields and reverting to normal state, he would be forever lost in a microsecond as the craft flashed by at translight hyperspeed. Infinity was a long ways to fall.

Electric discharges wavered blue around him. Occasionally he saw a flash in the direction of *Gantok*, when phasings happened momentarily to coincide. She must be shooting wildly, on the one-in-a-billion chance that some missile would be in exactly the right state when it passed through *Mercury* . . . or through van Rijn's stomach . . . no, through the volume of space where these things coexisted with different frequencies . . . must be precise. . . .

There was the fit-for-perdition hull plate. Clamp on the jack, bend the thing back toward some rough semblance of its proper shape . . . ah, heave ho . . . electric-powered hydraulics or not, it still took strength to do this; maybe some muscle remained under the blubber . . . lay out the reinforcing bars, secure them temporarily, unlimber your torch, slap down your glare filter . . . handle a flame and recall past years when he went hell-roaring in his own person . . . whoops, that lunge nearly tossed him off into God's great icebox!

He finished his job, reflected that the next ship of this model would need still heavier bracing, and crept back to the airlock, trying to ignore the aches that throbbed in his entire body. As he came inside, the rolling and plunging and racketing stopped. For an instant he wondered if he had been stricken deaf.

Torres' face, wet and haggard, popped into an intercom screen. Hoarsely, he said: "They've quit. They must realize their own boat will most likely go to pieces before ours—"

Van Rijn, who had heard him through a sonic pickup in his space helmet, straightened his bruised back and whooped. "Excellent! Now pull us up quick according to plan, you butterbrain!"

He felt the twisting sensation of reversion to normal state, and the hyperdrive thrum died away. Almost he lost his footing as *Mercury* flew off sidewise.

It had been Rentharik's last, desperate move, killing his oscillations, dropping solidly back into the ordinary condition of things where no speed can be greater than that of light. Had his opponent not done likewise, had the ships drawn apart at such an unnatural rate, stresses along the force-beams linking them would promptly have destroyed both, and he would have had that much vengeance. The Terran craft was, however, equipped with a detector coupled to an automatic cutoff, for just this possibility.

Torres barely averted a collision. At once he shifted *Mercury* around until her beams, unbreakably strong, held her within a few meters of *Gantok,* at a point where the weapons of the latter could not be brought to bear. If the Borthudian crew should be wild enough to suit up and try to cross the intervening small distance, to cut a way in and board, it would be no trick to flick them off into the deeps with a small auxiliary pressor.

Van Rijn bellowed mirth, hastened to discard his gear, and sought the bridge for a heart-to-heart talk with Rentharik. "—You is now enveloped in our hyperfield any time we switch it on, and it is strong enough to drag you along no matter what you do with your engines, understand? We is got several times your power. You better relax and let us take you with us peaceful, because if we get any suspicions about you, we will use our beams to pluck your vessel in small bits. Like they say on Earth, what is sauce for the stews is sauce for the pander. . . . Do not use bad language, please; my receiver is blushing." To his men: "Hokay, full speed ahead with this little minnow what thought it was a shark!"

A laser call as they entered the Antarean System brought a League cruiser out to meet them. The colony was worth that much protection against bandits, political agitators, and other imaginable nuisances. Though every planet here was barren, the innermost long since engulfed by the expansion of the great dying sun, sufficient mineral wealth existed on the outer worlds—together with a convenient location as a trade center for this entire sector—to support a human population equal to that of Luna. Van Rijn turned his prize over to the warcraft and let Torres bring the battered *Mercury* in. Himself, he slept a great deal, while Dorcas kept her ears covered. Though the Borthudians had, sanely, stayed passive, the strain of keeping alert for some further attempt of theirs had been considerable.

Torres had wanted to communicate with the prisoners, but van Rijn would not allow it. "No, no, my boy, we unmoralize them worse by refusing the light of our eyes. I want the good Captain Rentharik's fingernails chewed down to the elbow when I see him again."

Having landed, he invited himself to stay at the governor's mansion in Redsun City and make free use of wine cellar and concubines. Between banquets, he found time to check on local prices and raise the tag on pepper a millicredit per gram. The settlers would grumble, but they could afford it. Besides, were it not for him, their meals would be drab affairs, or else they'd have to synthesize their condiments at twice the cost, so didn't he deserve an honest profit?

After three days of this, he decided it was time to summon Rentharik. He lounged on the governor's throne in the high-pillared reception hall, pipe in right fist, bottle in left, small bells braided into his ringlets but merely a dirty bathrobe across his belly. One girl played on a shiverharp, one fanned him with peacock feathers, and one sat on an arm of the seat, giggling and dropping chilled grapes into his mouth. For the time being, he approved of the universe.

Gaunt and bitter between two League guardsmen, Rentharik advanced across the gleaming floor, halted before his captor, and waited.

"Ah, so. Greetings and salubrications," van Rijn boomed. "I trust you have had a pleasant stay? The local jails are much recommended, I am told."

"For your race, perhaps," the Borthudian said in dull anger. "My crew and I have been wretched."

"Dear me. My nose bleeds for you."

Pride spat: "More will bleed erelong, you pirate. His Mightiness will take measures."

"Your maggoty kinglet will take no measurements except of how far his chest is fallen," declared van Rijn. "If the civilized planets did not dare fight when he was playing buccaneer, he will not when the foot is in the other shoe. No, he will accept the facts and learn to love them."

"What are your immediate intentions?" Rentharik asked stoically.

Van Rijn stroked his goatee. "Well, now, it may be we can collect a little ransom, perhaps, eh? If not, the local mines are always short of labor, because conditions is kind of hard. Criminals get assigned to them. However, out of my sugar-sweet goodness, I let you choose one person, not yourself, what may go home freely and report what has happened. I will supply a boat what can make the trip. After that we negotiate, starting with rental on the boat."

Rentharik narrowed his eyes. "See here. I know how your vile mercantile society works. You do nothing that has no money return. You are not capable of it. And to equip a vessel like yours—able to seize a warship—must cost more than the vessel can ever hope to earn."

"Oh, very quite. It costs about three times as much. Of course, we gain some of that back from auctioning off our prizes, but I fear they is too specialized to raise high bids."

"So. We will strangle your Antares route. Do not imagine we will stop patrolling our sovereign realm. If you wish a struggle of attrition, we can outlast you."

"Ah, ah." Van Rijn waggled his pipestem. "That is what you cannot do, my friend. You can reduce our gains considerably, but you cannot eliminate them. Therefore we can continue our traffic so long as we choose. You see, each voyage nets an average thirty percent profit."

"But it costs three hundred percent of that profit to outfit a ship—"

"Indeed. But we are only special-equipping every *fourth* ship. That means we operate on a small margin, yes, but a little arithmetic should show you we can still scrape by in the black ink."

"Every fourth?" Rentharik shook his head, frankly puzzled. "What is your advantage? Out of every four encounters, we will win three."

"True. And by those three victories, you capture twelve slaves. The fourth time, we rope in twenty Borthudian spacemen. The loss of ships we can absorb, because it will not go on too long and will be repaid us. You see, you will never know beforehand which craft is going to be the one that can fight back. You will either have to disband your press gangs or quickly get them whittled away." Van Rijn swigged from his bottle. "Understand? You is up against loaded dice which will prong you edgewise unless you drop out of the game fast."

Rentharik crouched, as if to leap, and raged: "I learned, here, that your spacefolk will no longer travel through the Kossaluth. Do you think reducing the number of impressments by a quarter will change that resolution?"

Van Rijn demonstrated what it is to grin fatly. "If I know my spacefolk . . . why, of course. Because if you do continue to raid us, you will soon reduce yourselves to such few crews as you are helpless. Then you will *have* to deal with us, or else the League comes in and overthrows your whole silly hermit-kingdom system. That would be so quick and easy an operation, there would be no chance for the politicians at home to interfere.

"Our terms will include freeing of all slaves and big fat indemnities. Great big fat indemnities. They do right now, naturally, so the more prisoners you take in future, the worse it will cost you. Any man or woman worth salt can stand a couple years' service on your nasty rustbuckets, if this means afterward getting paid enough to retire on in luxuriance. Our main trouble will be fighting off the excessive volunteers."

He cleared his throat, buttered his tone, and went on: "Is you therefore not wise for making agreement right away? We will be very lenient if you do. Since you are then short of crews, you can send students to our academies at not much more than the usual fees. Otherwise we will just want a few minor trade concessions—"

"And in a hundred years, you will own us," Rentharik half-snarled, half-groaned.

"If you do not agree, by damn, we will own you in much less time than that. You can try impressing more of our people and bleed yourselves to death; then we come in and free them and take what is left of everything you had. Or you can leave our ships alone on their voyages—but then your subjects will soon know, and your jelly-built empire will break up nearly as quick, because how you going to keep us from delivering subversionists and weapons for rebels along the way? Or you can return your slaves right off, and make the kind of bargain with us what I have been pumping at you. In that case, you at least arrange that your ruling class loses power only, in an orderly way, and not their lives. Take your choice. You is well enough hooked that it makes no big matter to me."

The merchant shrugged. "You, personal," he continued, "you pick your delegate and we will let him go report to your chief swine. You might maybe pass on the word how Nicholas van Rijn of the Polesotechnic League does nothing without good reason, nor says anything what is not calm and sensible. Why, just the name of my ship could have warned you."

Rentharik seemed to shrivel. "How?" he whispered.

"Mercury," the man explained, "was the old Roman god of commerce, gambling . . . and, *ja,* thieves."

INTRODUCTION

❖ HOW TO BE ETHNIC IN
ONE EASY LESSON ❖

What Rennhi, her flightmates in the endeavor, and more
lately Hloch were able to seek out has been limited and
in great measure chance-blown. No scholar from Avalon
has yet prevailed over the time or the means to ransack
data banks on Terra itself. Yonder must abide records
more full by a cloud-height than those which have
reached the suns where Domain of Ythri and Terran
Empire come together.

It may be just as well. They would surely overwhelm
the writer of this book, whose aim is at no more than an
account of certain human events which helped bring
about the founding of the Stormgate Choth. Even the
fragmentary original material he has is more than he
can directly use. He rides among whatever winds blow,

175

choosing first one, then another, hoping that in this wise he may find the overall set of the airstream.

Here is a story of no large import, save that it gives a picture from within of Terran society when the Polesotechnic League was in its glory—and, incidentally, makes the first mention known to Hloch of a being who was to take a significant part in later history. The source is a running set of reminiscences written down through much of his life by James Ching, a spaceman who eventually settled on Catawrayannis. His descendants kept the notebooks and courteously made them available to Rennhi after she had heard of their existence. To screen a glossary of obscure terms, punch Library Central 254-0691.

—Hloch of the Stormgate Choth
The Earth Book of Stormgate

HOW TO BE ETHNIC IN ONE EASY LESSON

Adzel talks a lot about blessings in disguise, but this disguise was impenetrable. In fact, what Simon Snyder handed me was an exploding bomb.

I was hard at study when my phone warbled. That alone jerked me half out of my lounger. I'd set that instrument to pass calls from no more than a dozen people, to all of whom I'd explained that they shouldn't bother me about anything much less urgent than a rogue planet on a collision course.

You see, my preliminary tests for the Academy were coming up soon. Not the actual entrance exams—I'd face those a year hence—but the tests as to whether I should be allowed to apply for admission. You can't blame that policy on the Brotherhood. Not many regular spaceman's berths become available annually, and a hundred young Earthlings clamor for each of them. The ninety-nine who don't make it . . . well, mostly they try to get work with some company which will maybe someday assign them to a post somewhere outsystem; or they set their teeth and save their money till at last they can go as shepherded tourists.

At night, out above the ocean in my car, away from city glow, I'd look upward and be ripped apart by longing. As for the occasional trips to Luna—last time, several months before, I'd found my eyes running over at sight of that sky, when the flit was my sixteenth-birthday present.

And now tensor calculus was giving me trouble. No doubt the Education Central computer would have gotten monumentally bored, projecting the same stuff over and over on my screen, if it had been built to feel emotions. Is that why it hasn't been?

The phone announced: "Freeman Snyder."

You don't refuse your principal counselor. His or her word has too much to do with the evaluation of you as a potential student by places like the Academy. "Accept," I gulped. As his lean features flashed on: "Greeting, sir."

"Greeting, Jim," he said. "How are you?"

"Busy," I hinted.

"Indeed. You are a rather intense type, eh? The indices show you're apt to work yourself into the ground. A change of pace is downright necessary."

Why are we saddled with specialists who arbite our lives on the basis of a psychoprofile and a theory? If I'd been apprenticed to a Master Merchant of the Polesotechnic League instead, he wouldn't have given two snorts in vacuum about my "optimum developmental strategy." He'd have told me, "Ching, do this or learn that"; and if I didn't cut it satisfactorily, I'd be fired—or dead, because we'd be on strange worlds, out among the stars, the stars.

No use daydreaming. League apprenticeships are scarcer than hair on a neutron, and mostly filled by relatives. (That's less nepotism for its own sake than a belief that kin of survivor types are more likely to be the same than chance-met groundhugger kids.) I was an ordinary student bucking for an Academy appointment, from which I'd graduate to service on regular runs and maybe, at last, a captaincy.

"To be frank," Simon Snyder went on, "I've worried about your indifference to extracurricular activities. It doesn't make for an outgoing personality, you know. I've thought of an undertaking which should be right in your orbit. In addition, it'll be a real service, it'll bring real credit, to—" he smiled afresh to pretend he was joking while he intoned—"the educational complex of San Francisco Integrate."

"I haven't time!" I wailed.

"Certainly you do. You can't study twenty-four hours a day, even if a medic would prescribe the stim. Brains go stale. All work and no play, remember. Besides, Jim, this matter has its serious aspect. I'd like to feel I could endorse your altruism as well as your technological abilities."

I eased my muscles, let the lounger mold itself around me, and said in what was supposed to be a hurrah voice: "Please tell me, Freeman Snyder."

He beamed. "I knew I could count on you. You've heard of the upcoming Festival of Man."

"Haven't I?" Realizing how sour my tone was, I tried again. "I have."

He gave me a pretty narrow look. "You don't sound too enthusiastic."

"Oh, I'll tune in ceremonies and such, catch a bit of music and drama and whatnot, if and when the chance comes. But I've got to get these transformations in hyper-drive theory straight, or—"

"I'm afraid you don't quite appreciate the importance of the Festival, Jim. It's more than a set of shows. It's an affirmation."

Yes, I'd heard that often enough before—too dismally often. Doubtless you remember the line of argument the promoters used: "Humankind, gaining the stars, is in grave danger of losing its soul. Our extraterrestrial colonies are fragmenting into new nations, whole new cultures, to which Earth is scarcely a memory. Our traders, our explorers push ever outward, ever further away; and no missionary spirit drives them, nothing but lust for profit and adventure. Meanwhile the Solar Commonwealth is deluged with alien—nonhuman—influence, not only diplomats, entrepreneurs, students, and visitors, but the false glamour of ideas never born on man's true home—We grant we have learned much of value from these outsiders. But much else has been unassimilable or has had a disastrously distorting effect, especially in the arts. Besides, they are learning far more from us. Let us proudly affirm that fact. Let us hark back to our own origins, our own variousness. Let us strike new roots in the soil from which our forebears sprang."

A year-long display of Earth's past—well, it'd be colorful, if rather fakey most of the time. I couldn't take it more seriously than that. Space was where the future lay, I thought. At least, it was where I dreamed my personal future would lie. What were dead bones to me, no matter how fancy the costumes you put on them? Not that I scorned the past; even then, I wasn't so foolish. I just believed that what was worth saving would save itself, and the rest had better be let fade away quietly.

I tried to explain to my counselor: "Sure, I've been told about 'cultural pseudomorphosis' and the rest. Really, though, Freeman Snyder, don't you think the shoe is on the other foot? Like, well, I've got this friend from Woden, name of Adzel, here to learn planetology. That's a science we developed; his folk are primitive hunters, newly discovered by us. He talks human languages too—he's quick at languages—and lately he was converted to Buddhism and—Shouldn't the Wodenites worry about being turned into imitation Earthlings?"

My example wasn't the best, because you can only humanize a four-and-a-half-meter-long dragon to a limited extent. Whether he knew that or not (who can know all the raccs, all the worlds we've already found in our small corner of this wonderful cosmos?) Snyder wasn't impressed. He snapped, "The sheer variety of extraterrestrial influence is demoralizing. Now I want our complex to make a decent showing during the Festival. Every department, office, club, church, institution in the Integrate will take part. I want its schools to have a leading role."

"Don't they, sir? I mean, aren't projects under way?"

"Yes, yes, to a degree." He waved an impatient hand. "Far less than I'd expect from our youth. Too many of you are spacestruck—" He checked himself, donned his smile again, and leaned forward till his image seemed ready to fall out of the screen. "I've been thinking about what my own students might do. In your case, I have a first-class idea. You will represent San Francisco's Chinese community among us."

"What?" I yelped. "Bu—but—"

"A very old, almost unique tradition," he said. "Your people have been in this area for five or six hundred years."

"*My* people?" The room wobbled around me. "I mean . . . well, sure, my name's Ching and I'm proud of it. And maybe the, uh, the chromosome recombinations do make me look like those ancestors. But . . . half a thousand years, sir! If I haven't got blood in me of every breed of human being that ever lived, why, then I'm a statistical monstrosity!"

"True. However, the accident which makes you a throwback to your Mongoloid forebears is helpful. Few of my students are identifiably anything. I try to find roles for them, on the basis of surnames, but it isn't easy."

Yeh, I thought bitterly. *By your reasoning, everybody named Marcantonio should dress in a toga for the occasion, and everybody named Smith should paint himself blue.*

"There is a local ad hoc committee on Chinese-American activities," Snyder went on. "I suggest you contact them and ask for ideas and information. What can you present on behalf of our educational system? And then, of course, there's Library Central. It can supply more historical material than you could read in a lifetime. Do you good to learn a few subjects besides math, physics, xenology—" His grimace passed by. I gave him marks for sincerity: "Perhaps you can devise something, a float or the like, something which will call on your engineering ingenuity and knowledge. That would please them too, when you apply at the Academy."

Sure, I thought, *if it hasn't eaten so much of my time that I flunk these prelims.*

"Remember," Snyder said, "the Festival opens in barely three months. I'll expect progress reports from you. Feel free to call on me for help or advice at any time. That's what I'm here for, you know: to guide you in developing your whole self."

More of the same followed. I haven't the stomach to record it.

I called Betty Riefenstahl, but just to find out if I could come see her. Though holovids are fine for image and sound, you can't hold hands with one or catch a whiff of perfume and girl.

Her phone told me she wasn't available till evening. That gave me ample chance to gnaw my nerves raw. I couldn't flat-out refuse Snyder's pet notion. The right was mine, of course, and he wouldn't consciously hold a grudge; but neither would he speak as well as he might of my energy and team spirit. On the other hand, what did I know about Chinese civilization? I'd seen the standard sights; I'd read a classic or two in literature courses; and that was that. What persons I'd met over there were as modern-oriented as myself. (No pun, I hope!) And as for Chinese-Americans—

Vaguely remembering that San Francisco had once had special ethnic sections, I did ask Library Central. It screened a fleet of stuff about a district known as Chinatown. Probably contemporaries found that area picturesque. (Oh, treetop highways under the golden-red sun of Cynthia! Four-armed drummers who sound the mating call of Gorzun's twin moons! Wild wings above Ythri!) The inhabitants had celebrated a Lunar New Year with fireworks and a parade. I couldn't make out details—the photographs had been time-blurred when their information was recoded—and was too disheartened to plow through the accompanying text.

For me, dinner was a refueling stop. I mumbled something to my parents, who mean well but can't understand why I must leave the nice safe Commonwealth, and flitted off to the Riefenstahl place.

The trip calmed me a little. I was reminded that, to
outworlders like Adzel, the miracle was here. Light glimmered in a million earthbound stars across the hills, far
out over the great sheen of Bay and ocean; often it fountained upward in a many-armed tower, often gave way
to the sweet darkness of a park or ecocenter. A murmur
of machines beat endlessly through cool, slightly foggy
air. Traffic Control passed me so near a bus that I looked
in its canopy and saw the passengers were from the whole
globe and beyond—a dandified Lunarian, a stocky
blueskin of Alfzar, a spacehand identified by his Brotherhood badge, a journeyman merchant of the Polesotechnic League who didn't bother with any identification
except the skin weathered beneath strange suns, the go-
to-hell independence in his face, which turned me sick
with envy.

The Riefenstahls' apartment overlooked the Golden
Gate. I saw lights twinkle and flare, heard distant clangor
and hissing, where crews worked around the clock to
replicate an ancient bridge. Betty met me at the door.
She's slim and blonde and usually cheerful. Tonight she
looked so tired and troubled that I myself paid scant
attention to the briefness of her tunic.

"Sh!" she cautioned. "Let's don't say hello to Dad right
now. He's in his study, and it's very brown." I knew that
her mother was away from home, helping develop the
tape of a modern musical composition. Her father con-
ducted the San Francisco Opera.

She led me to the living room, sat me down, and
punched for coffee. A full-wall transparency framed her
where she continued standing, in city glitter and shimmer, a sickle moon with a couple of pinpoint cities visible
on its dark side, a few of the brightest stars. "I'm glad you
came, Jimmy," she said. "I need a shoulder to cry on."

"Like me," I answered. "You first, however."

"Well, it's Dad. He's ghastly worried. This stupid Festival—"

"Huh?" I searched my mind and found nothing except the obvious. "Won't he be putting on a, uh, Terrestrial piece?"

"He's expected to. He's been researching till every hour of the mornings, poor dear. I've been helping him go through playbacks—hundreds and hundreds of years' worth—and prepare synopses and excerpts to show the directors. We only finished yesterday, and I *had* to catch up on sleep. That's why I couldn't let you come earlier."

"But what's the problem?" I asked. "Okay, you've been forced to scan those tapes. But once you've picked your show, you just project it, don't you? At most, you may need to update the language. And you've got your mother to handle reprogramming."

Betty sighed. "It's not that simple. You see, they—his board of directors, plus the officials in charge of San Francisco's participation—they insist on a live performance."

Partly I knew what she was talking about, partly she explained further. Freeman Riefenstahl had pioneered the revival of in-the-flesh opera. Yes, he said, we have holographic records of the greatest artists; yes, we can use computers to generate original works and productions which no mortal being could possibly match. Yet neither approach will bring forth new artists with new concepts of a part, nor do they give individual brains a chance to create—and, when a million fresh ideas are flowing in to us from the galaxy, natural-born genius must create or else revolt.

"Let us by all means use technical tricks where they are indicated, as for special effects," Freeman Riefenstahl said. "But let us never forget that music is only alive in a living performer." While I don't claim to be very esthetic, I tuned in his shows whenever I could. They did have an excitement which no tape and no calculated stimulus interplay—no matter how excellent—can duplicate.

"His case is like yours," Betty told me near the start of our acquaintance. "We could send robots to space. Nevertheless men go, at whatever risk." That was when I stopped thinking of her as merely pretty.

Tonight, her voice gone bleak, she said: "Dad succeeded too well. He's been doing contemporary things, you know, letting the archives handle the archaic. Now they insist he won't be showing sufficient respect, as a representative of the Integrate, for the Human Ethos—unless he puts on a historic item, live, as the Opera Company's share of the Festival."

"Well, can't he?" I asked. "Sure, it's kind of short notice, same as for me. Still, given modern training methods for his cast—"

"Of course, of course," she said irritably. "But don't you see, a routine performance isn't good enough either? People today are conditioned to visual spectacles. At least, the directors claim so. And—Jimmy, the Festival is important, if only because of the publicity. If Dad's part in it falls flat, his contract may not be renewed. Certainly his effort would be hurt, to educate the public back to real music." Her tone and her head drooped. "And that'd hurt him."

She drew a breath, straightened, even coaxed a smile into existence. "Well, we've made our précis of suggestions," she said. "We're waiting to hear what the board decides, which may take days. Meanwhile, you need to tell me your woes." Sitting down opposite me: "Do."

I obeyed. At the end I grinned on one side of my face and remarked: "Ironic, huh? Here your father has to stage an ultraethnic production—I'll bet they'll turn handsprings for him if he can make it German, given a name like his—only he's not supposed to use technology for much except backdrops. And here I have to do likewise, in Chinese style, the flashier the better, only I really haven't time to apply the technology for making a firework fountain or whatever. Maybe he and I should pool our efforts."

"How?"

"I dunno." I shifted in the chair. "Let's get out of here, go someplace where we can forget this mess."

What I had in mind was a flit over the ocean or down to the swimmably warm waters off Baja, followed maybe by a snack in a restaurant featuring outsystem food. Betty gave me no chance. She nodded and said quickly, "Yes, I've been wanting to. A serene environment—Do you think Adzel might be at home?"

The League scholarship he'd wangled back on his planet didn't reach far on Earth, especially when he had about a ton of warmblooded mass to keep fed. He couldn't afford special quarters, or anything near the Clement Institute of Planetology. Instead, he paid exorbitant rent for a shack 'way down in the San Jose district. The sole public transportation he could fit into was a rickety old twice-a-day gyrotrain, which meant he lost hours commuting to his laboratory and live-lecture classes, waiting for them to begin and waiting around after they were finished. Also, I strongly suspected he was undernourished. I'd fretted about him ever since we met, in the course of a course in micrometrics.

He always dismissed my fears: "Once, Jimmy, I might well have chafed, when I was a prairie-galloping hunter. Now, having gained a minute measure of enlightenment, I see that these annoyances of the flesh are no more significant than we allow them to be. Indeed, we can turn them to good use. Austerities are valuable. As for long delays, why, they are opportunities for study or, better yet, meditation. I have even learned to ignore spectators, and am grateful for the discipline which that forced me to acquire."

We may be used to extraterrestrials these days. Nevertheless, he was the one Wodenite on this planet. And you take a being like that: four hoofed legs supporting a spike-backed, green-scaled, golden-bellied body and tail; torso, with arms in proportion, rising two meters to a crocodilian face, fangs, rubbery lips, bony ears, wistful brown eyes—you take that fellow and set him on a campus, in his equivalent of the lotus position, droning "*Om mani padme hum*" in a rich basso profundo, and see if you don't draw a crowd.

Serious though he was, Adzel never became a prig. He enjoyed good food and drink when he could get them, being especially fond of rye whiskey consumed out of beer tankards. He played murderous chess and poker. He sang, and sang well, everything from his native chants through human folk ballads on to the very latest spinnies. (A few things, such as *Eskimo Nell*, he refused to render in Betty's presence. From his avid reading of human history, he'd picked up anachronistic inhibitions.) I imagine his jokes often escaped me by being too subtle.

All in all, I was tremendously fond of him, hated the thought of his poverty, and had failed to hit on any way of helping him out.

I set my car down on the strip before his hut. A moldering conurb, black against feverish reflections off thickening fog, cast it into deep and sulfurous shadow. Unmuffled industrial traffic brawled around. I took a stun pistol from a drawer before escorting Betty outside.

Adzel's doorplate was kaput, but he opened at our knock. "Do come in, do come in," he greeted. Fluorolight shimmered gorgeous along his scales and scutes. Incense puffed outward. He noticed my gun. "Why are you armed, Jimmy?"

"The night's dark here," I said. "In a crime area like this—"

"Is it?" He was surprised. "Why, I have never been molested."

We entered. He waved us to mats on the floor. Those, and a couple of cheap tables, and bookshelves cobbled together from scrap and crammed with codexes as well as reels, were his furniture. An Old Japanese screen—repro, of course—hid that end of the single room which contained a miniature cooker and some complicated specially installed plumbing. Two scrolls hung on the walls, one showing a landscape and one the Compassionate Buddha.

Adzel bustled about, making tea for us. He hadn't quite been able to adjust to these narrow surroundings. Twice I had to duck fast before his tail clonked me. (I said nothing, lest he spend the next half-hour in apologies.) "I am delighted to see you," he boomed. "I gathered, however, from your call, that the occasion is not altogether happy."

"We hoped you'd help us relax," Betty replied. I myself felt a bit disgruntled. Sure, Adzel was fine people; but couldn't Betty and I relax in each other's company? I had seen too little of her these past weeks.

He served us. His pot held five liters, but—thanks maybe to that course in micrometrics—he could handle the tiniest cups and put on an expert tea ceremony. Appropriate silence passed. I fumed. Charming the custom might be; still, hadn't Oriental traditions caused me ample woe?

At last he dialled for *pipa* music, settled down before us on hocks and front knees, and invited: "Share your troubles, dear friends."

"Oh, we've been over them and over them," Betty said. "I came here for peace."

"Why, certainly," Adzel answered. "I am glad to try to oblige. Would you like to join me in a spot of transcendental meditation?"

That tore my patience apart. "No!" I yelled. They both stared at me. "I'm sorry," I mumbled. "But . . . chaos, everything's gone bad and—"

A gigantic four-digited hand squeezed my shoulder, gently as my mother might have done. "Tell, Jimmy," Adzel said low.

It flooded from me, the whole sad, ludicrous situation. "Freeman Snyder can't understand," I finished. "He thinks I can learn those equations, those facts, in a few days at most."

"Can't you? Operant conditioning, for example—"

"You know better. I can learn to parrot, sure. But I won't get the knowledge down in my bones where it belongs. And they'll set me problems which require original thinking. They must. How else can they tell if I'll be able to handle an emergency in space?"

"Or on a new planet." The long head nodded. "Yes-s-s."

"That's not for me," I said flatly. "I'll never be tagged by the merchant adventurers." Betty squeezed my hand. "Even freighters can run into grief, though."

He regarded me for a while, most steadily, until at last he rumbled: "A word to the right men—that does appear to be how your Technic civilization operates, no? *Zothkh.* Have you prospects for a quick performance of this task, that will allow you to get back soon to your proper work?"

"No. Freeman Snyder mentioned a float or display. Well, I'll have to soak up cultural background, and develop a scheme, and clear it with a local committee, and design the thing—which had better be spectacular as well as ethnic—and build it, and test it, and find the bugs in the design, and rebuild it, and—And I'm no artist anyhow. No matter how clever a machine I make, it won't look like much."

Suddenly Betty exclaimed: "Adzel, you know more about Old Oriental things than he does! Can't you make a suggestion?"

"Perhaps. Perhaps." The Wodenite rubbed his jaw, a sandpaper noise. "The motifs—Let me see." He hooked a book off a shelf and started leafing through it. "They are generally of pagan origin in Buddhistic, or for that matter Christian art. . . . *Gr-r-rrr'm.* . . . Betty, my sweet, while I search, won't you unburden yourself too?"

She twisted her fingers and gazed at the floor. I figured she'd rather not be distracted. Rising from my mat, I went to look over his shoulder—no, his elbow.

"My problem is my father's, actually," she began. "And maybe he and I already have solved it. That depends on whether or not one of the possibilities we've found is acceptable. If not—how much further can we research? Time's getting so short. He needs time to assemble a cast, rehearse, handle the physical details—" She noticed Adzel's puzzlement and managed a sort of chuckle. "Excuse me. I got ahead of my story. We—"

"Hoy!" I interrupted. My hand slapped down on a page. "What's that? . . . . Uh, sorry, Betty."

Her smile forgave me. "Have you found something?" She sprang to her feet.

"I don't know," I stammered, "b-b-but, Adzel, that thing in this picture could almost be you. What is it?"

He squinted at the ideograms. "The *lung*," he said.

"A dragon?"

"Western writers miscalled it thus." Adzel settled happily down to lecture us. "The dragon proper was a creature of European and Near Eastern mythology, almost always a destructive monster. In Chinese and related societies, contrariwise, these herpetoids represented beneficent powers. The *lung* inhabited the sky, the *li* the ocean, the *chiao* the marshes and mountains. Various other entities are named elsewhere. The *lung* was the principal type, the one which was mimed on ceremonial occasions—"

The phone warbled. "Would you please take that, Betty?" Adzel asked, reluctant to break off. "I daresay it's a notification I am expecting of a change in class schedules. Now, Jimmy, observe the claws on hind and forefeet Their exact number is a distinguishing characteristic of—"

"Dad!" Betty cried. Glancing sideways, I saw John Riefenstahl's mild features in the screen, altogether woebegone.

"I was hoping I'd find you, dear," he said wearily. I knew that these days she seldom left the place without recording a list of numbers where she could probably be reached.

"I've just finished a three-hour conference with the board chairman," her father's voice plodded. "They've vetoed every one of our proposals."

"Already?" she whispered. "In God's name, why?"

"Various reasons. They feel *Carmen* is too parochial in time and space; hardly anybody today would understand what motivates the characters. *Alpha of the Centaur* is about space travel, which is precisely what we're supposed to get away from. *La Traviata* isn't visual enough. *G . . . tterdämmerung*, they agree, has the Mythic Significance they want, but it's *too* visual. A modern audience wouldn't accept it unless we supply a realism of effects which would draw attention away from the live performers on whom it ought to center in a production that emphasizes Man. Et cetera, et cetera."

"They're full of nonsense!"

"They're also full of power, dear. Can you bear to run through more tapes?"

"I'd better."

"I beg your pardon, Freeman Riefenstahl," Adzel put in. "We haven't met but I have long admired your work. May I ask if you have considered Chinese opera?"

"The Chinese themselves will be doing that, Freeman—er—" The conductor hesitated.

"Adzel." My friend moved into scanner range. His teeth gleamed alarmingly sharp. "Honored to make your acquaintance, sir . . . ah . . . sir?"

John Riefenstahl, who had gasped and gone bloodless, wiped his forehead. "Eh-eh-excuse me," he stuttered. "I didn't realize you—That is, here I had Wagner on my mind, and then Fafner himself confronted me—"

I didn't know those names, but the context was obvious. All at once Betty and I met each other's eyes and let out a yell.

Knowing how Simon Snyder would react, I insisted on a live interview. He sat behind his desk, surrounded by his computers, communicators, and information retrievers, and gave me a tight smile.

"Well," he said. "You have an idea, Jim? Overnight seems a small time for a matter this important."

"It was plenty," I answered. "We've contacted the head of the Chinese-American committee, and he likes our notion. But since it's on behalf of the schools, he wants your okay."

" 'We'?" My counselor frowned. "You have a partner?"

"Chaos, sir, he *is* my project. What's a Chinese parade without a dragon? And what fake dragon can possibly be as good as a live one? Now we take this Wodenite, and just give him a wig and false whiskers, claws over his hoofs, lacquer on his scales—"

"A nonhuman?" The frown turned into a scowl. "Jim, you disappoint me. You disappoint me sorely. I expected better from you, some dedication, some application of your talents. In a festival devoted to your race, you want to feature an alien! No, I'm afraid I cannot agree—"

"Sir, please wait till you've met Adzel." I jumped from my chair, palmed the hall door, and called: "C'mon in."

He did, meter after meter of him, till the office was full of scales, tail, spikes, and fangs. He seized Snyder's hand in a gentle but engulfing grip, beamed straight into Snyder's face, and thundered: "How joyful I am at this opportunity, sir! What a way to express my admiration for terrestrial culture, and thus help glorify your remarkable species!"

"Um, well, that is," the man said feebly.

I had told Adzel that there was no reason to mention his being a pacifist. He continued: "I do hope you will approve Jimmy's brilliant idea, sir. To be quite frank, my motives are not unmixed. If I perform, I understand that the local restaurateurs' association will feed me during rehearsals. My stipend is exiguous and—" he licked his lips, two centimeters from Snyder's nose—"sometimes I get so hungry."

He would tell only the strict, if not always the whole truth. I, having fewer compunctions, whispered in my counselor's ear: "He is kind of excitable, but he's perfectly safe if nobody frustrates him."

"Well." Snyder coughed, backed away till he ran into a computer, and coughed again. "Well. Ah . . . yes. Yes, Jim, your concept is undeniably original. There is a—" he winced but got the words out—"a certain quality to it which suggests that you—" he strangled for a moment—"will go far in life."

"You plan to record that opinion, do you not?" Adzel asked. "In Jimmy's permanent file? At once?"

I hurried them both through the remaining motions. My friend, my girl, and her father had an appointment with the chairman of the board of the San Francisco Opera Company.

The parade went off like rockets. Our delighted local merchants decided to revive permanently the ancient custom of celebrating the Lunar New Year. Adzel will star in that as long as he remains on Earth. In exchange—since he brings in more tourist credits than it costs—he has an unlimited meal ticket at the Silver Dragon Chinese Food and Chop Suey Palace.

More significant was the production of Richard Wagner's *Siegfried*. At least, in his speech at the farewell performance, the governor of the Integrate said it was significant. "Besides the bringing back of a musical masterpiece too many centuries neglected," he pomped, "the genius of John Riefenstahl has, by his choice of cast, given the Festival of Man an added dimension. He has reminded us that, in seeking our roots and pride, we must never grow chauvinistic. We must always remember to reach forth the hand of friendship to our brother beings throughout God's universe," who might otherwise be less anxious to come spend their money on Earth.

The point does have its idealistic appeal, though. Besides, the show was a sensation in its own right. For years to come, probably, the complete Ring cycle will be presented here and there around the Commonwealth; and Freeman Riefenstahl can be guest conductor, and Adzel can sing Fafner, at top salary, any time they wish.

I won't see the end of that, because I won't be around. When everything had been settled, Adzel, Betty, and I threw ourselves a giant feast in his new apartment. After his fifth magnum of champagne, he gazed a trifle blurrily across the table and said to me:

"Jimmy, my affection for you, my earnest wish to make a fractional return of your kindness, has hitherto been baffled."

"Aw, nothing to mention," I mumbled while he stopped a volcanic hiccough.

"At any rate." Adzel wagged a huge finger. "He would be a poor friend who gave a dangerous gift." He popped another cork and refilled our glasses and his stein. "That is, Jimmy, I was aware of your ambition to get into deep space, and not as a plyer of routine routes but as a discoverer, a pioneer. The question remained, could you cope with unpredictable environments?"

I gaped at him. The heart banged in my breast. Betty caught my hand.

"You have convinced me you can," Adzel said. "True, Freeman Snyder may not give you his most ardent recommendation to the Academy. No matter. The cleverness and, yes, toughness with which you handled this problem—those convinced me, Jimmy, you are a true survivor type."

He knocked back half a liter before tying the star-spangled bow knot on his package: "Being here on a League scholarship, I have League connections. I have been in correspondence. A certain Master Merchant I know will soon be in the market for another apprentice and accepts what I have told him about you. Are you interested?"

I collapsed into Betty's arms. She says she'll find a way to follow me.

INTRODUCTION

◎ THE THREE-CORNERED WHEEL ◎ NOTE OF LEITMOTIF

Anybody not a scientific illiterate knew it was impossible to get power from the atomic nucleus. Then uranium fission came along.

It was easy to show that energy projectors—the "ray guns" of popular fiction—must necessarily be hotter at the source than at the target, and thus were altogether impractical. Then someone invented the laser.

Obviously spaceships must expel mass to gain velocity, and their crews must undergo acceleration pressure at all times when they were not in free fall, and must never demean themselves with daydreams about maneuvers akin to those of a water boat or an aircraft. Then people were iconoclastic enough to discover how to generate artificial positive and negative gravity fields.

The stars were plainly out of reach, unless one was willing to plod along slower than light. Einstein's equations

199

proved it beyond the ghost of a doubt. Then the quantum hyperjump was found, and suddenly faster-than-light ships were swarming across this arm of the galaxy.

One after another, the demonstrated impossibilities have evaporated, the most basic laws of nature have turned out to possess clauses in fine print, the prison bars of our capabilities have gone down before irreverent hacksaws. He would be rash indeed who claimed that there is any absolutely certain knowledge or any forever unattainable goal.

I am just that kind of fool. I hereby state, flatly and unequivocally, that some facts of life are eternal. They are human facts, to be sure. *Mutatis mutandis*, they probably apply to each intelligent race on each inhabited planet in the universe; but I do not insist on that point. What I do declare is that man, the child of Earth, lives by certain principles which are immutable.

They include:

1. Parkinson's Laws:
   (First) Work increases to occupy all organization available to do it. (Second) Expenditures rise with income.
2. Sturgeon's Revelation:
   Ninety percent of *everything* is crud.
3. Murphy's Law: Anything that can go wrong, will.
4. The Fourth Law of Thermodynamics:
   Everything takes longer and costs more.

My assertion is not so unguarded as may appear, because characteristics like these form part of my definition of man.

—Vance Hall
Commentaries on the Philosophy of Noah Arkwright

THE THREE-CORNERED WHEEL

※ I ※

"No!"

Rebo Legnor's-Child, Marchwarden of Gilrigor, sprang back from the picture as if it had come alive. "What are you thinking of?" he gasped. "Burn that thing! Now!" One hand lifted shakily toward the fire in the great brazier, whose flames relieved a little the gloom of the audience chamber. "Over there. I saw nothing and you showed me nothing. Do you understand?"

David Falkayn let fall the sheet of paper on which he had made the sketch. It fluttered to the table, slowly through an air pressure a fourth again as great as Earth's. "What—" His voice broke in a foolish squeak. Annoyance at that crowded out fear. He braced his shoulders and regarded the Ivanhoan squarely. "What is the matter?" he asked. "It is just a drawing."

"Of the *malkino*." Rebo shuddered. "And you not even belonging to our kind, let alone a Consecrate."

Falkayn stared at him, as if anyone of Terrestrial descent could read expressions on that unhuman face. Seen by the dull red sunlight slanting through narrow windows, Rebo looked more like a lion than a man, and not very much like either. The body was only roughly anthropoid: bipedal, two-armed, but short and thick in the torso, long and thick in the limbs, with a forward-leaning posture that reduced a sheer two meters of height to approximately Falkayn's level. The three fingers had one more joint than a man's, and narrow black nails; the thumbs were on the opposite side of the hands from those of Genus Homo; the feet were digitigrade. Mahogany fur covered the entire skin, but each hair bore tiny barbs, so that the effect was of rough plumage. The head was blocky and round-eared, the face flat, noseless, with breathing apertures below the angle of the great jaws and enormous green eyes above an astonishingly sensitive, almost womanlike mouth. But whatever impression that conveyed was overwhelmed by the tawny leonine mane which framed the countenance and spilled down the muscular back, and by the tufted tail that lashed the ankles. A pair of short scaly trousers and a leather baldric, from which hung a wicked-looking ax, enhanced the wild effect.

Nevertheless, Falkayn knew, inside that big skull was a brain as good as his own. The trouble was, it had not evolved on Earth. And when, in addition to every inborn strangeness, the mind was shaped by a culture that no man really understood . . . how much communication was possible?

The boy wet his lips. The dry cold air of Ivanhoe had chapped them. He didn't lay a hand on his blaster, but he became acutely aware of its comforting drag at his hip. Somehow he found words:

"I beg your pardon if I have given offense. You will understand that foreigners may often transgress through ignorance. Can you tell me what is wrong?"

Rebo's taut crouch eased a trifle. His eyes, seeing further into the red end of the spectrum than Falkayn's, probed corners which were shadows to the visitor. No one else stood on the floor or behind the grotesquely carved stone pillars. Only the yellow flames acrackle in the brazier, the acridity of smoke from unearthly wood, stirred in the long room. Outside—it seemed suddenly very far away—Falkayn heard the endless wind of the Gilrigor uplands go booming.

"Yes," the Marchwarden said, "I realize you acted unwittingly. And you, for your part, should not doubt that I remain friendly to you—not just because you are my guest at this moment, but because of the fresh breath you have brought to this stagnant land of ours."

"That we have perhaps brought," Falkayn corrected. "The future depends on whether we live or die, remember. And that in turn depends on your help." *Well put!* he congratulated himself. *Schuster ought to have heard that. Maybe then he'd stop droning at me about how I'll never make merchant status if I don't learn to handle words.*

"I will not be able to help you if they flay me," Rebo answered sharply. "Burn that thing, I say."

Falkayn squinted through the murk at his drawing. It showed a large flatbed wagon with eight wheels, to be drawn by a team of twenty fastigas. All the way from the spaceship to this castle, he had been aglow with visions of how awed and delighted the noble would be. He had seen himself, no longer Davy-this-and-Davy-that, hey-boy-c'mere, apprentice and unpaid personal servant to Master Polesotechnician Martin Schuster: but Falkayn of Hermes, a Prometheus come to Larsum with the gift of the wheel. *What's gone wrong?* he thought wildly; and then, with the bitterness common at his seventeen years: *Why does everything always go wrong?*

Nevertheless he crossed the floor of inlaid shells and cast the paper into the brazier. It flared up and crumbled to ash.

Turning, he saw that Rebo had relaxed. The Marchwarden poured himself a cupful of wine from a carafe on the table and tossed it off at a gulp. "Good," he rumbled. "I wish you could partake with me. It is distressful not to offer refreshment to a guest."

"You know that your foods would poison my race," Falkayn said. "That is one reason why we must transport the workmaker from Gilrigor to our ship, and soon. Will you tell me what is bad about the device I have illustrated? It can be easily built. Its kind—*wagons,* we call them—were among the most important things my people ever invented. They had much to do with our becoming more than—"

He checked himself just before he said "savages" or "barbarians." Rebo's hereditary job was to keep such tribes on their proper side of the Kasunian Mountains. Larsum was a civilized country, with agriculture, metallurgy, towns, roads, trade, a literate class.

But no wheels. Burdens went on the backs of citizens or their animals, by boat, by travois, by sledge in winter—never on wheels. Now that he thought about it, Falkayn remembered that not even rollers were employed.

"The idea is that round objects turn," he floundered.

Rebo traced a sign in the air. "Best not to speak of it." He changed his mind with soldierly briskness. "However, we must. Very well, then. The fact is that the *malkino* is too holy to be put to base use. The penalty for transgressing this law is death by flaying, lest God's wrath fall on the entire land."

Falkayn struggled with the language. The educator tapes aboard the *What Cheer* had given him fluency, but could not convey a better idea of semantic subtleties than the first expedition to Ivanhoe had gotten; and those men hadn't stayed many weeks. The word he mentally translated as "holy" implied more than dedication to spiritual purposes. There were overtones of potency, mana, and general ineffability. Never mind. "What does *malkino* mean?"

"A . . . a roundedness. I may not draw it for you, only a Consecrate may do that. But it is something perfectly round."

"Ah, I see. A *circle*, we would call it, or a *sphere* if solid. A wheel is circular. Well, I suppose we could make our wheels slightly imperfect."

"No." The maned head shook. "Until the imperfection became so gross that the wheels would not work anyway, the thing is impossible. Even if the Consecrates would allow it—and I know quite well they will not, as much from hostility to you as from dogma—the peasants would rise in horror and butcher you." Rebo's eyes glowed in the direction of Falkayn's gun. "Yes, I realize you have powerful, fire-throwing weapons. But there are only four of you. What avail against thousands of warriors, shooting from the cover of hills and woods?"

Falkayn hearkened back to what he had seen in Aesca, on his westward ride along the Sun's Way, and now in this stronghold. Architecture was based on sharp-cornered polygons. Furniture and utensils were square or oblong. The most ceremonial objects, like Rebo's golden wine goblet, went no further than to employ elliptical cross-sections, or mere arcs of true circles.

He felt ill with dismay. "Why?" he choked. "What makes a . . . a figure . . . so holy?"

"Well—" Rebo lowered himself uncomfortably to a chair, draping his tail over the rest across the back. He fiddled with his octagonal ax haft and didn't look at the other. "Well, ancient usage. I can read, of course, but I am no scholar. The Consecrates can tell you more. Still . . . the circle and the sphere are the signs of God. In a way, they are God. You see them in the sky. The sun and the moons are spheres. So is the world, however imperfect; and the Consecrates say that the planets have the same shape, and the stars are set inside the great ball of the universe. All the heavenly bodies move in circles. And, well, circle and sphere are the perfect shapes. Are they not? Everything perfect is a direct manifestation of God."

Remembering a little about Classical Greek philosophy —even if the human colony on Hermes had broken away from Earth and established itself as a grand duchy, it remained proud of its heritage and taught ancient history in the schools—Falkayn could follow that logic. His impulse was to blurt: "You're wrong! No planet or star is a true globe, and orbits are ellipses, and your damned little red dwarf sun isn't the center of the cosmos anyway. I've been out there and I know!" But Schuster had drilled enough caution into him that he checked himself. He'd accomplish nothing but to stiffen the enmity of the priests, and perhaps add the enmity of Rebo, who still wanted to be his friend.

How could he prove a claim that went against three or four thousand years of tradition? Larsum was a single country, cut off by mountain, desert, ocean, and howling savages from the rest of the world. It had no more than the vaguest rumors of what went on beyond its borders. From Rebo's standpoint, the only reasonable supposition was that the furless aliens with the beaks above their mouths had flown here from some distant continent. Reviewing the first expedition's reports of how upset and indignant the Consecrates at Aesca had gotten when told that its ship came from the stars, how hotly they had denied the possibility, Schuster had cautioned his fellows to avoid that topic. The only thing which mattered was to get the hell off this planet before they starved to death.

Falkayn's shoulders slumped. "My people have found in their travels that it does not pay to dispute the religious beliefs of others," he said. "Very well, I grant you wheels are forbidden. But then what can we do?"

Rebo looked up again with his disconcertingly intelligent gaze. He was no ham-headed medieval baron, Falkayn realized. His civilization was old, and the rough edges had been worn off its warrior class, off peasants and artisans and traders, as well as the priest-scribe-poet-artist-engineer-scientist Consecrates. Rebo Legnor's-Child might be likened to an ancient samurai, if any parallels to human history were possible. He'd grasped the principle of the wheel at once, and—

"Understand, I, and many of my breed, feel more than simply benevolent toward your kind," he said low. "When the first ship came, several years ago, a lightning flash went through the land. Many of us hoped it meant the end of . . . of certain irksome restrictions. Dealing with civilized outlanders should bring new knowledge, new powers, new ways of life, into this realm where nothing has changed for better than two millennia. I want most sincerely to help you, for my own gain as well as yours."

Besides the need for tact, Falkayn hadn't the heart to answer that the Polesotechnic League had no interest in trading with Larsum, or with any other part of Ivanhoe, There was nothing here that other worlds didn't produce better and cheaper. The first expedition had simply come in search of a place to establish an emergency repair depot, and this planet was simply the least unsalubrious one in this stellar neighborhood. The expedition had observed from orbit that Larsum possessed the most advanced culture. They landed, made contact, learned the language and a little bit of the folkways, then asked permission to erect a large building which none but visitors like themselves would be able to enter.

The request was grudgingly granted, less because of the metals offered in payment than because the Consecrates feared trouble if they refused. Even so, they demanded that the construction be well away from the capital; evidently they wanted to minimize the number of Larsans who might be contaminated by foreign ideas. Having completed the job and bestowed an arbitrary name on the planet, the expedition departed. Their data, with appropriate educator tapes, were issued to all ships that might take the Pleiades route. Everybody hoped that it would never be necessary to use the information. But luck had run out for the *What Cheer*.

Falkayn said only: "I do not see how you can help. What other way can that thing be moved, than on a wagon?"

"Could it not be taken apart, moved piece by piece, and put back together at your ship? I can supply a labor force."

"No." Damn! How do you explain the construction of a unitized thermonuclear generator to somebody who's never seen a waterwheel? You don't. "Except for minor attachments, it cannot be disassembled, at least not without tools which we do not carry."

"Are you certain that it weighs too much to be transported on skids?"

"Over roads like yours, yes, I think it does. If this were winter, perhaps a sledge would suffice. But we will be dead before snow falls again. Likewise, a barge would do, but no navigable streams run anywhere near, and we would not survive the time necessary to dig a canal."

Not for the first time, Falkayn cursed the depot builders, that they hadn't included a gravity sled with the other stored equipment. But then, every ship carried one or more gravity sleds. Who could have foreseen that the *What Cheer*'s would be out of commission? Or that she couldn't at least hop over to the building herself? Or, if anybody thought of such possibilities, they must have reasoned that a wagon could be made; the xenologists had noted that wheels were unknown, and never thought to ask if that was because of a law. A portable crane had certainly been provided, to load and unload whatever was needed for spaceship repair. In fact, so well stocked was the depot that it did not include food, because any crew who could limp here at all should be able to fix their craft in a few days.

"And I daresay no other vessel belonging to your nation will arrive in time to save you," Rebo said.

"No. The . . . the distances we cover in our travels are great beyond comprehension. We were bound for a

Poul Anderson

remote frontier world—country, if you prefer—to open certain negotiations about trade rights. To avoid competition, we left secretly. Nobody at our destination has any idea that we are coming, and our superiors at home do not expect us back for several months. By the time they begin to worry and start a search—and it will take weeks to visit every place where we might have landed—our food stocks will long have been exhausted. We carried minimal supplies, you see, in order to be heavily laden with valuables for—uh—"

"For bribes." Rebo made a sound that might correspond to a chuckle. "Yes. Well, then, we must think of something else. I repeat, I will do anything I can to help you. The building was erected here, rather than in some other marchland, because I insisted; and that was precisely because I hoped to see more of your voyagers." His hand went back to his ax. Falkayn had noticed before that the heads of implements were heat-shrunk to the handles. Now the reason came to him: rivets would be sacrilegious. The fingers closed with a snap and Rebo said harshly:

"I am as pious as the next person, but I cannot believe God meant the Consecrates to freeze every life in Larsum into an eternal pattern. There was an age of heroes once, before Ourato brought Uplands and Lowlands together beneath him. Such an age can come again, if the grip upon us is broken."

He seemed to realize he had said too much and added in haste, "Let us not speak of such high matters, though. The important thing is to get that workmaker to your wounded ship. If you and I can think of no lawful means, perhaps your comrades can. So take them back the word—the Marchwarden of Gilrigor cannot allow them to make a, a wagon; but he remains their well-wisher."

"Thank you," Falkayn mumbled. Abruptly the darkness of the room became stifling. "I had best start back tomorrow."

"So soon? You had a hard trip here, and a short and unhappy conversation. Aesca is so far off that a day or two of rest cannot make any difference."

Falkayn shook his head. "The sooner I return, the better. We have not much time to lose, you know."

A fresh fastiga—slightly larger than a horse, long-eared, long-snouted, feathery-furred, with a loud bray and a piny smell—waited in the cruciform courtyard. A remount and pack animal were strung behind. A guardsman held the leader's bridle. He wore a breastplate of reinforced leather, a helmeting network of iron-studded straps woven into his mane, and a broad-bladed spear across his back. Beyond him, lesser folk moved across the cobblestones: servants in livery of black and yellow shorts, drably clad peasants, a maneless female in a loose tunic. Around them bulked the four squat stone buildings that sheltered the household, linked by outer walls in which were the gates. At each corner of the square, a watchtower lifted its battlements into the deep greenish sky.

"Are you certain you do not wish an escort?" Rebo asked.

"There is no danger in riding alone, is there?" Falkayn replied.

"*Gr-rm* . . . no, I suppose not. I keep this region well patrolled. God speed you, then."

Falkayn shook hands, a Larsan custom, too. The Marchwarden's three long fingers and oppositely placed thumb fitted awkwardly into a human grasp. For a moment more they looked at each other.

The bulky garments Falkayn wore against the chill disguised his youthful slenderness. He was towheaded and blue-eyed, with a round face and a freckled snub nose that cost him much secret anguish. A baron's son from Hermes should look lean and dashing. To be sure, he was a younger son, and one who had gotten himself expelled from the ducal militechnic academy. The reason was harmless enough, a prank which had been traced to him by merest chance; but his father decided he had better seek his fortune elsewhere. So he had gone to Earth, and Martin Schuster of the Polesotechnic League had taken him on as an apprentice, and instead of the glamor and adventure which interstellar merchants were supposed to enjoy, there had been hard work and harder study. He had given a whoop when his master told him to ride here alone and arrange for local help. It was vastly disappointing that he couldn't stay awhile.

"Thank you for everything," he said. He swung himself into the saddle with less grace than he'd hoped, under a gravity fifteen percent greater than Earth's. The guard let go the bridle and he rode out the eastern gate.

A village nestled below the castle walls, cottages of dovetailed timber with sod roofs. Beyond them that highroad called the Sun's Way plunged downhill toward the distant Trammina Valley. It wasn't much of a road. The dirt surface was rough, weed-tufted, bestrewn with rocks which melting snows had carried down year after year from the upper slopes. Not far ahead, the path snaked around a tor and climbed again, steeply.

Falkayn glanced southward. The depot gleamed white on a ridge, like Heaven's gate before Lucifer. Otherwise he himself was the only sign of humankind. Coarse gray grass and thorny trees stretched over the hills, with here and there a flock of grazing beasts watched by a mounted herder. At his back, the Kasunian Mountains rose in harsh snow peaks, a wall across the world. One great moon hung ghostly above them. The ember-colored sun had just cleared the horizon toward which he rode.

Wind roared hollowly, thrusting at his face. He shivered. Ivanhoe was not terribly cold, in this springtime of the middle northern latitudes; the dense atmosphere gave considerable greenhouse effect. But the bloody light made him feel forever chilled. And the fastiga's cloven hooves beat the stones with a desolate sound.

Forgetting that he was Falkayn of Hermes, merchant prince, he pulled the radio transceiver from his pocket and thumbed the switch. Hundreds of kilometers away, an intercom buzzed. "Hullo," he said rather thinly. "Hullo, *What Cheer.* Anybody there?"

"*Si.*" Engineer Romulo Pasqual's voice came from the box. "Is that you, Davy *muchacho?*"

Falkayn was so glad of this little company that for once he didn't resent being patronized. "Yes. How's everything?"

"As before. Kirsh is brooding. Martin has gone to the temple again. He said it would probably be no use trying to talk them out of their prohibition on the wheel that you called us about last night. I?" Falkayn could almost see the Latin shrug. "I sit here and try to figure how we can move a couple tons of generator without wheels. A sort of giant stoneboat, *quizá?*"

"No. I thought of that, too, and discussed the notion with Rebo, when we spent a lot of the dark period hunting for ideas. Not over a road like this."

"Are you certain? If we hitch enough peasants and animals to the thing—"

"We can't get them. Rebo himself, if he drafted all the people and critters he can spare—remember, this is the planting season in a subsistence economy, and he also has to mount guard against the barbarians—he doubts if there'd be enough power to haul such a load over some of these upgrades."

"You said that quite a few of the *caballero* class were disgruntled with the priests. If they contributed, too—"

"It'd take a long time to arrange that, probably too long. Besides, Rebo thinks very few would dare go as far as he will, to help us. They may not like being tied hand and foot to Consecrate policy, when there's a whole world for them to spend their energies on. But quite apart from religious reverence, they're physically dependent on the Consecrates, who supply a good many technical and administrative services . . . and who can rouse the commoners against the wardens, if it ever came to an open break between the castes."

"So. Yes, Martin seemed to think much the same. We also were threshing this matter last night. . . . However, Davy, we should have at least a few score natives and a couple of hundred fastigas at our disposal, if Rebo is willing to help within the letter of the damned law. I swear they could move a stoneboat over any route. They might have to use winches—"

"Winches are a form of wheel," Falkayn reminded him.

"*Ay de mí,* so they are. Well, levers and dikes, then. The Mayans raised big pyramids without wheels. The task would not be as large, to skid the generator from Gilrigor to Aesca."

"Oh, sure, it could be done. But how long would it take? Come have a look at this so-called road. We'd be many months dead before the job was finished." Falkayn gulped. "How much food have we got if we ration ourselves? A hundred days' worth?"

"Something like that. Of course, we could live without eating for another month or two, I believe."

"Still not time enough to get your stoneboat across that distance. I swear it isn't."

"Well . . . no doubt you are right. You have inspected the terrain. It was only a rather desperate idea."

"Wagon transport is bad enough," Falkayn said. "I don't think that would make more than twenty kilometers per Earth-day in this area. Faster, of course, once we reached the lowlands, but I'd still estimate a month altogether."

"So slow? Well, yes, I suppose you are right. A rider needs more than a week. But this adds to our trouble. Martin is afraid that even if we can arrange something not forbidden by their law, the priests may have time to think of some new excuse for stopping us."

Falkayn's mouth tightened. "I wouldn't be surprised." His fright broke from him in a wail: "Why do they hate us so?"

"You should know that. Martin often talked to you while you rode westward."

"Yes. B-but I was sent off just a couple days after we landed. You three fellows have been on the scene, had a chance to speak with the natives, observe them—" Falkayn got his self-pity under control barely in time to avoid blubbering.

"The reason is plain," Pasqual said. "The Consecrates are the top crust of this petrified civilization. Change could only bring them down, however much it might improve the lot of the other classes. Then, besides self-interest, there is natural conservatism. Martin tells me theocracies are always hidebound. The Consecrates are smart enough to see that we newcomers represent a threat to them. Our goods, our ideas will upset the balance of society. So they will do everything they can to discourage more outworlders from coming."

"Can't you threaten revenge? Tell 'em a battleship will come and blow 'em to hell if they let us die."

"The first expedition told them a little too much of the true situation, I fear. Still, Martin may try such a bluff today. I do not know what he intends. But he has gotten . . . well, at least not very *un*friendly with some of the younger Consecrates, in the days since you left. Has he told you of his lectures to them? Do not surrender yet, *muchacho*."

Falkayn flushed indignantly. "I haven't," he snapped. "Don't you either."

Pasqual made matters worse by laughing. Falkayn signed off.

Anger faded before loneliness as the hours wore on. He hadn't minded the trip to Gilrigor Castle. That had been full of hope, and riding on animals purchased with gold from a wealthy Aescan, through an excitingly exotic land, was just what a merchant adventurer ought to do. But Rebo had smashed the hope, and now the countryside looked only dreary and sinister. Falkayn's mind whirled with plan after plan, each less practical than the last—recharging the accumulators by a hand-powered generator, airlifting with a balloon, making so many guns

that four men could stand off a million Larsans. . . .
Whenever he rejected a scheme, his father's mansion
and his mother's face rose up to make his eyes sting and
he clutched frantically after another idea.

There must be *some* way to move a big load without
wheels! What had he gone to school for? Physics, chemistry, biology, math, sociotechnics . . . damn everything,
here he was, child of a civilization that burned atoms and
traveled between the stars, and one stupid taboo was
about to kill him! But that was impossible. He was David
Falkayn, with his whole life yet to live. Death didn't
happen to David Falkayn.

The red sun climbed slowly up the sky. Ivanhoe had
a rotation period of nearly sixty hours. He stopped at
midday to eat and sleep awhile, and again shortly before
sunset. The landscape had grown still more bleak: nothing was to be seen now but hills, ravines, an occasional
brawling stream, wild pastures spotted with copses of
scrubby fringe-leaved trees, no trace of habitation.

He woke after some hours, crawled shivering from his
sleeping bag, started a campfire and opened a packet of
food. The smoke stung his nostrils. Antiallergen protected him against such slight contact with proteins made
deadly alien by several billion years of separate evolution.
He could even drink the local water. But nothing could
save him if he ate anything native. After swallowing his
rations, he readied the fastigas for travel. Because he was
still cold, he left the lead animal tethered and huddled
over the fire to store a little warmth in his body.

His eyes wandered upward. Earth and Hermes lay out
there—more than four hundred light-years away.

The second moon was rising, a mottled coppery disc
above the eastern scarps. Even without that help, one

could travel by night. For the stars swarmed and glittered, the seven giant Sisters so brilliant in their nebular hazes that they cast shadows, the lesser members of the cluster and the more distant suns of the galaxy filling the sky with their wintry hordes. A gray twilight overlay the world. Off in the west, the Kasunian snows seemed phosphorescent.

Hard to believe there could be danger in so much beauty. And in fact there seldom was. Nonetheless, when a spaceship ran on hyperdrive through a region where the interstellar medium was thicker than usual, there was a small but finite probability that one of her micro-jumps would terminate just where a bit of solid matter happened to be. If the difference in intrinsic velocities was great, it could do considerable damage. If, in addition, the lump was picked up in the space occupied by the nuclear fusion unit—well, that was what had happened to the *What Cheer.*

I suppose I'm lucky at that, Falkayn thought with a shudder. *The pebble could have ripped right through me.* Of course, then the others would have been all right, with no more than a job of hull patching to do. But at his age Falkayn didn't think that was preferable.

He had to admire the way Captain Mukerji had gotten them here. By commandeering every charged accumulator aboard ship, he'd kept the engines going as far as Ivanhoe. Landing on the last gasp of energy, by guess, God, and aerodynamics, took uncommon skill. Naturally, the sensible thing had been to make for Aesca, the capital, rather than directly for Gilrigor. One did not normally bypass local authorities, who might take offense and cause trouble. Who could have known that the trouble was already waiting there?

But now the spaceship sat, without enough ergs left in her power packs to lift a single gravity sled. The accumulators in the depot were insufficient for transportation; besides, they were needed for the repair tools. The spare atomic generator couldn't recharge anything until it had been installed in the ship, for it functioned integrally with engines and controls. And a thousand wheelless kilometers separated the two. . . .

Something stirred. One of the fastigas brayed. Falkayn's heart jumped into his gullet. He sprang erect with a hand on his blaster.

A native male trod into the little circle of firelight. His fur was fluffed out against the night cold and the breath steamed from below his jaws. Falkayn saw that he carried a rapier and—yes, by Judas, there was a circle emblazoned on his breastplate! The flames turned his great eyes into pools of restless red.

"What do you want?" Falkayn squeaked. Furiously, he reminded himself that the Ivanhoan's hands were extended empty in token of peace.

"God give you good evening," the deep voice answered. "I saw your camp from afar. I did not expect to find an outlander."

"N-n-nor I a Sanctuary guard."

"My corps travels widely on missions for the Consecrates. I hight Vedolo Pario's-Child."

"I, I . . . David, uh, David Falkayn's-Child."

"You have been on a visit to the Marchwarden, have you not?"

"Yes. As if you did not know!" Falkayn spat. *No, wait, watch your manners. We may still have a chance of talking the Consecrates into giving us a special dispensation about wheels.* "Will you join me?"

Vedolo hunkered, wrapping his tail about his feet. When Falkayn sat down again, the autochthon loomed over him on the other side of the flames, mane like a forested mountain against the Milky Way. "Yes," Vedolo admitted, "everyone in Aesca knew you were bound hither, to see if that which your fellows laid in the sealed building was still intact. I trust it was?"

Falkayn nodded. Nobody in the early Iron Age could break into an inertium-plated shed with a Nakamura lock. "And Marchwarden Rebo was most kind," he said.

"That is not surprising, from what we know of him. As I understand the matter, you must get certain spare parts from the building to repair your ship. Will Rebo, then, help you transport them to Aesca?"

"He would if he could. But the main thing we need is too heavy for any conveyance available to him."

"My Consecrate masters have wondered somewhat about that," Vedolo said. "They were shown around your vessel, at their own request, and the damaged section looked quite large."

That must have been after I left, Falkayn thought. *Probably Schuster was trying to ingratiate us with them. And I'll bet it misfired badly when they saw the circular shapes of things like meter dials—stiffened their hostility to us, even if they didn't say anything to him at the time.*

But how can this character know that, unless he followed me here? And why would he do so? What is this mission of his?

"Your shipmates explained that they had means of transport," Vedolo continued. "That makes me wonder why you returned this quickly, and alone."

"Well . . . we did have a device in mind, but there appear to be certain difficulties—"

Vedolo shrugged. "I have no doubt that folk as learned as you can overcome any problems. You have powers that we thought belonged only to angels—or to Anti-God—" He broke off and extended a hand. "Your flame weapons, for instance, which the earlier visitors demonstrated. I was not present in Aesca at the time, and have always been most curious about them. Is that a weapon at your belt? Might I see it?"

Falkayn went rigid. He could not interpret every nuance in the Larsan voices, so strangely unresonant for lack of a nasal chamber. But—"No!" he snapped.

The delicate lips curled back over sharp teeth. "You are less than courteous to a servant of God," Vedolo said.

"I . . . uh . . . the thing is dangerous. You might get hurt."

Vedolo raised an arm in the air and lowered it again. "Look at me," he said. "Listen carefully. There is much you do not understand, you bumptious invaders. I have something to tell you—"

In Ivanhoe's thick air, a human heard preternaturally well. Or perhaps it was only that Falkayn was strung wire taut, trembling and sweating with the sense of aloneness before implacable enmity. He heard the rustle out in the brush and flung himself aside as the bowstring sang. The arrow buried its eight-sided shaft in the earth where he had been.

Vedolo sprang up, sword flashing free. Falkayn rolled over. A thornbush raked his cheek. "Kill him!" Vedolo bawled and lunged at the human. Falkayn bounced erect. The rapier blade snagged his coat as he dodged. He got his blaster out and fired point blank.

Light flared hellishly for an instant. Vedolo went over in smoke, with a horrible squelch. Afterimages flew in rags before Falkayn's eyes. He stumbled toward his animals, which plunged and brayed in their panic. Through the dark he heard someone cry, "I cannot see, I cannot see, I am blinded!" The flash would have been more dazzling to Ivanhoans than to him. But they'd recover in a minute, and then they'd have much better night vision than he did.

"Kill his fastigas!" called another voice.

Falkayn fired several bolts. That should make their aim poor for a while longer, he thought in chaos. His lead animal reared and struck at him. Its eyeballs rolled, crimson against shadow-black in the streaming flame light. Falkayn sidestepped the hooves, got one hand on the bridle, and clubbed the long nose with his gun barrel. "Hold *still*, you brute," he sobbed. "It's your life, too."

Feet blundered through the brush. A lion head came into view. As he saw the human, the warrior yelled and threw a spear. It gleamed past, flattened shaft and iron head. Falkayn was too busy mounting to retaliate.

Somehow he got into the saddle. The remount shrieked as two arrows smote home in its belly. Falkayn cut it loose with a blaster shot.

"Get going!" he screamed. He struck heels into the sides of his beast. The fastiga broke into a rocking gallop, the pack animal behind at the end of its reins.

An ax hewed and missed. An arrow buzzed over his shoulder. Then he was beyond the assassins, back on the Sun's Way, westward bound again.

How many are there? it whirled in him. *Half a dozen? They must have left their own fastigas at a distance, so they could sneak up on me. I've got that much head start. But no remount anymore, and they certainly do.*

They were sent to waylay me, that's clear, to cause delay that might prove fatal while the others wondered what had happened and searched for me. They don't know about my radio. Not that that makes any difference now. They've got to catch me, before I get to Rebo's protection.

I wonder if I can beat them there.

With hysterical sardonicism: *Anyhow, I guess we can forget about that special dispensation.*

❀ III ❀

The *What Cheer* sat in a field a kilometer north of Aesca. By now thousands of local feet had tramped a path across it; the Ivanhoans were entirely humanlike in coming to gape at a novelty. But Captain Krishna Mukerji always rode into town.

"Really, Martin, you should, too," he said nervously. "Especially when the situation has all at once become so delicate. They don't consider it dignified for anyone of rank to arrive at the, er, the Sanctuary on foot."

"Dignity, schmignity," said Master Polesotechnician Schuster. "I should wear out my heart and my rump on one of those evil-minded animated derricks? I rode a horse once on Earth. I never repeat my mistakes." He waved a negligent hand. "Besides, I've already told the Consecrates, and anyone else that asked, the reason I go places on foot, and don't bother with ceremony, and talk friendly with low-life commoners, is that I've progressed beyond the need for outward show. That's a new idea here, simplicity as a virtue. It's got the younger Consecrates quite excited."

"Yes, I daresay this culture is most vulnerable to new ideas," Mukerji said. "There have been none for so long that the Larsans have no antibodies against them, so to speak, and can easily get feverish. . . . But the heads of the Sanctuary appear to realize this. If you cause too much disturbance with your comments and questions, they may not wait for us to starve. They may whip up an outright attack, casualties and the fear of a punitive expedition be damned."

"Don't worry," Schuster said. Another man in his position might have been offended; a first-year Polesotechnic cadet was taught not to clash head-on with the basics of an alien creature, and he had been a Master for two decades. But his face, broad and saber-nosed under sleek black hair, remained blandly smiling. "In all my conversations with these people, feeling them out, I've never yet challenged any of their beliefs. I don't intend to start now. In fact, I'm simply going to continue my seminar over there, as if we hadn't a care in the universe. To be sure, if I can steer the talk in a helpful direction—" He gathered a sheaf of papers and left the cabin: a short tubby man in vest and ruffled shirt, culottes and hose, as elegant as if he were bound for a reception on Earth.

Emerging from the air lock and heading down the gangway, he drew his mantle about him with a shiver. To avoid eardrum popping, the hull was kept at Ivanhoan air pressure, but not temperature. *Br-r-r,* he thought. *I don't presume to criticize the good Lord, but why did He make the majority of stars type M?*

The afternoon landscape reached somber, to his eyes, as far as he could see down the valley. Grainfields were turning bluish with the first young shoots of the year. Peasants, male, female, and young, hoed a toilsome way down those multitudinous rows. The square mud huts in which they lived stood at no great separation, for every farm was absurdly small. Nevertheless families did not outgrow the capacity of the land; disease and periodic famines kept the population stable. *To hell with any sentimental guff about cultural autonomy,* Schuster reflected. *This is one society that ought to be kicked apart.*

He reached the highroad and started toward the city. There was considerable traffic, food and raw materials coming from the hinterlands, handmade goods going back. Professional porters trotted under loads too heavy for Schuster even to think about. Fastigas dragged travois with vast bumping and clatter. A provincial Warden and his bodyguard galloped through, horns hooting, and the commoners jumped aside for their lives. Schuster waved to the troop as amiably as he did to everyone else that hailed him. No use standing on ceremony. In the couple of Earth-weeks since the ship landed, the Aescans had lost awe of the strangers. Humans were no weirder to them than the many kinds of angel and hobgoblin in which they believed, and seemed to be a good deal more mortal. True, they had remarkable powers; but then, so did any village wizard, and the Consecrates were in direct touch with God.

Not having been threatened by war in historical times, the city was unwalled. But its area was pretty sharply defined just the same, huts, tenements, and the mansions of the wealthy jammed close together along the contorted trails that passed for streets. Crowds moved by bazaars where shopkeepers' wives sang songs about their husbands' wares. Trousers and tunics, manes and fur, glowed where the red light slanted through shadows that were thick to Schuster's vision. The flat but deep Ivanhoan voices made a surf around him, overlaid by the shuffle of feet, clop of hooves, clangor from a smithy. Acrid stenches roiled in his nostrils.

It was a relief to arrive at one of the Three Bridges. When the Sanctuary guards had let him by, he walked alone. Only those who had business with the Consecrates passed here.

The Trammina River cut straight through town, oily with the refuse of a hundred thousand inhabitants. The bridges were arcs of a circle, soaring in stone to the island in the middle of the water. (Falkayn had relayed from Rebo the information that you were allowed to use up to one third of the sacred figure for an important purpose.) That island was entirely covered by the enormous step-sided pyramid of the Sanctuary. Buildings clustered on the lower terraces, graceful white structures with colonnaded porticos, where the Consecrates lived and worked. The upper pyramid held only staircases, leading to the top. There the Eternal Fire roared forth, vivid yellow tossing against the dusky-green sky. Obviously natural gas was being piped from some nearby well; but the citadel was impressive in every respect.

Except for what it cost those poor devils of peasants in forced labor and taxes, Schuster thought, *and what it's still costing them in liberty*. The fact that thousands of diverse barbarian cultures existed elsewhere on the planet proved that Pharaonism didn't come any more naturally to the Ivanhoans than it did to men.

White-robed Consecrates, most of their manes gray with age, and their blue-clad acolytes walked about the pyramid on their business, aloof in pride. Schuster's cheery greetings earned him little but frigid stares. He didn't let it bother him but bustled on to the fourth-step House of the Astrologers.

In a spacious room within, a score or so of the younger Consecrates sat around a table. "Good day, good day," Schuster beamed. "I trust I am not late?"

"No," said Herktaskor. A lean, intense-eyed being, he carried himself with something of the martial air of his Warden father. "Save that we have been eagerly awaiting the revelation you promised us this morning, when you borrowed that copy of the *Book of Stars*."

"Well, then," Schuster said, "let us get on with it." He went to the head of the table and spread out his papers. "I trust you have mastered those principles of mathematics that I explained to you in the past several days?"

A number of them looked unsure, but other shaggy heads nodded. "Indeed," said Herktaskor. His voice sank. "Oh, glorious!"

Schuster took out a fat cigar and got it going while he squinted at them. He had to hope they were telling the truth; for suddenly his little project, which had begun as a pastime, and in the vague hope of winning friends and sneaking some new concepts into this frozen society, had grown most terribly urgent. Last night Davy Falkayn radioed that shattering news about wheels being taboo, and now—

He thought, though, that Herktaskor was neither lying nor kidding himself. The Consecrate was brilliant in his way. And certainly there was a good foundation on which to build. Mathematics and observational astronomy were still live enterprises in Larsum. They had to be, when religion claimed that astrology was the means of learning God's will. Algebra and geometry had long been well developed. The step from them to basic calculus was really not large. Even dour Sketulo, the Chief of Sanctuary, had not objected to Schuster's organizing a course of lectures, as long as he stayed within the bounds of dogma. Quite apart from intellectual curiosity, it would be useful for the learned class to be able to calculate such things as the volumes and areas of unusual solids; it would make still tighter their grip on Larsum's economy.

"I planned to go on with the development of those principles," Schuster said. "But then I got to wondering if you might not be more interested in certain astrological implications. You see, by means of the calculus it is possible to predict where the moons and planets will be, far more accurately than hitherto."

Breath sucked in sharply between teeth. Even through the robes, the man could see how bodies tensed around the table.

"The *Book of Stars* gave me your tabulated observations, accumulated over many centuries," he went on. "These noontide hours I have weighed them in my mind." Actually, he had fed them to the ship's computer. "Here are the results of my calculations."

He drew a long breath of tobacco smoke. The muscles tightened in his belly. Every word must now be chosen with the most finicking care, for a wrong one could put a sword between his guts.

"I have hesitated to show you this," he said, "because at first glance it seems to contradict the Word of God as you have explained it to me. However, after pondering the question and studying the stars for an answer, I felt sure that you are intelligent enough to see the deeper truth behind deceptive appearances."

He paused. "Go on," Herktaskor urged.

"Let me approach the subject gradually. It is often a necessity of thought to assume something which one knows is not true. For example, the Consecrates as a whole possess large estates, manufactories, and other property. Title is vested in the Sanctuary. Now you know very well that the Sanctuary is neither a person nor a family. Yet for purposes of ownership, you act as if it were. Similarly, in surveying a piece of land, you employ plane trigonometry, though you know the world is actually round. . . ." He went on for some time, until he felt reasonably sure that everybody present understood the concept of a legal or mathematical fiction.

"What has this to do with astrology?" asked someone impatiently.

"I am coming to that," Schuster said. "What is the true purpose of your calculations? Is it not twofold? First, you wish to predict where the heavenly bodies will be with respect to each other at some given date, since this indicates what God desires you to do at that time. Second, you wish to uncover the grand plan of the heavens, since by studying God's works you may hope to learn more of His nature.

"Now as observations accumulated, your ancestors found it was not enough to assume that all the worlds, including this one, move in circles about the sun, and the moons in circles about this world, while the heavenly globe rotates around the whole. No, you had to picture these circles as having epicycles; and later it turned out that there must be epi-epicycles; and so on, until now for centuries the picture has been so complicated that the astrologers have given up hope of further progress."

"True," said one of them. "A hundred years ago, on just this account, Kurro the Wise suggested that God does not want us to understand the ultimate design of things too fully."

"Perhaps," Schuster said. "On the other hand, maybe God only wants you to use a different approach. A savage, trying to lift a heavy stone, might conclude that he is divinely forbidden to do so. But you lift it with a lever. In the same way, my people have discovered a sort of intellectual lever, by which we can pry more deeply into the motions of the heavenly bodies than we ever could by directly computing circles upon circles upon circles.

"The point is, however, that this requires us to employ a fiction. That is why I ask you not to be outraged when I lay that fiction before you. Granted, all motions in the sky are circular, since the circle is the token of God. But is it not permissible to assume, for purposes of calculation only, that they are not circular . . . and inquire into the consequences of that assumption?"

He started to blow a smoke ring but decided against it. "I must have a plain answer to that question," he said. "If such an approach is not permissible, then of course I shall speak no more."

But of course it was. After some argument and logic-chopping, Herktaskor ruled that it was not illegal to entertain a false hypothesis. Whereupon Schuster exposed his class to Kepler's laws and Newtonian gravitation.

That took hours. Once or twice Herktaskor had to roar down a Consecrate who felt the discussion was getting obscene. But on the whole, the class listened with admirable concentration and asked highly intelligent questions. This was a gifted species, Schuster decided; perhaps, intrinsically, more gifted than man. At least, he didn't know if any human audience, anywhere in space or time, would have grasped so revolutionary a notion so fast.

In the end, leaning wearily on the table, he tapped the papers before him and said from a roughened throat:

"Let me summarize. I have shown you a fiction, that the heavenly bodies move in ellipses under an inverse square law of attraction. With the help of the calculus, I have proved that the elliptical paths are a direct consequence of that law. Now here, in these papers, is a summary of my calculations on the basis of our assumption, about the actual heavenly motions as recorded in the *Book of Stars*. If you check them for yourselves, you will find that the data are explained without recourse to any epicycles whatsoever.

"Mind you, I have never said that the paths *are* anything but circular. I have only said that they may be *assumed* to be, and that this assumption simplifies astrological computation so much that predictions of unprecedented accuracy can now be made. You will wish to verify my claims and consult your superiors about their theological significance. Far be it from me to broadcast anything blasphemous.

"I got troubles enough," he added in Anglic.

There was no uproar when he left. His students were as wrung out as he. But later, when the implications began to sink in—

He returned to the ship. Pasqual met him in the wardroom. "Where have you been so long?" the engineer asked. "I was getting worried."

"At the lodge." Schuster threw himself into a chair with a sigh. "Whoof! Sabotage is hard work."

"Oh . . . I was asleep when you came back here for noon, and so did not tell you. While you were out this morning, Davy called in. He is on his way back."

"He might as well return, I suppose. We can't do anything until we get an okay from on high, and that'll take time."

"Too much time, maybe."

"And maybe not." Schuster shrugged. "Don't be like the nasty old man in a boat."

"Eh?"

"Asked, 'How do you know it will float?' Whereupon he said, 'Boo!' to the terrified crew and retired to the cabin to gloat. Be a good unko and fetch me a drink, will you, and then I'm going to retire myself."

"No supper?"

"A sandwich will do. We have to start rationing— remember?"

❀ IV ❀

The scanner alarm roused Schuster. He groaned out of his bunk and fumbled his way to the nearest viewscreen. What he saw brought him bolt awake.

A dozen Sanctuary guards sat mounted below the gangway. The light of moon and Pleiades glimmered on their spears. A pair of acolytes were helping a tall shape, gaunt in its robes, to dismount. Schuster would have known that white mane and disc-topped staff anywhere this side of the Coal Sack.

"*Oi, weh,*" he said. "Get your clothes on, chumlets. The local Pope wants an audience with us."

"Who?" Mukerji yawned.

"Sketulo, the Boss Consecrate, *in* person. Could be I've lit a bigger firecracker than I knew." Schuster scuttled back aft and threw on his own garments.

He was ready to receive the guest by the time that one had climbed to the air lock. "My master, you honor us beyond our worth," he unctuated. "Had we only known, we would have prepared a fitting—"

"Let us waste no time on hypocrisies," said the Larsan curtly. "I came so that we could talk in private, without fear of being overheard by underlings or fools." He gestured at Pasqual to close the inner door. "Dim your cursed lights."

Mukerji obeyed. Sketulo's huge eyes opened wide and smoldered on Schuster. "You being the captain here," he said, "I will see you alone."

The merchant lifted his shoulders and spread his palms at his shipmates but obediently led the way—in Larsum the place of honor was behind—to that cabin which served as his office on happier occasions. When its door had also been shut, he faced the other and waited.

Sketulo sat stiffly down on the edge of a lounger that had been adjusted to accommodate Ivanhoan bodies. His staff remained upright in one hand, its golden circle ashimmer in the wan light. Schuster lowered himself to a chair, crossed his legs, and continued to wait.

The old voice finally clipped: "When I gave you permission to instruct the young astrologers, I did not think even you would dare sow the seeds of heresy."

"My master!" Schuster protested in what he hoped would be interpreted as a shocked tone. "I did nothing of the sort."

"Oh, you covered yourself shrewdly, by your chatter of a fiction. But I have seldom seen anyone so agitated as those several Consecrates who came to me after you had left."

"Naturally the thought I presented was exciting—"

"Tell me." Sketulo pursed his wrinkled lips. "We will need considerable time to check your claims, of course; but does your hypothesis in truth work as well as you said?"

"Yes. Why should I discredit myself with boasts that can readily be disproven?"

"Thus I thought. Clever, clever . . ." The haggard head shook. "Anti-God has many ways of luring souls astray."

"But, my master, I distinctly told them this was a statement false to fact."

"So you did. You are reported to have said that it might, at best, be mathematically true, but this does not make it philosophically true." Sketulo leaned forward. Fiercely: "You must have known, however, that the question would soon arise whether there can be two kinds of truth, and that in any such contest, those whose lives are spent with observations and numbers will decide in the end that the mathematical truth is the only one."

I certainly did, Schuster thought. *It's exactly the point that got Galileo into trouble with the Inquisition, way back when on Earth.* A chill went through him. *I didn't expect you to see it this fast, though, you old devil.*

"By undermining the Faith thus subtly, you have confirmed my opinion that your kind are the agents of Anti-God," Sketulo declared. "You must not remain here."

Hope flared in Schuster. "Believe me, my master, we have no wish to do so! The sooner we can get what we need from our warehouse and be off, the happier we will be."

"Ah. But the others. When can we expect a third visit, a fourth, fleet after fleet?"

"Never, God willing. You were told by the first crew that arrived, we have no interest in trade—"

"So they said. And yet it was only a few short years before this vessel came. How do we know you tell the truth?"

You can't argue with a fanatic, Schuster thought, and kept silence. Sketulo surprised him again by changing the topic and asking in a nearly normal tone:

"How do you propose to move that great object hither?"

"Well, now, that is a good question, my master." Schuster's forehead went wet. He mopped it with his sleeve. "We have a way, but, uh, we have hesitated to suggest it—"

"I commanded that we be alone in order that we might both speak frankly."

Schuster sucked in a lungful of air, reached for a pad and penstyl, and explained about wagons.

Sketulo didn't move a muscle. When at length he spoke, it was only to say: "At certain most holy and secret rites, deep within the Sanctuary, there is that which is moved from one room to another by such means."

"We need not shock the populace," Schuster said. "Look, we can have sideboards, or curtains hanging down, or something like that, to hide the wheels."

Sketulo shook his head. "No. Almost everyone, as an unwitting child, has played with a round stick or stone. The barbarians beyond the Kasunian Range employ rollers. No doubt some of our own peasants do, furtively, when a heavy load must be moved and no one is watching. You could not deceive the more intelligent observers about what was beneath those covers; and they would tell the rest."

"But with official permission—"

"It may not be granted. God's law is plain. Even if you were given leave by the Sanctuary, most of the commoners would fear a curse. They would destroy you despite any injunctions of ours."

Since that was what Falkayn had quoted Rebo as saying, Schuster felt that perhaps Sketulo was telling the truth. Not that it mattered if he wasn't; he was obviously determined not to allow this thing.

The merchant sighed. "Well, then, my master, have you any other suggestion? Perhaps, if you would furnish enough laborers from the Consecrate estates, we could drag the workmaker here."

"This is the planting and cultivating season. We cannot spare so many hands, lest we have a famine later."

"Oh, now, my master, you and I have an identical interest: to get this ship off the ground. My associates at home can send you payment in metals, fabrics, and, yes, artificial food nourishing to your type of life."

Sketulo stamped the deck with his staff so it rang. His tone became a snarl: "We do not *want* your wares! We do not want you! The trouble you started today has snapped the last thread of my patience. If you perish here, despite that accursed rescue station, then God may well persuade your fellows that this is not a good place for such a station after all. At least, come what may, we will have done God's will here in Larsum . . . by giving not a finger's length of help to the agents of Anti-God!"

He stood up. His breath rasped harshly in the narrow metal space. Schuster rose, too, regarded him with a self-astonishing steadiness, and asked low: "Do I understand you rightly, then, my master, that you wish us to die?"

The unhuman head lifted stiffly over his. "Yes."

"Will your guard corps attack us, or would you rather stir mobs against us?"

Sketulo stood silent awhile. His eventual answer was reluctant: "Neither, unless you force our hand. The situation is complex. You know how certain elements of the

Warden and trader classes, not without influence, have been seduced into favoring somewhat your cause. Besides, although we could overcome you with sheer numbers, I am well aware that your weapons would cost us grievous losses—which might invite a barbarian invasion. So you may abide in peace awhile."

"Until you think of a safe way to cut our throats, hm?"

"Or until you starve. But from this moment you are forbidden to enter Aesca."

"*Nu?*" That would not be so good an idea anyway, with all those rooftops and alleys for an archer to snipe from. "Well—" Schuster's words trailed off. He wondered, momentarily frantic, if this mess was his fault, going so boldly forward, fatally misjudging the situation. . . . No. He hadn't foreseen Sketulo's precise reaction, but it was better to have everything out in the open. Had he known before what he did now, he wouldn't have sent Davy off alone. *Got to warn the kid to look out for assassins.* . . . He grinned one-sidedly. "At least we understand each other. Thanks for that."

For an instant more he toyed with the idea of taking the Larsan prisoner, a hostage. He dismissed it. That would be a sure way to provoke attack. Sketulo was quite willing to die for his faith. Schuster was equally willing to let him do so, but didn't want to be included in the deal. A wife and kids were waiting for him, very far away on Earth.

He led the old one to the air lock and watched him ride off. The sound of hooves fell hollow beneath the moon and the clustered stars.

❀ V ❀

It seemed to Falkayn that he had been riding through his whole life. Whatever might have happened before was a dream, a vapor somewhere in his emptied skull, unreal . . . reality was the ache in every cell of him, saddle sores, hunger, tongue gone wooden with thirst and eyelids sandpapery with sleeplessness, the fear of death battered out of him and nothing left but a sort of stupid animal determination to reach Gilrigor Castle, he couldn't always remember why.

He had made stops during the night, of course. A fastiga was tougher than a mule and swifter than a horse, but it must rest occasionally. Falkayn himself hadn't dared sleep, though, and saddled up again as soon as possible. Now his beasts were lurching along the road like drunks.

He turned his head—the neckbones creaked—and looked behind. His pursuers had been in sight ever since the first predawn paling of the sky made them visible. When was that—a century ago?—no, must be less than an hour, the sun wasn't aloft yet, though the blackness overhead had turned plum color and the Sisters were sunken below Kasunia's wall. There were four or five of them—hard to be sure in this twilight—only two kilometers behind him and closing the gap. Their spears made points of brightness among the shadows.

So close?

The knowledge rammed home. Energy spurted from some ultimate source, cleared his mind and whetted his senses. He felt the dawn wind on his cheeks, heard it sough in the wiry brush along the roadside and around the staggering hoofbeats of his mount, saw how the snow peaks in the west were reddening as they caught the first sunrays; he yanked the little transceiver from his pocket and slapped the switch over. "Hello!"

"Davy!" yelled Schuster's voice. "What's happened? You okay?"

"So far," Falkayn stammered. "N-not for long, I'm afraid."

"We been trying for hours to raise you."

He'd called the ship while he fled, to relate the circumstances, and contact was maintained until—"Guess I, I got so tired I just put the box away for a minute and then forgot about it. My animals are about to keel over. And . . . the Sanctuary boys are overhauling me."

"Any chance you can reach the castle before they get in bowshot?"

Falkayn bit his lip. "I doubt it. Can't be very far to go, a few kilometers, but—What can I do? Try to make a run for it on foot?"

"No, you'd be ridden down, shot in the back. I'd say make a stand."

"One of those bows, God, they've got almost the range of my gun, and they can attack me from every side at once. There's no cover here. Not even a clump of trees in sight."

"I know an old frontier stunt. Shoot your animals and use them for barricades."

"That won't protect me long."

"It may not have to. If you're as near the castle as you say, Ivanhoan eyes ought to spot flashes in the air from your shots. Anyhow, it's the only thing I can suggest."

"V-v-v—" Falkayn snapped his teeth together and held them that way for a second. "Very well."

Schuster's own voice turned uneven. "I wish to God I could be there to help you, Davy."

"I wouldn't mind if you were," Falkayn surprised himself by answering. Now that was more like how a man facing terrible odds ought to talk! "Uh, I'll have to pocket this radio again, but I'll leave the switch open. Maybe you can hear. Root for me, will you?"

He reined in and sprang to the ground. His fastigas stood passive, trembling in their exhaustion. Not without guilt feelings, he led the pack carrier around until it stood nose to tail with the mount. Quickly, then, he set his blaster to narrow beam and drilled their brains.

They collapsed awkwardly, like jointed dolls; a kind of sigh went from the loaded one, as if it were finally being allowed to sleep, but its eyes remained open and horribly fixed. Falkayn wrestled with the legs and necks, trying to make a wall that would completely surround him. Scant success . . . Panting, he looked eastward. His enemies had seen what he was about and broken into a trot, scattering right and left across the downs before they stopped to tether their spare animals. Five of them, all right.

The sun's disc peered over the ridges. *Wait, the more contrast, the more visible an energy flash will be.* Falkayn fired several times straight upward.

An arrow thunked into fastiga flesh. The boy went on his stomach and shot back. He missed the retreating rider. Crouching, he glared around the horizon. Another Larsan was drawing a bow at him, less than half a kilometer distant. He sighted carefully and squeezed trigger. The gun pointed a long blue-white finger. An instant later it said *crack!* and the Larsan dropped his bow and clutched at his left arm. Two other arrows came nastily near. Falkayn shot back, without hitting, but it did force the archers out of their own range for a little while, which was something.

He hadn't many charges left in the magazine, though. If the Consecrates' hired blades kept up their present tactics, compelling him to expend his ammunition—But did they know how little he had? No matter. They obviously were not going to quit before they finished their job. Unless he was lucky enough to drop them all, David Falkayn was probably done. He discovered he was accepting that fact soberly, not making much fuss about it one way or another, hoping mainly that he would be able to take some of them on hell road with him. *Rough on Mother and Dad, though,* he thought. *Rough on Marty Schuster, too. He'll have to tell them, if he lives.*

Two guards pounded down a grassy slope toward him, side by side. Their manes streamed in the air. When they were nearly in gunshot, they separated. Falkayn fired at one, who leaned so low simultaneously that the bolt missed. The other got off an arrow on a high trajectory. Falkayn shot at him, too, but he was already withdrawing on the gallop. The arrow smote, centimeters from Falkayn's right leg where he sprawled.

Nice dodge, he thought with the curious dispassion that had come upon him. *I wonder if they've met my kind of defensive maneuver before, or are just making a good response to something new? Wouldn't be surprised if that last was the case. They're brainy fellows, these Ivanhoans. While we, with our proud civilization, we can't respond to so simple a thing as a local taboo on wheels.*

Shucks, it should be possible to analyze the problem—

Two others were galloping close from the right. Falkayn narrowed his blaster beam as far as he could, to get maximum range, and shot with great care. He struck first one fastiga, then another: minor wounds, but painful.

Both animals reared. The riders got them under control again and wheeled away. Falkayn turned about in time to fire at the other two, but not in time to forestall their arrows. Misses on both sides.

—and figure out precisely what a wheel does, and then work out some other dodge that'll do the same thing.

Where was the fifth Larsan, the one who'd gotten winged? Wait . . . his fastiga stood riderless some distance off. But where was he? These bully boys weren't the type to call it a day just because of a disabled arm.

I got good grades in math and analytics. My discussants told me so. Now why can't I dredge something I learned back then, up into memory, and use it? I could solve the problem for an exam, I'll bet.

Most likely the wounded one was snaking through the taller bushes, trying to get so close that he could pounce and stab.

Of course, this isn't exactly an examination room. Analytical thinking doesn't come natural, most especially not when your life's involved, and it's very, very odd that I should begin on it at this precise moment. Maybe my subconscious smells an answer.

The four riders had gotten together for a conference. They looked like toys at this distance, near the top of a high ridge paralleling the road and sloping down to its edge. Falkayn couldn't hear anything but wind. The sun, fully risen now, made rippling violet shadows in the gray grass. The air was still cold; his breath smoked.

Let's see. A wheel is essentially a lever. But we've already decided that the other forms of lever aren't usable. Wait! A screw? No, how'd you apply it? If any such thing were practical for us, Romulo Pasqual would-d've thought of it by now.

How about cutting the wheel in slices, mounted separately? No, I remember suggesting that to Rebo, and he said it wouldn't do, because the whole ensemble viewed from the side would still have a circular outline.

The riders had evidently agreed on a plan. They unstrung their bows and fastened them carefully under the saddle girths. Then they started toward him, single file.

What else does a wheel do, besides supply mechanical advantage? Ideally, it touches the ground at only one point, and so minimizes friction. Is there some other shape which'll do the same? Sure, any number of 'em. But what good is an elliptical wheel?

Hey, couldn't you have a trick mounting, like an eccentric arm on an axle that was also elliptical, so the load would ride steady? M-m-m, no, I doubt if it's feasible, especially over roads as dreadful as this one, and nothing but muscle power available for traction. The system would soon be jolted to pieces.

The leading Sanctuary guard broke into a headlong gallop. Falkayn took aim and waited puzzledly for him to come in range of a beam wide enough to be surely lethal. The transceiver made muffled squawkings in Falkayn's pocket, but he hadn't the time for chatter.

Same objection, complexity, inefficiency, and fragility, applies to whatever else comes to mind, like say a tread-mill-powered caterpillar system. Perhaps Romulo can flange something up. But there ought to be a foolproof, easy answer.

Crouched against the neck of his fastiga, the leading guard was nearly in range. Yes, now *in* range! Falkayn fired. The blast took the animal full in the chest. It cartwheeled several meters more downhill, under its own momentum, before falling. Its rider had left the saddle at the moment it was struck, before the beam could seek him out. He hit the ground with acrobatic agility, rolled over, and disappeared in the brush.

By the time Falkayn saw what was intended, he had already shot the second. It crashed into the barrier of the first. The third rushed near, frightened but under control.

"Oh, no, you don't," the human rasped. "I'm not going to build your wall for you!" He let the other two pound by. As they slued about, exposing their riders to him, he had the bleak pleasure of killing an enemy. The fourth escaped out of range, jumped to earth, and ran toward the dead animals, leading his own but careful to stay on its far side.

Falkayn's bolts raked the slope, but he couldn't see his targets in the overgrowth and it was too moist in this spring season to catch fire. The third Larsan got to the barrier and slashed his fastiga's throat. It struggled, but hands reached from below to hold it there while it died.

So three warriors had made the course. Now they were ensconced behind a wall of their own, too thick for him to burn through, high enough for them to kneel behind and send arrows that would arch down onto him. Of course, their aim wouldn't be good—

The shafts began to rise. Falkayn made himself as small as possible and tried to burrow under one of his own slain fastigas.

Something which . . . which rolls, and holds its load steady, but isn't circular—

The arrows fell. Their points went hard into dirt and inert flesh. After some time of barrage, a leonine head lifted above the other barrier to see what had happened.

Falkayn, sensing a pause in the assault, rose to one knee and snapped a shot.

He ought to have hit, with a broad beam at such close range. But he didn't. The bolt struck the barricade and greasy smoke puffed outward. The Larsan dove for cover.

What made Falkayn's hand jerk was suddenly seeing the answer.

He snatched out the radio. "Hello!" he yelped. "Listen, I know what we can do!" .

"Anything, Davy," said Schuster like a prayer.

"Not for me. I mean to get you fellows out of here—"

The arrows hailed anew. Anguish ripped in Falkayn's left calf where he crouched. He stared at the shaft that skewered it, not really comprehending for a moment.

"Davy? You there?" Schuster cried across a thousand kilometers.

Falkayn swallowed hard. The wound didn't hurt too much, he decided. And the enemy had ceased fire again. They must be running low on ammo, too. The road was strewn with arrows.

"Listen carefully," he said to the box. It had fallen to the ground, and blood from his leg was trickling toward it. A dim part of him was interested to note that human blood in this light didn't have its usual brilliance but looked blackish red. The rate of flow indicated that no major vessel had been cut. "You know what a constant-width polygon is?" he asked.

A Larsan ventured another peek. When Falkayn didn't shoot, he rose to his feet for an instant and waved before dropping back to shelter. Falkayn was too busy to wonder what that meant.

"You hurt, Davy?" Schuster pleaded. "You don't sound so good. They still after you?"

"Shut up," Falkayn said. "I haven't much time. Listen. A figure of constant width is one that if you put it between two parallel lines, so they're tangent to it on opposite sides, and then revolve it, well, the lines stay tangent clear around the circumference. In other words, the width of the figure is the same along every line drawn from side to side through the middle. A circle is a member of that class, obviously. But—"

The Larsan whose left arm had been scorched to disability sprang from a clump of bushes along the road. There was a knife in his right hand. Falkayn caught the gleam in the corner of an eye, twisted about, and snatched for his blaster where it lay on the ground. The knife arm chopped through an arc. Falkayn shrieked as his own hand was pinned to earth.

"*Davy!*" Schuster cried.

Falkayn picked up the blaster with his left. The muzzle wavered back and forth. He shot and missed. The guard cleared the barrier at a jump, drawing his sword as he sprang. The blade swept around. Probably he had closed his eyes at the moment the gun went off, for he struck with accuracy. The weapon spun clear of Falkayn's lacerated grasp.

The human yanked out the knife that pinned him, surged to his feet, and attacked left-handed. His voice rose to a shout: "A circle's not the only one! You take an equi—"

His rush had brought him under the Larsan's guard. He stabbed, but the point slithered off the breastplate. The native shoved. Falkayn lurched backward. The guard poised his rapier.

"Equilateral triangle," Falkayn sobbed. "You draw arcs—"

A horn sounded. The guard recoiled with a snarl. On the hillside, an archer rose and sent a last arrow at Falkayn. But the human's hurt leg had given way. He went to his knees, and the shaft whirred where he had been.

Another arrow, from another direction, took the sword-wielder through the breast. He uttered a rather ghastly rattling cough and fell on top of a fastiga. The surviving Sanctuary agents pointed frantically at the circles on their cuirasses. But arrows stormed from the riders who galloped out of the west, and the episode was over.

Rebo Legnor's-Child drew rein at the head of his household warriors and sprang from the saddle in time for Falkayn to crumple into his arms.

❈ VI ❈

Mukerji entered the wardroom to find Schuster alone, laying out a hand of solitaire. "Where's Romulo?" he asked.

"Off in his own place, quietly going crazy," Schuster said. "He's trying to figure out what Davy was getting at just before—" He raised a face whose plumpness looked oddly pinched. "Heard anything from the kid?"

"No. I shall let you know the minute I do, of course. His set must still be on, I hear natives speak and move about. But not a word from him, and everyone else is probably afraid to answer the talking box."

"Oh, God. *I* sent him there."

"You could not have known there was any danger."

"I could know the ship was the safest place to be. I should have gone myself." Schuster stared blindly at his cards. "He was my apprentice."

Mukerji laid a hand on the merchant's shoulder. "You had no business on a routine mission like that. Fighting and all, it was routine. Your brains are needed here."

"What brains?"

"You must have some plan. What were you talking to that peasant about, a few hours before sunrise?"

"I bribed him with a trade knife to carry a message for me to the Sanctuary. Telling Herktaskor he should come out for a private conference. Second in command of the astrology department, you may recall; a very bright fellow, and I think more friendly than otherwise to us. At least, he doesn't have Sketulo's fanatical resistance to innovation." Schuster found he was laying a heart on a diamond, cursed, and scattered the cards with a sweep of his hand. "Obviously Rebo showed up, having seen the gun flashes, and dealt with Sketulo's killers. But did he come in time? Is Davy still alive?"

The scanner hooted. Both men leaped to their feet and ran out the door to the closest viewscreen. "Speak of the devil," Mukerji said. "Take over, Martin. I shall go back and hunch above the radio."

Schuster suppressed his inward turmoil and opened the air lock. A cold early-morning wind, laden with sharp odors, gusted at him. Herktaskor mounted the gangway and entered. His great form was muffled in a cloak, which he did not take off until the door had closed again. Beneath, he wore his robes. Evidently he hadn't wanted to be recognized on his way here.

"Greeting," said Schuster in a dull tone. "Thank you for coming."

"Your message left me scant choice," said the Consecrate. "For the good of Larsum and the Faith, I am bound to listen if you claim to have an important matter to discuss."

"Have you, ah, been forbidden to enter the ship?"

"No, but it is as well not to give the Chief the idea that he should forbid it." Herktaskor squinted against an illumination which he found blindingly harsh, though it had been reduced well below normal to conserve the small amount of charge left in the accumulators. Schuster led the being to his own cabin, dimmed the lights further, and offered the lounger.

They sat down and regarded each other for a silent while. At length Herktaskor said, "If you repeat this, I shall have to call you a liar. But having found you honorable"—that hurt a little; Schuster's plans were not precisely above-board—"I think you should know that many Consecrates feel Sketulo was wrong in immediately banning your new mathematics and astrology. Could he show by Scripture, tradition, or reasoning that they contravened the Word of God, then naturally the whole Sanctuary would have joined him in rejecting your teachings. But he has made no attempt to show it, has merely issued a flat decree."

"Are you permitted to argue with him about the matter?"

"Yes, the rule has always been that full-rank Consecrates may dispute freely within the bounds of doctrine. But we must obey the orders of our superiors as long as those are not themselves unlawful."

"I thought so. Well—" Schuster reached for a cigar. "Here is what I wanted to tell you. I wish the cooperation of the Sanctuary rather than its enmity. In order to win that cooperation, I would like to prove to you that we are no danger to the Faith, but may rather be the instruments of its furtherance. Then perhaps you can convince the others."

Herktaskor waited, impassive. Yet his eyes narrowed and seemed to kindle.

Schuster started the cigar and puffed ragged clouds. "The purpose of your astrology is to learn God's will and the plan on which He has constructed the universe. To me, this implies that the larger purpose of the Consecrates is to search out the nature of God, insofar as it may be understood by mortals. Your theologians have reached conclusions in the past. But are those conclusions final? May there not be much more to deduce?"

Herktaskor bowed his lion head and traced a solemn circle in the air. "There may. There must. Nothing of importance has been done in that field since the *Book of Domno* was written, but I myself have often speculated—Go on, I pray you."

"We newcomers are not initiates of your religion," Schuster said. "However, we, too, in our own fashion, have spent many centuries wondering about the divine. We, too, believe," *well, some of us,* "in a single God, immortal, omnipotent, omniscient . . . perfect . . . Who made all things. Now maybe our theology varies from yours at crucial points. But maybe not. May I compare views with you? If you can show me where my people have erred, I will be grateful and will, if I live, carry back the truth to them. If, on the other hand, I can show you, or merely suggest to you, points on which our thought has gone beyond yours, then you will understand, and can make your colleagues understand, that we outlanders are no menace, but rather a beneficial influence."

"I doubt that Sketulo and certain other stiff-minded Consecrates will ever concede that," Herktaskor said. His voice took on an edge. "Yet if a new truth were indeed revealed, and anyone dared deny it—" His fists unclenched. "I listen."

Schuster was not surprised. Every religion in Earth's past, no matter how exclusive in theory, had had influential thinkers who were willing to borrow ideas from contemporary rivals. He made himself as comfortable as possible. This would take a while.

"The first question I wish to raise," he said, "is why God created the universe. Have you any answer to that?"

Herktaskor started. "Why, no. The writings say only that He did. Dare we inquire into His reasons?"

"I believe so. See, if God is unbounded in every way, then He must have existed eternally before the world was. He is above everything finite. But thought and existence are themselves finite, are they not?"

"Well . . . well . . . yes. That sounds reasonable. Thought and existence as we know them, anyhow."

"Just so. I daresay your philosophers have argued whether the sound of a stone falling in the desert, unheard by any ears, is a real phenomenon." Herktaskor nodded. "It is an old conundrum, found on countless planets, I mean in many countries. In like manner, a God alone in utter limitlessness could not be be comprehended by thought nor described in words. No thinking, speaking creatures were there. Accordingly, in a certain manner of speaking, He did not exist. That is to say, His existence lacked an element of completion, the element of being observed and comprehended. But how can the existence of the perfect God be incomplete? Obviously it cannot. Therefore it was necessary for Him to bring forth the universe, that it might know Him. Do you follow me?"

Herktaskor's nod was tense. He had begun to breathe faster.

"Have I said anything thus far which contradicts your creed?" Schuster asked.

"No . . . I do not believe you have. Though this is so new—Go on!"

"The act of creation," Schuster said around his cigar, "must logically involve the desire to create, thought about the thing to be created, the decision to create, and the work of creation. Otherwise God would be acting capriciously, which is absurd. Yet such properties— desire, thought, decision, and work—are limited. They are inevitably focused on one creation, out of the infinite possibilities, and involve one set of operations. Thus the act of creation implies a degree of finitude in God. But this is unthinkable, even temporarily. Thus we have the paradox that He must create and yet He cannot. How shall this be resolved?"

"How do you resolve it?" Herktaskor breathed, looking a little groggy.

"Why, by deciding that the actual creation must have been carried out by ten intelligences known as the *Sephiroth*—"

"Hold on!" The Consecrate half rose. "There are no other gods, even lesser ones, and the *Book* does not credit the angels with making the world."

"Of course. Those I speak of are not gods or angels, they are separate manifestations of the One God, somewhat as the facets of a jewel are manifestations of it without being themselves jewels. God no doubt has infinitely many manifestations, but the ten *Sephiroth* are all that we have found logically necessary to explain the fact of creation. To begin with the first of them, the wish and idea of creation must have been coexistent with God from eternity. Therefore it contains the nine others which are required as attributes of that which is to be created—"

❦ ❦ ❦

Some hours later, Herktaskor said farewell. He walked like one in a daze. Schuster stood in the lock watching him go. He himself felt utterly exhausted.

If it turns out I've done this to him, to all of them, for nothing, may my own dear God forgive me.

Mukerji hurried from the wardroom. His feet clattered loudly on the deck. "Martin!" he yelled. "Davy's alive!"

Schuster spun on his heel. A wave of giddiness went through him, he leaned against the bulkhead and gasped weakly.

"His call came after you went off with that Brahmin," Mukerji said. "I don't know if I would do harm by interrupting you, so—Yes. He was wounded, hand and leg, nothing that won't heal, you know we need not worry about any local microbes. He fainted, and I imagine that he went directly from a swoon to a sleep. He could still only mumble when he called from Rebo's castle, said he would call back after he had gotten some more rest and explain his idea. Come, Romulo and I have already broken out a bottle to celebrate!"

"I could use that," Schuster said, and followed him.

After a few long swallows, he felt more himself. He set down his glass and gave the others a shaky grin. "Did you ever have anybody tell you you were not a murderer?" he asked. "That's how I'm feeling."

"Oh, come off it," Pasqual snorted. "You are not *that* responsible for your apprentices."

"No, maybe not, except I sent him where I could have gone myself—But he's okay, you say!"

"Without you here on the spot, that might make very little difference," Pasqual said. "Krish is just a spaceman and I just an engineer and Davy just a kid. We need somebody to scheme our way out of this hole. And you, *amigo mío*, are a schemer by trade."

"Well, Davy seems to have thought of something. What, I don't know." Schuster shrugged. "Or maybe I do know—some item I learned in school and forgot. He's closer to his school days."

"Assuming his idea is any good," Pasqual said with a return of worry. "I have not made any feasible plans myself, but believe me, I have thought of many harebrained ones."

"We'll have to wait and see. Uh, do you have any more details on the situation in Gilrigor?"

"Yes, I spoke directly with Rebo, after Davy had shown him how the radio works," Mukerji said. "The assassins were killed in his attack. He said he ordered that because he suspected they were indeed Sanctuary guards. If he had taken any of them prisoner, he would have been bound to release them again, or else face an awkward clash of wills between himself and Sketulo. And they would promptly have taken word back here. As it is, he has avoided the dilemma, and can claim his action was perfectly justified. At arrowshot distance, he could not see their insignia, and the natural assumption was that they were bandits—whom it is his duty to eradicate."

"Excellent." Schuster chuckled. "Rebo's a smart gazzer. If he finds an excuse not to send a messenger here, as I'm sure he can, we'll have gained several days before Sketulo wonders what's happened and sends someone else out to inquire—who's then got to get there and back, taking still more time. In other words, by keeping our mouths shut about the whole business, we turn his own delaying tactics on him." He looked around the table.

"And time is what we need right now, second only to haulage. Time for the Sanctuary to get so badly off balance, so embroiled internally, that no one can think up a new quasi-legal gimmick for stopping us."

"Be careful they are not driven to violence," Mukerji said.

"That's not too likely," Schuster replied. "The attempt on Davy was by stealth; I'm pretty sure Sketulo will disown his dead agents when the news breaks. Any decision to act with open illegality is tough for him, you see. It'd give people like Rebo much too good a talking point, or even an excuse to fight back. Besides, as I already remarked, time should now begin to work against the old devil."

Pasqual cocked his head at the merchant. "What have you been brewing?"

"Well—" Schuster reached for the bottle again. Liquor gurgled cheerily into his glass. "First off, as you know, I introduced Newtonian astronomy. I disguised it as a fictional hypothesis, but that just makes it sneakier, not any less explosive. Nobody can fool himself forever with a pretense this is only a fairy tale to simplify his arithmetic. Sooner or later, he'll decide the planetary orbits really are elliptical. And that knocks a major prop out from under his belief in the sacredness of circles, which in turn will repercuss like crazy on the rest of the religion. Sketulo foresaw as much, and right away he forbade any use of my ideas. This simply delays the inevitable, though. He can't stop his astrologers from thinking, and some of them from resenting the prohibition. That'll make tension in the Sanctuary, which'll occupy a certain amount of his time and energy, which'll therefore be diverted from the problem of how to burke us."

"Nice," Mukerji frowned, "but a little long range. The revolution might take fifty years to ripen."

"Admitted. The trend helps our cause, but not enough by itself. So today I got Herktaskor here. We talked theology."

"What? You can't upset a religion in an afternoon!"

"Oh, sure. I know that." Schuster took a drink. His grin broadened. "The *goyim* have been working on mine for two or three thousand years and got nowhere. I only pointed out certain logical implications of the local creed and suggested some of the answers to those implications which've been reached on Earth."

"So?" Pasqual asked wonderingly.

"Well, you know I'm interested in the history of science and philosophy, like to read about it and so forth. Because of this, as well as some family traditions, I've got a knowledge of the Kabbalah."

"*¿Qué es?*"

"The system of medieval Jewish theosophy. In one form or another, it had tremendous influence for centuries, even on Christian thought. But believe you me, it's the most fantastically complicated structure the human race ever built out of a few texts, a lot of clouds, and a logic that got the bit between its teeth. Jewish Orthodoxy never wanted any part of it—much too hairy, and among the Chasidim in particular it led to some wild emotional excesses.

"But it fits the Larsan system like a skin. For instance, in the Kabbalah there are ten subordinate emanations of God, who are the separate attributes of perfection. They're divided into three triads, each denoting one male and one female quality plus their union. There hasn't been much numerology here before now, but when I reminded Herktaskor that three points determine a circle, he gasped. Each of these triadic apices is identified with some part of the body of the archetypal man. One more *Sephirah* encircles the lot, which also accords nicely with Larsan symbolism, and the conjunction of them produced the universe. . . . Well, never mind details. It goes on to develop techniques of letter rearrangement by which the inner meaning of Scripture can be discovered, a doctrine of triple reincarnation, a whole series of demonologies and magical prescriptions, altogether magnificent, glittering nonsense that seduced some of the best minds Earth ever knew. I gave it to Herktaskor."

"And—?" Mukerji asked very softly.

"Oh, not all. That'd take months. I just told him the bare outlines. He may or may not come back for more. That hardly matters. The damage has been done. Larsan philosophy is still rather primitive, not ready to deal with such strong meat. Religion is theoretically a pure monotheism, in practice tainted with the ghosties and ghoulies of popular superstition, and no one so far has given its premises a really thorough examination. Yet theology does exist as a respectable enterprise. So the Consecrates are cocked and primed to go off, in an explosion of reinterpretations, reformations, counterreformations, revelations, new doctrines, fundamentalistic reactions, and every other kind of hooraw we humans have been through. As I've already said, the Kabbalah sure had that effect on Earth. In time, this should break up the Sanctuary and let some fresh air into Larsum."

Schuster sighed. "I'm afraid the process will be bloody," he finished. "If I didn't think it was for the long-range best, I wouldn't have done this thing, not even to save our lives."

Pasqual looked bewildered. "You are too subtle for me," he complained. "Will it?"

"If we can move that generator here within the next few weeks, I'm certain it will. Herktaskor is no fool, even if he is a natural-born theologian. After what happened about the calculus, he'll be discreet about who he picks to talk my ideas over with. But those are good brains in the Sanctuary, hungry to be used. If fact is denied them to work with, theory will serve. The notions will spread like a shock wave. Questions will soon be openly raised. Sketulo can't lawfully suppress discussion of that sort, and the others will be too heated up to obey an unlawful order. So he's going to have his hands full, that gazzer, for the rest of his life!"

❀ VII ❀

Rebo, Marchwarden of Gilrigor, reined in his fastiga on the crest of Ensum Hill. One hand, in an iron-knobbed gauntlet, pointed down the long slope. "Aesca," he said.

David Falkayn squinted through the day-gloom. To him the city was only a blot athwart the river's metal gleam. But a starpoint caught his eye, and his heart sprang within him. "Our ship," he breathed. "We are there."

Rebo peered across kilometers of fields and orchards. "No armed forces are gathered," he said. "I think I see the townsfolk beginning to swarm out, but no guards. Yet undoubtedly the Sanctuary has had word about us. So it is plain they do not intend to resist."

"Did you expect that—really?"

"I was not sure. That is why I brought so large a detachment of my own warriors." The cuirassed figure straightened in the saddle. The tail switched. "They would have been the ones breaking the law, had they tried to fight, so we would have had no compunctions. Not only the Wardens have chafed at the Consecrate bridle. My troop will be almost sorry not to bloody a blade this day."

"Not I." Falkayn shivered.

"Well," Rebo said, "peaceful or no, you have done more harm to them than I ever could. The world will not be the same again. So simple a thing as wagons—less toil, more goods moving faster, the age-old balance upset. And *I* will use some of that released power to overrun the Kasunians, which means I will be one to reckon with in the councils of the realm. Ever will your people be welcome in Gilrigor."

Falkayn dropped his glance, guiltily. "I cannot lie to you, my friend," he stumbled. "There may never be any more of us coming here."

"I had heard that," said Rebo, "and ignored it. Perhaps I did not wish to believe. No matter now." Pride rang in his tones. "One day our ships will come to you."

He raised his ax in signal. His riders deployed and the huge wagon lumbered over the ridge, drawn by twenty fastigas. The generator and crane lashed atop it glowed under the red sun.

The driver lowered his drag brake, a flat log, so the vehicle wouldn't get away from him on the downhill stretch. Groaning, squealing, banging, and rattling, the thing rocked onward.

It moved on eight rollers. They revolved between planks, the forward pair of which was adjustable by square pegs to permit turning. There were bumpers fore and aft to prevent their escape on an incline. As each roller emerged from the rear, two hooks caught two of the oblong metal eyes which ringed the grooves cut near either end of the log. These hooks were shrunk onto a pair of cross-braced, counter-weighted arms mounted high on the wagon bed. The arms were held in place by leather straps within a frame that stopped sidewise motion and pivoted on shapeless leather pads atop their posts. A couple of workers hauled lustily. The arms swung high. At the limit of their permissible arc, the carefully shaped hooks slipped out of the eyes and the roller fell onto a wooden roof that slanted downward to the front. Two other natives, equipped with peavies, stood there to make certain of its alignment. It boomed quickly between its guideboards and dropped to the road behind the front bumper. The wagon passed over it, the arms dipped in time to catch the next log, and the cycle began anew.

Each roller had three curved sides.

Draw an equilateral triangle, ABC. Put the point of your compasses on A and draw the arc BC. Move to B and describe AC, then to C and describe AB. Round off the corners. The resulting figure has constant width. It will roll between two parallel lines tangent to it maintaining that tangency for the whole revolution.

As a matter of fact, the class of constant-width polygons is infinite. The circle is merely a limiting case.

To be sure, Falkayn thought, the rollers on this Goldberg of his would wear down in time, approach the forbidden cross section and have to be replaced. Or would they? Someone like Rebo could argue that this proved the circle was actually the least perfect of all shapes, the degenerate product of a higher-order form. As if the poor old Consecrates didn't have theological problems enough!

He clucked to his mount and rode on ahead of the wagon, toward his ship.

INTRODUCTION

❁ A SUN INVISIBLE ❁
NOTES TOWARD A DEFINITION OF
RELATEDNESS

Before space flight it was often predicted that other planets would appeal strictly to the intellect. Even on Earthlike worlds, the course of biochemical evolution must be so different from the Terrestrial—since chance would determine which of many possible pathways was taken—that men could not live without special equipment. And as for intelligent beings, were we not arrogant to imagine that they would be so akin to us psychologically and culturally that we would find any common ground with them? The findings of the earliest extra-Solar expeditions seemed to confirm science in this abnegation of anthropomorphism.

Today the popular impression has swung to the opposite pole. We realize the galaxy is full of planets which, however exotic in detail, are as hospitable to us as ever Earth was. And we have all met beings who, no matter how unhuman their appearance, talk and act like one of our stereotypes. The Warrior, the Philosopher, the Merchant, the Old Space Ranger, we know in a hundred variant fleshly garments. We do business, quarrel, explore, and seek amusement with them as we might with any of our own breed. So is there not something fundamental in the pattern of Terrestrial biology and in Technic civilization itself?

No. As usual, the truth lies somewhere between the extremes. The vast majority of planets are in fact lethal environments for man. But on this account we normally pass them by, and so they do not obtrude very much on our awareness. Of those which possess free oxygen and liquid water, more than half are useless, or deadly, to us, for one reason or another. Yet evolution is not a random process. Natural selection, operating within the constraints of physical law, gives it a certain direction. Furthermore, so huge is the galaxy that the random variations which do occur closely duplicate each other on millions of worlds. Thus we have no lack of New Earths.

Likewise with the psychology of intelligent species. Most sophonts indeed possess basic instincts which diverge more or less from man's. With those of radically alien motivations we have little contact. Those we encounter on a regular basis are necessarily those whose bent is akin to ours; and again, given billions of planets, this bent is sure to be found among millions of races.

Of course, we should not be misled by superficial resemblances. The nonhuman remains nonhuman. He can only show us those facets of himself which we can understand. Thus he often seems to be a two-dimensional, even comic personality. But remember, we have the corresponding effect on him. It is just as well that the average human does not know on how many planets he is the standard subject of the bawdy joke.

Even so, most races have at least as much contrast between individuals—not to mention cultures—as Homo Sapiens does. Hence there is a degree of overlap. Often a man gets along better with some nonhuman being than he does with many of his fellowmen. "Sure," said a prospector on Quetzalcoatl, speaking of his partner, "he looks like a cross between a cabbage and a derrick. Sure, he belches H_2S and sleeps in a mud wallow, and his idea of fun is to spend six straight hours discussin' the whichness of the wherefore. But I can trust him—hell, I'd even leave him alone with my wife!"

—Noah Arkwright
An Introduction to Sophontology

A SUN INVISIBLE

❀ I ❀

The invaders had posted their fleet in standard patrol orbits. Otherwise they did nothing to camouflage themselves. It bespoke a confidence that chilled David Falkayn.

As his speedster neared Vanessa, he picked up ship after ship on his instruments. One passed so close that his viewscreens needed little magnification to show details. She was a giant, of Nova class, with only subtle outward indications that the hands which built her were not human. Her guns thrust across blackness and crowding constellations; sunlight blazed off her flanks; she was beautiful, arrogant, and terrifying.

Falkayn told himself he was not duly terrified. Himself wondered how big a liar he was.

His receiver buzzed, a call on the universal band. He flipped to Accept. The dial on the Doppler compensator indicated that the battleship was rapidly matching vectors with him. The image which looked out of the screen was—no, scarcely that of a Vanessan, but a member of the same species. It gabbled.

"Sorry, no spikka da—" Falkayn braked. Conquerors were apt to be touchy, and yonder chap sat aboard a vessel which could eat a continent with nuclear weapons and use his boat afterward for a toothpick. "I regret my ignorance of your various languages."

The Kraok honked. Evidently he, she, or yx did not know Anglic. Well, the interspeech of the Polesotechnic League . . . "*Loquerisne Latine?*"

The being reached for a vocalizer. Without such help, humans and Kraoka garbled each other's sounds rather badly. Adjusting it, the officer asked, "*Sprechen Sie Deutsch?*"

"Huh?" Falkayn's jaw hit his Adam's apple.

"*Ich haben die deutsche Sprache ein wenig gelehrt,*" said the Kraok with more pride than grammar, "*bei der grosse Kapitän.*"

Falkayn gripped tight to his pilot seat, and his sanity, and gaped.

Aside from being hostile, the creature was not an unpleasing sight. About two meters tall, the body resembled that of a slim tyrannosaur, if one can imagine tyrannosaurs with brown fur. From the back sprang a great, ribbed dorsal fin, partly folded but still shimmering iridescent. The arms were quite anthropoid, except for four-fingered hands where each digit had an extra joint. The head was round, with tufted ears, blunt muzzle, eyes smaller than a man's.

Clothing amounted to a brassard of authority, a pouch belt, and a sidearm. Falkayn could therefore search his memory and discover which of the three Kraokan sexes the officer belonged to: the so-called transmitter, which was fertilized by the male and in turn impregnated the female. *I should've guessed,* he thought, *even if the library on Garstang's didn't have much information on them. The males are short and meek and raise the young. The females are the most creative and make most of the decisions. The transmitters are the most belligerent.*

And right now are tracking me with guns. He felt altogether isolated. The throb and murmur of the boat, the odors of recycled air and his own sweat, his weight under the interior gee-field, were like an eggshell of life sensation around him. Outside lay starkness. The power of the League was distant by multiple parsecs, and these strangers had declared themselves its enemies.

"*Antworten Sie!*" demanded the Kraok.

Falkayn groped with half-forgotten bits of Yiddish that he had sometimes heard from Martin Schuster, during his apprenticeship. "*Ikh . . . veyss . . . nit keyn . . . Deitch,*" he said, as slowly and clearly as possible. "Get me . . . *ah mentsch* . . . uh, *zeit azay git.*" The other sat motionless. "Damn it, you've got humans with you," Falkayn said. "I know the name of one. Utah Horn. Understand? Utah Horn."

The Kraok switched him over to another, who squatted against a background of electronic apparatus. Unhuman tones whistled from an intercom. The new one turned to Falkayn.

"I know some Latin," yx said. In spite of a vocalizer, the accent was thick enough to spread on pumpernickel. "You identify."

Falkayn wet his lips. "I am the Polesotechnic League's factor on Garstang's," he said. "A messenger capsule brought me word about your, uh, advent. It said I had permission to come here."

"So." More whistles. "Indeed. One boat, unarmed, we allow to make landings at Elan-Trrl. You make trouble, we kill."

"Of course I won't," Falkayn promised, *unless I get a chance.* "I will proceed directly. Do you want my route plan?"

Yx did. The boat's pilot computer sent numbers to the battleship's. The track was approved. Maser beams flashed through space, alerting other vessels to keep an eye on the speedster. "You go," said the Kraok.

"But this Utah Horn—"

"Commander Horn see you when want to. Go." The screen blanked and Falkayn went. The acceleration strained his internal field compensators.

He gusted air from his lungs and stared outward. Hitherto, as he sped toward Thurman's Star, the view had been dominated by Beta Centauri, unwinking, almost intolerably brilliant across two-score light-years. But now the sun of Vanessa showed a visible disc. It wasn't that kind of type B supergiant: but nevertheless impressive, a white F_7, seething with prominences, shimmering with corona. If his shield screens should fail, its radiation would strike through the hull and destroy him.

Well, he gulped, *I wanted to be a dashing adventurer. So here I am, and mostly I want to dash.*

He stretched, opposed muscles to each other, worked out some of his tension. Then he felt hungry and went aft to build a sandwich; and when he had eaten and lit his pipe, a certain ebullience returned. For he was a bare twenty years old.

When he got his journeyman's papers, he was one of the youngest humans ever to do so. In large part, that was thanks to his role in the trouble on Ivanhoe. To set a similar record for a Master Merchant's certificate, he needed another exploit or two. Beljagor's message had made him whoop for glee.

Now it turned out that he was up against something more formidable than he had imagined. But he remained a scion of a baronial house in the Grand Duchy of Hermes. Mustn't let the side down, eh, what?

At a minimum, if he did nothing but convey word to Sector HQ about what had happened, that would bring him to the notice of the higher-ups. Maybe old Nick van Rijn himself would hear about this David Falkayn, who was so obviously being wasted in that dismal little outpost on Garstang's.

He practiced a reckless grin. It looked better than last year. While his face remained incurably snub-nosed, it had lost the chubbiness that used to distress him. And he was large and blond and rangy, he told himself, and had excellent taste in clothes and wine. Also women, he added, becoming more smug by the minute. If only he weren't the sole human on his assigned planet—Well, perhaps this mysterious Horn person had brought along some spare females. . . .

Vanessa grew in the vision ports, a reddish globe mottled with green and blue, sparked with reflections off the small seas. Falkayn wondered what the inhabitants called it. Being colonists themselves, whose civilization had not fallen apart during the long hiatus in Kraokan space travel as had happened on other settlements, they doubtless had a single language. Why hadn't Thurman done the usual thing in such cases, and put the native name of his discovery into the catalogues?

Quite probably because men couldn't wrap their larynxes around it. Or maybe he just felt like dubbing the planet "Vanessa." Judas, what a radium-plated opportunity an explorer had! What girl could possibly resist an offer to name a whole world for her?

Another warship in sentry orbit became discernible. Falkayn stopped dreaming.

⊗ ‖ ⊗

In the lost great days of their expansion, the Kraoka had never founded a city. The concept of so small a unit having an identity of its own—and composed of still lesser individual subunits, each with *its* separateness —was too alien to them. However, they did give names to the interconnected warrens they built at various sites. Falkayn's bible *(Terrestrial Pilot's Guide to the Beta Centauri Region)* informed him that Elan-Trrl, in any of several possible spellings, could be found in the middle northern latitudes, and was marked by a League radio beacon.

So crowded a microreel could say little about the planet. The only important hazards mentioned were ozone and ultraviolet. He got into a hooded coverall and donned a filter mask with goggles. The tiny spaceport swooped up at him. He landed and debarked.

For a moment he stood orienting himself, getting accustomed to strangeness. The sky overhead was cloudless, very pale blue, the sun too dazzling for him to look near. Colors seemed washed out in that cruel illumination. Beyond the port, hills rolled down to a lake from which irrigation canals seamed a landscape densely cultivated in bluish-green shrubs. Gnarled, feathery-leaved trees grew along the canal banks and high-prowed motorboats glided on the water. The agricultural machines in the fields, and the occasional gravity craft that flitted overhead, must have been imported by League traders. On the horizon there bulked a dry brown mountain range.

Falkayn felt heavy, under the pull of one-point-two gees. A wind boomed around him, casting billows of heat. But in this parched air he wasn't grossly uncomfortable.

On the other side of the port, Elan-Trrl lifted bulbous towers. Their gray stone was blurred in outline, from millennia of weathering. He didn't see much traffic; mainly underground, he believed. His eyes went gratefully to the homelike steel-and-vitryl facades of the League compound at the edge of the space field. They wavered in the heat shimmers.

Two vessels rested near his. One was a stubby Holbert, evidently Beljagor's; the second, lean and armed, modeled after a Terrestrial chaser, must belong to the invaders. Several Kraoka stood guard in her shade. They must have been told to expect Falkayn, for they made no move toward him. Nor did they speak. As he walked to the compound, he felt their eyes bore at his back. His boots made a loud, lonely noise beneath the wind.

The door of the factor's quarters opened for him. The air in the lobby was no less hot and sere than outside, the light scarcely less harsh. But naturally the League would put someone from an F-type star here. Falkayn began to think more kindly about cool green Garstang's. And why hadn't this Beljagor unko come out to meet him?

An intercom said, "Down the hall to your right," in Latin and a gravelly bass.

Falkayn proceeded to the main office. Beljagor sat behind his desk, puffing a cigar. Above him hung the emblem of the Polesotechnic League, an early Caravel spaceship on a sunburst and the motto *All the Traffic Will Bear.* Computers, vocascribes, and other equipment were familiar, too. The boss was not. Falkayn had never met anyone from Jaleel before.

"So there you are," Beljagor said. "Took you long enough."

Falkayn stopped and looked at him. The factor was somewhat anthropoid. That is, his stocky form sported two legs, two arms, one head, and no tail. But he was little over a meter tall; his feet each had three thick toes, his hands three mutually opposed fingers; the kilt which was his solitary garment revealed gray scales and yellow abdomen. His nose could best be likened to a tapir's snout, his ears to a sort of bat wings. A bunch of carroty cilia sprouted from the top of his pate, a pair of fleshy chemosensor tendrils from above his eyes. Those eyes were as small as a Kraok's; animals which see a ways into the ultraviolet and don't use the red end of man's spectrum have no need for large orbs.

As if for comparison, a Vanessan squatted on yxs—no, her this time—tail before the desk. Beljagor gestured with his cigar. "This here is Quillipup, my chief liaison officer. And you are . . . what is your silly name, now?"

"David Falkayn!" The newcomer could do nothing but snap a bit, when he was a mere journeyman face to face with a Master.

"Well, sit. Have a beer? You Earthtypes dehydrate easy."

Falkayn decided Beljagor wasn't such a bad fellow after all. "Thank you, sir." He folded his lean frame into a lounger.

The Jaleelan ordered through his intercom. "Have any trouble on your way?" he asked.

"No."

"I didn't expect you would. You're not worth bothering with. Also, Horn wanted you to come, and he seems to rank high in their fleet." Beljagor shrugged. "Can't say I wanted you myself. An unlicked cub! If there'd been an experienced man anywhere nearby, we might have gotten something done."

Falkayn swallowed another chunk of pride. "Regrets, sir. But when the League has only been operating hereabouts for a few decades—I'm not sure what you have in mind. Your message just said the Thurmanian System had been invaded by a force of Kraoka who're ordering the League out of the whole Beta Centauri region."

"Well, somebody has to go warn HQ," Beljagor grunted, "and I won't myself. That is, I figure to stay here and stall, maybe even argue them into changing their minds. Your own post won't miss *you*." He fumed in silence for a while. "First, though, before you leave, I want you to try and make a few elementary observations. That's why I sent to Garstang's for help, instead of Roxlatl. Snarfen is probably ten times as able as you—he being a Master—but you are a human and there are humans in high positions among the Antoranites. Like Horn, who said he'd want to interview you, after I mentioned your origin. So maybe you can get a line on what's going on. Takes one member of your ridiculous race to understand another, I always say."

Falkayn stuck grimly to the point. "The Antoranites . . . sir?"

"The invaders call their base Antoran. They won't describe it beyond the name."

Falkayn glanced at Quillipup. "Don't you have some idea where they come from?" he asked.

"No," said the Kraok into her vocalizer. "It can be no world that the Race was known to have settled. But records are incomplete."

"I don't understand how—"

"I shall explain. Ages before your species or Master Beljagor's were aught but savages, our great ancestors on Kraokanan—"

"Yes, I know about them."

"Don't interrupt your superiors, cub," Beljagor growled. "Besides, I'm not sure you do know the history. And won't hurt you to hear it again, whether or not you've waded through a book or two." His nose twitched in disdain. "You're with Solar Spice & Liquors, right? They don't deal here. Nothing for them. As far as interstellar trade goes, Vanessa doesn't produce anything but drugs and fluorescents that aren't useful to your type of life. Me, I'm not only here as agent for General Motors of Jaleel, I often represent other companies from similar planets. So I have to know the situation inside out. Go on, Quillipup."

"Now you are interrupting," sulked the Vanessan.

"When I speak, it's not an interruption, it's an enlightenment. Go on, I said. Make it short. None of your damned singing chronicles, you hear?"

"The majesty of the Race cannot well be conveyed without the Triumph Ballads."

"Stuff the majesty of the Race! Carry on."

"Oh, well, he probably could not appreciate the splendor anyway."

Falkayn gritted his teeth. Where the hell was that promised beer?

"Thousands upon thousands of years ago, then," Quillipup began, "the Race mastered space flight and set forth to colonize among the stars. Long and mighty was that striving, and the tales of the hero-crews echo down the ages. As for example, Ungn—"

"Vector back," ordered Beljagor, for Quillipup seemed about to burst into song.

Falkayn wondered if her bragging was due to an inferiority complex. The fact of the matter was that the Kraoka never had learned how to build a hyperdrive engine. Everything must be done at sublight speeds: decades or centuries, from star to star. And then only the bright F-types, which are comparatively rare, were reasonable goals. Smaller suns, like Sol, were too cool and dim, too poor in the ultraviolet radiation on which a high-energy biochemistry depended. Bigger ones like Beta Centauri—indeed, any above F_5 in the main sequence—lacked planets. The Kraoka were lucky to have found fourteen new systems they could use.

"Try to imagine the ancestral achievement," Quillipup urged. "Not merely did they cross the unthinkable interstellar abysses, they often transformed the atmosphere and ecology of entire worlds, to make them habitable. Never another species has gained the skill in that art which they possessed."

Well, naturally not, Falkayn thought. Modern spacefarers had no reason to be planetary engineers. If they didn't like a globe, they flitted off to look for another. Sublight travelers could not be so choosy.

He must admit that the Kraokan past had a certain grandeur. Men would hardly have mounted so vast a project for so long; they had more individual but less racial pride.

"When the Dark Ages descended," Quillipup said, "we remembered. Whatever else slipped from our grasp, we were yet able to look into the night sky and know what stars shone upon our kindred."

According to what Falkayn had read, the collapse had been gradual but inevitable. The sphere of operations simply became too big for expeditions so slow; it grew too costly, in time and labor and resources, to attain the next white sun. Thus exploration ended.

And likewise did trade between the colonies. It couldn't be made to pay. The Polesotechnic League exists merely because—given hyperdrive and gravity control—interstellar freight costs less for numberless planetary products than manufacture at home would cost. Though the ancient Kraoka had lacked a profit motive, they were not exempt from the laws of economics.

So they built no more star ships. In time, most of the colonies even quit interplanetary travel. Several fell into chaos and ultimate barbarism. Vanessa was luckier: civilization persisted, ossified and changeless but on a fairly high technological level, for some three hundred centuries. Then Thurman came. And now the Kraoka again had news from their lost brothers and dreamed of reunifying the Race.

Which required money. A spaceship is not exactly cheap, and the League is no charitable organization. Let the Vanessans accumulate sufficient credit, and shipyards elsewhere in the galaxy would be glad to take their orders. But not before.

Falkayn grew aware that Quillipup was droning on about more immediately significant business.

"—neither chronicle nor tradition identifies a world that might be Antoran. Phonetic analysis of clandestinely recorded speech, and certain details of custom that have been observed, suggest that the planet was settled from Dzua. But Dzua was one of the first worlds on which civilization disintegrated, and no record remains of enterprises which might once have begun there. Antoran must, accordingly, be a fifteenth colony, forgotten at home and never mentioned to the rest of us."

"Are you sure?" Falkayn ventured. "I mean, could one of the known Kraokan planets not have—"

"Certainly not," Beljagor said. "I've been on all of them and I know their capabilities. A fleet like this one—and I was taken into space, shown how big a fleet it is and what it can do—it can't be built without more industry than anybody could hide."

"The invaders . . . what have they said?"

"Not a clue-giving word, I told you. They don't belong to your blabbermouth species. Kraoka have too much tribal-identity instinct to break security."

"They must at least have explained their reasons."

"Oh, that. Yes. They're hell-bent to reestablish the old society, as an empire this time. And they want the League out of the entire region because they say we're a bunch of dominators, exploiters, corrupters of the pure tradition, and I don't know what stinking else."

Falkayn stole a look at Quillipup. He couldn't read expressions on her face, but the dorsal fin—a body-cooling surface—was erecting itself and the tail switched. Vanessa had offered no resistance to the take-over. Quite probably Quillipup would not be a bit sorry if her present employers got booted out.

The human said carefully, "Well, sir, in a way they're justified, aren't they? This is their home, not ours. We've done nothing for the Kraoka that we didn't make a fat profit on. And if they want to deal with us, they have to change a high, ancient culture—"

"Your idealism pierces me to the core; I won't say in what part of my anatomy," Beljagor sneered. "What matters is that the League stands to lose a megawhopping amount of money. All our facilities in the region are to be confiscated, you hear? So they'll get our trade with the cooler stars, too. And I don't think they'll stop there, either. Those humans who're with them, what do *they* want?"

"Well . . . yes," Falkayn conceded. There was no denying that his own species was among the most predatory in the universe. "Your message mentioned somebody called Utah Horn. That does sound pretty, uh, Wild West and bandit-like."

"I'll notify him you're here," Beljagor said. "He wants to talk with a League official of his own race. Well, he'll have to settle for you. I wish I could hope you'll manage to worm something out of him."

A server floated in with bottles. "Here's the beer," Beljagor announced. The machine opened two, Quillipup curtly declining a third. Her sinews were taut and her tail lashed the clawed feet.

"*Ad fortunam tuam,*" Beljagor said with no great sincerity, and tossed off half a liter.

Falkayn opened his mask at the mouth and did the same. Then he spouted the liquid back, choked, coughed, and fought not to vomit.

"Huh?" Beljagor stared. "What in the nine pustulant hells—? Oh, I see. I forgot your breed can't stand Jaleelan proteins." He slapped his thigh with a pistol noise. "Haw, haw, haw!"

❀ ‖ ❀

Humans being as ubiquitous as they are, nearly every League outpost on a nonterrestroid planet includes a suite conditioned and stocked for such visitors. Falkayn had been afraid that those Antoranite officers who were of his lineage would have taken the quarters over, leaving him to twiddle his thumbs in the cramped speedster. But they preferred their spaceships, he learned. Perhaps they were wary of booby traps. He was free to twiddle his thumbs in a series of rooms.

His phone chimed as Vanessa's nineteen-hour day was drawing to a close. A man in a form-fitting green uniform looked out of the screen. His features were hard, moustached, and so deeply tanned that at first Falkayn took him for an African. "You are the one from the other Polesotechnic station?" he asked. He spoke coldly, with a guttural accent.

"Yes. David Falkayn. And you're Commander Horn?"

"No. Captain Blanck, in charge of security. Since Commander Horn is to have a conference with you, I am making safe arrangements."

"I'm not quite sure what we are to confer about."

Blanck cracked a smile. It seemed to hurt his face. "Nothing very definite, Freeman Falkayn. We wish certain messages conveyed by you to the League. Otherwise, shall we say that it is mutually advantageous to get some personal impressions of each other, uncomplicated by inherent differences between species. Antoran will fight if need be, but would rather not. Commander Horn wishes to persuade you that we are no monsters, nor engaged in an unreasonable cause. It is hoped that you in turn can convince your superiors."

"Um-m-m . . . okay. Where and when?"

"I think best in your billet. We assume you are not so stupid as to attempt any breach of truce."

"With a war fleet sitting right over my head? Don't worry!" Falkayn considered. "How about dinner here?

I've checked the supplies, and they're better than anything a spaceship is likely to have."

Blanck agreed, set the time for an hour hence, and switched off. Falkayn got the kitchen servers busy. The fact that he was to dine with an enemy did not mean he couldn't dine well. Of course, a space cowboy like Utah Horn wouldn't know caviar from buckshot; but Falkayn was prepared to savor for two.

While he dressed, in a formal gold outfit, he lined up his thoughts. There didn't seem to be many humans with the invaders, but they all seemed to be key personnel. No doubt they were the ones who had originally shown the Antoranites how to build warcraft and were the experienced strategists and tacticians of the whole shebang. Horn was willing to come here because a fellow human taken aboard a ship might observe too much, critical little details which would have escaped Beljagor. But Falkayn could try to pump him. . . .

A tender landed from the orbiting flotilla. Dusk had fallen, and Falkayn could barely see that a single human walked toward his lodgings, accompanied by four Kraokan guards. Those took stations at the entrance.

A minute passed while his guest waited in the air lock for ozone to be converted; then Falkayn activated the inner door. The Antoranite had just hung up a filter mask. Falkayn lurched.

"What?" he yelled.

She couldn't be many years older than himself. The uniform was snug around a figure which would have stunned him even if he had not been celibate for months. Blue-black hair fell softly to her shoulders past enormous hazel eyes, tip-tilted nose, the most delightful mouth he had ever—

"But, but, but," he said.

She turned Blanck's accent to music. "Freeman Falkayn? I am Commander Horn."

"*Utah* Horn?"

"Yes, that is correct, Jutta Horn of Neuheim. You are surprised?"

Falkayn nodded in a blackjacked fashion.

"You see, Neuheim's population being small, any who happen to have some ability must help. Besides, my father was the man who discovered the lost planet and began this whole crusade. The Kraoka, with their feeling for ancestry, revere me on that account; and moreover, they are used to thinking of females as leaders. So I am doubly useful: any orders transmitted by me are sure to be obeyed to the letter. You must have met women spacers before now."

"Uh, it's only that, uh—" *I get it. When he dictated his letter to me, Beljagor was using a 'scribe adjusted for Anglic spelling. Quite understandable, when so few people speak German anymore. He did use the masculine pronoun for her. But either he didn't happen to meet her personally, or he's too contemptuous of humans to bother noticing their sex.*

The loss is entirely his.

Falkayn collected himself, smiled his largest smile and bowed his most sweeping bow. "I wish I could be so pleasantly surprised every time," he purred. "Welcome, Commander. Do sit down. What would you like to drink?"

She looked doubtful. "I am not sure if I ought."

"Come, come. A dinner without an aperitif is like a—ahem!—a day without sunshine." He had almost said, "A bed without a girl," but that might be rushing matters.

"*Ach*, I am not familiar with these things."

"High time you became so, then." Falkayn told the nearest server to bring old-fashioneds. He preferred a martini himself, by several light-years, but if her palate was uneducated she'd drink more of something sweet.

She settled primly on a chair. He saw that her wrist communicator was energized, doubtless transmitting to the guards outside. If they heard anything suspicious, they would break in. Still, they wouldn't catch the nuances of what Falkayn was feverishly planning.

He sat down, too. She refused a cigarette. "You must not have had a chance to be corrupted by civilization," he laughed.

"No," she agreed, deadpan. "I was born and raised on Neuheim. My sole visits beyond the system, until now, were to unexplored stars in the course of training cruises."

"What is this Neuheim?"

"Our planet. A part of the Antoranite System."

"Eh? You mean Antoran is a star?"

Jutta Horn bit her lip. "I did not know you had the opposite impression."

In spite of her nearness, or maybe because of being stimulated thereby, Falkayn's mind leaped. "Ah-ha!" he grinned. "This tells me something. We took for granted that the Antoranites were from a single planet and their human allies simply adventurers. Earthmen don't call themselves Solarians. But Earthmen and Martians do collectively. Ergo, there's more than one inhabited planet going around Antoran. Your Neuheim; and how many Kraokan worlds?"

"No matter!" she clipped.

He waved his hand. "I'm sorry if I've disturbed you. Here are our cocktails. Let's drink to a better understanding between us."

She sipped, hesitantly at first, then with frank enjoyment. "You are more friendly than I had expected," she said.

"How could I be otherwise toward you, my lady?" She blushed and fluttered her lashes, yet obviously she was not playing coquette. He eased off; never embarrass your target. "We're discussing our differences like two civilized people, trying to reach a compromise. Aren't we?"

"What authority have you to sign treaties?" She might never have been in civilization, but she had been taught how it worked.

"None," Falkayn said. "As the man on the spot, though, I can make recommendations that will have considerable weight."

"You look so young to be so important," she murmured.

"Oh, well," said Falkayn modestly, "I've knocked around a bit, you know. Had the chance to do this and that. Let's talk about you."

She took his pronoun for plural and started off on what must be a prepared lecture.

Antoran did indeed have planets which the Kraoka of Dzua had once colonized. Though the settlers perforce gave up star travel, they had maintained interplanetary commerce down the millennia, keeping more technology than Vanessa did.

Forty-odd years ago, Robert Horn of Nova Germania was being chased by a League cruiser. He laid a course to throw the pursuer off his trail—the old star-dodge maneuver—and thus passed so near Antoran that he detected radio emissions. Later he slipped back to investigate and discovered the planets.

"Yes, he was an outlaw," his daughter said defiantly. "He was a leader in the Landholders' Revolt . . . so good, so effective, that afterward they dared not give him amnesty."

Falkayn had heard vaguely about the matter. Something to do with a conspiracy among Nova Germania's first families, descendants of the original pioneers, to get back the power that a new constitution had taken away from them. And, yes, the League was involved; the republican government offered better trading concessions than the Landholders had granted in their day. No wonder that this girl was busily doing the League all the dirt she could.

He smiled and refilled her glass. "I can sympathize," he said. "Being from Hermes, you see. Aristocracy's far and away my favorite system."

Her eyes widened. "You are *adel*—nobly born?"

"Younger son," Falkayn said, modest again. He did not add that he'd been shipped to Earth for his education because he kept kicking over the traces which an aristocrat was expected to carry. "Do go on. You fascinate me."

"The Antoranite System includes one planet which the Kraoka had modified for habitability, but which was too far out, too cold and dark, to be really worth their while. For humans it is better. That is my world, Neuheim."

Hm, Falkayn thought. This implied at least one planet further inward which did provide a good Kraokan environment. Very possibly more than one; a war fleet as big as Beljagor claimed he had seen can't be built in a hurry without a lot of population and resources. But this in turn implied a large sun with a wide biothermal zone.

Which didn't make sense! Every F-type star in this region had been visited by League surveyors; likewise the G-types; and there definitely was no such system as—

"My father returned in secret to Nova Germania," Jutta Horn said. "He got recruits there and elsewhere. The whole world of Neuheim was given them in exchange for their help."

I feel pretty sure they planted the idea of conquest in the first place, Falkayn reflected. *Yeh, I can guess how Kraoka might fall for the concept of a reunified Vaterland. And given enough anti-League propaganda, they might well come to believe that the only way to get unification is to expel us first.*

"So Germanian engineers showed the Antoranites how to make hyperdrive ships," he said; "and Germanian officers trained the crews; and Germanian secret agents kept track of events outsystem—my, you've been busy."

She nodded. Two drinks blurred her tone a little. "That is true. Everything comes second to the crusade. Afterward we can relax. How I look forward!"

"Why not start right away?" Falkayn asked. "Why fight the League? We've no objection to the Kraoka building a star marine at their own expense, nor to any social arrangements you've made on Neuheim."

"After the way the League meddled in the past?" she challenged.

"Yes, granted, we do, now and then, when our interests are threatened. But still, Jutta"—there, he'd established a first-name relationship—"the Polesotechnic League is not a state, not even a government. It's nothing but a mutual-benefit association of interstellar merchants, who're probably more wolfish toward each other than toward anybody outside."

"Power is the one basis of negotiation," she said, turning Clausewitzian. "When we and our allies have secured this region, then perhaps we will allow you to operate here again . . . under our rules. Otherwise you could too easily impose your will on us, if we did not happen to desire the same things as you."

"The League isn't going to take this lying down," he warned.

"I think the League had better do so," she retorted. "We are here, in the region, with interior lines of communication. We can strike from space, anywhere. A League war fleet must come across many parsecs. It will find its bases demolished. And it will not know where our home planets are!"

Falkayn backed off in haste. He didn't want her in that mood. "You certainly have a tremendous advantage," he said. "The League can muster forces greater by orders of magnitude—surely you realize that—but the League may well decide that the cost of defeating you would be greater than any possible gain in doing so."

"Thus my father calculated before he died. Merchants, who lust for nothing but money, can be cowed. *Adelsvolk* are different. They live for an ideal, not for economics."

I wish to hell you'd had a chance to stick that pretty nose out of your smug, ingrown little kingdom and see what working aristocrats are like, Falkayn thought. Aloud: "Well, now, Jutta, I can't quite agree. Remember, I'm both a merchant and a nobleman's son. The psychologies aren't so unlike. A peer has to be a politician, with everything that that entails, or he's no good. And a merchant has to be an idealist."

"What?" She blinked in startlement. "How?"

"Why, you don't think we work for money alone, do you? If that were the object, we'd stay safe and snug at home. No, it's adventure, new horizons, life's conquest of inanimate nature—the universe itself, the grandest enemy of all."

She frowned, but she was softened. "I do not understand, quite."

"Suppose I give you a few examples—"

✸ IV ✸

Dinner was served in the roof turret, which had a view like being outdoors. By night Vanessa took on beauty. Both moons were aloft, small and swift, turning the land to a fantasy of dim silver and moving shadows. The lake gleamed, the native towers looked like giant blossoms. Overhead the sky was splendid with stars, Beta Centauri the king jewel, its blue radiance matching the moons'.

And glowpanels caressed Jutta's sun-browned cheeks with their own light; and Beethoven's Seventh lilted softly from a speaker; and bubbles danced in the champagne glasses. Dinner had made its stately progression from hors d'oeuvres and consommé through fish, roast, and salad, to petits fours and now cheeses. Falkayn had kept the magnum flash busy. Not that either party was drunk—Jutta, alas, had so far kept her wits patriotically about her—but they both felt more than cheerful.

"Tell me other things," she urged. "You have had such a wonderful existence, David. Like the hero of an ancient saga—but this is now, which makes it twice as good."

"Let me think," he said, giving her a refill. "Maybe the time I cracked up on a rogue planet?"

"A what?"

"Free planet, sunless. More of them floating around in space than there are stars. The smaller the body, you see, the likelier it was to form when the galaxy coalesced. Normally you find them in groups . . . to be honest, you don't normally find them, because space is big and they are little and dark. But by sheer chance, on the way from Tau Ceti to 70 Ophiuchi, I—"

The adventure had, in fact, happened to somebody else. So had most of the stories Falkayn had been relating. But he saw no reason to spoil a good yarn with pedantry.

Besides, she continued to sip, in an absentminded and unsuspecting way, while he talked.

"—and finally I replenished my air by boiling and processing frozen gases. And was I glad to leave!"

"I should think so." She shivered. "Space is bleak. Lovely but bleak. I like planets better." She gazed outward. "The night here is different from home. I don't know which I like best, Neuheim or Vanessa. After dark, I mean," she added, with a slightly wobbling laugh. "None of the Kraokan worlds are pleasant by day."

"None whatsoever? You must have seen quite a variety, with three of them for neighbors."

"Five," she corrected. Her hand went to her mouth. "*Lieber Gott!* I didn't mean to tell."

He chuckled, though inwardly he thrummed with a new excitement. Judas! Five planets—six, counting Neuheim —in the thermal zone where water was liquid . . . around one star! "It doesn't make any practical difference," he said, "when you've evidently found some way to make your whole system invisible. I'd like to know more about you, that's all, and I can't unless you tell me something about your home." He reached across the table and patted her hand. "That's what gave you your dreams, your hopes—your charm, if I may say so. Neuheim must be a paradise."

"No, it is a hard world for humans," she answered earnestly. "In my own lifetime, we have had to move entire villages toward the poles as the planet swung closer to the sun. Even the Kraoka have their troubles for similar reasons." She pulled free of his touch. "But I am talking of what I shouldn't."

"Very well, let's keep to harmless things," he said. "You mentioned that the nights were different at home. In what way?"

"Oh . . . different constellations, of course. Not greatly, but enough to notice. And then, because of the auroras, we never see the stars so clearly as here, from any location. I *must* not say more. You are far too observing, Davy. Tell me, instead, about your Hermes." She smiled irresistibly. "I would like to know where your own dreams come from."

Nothing loath, Falkayn spoke of mountains, virgin wilderness, plains darkened by horned herds, surf-bathing at Thunderstrands—"What does that mean, Davy?"

"Why, bathing in the surf. You know, the waves caused by tidal action." He decided to disarm her suspicions with a joke. "Now, my poor innocent, you've given yourself away again. You imply Neuheim doesn't have tides."

"No harm in that," she said. "True, we have not any moon. The oceans are like huge, still lakes."

"Doesn't the sun—" He checked himself.

"Not so far away as it is, a tiny point of fire, I can't get used to the disc here." Abruptly Jutta set down her glass. "Listen," she said, "you are either very young and sweet or you are clever as Satan."

"Why not both?"

"I cannot take the chance." She rose. "Best I leave now. I made a mistake to come."

"What?" He scrambled to his own feet. "But the evening's hardly begun. I thought we'd go back to the living room and relax with some more music." The *Liebestod*, for instance.

"No." Distress and determination chased each other across her face. "I enjoy myself too much. I forget to guard my tongue. Take to the League this word from us. Before they can marshal against us, we will have the Kraokan stars, and more. But if the League will be reasonable, *ja*, perhaps we can discuss trade treaties." Her eyes dropped. She flushed. "I would like if you could return."

God damn all politics! Falkayn groaned. He got nowhere trying to change her mind, and finally had to see her to the door. There he kissed her hand . . . and before he could build on that beginning, she had whispered good night, and was outside.

He poured himself a stiff whisky, lit his pipe, and flung himself into a lounger. None were an adequate substitute.

Rats! he brooded. *Giant mutant rats! She'll have me hustled off the planet right away, tomorrow dawn, before I can use any information I might have gathered.*

Well, at least there'll be girls at Sector HQ. And maybe, eventually, I'll find myself back here.

As a journeyman assistant, and Jutta will be at the social apex of an interstellar empire. She wouldn't snub me on that account, but what chance would we ever have to get together?

He puffed hard and scowled at a repro of a Hokusai portrait, an old man, which hung opposite him. The old man smiled back till Falkayn wanted to punch him in the nose.

The long-range significance of the Neuheimer scheme was far nastier than several gigacredits' loss to the merchant princes, Falkayn saw. Suppose it did succeed. Suppose the mighty Polesotechnic League was defied and defeated, and the Kraokan Empire was established. Well, the Kraoka by themselves might or might not be content to stop at that point and settle down to peaceful relationships with everybody else. In any event, they were no direct threat to the human race; they didn't want the same kind of real estate.

But the Neuheimer humans—Already they spoke of themselves as crusaders. Consider the past history of Homo self-styled Sapiens and imagine what so spectacular a success would do to a bunch of ideologically motivated militarists! Oh, the process would be slow; they'd have to increase their numbers, and enlarge their industrial base, and get control of every man-useful planet in this neighborhood. But eventually, for power, and glory, and upset of the hated merchants, and advancement of a Way of Life—war.

The time to squelch them was now. A good healthy licking would discredit the Landholders; peace, mercantilism, and cooperation with others (or, at least, simple cutthroat economic competition) would become fashionable on Neuheim; and, incidentally, a journeyman who played a significant part in that outcome would expect early certification as a Master Merchant.

Whereas a mere bearer of bad tidings—

"All right," Falkayn muttered. "Step One in the squelching process: Find their damned planetary system!"

They couldn't hope to keep its location secret forever. Just long enough to secure a grip on this region; and given the destructive power of a space fleet, that needn't be very long. While it remained hidden, though, the source of their strength was quite efficiently protected. Hence their entire effort could go into purely offensive operations, which gave them a military capability far out of proportion to their actual force.

Nonetheless, if the League should decide to fight, the League would win. No question about that. In the course of the war, the secret was bound to be discovered, one way or another. And then—nuclear bombardment from space—*No!*

The Landholders were gambling that the League, rather than start an expensive battle for a prize that would certainly be ruined in the course of the fighting, would vote to cut its losses and come to terms. Antoran being hidden, the bet looked fairly good. But no matter how favorable the odds, only fanatics played with entire living worlds for stakes. Poor Jutta! What foul company she was mixed up in. How he'd like to introduce her to some decent people.

Okay, then, where was the silly star?

Someplace not far off. Jutta had betrayed nothing by admitting that the constellations at home were almost like the constellations here. The ancient Kraoka could not have traveled any enormous ways, as interstellar distances go. Also, the home base must be in this territory so that its fleet could exploit the advantage of interior communications.

And Antoran must be large and bright, no later in the main sequence than, say, G_0. Yet . . . every possible sun was already eliminated by information the League had long possessed.

Unless—wait a minute—could it be hidden by a thick nebulosity?

No. There'd still be radio indications. And Jutta had spoken of seeing stars from her home.

Aurora. Hm. She'd mentioned the necessity for certain villagers to migrate toward the poles, as her planet got too near its primary. Which meant their original settlements were a good bit further toward the equator. Even so, auroras had been conspicuous: everywhere you went, she'd said. This, again, suggested a highly energetic sun.

Funny, about the eccentric orbit. More than one planet in the system, too, with the same problem. Unheard of. You'd almost think that—

Falkayn sat bolt upright. His pipe dropped from his jaws to his lap. "Holy . . . hyper . . . Judas," he gasped.

Thereafter he thought most furiously. He did not come back to himself until the coals from his pipe set fire to his trousers.

❁ ❁ ❁

❁ V ❁

The door to Beljagor's place, offices-cum-residence, barely had time to get out of Falkayn's way. But as he entered the lobby, he skidded to a stop. In a small room opening on this, two Kraoka were talking. One was armed and brassarded, an invader. The other was Quillipup. They froze.

"Greetings," said the liaison agent after a pause. "What brings you here?"

"I want to see your boss," Falkayn answered.

"I believe he is asleep," Quillipup said.

"Too bad." Falkayn started down the hall.

"Stop!" Quillipup bounded after him. "I told you he is asleep."

"And I told you it's a pity he has to be wakened," Falkayn rapped.

Quillipup regarded him. Her dorsal fin rose. The Antoranite glided close behind, hand not far from blaster.

"What have you to say which is so urgent?" Quillipup asked slowly.

Falkayn gave her eyeball for eyeball and responded, "What's so urgent for you, that it can't wait till Beljagor has risen?"

Silence, under the icy white light. Falkayn grew aware of blood pounding in his ears. His skin prickled. That energy gun looked too businesslike for his taste. But Quillipup turned on her heel, without a word, and led her companion back to the office. Falkayn let out a hard-held breath and continued on his way.

He hadn't been told where in the building the factor lived, but the layout of places like this was pretty standardized. The suite door was locked. He buzzed. Nothing happened. He buzzed again.

The scanner must have a screen in the bedroom, because the voice from the annunciator rasped, "You! Do you suppose I'd get up for a pestilential human?"

"Yes," Falkayn said. "Urgent."

"Urgent that you jump off the nearest cliff, right. And a bad night to you." The speaker clicked off.

That adjective "urgent" was being overworked, Falkayn decided. He leaned on the buzzer.

"Stop your infernal racket!" howled Beljagor.

"Sure, when you let me in," Falkayn said. *Click.*

Falkayn whistled "The Blue Danube" to pass the time while he leaned on the buzzer.

The door flew open. Beljagor bounced forth. Falkayn was interested to note that the Jaleelan slept in pajamas, bright purple ones. "You insolent whelp!" the factor bawled. "Get out of here!"

"Yes, sir," Falkayn said. "You come, too."

"What?"

"I have to show you something in my space boat."

Beljagor's eyes turned red. His tendrils stood erect. He drank air until his small round form seemed ready to explode.

"Please, sir," Falkayn begged. "You've got to. It's terribly important."

Beljagor cursed and swung a fist.

Falkayn sidestepped the blow, picked up the Master Merchant by collar and trousers, and bore him kicking and yelling down the hall. "I told you you had to come," the journeyman said patiently.

The two Kraoka in the lobby had left, and those on sentry-go at the warship made no move to interfere. Maybe, behind furry poker faces, they enjoyed the sight. Falkayn had left the gangway ramp extruded from his speedster but had put a recognition lock on the entrance. It opened for him. He carried Beljagor inside, set him down, and waited for the storm to break.

The Jaleelan spoke no word, only looked at him. His snout quivered a little.

"Okay," Falkayn sighed. "You don't accept my apologies. You'll have my certificate revoked. You'll strangle me with my own guts. Anything else?"

"I suppose you have an explanation," Beljagor said like fingernails going quite slowly over a blackboard.

"Yes, sir. The business won't wait. And I didn't dare speak anyplace but here. Your Quillipup is acting far too friendly with the self-appointed liberators. Be no trick for her to bug your quarters."

What ozone had come in with them—less than by day—must have been processed into oxygen by now. Falkayn slipped off his filter mask. Beljagor mumbled something about Earth-type atmosphere being good for naught except breaking wind. Otherwise, though, the factor had cooled off astonishingly fast. "Talk, cub," he ordered.

"You see," Falkayn said, "I know where Antoran is."

"Heh?" Beljagor jumped several centimeters in the pilot chair he occupied.

"They'd never let me go if they found out I know," Falkayn continued. He leaned back against a bulkhead. His gaze drifted beyond the viewpoints. Both moons had set, and Beta Centauri ruled heaven. "As is, you'll have to come, too."

"What? Impossible! If you think I'll abandon the property of General Motors to a gang of pirates—"

"They'll doubtless send you packing before long in any event," Falkayn said. "Admit that. You just hate to surrender. But we've got to take the bull by the tail and look the situation squarely in the face."

"What do you mean, you know where Antoran is?" Beljagor spluttered. "Did you swallow something the Horn creature told you for a joke?"

"No, sir, she didn't intend to give me any information. Only, well, she was raised in an isolated, dedicated, Spartan society. She wasn't equipped to handle me." Falkayn grinned. "Figuratively, I mean, not literally. Her fellows didn't allow for the effects of alcohol and smooth talk. Not used to such things themselves, I imagine. Could be they also counted on my being so overbowled by her looks that I'd merely gawk and listen to her. They seem to be a very romantic bunch. Dangerous as hell, but romantic."

"Well? Well? What did Horn say?"

"Little items. They gave the show away, though. Like, Antoran isn't a planet but a star. And just one star hereabouts can possibly fit the data." Falkayn let Beljagor rumble for a moment before he pointed skyward and said, "Beta Centauri."

The factor did explode. He hopped around the cabin, flapping his arms and raving. Falkayn filed the choicer epithets in his memory for later use.

At last Beljagor was sufficiently calm to stand in one spot, raise a finger, and say, "You unutterable imbecile, for your information, Beta is a type B blue giant. People knew before space flight began, giant suns don't have planets. Angular momentum per unit mass proved as much. After the hyperdrive came along, direct expeditions to any number of them clinched the matter. Even supposing, somehow, one did acquire satellites, those satellites never would get habitable. Giant stars burn hydrogen so fast their existence is measured in millions of years. Millions, you hear, not billions. Beta Centauri can hardly be ten million years old. More than half its stable lifetime is past. It'll go supernova and become a white dwarf. Life'd have no chance to evolve before the planets were destroyed. Not that there are any, I repeat. The reason for only the smaller suns having planets is understood. A big protostar, condensing from the interstellar medium, develops too intense a gravitational field for the secondary condensation process to take place outside it.

"I thought even humans learned so much elementary astrophysics in the first grade of school. I was wrong. Now you know."

His voice rose to a scream. *"And for this you got me out of bed!"*

Falkayn moved to block the cabin exit. "But I do know," he said. "Everybody does. The Antoranites have based their whole strategy on our preconception. They figure by the time we discover Beta Centauri is a freak case, they'll control the whole region."

Beljagor hurled himself back into the pilot chair, folded his arms, and grated, "Well, get the farce over with, since you must."

"Here are the facts," Falkayn said. He ticked them off. "One, the Antoranite System was colonized by Kraoka, who couldn't and didn't settle on planets with suns as cool as Sol. Two, Antoran has six planets in the liquid-water zone. No matter how you arrange their orbits, that zone has to be mighty broad—which indicates a correspondingly luminous star. Three, the outermost of those six planets is too cold and weakly irradiated for Kraokan comfort, but suits humans fairly well. Yet it has brilliant auroras even in the temperate zones. For that, you need a sun which shoots out some terrifically energetic particles: again, a giant.

"Four, this human planet, Neuheim, is far out. The proof lies in three separate facts, (a) From Neuheim, the sun doesn't have a naked-eye disc, (b) There are no solar tides worth mentioning, (c) The year is long, I figure something like two Earth centuries. I know the year is long, because Jutta let slip that her people had to shift some towns poleward a while back. Orbital eccentricity was making the lower latitudes too hot, maybe also too much UV was penetrating the ozone layer in those parts and making poisonous concentrations of ozone at the surface, like here. Nevertheless, the original human settlement was forty years ago. In other words, Neuheim's radius vector changes at so leisurely a rate that it was worth sitting down in areas which the colonists knew would have to be abandoned later. I suppose they wanted to exploit local minerals.

"Okay. In spite of its enormous distance from the primary, Neuheim *is* habitable, if you don't mind getting a deep suntan. What kind of star can buck the inverse-square law on so grand a scale? What but a blue giant! And Beta Centauri is the only blue giant close by."

He stopped, hoarse and in need of beer. Beljagor sat like a graven image, assuming that anybody would want to grave such an image, while the minutes stretched. A space boat whined overhead, an enemy craft on an unknown errand.

Finally, tonelessly, Beljagor asked, "How could there be planets?"

"I've worked that out," Falkayn replied. "A freak, as I remarked before, perhaps the only case in the universe, but still possible. The star captured a mess of rogue planets."

"Nonsense. Single bodies can't make captures." But Beljagor didn't yell his objection.

"Granted. Here's what must have happened. Beta was condensing, with a massive nucleus already but maybe half its mass still spread over God knows how many astronomical units, as a nebular cloud. A cluster of rogue planets passed through. Beta's gravity field swung them around. But because of friction with the nebula, they didn't recede into space again. Energy loss, you see, converting hyperbolic orbits into elliptical ones. Could be that there was also a secondary center of stellar condensation, which later spiraled into the main mass. Two bodies can certainly make captures. But I think friction alone would serve.

"The elliptical orbits were almighty eccentric, of course. Friction smoothed them out some. But Jutta admitted that to this day the planets have paths eccentric enough to cause weather trouble. Which is not the normal case either, you recall. Makes another clue for us."

"Hm-m-m." Beljagor tugged his nose and pondered.

"The planets would've exuded gases and water vapor in the early stages of their existence, through vulcanism, like any other substellar globes," Falkayn plowed on. "The stuff froze in space. But Beta unfroze it.

"I don't know how the Kraoka of Dzua learned what the situation was. Maybe they simply didn't know that blue giants don't have planets. Or maybe they sent a telemetric probe for astrophysical research, and it informed them. Anyhow, they discovered Beta had five potentially good worlds plus one that was marginal for them. So they colonized. Sure, the planets were sterile, with poisonous atmospheres. But the ancient Kraoka were whizzes at environmental engineering. You can sketch for yourself what they did: seeded the air with photosynthetic spores to convert it, released other forms of life to consume the primeval organic matter and form the basis of an ecology, etcetera. Under those conditions, microbes would multiply exponentially, and it'd take no more than a few centuries for a world to become habitable."

Falkayn shrugged. "Beta will blow up and destroy their work in five or ten million years," he finished. "But that's ample time for anyone, hey?"

"Yes," Beljagor said low.

He raised his head, looked directly at the man, and said, "If this be true, we've got to tell the League. A war fleet that went straight to Beta should catch the enemy by complete surprise. Once the home planets were hostage to us, obviously there'd be no fighting."

"Uh-huh." Falkayn suppressed a yawn. Weariness was beginning to overtake him.

"But this is only a hypothesis," Beljagor said. "Your evidence is all hearsay. Horn could've been putting you on. The League can't base a whole operation on an idea which may turn out wrong. That'd be ruinous. We need positive proof."

"Right," Falkayn nodded. "So we'll both go, in our separate boats. You can easily make some excuse for having changed your mind about staying here. They won't suspect a thing if you throw a temper tantrum and storm off into space."

Beljagor grew rigid. "What are you saying? I'm the most patient, long-suffering entity in this cosmos."

"Huh?"

"When I think of what I have to put up with, impertinence like yours, stupidity, greed, thievishness, lack of appreciation—" Beljagor's tone mounted to a dull roar. Falkayn smothered a second yawn.

"Well, such is my life," said the factor as a coda. "I'll think of something. What do you propose after we take off?"

"We'll start ostensibly for HQ," Falkayn said. "Once we're out of detector range, we'll head toward Beta. We'll stop at a safe distance. You wait. I'll run in close to the star and make observations. Then I'll come back to you and we really will skite for friendlier country."

"Why the separate excursion?"

"I might get caught. In that case—if I haven't rejoined you by the agreed time—you can tell the League what we do know and suggest they investigate Beta themselves."

"Hm. Ha. Correct. But why do you volunteer for the dangerous part? I doubt that you're competent."

"Sir," Falkayn said tiredly, "I may be young, but I can handle instruments. This speedster is built for humans—you couldn't operate her efficiently—and she's better adapted to a quick job of spying than your craft. So I'm elected. Besides," he added, "if I get clobbered, I'm a mere journeyman, a human at that. You're a Master Merchant from Jaleel."

His sarcasm went to waste. Beljagor sprang erect with tears starting from his porcine eyes. "Right!" he cried, choked by emotion. "How noble of you to admit it!" He wrung Falkayn's hand. "Please don't think badly of me. I may be loud now and then—I may talk rough when my patience wears thin—but believe me, I've got no prejudice against your race. Humans have fine qualities. Why, some of my best friends are human!"

⊛ VI ⊛

Danger began about one light-year from goal: the distance within which the instantaneous space-time pulses emitted by a vessel in hyperdrive are detectable. Beljagor's boat lay outside that radius, her own detectors wide open. Not that there was any measurable chance of a speck like her being found by accident. Falkayn would have trouble enough making rendezvous, knowing her location. But if Beljagor observed the "wake" of another ship, he would be careful not to start his own secondary engines until the stranger was safely remote again.

Falkayn had no like choice. At full quasi-speed, he drove straight for Beta Centauri.

The sun grew and grew before him. Under magnification, he could see the disc, seething with nuclear storms, raging with billion-kilometer prominences, hell-blue and terrible. Eleven times the mass of Sol; fourteen hundred times the luminosity; across a full hundred and ninety light-years, one of the brightest stars in Earth's sky. He tried to whistle a tune, but the sound was too small and scared.

Inward. Inward. Now he could start the cameras. Photographing the viewscreens, which compensated for aberration and Doppler effect, they pictured a stable background of constellations. Planets, though, registered as meteorite streaks—yes, here! Falkayn changed course and repeated his observations. Before long he had the triangulation data to feed his computer.

He'd only spotted a few of the captured worlds, not all of them possible habitations. What he had was sufficient, however, especially when one turned out to be approximately thirty-seven astronomical unit: from the sun, the right distance and the right diameter for Neuheim. And, uh-huh, his detectors showed hypervibrations crisscrossing local space, comings and goings among the stars.

One indication was too damn near for his liking, and getting nearer. A patrol craft must have sniffed his trail and be on her way to investigate. Well, she'd have to be fiendish fast to catch this little beauty of his!

She was.

As he fled spaceward, Falkayn watched the intensity readings creep higher. He scowled, puffed his pipe, and figured. He could rendezvous with Beljagor before he was overhauled, but then the Antoranite would be within a light-year of them, and get a fix on both.

Well, they could separate. . . .

A second needle flickered on the detector panel. Falkayn said bad words. Another ship was closing in. Extrapolating directions and rates of amplitude increase, he found that Number Two couldn't run him down—but could snag Beljagor's ambling Holbert.

So. The thing to do was switch off the secondaries and lie doggo, hidden by the sheer vastness of space. . . . Uh-uh. If those fellows knew their business, they'd identify the point where he stopped—at this range—within several million kilometers. They'd also go sublight, and home on the neutrino emission of his power plant. Or simply finger him with a radar sweep.

"Brother," Falkayn told himself, "you've had it, with pineapples."

He looked into the glory which was space, sun after sun until suns grew so thick that they melted into the great argent flood of the Milky Way. He remembered how light is trapped in the leaves of a wind-tossed tree; and how good the beer had tasted in a funny little Swiss tavern; and how often he had laughed among friends; and how a woman felt; and he sensed an utter lack of ambition to be a hero.

Don't irritate them. Surrender. Otherwise they'll phase in to your hyperjump frequency and put a warhead between your ears.

Beljagor could still report to the League, after the enemy had returned home. Of course, then he'd have no confirmation of Beta Centauri's nature. Falkayn's not showing up was inadequate proof, when he could have come to grief in any number of ways. So the League must send spies of its own, who would also be detected. Using ultrafast ships, they'd get away, but the enemy would be alerted and would mount strong guard on his home country. If war then came, it would be more savage than one dared think about, whole planets might be incinerated, Jutta be blown to incandescent gas, Falkayn himself—Judas!

Why wasn't there faster-than-light radio, so he could beam a message to the factor before he must stop? Damn the laws of physics!

The boat hummed and quivered with driving energies. Falkayn was maddeningly aware of thirst, an itch between his shoulder blades, a need for a haircut. This was no time to be human. *Think, blast you.*

He couldn't. He prowled the cabin, smoked his tongue leathery, forced down a plateful of rations, and came back to gloom at the detectors. Until finally he said, "To hell with this," killed his last bottle of Scotch and went to sleep.

He awoke some hours later, and there was his solution. For a while he lay staring at the overhead, awed by his genius. But according to computation, he'd soon reach Beljagor. Which meant he was in detection range right now, and the Jaleelan was certainly cursing a Beta-colored streak as he watched his own instruments. He'd not be asleep under these circumstances—not him.

"No time like the present," Falkayn said, thus proving his originality had limits. He sprang from his bunk and started scribbling notes.

"Okay, chum." He settled into the pilot chair. Switch off the secondaries and go sublight. One minute later, switch them back on. Thirty seconds later, off again. One minute later, on again.

Polesotechnic pulse code. The needles of whichever detectors were tuned on him must be jumping back and forth, dash-dot-dash-dash-dot. HYPOTHESIS CONFIRMED. F. Repeat the cycle, to be sure Beljagor noticed. And again. Let him wonder if the F was anything but an initial. He'd get the rest of the idea, which was all that mattered. God willing, the Antoranites would not; this particular code was kept secret.

The engines began objecting to abuse. Falkayn whiffed scorched insulation and heard an ominous whine in the power hum. He switched vectors, taking off at a sharp angle to his former path, and drove steadily.

Arithmetic showed that when Enemy Number One pulled alongside him, they'd be well over a light-year from Beljagor. So would Enemy Number Two, who was obligingly coming about also. Falkayn left the board on automatic, showered, dressed in his fanciest clothes, and fixed a leisurely breakfast.

Next he destroyed his photographs, registry, route papers, and certain parts of his log, and did an artistic job of forging substitutes. League vessels are equipped for a variety of emergencies.

The Antoranite hove close, a Comet class with wicked-looking guns. Her probelight flashed the command to halt. Falkayn obeyed. The other went sublight likewise, matched kinetic velocities, and lay at a cautious distance. The radio buzzed. Falkayn accepted.

A long-jawed human officer type with a chestful of ribbons glared from the screen. "Hello," Falkayn said. "Do you speak Anglic or Latin?"

"*Ja,*" said the man. He picked the former. "Yourself identify."

"PL speedster *Greased Lightning* out of Tricorn for Hopewell, journeyman Sebastian Tombs aboard solo. And who might you be?"

"Neuheim warship *Graf Helmuth Karl Bernhard von Moltke*, Landholder Otto von Lichtenberg commanding, *Oberleutnant* Walter Schmitt speaking."

"Neuheim? Where the devil is Neuheim? Never heard of it."

"Vot iss your purpose? Vy haff you tried to escape?"

"My purpose," Falkayn said, "is a trip from my post on Tricorn to ask for some emergency supplies from the Polesotechnic station on Hopewell. We had a flood and it rather messed us up. As for why I ran from you, good Lord, when strangers start chasing a fellow, what do you expect him to do?"

"You assumed ve vas unfriendly," Schmitt said, more in anger than in sorrow. "Maybe you iss unfriendly to us, ha?"

"No, ha. If you consult your navigation tables, you'll find Beta Centauri is almost directly between Tricorn and Hopewell. And I was bound for Hopewell, instead of some closer post, because Hopewell is the nearest planet where I can be sure of getting the stuff we need. Zipping past Beta, I noticed a roughness in the engines." It was there yet, thanks to his using them for a radio. "To check the vector control, I changed course a few times, as you probably noticed. Then all at once, whoosh, here I detected a ship headed for me where no ship ought to be. Perhaps you were a harmless scientific expedition, anxious for a gabfest. But I wasn't about to chance it. Pirates exist, you know. I skedaddled. My engines began spontaneously popping in and out of secondary. I got the Lauritzens fixed and tried a change of course, hoping you'd understand I didn't want company and leave me alone. No luck. So here we are."

Falkayn donned an indignant look and pounded the pilot board. "Seems like you're the one who has explaining to do," he barked. "What is this Neuheim comedy? Why are warships hanging around a blue giant? What's the idea, taking off after a harmless passerby? The Polesotechnic League is going to hear about this!"

"Perhaps," said Schmitt. "Shtand by to be boarded."

"Damnation, you have no right—"

"Ve haff several nuclear cannon zeroed on you. Gifs t'at a right?"

"It does," Falkayn sighed.

He cooperated in linking air locks by a gangtube. Schmitt entered with a squad, who pointed their rifles at him, and demanded to see his papers.

Presently: "Fery vell, Herr Tombs. Might be you are honest. I do not know. Ve haff our orders. It vill be necessary to intern you on Neuheim."

"What?" Falkayn bellowed. He held his breath till he turned scarlet and his eyes popped. "Do you realize who I am? I'm a certified member of the Polesotechnic League!"

"Too bad for you," Schmitt said. "Come along." He grabbed Falkayn's wrist.

Falkayn yanked it back, drew himself straight, and blessed his father for teaching him the proper mannerisms. "Sir," he said, and liquid helium dripped from every word, "if I am to be a prisoner, I protest the illegality but I must yield. Nevertheless, there is such a thing as the laws of war. Furthermore, I am heir apparent to the Barony of Dragonshaw, United Kingdom of New Asia and Radagach. You will treat me with the respect according to my station!"

Schmitt paled. He clicked his heels, bowed, and followed with a salute. *"Jawohl, mein Herr,"* he gasped. "I
beg for your most gracious pardon. If you had seen fit
to tell me more earlier—Landholder von Lichtenberg
vill be reqvesting t'e honor uff your pressence at tea."

❈ VII ❈

Schloss Graustein was not the worst place in the cosmos
to be a prisoner. Though gaunt and drafty on its high
ridge, it was surrounded by forests where the hunting
was excellent. The food was heavy but edible, and the
local beer superb. Landholder Graustein did his best to
make the distinguished, if compulsory, guest feel at
home. During long conversations and occasional guided
tours of the planet, Falkayn spotted interesting commercial opportunities, once the region had been pacified.

Unless—He didn't want to contemplate the alterna-
tive. And after some weeks, time began to hang as leaden
as the knackwurst.

Thus Falkayn was quite happy when a servant knocked
at the door of his suite and announced a visitor. But then
she stepped through. He had never thought she would
be an unwelcome sight.

"Jutta," he whispered.

She closed the door behind her and regarded him for
a still moment. Dark wood and granite panels framed
her where she stood vivid under the fluorolight. She was
in mufti, and if he had thought her beautiful when uni-
formed, he must now multiply by an astronomical factor.
"So it is indeed you," she said.

"P-p-please sit down," he managed. She remained
standing. Her features were stony, her voice flat.

"Those idiots took for granted you were what you claimed, a merchant who simply chanced to pass by and saw too much. They never interrogated you in depth, never notified the fleet command. I only heard of you yesterday, in conversation with Landholder von Lichtenberg, after I came home on leave. The description—" Words trailed off.

Falkayn rallied his courage. "A stratagem of war, my dear," he said gently. "Not a war that my side began, either."

"What have you done?"

He told his pulse to decelerate, took out his pipe, and made a production of loading and kindling it. "You can squirt me full of babble juice, so I might as well Tell All," he smiled. "I guessed the truth and went for a look to make certain."

"That funny little being who left about the same time as you did . . . he knew?"

Falkayn nodded. "He's reported to HQ long ago. If the League is half as realistic as I think, a battle fleet you can't hope to resist is on its way right now."

She clenched one hand over another. Tears stood in her eyes. "What follows?"

"They should head straight here. I expect them any day. You've nothing in the Beta System except a few patrollers; the rest of your navy is spread over a dozen stars, right? The League doesn't want to bombard planets, but in this case—" She uttered anguish. He went quickly to her, took both those hands, and said, "No, no. *Realpolitik,* Remember? The object of war is not to destroy the enemy but to impose your will on him. Why should we kill people that we might sell things to? We'll simply take the Beta System prisoner and then bargain about its release.

"I don't make policy, but I can predict what'll happen. The League will demand you disband your armed forces, down to a normal defense level. And, naturally, we'll want to keep our trade concessions. But that's all. Now that some Kraoka have starships, they can go ahead and unify, as long as they do it peacefully. We'd hoped to sell them a cargo and passenger fleet, at a huge markup, but that hope isn't worth fighting for—you do have bargaining power yourselves, in your own capabilities for making trouble, you know. Neuheim can keep any social order it wants. Why not? If you try to maintain this wretched autarchy, you'll be depriving yourselves of so much that inside of ten years your people will throw out the Landholders and yell for us."

He chucked her under the chin. "I understand," he said. "It's tough when a dream dies. But why should you, your whole life, carry your father's grudges?"

She surrendered to tears. He consoled her, and a private hope began to grow in him.

Not that he was in the market for a wife. Judas! At his age? However—

Afterward they found themselves on the balcony. Night had fallen, the auroral night where vast banners shook red and green across the sky, dimming the stars, and the mountain swooped down to a forest which breathed strange sweet odors back upward. Wineglasses were in their hands, and she stood close to him.

"You can report who I am," he said, "and cause me to have an unpleasant time, maybe even be shot." Pale in the shuddering light, her face lost its look of happiness and he heard the breath suck between her teeth. "Your duty, according to the articles of war," he continued. "And it won't make one bit of difference, it'll be too late—except that the League protects its own and will take a stiff price for me."

"What choice have I?" she pleaded.

He flashed a well-rehearsed grin. "Why, to keep your lovely mouth shut, tell everybody you were mistaken and Sebastian Tombs has nothing to do with that Falkayn character. When peace comes—well, you're quite influential on this planet. You could do a lot to help your people adjust."

"And become merchants?" she said, in a dying flare of scorn.

"I remarked once," he said, "that we aren't really so ignoble. We're after a profit, yes. But even a knight must eat, and *our* bread doesn't come from slaves or serfs or anyone who had to be killed. Look beyond those lights. They're fine, sure, but how about the stars on the other side?"

She caught his arm. He murmured, as best he could in Latin, *"Thy merchants chase the morning down the sea . . ."* and when she turned questioning to him he added, low in the dusk,

> *"Their topmasts gilt by sunset, though their sails*
> *   be whipped to rags,*
> *Who raced the wind around the world go reeling*
> *   home again,*
> *With ivory, apes, and peacocks loaded, memories*
> *   and brags,*
> *To sell for this high profit: knowing fully they are*
> *   Men!"*

"Oh-h-h," he heard.

And to think he'd resented his schoolmasters, when he was a kid on Hermes, making him read Flecker and Sanders in the original.

"I will not tell anyone," she said.

And: "May I stay here for a while?"

Falkayn was downright regretful a week later, when the League fleet arrived to rescue him.

INTRODUCTION

❖ THE SEASON OF FORGIVENESS ❖

The following story was also written by Judith Dalmady/
Lundgren for the periodical *Morgana*. She based it upon
an incident whereof her father had told her, he having
gotten the tale from one of the persons directly concerned when he was an entrepreneur in those parts.
Hloch includes it, first, because it shows more than the
usual biographies do of a planet on which Falkayn had,
earlier, had a significant adventure. Second, it gives yet
another glimpse into a major human faith, alive unto this
year and surely of influence upon him and his contemporaries.

—Hloch of the Stormgate Choth
The Earth Book of Stormgate

THE SEASON OF FORGIVENESS

It was a strange and lonely place for a Christmas celebration —the chill planet of a red dwarf star, away off in the Pleiades region, where half a dozen humans laired in the ruins of a city which had been great five thousand years ago, and everywhere else reached wilderness.

"No!" said Master Trader Thomas Overbeck. "We've got too much work on our hands to go wasting man-hours on a piece of frivolity."

"It isn't, sir," answered his apprentice, Juan Hernandez. "On Earth it's important. You have spent your life on the frontier, so perhaps you don't realize this."

Overbeck, a large blond man, reddened. "Seven months here, straight out of school, and you're telling me how to run my shop? If you've learned all the practical technique I have to teach you, why, you may as well go back on the next ship."

Juan hung his head. "I'm sorry, sir. I meant no disrespect."

Standing there, in front of the battered desk, against a window which framed the stark, sullenly lit landscape and a snag of ancient wall, he seemed younger than his sixteen Terrestrial years, slight, dark-haired, big-eyed. The company-issue coverall didn't fit him especially well. But he was quick-witted, Overbeck realized; he had to be, to graduate from the Academy that soon. And he was hardworking, afire with eagerness. The merchants of the League operated over so vast and diverse a territory that promising recruits were always in short supply.

That practical consideration, as well as a touch of sympathy, made the chief growl in a milder tone: "Oh, of course I've no objection to any small religious observance you or the others may want to hold. But as for doing more—" He waved his cigar at the scene outside. "What does it mean, anyway? A date on a chronopiece. A chronopiece adjusted for Earth! Ivanhoe's year is only two-thirds as long; but the globe takes sixty hours to spin around once; and to top it off, this is local summer, even if you don't dare leave the dome unless you're bundled to the ears. You see, Juan, I've got the same right as you to repeat the obvious."

His laughter boomed loud. While the team kept their living quarters heated, they found it easiest to maintain ambient air pressure, a fourth again as high as Terrestrial standard. Sound carried strongly. "Believe it or not," he finished, "I do know something about Christmas traditions, including the very old ones. You want to decorate the place and sing 'Jingle Bells'? That's how to make 'em ridiculous!"

"Please, no, sir," Juan said. "Also on Earth, in the southern hemisphere the feast comes at summer. And nobody is sure what time of year the Nativity really happened." He knotted his fists before he plunged on. "I thought not of myself so much, though I do remember how it is in my home. But that ship will come soon. I'm told small children are aboard. Here will be a new environment for them, perhaps frightening at first. Would we not help them feel easy if we welcomed them with a party like this?"

"Hm." Overbeck sat still a minute, puffing smoke and tugging his chin. His apprentice had a point, he admitted.

Not that he expected the little ones to be anything but a nuisance as far as he himself was concerned. He'd be delighted to leave them behind in a few more months, when his group had ended its task. But part of that task was to set up conditions which would fit the needs of their successors. The sooner those kids adjusted to life here, the sooner the parents could concentrate on their proper business.

And that was vital. Until lately, Ivanhoe had had no more than a supply depot for possible distressed spacecraft. Then a scientific investigator found the *adir* herb in the deserts of another continent. It wouldn't grow outside its own ecology; and it secreted materials which would be valuable starting points for several new organic syntheses. In short, there was money to be gotten. Overbeck's team was assigned to establish a base, make friends with the natives, learn their ways and the ways of their country, and persuade them to harvest the plant in exchange for trade goods.

That seemed fairly well in order now, as nearly as a man could judge amidst foreignness and mystery. The time looked ripe for putting the trade on a regular basis. Humans would not sign a contract to remain for a long stretch unless they could bring their families. Nor would they stay if the families grew unhappy.

And Tom Overbeck wouldn't collect his big, fat bonus until the post had operated successfully for five standard years.

Wherefore the Master Trader shrugged and said, "Well, okay. If it doesn't interfere too much with work, go ahead."

He was surprised at how enthusiastically Ram Gupta, Nikolai Sarychev, Mamoru Noguchi, and Philip Feinberg joined Juan's project. They were likewise young, but not boys; and they had no common faith. Yet together they laughed a lot as they made ready. The rooms and passageways of the dome filled with ornaments cut from foil or sheet metal, twisted together from color-coded wire, assembled from painted paper. Smells of baking cookies filled the air. Men went about whistling immemorial tunes.

Overbeck didn't mind that they were cheerful. That was a boost to efficiency, in these grim surroundings. He argued a while when they wanted to decorate outdoors as well, but presently gave in.

After all, he had a great deal else to think about.

A couple of Ivanhoan days after their talk, he was standing in the open when Juan approached him. The apprentice stopped, waited, and listened, for his chief was in conversation with Raffak.

The dome and sheds of the human base looked oddly bright, totally out of place. Behind them, the gray walls of Dahia lifted sheer, ten meters to the parapets, overtopped by bulbous-battlemented watchtowers. They were less crumbled than the buildings within. Today's dwindled population huddled in what parts of the old stone mansions and temples had not collapsed into rubble. A few lords maintained small castles for themselves, a few priests carried on rites behind porticos whose columns were idols, along twisting dusty streets. Near the middle of town rose the former Imperial palace. Quarried for centuries, its remnants were a colossal shapelessness.

The city dwellers were more quiet than humans. Not even vendors in their flimsy booths cried their wares. Most males were clad in leather kilts and weapons, females in zigzag-patterned robes. The wealthy and the military officers rode on beasts which resembled narrow-snouted, feathery-furred horses. The emblems of provinces long lost fluttered from the lances they carried. Wind, shrill in the lanes, bore sounds of feet, hoofs, groaning cartwheels, an occasional call or the whine of a bone flute.

A human found it cold. His breath smoked into the dry air. Smells were harsh in his nostrils. The sky above was deep purple, the sun a dull ruddy disc. Shadows lay thick; and nothing, in that wan light, had the same color as it did on Earth.

The deep tones of his language rolled from Raffak's mouth. "We have made you welcome, we have given you a place, we have aided you by our labor and counsel," declared the speaker of the City Elders.

"You have . . . for a generous payment," Overbeck answered.

"You shall not, in return, exclude Dahia from a full share in the wealth the *adir* will bring." A four-fingered hand, thumb set oppositely to a man's, gestured outward. Through a cyclopean gateway showed a reach of dusky-green bush, part of the agricultural hinterland. "It is more than a wish to better our lot. You have promised us that. But Dahia was the crown of an empire reaching from sea to sea. Though it lies in wreck, we who live here preserve the memories of our mighty ancestors, and faithfully serve their gods. Shall desert-prowling savages wax rich and strong, while we descendants of their over-lords remain weak—until they become able to stamp out this final spark of glory? Never!"

"The nomads claim the wild country," Overbeck said. "No one has disputed that for many centuries."

"Dahia disputes it at last. I came to tell you that we have sent forth emissaries to the Black Tents. They bore our demand that Dahia must share in the *adir* harvest."

Overbeck, and a shocked Juan, regarded the Ivanhoan closely. He seemed bigger, more lionlike than was right. His powerful, long-limbed body would have loomed a full two meters tall did it not slant forward. A tufted tail whipped the bent legs. Mahogany fur turned into a mane around the flat face. That face lacked a nose—breathing was through slits beneath the jaws—but the eyes glowed green and enormous, ears stood erect, teeth gleamed sharp.

The human leader braced himself, as if against the drag of a gravity slightly stronger than Earth's, and stated: "You were foolish. Relations between Dahia and the nomads are touchy at best, violent at worst. Let war break out, and there will be no *adir* trade. Then Dahia too will lose."

"Lose material goods, maybe," Raffak said. "Not honor."

"You have already lost some honor by your action. You knew my people had reached agreement with the nomads. Now you Elders seek to change that agreement

before consulting us." Overbeck made a chopping gesture which signified anger and determination. "I insist
on meeting with your council."

After an argument, Raffak agreed to this for the next
day, and stalked off. Hands jammed into pockets, Overbeck stared after him. "Well, Juan," he sighed, "there's
a concrete example for you, of how tricky this business
of ours can get."

"Might the tribes really make trouble, sir?" wondered
the boy.

"I hope not." Overbeck shook his head. "Though how
much do we know, we Earthlings, as short a while as
we've been here? Two whole societies, each with its own
history, beliefs, laws, customs, desires—in a species that
isn't human!"

"What do you suppose will happen?"

"Oh, I'd guess the nomads will refuse flat-out to let
the Dahians send gathering parties into their territory.
Then I'll have to persuade the Dahians all over again, to
let nomads bring the stuff here. That's what happens
when you try to make hereditary rivals cooperate."

"Couldn't we base ourselves in the desert?" Juan
asked.

"It's better to have a large labor force we can hire at
need, one that stays put," Overbeck explained. "Besides,
well—" He looked almost embarrassed. "We're after a
profit, yes, but not to exploit these poor beings. An *adir*
trade would benefit Dahia too, both from the taxes levied
on it and from developing friendlier relations with the
tribesfolk. In time, they could start rebuilding their civilization here. It was great once, before its civil wars and
the barbarian invasions that followed." He paused.
"Don't ever quote me to them."

"Why not, sir? I should think—"

"*You* should. I doubt they would. Both factions are proud and fierce. They might decide they were being patronized, and resent it in a murderous fashion. Or they might get afraid we intend to undermine their martial virtues, or their religions, or something." Overbeck smiled rather grimly. "No, I've worked hard to keep matters simple, on a level where nobody can misunderstand. In native eyes, we Earthlings are tough but fair. We've come to build a trade that will pay off for us, and for no other reason. It's up to them to keep us interested in remaining, which we won't unless they behave. That attitude, that image is clear enough, I hope, for the most alien mind to grasp. They may not love us, but they don't hate us either, and they're willing to do business."

Juan swallowed and found no words.

"What'd you want of me?" Overbeck inquired.

"Permission to go into the hills, sir," the apprentice said. "You know those crystals along Wola Ridge? They'd be beautiful on the Christmas tree." Ardently: "I've finished all my jobs for the time being. It will only take some hours, if I can borrow a flitter."

Overbeck frowned. "When a fight may be brewing? The Black Tents are somewhere that way, last I heard."

"You said, sir, you don't look for violence. Besides, none of the Ivanhoans have a grudge against us. And they respect our power. Don't they? Please!"

"I aim to preserve that state of affairs." Overbeck pondered. "Well, shouldn't be any risk. And, hm-m-m, a human going out alone might be a pretty good demonstration of confidence. . . . Okay," he decided. "Pack a blaster. If a situation turns ugly, don't hesitate to use it. Not that I believe you'll get in any scrape, or I wouldn't let you go. But—" He shrugged. "There's no such thing as an absolutely safe bet."

Three hundred kilometers north of Dahia, the wilderness was harsh mountainsides, deep-gashed canyons, umber crags, thinly scattered thorn-shrubs and wind-gnarled trees with ragged leaves. Searching for the mineral which cropped here and there out of the sandy ground, Juan soon lost sight of his flitter. He couldn't get lost from it himself. The aircraft was giving off a radio signal, and the transceiver in his pocket included a directional meter for homing on it. Thus he wandered further than he realized before he had collected a bagful.

However slowly Ivanhoe rotates, its days must end. Juan grew aware of how low the dim red sun was, how long and heavy the shadows. Chilliness had turned to a cold which bit at his bare face. Evening breezes snickered in the brush. Somewhere an animal howled. When he passed a rivulet, he saw that it had begun to freeze.

I'm in no trouble, he thought, *but I am hungry, and late for supper, and the boss will be annoyed.* Even now, it was getting hard for him to see. His vision was meant for bright, yellow-white Sol. He stumbled on rocks. Had his radio compass not been luminous-dialed, he would have needed a flashbeam to read it.

Nevertheless he was happy. The very weirdness of this environment made it fascinating; and he could hope to go on to many other worlds. Meanwhile, the Christmas celebration would be a circle of warmth and cheer, a memory of home—his parents, his brother and two sisters, Tío Pepe and Tía Carmen, the dear small Mexican town and the laughter as children struck at a *piñata*—

"*Raielli, Erratan!*"

Halt, Earthling! Juan jarred to a stop.

He was near the bottom of a ravine, which he was crossing as the most direct way to the flitter. The sun lay hidden behind one wall of it, and dusk filled the heavens. He could just make out boulders and bushes, vague in the gloom.

Then metal caught what light there was in a faint glimmer. He saw spearheads and a single breastplate. The rest of the warriors had only leather harness. They were blurs around him, save where their huge eyes gleamed like their steel.

Juan's heart knocked. *These are friends!* he told himself. *The People of the Black Tents are anxious to deal with us—Then why did they wait here for me? Why have a score of them risen out of hiding to ring me in?*

His mouth felt suddenly parched. He forced it to form words, as well as it could imitate the voice of an Ivanhoan. City and wilderness dwellers spoke essentially the same language. "G-greeting." He remembered the desert form of salutation. "I am Juan Sancho's-child, called Hernandez, pledged follower of the merchant Thomas William's-child, called Overbeck, and am come in peace."

"I am Tokonnen Undassa's-child, chief of the Elassi Clan," said the lion-being in the cuirass. His tone was a snarl. "We may no longer believe that any Earthling comes in peace."

"What?" cried Juan. Horror smote him. "But we do! How—"

"You camp among the City folk. Now the City demands the right to encroach on our land. . . . Hold! I know what you carry."

Juan had gripped his blaster. The natives growled. Spears drew back, ready to throw. Tokonnen confronted the boy and continued:

"I have heard tell about weapons like yours. A fire-beam, fiercer than the sun, springs forth, and rock turns molten where it strikes. Do you think a male of Elassi fears that?" Scornfully: "Draw it if you wish."

Juan did, hardly thinking. He let the energy gun dangle downward in his fingers and exclaimed, "I only came to gather a few crystals—"

"If you slay me," Tokonnen warned, "that will prove otherwise. And you cannot kill more than two or three of us before the spears of the rest have pierced you. We know how feebly your breed sees in the least of shadows."

"But what do you *want?*"

"When we saw you descend, afar off, we knew what we wanted—you, to hold among us until your fellows abandon Dahia."

Half of Juan realized that being kept hostage was most likely a death sentence for him. He couldn't eat Ivanhoan food; it was loaded with proteins poisonous to his kind of life. In fact, without a steady supply of antiallergen, he might not keep breathing. How convince a barbarian herder of that?

The other half pleaded, "You are being wild. What matter if a few City dwellers come out after *adir?* Or . . . you can tell them 'no.' Can't you? We, we Earthlings—we had nothing to do with the embassy they sent"

"We dare not suppose you speak truth, you who have come here for gain," Tokonnen replied. "What is our freedom to you, if the enemy offers you a fatter bargain?

And we remember, yes, across a hundred generations we remember the Empire. So do they in Dahia. They would restore it, cage us within their rule or drive us into the badlands. Their harvesters would be their spies, the first agents of their conquest. This country is ours. It is strong with the bones of our fathers and rich with the flesh of our mothers. It is too holy for an Imperial foot to tread. You would not understand this, merchant."

"We mean you well," Juan stammered. "We'll give you things—"

Tokonnen's mane lifted haughtily against darkling cliff, twilit sky. From his face, unseen in murk, the words rang: "Do you imagine things matter more to us than our liberty or our land?" Softer: "Yield me your weapon and come along. Tomorrow we will bring a message to your chief."

The warriors trod closer.

There went a flash through Juan. He knew what he could do, must do. Raising the blaster, he fired straight upward.

Cloven air boomed. Ozone stung with a smell of thunderstorms. Blue-white and dazzling, the energy beam lanced toward the earliest stars.

The Ivanhoans yelled. By the radiance, Juan saw them lurch back, drop their spears, clap hands to eyes. He himself could not easily look at that lightning bolt. They were the brood of a dark world. Such brilliance blinded them.

Juan gulped a breath and ran.

Up the slope! Talus rattled underfoot. Across the hills beyond! Screams of wrath pursued him.

The sun was now altogether down, and night came on apace. It was less black than Earth's, for the giant stars of the Pleiades cluster bloomed everywhere aloft, and the nebula which enveloped them glowed lacy across heaven. Yet often Juan fell across an unseen obstacle. His pulse roared, his lungs were aflame.

It seemed forever before he glimpsed his vehicle. Casting a glance behind, he saw what he had feared, the warriors in pursuit. His shot had not permanently damaged their sight. And surely they tracked him with peripheral vision, ready to look entirely away if he tried another flash.

Longer-legged, born to the planet's gravity, they over-hauled him, meter after frantic meter. To him they were barely visible, bounding blacknesses which often disap-peared into the deeper gloom around. He could not have hoped to pick them all off before one of them got to range, flung a spear from cover, and struck him.

Somehow, through every terror, he marveled at their bravery.

Run, run.

He had barely enough of a head start. He reeled into the hull, dogged the door shut, and heard missiles clatter on metal. Then for a while he knew nothing.

When awareness came back, he spent a minute giving thanks. Afterward he dragged himself to the pilot chair. *What a scene!* passed across his mind. And, a crazy chuckle: *The old definition of adventure. Somebody else having a hard time a long ways off.*

He slumped into the seat. The vitryl port showed him a sky turned wonderful, a land of dim slopes and sharp ridges—He gasped and sat upright. The Ivanhoans were still outside.

They stood leaning on their useless spears or clinging to the hilts of their useless swords, and waited for what-ever he would do. Shakily, he switched on the sound amplifier and bullhorn. His voice boomed over them: "What do you want?"

Tokonnen's answer remained prideful. "We wish to know your desire, Earthling. For in you we have met a thing most strange."

Bewildered, Juan could merely respond with, "How so?"

"You rendered us helpless," Tokonnen said. "Why did you not at once kill us? Instead, you chose to flee. You must have known we would recover and come after you. Why did you take the unneeded risk?"

"You *were* helpless," Juan blurted. "I couldn't have . . . hurt you . . . especially at this time of year."

Tokonnen showed astonishment. "Time of year? What has that to do with it?"

"Christmas—" Juan paused. Strength and clarity of mind were returning to him. "You don't know about that. It's a season which, well, commemorates one who came to us Earthlings, ages ago, and spoke of peace as well as much else. For us, this is a holy time." He laid hands on controls. "No matter. I only ask you believe that we don't mean you any harm. Stand aside. I am about to raise this wagon."

"No," Tokonnen said. "Wait. I ask you, wait." He was silent for a while, and his warriors with him. "What you have told us—We must hear further. Talk to us, Earthling."

Once he had radioed that he was safe, they stopped worrying about Juan at the base. For the next several hours, the men continued their jobs. It was impossible for them to function on a sixty-hour day, and nobody tried. Midnight had not come when they knocked off.

Recreation followed. For four of them, this meant preparing their Christmas welcome to the ship.

As they worked outdoors, more and more Dahians gathered, fascinated, to stand silently around the plaza and watch. Overbeck stepped forth to observe the natives in his turn. Nothing like this had ever happened before.

A tree had been erected on the flagstones. Its sparse branches and stiff foliage did not suggest an evergreen; but no matter, it glittered with homemade ornaments and lights improvised from electronic parts. Before it stood a manger scene that Juan had constructed. A risen moon, the mighty Pleiades, and the luminous nebular veil cast frost-cold brilliance. The beings who encompassed the square, beneath lean houses and fortress towers, formed a shadow-mass wherein eyes glimmered.

Feinberg and Gupta decorated. Noguchi and Sarychev, who had the best voices, rehearsed. Breath from their song puffed white.

"O little town of Bethlehem,
How still we see thee lie—"

A muted "A-a-ahhh!" rose from the Dahians, and Juan landed his flitter.

He bounded forth. Behind him came a native in a steel breastplate. Overbeck had awaited this since the boy's last call. He gestured to Raffak, speaker of the Elders. Together, human and Ivanhoan advanced to greet human and Ivanhoan.

Tokonnen said, "It may be we misjudged your intent, City folk. The Earthling tells me we did."

"And his lord tells me we of Dahia pushed forward too strongly," Raffak answered. "That may likewise be."

Tokonnen touched sword-hilt and warned, "We shall yield nothing which is sacred to us."

"Nor we," said Raffak. "But surely our two people can reach an agreement. The Earthlings can help us make terms."

"They should have special wisdom, now in the season of their Prince of Peace."

"Aye. My fellows and I have begun some hard thinking about that."

"How do you know of it?"

"We were curious as to why the Earthlings were making beauty, here where we can see it away from the dreadful heat," Raffak said. "We asked. In the course of this, they told us somewhat of happenings in the desert, which the far-speaker had informed them of."

"It is indeed something to think about," Tokonnen nodded. "They, who believe in peace, are more powerful than us."

"And it was war which destroyed the Empire. But come," Raffak invited. "Tonight be my guest. Tomorrow we will talk."

They departed. Meanwhile the men clustered around Juan. Overbeck shook his hand again and again. "You're a genius," he said. "I ought to take lessons from you."

"No, please, sir," his apprentice protested. "The thing simply happened."

"It wouldn't have, if I'd been the one who got caught."

Sarychev was puzzled. "I don't quite see what did go on," he confessed. "It was good of Juan to run away from those nomads, instead of cutting them down when he had the chance. However, that by itself can't have turned them meek and mild." .

"Oh, no." Overbeck chuckled. His cigar end waxed and waned like a variable star. "They're as ornery as ever—same as humans." Soberly: "The difference is, they've become willing to listen to us. They can take our ideas seriously, and believe we'll be honest brokers, who can mediate their quarrels."

"Why could they not before?"

"My fault, I'm afraid. I wasn't allowing for a certain part of Ivanhoan nature. I should have seen. After all, it's part of human nature too."

"What is?" Gupta asked.

"The need for—" Overbeck broke off. "You tell him, Juan. You were the one who did see the truth."

The boy drew breath. "Not at first," he said. "I only found I could not bring myself to kill. Is Christmas not when we should be quickest to forgive our enemies? I told them so. Then . . . when suddenly their whole attitude changed . . . I guessed what the reason must be." He searched for words. "They knew—both Dahians and nomads knew—we are strong; we have powers they can't hope to match. That doesn't frighten them. They have to be fearless, to survive in as bleak a country as this.

"Also, they have to be dedicated. To keep going through endless hardship, they must believe in something greater than themselves, like the Imperial dream of Dahia or the freedom of the desert. They're ready to die for those ideals.

"We came, we Earthlings. We offered them a fair, profitable bargain. But nothing else. We seemed to have no other motive than material gain. They could not understand this. It made us too peculiar. They could never really trust us.

"Now that they know we have our own sacrednesses, well, they see we are not so different from them, and they'll heed our advice."

Juan uttered an unsteady laugh. "What a long lecture, no?" he ended. "I'm very tired and hungry. Please, may I go get something to eat and afterward to bed?"

As he crossed the square, the carol followed him:

"—The hopes and fears of all the years
Are met in thee tonight."

INTRODUCTION

❂ THE MAN WHO COUNTS ❂

A full sky-dance portraying Nicholas van Rijn needs the space of a small book. Several historical novels wherein he figures exist, and maychance you will wish to screen them. For the purpose which his Wyvan gave him, Hloch chooses the following. This is partly because van Rijn is more central in it than in others; partly because the consequences had some importance to Falkayn's home world; and partly because winged sophonts have a special interest for us, rare as they are. In addition, Diomedes, freak among planets, helps remind of the awesome unforeseeability of the universe, a fact before which starfaring races must humble their very death-pride.

While this tale appears to be reasonably factual, its source is uncertain. Original publication was either on Terra or Hermes; separate authors and dates are given on those two worlds, and Rennhi did not feel the matter was worth pursuing further.

—Hloch of the Stormgate Choth
The Earth Book of Stormgate

THE MAN WHO COUNTS

❁ I ❁

Grand Admiral Syranax hyr Urnan, hereditary Commander-in-chief of the Fleet of Drak'ho, Fisher of the Western Seas, Leader in Sacrifice, and Oracle of the Lodestar, spread his wings and brought them together again in an astonished thunderclap. For a moment, it snowed papers from his desk.

"No!" he said. "Impossible! There's some mistake."

"As my Admiral wills it." Chief Executive Officer Delp hyr Orikan bowed sarcastically. "The scouts saw nothing."

Anger crossed the face of Captain T'heonax hyr Urnan, son of the Grand Admiral and therefore heir apparent. His upper lip rose until the canine tushes showed, a white flash against the dark muzzle.

"We have no time to waste on your insolence, Executive Delp," he said coldly. "I would advise my father to dispense with an officer who has no more respect."

Under the embroidered cross-belts of office, Delp's big frame tautened. Captain T'heonax glided one step toward him. Tails curled back and wings spread, instinctive readiness for battle, until the room was full of their bodies and their hate. With a calculation which made it seem accidental, T'heonax dropped a hand to the obsidian rake at his waist. Delp's yellow eyes blazed and his fingers clamped on his own tomahawk.

Admiral Syranax's tail struck the floor. It was like a fire-bomb going off. The two young nobles jerked, remembered where they were, and slowly, muscle by muscle laying itself back to rest under the sleek brown fur, they relaxed.

"Enough!" snapped Syranax. "Delp, your tongue will flap you into trouble yet. T'heonax, I've grown bored with your spite. You'll have your chance to deal with personal enemies, when I am fish food. Meanwhile, spare me my few able officers!"

It was a firmer speech than anyone had heard from him for a long time. His son and his subordinate recalled that this grizzled, dim-eyed, rheumatic creature had once been the conqueror of the Maion Navy—a thousand wings of enemy leaders had rattled grisly from the mastheads—and was still their chief in the war against the Flock. They assumed the all-fours crouch of respect and waited for him to continue.

"Don't take me so literally, Delp," said the admiral in a milder tone. He reached to the rack above his desk and got down a long-stemmed pipe and began stuffing it with flakes of dried sea driss from the pouch at his waist. Meanwhile, his stiff old body fitted itself more comfortably into the wood-and-leather seat. "I was quite surprised, of course, but I assume that our scouts still know how to use a telescope. Describe to me again exactly what happened."

"A patrol was on routine reconnaissance about thirty obdisai north-north-west of here," said Delp with care. "That would be in the general area of the island called . . . I can't pronounce that heathenish local name, sir; it means Banners Flew."

"Yes, yes," nodded Syranax. "I have looked at a map now and then, you know."

T'heonax grinned. Delp was no courtier. That was Delp's trouble. His grandfather had been a mere Sailmaker, his father never advanced beyond the captaincy of a single raft. That was after the family had been ennobled for heroic service at the Battle of Xarit'ha, of course—but they had still been very minor peers, a tarry-handed lot barely one cut above their own crewfolk.

Syranax, the Fleet's embodied response to these grim days of hunger and uprooting, had chosen officers on a basis of demonstrated ability, and nothing else. Thus it was that simple Delp hyr Orikan had been catapulted in a few years to the second highest post in Drak'ho. Which had not taken the rough edges off his education, or taught him how to deal with *real* nobles.

If Delp was popular with the common sailors, he was all the more disliked by many aristocrats—a parvenu, a boor, with the nerve to wed a sa Axollon! Once the old admiral's protecting wings were folded in death—

T'heonax savored in advance what would happen to Delp hyr Orikan. It would be easy enough to find some nominal charge.

The executive gulped. "Sorry, sir," he mumbled. "I didn't mean . . . we're still so new to this whole sea . . . well. The scouts saw this drifting object. It was like nothing ever heard of before. A pair of 'em flew back to report and ask for advice. I went to look for myself. Sir, it's true!"

"A floating object—six times as long as our longest canoe—like ice, and yet not like ice—" The admiral shook his gray-furred head. Slowly, he put dry tinder in the bottom of his firemaker. But it was with needless violence that he drove the piston down into the little hardwood cylinder. Removing the rod again, he tilted fire out into the bowl of his pipe, and drew deeply.

"The most highly polished rock crystal might look a bit like that stuff, sir," offered Delp. "But not so bright. Not with such a *shimmer*."

"And there are animals scurrying about on it?"

"Three of them, sir. About our size, or a little bigger, but wingless and tailless. Yet not just animals either . . . I think . . . they seem to wear clothes and—I don't think the shining thing was ever intended as a boat, though. It rides abominably, and appears to be settling."

"If it's not a boat, and not a log washed off some beach," said T'heonax, "then where, pray tell, is it from? The Deeps?"

"Hardly, captain," said Delp irritably. "If that were so, the creatures on it would be fish or sea mammals or—well, adapted for swimming, anyway. They're not. They look like typical flightless land forms, except for having only four limbs."

"So they fell from the sky, I presume?" sneered T'heonax.

"I wouldn't be at all surprised," said Delp in a very low voice. "There isn't any other direction left."

T'heonax sat up on his haunches, mouth falling open. His father only nodded.

"Very good," murmured Syranax. "I'm pleased to see a little imagination around here."

"But where did they fly *from*?" exploded T'heonax.

"Perhaps our enemies of Lannach would have some account of it," said the admiral. "They cover a great deal more of the world every year than we do in many generations; they meet a hundred other barbarian flocks down in the tropics and exchange news."

"And females," said T'heonax. He spoke in that mixture of primly disapproving voice and lickerish overtones with which the entire Fleet regarded the habits of the migrators.

"Never mind that," snapped Delp.

T'heonax bristled. "You deck-swabber's whelp, do you dare—"

"Shut up!" roared Syranax.

After a pause, he went on: "I'll have inquiries made among our prisoners. Meanwhile, we had better send a fast canoe to pick up these beings before that object they're on founders."

"They may be dangerous," warned T'heonax.

"Exactly," said his father. "If so, they're better in our hands than if, say, the Lannach'honai should find them and make an alliance. Delp, take the *Nemnis*, with a reliable crew, and crowd sail on her. And bring along that fellow we captured from Lannach, what's his name, the professional linguist—"

"Tolk?" The executive stumbled over the unfamiliar pronunciation.

"Yes. Maybe he can talk to them. Send scouts back to report to me, but stand well off the main Fleet until you're sure that the creatures are harmless to us. Also till I've allayed whatever superstitious fears about sea demons there are in the lower classes. Be polite if you can, get rough if you must. We can always apologize later . . . or toss the bodies overboard. Now, jump!"

Delp jumped.

❀ II ❀

Desolation walled him in.

Even from this low, on the rolling, pitching hull of the murdered skycruiser, Eric Wace could see an immensity of horizon. He thought that the sheer size of that ring, where frost-pale heaven met the gray which was cloud and storm-scud and great marching waves, was enough to terrify a man. The likelihood of death had been faced before, on Earth, by many of his forebears; but Earth's horizon was not so remote.

Never mind that he was a hundred-odd light-years from his own sun. Such distances were too big to be understood: they became mere numbers, and did not frighten one who reckoned the pseudo-speed of a secondary-drive spaceship in parsecs per week.

Even the ten thousand kilometers of open ocean to this world's lone human settlement, the trading post, was only another number. Later, if he lived, Wace would spend an agonized time wondering how to get a message across that emptiness. But at present he was too occupied with keeping alive.

But the breadth of the planet was something he could see. It had not struck him before, in his eighteen-month stay; but then he had been insulated, psychologically as well as physically, by an unconquerable machine technology. Now he stood alone on a sinking vessel, and it was twice as far to look across chill waves to the world's rim as it had been on Earth.

The skycruiser rolled under a savage impact. Wace lost his footing and slipped across curved metal plates. Frantic, he clawed for the light cable which lashed cases of food to the navigation turret. If he went over the side, his boots and clothes would pull him under like a stone. He caught it in time and strained to a halt. The disappointed wave slapped his face, a wet salt hand.

Shaking with cold, Wace finished tucking the last box into place and crawled back toward the entry hatch. It was a miserable little emergency door, but the glazed promenade deck, on which his passengers had strolled while the cruiser's gravbeams bore her through the sky, was awash, its ornate bronzed portal submerged.

Water had filled the smashed engine compartment when they ditched. Since then it had been seeping around twisted bulkheads and strained hull plates, until the whole thing was about ready for a last long dive to the sea bottom.

Wind passed gaunt fingers through his drenched hair and tried to hold open the hatch when he wanted to close it after him. He had a struggle against the gale . . . Gale? Hell, no! It had only the velocity of a stiffish breeze—but with six times the atmospheric pressure of Earth behind it, that breeze struck like a Terrestrial storm. Damn PLC 2987165 II! Damn the PL itself, and damn Nicholas van Rijn, and most particularly damn Eric Wace for being fool enough to work for the Company!

Briefly, while he fought the hatch, Wace looked out over the coaming as if to find rescue. He glimpsed only a reddish sun, and great cloud-banks dirty with storm in the north, and a few specks which were probably natives.

Satan fry those natives on a slow griddle, that they did not come to help! Or at least go decently away while the humans drowned, instead of hanging up there in the sky to gloat!

"Is all in order?"

Wace closed the hatch, dogged it fast, and came down the ladder. At its foot, he had to brace himself against the heavy rolling. He could still hear waves beat on the hull, and the wind-yowl.

"Yes, my lady," he said. "As much as it'll ever be."

"Which isn't much, not?" Lady Sandra Tamarin played her flashlight over him. Behind it, she was only another shadow in the darkness of the dead vessel. "But you look a saturated rat, my friend. Come, we have at least fresh clothes for you."

Wace nodded and shrugged out of his wet jacket and kicked off the squelching boots. He would have frozen up there without them—it couldn't be over five degrees C.—but they seemed to have blotted up half the ocean. His teeth clapped in his head as he followed her down the corridor.

He was a tall young man of North American stock, ruddy-haired, blue-eyed, with bluntly squared-off features above a well-muscled body. He had begun as a warehouse apprentice at the age of twelve, back on Earth, and now he was the Solar Spice & Liquors Company's factor for the entire planet known as Diomedes. It wasn't exactly a meteoric rise—van Rijn's policy was to promote according to results, which meant that a quick mind, a quick gun, and an eye firmly held to the main chance were favored. But it had been a good solid career, with a future of posts on less isolated and unpleasant worlds, ultimately an executive position back Home and—and what was the use, if alien waters were to eat him in a few hours more?

At the end of the hall, where the navigation turret poked up, there was again the angry copper sunlight, low in the wan smoky-clouded sky, south of west as day declined. Lady Sandra snapped off her torch and pointed to a coverall laid out on the desk. Beside it were the outer garments, quilted, hooded, and gloved, he would need before venturing out again into the pre-equinoctial springtime. "Put on everything," she said. "Once the boat starts going down, we will have to leave in a most horrible hurry."

"Where's Freeman van Rijn?" asked Wace.

"Making some last-minute work on the raft. That one is a handy man with the tools, not? But then, he was once a common space-hand."

Wace shrugged and waited for her to leave.

"Change, I told you," she said.

"But—"

"Oh." A thin smile crossed her face. "I thought not there was a nudity taboo on Earth."

"Well . . . not exactly, I guess, my lady . . . but after all, you're a noble born, and I'm only a trader—"

"From republican planets like Earth come the worst snobs of all," she said. "Here we are all human beings. Quickly, now, change. I shall turn my back if you desire so."

Wace scrambled into the outfit as fast as possible. Her mirth was an unexpected comfort to him. He considered what luck always appeared to befall that pot-bellied old goat van Rijn.

It wasn't right!

The colonists of Hermes had been, mostly, a big fair stock, and their descendants had bred true: especially the aristocrats, after Hermes set up as an autonomous grand duchy during the Breakup. Lady Sandra Tamarin was nearly as tall as he, and shapeless winter clothing did not entirely hide the lithe full femaleness of her. She had a face too strong to be pretty—wide forehead, wide mouth, snub nose, high cheekbones—but the large smoky-lashed green eyes, under heavy dark brows, were the most beautiful Wace had ever seen. Her hair was long, straight, ash-blond, pulled into a knot at the moment but he had seen it floating free under a coronet by candlelight—

"Are you quite through, Freeman Wace?"

"Oh . . . I'm sorry, my lady. I got to thinking. Just a moment!" He pulled on the padded tunic, but left it unzipped. There was still some human warmth lingering in the hull. "Yes. I beg your pardon."

"It is nothing." She turned about. In the little space available, their forms brushed together. Her gaze went out to the sky. "Those natives, are they up there yet?"

"I imagine so, my lady. Too high for me to be sure, but they can go up several kilometers with no trouble at all."

"I have wondered, Trader, but got no chance to ask. I thought not there could be a flying animal the size of a man, and yet these Diomedeans have a six-meter span of bat wings. How?"

"At a time like *this* you ask?"

She smiled. "We only wait now for Freeman van Rijn. What else shall we do but talk of curious things?"

"We . . . help him . . . finish that raft soon or we'll all go under!"

"He told me he has just batteries enough for one cutting torch, so anyone else is only in the way. Please continue talking. The highborn of Hermes have their customs and taboos, also for the correct way to die. What else is man, if not a set of customs and taboos?" Her husky voice was light, she smiled a little, but he wondered how much of it was an act.

He wanted to say: We're down in the ocean of a planet whose life is poison to us. There is an island a few score kilometers hence, but we only know its direction vaguely. We may or may not complete a raft in time, patched together out of old fuel drums, and we may or may not get our human-type rations loaded on it in time, and it may or may not weather the storm brewing yonder in the north. Those were natives who swooped low above us a few hours ago, but since then they have ignored us . . . or watched us . . . anything except offer help.

Someone hates you or old van Rijn, he wanted to say. Not me, I'm not important enough to hate. But van Rijn is the Solar Spice & Liquors Company, which is a great power in the Polesotechnic League, which is *the* great power in the known galaxy. And you are the Lady Sandra Tamarin, heiress to the throne of an entire planet, if you live; and you have turned down many offers of marriage from its decaying, inbred aristocracy, publicly preferring to look elsewhere for a father for your children, that the next Grand Duke of Hermes may be a man and not a giggling clothes horse; so no few courtiers must dread your accession.

Oh, yes, he wanted to say, there are plenty of people who would gain if either Nicholas van Rijn or Sandra Tamarin failed to come back. It was a calculated gallantry for him to offer you a lift in his private ship, from Antares where you met, back to Earth, with stopovers at interesting points along the way. At the very least, he can look for trade concessions in the Duchy. At best . . . no, hardly a formal alliance; he has too much hell in him; even you—most strong and fair and innocent—would never let him plant himself on the High Seat of your fathers.

But I wander from the subject, my dear, he wanted to say; and the subject is, that someone in the spaceship's crew was bribed. The scheme was well-hatched; the someone watched his chance. It came when you landed on Diomedes, to see what a really new raw planet is like, a planet where even the main continental outlines have scarcely been mapped, in the mere five years that a spoonful of men have been here. The chance came when I was told to ferry you and my evil old boss to those sheer mountains, halfway around this world, which have been noted as spectacular scenery. A bomb in the main generator . . . a slain crew, engineers and stewards gone in the blast, my co-pilot's skull broken when we ditched in the sea, the radio shattered . . . and the last wreckage is going to sink long before they begin to worry at Thursday Landing and come in search of us . . . and assuming we survive, is there the slightest noticeable chance that a few skyboats, cruising a nearly unmapped world twice the size of Earth, will happen to see three human fly-specks on it?

Therefore, he wanted to say, since all our schemings and posturings have brought us merely to this, it would be well to forget them in what small time remains, and kiss me instead.

But his throat clogged up on him, and he said none of it.

"So?" A note of impatience entered her voice. "You are very silent, Freeman Wace."

"I'm sorry, my lady," he mumbled. "I'm afraid I'm no good at making conversation under . . . uh, these circumstances."

"I regret I have not qualifications to offer to you the consolations of religion," she said with a hurtful scorn.

A long gray-bearded comber went over the deck outside and climbed the turret. They felt steel and plastic tremble under the blow. For a moment, as water sheeted, they stood in a blind roaring dark.

Then, as it cleared, and Wace saw how much farther down the wreck had burrowed, and wondered if they would even be able to get van Rijn's raft out through the submerged cargo hatch, there was a whiteness that snatched at his eye.

First he didn't believe it, and then he wouldn't believe because he dared not, and then he could no longer deny it.

"Lady Sandra." He spoke with immense care; he *must* not scream his news at her like any low-born Terrestrial.

"Yes?" She did not look away from her smoldering contemplation of the northern horizon, empty of all but clouds and lightning.

"There, my lady. Roughly southeast, I'd guess . . . sails, beating upwind."

"*What?*" It was a shriek from her. Somehow, that made Wace laugh aloud.

"A boat of some kind," he pointed. "Coming this way."

"I didn't know the natives were sailors," she said, very softly.

"They aren't, my lady—around Thursday Landing," he replied. "But this is a big planet. Roughly four times the surface area of Earth, and we only know a small part of one continent."

"Then you know not what they are like, these sailors?"

"My lady, I have no idea."

❀ III ❀

Nicholas van Rijn came puffing up the companionway at their shout. "Death and damnation!" he roared. "A boat, do you say, *ja?* Better for you it is a shark, if you are mistaken. By damn!" He stumped into the turret and glared out through salt-encrusted plastic. The light was dimming as the sun went lower and the approaching storm clouds swept across its ruddy face. "So! Where is it, this pestilential boat?"

"There, sir," said Wace. "That schooner—"

"Schooner! Schnork! Powder and balls, you cement head, that is a yawl rig . . . no, wait, by damn, there is a furled square sail on the mainmast too, and, yes, an outrigger—*Ja*, the way she handles, she must have a regular rudder—Good saints help us! A bloody-be-damned-to-blazes dugout!"

"What else do you expect, on a planet without metals?" said Wace. His nerves were worn too thin for him to remember the deference due a merchant prince.

"Hm-m-m . . . coracles, maybe so, or rafts or catamarans—Quick, dry clothes! Too cold it is for brass monkeys!"

Wace grew aware that van Rijn was standing in a puddle, and that bitter sea water streamed from his waist and legs. The storeroom where he had been at work must have been awash for—for hours!

"I know where they are, Nicholas." Sandra loped off down the corridor. It slanted more ominously every minute, as the sea pushed in through a ruined stern.

Wace helped his chief off with the sopping coverall. Naked, van Rijn suggested . . . what was that extinct ape? . . . a gorilla, two meters tall, hairy and huge-bellied, with shoulders like a brick warehouse, loudly bawling his indignation at the cold and the damp and the slowness of assistants. But rings flashed on the thick fingers and bracelets on the wrists, and a little St. Dismas medal swung from his neck. Unlike Wace, who found a crew cut and a clean shave more practical, van Rijn let his oily black locks hang curled and perfumed in an archaic mode, flaunted a goatee on his triple chin and intimidating waxed mustaches beneath the great hook nose.

He rummaged in the navigator's cabinet, wheezing, till he found a bottle of rum. "Ahhh! I knew I had the devil-begotten thing stowed somewhere." He put it to his frog-mouth and tossed off several shots at a gulp. "Good! Fine! Now maybe we can begin to be like self-respectful humans once more, *nie?*"

He turned about, majestic and globular as a planet, when Sandra came back. The only clothes she could find to fit him were his own, a peacock outfit of lace-trimmed shirt, embroidered waistcoat, shimmersilk culottes and stockings, gilt shoes, plumed hat, and holstered blaster. "Thank you," he said curtly. "Now, Wace, while I dress, in the lounge you will find a box of Perfectos and one small bottle applejack. Please to fetch them, then we go outside and meet our hosts."

"Holy St. Peter!" cried Wace. "The lounge is under water!"

"Ah?" Van Rijn sighed, woebegone. "Then you need only get the applejack. Quick, now!" He snapped his fingers.

Wace said hastily: "No time, sir. I still have to round up the last of our ammunition. Those natives could be hostile."

"If they have heard of us, possible so," agreed van Rijn. He began donning his natural-silk underwear.

"*Brrrr!* Five thousand candles I would give to be back in my office in Jakarta!"

"To what saint do you make the offer?" asked Lady Sandra.

"St. Nicholas, natural—my namesake, patron of wanderers and—"

"St. Nicholas had best get it in writing," she said.

Van Rijn purpled; but one does not talk back to the heiress apparent of a nation with important trade concessions to offer. He took it out by screaming abuse after the departing Wace.

It was some time before they were outside. Van Rijn got stuck in the emergency hatch and required pushing, while his anguished basso obscenities drowned the nearing thunder. Diomedes' period of rotation was only twelve and a half hours, and this latitude, thirty degrees north, was still on the winter side of equinox; so the sun was toppling seaward with dreadful speed. They clung to the lashings and let the wind claw them and the waves burst over them. There was nothing else they could do.

"It is no place for a poor old fat man," snuffled van Rijn. The gale ripped the words from him and flung them tattered over the rising seas. His shoulder-length curls flapped like forlorn pennons. "Better I should have stayed at home in Java where it is warm, not lost my last few pitiful years out here."

Wace strained his eyes into the gloom. The dugout had come near. Even a landlubber like himself could appreciate the skill of its crew, and van Rijn was loud in his praises. "I nominate him for the Sunda Yacht Club, by damn, yes, and enter him in the next regatta and make bets!"

It was a big craft, more than thirty meters long, with an elaborate stempost, but dwarfed by the reckless spread of its blue-dyed sails. Outrigger or no, Wace expected it to capsize any moment. Of course, a flying species had less to worry about if that should happen than—

"The Diomedeans." Sandra's tone was quiet in his ear, under shrill wind and booming waters. "You have dealt with them for a year and a half, not? What can we await for from them?"

Wace shrugged. "What could we expect from any random tribe of humans, back in the Stone Age? They might be poets, or cannibals, or both. All I know is the Tyrlanian Flock, who are migratory hunters. They always stick by the letter of their law—not quite so scrupulous about its spirit, of course, but on the whole a decent tribe."

"You speak their language?"

"As well as my human palate and Techno-Terrestrial culture permit me to, my lady. I don't pretend to understand all their concepts, but we get along—" The broken hull lurched. He heard some abused wall rend, and the inward pouring of still more sea, and felt the sluggishness grow beneath his feet. Sandra stumbled against him. He saw that the spray was freezing in her brows.

"That does not mean I'll understand the local language," he finished. "We're farther from Tyrlan than Europe from China."

The canoe was almost on them now. None too soon: the wreck was due to dive any minute. It came about, the sails rattled down, a sea anchor was thrown and brawny arms dug paddles into the water. Swiftly, then, a Diomedean flapped over with a rope. Two others hovered close, obviously as guards. The first one landed and stared at the humans.

Tyrlan being farther north, its inhabitants had not yet returned from the tropics and this was the first Diomedean Sandra had encountered. She was too wet, cold, and weary to enjoy the unhuman grace of his movements, but she looked very close. She might have to dwell with this race a long time, if they did not murder her.

He was the size of a smallish man, plus a thick meter-long tail ending in a fleshy rudder and the tremendous chiropteral wings folded along his back. His arms were set below the wings, near the middle of a sleek otterlike body, and looked startlingly human, down to the muscular five-fingered hands. The legs were less familiar, bending backward from four-taloned feet which might almost have belonged to some bird of prey. The head, at the end of a neck that would have been twice too long on a human, was round, with a high forehead, yellow eyes with nictitating membranes under heavy brow ridges, a blunt-muzzled black-nosed face with short cat-whiskers, a big mouth and the bearlike teeth of a flesh-eater turned omnivore. There were no external ears, but a crest of muscle on the head helped control flight. Short, soft brown fur covered him; he was plainly a male mammal.

He wore two belts looped around his "shoulders," a third about his waist, and a pair of bulging leather pouches. An obsidian knife, a slender flint-headed ax, and a set of bolas were hung in plain view. Through the thickening dusk, it was hard to make out what his wheeling comrades bore for weapons—something long and thin, but surely not a rifle, on this planet without copper or iron. . . .

Wace leaned forward and forced his tongue around the grunting syllables of Tyrlanian: "We are friends. Do you understand me?"

A string of totally foreign words snapped at him. He shrugged, ruefully, and spread his hands. The Diomedean moved across the hull—bipedal, body slanted forward to balance wings and tail—and found the stud to which the humans' lashings were anchored. Quickly, he knotted his own rope to the same place.

"A bowline," said van Rijn, almost quietly. "It makes me homesick."

At the other end of the line, they began to haul the canoe closer. The Diomedean turned to Wace and pointed at his vessel. Wace nodded, realized that the gesture was probably meaningless here, and took a precarious step in that direction. The Diomedean caught another rope flung to him. He pointed at it, and at the humans, and made gestures.

"I understand," said van Rijn. "Nearer than this they dare not come. Too easy their boat gets smashed against us. We get this cord tied around our bodies, and they haul us across. Good St. Christopher, what a thing to do to a poor creaky-boned old man!"

"There's our food, though," said Wace.

The skycruiser jerked and settled deeper. The Diomedean jittered nervously.

"No, no!" shouted van Rijn. He seemed under the impression that if he only bellowed loudly enough, he could penetrate the linguistic barrier. His arms windmilled. "*Nie!* Never! Do you not understand, you oatmeal brains? Better to guggle down in your pestbegotten ocean than try eating your food. We die! Bellyache! Suicide!" He pointed at his mouth, slapped his abdomen, and waved at the rations.

Wace reflected grimly that evolution was too flexible. Here you had a planet with oxygen, nitrogen, hydrogen, carbon, sulfur . . . a protein biochemistry forming genes, chromosomes, cells, tissues . . . protoplasm by any reasonable definition . . . and the human who tried to eat a fruit or steak from Diomedes would be dead ten minutes later of about fifty lethal allergic reactions. These just weren't the *right* proteins. In fact, only immunization shots prevented men from getting chronic hay fever, asthma, and hives, merely from the air they breathed or the water they drank.

He had spent many cold hours today piling the cruiser's food supplies out here, for transference to the raft. This luxury atmospheric vessel had been carried in van Rijn's spaceship, ready-stocked for extended picnic orgies when the mood struck him. There was enough rye bread, sweet butter, Edam cheese, lox, smoked turkey, dill pickles, fruit preserves, chocolate, plum pudding, beer, wine, and God knew what else, to keep three people going for a few months.

The Diomedean spread his wings, flapping them to maintain his footing. In the wan stormy light, the thumbs-turned-claws on their leading edge seemed to whicker past van Rijn's beaky face like a mowing machine operated by some modernistic Death. The merchant waited stolidly, now and then aiming a finger at the stacked cases. Finally the Diomedean got the idea, or simply gave in. There was scant time left. He whistled across to the canoe. A swarm of his fellows came over, undid the lashings and began transporting boxes. Wace helped Sandra fasten the rope about her. "I'm afraid it will be a wet haul, my lady," he tried to smile.

She sneezed. "So this is the brave pioneering between the stars! I will have a word or two for my court poets when I get home . . . if I do."

When she was across, and the rope had been flown back, van Rijn waved Wace ahead. He himself was arguing with the Diomedean chief. How it was done without a word of real language between them, Wace did not know, but they had reached the stage of screaming indignation at each other. Just as Wace set his teeth and went overboard, van Rijn sat mutinously down.

And when the younger man made his drowned-rat arrival on board the canoe, the merchant had evidently won his point. A Diomedean could air-lift about fifty kilos for short distances. Three of them improvised a rope sling and carried van Rijn over, above the water.

He had not yet reached the canoe when the sky-cruiser sank.

❧ IV ❧

The dugout held about a hundred natives, all armed, some wearing helmets and breastplates of hard laminated leather. A catapult, just visible through the dark, was mounted at the bows; the stern held a cabin, made from sapling trunks chinked with seaweed, that towered up almost like the rear end of a medieval caravel. On its roof, two helmsmen strained at the long tiller.

"Plain to see, we have found a navy ship," grunted van Rijn. "Not so good, that. With a trader, I can talk. With some pest-and-pox officer with gold braids on his brain, him I can only shout." He raised small, close-set eyes to a night heaven where lightning ramped. "I am a poor old sinner," he shouted, "but this I have not deserved! Do you hear me?"

After a while the humans were prodded between lithe devil-bodies, toward the cabin. The dugout had begun to run before the gale, on two reef points and a jib. The roll and pitch, clamor of waves and wind and thunder, had receded into the back of Wace's consciousness. He wanted only to find some place that was dry, take off his clothes and crawl into bed and sleep for a hundred years.

The cabin was small. Three humans and two Diomedeans left barely room to sit down. But it was warm, and a stone lamp hung from the ceiling threw a dim light full of grotesquely moving shadows.

The native who had first met them was present. His volcanic-glass dagger lay unsheathed in one hand, and he held a wary lion-crouch; but half his attention seemed aimed at the other one, who was leaner and older, with flecks of gray in the fur, and who was tied to a corner post by a rawhide leash.

Sandra's eyes narrowed. The blaster which van Rijn had lent her slid quietly to her lap as she sat down. The Diomedean with the knife flicked his gaze across it, and van Rijn swore. "You little all-thumbs brain, do you let him see what is a weapon?"

The first autochthon said something to the leashed one. The latter made a reply with a growl in it, then turned to the humans. When he spoke, it did not sound like the same language.

"So! An interpreter!" said van Rijn. "You speakee Angly, ha? Haw, haw, haw!" He slapped his thigh.

"No, wait. It's worth trying." Wace dropped into Tyrlanian: "Do you understand me? This is the only speech we could possibly have in common."

The captive raised his head-crest and sat up on his hands and haunches. What he answered was *almost* familiar. "Speak slowly, if you will," said Wace, and felt sleepiness drain out of him.

Meaning came through, thickly: "You do not use a version (?) of the Carnoi that I have heard before."

"Carnoi—" Wait, yes, one of the Tyrlanians had mentioned a confederation of tribes far to the south, bearing some such name. "I am using the tongue of the folk of Tyrlan."

"I know not that race (?). They do not winter in our grounds. Nor do any Carnoi as a regular (?) thing, but now and then when all are in the tropics (?) one of them happens by, so—" It faded into unintelligibility.

The Diomedean with the knife said something, impatiently, and got a curt answer. The interpreter said to Wace:

"I am Tolk, a *mochra* of the Lannachska—"

"A what of the what?" said Wace.

It is not easy even for two humans to converse, when it must be in different patois of a language foreign to both. The dense accents imposed by human vocal cords and Diomedean ears—they heard farther into the subsonic, but did not go quite so high in pitch, and the curve of maximum response was different—made it a slow and painful process indeed. Wace took an hour to get a few sentences' worth of information.

Tolk was a linguistic specialist of the Great Flock of Lannach; it was his function to learn every language that came to his tribe's attention, which were many. His title might, perhaps, be rendered Herald, for his duties included a good deal of ceremonial announcements and he presided over a corps of messengers. The Flock was at war with the Drak'honai, and Tolk had been captured in a recent skirmish. The other Diomedean present was named Delp, and was a high-ranking officer of the Drak'honai.

Wace postponed saying much about himself, less from a wish to be secretive than from a realization of how appalling a task it would be. He did ask Tolk to warn Delp that the food from the cruiser, while essential to Earthlings, would kill a Diomedean.

"And why should I tell him that?" asked Tolk, with a grin that was quite humanly unpleasant.

"If you don't," said Wace, "it may go hard with you when he learns that you did not."

"True." Tolk spoke to Delp. The officer made a quick response.

"He says you will not be harmed unless you yourselves make it necessary," explained Tolk. "He says you are to learn his language so he can talk with you himself."

"What was it now?" interrupted van Rijn.

Wace told him. Van Rijn exploded. "What? What does he say? Stay here till—Death and wet liver! I tell that filthy toad—" He half-rose to his feet. Delp's wings rattled together. His teeth showed. The door was flung open and a pair of guards looked in. One of them carried a tomahawk, another had a wooden rake set with chips of flint.

Van Rijn clapped a hand to his gun. Delp's voice crackled out. Tolk translated: "He says to be calm."

After more parley, and with considerable effort and guesswork on Wace's part: "He wishes you no harm, but he must think of his own people. You are something new. Perhaps you can help him, or perhaps you are so harmful that he dare not let you go. He must have time to find out. You will remove all your garments and implements, and leave them in his charge. You will be provided other clothing, since it appears you have no fur."

When Wace had interpreted for van Rijn, the merchant said, surprisingly at ease: "I think we have no choice just now. We can burn down many of them, *ja*. Maybe we can take the whole boat. But we cannot sail it all the way home by ourselves. If nothing else, we would starve en route, *nie*? Were I younger, yes, by good St. George, I would fight on general principles. Single-handed I would take him apart and play a xylophone on his ribs, and try to bluster his whole nation into helping me. But now I am too old and fat and tired. It is hard to be old, my boy—"

He wrinkled his sloping forehead and nodded in a wise fashion. "But, where there are enemies to bid against each other, that is where an honest trader has a chance to make a little bit profit!"

❀ V ❀

"First," said Wace, "you must understand that the world is shaped like a ball."

"Our philosophers have known it for a long time," said Delp complacently. "Even barbarians like the Lannach'-honai have an idea of the truth. After all, they cover thousands of obdisai every year, migrating. We're not so mobile, but we had to work out an astronomy before we could navigate very far."

Wace doubted that the Drak'honai could locate them-selves with great precision. It was astonishing what their neolithic technology had achieved, not only in stone but in glass and ceramics; they even molded a few synthetic resins. They had telescopes, a sort of astrolabe, and navi-gational tables based on sun, stars, and the two small moons. However, compass and chronometer require iron, which simply did not exist in any noticeable quantity on Diomedes.

Automatically, he noted a rich potential market. The primitive Tyrlanians were avid for simple tools and weapons of metal, paying exorbitantly in the furs, gems, and pharmaceutically useful juices which made this planet worth the attention of the Polesotechnic League. The Drak'honai could use more sophisticated amenities, from clocks and slide rules to Diesel engines—and were able to meet proportionately higher prices.

He recollected where he was: the raft *Gerunis,* headquarters of the Chief Executive Officer of the Fleet; and that the amiable creature who sat on the upper deck and talked with him was actually his jailer.

How long had it been since the crash—fifteen Diomedean days? That would be more than a week, Terrestrial reckoning. Several percent of the Earthside food was already eaten.

He had lashed himself into learning the Drak'ho tongue from his fellow-prisoner Tolk. It was fortunate that the League had, of necessity, long ago developed the principles by which instruction could be given in minimal time. When properly focused, a trained mind need only be told something once. Tolk himself used an almost identical system; he might never have seen metal, but the Herald was semantically sophisticated.

"Well, then," said Wace, still haltingly and with gaps in his vocabulary, but adequately for his purposes, "do you know that this world-ball goes around the sun?"

"Quite a few of the philosophers believe that," said Delp. "I'm a practical (?) one myself, and never cared much one way or another."

"The motion of your world is unusual. In fact, in many ways this is a freak place. Your sun is cooler and redder than ours, so your home is colder. This sun has a *mass* . . .

what do you say? . . . not much less than that of our own;
and it is about the same distance. Therefore Diomedes,
as we call your world, has a year only somewhat longer
than our Earth's. Seven hundred eighty-two Diomedean
days, isn't it? Diomedes has more than twice the diameter of Earth, but lacks the heavy materials found in most
worlds. Therefore its *gravity*—hell!—therefore I only
weigh about one-tenth more here than I would at home."

"I don't understand," said Delp.

"Oh, never mind," said Wace gloomily.

The planetographers were still puzzling about Diomedes. It didn't fall into either of the standard types, the
small hard ball like Earth or Mars, or the gas giant with
a collapsed core like Jupiter or 61 Cygni C. It was intermediate, with a mass of 4.75 Earths; but its overall density was only half as much. This was due to the nearly
total absence of all elements beyond calcium.

There was one sister freak, uninhabitable; the
remaining planets were more or less normal giants, the
sun a G8 dwarf not very different from other stars of
that size and temperature. It was theorized that because
of some improbable turbulence, or possibly an odd magnetic effect—a chance-created cosmic mass spectrograph
—no heavy elements had occurred in the local section
of the primordial gas cloud . . . But why hadn't there at
least been a density-increasing molecular collapse at the
center of Diomedes? Sheer mass-pressure ought to have
produced degeneracy. The most plausible answer to that
was, the minerals in the body of this world were not
normal ones, being formed in the absence of such elements as chromium, manganese, iron, and nickel. Their
crystal structure was apparently more stable than, say,

olivine, the most important of the Earth materials con-
densed by pressure—

The devil with it!

"Never mind that weight stuff," said Delp. "What's so
unusual about the motion of Ikt'hanis?" It was his name
for this planet, and did not mean "earth" but—in a language where nouns were compared—could be translated
"Oceanest," and was feminine.

Wace needed time to reply; the technicalities outran
his vocabulary.

It was merely that the axial tilt of Diomedes was almost
ninety degrees, so that the poles were virtually in the
ecliptic plane. But that fact, coupled with the cool ultra-
violet-poor sun, had set the pattern of life.

At either pole, nearly half the year was spent in total
night. The endless daylight of the other half did not really
compensate; there were polar species, but they were
unimpressive hibernators. Even at forty-five degrees latitude, a fourth of the year was darkness, in a winter grim-
mer than Earth had ever seen. That was as far north or
south as any intelligent Diomedeans could live; the
annual migration used up too much of their time and
energy, and they fell into a stagnant struggle for existence
on the paleolithic level.

Here, at thirty degrees north, the Absolute Winter
lasted one-sixth of the year—a shade over two Terrestrial
months—and it was only (!) a few weeks' flight to the
equatorial breeding grounds and back during that time.
Therefore the Lannachska were a fairly cultivated people. The Drak'honai were originally from even farther
south—

But you could only do so much without metals. Of
course, Diomedes had abundant magnesium, beryllium,

and aluminum, but what use was that unless you first developed electrolytic technology, which required copper or silver?

Delp cocked his head. "You mean it's always equinox on your Eart'?"

"Well, not quite. But by your standards, very nearly!"

"So that's why you haven't got wings. The Lodestar didn't give you any, because you don't need them."

"Uh . . . perhaps. They'd have been no use to us, anyway. Earth's air is too thin for a creature the size of you or me to fly under its own power."

"What do you mean, thin? Air is . . . is air."

"Oh, never mind. Take my word for it."

How did you explain gravitational potential to a non-human whose mathematics was about on Euclid's level? You could say: "Look, if you go sixty-three hundred kilometers upward from the surface of Earth, the attraction has dropped off to one-fourth; but you must go thirteen thousand kilometers upward from Diomedes to diminish its pull on you correspondingly. Therefore Diomedes can hold a great deal more air. The weaker solar radiation helps, to be sure, especially the relatively less ultraviolet. But on the whole, gravitational potential is the secret.

"In fact, so dense is this air that if it held proportionate amounts of oxygen, or even of nitrogen, it would poison me. Luckily, the Diomedean atmosphere is a full seventy-nine percent neon. Oxygen and nitrogen are lesser constituents: their partial pressures do not amount to very much more than on Earth. Likewise carbon dioxide and water vapor."

But Wace said only: "Let's talk about ourselves. Do you understand that the stars are other suns, like yours, but immensely farther away; and that Earth is a world of such a star?"

"Yes. I've heard the philosophers wonder—I'll believe you."

"Do you realize what our powers are, to cross the space between the stars? Do you know how we can reward you for your help in getting us home, and how our friends can punish you if you keep us here?"

For just a moment, Delp spread his wings, the fur bristled along his back and his eyes became flat yellow chips. He belonged to a proud folk.

Then he slumped. Across all gulfs of race, the human could sense how troubled he was:

"You told me yourself, Eart'ho, that you crossed The Ocean from the west, and in thousands of obdisai you didn't see so much as an island. It bears our own explorings out. We couldn't possibly fly that far, carrying you or just a message to your friends, without some place to stop and rest between times."

Wace nodded, slowly and carefully. "I see. And you couldn't take us back in a fast canoe before our food runs out."

"I'm afraid not. Even with favoring winds all the way, a boat is so much slower than wings. It'd take us half a year or more to sail the distance you speak of."

"But there must be *some* way—"

"Perhaps. But we're fighting a hard war, remember. We can't spare much effort or many workers for your sake.

"I don't think the Admiralty even intends to try."

❧ VI ❧

To the south was Lannach, an island the size of Britain. From it Holmenach, an archipelago, curved northward for some hundreds of kilometers, into regions still wintry. Thus the islands acted as boundary and shield: defining the Sea of Achan, protecting it from the great cold currents of The Ocean.

Here the Drak'honai lay.

Nicholas van Rijn stood on the main deck of the *Gerunis*, glaring eastward to the Fleet's main body. The roughly woven, roughly fitted coat and trousers which a Sailmaker had thrown together for him irritated a skin long used to more expensive fabrics. He was tired of sugar-cured ham and brandied peaches—though when such fare gave out, he would begin starving to death. The thought of being a captured chattel whose wishes nobody need consult was pure anguish. The reflection on how much money the company must be losing for lack of his personal supervision was almost as bad.

"Bah!" he rumbled. "If they would make it a goal of their policy to get us home, it could be done."

Sandra gave him a weary look. "And what shall the Lannachs be doing while the Drak'honai bend all their efforts to return us?" she answered. "It is still a close thing, this war of theirs. Drak'ho could lose it yet."

"Satan's hoof-and-mouth disease!" He waved a hairy fist in the air. "While they squabble about their stupid little territories, the Solar Spice & Liquors is losing a million credits a day!"

"The war happens to be a life-and-death matter for both sides," she said.

"Also for us. *Nie?*" He fumbled after a pipe, remembered that his meerschaums were on the sea bottom, and groaned. "When I find who it was stuck that bomb in my cruiser—" It did not occur to him to offer excuses for getting her into this. But then, perhaps it was she who had indirectly caused the trouble. "Well," he finished on a calmer note, "it is true we must settle matters here, I think. End the war for them so they can do important business like getting me home."

Sandra frowned across the bright sun-blink of waters. "Do you mean help the Drak'honai? I do not care for that so much. They are the aggressors. But then, they saw the wives and little ones hungry—" She sighed. "It is hard to unravel. Let such be so, then."

"Oh, no!" Van Rijn combed his goatee. "We help the other side. The Lannachska."

"What!" She stood back from the rail and dropped her jaw at him. "But . . . but—"

"You see," explained van Rijn, "I know a little something about politics. It is needful for an honest business-man seeking to make him a little hard-earned profit, else some louse-bound politician comes and taxes it from him for some idiot school or old-age pension. The politics here is not so different from what we do out in the galaxy. It is a culture of powerful aristocrats, this Fleet, but the balance of power lies with the throne—the Admiralty. Now the admiral is old, and his son the crown prince has more to say than is rightful. I waggle my ears at gossip—they forget how much better we hear than they, in this pea-soup-with-sausages atmosphere. I know. He is a hard-cooked one, him that T'heonax.

"So we help the Drak'honai win over the Flock. So what? They are already winning. The Flock is only mak-ing guerrilla now, in the wild parts of Lannach. They are still powerful, but the Fleet has the upper hand, and need only maintain *status quo* to win. Anyhow, what can we, who the good God did not offer wings, do at guerril-las? We show T'heonax how to use a blaster, well, how do we show him how to find somebodies to use it on?"

"Hm-m-m . . . yes." She nodded, stiffly. "You mean that we have nothing to offer the Drak'honai, except trade and treaty later on, if they get us home."

"Just so. And what hurry is there for them to meet the League? They are natural wary of unknowns like us from Earth. They like better to consolidate themselves in their new conquest before taking on powerful strangers, *nie?* I hear the scuttled butt, I tell you; I know the trend of thought about us. Maybe T'heonax lets us starve, or cuts our throats. Maybe he throws our stuff overboard and says later he never heard of us. Or maybe, when a League boat finds him at last, he says *ja,* we pulled some humans from the sea, and we was good to them, but we could not get them home in time."

"But could they—actually? I mean, Freeman van Rijn, how would *you* get us home, with any kind of Diomedean help?"

"Bah! Details! I am not an engineer. Engineers I hire. My job is not to do what is impossible, it is to make others do it for me. Only how can I organize things when I am only a more-than-half prisoner of a king who is not interested in meeting my peoples? Hah?"

"Whereas the Lannach tribe is hard pressed and will let you, what they say, write your own ticket. Yes." Sandra laughed, with a touch of genuine humor. "Very good, my friend! Only one question now, how do we get to the Lannachs?"

She waved a hand at their surroundings. It was not an encouraging view.

The *Gerunis* was a typical raft: a big structure, of light tough balsalike logs lashed together with enough open space and flexibility to yield before the sea. A wall of uprights, pegged to the transverse logs, defined a capacious hold and supported a main deck of painfully trimmed planks. Poop and forecastle rose at either end, their flat decks bearing artillery and, in the former case, the outsize tiller. Between them were seaweed-thatched cabins for storage, workshops, and living quarters. The overall dimensions were about sixty meters by fifteen, tapering toward a false bow which provided a catapult platform and some streamlining. A foremast and mainmast each carried three big square sails, a lateen-rigged mizzen stood just forward of the poop. Given a favoring wind—remembering the force of most winds on this planet—the seemingly awkward craft could make several knots, and even in a dead calm it could be rowed.

It held about a hundred Diomedeans plus wives and children. Of those, ten couples were aristocrats, with private apartments in the poop; twenty were ranking sailors, with special skills, entitled to one room per family in the main-deck cabins; the rest were common deckhands, barracked into the forecastle.

Not far away floated the rest of this squadron. There were rafts of various types, some primarily dwelling units like the Gerunis, some triple-decked for cargo, some bearing the long sheds in which fish and seaweed were processed. Often several at a time were linked together to form a little temporary island. Moored to them, or patrolling between, were the outrigger canoes. Wings beat in the sky, where aerial detachments kept watch for an enemy: full-time professional warriors, the core of Drak'ho's military strength.

Beyond this outlying squadron, the other divisions of the Fleet darkened the water as far as a man's eyes would reach. Most of them were fishing. It was brutally hard work, where long nets were trolled by muscle power. Nearly all a Drak'ho's life seemed to go to back-bending labor. But out of these fluid fields they were dragging a harvest which leaped and flashed.

"Like fiends they must drive themselves," observed van Rijn. He slapped the stout rail. "This is tough wood, even when green, and they chew it smooth with stone and glass tools! Some of these fellows I would like to hire, if the union busybodies can be kept away from them."

Sandra stamped her foot. She had not complained at danger of death, cold and discomfort and the drudgery of Tolk's language lessons filtered through Wace. But there are limits. "Either you talk sense, Freeman, or I go somewhere else! I asked you how we get away from here."

"We get rescued by the Lannachska, of course," said van Rijn. "Or, rather, they come steal us. Yes, so-fashion will be better. Then, if they fail, friend Delp cannot say it is our fault we are so desired by all parties."

Her tall form grew rigid. "What do you mean? How are they to know we are even here?"

"Maybe Tolk will tell them."

"But Tolk is even more a prisoner than we, not?"

"So. However—" van Rijn rubbed his hands. "We have a little plan made. He is a good head, him. Almost as good as me."

Sandra glared. "And will you deign to tell me how you plotted with Tolk, under enemy surveillance, when you cannot even speak Drak'ho?"

"Oh, I speak Drak'ho pretty good," said van Rijn blandly. "Did you not just hear me admit how I eavesdrop on all the palaver aboard? You think just because I make so much trouble, and still sit hours every day taking special instruction from Tolk, it is because I am a dumb old bell who cannot learn so easy? Horse maneuvers! Half the time we mumble together, he is teaching me his own Lannach lingo. Nobody on this raft knows it, so when they hear us say funny noises they think maybe Tolk tries words of Earth language out, ha? They think he despairs of teaching me through Wace and tries himself to pound some Drak'ho in me. Ho, ho, they are bamboozles, by damn! Why, yesterday I told Tolk a dirty joke in Lannachamael. He looked very disgusted. There is proof that poor old van Rijn is not fat between the ears. We say nothing of the rest of his anatomy."

Sandra stood quiet for a bit, trying to understand what it meant to learn two nonhuman languages simultaneously, one of them forbidden.

"I do not see why Tolk looks disgusted," mused van Rijn. "It was a good joke. Listen: there was a salesman who traveled on one of the colonial planets, and—"

"I can guess why," interrupted Sandra hastily. "I mean . . . why Tolk did not think it was a funny tale. Er . . . Freeman Wace was explaining it to me the other day. Here on Diomedes they have not the trait of, um, constant sexuality. They breed once each year only, in the tropics. No families in our sense. They would not think our"—she blushed—"our all-year-around interest in these questions was very normal or very polite."

Van Rijn nodded. "All this I know. But Tolk has seen somewhat of the Fleet, and in the Fleet they do have marriage, and get born at any time of year, same like humans."

"I got that impression," she answered slowly, "and it puzzles me. Freeman Wace said the breeding cycle was in their, their heredity. Instinct, or glands, or what it now is called. How *could* the Fleet live differently from what their glands dictate?"

"Well, they do." Van Rijn shrugged massive shoulders. "Maybe we let some scientist worry about it for a thesis later on, hah?"

Suddenly she gripped his arm so he winced. Her eyes were a green blaze. "But you have not said . . . what is to happen? How is Tolk to get word about us to Lannach? What do we do?"

"I have no idea," he told her cheerily. "I play with the ear."

He cocked a beady eye at the pale reddish overcast. Several kilometers away, enormously timbered, bearing what was almost a wooden castle, floated the flagship of all Drak'ho. A swirl of bat wings was lifting from it and streaming toward the *Gerunis*. Faintly down the sky was borne the screech of a blown sea shell.

"But I think maybe we find out quick," finished van Rijn, "because his rheumatic majesty comes here now to decide about us."

❧ VII ❧

The admiral's household troops, a hundred full-time warriors, landed with beautiful exactness and snapped their weapons to position. Polished stone and oiled leather caught the dull light like sea-blink; the wind of their wings roared across the deck. A purple banner trimmed with scarlet shook loose, and the *Gerunis* crew, respectfully crowded into the rigging and on the forecastle roof, let out a hoarse ritual cheer.

Delp hyr Orikan advanced from the poop and crouched before his lord. His wife, the beautiful Rodonis sa Axollon, and his two young children came behind him, bellies to the deck and wings over eyes. All wore the scarlet sashes and jeweled arm-bands which were formal dress.

The three humans stood beside Delp. Van Rijn had vetoed any suggestion that they crouch, too. "It is not right for a member of the Polesotechnic League, he should get down on knees and elbows. Anyway I am not built for it."

Tolk of Lannach sat haughty next to van Rijn. His wings were tucked into a net and the leash on his neck was held by a husky sailor. His eyes were as bleak and steady on the admiral as a snake's.

And the armed young males who formed a rough honor guard for Delp their captain had something of the same chill in their manner—not toward Syranax, but toward his son, the heir apparent on whom the admiral leaned. Their spears, rakes, tomahawks, and wood-bayoneted blowguns were held in a gesture of total respect: nevertheless, the weapons were held.

Wace thought that van Rijn's out-size nose must have an abnormal keenness for discord. Only now did he himself sense the tension on which his boss had obviously been counting.

Syranax cleared his throat, blinked, and pointed his muzzle at the humans. "Which one of you is captain?" he asked. It was still a deep voice, but it no longer came from the bottom of the lungs, and there was a mucous rattle in it.

Wace stepped forward. His answer was the one van Rijn had, hastily and without bothering to explain, commanded that he give: "The other male is our leader, sir. But he does not speak your language very well as yet. I myself still have trouble with it, so we must use this Lannach'ho prisoner to interpret."

T'heonax scowled. "How should he know what you want to say to us?"

"He has been teaching us your language," said Wace. "As you know, sir, foreign tongues are his main task in life. Because of this natural ability, as well as his special experience with us, he will often be able to guess what we may be trying to say when we search for a word."

"That sounds reasonable." Syranax's gray head wove about. "Yes."

"I wonder!" T'heonax gave Delp an ugly look. It was returned in spades.

"So! By damn, now I talk." Van Rijn rolled forward. "My good friend . . . um . . . er . . . *pokker,* what is the word?—my admiral, we, ahem, we talk-um like good brothers—good brothers, is that how I say-um, Tolk—?"

Wace winced. Despite what Sandra had whispered to him, as they were being hustled here to receive the visitors, he found it hard to believe that so ludicrous an accent and grammar were faked.

And why?

Syranax stirred impatiently. "It may be best if we talked through your companion," he suggested.

"Bilge and barnacles!" shouted van Rijn. "Him? No, no, me talk-um talky-talk self. Straight, like, um, er, what-is-your-title. We talk-um like brothers, ha?"

Syranax sighed. But it did not occur to him to overrule the human. An alien aristocrat was still an aristocrat, in the eyes of this caste-ridden society, and as such might surely claim the right to speak for himself.

"I would have visited you before," said the admiral, "but you could not have conversed with me, and there was so much else to do. As they grow more desperate, the Lannach'honai become more dangerous in their raids

and ambushes. Not a day goes by that we do not have
at least a minor battle."

"Hm-m-m?" van Rijn counted off the declension-com-
parison on his fingers. "*Xammagapai* . . . let me see, *xam-
magan, xammagai* . . . oh, yes. A small fight! I make-um
see no fights, old admiral—I mean, honored admiral."

T'heonax bristled. "Watch your tongue, Eart'ho!" he
clipped. He had been over frequently to stare at the
prisoners, and their sequestered possessions were in his
keeping. Little awe remained—but then, Wace decided,
T'heonax was not capable of admitting that a being could
possibly exist in any way superior to T'heonax.

"And yours, son," murmured Syranax. To van Rijn:
"Oh, they would scarcely venture this far out. I mean
our positions on the mainland are constantly harassed."

"Yes," nodded the Terrestrial, rather blankly.

Syranax lay down on the deck in an easy lion-pose.
T'heonax remained standing, taut in Delp's presence. "I
have, of course, been getting reports about you," went
on the admiral. "They are, ah, remarkable. Yes, remarkable. It's alleged you came from the stars."

"Stars, yes!" van Rijn's head bobbed with imbecilic
eagerness. "We from stars. Far far away."

"Is it true also that your people have established an
outpost on the other shore of The Ocean?"

Van Rijn went into a huddle with Tolk. The Lannacha
put the question into childish words. After several explanations, van Rijn beamed. "Yes, yes, we from across
Ocean. Far far away."

"Will your friends not come in search of you?"

"They look-um, yes, they look-um plenty hard. By Joe!
Look-um all over. You treat-um us good or our friends
find out and—" Van Rijn broke off, looking dismayed,
and conferred again with Tolk.

"I believe the Eart'ho wishes to apologize for tactlessness," explained the Herald dryly.

"It may be a truthful kind of tactlessness," observed
Syranax. "If his friends can, indeed, locate him while he
is still alive, much will depend on what kind of treatment
he received from us. Eh? The problem is, can they find
him that soon? What say, Eart'ho?" He pushed the last
question out like a spear.

Van Rijn retreated, lifting his hands as if to ward off
a blow. "Help!" he whined. "You help-um us, take us
home, old admiral . . . honored admiral . . . we go home
and pay-um many many fish."

T'heonax murmured in his father's ear: "The truth
comes out—not that I haven't suspected as much
already. His friends have no measurable chance of finding him before he starves. If they did, he wouldn't be
begging us for help. He'd be demanding whatever struck
his fancy."

"*I* would have done that in all events," said the admiral. "Our friend isn't very experienced in these matters,
eh? Well, it's good to know how easily truth can be
squeezed out of him."

"So," said T'heonax contemptuously, not bothering to
whisper, "the only problem is, to get some value out of
the beasts before they die."

Sandra's breath sucked sharply in. Wace grasped her
arm, opened his mouth, and caught van Rijn's hurried
Anglic murmur: "Shut up! Not a word, you bucket head!"
Whereupon the merchant resumed his timid smile and
attitude of straining puzzlement.

"It isn't right!" exploded Delp. "By the Lodestar, sir,
these are guests—not enemies—we can't just *use* them!"

"What else would you do?" shrugged T'heonax.

His father blinked and mumbled, as if weighing the arguments for both sides. Something like a spark jumped between Delp and T'heonax. It ran along the ranked lines of *Gerunis* crew-folk and household troopers as an imperceptible tautening, the barest ripple of muscle and forward slant of weapons.

Van Rijn seemed to get the drift all at once. He recoiled operatically, covered his eyes, then went to his knees before Delp. "No, no!" he screamed. "You take-um us home! You help-um us, we help-um you! You remember say how you help-um us if we help-um you!"

"What's this?"

It was a wild-animal snarl from T'heonax. He surged forward. "You've been bargaining with them, have you?"

"What do you mean?" The executive's teeth clashed together, centimeters from T'heonax's nose. His wing-spurs lifted like knives.

"What sort of help were these creatures going to give you?"

"What do you think?" Delp flung the gage into the winds, and crouched waiting.

T'heonax did not quite pick it up. "Some might guess you had ideas of getting rid of certain rivals within the Fleet," he purred.

In the silence which fell across the raft, Wace could hear how the dragon shapes up in the rigging breathed more swiftly. He could hear the creak of timbers and cables, the slap of waves and the low damp mumble of wind. Almost, he heard obsidian daggers being loosened in their sheaths.

If an unpopular prince finds an excuse to arrest a subordinate whom the commoners trust, there are likely going to be men who will fight. It was not otherwise here on Diomedes.

Syranax broke the explosive quiet. "There's some kind of misunderstanding," he said loudly. "Nobody is going to charge anyone with anything on the basis of this wing-less creature's gabble. What's the fuss about? What could he possibly do for any of us, anyway?"

"That remains to be seen," answered T'heonax. "But a race which can fly across The Ocean in less than an equinoctial day must know some handy arts."

He whirled on a quivering van Rijn. With the relish of the inquisitor whose suspect has broken, he said curtly: "Maybe we can get you home somehow if you help us. We are not sure how to get you home. Maybe your stuff can help us get you home. You show us how to use your stuff."

"Oh, yes!" said van Rijn. He clasped his hands and waggled his head. "Oh, yes, good sir, I do you want-um."

T'heonax clipped an order. A Drak'ho slithered across the deck with a large box. "I've been in charge of these things," explained the heir. "Haven't tried to fool with it, except for a few knives of that shimmery substance—" Momentarily, his eyes glowed with honest enthusiasm. "You've never *seen* such knives, father! They don't hack or grind, they slice! They'll carve seasoned wood!"

He opened the box. The ranking officers forgot dignity and crowded around. T'heonax waved them back. "Give this blubberpot room to demonstrate," he snapped. "Bowmen, blowgunners, cover him from all sides. Be ready to shoot if necessary."

Van Rijn took out a blaster.

"You mean to fight your way clear?" hissed Wace. "You can't!" He tried to step between Sandra and the menace of weapons which suddenly ringed them in. "They'll fill us with arrows before—"

"I know, I know," growled van Rijn *sotto voce*. "When will you young pridesters learn, just because he is old and lonely, the boss does not yet have teredos in the brain? You keep back, boy, and when trouble breaks loose, hit the deck and dig a hole."

"What? But—"

Van Rijn turned a broad back on him and said in broken Drak'ho, with servile eagerness: "Here a . . . how you call it? . . . thing. It make fire. It burn-um holes, by Joe."

"A portable flame thrower—that small?" For a moment, an edge of terror sharpened T'heonax's voice.

"I told you," said Delp, "we can gain more by dealing honorably with them. By the Lodestar, I think we could get them home, too, if we really tried!"

"You might wait till I'm dead, Delp, before taking the Admiralty," said Syranax. If he meant it as a joke, it fell like a bomb. The nearer sailors, who heard it, gasped. The household warriors touched their bows and blowguns. Rodonis sa Axollon spread her wings over her children and snarled. Deckhand females, jammed into the forecastle, let out a whimper of half-comprehending fear.

Delp himself steadied matters. "Quiet!" he bawled. "Belay there! Calm down! By all the devils in the Rainy Stars, have these creatures driven us crazy?"

"See," chattered van Rijn, "take *blaster* . . . we call-um *blaster* . . . pull-um here—"

The ion beam stabbed out and crashed into the mainmast. Van Rijn yanked it away at once, but it had already made a gouge centimeters deep in that tough wood. Its blue-white flame licked across the deck, whiffed a coiled cable into smoke, and took a section out of the rail, before he released the trigger.

The Drak'honai roared!

It was minutes before they had settled back into the shrouds or onto the decks; curiosity seekers from nearby craft still speckled the sky. However, they were technologically sophisticated in their way. They were excited rather than frightened.

"Let me see that!" T'heonax snatched at the gun.

"Wait, Wait, good sir, wait." Van Rijn snapped open the chamber, in a set of movements screened by his thick hands, and popped out the charge. "Make-um safe first. There."

T'heonax turned it over and over. "What a weapon!" he breathed. "What a *weapon*!"

Standing there in a frosty sweat, waiting for van Rijn to spoon up whatever variety of hell he was cooking, Wace still managed to reflect that the Drak'honai were overestimating. Natural enough, of course. But a gun of this sort would only have a serious effect on ground-fighting tactics—and the old sharper was coolly disarming all the blasters anyway, no uninstructed Diomedean was going to get any value from them—

"I make safe," van Rijn burbled. "One, two, three, four, five I make safe. . . . Four? Five? Six?" He began turning over the piled-up clothes, blankets, heaters, campstove, and other equipment "Where other three blasters?"

"What other three?" T'heonax stared at him.

"We have six." Van Rijn counted carefully on his fingers. "*Ja*, six. I give-um all to good sir Delp here."

"WHAT?"

Delp leaped at the human, cursing. "That's a lie! There were only three, and you've got them here!"

"Help!" Van Rijn scuttled behind T'heonax. Delp's body clipped the admiral's son. Both Drak'honai went over in a whirl of wings and tails.

"He's plotting mutiny!" screamed T'heonax.

Wace threw Sandra to the deck and himself above her. The air grew dense with missiles.

Van Rijn turned ponderously to grab the sailor in charge of Tolk. But that Drak'ho had already sprung away to Delp's defense. Van Rijn had only to peel off the imprisoning net.

"Now," he said in fluent Lannachamael, "go bring an army to fetch us out of here. Quick, before someone notices!"

The Herald nodded, threshed his wings, and was gone into a sky where battle ran loose.

Van Rijn stooped over Wace and Sandra. "This way," he panted under the racket. A chance tail-buffet, as a sailor fought two troopers, brought a howl from him. "Thunder and lightning! Pest and poison ivy!" He wrestled Sandra to her feet and hustled her toward the comparative shelter of the forecastle.

When they stood inside its door, among terrified females and cubs, looking out at the fight, he said:

"It is a pity that Delp will go under. He has no chance. He is a decent sort; we could maybe have done business."

"All saints in Heaven!" choked Wace. "You touched off a civil war just to get your messenger away?"

"You know perhaps a better method?" asked van Rijn.

❂ VIII ❂

When Commander Krakna fell in battle against the invaders, the Flock's General Council picked one Trolwen to succeed him. They were the elders, and their choice comparatively youthful, but the Lannachska thought it only natural to be led by young males. A commander needed the physical stamina of two, to see them through a hard and dangerous migration every year; he seldom lived to grow feeble. Any rash impulses of his age were curbed by the General Council itself, the clan leaders who had grown too old to fly at the head of their squadron-septs and not yet so old and weak as to be left behind on some winter journey.

Trolwen's mother belonged to the Trekkan group, a distinguished bloodline with rich properties on Lannach; she herself had added to that wealth by shrewd trading. She guessed that his father was Tornak of the Wendru—not that she cared especially, but Trolwen looked noticeably like that fierce warrior. However, it was his own record as a clan-elected officer, in storm and battle and negotiation and everyday routine, which caused the Council to pick him as leader of all the clans. In the ten-days since, he had been the chief of a losing cause; but possibly his folk were pressed back into the uplands more slowly than would have happened without him.

Now he led a major part of the Flock's fighting strength out against the Fleet itself.

Vernal equinox was barely past, but already the days lengthened with giant strides; each morning the sun rose farther north, and a milder air melted the snows until Lannach's dales were a watery brawling. It took only one hundred thirty days from equinox to Last Sunrise—thereafter, during the endless light of High Summer, there would be nothing but rain or mist to cover an attack.

And if the Drakska were not whipped by autumn, reflected Trolwen grimly, there would be no point in trying further; the Flock would be done.

His wings thrust steadily at the sky, the easy strength-hoarding beat of a wanderer born. Under him reached a broken white mystery of cloud, with the sea far beneath it peering through in a glimmer like polished glass; overhead lay a clear violet-blue roof, the night and the stars. Both moons were up, hasty Flichtan driving from horizon to horizon in a day and a half, Nua so much slower that her phases moved more rapidly than herself. He drew the cold, flowing darkness into his lungs, felt the thrust in muscles and the ripple in fur, but without the sensuous enjoyment of an ordinary flight.

He was thinking too hard about killing.

A commander should not show indecision, but he was young and gray. Tolk the Herald would understand. "How shall we know that these beings are on the same raft as when you left?" he asked. He spoke in the measured, breath-conserving rhythm of a route flight. The wind muttered beneath his words.

"We cannot be sure, of course, Flockchief," replied Tolk. "But the fat one considered that possibility, too. He said he would manage, somehow, to be out on deck in plain view every day at sunrise."

"Perhaps, though," worried Trolwen, "the Draka authorities will have locked him away, suspecting his help in your escape."

"What he did was probably not noticed in the turmoil," said Tolk.

"And perhaps he cannot help us after all." Trolwen shivered. The Council had spoken strongly against this raid: too risky, too many certain casualties. The turbulent clans had roared their own disapproval. He had had difficulty persuading them.

And if it turned out he was throwing away lives on something as grotesque as this, for no good purpose—Trolwen was as patriotic as any young male whose folk have been cruelly attacked; but he was not unconcerned about his own future. It had happened in the past that commanders who failed badly were read forever out of the Flock, like any common thief or murderer.

He flew onward.

A chill thin light had been stealing into the sky for a time. Now the higher clouds began to flush red, and a gleam went over the half-hidden sea. It was crucial to reach the Fleet at just about this moment, enough light to see what to do and not enough to give the enemy ample warning.

A Whistler, with the slim frame and outsize wings of adolescence, emerged from a fog-bank. The shrill notes of his lips carried far and keenly. Tolk, who as Chief Herald guided the education of these messenger-scouts, cocked his head and nodded. "We guessed it very well," he said calmly. "The rafts are only five buaska ahead."

"So I hear." Tension shook Trolwen's voice. "Now—"

He broke off. More of the youths were beating upwind into view, faster than an adult could fly. Their whistles wove into an exuberant battle music. Trolwen read the code like his own speech, clamped jaws together, and waved a hand at his standard bearer. Then he dove.

As he burst through the clouds, he saw the Fleet spread enormous, still far below him but covering the waters, from those islands called The Pups to the rich eastern driss banks. Decks and decks and decks cradled on a purplish-gray calm, masts raked upward like teeth, the dawn-light smote the admiral's floating castle and burned off his banner. There was an explosion skyward from rafts and canoes, as the Drak'honai heard the yells of their own sentries and went to arms.

Trolwen folded his wings and stooped. Behind him, in a wedge of clan-squadrons, roared three thousand Lannacha males. Even as he fell, he glared in search— where was that double-cursed Eart'a monster—*there!* The distance-devouring vision of a flying animal picked out three ugly shapes on a raft's quarterdeck, waving and jumping about.

Trolwen spread his wings to brake. "Here!" he cried. The standard bearer glided to a stop, hovered, and unfurled the red flag of Command. The squadrons changed from wedge to battle formation, peeled off, and dove for the raft.

The Drakska were forming their own ranks with terrifying speed and discipline. "All smoke-snuffing gods!" groaned Trolwen. "If we could just have used a single squadron—a raid, not a full-scale battle—"

"A single squadron could hardly have brought the Eart'ska back alive, Flockchief," said Tolk. "Not from the very core of the enemy. We have to make it seem . . . not worth their while . . . to keep up the engagement, when we retreat."

"They know ghostly well what we've come for," said Trolwen. "Look how they swarm to that raft!"

The Flock troop had now punched through a shaken line of Draka patrols and reached water surface. One detachment attacked the target vessel, landed in a ring around the humans and then struck out to seize the entire craft. The rest stayed airborne to repel the enemy's counter-assault.

It was simple, clumsy ground fighting on deck. Both sides were similarly equipped: weapon technology seems to diffuse faster than any other kind. Wooden swords set with chips of flint, fire-hardened spears, clubs, daggers, tomahawks, struck small wicker shields and leather harness. Tails smacked out, talons ripped, wings buffeted and cut with horny spurs, teeth closed in throats, fists battered on flesh. Hard-pressed, a male would fly upward—there was little attempt to keep ranks, it was a free-for-all. Trolwen had no special interest in that phase of the battle: having landed superior numbers, he knew he could take the raft, if only his aerial squadrons could keep the remaining Drakska off.

He thought—conventionally, in the wake of a thousand bards—how much like a dance a battle in the air was: intricate, beautiful, and terrible. To co-ordinate the efforts of a thousand or more warriors awing reached the highest levels of art.

The backbone of such a force was the archers. Each gripped a bow as long as himself in his foot talons, drew the cord with both hands and let fly, plucked a fresh arrow from the belly quiver with his teeth and had it ready to nock before the string snapped taut. Such a corps, trained almost from birth, could lay down a curtain which none might cross alive. But after the whistling death was spent, as it soon was, they must stream back to the bearers for more arrows. That was the most vulnerable aspect of their work, and the rest of the army existed to guard it.

Some cast bolas, some the heavy sharp-edged boomerang, some the weighted net in which a wing-tangled foe could plunge to his death. Blowguns were a recent innovation, observed among foreign tribes in the tropical meeting places. Here the Drakska were ahead: their guns had a bolt-operated repeater mechanism and fire-hardened wooden bayonets. Also, the separate military units in the Fleet were more tightly organized.

On the other hand, they still relied on an awkward set of horn calls to integrate their entire army. Infinitely more flexible, the Whistler corps darted from leader to leader, weaving the Flock into one great wild organism.

Up and down the battle ramped, while the sun rose and the clouds broke apart and the sea grew red-stained. Trolwen clipped his orders: Hunlu to reinforce the upper right flank, Torcha to feint at the admiral's raft while Srygen charged on the opposite wing—

But the Fleet was here, thought Trolwen bleakly, with all its arsenals: more missiles than his fliers, who were outnumbered anyway, could ever have carried. If this fight wasn't broken off soon—

The raft with the Eart'ska had now been seized. Draka canoes were approaching to win it back. One of them opened up with fire weapons: the dreaded, irresistible burning oil of the Fleet, pumped from a ceramic nozzle; catapults throwing vases of the stuff which exploded in gouts of flame on impact. Those were the weapons which had annihilated the boats owned by the Flock, and taken its coastal towns. Trolwen cursed with a reflex anguish when he saw.

But the Eart'ska were off the raft, six strong porters carrying each one in a specially woven net. By changing bearers often, those burdens could be taken to the Flock's mountain stronghold. The food boxes, hastily dragged up from the hold, were less difficult—one porter to each. A Whistler warbled success.

"Let's go!" Orders rattled from Trolwen, his messengers swooped to the appropriate squadrons. "Hunlu and

Srygen, close ranks about the bearers; Dwarn fly above with half his command, the other half guard the left wing. Rearguards—"

The morning was perceptibly further along before he had disengaged. His nightmare had been that the larger Fleet forces would pursue. A running battle all the way home could have snapped the spine of his army. But as soon as he was plainly in retreat, the enemy broke contact and retired to decks.

"As you predicted, Tolk," panted Trolwen.

"Well, Flockchief," said the Herald with his usual calm, "they themselves wouldn't be anxious for such a melee. It would overextend them, leave their rafts virtually defenseless—for all they know, your whole idea was to lure them into such a move. So they have merely decided that the Eart'ska aren't worth the trouble and risk: an opinion which the Eart'ska themselves must have been busily cultivating in them."

"Let's hope it's not a correct belief. But however the gods decree, Tolk . . . you still foresaw this outcome. Maybe you should be Commander."

"Oh, no. Not I. It was the fat Eart'ska who predicted this—in detail."

Trolwen laughed, "Perhaps, then, he should command."

"Perhaps," said Tolk, very thoughtfully, "he will."

❈ IX ❈

The northern coast of Lannach sloped in broad valleys to the Sea of Achan; and here, in game-filled forests and on grassy downs, had arisen those thorps in which the

Flock's clans customarily dwelt. Where Sagna Bay made its deep cut into the land, many such hamlets had grown together into larger units. Thus the towns came to be, Ulwen and flinty Mannenach and Yo of the Carpenters.

But their doors were broken down and their roofs burned open; Drak'ho canoes lay on Sagna's beaches, Drak'ho war-bands laired in empty Ulwen and patrolled the Anch Forest and rounded up the hornbeast herds emerging from winter sleep on Duna Brae.

Its boats sunk, its houses taken, and its hunting and fishing grounds cut off, the Flock retired into the uplands. On the quaking lava slopes of Mount Oborch or in the cold canyons of the Misty Mountains, there were a few small settlements where the poorer clans had lived. The females, the very old and the very young could be crowded into these; tents could be pitched and caves occupied. By scouring this gaunt country from Haik Heath to the Ness, and by going often hungry, the whole Flock could stay alive for a while longer.

But the heart of Lannach was the north coast, which the Drak'honai now forbade. Without it, the Flock was nothing, a starveling tribe of savages . . . until autumn, when Birthtime would leave them altogether helpless.

"It is not well," said Trolwen inadequately.

He strode up a narrow trail, toward the village—what was its name now? Salmenbrok—which perched on the jagged crest above. Beyond that, dark volcanic rock still streaked with snowfields climbed dizzily upward to a crater hidden in its own vapors. The ground shivered underfoot, just a bit, and van Rijn heard a rumble in the guts of the planet.

Poor isostatic balance . . . to be expected under these low-density conditions . . . a geologic history of overly-rapid change, earthquake, eruption, flood, and new lands coughed up from the sea bottom in a mere thousand decades . . . hence, in spite of all the water, a catastrophically uneven climate—

He wrapped the stinking fur blanket they had given him more closely around his rough-coated frame, blew on numbed hands, peered into the damp sky for a glimpse of sun, and swore.

This was no place for a man his age and girth. He should be at home, in his own deeply indented armchair, with a good cigar, a tall drink and the gardens of Jakarta flaming around him. For a moment, the remembrance of Earth was so sharp that he snuffled in self-pity. It was bitter to leave his bones in this nightmare land, when he had thought to pull Earth's soft green turf about his weary body. . . . Hard and cruel, yes, and every day the company must be getting deeper into the red ink without him there to oversee! That hauled him back to practicalities.

"Let me get this all clear in my head," he requested. He found himself rather more at home in Lannachamael than he had been—even without faking—in the Drak'ho speech. Here, by chance, the grammar and the guttural noises were not too far from his mother tongue. Already he approached fluency.

"You came back from your migration and found the enemy was here waiting for you?" he continued.

Trolwen jerked his head in a harsh and painful gesture. "Yes. Hitherto we had only known vaguely of their existence; their home regions are well to the southeast of ours. We knew they had been forced to leave because suddenly the trech—the fish which are the mainstay of their diet—had altered their own habits, shifting from Draka waters to Achan. But we had no idea the Fleet was bound for our country."

Van Rijn's long hair swished, lank and greasy-black, the careful curls all gone out of it, as he nodded. "It is like home history. In the Middle Ages on Earth, when the herring changed their ways for some begobbled herring reason, it would change the history of maritime countries. Kings would fall, by damn, and wars would be fought over the new fishing grounds."

"It has never been of great importance to us," said Trolwen. "A few clans in the Sagna region have . . . had small dugouts and got much of their food with hook and line. None of this beast-labor the Drakska go through, dragging those nets, even if they do pull in more fish! But for our folk generally, it was a minor thing. To be sure, we were pleased, several years ago, when the trech appeared in great numbers in the Sea of Achan. It is large and tasty, its oil and bones have many uses. But it was not such an occasion for rejoicing as if . . . oh, as if the wild hornbeasts had doubled their herds overnight."

His fingers closed convulsively on the handle of his tomahawk. He was, after all, quite young. "Now I see the gods sent the trech to us in anger and mockery. For the Fleet followed the trech."

Van Rijn paused on the trail, wheezing till he drowned out the distant lava rumbles. "Whoof! Hold it there, you! Not so like a God-forgotten horse race, if you please—Ah. If the fish are not so great for you, why not let the Fleet have the Achan waters?"

It was, he knew, not a true question: only a stimulus. Trolwen delivered himself of several explosive obscenities before answering, "They attacked us the moment we came home this spring. They had already occupied our coastlands! And even had they not done so, would you let a powerful horde of . . . strangers . . . whose very habits are alien and evil . . . would you let them dwell at your windowsill? How long could such an arrangement last?"

Van Rijn nodded again. Just suppose a nation with tyrant government and filthy personal lives were to ask for the Moon, on the grounds that they needed it and it was not of large value to Earth—Personally, he could afford to be tolerant. In many ways, the Drak'honai were closer to the human norm than the Lannachska. Their master-serf culture was a natural consequence of economics: given only neolithic tools, a raft big enough to support several families represented an enormous capital investment. It was simply not possible for disgruntled individuals to strike out on their own; they were at the mercy of the State. In such cases, power always concentrates in the hands of aristocratic warriors and intellectual priesthoods; among the Drak'honai, those two classes had merged into one.

The Lannachska, on the other hand—more typically Diomedean—were primarily hunters. They had very few highly specialized craftsmen; the individual could survive using tools made by himself. The low calorie/area factor of a hunting economy made them spread out thin over a large region, each small group nearly independent of the rest. They exerted themselves in spasms, during the chase for instance; but they did not have to toil day after day until they nearly dropped, as the common netman or oarsman or deckhand must in the Fleet—hence there was no economic justification on Lannach for a class of bosses and overseers.

Thus, their natural political unit was the little matrilineal clan. Such semiformal blood groups, almost free of government, were rather loosely organized into the

Great Flock. And the Flock's *raison d'etre*—apart from minor inter-sept business at home—was simply to increase the safety of all when every Diomedean on Lannach flew south for the winter.

Or came home to war!

"It is interesting," murmured van Rijn, half in Anglic. "Among our peoples, like on most planets, only the agriculture folk got civilized. Here they make no farms at all: the big half-wild hornbeast herds is closest thing, *nie?* You hunt, berry-pick, reap wild grain, fish a little—yet some of you know writing and make books; I see you have machines and houses, and weave cloth. Could be, the every-year stimulus of meeting foreigners in the tropics gives you ideas?"

"What?" asked Trolwen vaguely.

"Nothings. I just wondered, me, why—since life here is easy enough so you have time for making civilization —you do not grow so many you eat up all your game and chop down all your woods. That is what we called a successful civilization back on Earth."

"Our numbers do not increase fast," said Trolwen. "About three hundred years ago, a daughter Flock was formed and moved elsewhere, but the increase is very slow. We lose so many on the migrations, you see—storm, exhaustion, sickness, barbarian attack, wild animals, sometimes cold or famine—" He hunched his wings, the Diomedean equivalent of a shrug.

"Ah-ha! Natural selection. Which is all well and good, if nature is obliging to pick you for survival. Otherwise gives awful noises about tragedy." Van Rijn stroked his goatee. The chins beneath it were getting bristly as his last application of antibeard enzyme wore off. "So. It does give one notion of what made your race get brains.

Hibernate or migrate! And if you migrate, then be smart enough to meet all kinds trouble, by damn."

He resumed his noisy walk up the trail. "But we got our troubles of now to think about, especially since they are too the troubles belonging with Nicholas van Rijn. Which is not to be stood. Hmpf! Well, now, tell me more. I gather the Fleet scrubbed its decks with you and kicked you up here where the only flat country is the map. You want home to the lowlands again. You also want to get rid of the Fleet."

"We gave them a good fight," said Trolwen stiffly. "We still can—and will, by my grandmother's ghost! There were reasons why we were defeated so badly. We came tired and hungry back from ten-days of flight; one is always weak at the end of the springtime journey home. Our strongholds had already been occupied. The Draka flamethrowers set afire such other defenses as we contrived, and made it impossible for us to fight them on the water, where their real strength lies."

His teeth snapped together in a carnivore reflex. "And we have to overcome them soon! If we don't we are finished. And they know it!"

"I am not clear over this yet," admitted van Rijn. "The hurry is that all your young are born the same time, *nie?*"

"Yes." Trolwen topped the rise and waited beneath the walls of Salmenbrok for his puffing guest.

Like every Lannachska settlement, it was fortified against enemies, animal or intelligent. There was no stockade—that would be pointless here where all the higher life-forms had wings. An average building was roughly in the shape of an ancient Terrestrial block-house. The ground floor was doorless and had mere slits for windows; entrance was through an upper story or a trap in the thatched roof. A hamlet was fortified not by outer walls but by being woven together with covered bridges and underground passages.

Up here, above timberline, the houses were of undressed stone mortared in place, rather than the logs more common among the valley clans. But this thorp was solidly made, furnished with a degree of comfort that indicated how bountiful the lowlands must be.

Van Rijn took time to admire such features as wooden locks constructed like Chinese puzzles, a wooden lathe set with a cutting edge of painstakingly fractured diamond, and a wooden saw whose teeth were of renewable volcanic glass. A communal windmill ground nuts and wild grain, as well as powering numerous smaller machines; it included a pump which filled a great stone basin in the overhanging cliff with water, and the water could be let down again to keep the mill turning when there was no wind. He even saw a tiny sail-propelled railroad, with wooden-wheeled basketwork carts running on iron-hard wooden rails. It carried flint and obsidian from the local quarries, timber from the forests, dried fish from the lowlands, handicrafts from all the island. Van Rijn was delighted.

"So!" he said. "Commerce! You are fundamentally capitalists. Ha, by damn, I think soon we do some business!"

Trolwen shrugged. "There is nearly always a strong wind up here. Why should we not let it take our burdens? Actually, all the apparatus you see took many lifetimes to complete—we're not like those Drakska, wearing themselves out with labor."

Salmenbrok's temporary population crowded about the human, with mumbling and twittering and wing-flapping, the cubs twisting around his legs and their mothers shrieking at them to come back. "Ten thousand purple devils!" he choked. "They think maybe I am a politician to kiss their brats, ha?"

"Come this way," said Trolwen. "Toward the Males' Temple—females and young may not follow, they have their own." He led the way along another path, making an elaborate salute to a small idol in a niche on the trail. From its crudity, the thing had been carved centuries ago. The Flock seemed to have only a rather incoherent polytheism for religion, and not to take that very seriously these days; but it was as strict about ritual and tradition as some classic British regiment—which, in many ways, it resembled.

Van Rijn trudged after, casting a glance behind. The females here looked little different from those in the Fleet: a bit smaller and slimmer than the males, their wings larger but without a fully developed spur. In fact, racially the two folk seemed identical.

And yet, if all that the company's agents had learned about Diomedes was not pure gibberish, the Drak'honai represented a biological monstrousness. An impossibility!

Trolwen followed the man's curious gaze, and sighed. "You can notice nearly half our nubile females are expecting their next cub."

"Hm-m-m. *Ja*, there is your problem. Let me see if I understand it right. Your young are all born at the fall equinox—"

"Yes. Within a few days of each other; the exceptions are negligible."

"But it is not so many ten-days thereafter you must leave for the south. Surely a new baby cannot fly?"

"Oh, no. It clings to the mother all the way; it is born with arms able to grasp hard. There is no cub from the preceding year; a nursing female does not get pregnant. Her two-year-old is strong enough to fly the distance, given rest periods in which it rides on someone's back—though that's the age group where we suffer the most loss. Three-year-olds and above need only be guided and guarded: their wings are quite adequate."

"But this makes much trouble for the mother, not so?"

"She is assisted by the half-grown clan members, or the old who are past childbearing but not yet too old to survive the journey. And the males, of course, do all the hunting, scouting, fighting, and so forth."

"So. You come to the south. I hear told it makes easy to live there, nuts and fruits and fish to scoop from the water. Why do you come back?"

"This is our home," said Trolwen simply.

After a moment: "And, of course, the tropic islands could never support the myriads which gather there each midwinter—twice a year, actually. By the time the migrants are ready to leave, they have eaten that country bare."

"I see. Well, keep on. In the south, at solstice time, is when you rut."

"Yes. The desire comes on us—but you know what I mean."

"Of course," said van Rijn blandly.

"And there are festivals, and trading with the other tribes . . . frolic or fight—" The Lannacha sighed. "Enough. Soon after solstice, we return, arriving here sometime before equinox, when the large animals on which we chiefly depend have awoken from their winter sleep and put on a little flesh. There you have the pattern of our lives, Eart'ho."

"It sounds like fun, if I was not too old and fat." Van Rijn blew his nose lugubriously. "Do not get old, Trolwen. It is so lonesome. You are lucky, dying on migration when you grow feeble, you do not live wheezy and helpless with nothing but your dear memories, like me."

"I'm not likely to get old as matters stand now," said Trolwen.

"When your young are born, all at once in the fall . . . *ja*," mused van Rijn, "I can see how then is time for nothing much but obstetrics. And if you have not food and shelter and such helps ready, most of the young die—"

"They are replaceable," said Trolwen, with a degree of casualness that showed he was, after all, not just a man winged and tailed. His tone sharpened. "But the females who bear them are more vital to our strength. A recent mother must be properly rested and fed, you understand, or she will never reach the south—and consider what a part of our total numbers are going to become mothers. It's a question of the Flock's survival as a nation! And those filthy Drakska, breeding the year round like . . . like fish. . . . *No!*"

"No indeed," said van Rijn. "Best we think of somethings very fast, or I grow very hungry, too."

"I spent lives to rescue you," said Trolwen, "because we all hoped you would think of something yourself."

"Well," said van Rijn, "the problem is to get word to my own people at Thursday Landing. Then they come here quick, by damn, and I will tell them to clean up on the Fleet."

Trolwen smiled. Even allowing for the unhuman shape of his mouth, it was a smile without warmth or humor. "No, no," he said. "Not that easily. I dare not, cannot spare the folk, or the time and effort, in some crazy attempt to cross The Ocean . . . not while Drak'ho has us by the throat. Also—forgive me—how do I know that you will be interested in helping us, once you are able to go home again?"

He looked away from his companion, toward the porti-coed cave that was the Males' Temple. Steam rolled from its mouth, there was the hiss of a geyser within.

"I myself might have decided otherwise," he added abruptly, in a very low voice. "But I have only limited powers—any plan of mine—the Council—do you see? The Council is suspicious of three wingless monsters. It thinks . . . we know so little about you . . . our only sure hold on you is your own desperation . . . the Council will allow no help to be brought for you until the war is over."

Van Rijn lifted his shoulders and spread his hands. "Confidential, Trolwen, boy, in their place I would do the same."

❧ X ❧

Now darkness waned. Soon there would be light nights, when the sun hovered just under the sea and the sky was like white blossoms. Already both moons could be seen in full phase after sunset. As Rodonis stepped from her cabin, swift Sk'huanax climbed the horizon and swung up among the many stars toward slow and patient Lykaris. Between them, She Who Waits and He Who Pursues cast a shuddering double bridge over broad waters.

Rodonis was born to the old nobility, and had been taught to smile at Moons worship. Good enough for the

common sailors, who would otherwise go back to their
primitive bloody sacrifices to Aeak'ha-in-the-Deeps, but
really, an educated person knew there was only the
Lodestar. . . . Nevertheless, Rodonis went down on the
deck, hooded herself with her wings, and whispered her
trouble to bright mother Lykaris.

"A song do I pledge you, a song all for yourself, to be
made by the Fleet's finest bards and sung in your honor
when next you hold wedding with He Who Pursues you.
You will not wed Him again for more than a year, the
astrologues tell me; there will be time enough to fashion
a song for you which shall live while the Fleet remains
afloat, O Lykaris: if but you will spare me my Delp."

She did not address Sk'huanax the Warrior, any more
than a male Drak'ho would have dreamed of petitioning
the Mother. But she said to Lykaris in her mind, that
there could be no harm in calling to his attention the
fact that Delp was a brave person who had never omitted
the proper offerings.

The moons brightened. A bank of cloud in the west
bulked like frosty mountains. Far off stood the ragged
loom of an island, and she could hear pack ice cough in
the north. It was a big strange seascape, this was not the
clear green Southwater whence starvation had driven the
Fleet and she wondered if Achan's gods would ever let
the Drak'honai call it home.

The *lap-lap* of waves, creaking timbers, cables that
sang as the dew tautened them, wind-mumble in
shrouds, a slatting sail, the remote plaintiveness of a flute
and the nearer homely noises from this raft's own forecastle, snores and cub-whimpers and some couple's satisfied grunt . . . were a strong steady comfort in this cold
emptiness named Achan Sea. She thought of her own

young, two small furry shapes in a richly tapestried bed, and it gave her the remaining strength needed. She spread her wings and mounted the air.

From above, the Fleet at night was all clumps of shadow, with the rare twinkle of firepots where some crew worked late. Most were long abed, worn out from a day of dragging nets, manning sweeps and capstans, cleaning and salting and pickling the catch, furling and unfurling the heavy sails of the rafts, harvesting driss and fruitweed, felling trees and shaping timber with stone tools. A common crew member, male or female, had little in life except hard brutal labor. Their recreations were almost as coarse and violent: the dances, the athletic contests, the endless lovemaking, the bawdy songs roared out from full lungs over a barrel of seagrain beer.

For a moment, as such thoughts crossed her mind, Rodonis felt pride in her crewfolk. To the average noble, a commoner was a domestic animal, ill-mannered, unlettered, not quite decent, to be kept in line by whip and hook for his own good. But flying over the great sleeping beast of a Fleet, Rodonis sensed its sheer vigor, coiled like a snake beneath her—these were the lords of the sea, and Drak'ho's haughty banners were raised on the backs of Drak'ho's lusty deckhands.

Perhaps it was simply that her own husband's ancestors had risen from the forecastle not many generations back. She had seen him help his crew often enough, working side by side with them in storm or fish run; she had learned it was no disgrace to swing a quernstone or set up a massive loom for herself.

If labor was pleasing to the Lodestar, as the holy books said, then why should Drak'ho nobles consider it distasteful? There was something bloodless about the old families, something not quite healthy. They died out, to be replaced from below, century after century. It was well-known that deckhands had the most offspring, skilled handicrafters and full-time warriors rather less, hereditary officers fewest of all. Why, Admiral Syranax had in a long life begotten only one son and two daughters. She, Rodonis, had two cubs already, after a mere four years of marriage.

Did this not suggest that the high Lodestar favored the honest person working with honest hands?

But no . . . those Lannach'honai all had young every other year, like machinery, even though many of the tykes died on migration. And the Lannach'honai did not work: not really: they hunted, herded, fished with their effeminate hooks, they were vigorous enough but they never stuck to a job through hours and days like a Drak'ho sailor . . . and, of course, their habits were just disgusting. *Animal!* A couple of ten-days a year, down in the twilight of equatorial solstice, indiscriminate lust, and that was all. For the rest of your life, the father of your cub was only another male to you—not that you knew who he was anyway, you hussy!—and at home there was no modesty between the sexes, there wasn't even much distinction in everyday habits, because there was no more desire. Ugh!

Still, those filthy Lannach'honai had flourished, so maybe the Lodestar did not care. . . . No, it was too cold a thought, here in the night wind under ashen Sk'huanax. Surely the Lodestar had appointed the Fleet an instrument, to destroy those Lannach beasts and take the country they had been defiling.

Rodonis' wings beat a little faster. The flagship was close now, its turrets like mountain peaks in the dark.

There were many lamps burning, down on deck or in shuttered rooms. There were warriors cruising endlessly above and around. The admiral's flag was still at the masthead, so he had not yet died; but the death watch thickened hour by hour.

Like carrion birds waiting, thought Rodonis with a shudder.

One of the sentries whistled her to a hover and flapped close. Moonlight glistened on his polished spearhead. "Hold! Who are you?"

She had come prepared for such a halt, but briefly, the tongue clove to her mouth. For she was only a female, and a monster laired beneath her.

A gust of wind rattled the dried things hung from a yardarm: the wings of some offending sailor who now sat leashed to an oar or a millstone, if he still lived. Rodonis thought of Delp's back bearing red stumps, and her anger broke loose in a scream:

"Do you speak in that tone to a sa Axollon?"

The warrior did not know her personally, among the thousands of Fleet citizens, but he knew an officer-class scarf; and it was plain to see that a life's toil had never been allowed to twist this slim-flanked body.

"Down on the deck, scum!" yelled Rodonis. "Cover your eyes when you address me!"

"I . . . my lady," he stammered, "I did not—"

She dove directly at him. He had no choice but to get out of the way. Her voice cracked whip-fashion, trailing her: "Assuming, of course, that your boatswain has first obtained my permission for you to speak to me."

"But . . . but . . . but—" Other fighting males had come now, to wheel as helplessly in the air. Such laws did exist; no one had enforced them to the letter for centuries, but—

An officer on the main deck met the situation when Rodonis landed. "My lady," he said with due deference, "it is not seemly for an unescorted female to be aboard at all, far less to visit this raft of sorrow."

"It is necessary," she told him. "I have a word for Captain T'heonax which will not wait."

"The captain is at his honored father's bunkside, my lady. I dare not—"

"Let it be your teeth he has pulled, then, when he learns that Rodonis sa Axollon could have forestalled another mutiny!"

She flounced across the deck and leaned on the rail, as if brooding her anger above the sea. The officer gasped. It was like a tail-blow to the stomach. "My lady! At once . . . wait, wait here, only the littlest of moments—Guard! Guard, there! Watch over my lady. See that she lacks not." He scuttled off.

Rodonis waited. Now the real test was coming.

There had been no problem so far. The Fleet was too shaken; no officer, worried ill, would have refused her demand when she spoke of a second uprising.

The first had been bad enough. Such a horror, an actual revolt against the Lodestar's own Oracle, had been unknown for more than a hundred years . . . and with a war to fight at the same time! The general impulse had been to deny that anything serious had happened at all. A regrettable misunderstanding . . . Delp's folk misled, fighting their gallant, hopeless fight out of loyalty to their captain . . . after all, you couldn't expect ordinary sailors to understand the more modern principle, that the Fleet and its admiral transcended any individual raft—

Harshly, her tears at the time only a dry memory, Rodonis rehearsed her interview with Syranax, days ago.

"I am sorry, my lady," he had said. "Believe me, I am sorry. Your husband was provoked, and he had more justice on his side than T'heonax. In fact, I know it was just a fight which happened, not planned, only a chance spark touching off old grudges, and my own son mostly to blame."

"Then let your son suffer for it!" she had cried.

The gaunt old skull wove back and forth, implacably. "No. He may not be the finest person in the world, but he is my son. And the heir. I haven't long to live, and wartime is no time to risk a struggle over the succession. For the Fleet's sake, T'heonax must succeed me without argument from anyone; and for this, he must have an officially unstained record."

"But why can't you let Delp go too?"

"By the Lodestar, if I could! But it's not possible. I can give everyone else amnesty, yes, and I will. But there must be one to bear the blame, one on whom to vent the pain of our hurts. Delp has to be accused of engineering a mutiny, and be punished, so that everybody else can say, 'Well, we fought each other, but it was all his fault, so now we can trust each other again.'"

The admiral sighed, a tired breath out of shrunken lungs. "I wish to the Lodestar I didn't have to do this. I wish . . . I'm fond of you too, my lady. I wish we could be friends again."

"We can," she whispered, "if you will set Delp free."

The conqueror of Maion looked bleakly at her and said: "No. And now I have heard enough."

She had left his presence.

And the days passed, and there was the farcical nightmare of Delp's trial, and the nightmare of the sentence passed on him, and the nightmare of waiting for its execution. The Lannach'ho raid had been like a moment's waking from fever-dreams: for it was sharp and real, and your shipmate was no longer your furtive-eyed enemy but a warrior who met the barbarian in the clouds and whipped him home from your cubs!

Three nights afterward, Admiral Syranax lay dying. Had he not fallen sick, Delp would now be a mutilated slave, but in this renewed tension and uncertainty, so controversial a sentence was naturally stayed.

Once T'heonax had the Admiralty, thought Rodonis in a cold corner of her brain, there would be no more delay. Unless—

"Will my lady come this way?"

They were obsequious, the officers who guided her across the deck and into the great gloomy pile of logs. Household servants, pattering up and down windowless corridors by lamplight, stared at her in a kind of terror. Somehow, the most secret things were always known to the forecastle, immediately, as if smelled.

It was dark in here, stuffy, and silent. *So* silent. The sea is never still. Only now did Rodonis realize that she had not before, in all her life, been shut away from the sound of waves and timber and cordage. Her wings tensed, she wanted to fly up with a scream.

She walked.

They opened a door for her; she went through, and it closed behind her with sound-deadening massiveness. She saw a small, richly furred and carpeted room, where many lamps burned. The air was so thick it made her dizzy. T'heonax lay on a couch watching her, playing with one of the Eart'ho knives. There was no one else.

"Sit down," he said.

She squatted on her tail, eyes smoldering into his as if they were equals.

"What did you wish to say?" he asked tonelessly.

"The admiral your father lives?" she countered.

"Not for long, I fear," he said. "Aeak'ha will eat him before noon." His eyes went toward the arras, haunted. "How long the night is!"

Rodonis waited.

"Well?" he said. His head swung back, snakishly. A rawness was in his tone. "You mentioned something about . . . another mutiny?"

Rodonis sat straight up on her haunches. Her crest grew stiff. "Yes," she replied in a winter voice. "My husband's crew have not forgotten him."

"Perhaps not," snapped T'heonax. "But they've had sufficient loyalty to the Admiralty drubbed into them by now."

"Loyalty to Admiral Syranax, yes," she told him. "But that was never lacking. You know as well as I, what happened was no mutiny . . . only a riot, by males who were against you. Syranax they have always admired, if not loved.

"The *real* mutiny will be against his murderer."

T'heonax leaped.

"What do you mean?" he shouted. "Who's a murderer?"

"You are." Rodonis pushed it out between her teeth. "You have poisoned your father."

She waited then, through a time which stretched close to breaking. She could not tell if the notoriously violent male she faced would kill her for uttering those words.

Almost, he did. He drew back from her when his knife touched her throat. His jaws clashed shut again, he leaped onto his couch and stood there on all fours with back arched, tail rigid and wings rising.

"Go on," he hissed. "Say your lies. I know well enough how you hate my whole family, because of that worthless husband of yours. All the Fleet knows. Do you expect them to believe your naked word?"

"I never hated your father;" said Rodonis, not quite steadily, death had brushed very close. "He condemned Delp, yes. I thought he did wrongly, but he did it 'for the Fleet, and I . . . I am of officer kindred myself. You recall, on the day after the raid I asked him to dine with me, as a token to all that the Drak'honai must close ranks."

"So you did," sneered T'heonax. "A pretty gesture. I remember how hotly spiced the guests said the food was. And the little keepsake you gave him, that shining disk from the Eart'ho possessions. Touching! As if it were yours to give. Everything of theirs belongs to the Admiralty."

"Well, the fat Eart'ho had given it to me himself," said Rodonis. She was deliberately leading the conversation into irrelevant channels, seeking to calm them both. "He had recovered it from his baggage, he said. He called it a *coin* . . . an article of trade among his people . . . thought I might like it to remember him by. That was just after the . . . the riot . . . and just before he and his companions were removed from the *Gerunis* to that other raft."

"It was a miser's gift," said T'heonax. "The disk was quite worn out of shape—Bah!" His muscles bunched again. "Come. Accuse me further, if you dare."

"I have not been altogether a fool," said Rodonis. "I have left letters, to be opened by certain friends if I do not return. But consider the facts, T'heonax. You are an ambitious male, and one of whom most persons are willing to think the worst. Your father's death will make you

Admiral, the virtual owner of the Fleet—how long you must have chafed, waiting for this! Your father is dying, stricken by a malady unlike any known to our chirurgeons: not even like any known poison, so wildly does it destroy him. Now it is known to many that the raiders did not manage to carry off every bit of the Eart'ho food: three small packets were left behind. The Eart'honai frequently and publicly warned us against eating any of their rations. And you have had charge of all the Eart'ho things!"

T'heonax gasped.

"It's a lie!" he chattered. "I don't know ... I haven't ... I never—Will anyone believe I, anyone, could do such a thing ... poison ... to his own father?"

"Of you they will believe it," said Rodonis.

"I swear by the Lodestar—!"

"The Lodestar will not give luck to a Fleet commanded by a parricide. There will be mutiny on that account alone, T'heonax."

He glared at her, wild and panting. "What do you want?" he croaked.

Rodonis looked at him with the coldest gaze he had ever met. "I will burn those letters," she said, "and will keep silence forever. I will even join my denials to yours, should the same thoughts occur to someone else. But Delp must have immediate, total amnesty."

T'heonax bristled and snarled at her.

"I could fight you," he growled. "I could have you arrested for treasonable talk, and kill anyone who dared—"

"Perhaps," said Rodonis. "But is it worth it? You might split the Fleet open and leave us all a prey to the Lannach'honai. All I ask is my husband back."

"For that, you would threaten to ruin the Fleet?"

"Yes," she said.

And after a moment: "You do not understand. You males make the nations and wars and songs and science, all the little things. You imagine you are the strong practical sex. But a female goes again and yet again under death's shadow, to bring forth another life. We are the hard ones. We have to be."

Theonax huddled back, shivering.

"Yes," he whispered at last, "yes, curse you, shrivel you, yes, you can have him. I'll give you an order now, this instant. Get his rotten feet off my raft before dawn, d'you hear? But I did not poison my father." His wings beat thunderous, until he lifted up under the ceiling and threshed there, trapped and screaming. "I *didn't!*"

Rodonis waited.

Presently she took the written order, and left him, and went to the brig, where they cut the ropes that bound Delp hyr Orikan. He lay in her arms and sobbed. "I will keep my wings, I will keep my wings—"

Rodonis sa Axollon stroked his crest, murmured to him, crooned to him, told him all would be well now, they were going home again, and wept a little because she loved him.

Inwardly she held a chill memory, how old van Rijn had given her the coin but warned her against . . . what had he said? . . . heavy metal poisoning. "To you, iron, copper, tin is unknown stuffs. I am not a chemist, me; chemists I hire when chemicking is needful; but I think better I eat a shovelful arsenic than one of your cubs try teething on this piece money, by damn!"

And she remembered sitting up in the dark, with a stone in her hand, grinding and grinding the coin, until there was seasoning for the unbendable admiral's dinner.

Afterward she recollected that the Eart'ho was not supposed to have such mastery of her language. It occurred to her now, like a shudder, that he could very well have left that deadly food behind on purpose, in hopes it might cause trouble. But how closely had he foreseen the event?

❀ XI ❀

Guntra of the Enklann sept came in through the door. Eric Wace looked wearily up. Behind him, hugely shadowed between rush lights, the mill was a mumble of toiling forms.

"Yes?" he sighed.

Guntra held out a broad shield, two meters long, a light sturdy construction of wicker on a wooden frame. For many ten-days she had supervised hundreds of females and cubs as they gathered and split and dried the reeds, formed the wood, wove the fabric, assembled the unit. She had not been so tired since homecoming. Nevertheless, a small victory dwelt in her voice: "This is the four thousandth, Councilor." It was not his title, but the Lannacha mind could hardly imagine anyone without definite rank inside the Flock organization. Considering the authority granted the wingless creatures, it fell most naturally to call them Councilors.

"Good." He hefted the object in hands grown calloused. "A strong piece of work. Four thousand are more than enough; your task is done, Guntra."

"Thank you." She looked curiously about the transformed mill. Hard to remember that not so long ago it had existed chiefly to grind food.

Angrek of the Trekkans came up with a block of wood in his grasp. "Councilor," he began, "I—" He stopped. His gaze had fallen on Guntra, who was still in her early middle years and had always been considered handsome.

Her eyes met his. A common smokiness lit them. His wings spread and he took a stiff step toward her.

With a gasp, almost a sob, Guntra turned and fled. Angrek stared after her, then threw his block to the floor and cursed.

"What the devil?" said Wace.

Angrek beat a fist into his palm. "Ghosts," he muttered. "It must be ghosts . . . unrestful spirits of all the evildoers who ever lived . . . possessing the Drakska, and now come to plague us!"

Another pair of bodies darkened the door, which stood open to the short pale night of early summer. Nicholas van Rijn and Tolk the Herald entered.

"How goes it, boy?" boomed van Rijn. He was gnawing a nitro-packed onion; the gauntness which had settled on Wace, even on Sandra, had not touched him. But then, thought Wace bitterly, the old blubberbucket didn't work. All he did was stroll around and talk to the local bosses and complain that things weren't proceeding fast enough.

"Slowly, sir." The younger man bit back words he would rather have said. *You bloated leech, do you expect to be carried home by my labor and my brains, and fob me off with another factor's post on another hell-planet?*

"It will have to be speeded, then," said van Rijn. "We cannot wait so long, you and me."

Tolk glanced keenly at Angrek. The handicrafter was still trembling and whispering charms. "What's wrong?" he asked.

"The . . . an influence." Angrek covered his eyes. "Herald," he stammered, "Guntra of the Enklann was here just now, and for a moment we . . . we desired each other."

Tolk looked grave, but spoke without reproof. "It has happened to many. Keep it under control."

"But what *is* it, Herald? A sickness? A judgment? What have I done?"

"These unnatural impulses aren't unknown," said Tolk. "They crop up in most of us, every once in a while. But of course, one doesn't talk about it; one suppresses it, and does his or her best to forget it ever happened." He scowled. "Lately there has been more of such hankering than usual. I don't know why. Go back to your work and avoid females."

Angrek drew a shaky breath, picked up his piece of wood, and nudged Wace. "I wanted your advice; the shape here doesn't seem to me the best for its purpose—"

Tolk looked around. He had just come back from a prolonged journey, cruising over his entire homeland to bear word to scattered clans. "There has been much work done here," he said.

"*Ja,*" nodded van Rijn complacently. "He is a talented engineer, him my young friend. But then, the factor on a new planet had pest-bedamned better be a good engineer."

"I am not so well acquainted with the details of his schemes."

"My schemes," corrected van Rijn, somewhat huffily. "I tell him to make us weapons. All he does then is make them."

"All?" asked Tolk dryly. He inspected a skeletal framework. "What's this?"

"A repeating dart-thrower; a machine gun, I call it. See, this walking beam turns this spurred fly wheel. Darts are fed to the wheel on a belt—s-s-so—and tossed off fast: two or three in an eye-wink, at least. The wheel is swivel-mounted to point in any direction. It is an old idea, really, I think Miller or de Camp or someone first built it long ago. But it is one hard damn thing to face in battle."

"Excellent," approved Tolk. "And that over there?"

"We call it a ballista. It is like the Drak'ho catapults, only more so. This throws large stones, to break down a wall or sink a boat. And here—*ja*." Van Rijn picked up the shield Guntra had brought. "This is not so good advertising copy, maybe, but I think it means a bit more for us than the other machineries. A warrior on the ground wears one on his back."

"Mm-m-m . . . yes, I see where a harness would fit . . . it would stop missiles from above, eh? But our warrior could not fly while he wore it."

"Just so!" roared van Rijn. "Just bloody-be-so! That is the troubles with you folk on Diomedes. Great balls of cheese! How you expect to fight a real war with nothing but air forces, ha? Up here in Salmenbrok, I spend all days hammering into stupid officer heads, it is infantry takes and holds a position, by damn! And then officers have to beat it into the ranks, and practice them—gout of Judas! It is not time enough! In these few ten-days, I have to try make what needs years!"

Tolk nodded, almost casually. Even Trolwen had needed time and argument before he grasped the idea of a combat force whose main body was deliberately restricted to ground operations. It was too alien a concept. But the Herald said only: "Yes. I see your reasoning. It is the strong points which decide who holds

Lannach, the fortified towns that dominate a countryside from which the food comes. And to take the town back, we will need to dig our way in."

"You think smartly," approved van Rijn. "In Earth history, it took some peoples a long time to learn there is no victory in air power alone."

"There are still the Drakska fire weapons," said Tolk. "What do you plan to do about them? My whole mission, these past ten-days, has been largely to persuade the outlying septs to join us. I gave them your word that the fire could be faced, that we'd even have flamethrowers and bombs of our own. I'd better have been telling the truth."

He looked about. The mill, converted to a crude factory, was too full of winged laborers for him to see far. Nearby, a primitive lathe, somewhat improved by Wace, was turning out spearshafts and tomahawk handles. Another engine, a whirling grindstone, was new to him: it shaped ax heads and similar parts, not as good as the handmade type but formed in wholesale lots. A drop hammer knocked off flint and obsidian flakes for cutting edges; a circular saw cut wooden members; a rope-twisting machine spun faster than the eye could follow. All of it was belt-powered from the great millwheels—all of it ludicrously haywired and cranky—but it spat forth the stuff of war faster than Lannach could use, filling whole bins with surplus armament.

"It is remarkable," said Tolk. "It frightens me a little."

"I made a new way of life here," said van Rijn expansively. "It is not this machine or that one which has already changed your history beyond changing back. It is the basic idea I have introduced: mass production."

"But the fire—"

"Wace has also begun to make us fire weapons. Sulfur they have gathered from Mount Oborch, and there are oil pools from which we are getting nice arsonish liquids. Distillation, that is another art the Drak'ho have had and you have not. Now we will have some Molotov cocktails for our own selves."

The human scowled. "But there is one thing true, my friend. We have not time to train your warriors like they should be to use this material. Soon I starve; soon your females get heavy and food must be stored." He heaved a pathetic sigh. "Though I am long dead before you folks have real sufferings."

"Not so," said Tolk grimly. "We have almost half a year left before Birthtime, true. But already we are weakened by hunger, cold, and despair. Already we have failed to perform many ceremonies—"

"Blast your ceremonies!" snapped van Rijn. "I say it is Ulwen town we should take first, where it sits so nice overlooking Duna Brae that all the hornbeasts live at. If we have Ulwen, you have eats enough, also a strong point easy to defend. But no, Trolwen and the Council say we must strike straight for Mannenach, leaving Ulwen enemy-held in our rear, and going down clear to Sagna Bay where their rafts can get at us. For why? So you can hold some blue-befungused rite there!"

"You cannot understand," said Tolk gently. "We are too different. Even I, whose life's work it has been to deal with alien peoples, cannot grasp your attitude. But our life is the cycle of the year. It is not that we take the old gods so seriously any more—but their rituals, the rightness and decency of it all, the *belonging*—" He looked upward, into the shadow-hidden roof, where the wind hooted and rushed about the busy millwheels. "No,

I don't believe that ancestral ghosts fly out there of nights. But I do believe that when I welcome High Summer back at the great rite in Mannenach, as my forebears have done for as long as there has been a Flock . . . then I am keeping the Flock itself alive."

"Bah!" Van Rijn extended a dirt-encrusted hand to scratch the matted beard which was engulfing his face. He couldn't shave or wash: even given antiallergen shots, human skin wouldn't tolerate Diomedean soap. "I tell you why you have all this ritual. First, you are a slave to the seasons, more even than any farmer on Earth back in our old days. Second, you must fly so much, and leave your homes empty all the dark time up here, that ritual is your most precious possession. It is the only thing you have not weighing too much to be carried with you everywhere."

"That's as may be," said Tolk. "The fact remains. If there is any chance of greeting the Full Day from Mannenach Standing Stones, we shall take it. The extra lives which are lost because this may not be the soundest strategy, will be offered in gladness."

"If it does not cost us the whole befouled war." Van Rijn snorted. "Devils and dandruff! My own chaplain at home, that pickle face, is not so fussy about what is proper. Why, that poor young fellow there was near making suicide now, just because he got a little bit excited over a wench out of wenching season, *nie?*"

"It isn't done," said Tolk stiffly. He walked from the shop. After a moment, van Rijn followed.

Wace settled the point of discussion with Angrek, checked operations elsewhere, swore at a well-meaning young porter who was storing volatile petroleum fractions beside the hearth, and left. His feet were heavy at the end of his legs. It was too much for one man to do, organizing, designing, supervising, trouble-shooting —Van Rijn seemed to think it was routine to lift neolithic hunters into the machine age in a few weeks. He ought to try it himself! It might sweat some of the lard off the old hog.

The nights were so short now, only a paleness between two red clouds on a jagged horizon, that Wace no longer paid any heed to the time. He worked until he was ready to drop, slept a while, and went back to work.

Sometimes he wondered if he had ever felt rested . . . and clean, and well fed, and comforted in his aloneness.

Morning smoldered on northerly ridges, where a line of volcanoes smeared wrathful black across the sun. Both moons were sinking, each a cold coppery disk twice the apparent size of Earth's Luna. Mount Oborch shivered along giant flanks and spat a few boulders at the pallid sky. The wind came galing, stiff as an iron bar pressed against Wace's suddenly chilled back. Salmenbrok village huddled flinty barren under its loud quick thrust.

He had reached the ladder made for him, so he could reach the tiny loft-room he used, when Sandra Tamarin came from behind the adjoining tower. She paused, one hand stealing to her face. He could not hear what she said, in the blustery air.

He went over to her. Gravel scrunched under the awkward leather boots a Lannacha tailor had made him. "I beg your pardon, my lady?"

"Oh . . . it was nothing, Freeman Wace." Her green gaze came up to meet his, steadily and proudly, but he saw a redness steal along her cheeks. "I only said . . . good morning."

"Likewise." He rubbed sandy-lidded eyes. "I haven't seen you for some time, my lady. How are you?"

"Restless," she said. "Unhappy. Will you talk to me for a little, perhaps?"

They left the hamlet behind and followed a dim trail upward, through low harsh bushes breaking into purple bloom. High above them wheeled a few sentries, but those were only impersonal specks against heaven. Wace felt his heartbeat grow hasty.

"What have you been doing?" he asked.

"Nothing of value. What can I do?" She stared down at her hands. "I try, but I have not the skills, not like you the engineer or Freeman van Rijn."

"Him?" Wace shrugged. No doubt the old goat had found plenty of chance to brag himself up, as he lounged superfluous around Salmenbrok. "It—" He stopped, groping after words. "It's enough just to have my lady present."

"Why, Freeman!" She laughed, with genuine half-amused pleasure and no coyness at all. "I never thought you so gallant in the words."

"Never had much chance to be, my lady," he murmured, too tired and strength-emptied to keep up his guard.

"Not?" She gave him a sideways look. The wind laid its fingers in her tightly braided hair and unfurled small argent banners of it. She was not yet starved, but the bones in her face were standing out more sharply; there was a smudge on one cheek and her garments were clumsy baggings hurled together by a tailor who had never seen a human frame before. But somehow, stripped thus of queenliness, she seemed to him more beautiful than erstwhile—perhaps because of being

closer? Because her poverty said with frankness that she
was only human flesh like himself?

"No," he got out between stiff lips.

"I do not understand," she said.

"Your pardon, my lady. I was thinking out loud. Bad
habit. But one does, on these outpost worlds. You see
the same few men so often that they stop being company;
you avoid them—and, of course, we're always
undermanned, so you have to go out by yourself on various jobs, maybe for weeks at a time. Why am I saying
all this? I don't know. Dear God, how tired I am!"

They paused on a ridge. At their feet was a cliff tumbling through hundreds of meters down to a foam-white
river. Across the canyon were mountains and mountains,
their snows tinged bloody by the sun. The wind came
streaking up the dales and struck the humans in the face.

"I see. Yes, it clears for me." Sandra regarded him
with grave eyes. "You have had to work hard your whole
life. There has not been time for the pleasures, the
learned manners and culture. Not?"

"No time at all, my lady," he said. "I was born in the
slums, one kilometer from the old Triton Docks. Nobody
but the very poor would live that close to a spaceport,
the traffic and stinks and earthquake noise . . . though
you got used to it, till it was a part of you, built into
your bones. Half my playmates are now dead or in jail,
I imagine, and the other half are scrabbling for the occasional half-skilled hard-and-dirty job no one else wants.
Don't pity me, though. I was lucky. I got apprenticed to
a fur wholesaler when I was twelve. After two years,
I'd made enough contacts to get a hard-and-dirty job
myself—only this was on a spaceship, fur-trapping expedition to Rhiannon. I taught myself a little something in

odd moments, and bluffed about the rest I was supposed to know, and got a slightly better job. And so on and so on, till they put me in charge of this outpost . . . a very minor enterprise, which may in time become moderately profitable but will never be important. But it's a stepping stone. So here I am, on a mountain top with all Diomedes below me, and what's next?"

He shook his head, violently, wondering why his reserve had broken down. Being so exhausted was like a drunkenness. But more to it than that . . . no, he was *not* fishing for sympathy . . . down underneath, did he want to find out if she would understand? If she could?

"You will get back," she said quietly. "Your kind of man survives."

"Maybe!"

"It is heroic, what you have done already." She looked away from him, toward the driving clouds around Oborch's peak. "I am not certain anything can stop you. Except yourself."

"I?" He was beginning to be embarrassed now, and wanted to talk of other things. He plucked at his bristly red beard.

"Yes. Who else can? You have come so far, so fast. But why not stop? Soon, perhaps here on this mountain, must you not ask yourself how much farther it is worth going?"

"I don't know. As far as possible, I guess."

"Why? Is it necessary to become great? Is it not enough to be free? With your talent and experience, you can make good-enough monies on many settled planets where men are more at home than here. Like Hermes, *exemplia*. In this striving to be rich and powerful, is it not merely that you want to feed and shelter the little boy who once cried himself hungry to sleep back in Triton Docks? But that little boy you can never comfort, my friend. He died long ago."

"Well . . . I don't know . . . I suppose one day I'll have a family. I'd want to give my wife more than just a living; I'd want to leave my children and grandchildren enough resources to go on—to stand off the whole world if they have to—"

"Yes. So. I think maybe—" he saw, before she turned her head from him, how the blood flew up into her face—"the old fighting Dukes of Hermes were like so. It would be well if we had a breed of men like them again—" Suddenly she began walking very fast down the path. "Enough. Best we return, not?"

He followed her, little aware of the ground he trod.

❈ XII ❈

When the Lannachska were ready to fight, they were called to Salmenbrok by Tolk's Whistlers until the sky darkened with their wings. Then Trolwen made his way through a seethe of warriors to van Rijn.

"Surely the gods are weary of us," he said bitterly. "Near always, at this time of year, there are strong south winds." He gestured at a breathless heaven. "Do you know a spell for raising dead breezes?"

The merchant looked up, somewhat annoyed. He was seated at a table outside the wattle-and-clay hut they had built for him beyond the village—for he refused to climb ladders, or sleep in a damp cave—dicing with Corps Captain Srygen for the beryl-like gemstones which were a local medium of exchange. The number of species in the galaxy which have independently invented some form of African golf is beyond estimation.

"Well," he snapped, "and why must you have your tail fanned? . . . Ah, seven! No, pox and pills, I remember, here seven is not a so good number. Well, we try again." The three cubes clicked in his hand and across the table. "Hm-m-m, seven again." He scooped up the stakes. "Double or nothings?"

"The ghost-eaters take it!" Srygen got up. "You've been winning too motherless often for my taste."

Van Rijn surged to his own feet like a broaching whale. "By damn, you take that back or—"

"I said nothing challengeable," Srygen told him coldly. "You implied it. I am insulted, myself!"

"Hold on there," growled Trolwen. "What do you think this is, a beer feast? Eart'a, all the fighting forces of Lannach are now gathered on these hills. We cannot feed them here very long. And yet, with the new weapons loaded on the railway cars, we cannot stir until we get a south wind. What to do?"

Van Rijn glared at Srygen. "I said I was insulted. I do not think so good when I am insulted."

"I am sure the captain will apologize for any unintended offense," said Trolwen, with a red-shot look at them both.

"Indeed," said Srygen. He spoke it like pulling teeth.

"So." Van Rijn stroked his beard. "Then to prove you make no doubt about my honesties, we throw once more, *nie?* Double or nothings."

Srygen snatched the dice and hurled them. "Ah, a six you have," said van Rijn. "It is not so easy to beat. I am afraid I have already lost. It is not so simple to be a poor tired hungry old man, far away from his home and from the Siamese cats who are all he has to love him for himself, not just his monies. . . . Tum-te-tum-te-tum. . . . Eight! A two, a three, a three! Well, well, well!"

"Transport," said Trolwen, hanging on to his temper by a hair. "The new weapons are too heavy for our porters. They have to go by rail. Without a wind, how do we get them down to Sagna Bay?"

"Simple," said van Rijn, counting his take. "Till you get a good wind, tie ropes to the cars and all these so-husky young fellows pull."

Srygen blew up. "A free clan male, to drag a car like a . . . like a *Draka?*" He mastered himself and choked: "It isn't done."

"Sometimes," said van Rijn, "these things must be done." He scooped up the jewels, dropped them into a purse, and went over to a well. "Surely you have some disciplines in this Flock."

"Oh . . . yes . . . I suppose so—" Trolwen's unhappy gaze went downslope to the brawling, shouting winged tide which had engulfed the village. "But sustained labor like that has always . . . long before the Drakska came . . . always been considered—perverted, in a way—it is not exactly forbidden, but one does not do it without the most compelling necessity. To labor in *public*—No!"

Van Rijn hauled on the windlass. "Why not? The Drak'honai, them, make all kinds tiresome preachments about the dignity of labor. For them it is needful; in their way of life, one must work hard. But for you? Why must one *not* work hard in Lannach?"

"It isn't right," said Srygen stiffly. "It makes us like some kind of animal."

Van Rijn pulled the bucket to the well coping and took a bottle of Earthside beer from it. "Ahhh, good

and cold . . . hm-m-m, possibly too cold, damn all places
without thermostatted coolers—" He opened the bottle
on the stone curb and tasted. "It will do. Now, I have
made travels, and I find that everywhere the manners
and morals of peoples have some good reason at bottom.
Maybe the race has forgotten why was a rule made in
the first place, but if the rule does not make some sense,
it will not last many centuries. Follows then that you do
not like prolonged hard work, except to be sure migration, because it is not good for you for some reason. And
yet it does not hurt the Drak'honai too much. Paradox!"

"Unlawfulness take your wonderings," snarled Trolwen. "It was your idea that we make all this newfangled
apparatus, instead of fighting as our males have always
fought. Now, how do we get it down to the lowlands
without demoralizing the army?"

"Oh, that!" Van Rijn shrugged. "You have
sports—contests—*nie?*"

"Of course."

"Well, you explain these cars must be brought with us
and, while it is not necessary we leave at once—"

"But it is! We'll starve if we don't!"

"My good young friend," said van Rijn patiently, "I
see plain you have much to learn about politics. You
Lannachska do not understand lying, I suppose because
you do not get married. You tell the warriors, I say, that
we can wait for a south wind all right but you know they
are eager to come to grips with the foe and therefore
they will be invited to play a small game. Each clan will
pull so and so many cars down, and we time how fast it
goes and make a prize for the best pullers."

"Well, I'll be accursed," said Srygen.

Trolwen nodded eagerly. "It's just the sort of thing
that gets into clan traditions—"

"You see," explained van Rijn, "it is what we call semantics on Earth. I am old and short with breath, so I can look unprejudiced at all these footballs and baseballs and potato races, and I know that a game is hard work you are not required to do."

He belched, opened another bottle, and took a half-eaten salami from his purse. The supplies weren't going to last very much longer.

⊛ XIII ⊛

When the expedition was halfway down the Misty Mountains, their wind rose behind them. A hundred warriors harnessed to each railway car relaxed and waited for the timers whose hourglasses would determine the winning team.

"But they are not all so dim in the brain, surely," said Sandra.

"Oh, no," answered Wace. "But those who were smart enough to see through Old Nick's scheme were also smart enough to see it was necessary, and keep quiet."

He huddled in a mordant blast that drove down alpine slopes to the distant cloudy green of hills and valleys, and watched the engineers at work. A train consisted of about thirty light little cars roped together, with a "locomotive" at the head and another in the middle. These were somewhat more sturdily built, to support two high masts with square sails. Given wood of almost metallic hardness, plus an oil-drip over the wheels in lieu of ball bearings, plus the hurricane thrust of Diomedean winds, the system became practical. You didn't get up much speed, and you must often wait for a following wind, but this was not a culture bound to hourly schedules.

"It's not too late for you to go back, my lady," said Wace. "I can arrange an escort."

"No." She laid a hand on the bow which had been made for her—no toy, a 25–kilo killing tool such as she had often hunted with in her home forests. Her head lifted, the silver-pale hair caught chill ruddy sunlight and threw back a glow to this dark immensity of cliffs and glaciers. "Here we stand or here we die. It would not be right for a ruler born to stay home."

Van Rijn hawked. "Trouble with aristocrats," he muttered. "Bred for looks and courage, not brains. Now *I* would go back, if not needed here to show I have confidence in my own plans."

"Do you?" asked Wace skeptically.

"Let be with foolishness," snorted van Rijn. "Of course not." He trudged back to the staff car which had been prepared for him: at least it had walls, a roof, and a bunk. The wind shrieked down ringing stony canyons, he leaned against it with his entire weight. Overhead swooped and soared the squadrons of Lannach.

Wace and Sandra each had a private car, but she asked him to ride down with her. "Forgive me if I make dramatics, Eric, but we may be killed and it is lonely to die without a human hand to hold." She laughed, a little breathlessly. "Or at least we can talk."

"I'm afraid—" He cleared a tightened throat. "I'm afraid, my lady, I can't converse as readily as . . . Freeman van Rijn."

"Oh," she grinned, "that was what I meant. I said *we* can talk, not him only."

Nevertheless, when the trains got into motion, she grew quiet as he.

Lacking their watches they could scarcely even guess how long the trip took. High summer had almost come to Lannach; once in twelve and a half hours, the sun scraped the horizon north of west, but there was no more real night. Wace watched the kilometers click away beneath him; he ate, slept, spoke desultorily with Sandra or with young Angrek who served as her aide, and the great land flattened into rolling valleys and forests of low fringe-leaved trees, and the sea came near.

Now and again a hotbox or a contrary wind delayed the caravan. There was restlessness in the ranks: they were used to streaking in a day from the mountains to the coast, not to wheeling above this inchworm of a railway. Drak'honai scouts spied them from afar, inevitably, and a detachment of rafts lumbered into Sagna Bay with powerful reinforcements. Raids probed the flanks of the attackers. And still the trains must crawl.

In point of fact, there were eight Diomedean revolutions between the departure from Salmenbrok and the Battle of Mannenach.

The harbor town lay on the Sagna shore, well in from the open sea and sheltered by surrounding wooded hills. It was a gaunt grim-looking complex of stone towers, tightly knitted together with the usual tunnels and enclosed bridges, talking in the harsh tones of half a dozen big windmills. It overlooked a small pier, which the Drak'honai had been enlarging. Beyond, dark on the choppy brown waters, rocked two score enemy craft.

As his train halted, Wace jumped from Sandra's car. There was nothing to shoot at yet: Mannenach revealed only a few peaked roofs thrusting above the grassy ridge before him. Even against the wind, he could hear the thunder of wings as the Drak'honai lifted from the town, twisting upward in a single black mass like some tornado made flesh. But heaven was thick with Lannachska above him, and the enemy made no immediate attack.

His heart thumped, runaway, and his mouth was too dry for him to speak. Almost hazily, he saw Sandra beside him. A Diomedean bodyguard under Angrek closed around in a thornbush of spears.

The girl smiled. "This is a kind of relief," she said. "No more sitting and worrying, only to do what we can, not?"

"Not indeed!" puffed van Rijn, stumping toward them. Like the other humans, he had arranged for an ill-fitting cuirass and helmet of laminated hard leather above the baggy malodorous native clothes. But he wore two sets of armor, one on top of the other, carried a shield on his left arm, had deputed two young warriors to hold another shield over him like a canopy, and bore a tomahawk and a beltful of stone daggers. "Not if I can get out of it, by damn! You go ahead and fight. I will be right behind you—as far behind as the good saints let."

Wace found his tongue and said maliciously: "I've often thought there might be fewer wars among civilized races, if they reverted to this primitive custom that the generals are present at the battles."

"Bah! Ridiculous! Just as many wars, only using generals who have guts more than brains. I think cowards make the best strategists, stands to reason, by damn. Now I stay in my car." Van Rijn stalked off, muttering.

Trolwen's newly-formed field artillery corps were going frantic, unloading their clumsy weapons from the trains and assembling them while squads and patrols skirmished overhead. Wace cursed—here was something he could do!—and hurried to the nearest confusion. "Hoy, there! Back away! What are you trying to do? Here, you,

you, you, get up in the car and unlash the main frame . . . that piece *there,* you clothead!" After a while, he almost lost consciousness of the fighting that developed around him.

The Mannenach garrison and its sea-borne reinforcements had begun with cautious probing, a few squadrons at a time swooping to flurry briefly with some of the Lannachska flying troops and then pull away again toward the town. Drak'ho forces here were outnumbered by a fair margin; Trolwen had reasoned correctly that no admiral would dare leave the main Fleet without a strong defense while Lannach was still formidable. In addition, the sailors were puzzled, a little afraid, at the unprecedented attacking formations.

Fully half the Lannachska were ranked on the ground, covered by rooflike shields which would not even permit them to fly! Never in history had such a thing been known!

During an hour, the two hordes came more closely to grips. Much superior in the air, the Drak'honai punched time after time through Trolwen's fliers. But integrated by the Whistler corps, the aerial troops closed again, fluidly. And there was little profit in attacking the Lannachska infantry—those awkward wicker shields trapped edged missiles, sent stones rebounding, an assault from above was almost ignored.

Arrows were falling thickly when Wace had his last fieldpiece assembled. He nodded at a Whistler, who whirled up immediately to bear the word to Trolwen. From the commander's position, where he rode a thermal updraft, came a burst of messengers—banners broke out on the ground, war whoops tore through the wind, it was the word to advance!

Ringed by Angrek's guards, Wace remained all too well aware that he was at the forefront of an army. Sandra went beside him, her lips untense. On either hand stretched spear-jagged lines of walking dragons. It seemed like a long time before they had mounted the ridge.

One by one, Drak'honai officers realized . . . and yelled their bafflement.

These stolid ground troops, unassailable from above, unopposed below, were simply pouring over the hill to Mannenach's walls, trundling their siege tools. When they arrived there, they got to work.

It became a gale of wings and weapons. The Drak'honai plunged, hacked and stabbed at Trolwen's infantry—and were in their turn attacked from above, as his fliers whom they had briefly dispersed resumed formation. Meanwhile, *crunch, crunch, crunch*, rams ate at Mannenach; detachments on foot went around the town and down toward the harbor.

"Over there! Hit 'em again!" Wace heard all at once that he was yelling.

Something broke through the chaos overhead. An arrow-filled body crashed to earth. A live one followed it, a Drak'ho warrior with the air pistol-cracking under his wings. He came low and fast; one of Angrek's lads thrust a sword at him, missed, and had his brains spattered by the sailor's tomahawk.

Without time to know what had happened, Wace saw the creature before him. He struck, wildly, with his own stone ax. A wing-buffet knocked him to the ground. He bounced up, spitting blood, as the Drak'ho came about and dove again. His hands were empty—Suddenly the Drak'ho screamed and clawed at an arrow in his throat, fluttered down and died.

Sandra nocked a fresh shaft. "I told you I would have some small use today," she said.

"I—" Wace reeled where he stood, looking at her.

"Go on," she said. "Help them break through. I will guard."

Her face was even paler than before, but there was a green in her eyes which burned.

He spun about and went back to directing his sappers. It was plain now that battering rams had been a mistake; they wouldn't get through mortared walls till Matthewsmas. He took everyone off the engines and put them to helping those who dug. With enough wooden shovels—or bare hands—they'd be sure to strike a tunnel soon.

From somewhere near, there lifted a clatter great enough to drown out the straggle around him. Wace jumped up on a ram's framework and looked over the heads of his engineers.

A body of Drak'honai had resorted to the ground themselves. They were not drilled in such tactics; but then, the Lannachska had had only the sketchiest training. By sheer sustained fury the Drak'honai were pushing their opponents back. From Trolwen's airy viewpoint, thought Wace, there must be an ugly dent in the line.

Where the devil were the machine guns?

Yes, here came one, bouncing along on a little cart. Two Lannachska began pumping the flywheel, a third aimed and operated the feed. Darts hosed across the Drak'honai. They broke up, took to the sky again. Wace hugged Sandra and danced her across the field.

Then hell boiled over on the roofs above him. His immediate corps had finally gotten to an underground passage and made it a way of entry. Driving the enemy before them, up to the top floors and out, they seized this one tower in a rush.

"Angrek!" panted Wace. "Get me up there!" Someone lowered a rope. He swarmed up it, with Sandra close behind. Standing on the ridgepole, he looked past stony parapets and turning millwheels, down to the bay. Trolwen's forces had taken the pier without much trouble. But they were getting no farther: a steady hail of firestreams, oil bombs, and catapult missiles from the anchored rafts staved them off. Their own similar armament was outranged.

Sandra squinted against the wind, shifted north to lash her eyes to weeping, and pointed. "Eric—do you recognize that flag, on the largest of the vessels there?"

"Hm-m-m . . . let me see . . . yes, I do. Isn't that our old chum Delp's personal banner?"

"So it is. I am not sorry he has escaped punishment for the riot we made. But I would rather have someone else to fight, it would be safer."

"Maybe," said Wace. "But there's work to do. We have our toe hold in the city. Now we'll have to beat down doors and push out the enemy—room by room—and you're staying here!"

"I am not!"

Wace jerked his thumb at Angrek. "Detail a squad to take the lady back to the trains," he snapped.

"No!" yelled Sandra.

"You're too late," grinned Wace. "I arranged for this before we ever left Salmenbrok."

She swore at him—then suddenly, softly, she leaned over and murmured beneath the wind and the warshrieks: "Come back hale, my friend."

He led his troopers into the tower.

Afterward he had no clear memory of the fight. It was a hard and bloody operation, ax and knife, tooth and fist, wing and tail, in narrow tunnels and cavelike rooms. He took blows, and gave them; once, for several seconds, he lay unconscious, and once he led a triumphant break-through into a wide assembly hall. He was not fanged, winged, or caudate himself, but he was heavier than any Diomedean; his blows seldom had to be repeated.

The Lannachska took Mannenach because they had—not training enough to make them good ground fighters—but enough to give them the *concept* of battle with immobilized wings. It was as revolting to Diomedean instincts as the idea of fighting with teeth alone, hands bound, would be to a human; unprepared for it, the Drak'honai bolted and ran ratlike down the tunnels in search of open sky.

Hours afterward, staggering with exhaustion, Wace climbed to a flat roof at the other end of town. Tolk sat there waiting for him.

"I think . . . we have . . . it all now," gasped the human.

"And yet not enough," said Tolk haggardly. "Look at the bay."

Wace grabbed the parapet to steady himself.

There was no more pier, no more sheds at the waterfront—it all stood in one black smoke. But the rafts and canoes of Drak'ho had edged into the shallows, forming a bridge to shore; and over this the sailors were dragging dismounted catapults and flamethrowers.

"They have too good a commander," said Tolk. "He has gotten the idea too fast, that our new methods have their own weaknesses."

"What is . . . Delp . . . going to do?" whispered Wace.

"Stay and see," suggested the Herald. "There is no way for us to help."

The Drak'honai were still superior in the air. Looking up toward a sky low and gloomy, rain clouds driving across angry gunmetal waters, Wace saw them moving to envelop the Lannacha air cover.

"You see," said Tolk, "it is true that their fliers cannot do much against our walkers—but the enemy chief has realized that the converse is also true."

Trolwen was too good a tactician himself to be cut up in such a fashion. Fighting every centimeter, his fliers retreated. After a while there was nothing in the sky but gray wrack.

Down on the ground, covered by arcing bombardment from the rafts, the sailors were setting up their mobile artillery. They had more of it than the Lannachska, and were better shots. A few infantry charges broke up in bloody ruin.

"Our machine guns they do not possess, of course," said Tolk. "But then, we do not have enough to make the difference."

Wace whirled on Angrek, who had joined him. "Don't stand here!" he cried. "Let's get down—rally our folk—seize those—It can be done, I tell you!"

"Theoretically, yes." Tolk nodded his lean head. "I can see where a person on the ground, taking advantage of every bit of cover, might squirm his way up to those catapults and flamethrowers, and tomahawk the operators. But in practice—well, we do not have such skill."

"Then what would you do?" groaned Wace.

"Let us first consider what will assuredly happen," said Tolk. "We have lost our trains; if not captured, they will be fired presently. Thus our supplies are gone. Our forces have been split, the fliers driven off, we ground-lings left here. Trolwen cannot fight his way back to us,

being outnumbered. We at Mannenach do outnumber
our immediate opponents by quite a bit. But we cannot
face their artillery.

"Therefore, to continue the fight, we must throw away
our big shields and other new-fangled items, and revert
to conventional air tactics. But this infantry is not well
equipped for normal combat: we have few archers, for
instance. Delp need only shelter on the rafts, behind his
fire weapons, and for all our greater numbers we'll be
unable to touch him. Meanwhile he will have us pinned
here, cut off from food and material. The excess war
goods your mill produced are valueless lying up in Salmenbrok. And there will certainly be strong reinforcements from the Fleet."

"To hell with that!" shouted Wace. "We have the
town, don't we? We can hold it against them till they rot!"

"What can we eat while they are rotting?" said Tolk.
"You are a good craftsman, Eart'a, but no student of war.
The cold fact is, that Delp managed to split our forces,
and therefore he has already won. I propose to cut our
losses by retreating now, while we still can."

And then suddenly his manner broke, and he stooped
and covered his eyes with his wings. Wace saw that the
Herald was growing old.

❀ XIV ❀

There was dancing on the decks, and jubilant chants rang
across Sagna Bay to the enfolding hills. Up and down
and around, in and out, the feet and the wings interwove
till timbers trembled. High in the rigging, a piper skirled
their melody; down below, a great overseer's drum which

set the pace of the oars now thuttered their stamping rhythm. In a ring of wing-folded bodies, sweat-gleaming fur and eyes aglisten, a sailor whirled his female while a hundred deep voices roared the song:

> " . . . A-sailing, a-sailing,
> a-sailing to the Sea of Beer,
> fair lady, spread your sun-bright wings
> and sail with me!"

Delp walked out on the poop and looked down at his folk.

"We'll have many a new soul in the Fleet, sixty ten-days hence," he laughed.

Rodonis held his hand, rightly: "I wish—" she began.

"Yes?"

"Sometimes . . . oh, it's nothing—" The dancing pair fluttered upward, and another couple sprang out to beat the deck in their place; planks groaned under one more huge ale barrel, rolled forth to celebrate victory. "Sometimes I wish we could be like them."

"And live in the forecastle?" said Delp dryly.

"Well, no . . . of course not—"

"There's a price on the apartment, and the servants, and the bright clothes and leisure," said Delp. His eyes grew pale. "I'm about to pay some more of it."

His tail stroked briefly over her back, then he beat wings and lifted into the air. A dozen armed males followed him. So did the eyes of Rodonis.

Under Mannenach's battered walls the Drak'ho rafts lay crowded, the disorder of war not yet cleaned up in the haste to enjoy a hard-bought victory. Only the full-time warriors remained alert, though no one else would need much warning if there should be an attack. It was the boast of the forecastle that a Fleet sailor, drunk and with a female on his knee, could outfight any three foreigners sober.

Delp, flapping across calm waters under a high cloudless day-sky, found himself weighing the morale value of such a pride against the sharp practical fact that a Lannach'ho fought like ten devils. The Drak'honai had won *this* time.

A cluster of swift canoes floated aloof, the admiral's standard drooping from one garlanded masthead. T'heonax had come at Delp's urgent request, instead of making him go out to the main Fleet—which might mean that T'heonax was prepared to bury the old hatred. (Rodonis would tell her husband nothing of what had passed between them, and he did not urge her; but it was perfectly obvious she had forced the pardon from the heir in some way.) Far more likely, though, the new admiral had come to keep an eye on this untrusted captain, who had so upset things by turning the holding operation on which he had been contemptuously ordered, into a major victory. It was not unknown for a field commander with such prestige to hoist the rebel flag and try for the Admiralty.

Delp, who had no respect for T'heonax but positive reverence for the office, bitterly resented that imputation.

He landed on the outrigger as prescribed and waited until the Horn of Welcome was blown on board. It took longer than necessary. Swallowing anger, Delp flapped to the canoe and prostrated himself.

"Rise," said T'heonax in an indifferent tone. "Congratulations on your success. Now, you wished to confer with me?" He patted down a yawn. "Please do."

Delp looked around at the faces of officers, warriors, and crewfolk. "In private, with the admiral's most trusted advisors, if it please him," he said.

"Oh? Do you consider what you have to say is that important?" Theonax nudged a young aristocrat beside him and winked.

Delp spread his wings, remembered where he was, and nodded. His neck was so stiff it hurt. "Yes, sir, I do," he got out.

"Very well." Theonax walked leisurely toward his cabin.

It was large enough for four, but only the two of them entered, with the young court favorite, who lay down and closed his eyes in boredom. "Does not the admiral wish advice?" asked Delp.

Theonax smiled. "So you don't intend to give me advice yourself, captain?"

Delp counted mentally to twenty, unclenched his teeth, and said:

"As the admiral wishes. I've been thinking about our basic strategy, and the battle here has rather alarmed me—"

"I didn't know you were frightened."

"Admiral, I . . . never mind! Look here, sir, the enemy came within two fishhooks of beating us. They had the town. We've captured weapons from them equal or superior to our own, including a few gadgets I've never seen or heard of . . . and in incredible quantities, considering how little time they had to manufacture the stuff. Then too, they had these abominable new tactics, ground fighting—not as an incidental, like when we board an enemy raft, but as the main part of their effort!

"The only reason they lost was insufficient co-ordination between ground and air, and insufficient flexibility. They should have been ready to toss away their shields and take to the air in fully equipped squadrons at an instant's notice.

"And I don't think they'll neglect to remedy that fault, if we give them the chance."

T'heonax buffed his nails on a sleek-furred arm and regarded them critically. "I don't like defeatists," he said.

"Admiral, I'm trying not to underestimate them. It's pretty clear they got all these new ideas from the Eart'ho-nai. What else do the Eart'honai know?"

"Hm-m-m. Yes." T'heonax raised his head. A moment's uneasiness flickered in his gaze. "True. What do you propose?"

"They're off balance now," said Delp with rising eagerness. "I'm sure the disappointment has demoralized them. And of course, they've lost all that heavy equipment. If we hit them hard, we can end the war. What we must do is inflict a decisive defeat on their entire army. Then they'll have to give up, yield this country to us or die like insects when their birthing time comes."

"Yes." T'heonax smiled in a pleased way. "Like insects. Like dirty, filthy insects. We won't let them emigrate, captain."

"They deserve their chance," protested Delp.

"That's a question of high policy, captain, for me to decide."

"I'm . . . sorry, sir." After a moment: "But will the admiral, then, assign the bulk of our fighting forces to . . . to some reliable officer, with orders to hunt out the Lannach'honai?"

"You don't know just where they are?"

"They could be almost anywhere in the uplands, sir. That is, we have prisoners who can be made to guide us and give some information; Intelligence says their head-quarters is a place called Psalmenbrox. But of course they can melt into the land." Delp shuddered. To him, whose world had been lonely islands and flat sea horizon, horror dwelt in the tilted mountains. "It has infinite cover to hide them. This will be no easy campaign."

"How do you propose to wage it at all?" asked T'heonax querulously. He did not like to be reminded, on top of a victory celebration and a good dinner, that there was still much death ahead of him.

"By forcing them to meet us in an all-out encounter, sir. I want to take our main fighting strength, and some native guides compelled to help us, and go from town to town up there, systematically razing whatever we find, burning the woods and slaughtering the game. Give them no chance for the large battues on which they must depend to feed their females and cubs. Sooner or later, and probably sooner, they will have to gather every male and meet us. That's when I'll break them."

"I see." T'heonax nodded. Then, with a grin: "And if they break you?"

"They won't."

"It is written: 'The Lodestar shines for no single nation.' "

"The admiral knows there's always some risk in war. But I'm convinced there's less danger in my plan than in hanging about down here, waiting for the Eart'honai to perfect some new devilment."

T'heonax's forefinger stabbed at Delp. "Ah-hah! Have you forgotten, their food will soon be gone? We can count them out."

"I wonder—"

"Be quiet!" shrilled T'heonax.

After a little time, he went on: "Don't forget, this enormous expeditionary force of yours would leave the Fleet ill defended. And without the Fleet, the rafts, we ourselves are finished."

"Oh, don't be afraid of attack, sir—" began Delp in an eager voice.

"Afraid!" T'heonax puffed himself out. "Captain, it is treason to hint that the admiral is a . . . is not fully competent."

"I didn't mean—"

"I shall not press the matter," said T'heonax smoothly. "However, you may either make full abasement, craving my pardon, or leave my presence."

Delp stood up. His lips peeled back from the fangs; the race memory of animal forebears who had been hunters bade him tear out the other's throat. T'heonax crouched, ready to scream for help.

Very slowly, Delp mastered himself. He half-turned to go. He paused, fists jammed into balls and the membrane of his wings swollen with blood.

"Well?" smiled T'heonax.

Like an ill-designed machine, Delp went down on his belly. "I abase myself," he mumbled. "I eat your offal. I declare that my fathers were the slaves of your fathers. Like a netted fish, I gasp for pardon."

T'heonax enjoyed himself. The fact that Delp had been so cleverly trapped between his pride and his wish to serve the Fleet made it all the sweeter.

"Very good, captain," said the admiral when the ceremony was done. "Be thankful I didn't make you do this publicly. Now let me hear your argument. I believe you were saying something about the protection of our rafts."

"Yes . . . yes, sir. I was saying . . . the rafts need not fear the enemy."

"Indeed? True, they lie well out at sea, but not too far to reach in a few hours. What's to prevent the Flock army from assembling, unknown to you, in the mountains, then attacking the rafts before you can come to our help?"

"I would only hope they do so, sir." Delp recovered a little enthusiasm. "But I'm afraid their leadership isn't that stupid. Since when . . . I mean . . . at no time in naval history, sir, has a flying force, unsupported from the water, been able to overcome a fleet. At best, and at heavy cost, it can capture one or two rafts . . . temporarily, as in the raid when they stole the Eart'honai. Then the other vessels move in and drive it off. You see, sir, fliers can't use the engines of war, catapults and flamethrowers and so on, which alone can reduce a naval organization. Whereas the raft crews can stand under shelters and fire upward, picking the fliers off at leisure."

"Of course." T'heonax nodded. "All this is so obvious as to be a gross waste of my time. But your idea is, I take it, that a small cadre of guards would suffice to hold off a Lannach'ho attack of any size."

"And, if we're lucky, keep the enemy busy out at sea till I could arrive with our main forces. But as I said, sir, they must have brains enough not to try it."

"You assume a great deal, captain," murmured T'heonax. "You assume, not merely that I will let you go into the mountains at all, but that I will put you in command."

Delp bent his head and drooped his wings. "Apology, sir."

"I think . . . yes, I think it would be best if you just stayed here at Mannenach with your immediate flotilla."

"As the admiral wishes. Will he consider my plan, though?"

"Aeak'ha eat you!" snarled T'heonax. "I've no love for you, Delp, as well you know; but your scheme is good, and you're the best one to carry it through. I shall appoint you in charge."

Delp stood as if struck with a maul.

"Get out," said T'heonax. "We will have an official conference later."

"I thank my lord admiral—"

"Go, I said!"

When Delp had gone, T'heonax turned to his favorite. "Don't look so worried," he said. "I know what you're thinking. The fellow will win his campaign, and become still more popular, and somewhere along the line he will get ideas about seizing the Admiralty."

"I only wondered how my lord planned to prevent that," said the courtier.

"Simple enough." T'heonax grinned. "I know his type. As long as the war goes on, we've no danger of rebellion from him. So, let him break the Lannach'honai as he wishes. He'll pursue their remnants, to make sure of finishing the job. And in that pursuit—a stray arrow from somewhere—most regrettable—these things are easy to arrange. Yes."

❁ XV ❁

This atmosphere carried the dust particles which are the nuclei of water condensation to a higher, hence colder altitude. Thus Diomedes had more clouds and precipitation of every kind than Earth. On a clear night you saw fewer stars; on a foggy night you did not see at all.

Mist rolled up through stony dales, until the young High Summer became a dripping chill twilight. The hordes lairing about Salmenbrok mumbled in their hunger and hopelessness: now the sun itself had withdrawn from them.

No campfires glowed; the wood of this region had all been burned. And the hinterland had been scoured clean of game, unripe wild grains, the very worms and insects, eaten by these many warriors. Now, in an eerie dank dark, only the wind and the rushing glacial waters lived . . . and Mount Oborch, sullenly prophesying deep in the earth.

Trolwen and Tolk went from the despair of their chieftains, over narrow trails where fog smoked and the high thin houses stood unreal, to the mill where the Eart'-ska worked.

Here alone, it seemed, existence remained—fires still burned, stored water came down flumes to turn the wind-abandoned wheels, movement went under flickering tapers as lathes chattered and hammers thumped. Somehow, in some impossible fashion, Nicholas van Rijn had roared down the embittered protests of Angrek's gang, and their factory was at work.

Working for what? thought Trolwen, in a mind as gray as the mist.

Van Rijn himself met them at the door. He folded massive arms on hairy breast and said: "How do you, my friends? Here it goes well, we have soon a many artillery pieces ready."

"And what use will they be?" said Trolwen. "Oh, yes, we have enough to make Salmenbrok well-nigh impregnable. Which means, we could hole up here and let the enemy ring us in till we starve."

"Speak not to me of starving." Van Rijn fished in his pouch, extracted a dry bit of cheese, and regarded it mournfully. "To think, this was not so long ago a rich delicious Swiss. Now, not to rats would I offer it." He stuffed it into his mouth and chewed noisily. "My problem of belly stoking is worse than yours. *Imprimis,* the high boiling point of water here makes this a world of very bad cooks, with no idea about controlled temperatures. *Secundus,* did your porters haul me through the air, that long lumpy way from Mannenach, to let me hunger into death?"

"I could wish we'd left you down there!" flared Trolwen.

"No," said Tolk. "He and his friends have striven, Flockchief."

"Forgive me," said Trolwen contritely. "It was only . . . I got the news . . . the Drak'honai have just destroyed Eiseldrae."

"An empty town, *nie?*"

"A holy town. And they set afire the woods around it." Trolwen arched his back. "This can't go on! Soon, even if we should somehow win, the land will be too desolated to support us."

"I think still you can spare a few forests," said van Rijn. "This is not an overpopulated country."

"See here," said Trolwen in a harshening tone, "I've borne with you so far. I admit you're essentially right: that to fare out with all our power, for a decisive battle with the massed enemy, is to risk final destruction. But to sit here, doing nothing but make little guerrilla raids on their outposts, while they grind away our nation—that is to make certain we are doomed."

"We needed time," said van Rijn. "Time to modify the extra field pieces, making up for what we lost at Mannenach."

"Why? They're not portable, without trains. And to make matters worse, that motherless Delp has torn up the rails!"

"Oh, yes, they are portable. My young friend Wace has done a little redesigning. Knocked down, with females and cubs to help, everyone carrying a single small piece or two—we can tote a heavy battery of weapons, by damn!"

"I know. You've explained all this before. And I repeat: what will we use them against? If we set them up at some particular spot, the Drak'honai need only avoid that spot. And we can't stay very long in any one place, because our numbers eat it barren." Trolwen drew a breath. "I did not come here to argue, Eart'a. I came from the General Council of Lannach, to tell you that Salmenbrok's food is exhausted—and so is the army's patience. We *must* go out and fight!"

"We shall," said van Rijn imperturbably. "Come, I will go talk at these puff-head councilors."

He stuck his head in the door: "Wace, boy, best you start to pack what we have. Soon we transport it."

"I heard you," said the younger man.

"Good. You make the work here, I make the politicking, so it goes along fine, *nie?*" Van Rijn rubbed shaggy fists, beamed, and shuffled off with Trolwen and Tolk.

Wace stared after him, into the blind fog-wall. "Yes," he said. "That's how it has been. We work, and he talks. Very equitable!"

"What do you mean?" Sandra raised her head from the table at which she sat marking gun parts with a small paintbrush. A score of females were working beside her.

"What I said. I wonder why I don't say it to his face. I'm not afraid of that fat parasite, and I don't want his

mucking paycheck any more." Wace waved at the mill
and its sooty confusion. "Do this, do that, he says, and
then strolls off again. When I think how he's eating food
which would keep *you* alive—"

"You do not understand?" She stared at him for a
moment. "No, I think maybe you have been too busy,
all the time here, to stop and think. And before then,
you were a small-job man without the art of government, not?"

"What do you mean?" he echoed her. He regarded
her with eyes washed-out and bleared by fatigue.

"Maybe later. Now we must hurry. Soon we will leave
this town, and everything must be set to go."

This time she had found a place for her hands, in the
ten or fifteen Earth-days since Mannenach. Van Rijn
had demanded that everything—the excess war materiel,
which there had luckily not been room enough to take
down to battle—be made portable by air. That involved a
certain amount of modification, so that the large wooden
members could be cut up into smaller units, for reassem-
bly where needed. Wace had managed that. But it would
all be one chaos at journey's end, unless there was a
system for identifying each item. Sandra had devised the
markings and was painting them on.

Neither she nor Wace had stopped for much sleep.
They had not even paused to wonder greatly what use
there would be for their labor.

"Old Nick did say something about attacking the Fleet
itself," muttered Wace. "Has he gone uncon? Are we
supposed to land on the water and assemble our catapults?"

"Perhaps," said Sandra. Her tone was serene. "I do
not worry so much any more. Soon it will be decided . . .
because we have food for just four Earth-weeks or less."

"We can last at least two months without eating at all," he said.

"But we will be weak." She dropped her gaze. "Eric—"

"Yes?" He left his mill-powered obsidian-toothed circular saw, and came over to stand above her. The dull rush light caught drops of fog in her hair, they gleamed like tiny jewels.

"Soon . . . it will make no matter what I do . . . there will be hard work, needing strength and skill I have not . . . maybe fighting, where I am only one more bow, not a very strong bow even." Her fingernails whitened where she gripped her brush. "So when it comes to that, I will eat no more. You and Nicholas take my share."

"Don't be a fool," he said hoarsely.

She sat up straight, turned around and glared at him. Her pale cheeks reddened. "Do you not be the fool, Eric Wace," she snapped. "If I can give you and him just one extra week where you are strong—where your hunger does not keep you from even thinking clearly—then it will be myself I save too, perhaps. And if not, I have only lost one or two worthless weeks. Now get back to your machine!"

He watched her, for some small while, and his heart thuttered. Then he nodded and returned to his own work.

And down the trails to an open place of harsh grass, where the Council sat on a cliff's edge, van Rijn picked his steadily swearing way.

The elders of Lannach lay like sphinxes against a skyline gone formless gray, and waited for him. Trolwen went to the head of the double line, Tolk remained by the human.

"In the name of the All-Wise, we are met," said the commander ritually. "Let sun and moons illumine our minds. Let the ghosts of our grandmothers lend us their guidance. May I not shame those who flew before me, nor those who come after." He relaxed a trifle. "Well, my officers, it's decided we can't stay here. I've brought the Eart'a to advise us. Will you explain the alternatives to him?"

A gaunt, angry-eyed old Lannacha hunched his wings and spat: "First, Flockchief, why is he here at all?"

"By the commander's invitation," said Tolk smoothly.

"I mean . . . Herald, let's not twist words. You know what I mean. The Mannenach expedition was undertaken at his urging. It cost us the worst defeat in our history. Since then, he has insisted our main body stay here, idle, while the enemy ravages an undefended land. I don't see why we should take his advice."

Trolwen's eyes were troubled. "Are there further challenges?" he asked, in a very low voice.

An indignant mumble went down the lines. "Yes . . . yes . . . yes . . . let him answer, if he can."

Van Rijn turned turkey red and began to swell like a frog.

"The Eart'a has been challenged in Council," said Trolwen. "Does he wish to reply?"

He sat back then, waiting like the others.

Van Rijn exploded.

"Pest and damnation! Four million worms cocooning in hell! How long am I to be saddled with stupid ungratefuls? How many politicians and brass hats have You Up There plagued this universe with?" He waved his fists in the air and screamed. "Satan and sulfur! It is not to be stood! If you are all so hot to make suicides for yourselves, why does poor old van Rijn have to hold on to

your coat tails the whole time? *Perbacco,* you stop
insulting me or I stuff you down your own throats!" He
advanced like a moving mountain, roaring at them. The
nearest councilors flinched away.

"Eart'a . . . sir . . . officer . . . please!" whispered Trolwen.

When he had them sufficiently browbeaten, van Rijn
said coldly: "All rights. I tell you, by damn. I give you
good advices and you stupid them up and blame
me—but I am a poor patient old man, not like when I
was young and strong no, I suffer it with Christian meek-
ness and keep on giving you good advices.

"I warned you and I warned you, do not hit Mannenach first, I warned you. I told you the rafts could come
right up to its walls, and the rafts are the strength of the
Fleet. I got down on these two poor old knees, begging
and pleading with you first to take the key upland towns,
but no, you would not listen to me. And still we *had*
Mannenach, but the victory was stupided away . . . oh, if
I had wings like an angel, so I could have led you in
person! I would be cock-a-doodle-dooing on the admiral's masthead this moment, by holy Nicolai miter! That
is why you take my advices, by damn—no, you take my
orders! No more backward talking from you, or I wash
my hands with you and make my own way home. From
now on, if you want to keep living, when van Rijn says
frog, you jump. Understanding?"

He paused. He could hear his own asthmatic
wheezes . . . and the far unhappy mumble of the camp,
and the cold wet clinking of water down alien rocks . . .
nothing more in all the world.

Finally Trolwen said in a weak voice: "If . . . if the
challenge is considered answered . . . we shall resume
our business."

No one spoke.

"Will the Eart'a take the word?" asked Tolk at last. He alone appeared self-possessed, in the critical glow of one who appreciates fine acting.

"*Ja.* I will say, I know we cannot remain here any more. You ask why I kept the army on leash and let Captain Delp have his way." Van Rijn ticked it off on his fingers. "*Imprimis,* to attack him directly is what he wants; he can most likely beat us, since his force is bigger and not so hungry or discouraged. *Secundus,* he will not advance to Salmenbrok while we are all here, since we could bushwhack him; therefore, by staying put the army has gained me a chance to make ready our artillery pieces. *Tertius,* it is my hope that by this delay while I had the mill going, we have won the means of victory."

"What?" It barked from the throat of a councilor who forgot formalities.

"Ah." Van Rijn laid a finger to his imposing nose and winked. "We shall see. Maybe now you think even if I am a pitiful old weak tired man who should be in bed with hot toddies and a good cigar, still a Polesotechnic merchant is not just to sneeze at. So? Well, then. I propose we leave this land and head north."

A hubbub broke loose. He waited patiently for it to subside.

"Order!" shouted Trolwen. "Order!" He slapped the hard earth with his tail. "Quiet, there, officers! . . . Eart'a, there has been some talk of abandoning Lannach altogether—more and more of it, indeed, as our folk lose heart. We could still reach Swampy Kilnu in time to . . . to save most of our females and cubs at Birthtime. But it would be to give up our towns, our fields and forests—everything we have, everything our forebears labored for hundreds of years to create—to sink back into savagery, in a dark fever-haunted jungle, to become nothing—I myself will die in battle before making such a choice."

He drew a breath and hurled out: "But Kilnu is, at least, to the south. North of Achan, there is still ice!"

"Just so," said van Rijn.

"Would you have us starve and freeze on the Dawrnach glaciers? We can't land any further south than Dawrnach; the Fleet's scouts would be certain to spot us anywhere in Holmenach. Unless you want to fight the last fight in the archipelago—?"

"No," said van Rijn. "We should sneak up to this Dawrnach place. We can pack a lunch—take maybe a ten-days' worth of food and fuel with us, as well as the armament—*nie*?"

"Well . . . yes . . . but even so—Are you suggesting we should attack the Fleet itself, the rafts, from the north? It would be an unexpected direction. But it would be just as hopeless."

"Surprise we will need for my plan," said van Rijn. "*Ja.* We cannot tell the army. One of them might be captured in some skirmish and made to tell the Drak'honai. Best maybe I not even tell you."

"Enough!" said Trolwen. "Let me hear your scheme."

Much later: "It won't work. Oh, it might well be technically feasible. But it's a political impossibility."

"Politics!" groaned van Rijn. "What is it this time?"

"The warriors . . . yes, and the females too, even the cubs, since it would be our whole nation which goes to Dawrnach. They must be told why we do so. Yet the whole scheme, as you admit, will be ruined if one person falls into enemy hands and tells what he knows under torture."

"But he need not know," said van Rijn. "All he need be told is, we spend a little while gathering food and wood to travel with. Then we are to pack up and go some other place, he has not been told where or why."

"We are not Drakska," said Trolwen angrily. "We are a free folk. I have no right to make so important a decision without submitting it to a vote."

"Hm-m-m maybe you could talk to them?" Van Rijn tugged his mustaches. "Orate at them. Persuade them to waive their right to know and help decide. Talk them into following you with no questions."

"No," said Tolk. "I'm a specialist in the arts of persuasion, Eart'a, and I've measured the limits of those arts. We deal less with a Flock now than a mob—cold, hungry, without hope, without faith in its leaders, ready to give up everything—or rush forth to blind battle—they haven't the morale to follow anyone into an unknown venture."

"Morale can be pumped in," said van Rijn. "I will try."

"*You!*"

"I am not so bad at oratings, myself, when there is need. Let me address them."

"They . . . they—" Tolk stared at him. Then he laughed, a jarringly sarcastic note. "Let it be done, Flock-chief. Let's hear what words this Eart'a can find, so much better than our own."

And an hour later, he sat on a bluff, with his people a mass of shadow below him, and he heard van Rijn's bass come through the fog like thunder:

" . . . I say only, think what you have here, and what they would take away from you:

"This royal throne of kings, this sceptr'd isle,
This earth of majesty, this seat of Mars,
This other Eden, demi-paradise,
This fortress built by Nature for herself
Against infection and the hand of war,
This happy breed . . ."

"I don't comprehend all those words," whispered Tolk.

"Be still!" answered Trolwen. "Let me hear." There were tears in his eyes; he shivered.

" . . . This blessed plot, this earth, this realm, this Lannach . . ."

The army beat its wings and screamed.

Van Rijn continued through adaptations of Pericles' funeral speech, "Scots Wha' Hae," and the Gettysburg Address. By the time he had finished discussing St. Crispin's Day, he could have been elected commander if he chose.

◈ XVI ◈

The island called Dawrnach lay well beyond the archipelago's end, several hundred kilometers north of Lannach. However swiftly the Flock flew, with pauses for rest on some bird-shrieking skerry, it was a matter of Earth-days to get there, and a physical nightmare for humans trussed in carrying nets. Afterward Wace's recollections of the trip were dim.

When he stood on the beach at their goal, his legs barely supporting him, it was small comfort.

High Summer had come here also, and this was not too far north; still, the air remained wintry and Tolk said no one had ever tried to live here. The Holmenach islands deflected a cold current out of The Ocean, up into the Iceberg Sea, and those bitter waters flowed around Dawrnach.

Now the Flock, wings and wings and wings dropping down from the sky until they hid its roiling grayness, had reached journey's conclusion: black sands, washed by heavy dark tides and climbing sheer up through permanent glaciers to the inflamed throat of a volcano. Thin straight trees were sprinkled over the lower slopes, between quaking tussocks; there were a few sea birds, to dip above the broken offshore ice-floes; otherwise the hidden sun threw its clotted-blood light on a sterile country.

Sandra shuddered. Wace was shocked to see how thin she had already grown. And now that they were here, in the last phase of their striving—belike of their lives—she intended to eat no more.

She wrapped her stinking coarse jacket more tightly about her. The wind caught snarled pale elflocks of her hair and fluttered them forlorn against black igneous cliffs. Around her crouched, walked, wriggled, and flapped ten thousand angry dragons: whistles and gutturals of unhuman speech, the cannon-crack of leathery wings, overrode the empty wind-whimper. As she rubbed her eyes, pathetically like a child, Wace saw that her once beautiful hands were bleeding where they had clung to the net, and that she shook with weariness.

He felt his heart twisted, and moved toward her. Nicholas van Rijn got there first, fat and greasy, with a roar for comfort: "So, by jolly damn, now we are here and soon I get you home again to a hot bath. Holy St. Dismas, right now I smell you three kilometers upwind!"

Lady Sandra Tamarin, heiress to the Grand Duchy of Hermes, gave him a ghostly smile. "If I could rest for a little—" she whispered.

"*Ja, ja,* we see." Van Rijn stuck two fingers in his mouth and let out an eardrum-breaking blast. It caught Trolwen's attention. "You there! Find her here a cave or something and tuck her in."

"I?" Trolwen bridled. "I have the Flock to see to!"

"You heard me, pot head." Van Rijn stumped off and buttonholed Wace. "Now, then. You are ready to begin work? Round up your crew, however many you need to start."

"I—" Wace backed away. "Look here, it's been I don't know how many hours since our last stop, and—"

Van Rijn spat. "And how many weeks makes it since I had a smoke or even so much a little glass Genever, ha? You have no considerations for other people." He pointed his beak heavenward and screamed: "Do I have to do everything? Why have You Up There filled up the galaxy with no-good loafers? It is not to be stood!"

"Well . . . well—" Wace saw Trolwen leading Sandra off, to find a place where she could sleep, forgetting cold and pain and loneliness for a few niggard hours. He struck a fist into his palm and said: "All right! But what will you be doing?"

"I must organize things, by damn. First I see Trolwen about a gang to cut trees and make masts and yards and oars. Meanwhiles all this canvas we have brought along has got to somehow be made in sails; and there are the riggings; and also we must fix up for eating and shelter—Bah! These is details. It is not right I should be bothered. Details, I hire ones like you for."

"Is life anything but details?" snapped Wace.

Van Rijn's small gray eyes studied him for a moment. "So," rumbled the merchant, "it gives back talks from you too, ha? You think maybe just because I am old and weak, and do not stand so much the hardships like when I was young . . . maybe I only leech off your work, *nie?* Now is too small time for beating sense into your head. Maybe you learn for yourself." He snapped his fingers. "Jump!"

Wace went off, damning himself for not giving the old pig a fist in the stomach. He would, too, come the day! Not now . . . unfortunately, van Rijn had somehow oozed into a position where it was him the Lannachska looked up to . . . instead of Wace, who did the actual work—Was that a paranoid thought? No.

Take this matter of the ships, for instance. Van Rijn had pointed out that an island like Dawrnach, loaded with pack ice and calving glaciers, afforded plenty of building material. Stone chisels would shape a vessel as big as any raft in the Fleet, in a few hours' work. The most primitive kind of blowtorch, an oil lamp with a bellows, would smooth it off. A crude mast and rudder could be planted in holes cut for the purpose: water, refreezing, would be a strong cement. With most of the Flock, males, females, old, young, made one enormous labor force for the project, a flotilla comparable in numbers to the whole Fleet could be made in a week.

If an engineer figured out all the practical procedure. How deep a hole to step your mast in? Is ballast needed? Just how do you make a nice clean cut in an irregular ice block hundreds of meters long? How about smoothing the bottom to reduce drag? The material was rather friable; it could be strengthened considerably by dashing bucketsful of mixed sawdust and sea water over the finished hull, letting this freeze as a kind of armor—but what proportions?

There was no time to really test these things. Somehow, by God and by guess, with every element against him, Eric Wace was expected to produce.

And van Rijn? What did van Rijn contribute? The basic idea, airily tossed off, apparently on the assumption that Wace was Aladdin's jinni. Oh, it was quite a flash of imaginative insight, no one could deny that. But imagination is cheap.

Anyone can say: "What we need is a new weapon, and we can make it from such-and-such unprecedented materials." But it will remain an idle fantasy until somebody shows up who can figure out *how* to make the needed weapon.

So, having enslaved his engineer, van Rijn strolled around, jollying some of the Flock and bullying some of the others—and when he had them all working their idiotic heads off, he rolled up in a blanket and went to sleep!

❈ XVII ❈

Wace stood on the deck of the *Rijstaffel* and watched his enemy come over the world's rim.

Slowly, he reached into the pouch at his side. His hand closed on a chunk of stale bread and a slab of sausage. It was the last Terrestrial food remaining: for Earth-days, now, he had gone on a still thinner ration than before, so that he could enter this battle with something in his stomach.

He found that he didn't want it after all.

Surprisingly little cold breathed up from underfoot. The warm air over the Sea of Achan wafted the ice-chill away. He was less astonished that there had been no appreciable melting in the week he estimated they had been creeping southward; he knew the thermal properties of water.

Behind him, primitive square sails, lashed to yardarms of green wood on overstrained one-piece masts, bellied in the north wind. These ice ships were tubby, but considerably less so than a Drak'ho raft; and with some unbelievable talent for tyranny, van Rijn had gotten reluctant Lannachska to work under frigid sea water, cutting the bottoms into a vaguely streamlined shape. Now, given the power of a Diomedean breeze, Lannach's war fleet waddled through Achan waves at a good five knots.

Though the hardest moment, Wace reflected, had not been while they worked their hearts out to finish the craft. It had come afterward, when they were almost ready to leave and the winds turned contrary. For a period measured in Earth-days, thousands of Lannachska huddled soul-sick under freezing rains, ranging after fish and bird rookeries to feed cubs that cried with hunger. Councilors and clan leaders had argued that this was a war on the Fates: there could be no choice but to give up and seek out Swampy Kilnu. Somehow, blustering, whining, pleading, promising—in a few cases, bribing with what he had won at dice—van Rijn had held them on Dawrnach.

Well—it was over with.

The merchant came out of the little stone cabin, walked over the gravel-strewn deck past crouching war-engines and heaped missiles, till he reached the bows where Wace stood.

"Best you eat," he said. "Soon gives no chance."

"I'm not hungry," said Wace.

"So, no?" Van Rijn grabbed the sandwich out of his fingers. "Then, by damn, I am!" He began cramming it between his teeth.

Once again he wore a double set of armor, but he had chosen one weapon only for this occasion, an outsize stone ax with a meter-long handle. Wace carried a smaller tomahawk and a shield. Around the humans, it bristled with armed Lannachska.

"They're making ready to receive us, all right," said Wace. His eyes sought out the gaunt enemy war-canoes, beating upwind.

"You expected a carpet with acres and acres, like they say in America? I bet you they spotted us from the air hours ago. Now they send messengers hurry-like back to their army in Lannach." Van Rijn held up the last fragment of meat, kissed it reverently, and ate it.

Wace's eyes traveled backward. This was the flagship—chosen as such when it turned out to be the fastest—and had the forward position in a long wedge. Several score grayish-white, ragged-sailed, helter-skelter little vessels wallowed after. They were outnumbered and outgunned by the Drak'ho rafts, of course; they just had to hope the odds weren't too great. The much lower freeboard did not matter to a winged race, but it would be important that their crews were not very skilled sailors—

But at least the Lannachska were fighters. Winged tigers by now, thought Wace. The southward voyage had rested them, and trawling had provided the means to feed them, and the will to battle had kindled again. Also, though they had a smaller navy, they probably had more warriors, even counting Delp's absent army.

And they could afford to be reckless. Their females and young were still on Dawrnach—with Sandra, grown so white and quiet—and they had no treasures along to worry about. For cargo they bore just their weapons and their hate.

From the clouds of airborne, Tolk the Herald came down. He braked on extended wings, slithered to a landing, and curved back his neck swan-fashion to regard the humans.

"Does it all go well down here?" he asked.

"As well as may be," said van Rijn. "Are we still bearing on the pest-rotten Fleet?"

"Yes. It's not many buaska away now. Barely over your sea-level horizon, in fact; you'll raise it soon. They're using sail and oars alike, trying to get out of our path, but they'll not achieve it if we keep this wind and those canoes don't delay us."

"No sign of the army in Lannach?"

"None yet. I daresay what's-his-name . . . the new admiral that we heard about from those prisoners . . . has messengers scouring the mountains. But that's a big land up there. It will take time to locate him." Tolk snorted professional scorn. "Now *I* would have had constant liaison, a steady two-way flow of Whistlers."

"Still," said van Rijn, "we must expect them soon, and then gives hell's safety valve popping off."

"Are you certain we can—"

"I am certain of nothings. Now get back to Trolwen and oversee."

Tolk nodded and hit the air again.

Dark purplish water curled in white feathers, beneath a high heaven where clouds ran like playful mountains, tinted rosy by the sun. Not many kilometers off, a small island rose sheer; through a telescope, Wace could count the patches of yellow blossom nodding under tall bluish conifers. A pair of young Whistlers dipped and soared over his head, dancing like the clan banners being unfurled in the sky. It was hard to understand that the slim carved boats racing so near bore fire and sharpened stones.

"Well," said van Rijn, "here begins our fun. Good St. Dismas, stand by me now."

"St. George would be a little more appropriate, wouldn't he?" asked Wace.

"You may think so. Me, I am too old and fat and cowardly to call on Michael or George or Olaf or any like those soldierly fellows. I feel more at home, me, with saints not so bloody energetic, Dismas or my own good namesake who is so kind to travelers."

"And is also the patron of highway men," remarked Wace. He wished his tongue wouldn't get so thick and dry on him. He felt remote, somehow . . . not really afraid . . . but his knees were rubbery.

"Ha!" boomed van Rijn. "Good shootings, boy!" The forward ballista on the *Rijstaffel*, with a whine and a thump, had smacked a half-ton stone into the nearest canoe. The boat cracked like a twig; its crew whirled up, a squad from Trolwen's aerial command pounced, there was a moment's murderous confusion and then the Drak'honai had stopped existing.

Van Rijn grabbed the astonished ballista captain by the hands and danced him over the deck, bawling out,

"Du bist mein Sonnenschein, mein einzig Sonnenschein, du machst mir fröhlich—"

Another canoe swung about, close-hauled. Wace saw its flamethrower crew bent over their engine and hurled himself flat under the low wall surrounding the ice deck.

The burning stream hit that wall, splashed back, and spread itself on the sea. It could not kindle frozen water, nor melt enough of it to notice. Sheltered amidships, a hundred Lannacha archers sent an arrow-sleet up, to arc under heaven and come down on the canoe.

Wace peered over the wall. The flamethrower pump-man seemed dead, the hoseman was preoccupied with a transfixed wing . . . no steersman either, the canoe's boom slatted about in a meaningless arc while its crew huddled—"Dead ahead!" he roared. "Ram them!"

The Lannacha ship trampled the dugout underfoot.

Drak'ho canoes circled like wolves around a buffalo herd, using their speed and maneuverability. Several darted between ice vessels, to assail from the rear; others went past the ends of the wedge formation. It was not quite a one-sided battle—arrows, catapult bolts, flung stones, all hurt Lannachska; oil jugs arced across the water, exploding on ice decks; now and then a fire stream ignited a sail.

But winged creatures with a few buckets could douse burning canvas. During that entire phase of the engagement, only one Lannacha craft was wholly dismasted, and its crew simply abandoned it, parceling themselves out among other vessels. Nothing else could catch fire, except live flesh, which has always been the cheapest article in war.

Several canoes, converging on a single ship, tried to board. They were nonetheless outnumbered, and paid heavily for the attempt. Meanwhile Trolwen, with absolute air mastery, swooped and shot and hammered.

Drak'ho's canoes scarcely hindered the attack. The dugouts were rammed, broken, set afire, brushed aside by their unsinkable enemy.

By virtue of being first, of having more or less punched through the line, the *Rijstaffel* met little opposition. What there was, was beaten off by catapult, ballista, fire pot, and arrows: long-range gunnery. The sea itself burned and smoked behind; ahead lay the great rafts.

When those sails and banners came into view, Wace's dragon crewmen began to sing the victory song of the Flock.

"A little premature, aren't they?" he cried above the racket.

"Ah," said van Rijn quietly, "let them make fun for now. So many will soon be down, blind among the fishes, *nie?*"

"I suppose—" Hastily, as if afraid of what he had done merely to save his own life, Wace said: "I like that melody, don't you? It's rather like some old American folk songs. *John Harty*, say."

"Folk songs is all right if you should want to play you are Folk in great big capitals," snorted van Rijn. "I stick with Mozart, by damn."

He stared down into the water, and a curious wistfulness tinged his voice. "I always hoped maybe I would understand Bach some day, before I die, old Johann Sebastian who talked with God in mathematics. I have not the brains, though, in this dumb old head. So maybe I ask only one more chance to listen at *Eine Kleine Nachtmusik.*"

There was an uproar in the Fleet. Slowly and ponderously, churning the sea with spider-leg oars, the rafts were giving up their attempt at evasion. They were pulling into war formation.

Van Rijn waved angrily at a Whistler. "Quick! You get upstairs fast, and tell that crockhead Trolwen not to bother air-covering us against the canoes. Have him attack the rafts. Keep them busy, by hell! Don't let messengers flappity-flap between enemy captains so they can organize!"

As the young Lannacha streaked away, the merchant tugged his goatee—almost lost by now in a dirt-stiffened beard—and snarled: "Great hairy honeypots! How long do I have to do all the thinkings? Good St. Nicholas, you bring me an officer staff with brains between the ears, instead of clabbered oatmeal, and I build you a cathedral on Mars! You hear me?"

"Trolwen is in the midst of a fight up there," protested Wace. "You can't expect him to think of everything."

"Maybe not," conceded van Rijn grudgingly. "Maybe I am the only one in the galaxy who makes no mistakes."

Horribly near, the massed rafts became a storm when Trolwen took his advice. Bat-winged devils sought each other's lives through one red chaos. Wace thought his own ships' advance must be nearly unnoticed in that whirling, shrieking destruction.

"They're *not* getting integrated!" he said, beating his fist on the wall. "Before God, they're not!"

A Whistler landed, coughing blood; there was a monstrous bruise on his side. "Over yonder . . . Tolk the Herald says . . . empty spot . . . drive wedge in Fleet—" The thin body arced and then slid inertly to the deck. Wace stooped, taking the unhuman youth in his arms. He heard blood gurgle in lungs pierced by the broken ends of ribs.

"Mother, mother," gasped the Whistler. "He hit me with an ax. Make it stop hurting, mother."

Presently he died.

Van Rijn cursed his awkward vessel into a course change—not more than a few degrees, it wasn't capable of more, but as the nearer rafts began to loom above the ice deck, it could be seen that there was a wide gap in their line. Trolwen's assault had so far prevented its being closed. Red-stained water, littered with dropped spears and bows, pointed like a hand toward the admiral's floating castle.

"In there!" bawled van Rijn. "Clobber them! Eat them for breakfast!"

A catapult bolt came whirring over the wall, ripped through his sleeve and showered ice chips where it struck. Then three streams of liquid fire converged on the *Rijstaffel*.

Flame fingers groped their way across the deck, one Lannacha lay screaming and charring where they had touched him, and found the sails. It was no use to pour water this time: oil-drenched, mast and rigging and canvas became one great torch.

Van Rijn left the helmsman he had been swearing at and bounded across the deck, slipped where some of it had melted, skated on his broad bottom till he fetched up against a wall, and crawled back to his feet calling down damnation on the cosmos. Up to the starboard shrouds he limped, and his stone ax began gnawing the cordage. "Here!" he yelled. "Fast! Help me, you jellybones! Quick, have you got fur on the brain, quick before we drift past!"

Wace, directing the ballista crew, which was stoning a nearby raft, understood only vaguely. Others were more ready than he. They swarmed to van Rijn and hewed. He himself sought the racked oil bombs and broke one at the foot of the burning mast.

Its socket melted, held up only by the shrouds, the enormous torch fell to port when the starboard lines were slashed. It struck the raft there; flames ran from it, beating back frantic Drak'ho crewmen who would push it loose; rigging caught; timbers began to char. As the *Rijstaffel* drifted away, that enemy vessel turned into a single bellowing pyre.

Now the ice ship was nearly uncontrollable, driven by momentum and chance currents deeper into the confused Fleet. But through the gap which van Rijn had so ardently widened, the rest of the Lannacha craft pushed. War-flames raged between floating monsters—but wood will burn and ice will not.

Through a growing smoke-haze among darts and arrows that rattled down from above, on a deck strewn with dead and hurt but still filled by the revengeful hale, Wace trod to the nearest bomb crew. They were preparing to ignite another raft as soon as the ship's drift brought them into range.

"No," he said.

"What?" The captain turned a sooty face to him, crest adroop with weariness. "But sir, they'll be pumping fire at us!"

"We can stand that," said Wace. "We're pretty well sheltered by our walls. I don't want to burn that raft. I want to capture it!"

The Diomedean whistled. Then his wings spread and his eyes flared and he asked: "May I be the first on board it?"

Van Rijn passed by, hefting his ax. He could not have heard what was said, but he rumbled: "*Ja.* I was just about to order this. We can use us a transportation that maneuvers."

The word went over the ship. Its slippery deck darkened with armed shapes that waited. Closer and closer, the wrought ice-floe bore down on the higher and more massive raft. Fire, stones, and quarrels reached out for the Lannachska. They endured it, grimly. Wace sent a Whistler up to Trolwen to ask for help; a flying detachment silenced the Drak'ho artillery with arrows.

Trolwen still had overwhelming numerical superiority. He could choke the sky with his warriors, pinning the Drak'honai to their decks to await sea-borne assault. So far, thought Wace, Diomedes' miserly gods had been smiling on him. It couldn't last much longer.

He followed the first Lannacha wave, which had flown to clear a bridgehead on the raft. He sprang from the ice-floe when it bumped to a halt, grasped a massive timber, and scrambled up the side. When he reached the top and unlimbered his tomahawk and shield, he found himself in a line of warriors. Smoke from the burnings elsewhere stung his eyes; only indistinctly did he see the defending Drak'honai, pulled into ranks ahead of him and up on the higher decks.

Had the yelling and tumbling about overhead suddenly redoubled?

A stumpy finger tapped him. He turned around to meet van Rijn's porcine gaze.

"Whoof and whoo! What for a climb that was! Better I should have stayed, *nie?* Well, boy, we are on our own now. Tolk just sent me word, the whole Drak'ho Expeditionary Force is in sight and lolloping hereward fast."

❈ XVIII ❈

Briefly, Wace felt sick. Had it all come to this, a chipped flint in his skull after Delp's army had beaten off the Lannachska?

Then he remembered standing on the cold black beach of Dawrnach, shortly before they sailed, and wondering aloud if he would ever again speak with Sandra. "I'll have the easy part if we lose," he had said. "It'll be over quickly enough for me. But you—"

She gave him a look that brimmed with pride, and answered: "What makes you think you can lose?"

He hefted his weapon. The lean winged bodies about him hissed, bristled, and glided ahead.

These were mostly troopers from the Mannenach attempt; every ice ship bore a fair number who had been taught the elements of ground fighting. And on the whole trip south to find the Fleet, van Rijn and the Lannacha captains had exhorted them: "Do not join our aerial forces. Stay on the decks when we board a raft. This whole plan hinges on how many rafts we can seize or destroy. Trolwen and his air squadrons will merely be up there to support you."

The idea took root reluctantly in any Diomedean brain. Wace was not at all certain it wouldn't die within the next hour, leaving him and van Rijn marooned on hostile timbers while their comrades soared up to a pointless sky battle. But he had no choice, save to trust them now.

He broke into a run. The screech that his followers let out tore at his eardrums.

Wings threshed before him. Instinctively, the untrained Drak'ho lines were breaking up. Through geological eras, the only sane thing for a Diomedean to do had been to get above an attacker. Wace stormed on where they had stood.

Lifting from all the raft, enemy sailors stooped on these curious unflying adversaries. A Lannacha forgot himself, flapped up, and was struck by three meteor bodies. He was hurled like a broken puppet into the sea. The Drak'honai rushed downward.

And they met spears which snapped up like a picket fence. No few of Lannach's one-time ground troopers had rescued their basketwork shields from the last retreat and were now again transformed into artificial turtles. The rest fended off the aerial assault—and the archers made ready.

Wace heard the sinister whistle rise behind him, and saw fifty Drak'honai fall.

Then a dragon roared in his face, striking with a knife-toothed rake. Wace caught the blow on his shield. It shuddered in his left arm, numbing the muscles. He lashed out a heavy-shod foot, caught the hard belly and heard the wind leave the Drak'ho. His tomahawk rose and fell with a dull chopping sound. The Diomedean fluttered away, pawing at a broken wing.

Wace hurried on. The Drak'honai, stunned by the boarding party's tactics, were now milling around overhead out of bowshot. Females snarled in the forecastle doors, spreading wings to defend their screaming cubs. They were ignored: the object was to capture the raft's artillery.

Someone up there must have seen what was intended. His hawk-shriek and hawk-stoop were ended by a Lannacha arrow; but then an organized line peeled off the Drak'honai mass, plummeted to the forecastle deck, and took stance before the main battery of flamethrowers and ballistae.

"So!" rumbled van Rijn. "They make happy fun games after all. We see about this!"

He broke into an elephantine trot, whirling the great mallet over his head. A slingstone bounced off his leather-decked abdomen, an arrow ripped along one cheek, blowgun darts pincushioned his double cuirass. He got a boost from two winged guards, up the sheer ladderless bulkhead of the forecastle. Then he was in among the defenders.

"*Je maintiendrai!*" he bawled, and stove in the head of the nearest Drak'ho. "*God send the right!*" he shouted, stamping on the shaft of a rake that clawed after him. "*Fram, fram, Kristmenn, Krossmenn, Kongsmenn!*" he bellowed, drumming on the ribs of three warriors who ramped close. "*Heineken's Bier!*" he trumpeted, turning to wrestle with a winged shape that fastened onto his back, and wringing its neck.

Wace and the Lannachska joined him. There was an interval with hammer and thrust and the huge bone-breaking buffets of wing and tail. The Drak'honai broke. Van Rijn sprang to the flamethrower and pumped. "Aim the hose!" he panted. "Flush them out, you rust-infested heads!" A gleeful Lannacha seized the ceramic nozzle, pressed the hardwood ignition piston, and squirted burning oil upward.

Down on the lower decks, ballistae began to thump, catapults sang and other flamethrowers licked. A party from the ice ship reassembled one of their wooden machine guns and poured darts at the last Drak'ho counter-erassault.

A female shape ran from the forecastle. "It's our husbands they kill!" she shrieked. "Destroy them!"

Van Rijn leaped off the upper deck, a three-meter fall. Planks thundered and groaned when he hit them.

Puffing, waving his arms, he got ahead of the frantic creature. "Get back!" he yelled in her own language. "Back inside! Shoo! Scat! Want to leave your cubs unprotected? I eat young Drak'honai! With horseradish!"

She wailed and scuttled back to shelter. Wace let out a gasp. His skin was sodden with sweat. It had not been too serious a danger, perhaps . . . in theory, a female mob could have been massacred under the eyes of its young . . . but who could bring himself to that? Not Eric Wace, certainly. Better give up and take one's spear thrust like a gentleman.

He realized, then, that the raft was his.

Smoke still thickened the air too much for him to see very well what was going on elsewhere. Now and then, through a breach in it, appeared some vision: a raft set unquenchably afire, abandoned; an ice vessel, cracked, dismasted, arrow-swept, still bleakly slugging it out; another Lannacha ship laying to against a raft, another boarding party; the banner of a Lannacha clan blowing in sudden triumph on a foreign masthead. Wace had no idea how the sea fight as a whole was going—how many ice craft had been raked clean, deserted by discouraged crews, seized by Drak'ho counterattack, left drifting uselessly remote from the enemy.

It had been perfectly clear, he thought—van Rijn had said it bluntly enough to Trolwen and the Council—that the smaller, less well equipped, virtually untrained Lannacha navy would have no chance whatsoever of decisively whipping the Fleet. The crucial phase of this battle was not going to involve stones or flames.

He looked up. Beyond the spars and lines, where the haze did not reach, heaven lay unbelievably cool. The formations of war, weaving in and about, were so far above him that they looked like darting swallows.

Only after minutes did his inexpert eyes grasp the picture.

With most of his force down among the rafts, Trolwen was ridiculously outnumbered in the air as soon as Delp arrived. On the other hand, Delp's folk had been flying for hours to get here; they were no match individually for well-rested Lannachska. Realizing this, each commander used his peculiar advantage: Delp ordered unbreakable mass charges, Trolwen used small squadrons which swooped in, snapped wolfishly, and darted back again. The Lannachska retreated all the time, except when Delp tried to send a large body of warriors down to relieve the rafts. Then the entire, superbly integrated air force at Trolwen's disposal would smash into that body. It would disperse when Delp brought in reinforcements, but it had accomplished its purpose—to break up the formation and checkrein the seaward movement.

So it went, for some timeless time in the wind under the High Summer sun. Wace lost himself, contemplating the terrible beauty of death winged and disciplined. Van Rijn's voice pulled him grudgingly back to luckless unflying humanness.

"Wake up! Are you making dreams, maybe, like you stand there with your teeth hanging out and flapping in the breeze? Lightnings and Lucifer! If we want to keep this raft, we have to make some use with it, by damn. You boss the battery here and I go tell the helmsman what to do. So!" He huffed off, like an ancient steam locomotive in weight and noise and sootiness.

They had beaten off every attempt at recapture, until the expelled crew went wrathfully up to join Delp's legions. Now, awkwardly handling the big sails, or ordered protestingly below to the sweeps, van Rijn's gang got their new vessel into motion. It grunted its way across a roiled, smoky waste of water, until a Drak'ho craft loomed before it. Then the broadsides cut loose, the arrows went like sleet, and crew locked with crew in troubled air midway between the thuttering rafts.

Wace stood his ground on the foredeck, directing the fire of its banked engines: stones, quarrels, bombs, oils-treams, hurled across a few meters to shower splinters and char wood as they struck. Once he organized a bucket brigade, to put out the fire set by an enemy hit. Once he saw one of his new catapults, and its crew, smashed by a two-ton rock, and forced the survivors to lever that stone into the sea and rejoin the fight. He saw how sails grew tattered, yards sagged drunkenly, bodies heaped themselves on both vessels after each clumsy round. And he wondered, in a dim part of his brain, why life had no more sense, anywhere in the known universe, than to be forever tearing itself.

Van Rijn did not have the quality of crew to win by sheer bombardment, like a neolithic Nelson. Nor did he especially want to try boarding still another craft; it was all his little tyro force could do to man and fight this one. But he pressed stubbornly in, holding the helmsmen to their collision course, going below-decks himself to keep exhausted Lannachska at their heavy oars. And his raft wallowed its way through a firestorm, a stonestorm, a storm of living bodies, until it was almost on the enemy vessel.

Then horns hooted among the Drak'honai, their sweeps churned water and they broke from their place in the Fleet's formation to disengage.

Van Rijn let them go, vanishing into the hazed masts and cordage that reached for kilometers around him. He stumped to the nearest hatch, went down through the poop-deck cabins and so out on the main deck. He rubbed his hands and chortled. "Aha! We gave him a little scare, eh, what say? He'll not come near any of our boats soon again, him!"

"I don't understand, Councilor," said Angrek, with immense respect. "We had a smaller crew, with far less skill. He ought to have stayed put, or even moved in on us. He could have wiped us out, if we didn't abandon ship altogether."

"Ah!" said van Rijn. He wagged a sausagelike finger. "But you see, my young and innocent one, he is carrying females and cubs, as well as many valuable tools and other goods. His whole life is on his raft. He dare not risk its destruction; we could so easy set it hopeless afire, even if we can't make capture. Ha! It will be a frosty morning in hell, when they outthink Nicholas van Rijn, by damn!"

"Females—" Angrek's eyes shifted to the forecastle. A lickerish light rose in them.

"After all," he murmured, "it's not as if they were *our* females—"

A score or more Lannachska were already drifting in that same direction, elaborately casual—but their wings were held stiff and their tails twitched. It was noteworthy that more of the recent oarsmen were in that group than any other class.

Wace came running to the forecastle's edge. He leaned over it, cupped his hands and shouted: "Freeman van Rijn! Look upstairs!"

"So." The merchant raised pouched little eyes, blinked, sneezed, and blew his craggy nose. One by one, the Lannachska resting on scarred bloody decks lifted their own gaze skyward. And a stillness fell on them.

Up there, the struggle was ending.

Delp had finally assembled his forces into a single irresistible mass and taken them down as a unit to sea level. There they joined the embattled raft crews—one raft at a time. A Lannachska boarding party, so suddenly and grossly outnumbered, had no choice but to flee, abandon even its own ice ship, and go up to Trolwen.

The Drak'honai made only one attempt to recapture a raft which was fully in Lannacha possession. It cost them gruesomely. The classic dictum still held, that purely airborne forces were relatively impotent against a well-defended unit of the Fleet.

Having settled in this decisive manner exactly who held every single raft, Delp reorganized and led a sizable portion of his troops aloft again to engage Trolwen's augmented air squadrons. If he could clear them away, then, given the craft remaining to Drak'ho plus total sky domination, Delp could regain the lost vessels.

But Trolwen did not clear away so easily. And, while naval fights went on below, a vicious combat traveled through the clouds. Both were indecisive.

Such was the overall view of events, as Tolk related it to the humans an hour or so later. All that could be seen from the water was that the sky armies were separating. They hovered and wheeled, dizzyingly high overhead, two tangled masses of black dots against ruddy-tinged cloud banks. Doubtless threats, curses, and boasts were tossed across the wind between them, but there were no more arrows.

"What is it?" gasped Angrek. "What's happening up there?"

"A truce, of course," said van Rijn. He picked his teeth with a fingernail, hawked, and patted his abdomen complacently. "They was making nowheres, so finally Tolk got someone through to Delp and said let's talk this over, and Delp agreed."

"But—we can't—you can't bargain with a Draka! He's not . . . he's *alien!*"

A growl of goose-pimpled loathing assent went along the weary groups of Lannachska.

"You can't reason with a filthy wild animal like that," said Angrek. "All you can do is kill it. Or it will kill you!"

Van Rijn cocked a brow at Wace, who stood on the deck above him, and said in Anglic: "I thought maybe we could tell them now that this truce is the only objective of all our fighting so far—but maybe not just yet, *nie?*"

"I wonder if we'll ever dare admit it," said the younger man.

"We will have to admit it, this very day, and hope we do not get stuffed alive with red peppers for what we say. After alls, we did make Trolwen and the Council agree. But then, they are very hard-boiled-egg heads, them." Van Rijn shrugged. "Comes now the talking. So far we have had it soft. This is the times that fry men's souls. Ha! Have you got the nerve to see it through?"

❧ XIX ❧

Approximately one tenth of the rafts lumbered out of the general confusion and assembled a few kilometers away. They were joined by such ice ships as were still in service. The decks of all were jammed with tensely waiting warriors. These were the vessels held by Lannach.

Another tenth or so still burned, or had been torn and beaten by stonefire until they were breaking up under Achan's mild waves. These were the derelicts, abandoned by both nations. Among them were many dugouts, splintered, broken, kindled, or crewed only by dead Drak'honai.

The remainder drew into a mass around the admiral's castle. This was no group of fully manned, fully equipped rafts and canoes; no crew had escaped losses, and a good many vessels were battered nearly into uselessness. If the Fleet could get half their normal fighting strength back into action, they would be very, very lucky.

Nevertheless, this would be almost three times as many units as the Lannachska now held *in toto*. The numbers of males on either side were roughly equal; but, with more cargo space, the Drak'honai had more ammunition. Each of their vessels was also individually superior: better constructed than an ice ship, better crewed than a captured raft.

In short, Drak'ho still held the balance of power.

As he helped van Rijn down into a seized canoe, Tolk said wryly: "I'd have kept my armor on if I were you, Eart'a. You'll only have to be laced back into it, when the truce ends."

"Ah." The merchant stretched monstrously, puffed out his stomach, and plumped himself down on a seat. "Let us suppose, though, the armistice does not break. Then I will have been wearing that bloody-be-smeared corset all for nothings."

"I notice," added Wace, "neither you nor Trolwen are cuirassed."

The commander smoothed his mahogany fur with a nervous hand. "That's for the dignity of the Flock," he muttered. "Those muck-walkers aren't going to think I'm afraid of them."

The canoe shoved off, its crew bent to the oars, it skipped swiftly over wrinkled dark waters. Above it dipped and soared the rest of the agreed-on Lannacha guard, putting on their best demonstration of parade flying for the edification of the enemy. There were about a hundred all told. It was comfortlessly little to take into the angered Fleet.

"I don't expect to reach any agreement," said Trolwen. "No one can—with a mind as foreign as theirs."

"The Fleet peoples are just like you," said van Rijn. "What you need is more brotherhood, by damn. You should bash in their heads without this race prejudice."

"Just like *us?*" Trolwen bristled. His eyes grew flat glass-yellow. "See here, Eart'a—"

"Never mind," said van Rijn. "So they do not have a rutting season. So you think this is a big thing. All right. I got some thinkings to make of my own. Shut up."

The wind ruffled waves and strummed idly on rigging. The sun struck long copper-tinged rays through scudding cloudbanks, to walk on the sea with fiery footprints. The air was cool, damp, smelling a little of salty life. It would not be an easy time to die, thought Wace. Hardest of all, though, to forsake Sandra, where she lay dwindling under the ice cliffs of Dawrnach. *Pray for my soul, beloved, while you wait to follow me. Pray for my soul.*

"Leaving personal feelings aside," said Tolk, "there's much in the commander's remarks. That is, a folk with lives as alien to ours as the Drakska will have minds equally alien. I don't pretend to follow the thoughts of you, Eart'ska: I consider you my friends, but let's admit it, we have very little in common. I only trust you because your immediate motive—survival—has been made so clear to me. When I don't quite follow your reasoning, I can safely assume that it is at least well-intentioned.

"But the Drakska, now—how can they be trusted? Let's say that a peace agreement is made. How can we know they'll keep it? They may have no concept of honor at all, just as they lack all concept of sexual decency. Or, even if they do intend to abide by their oaths, are we sure the words of the treaty will mean the same thing to them as to us? In my capacity of Herald, I've seen many semantic misunderstandings between tribes with different languages. So what of tribes with different instincts?

"Or I wonder . . . can we even trust ourselves to keep such a pledge? We do not hate anyone merely for having fought us. But we hate dishonor, perversion, uncleanliness. How can we live with ourselves, if we make peace with creatures whom the gods must loathe?"

He sighed and looked moodily ahead to the nearing rafts.

Wace shrugged. "Has it occurred to you, they are thinking very much the same things about you?" he retorted.

"Of course they are," said Tolk. "That's yet another hailstorm in the path of negotiations."

Personally, thought Wace, *I'll be satisfied with a temporary settlement. Just let them patch up their differences long enough for a message to reach Thursday Landing.* (How?) *Then they can rip each other's throats out for all I care.*

He glanced around him at the slim winged forms, and thought of work and war, torment and triumph—yes, and now and then some laughter or a fragment of song—shared. He thought of high-hearted Trolwen, philosophic Tolk, earnest young Angrek, he thought of brave kindly Delp and his wife Rodonis, who was so much more a lady than many a human female he had known. And the small furry cubs which tumbled in the dust or climbed into his lap . . . *No,* he told himself, *I'm wrong. It means a great deal to me, after all, that this war should be permanently ended.*

The canoe slipped in between towering raft walls. Drak'ho faces looked stonily down on it. Now and then someone spat into its wake. They were all very quiet.

The unwieldy pile of the flagship loomed ahead. There were banners strung from the mastheads, and a guard in bright regalia formed a ring enclosing the main deck. Just before the wooden castle, sprawled on furs and cushions, Admiral T'heonax and his advisory council waited. To one side stood Captain Delp with a few personal guards, in war-harness still sweaty and unkempt.

Total silence lay over them as the canoe came to a halt and made fast to a bollard. Trolwen, Tolk, and most of the Lannacha troopers flew straight up to the deck. It was minutes later, after much pushing, panting, and swearing, that the humans topped that mountainous hull.

Van Rijn glowered about him. "What for hospitality!" he snorted in the Drak'ho language. "Not so much as one little rope let down to me, who is pushing my poor old tired bones to an early grave all for your sakes. Before Heaven, it is hard! It is hard! Sometimes I think I give up, me, and retire. Then where will the galaxy be? Then you will all be sorry, when it is too late."

T'heonax gave him a sardonic stare. "You were not the best behaved guest the Fleet has had, Eart'ho," he answered. "I've a great deal to repay you. Yes. I have not forgotten."

Van Rijn wheezed across the planks to Delp, extending his hand. "So our intelligences was right, and it was you doing all the works," he blared. "I might have been sure. Nobody else in this Fleet has so much near a gram of brains. I, Nicholas van Rijn, compliment you with regards."

T'heonax stiffened and his councilors, rigid in braid and sash, looked duly shocked at this ignoring of the admiral. Delp hung back for an instant. Then he took van Rijn's hand and squeezed it, quite in the Terrestrial manner.

"Lodestar help me, it is good to see your villainous fat face again," he said. "Do you know how nearly you cost me my . . . everything? Were it not for my lady—"

"Business and friendship we do not mix," said van Rijn airily. "Ah, yes, good Vrouw Rodonis. How is she and all the little ones? Do they still remember old Uncle Nicholas and the bedtime stories he was telling them, like about the—"

"If you please," said T'heonax in an elaborate voice, "we will, with your permission, carry on. Who shall interpret? Yes, I remember you now, Herald." An ugly look. "Your attention, then. Tell your leader that this parley was arranged by my field commander, Delp hyr Orikan, without even sending a messenger down here to consult me. I would have opposed it had I known. It was neither prudent nor necessary. I shall have to have these decks scrubbed where barbarians have trod. However, since the Fleet is bound by its honor—you do have a word for honor in your language, don't you?—I will hear what your leader has to say."

Tolk nodded curtly and put it into Lannachamael. Trolwen sat up, eyes kindling. His guards growled, their hands tightened on their weapons. Delp shuffled his feet unhappily, and some of T'heonax's captains looked away in an embarrassed fashion.

"Tell him," said Trolwen after a moment, with bitter precision, "that we will let the Fleet depart from Achan at once. Of course, we shall want hostages."

Tolk translated. T'heonax peeled lips back from teeth and laughed. "They sit here with their wretched handful of rafts and say this to us?" His courtiers tittered an echo.

But his councilors, who captained his flotillas, remained grave. It was Delp who stepped forward and said: "The admiral knows I have taken my share in this war. With these hands, wings, this tail, I have killed enemy males; with these teeth, I have drawn enemy blood. Nevertheless I say now, we'd better at least listen to them."

"What?" T'heonax made round eyes. "I hope you are joking."

Van Rijn rolled forth. "I got no time for fumblydiddles," he boomed. "You hear me, and I put it in millicredit words so some two-year-old cub can explain it to you. Look out there!" His arm waved broadly at the sea. "We have rafts. Not so many, perhaps, but enough. You make terms with us, or we keep on fighting. Soon it is you who do not have enough rafts. So! Put that in your pipe and stick it!"

Wace nodded. Good. Good, indeed. Why had that Drak'ho vessel run from his own lubber-manned prize? It was willing enough to exchange long-range shots, or to grapple sailor against sailor in the air. It was not willing to risk being boarded, wrecked, or set ablaze by Lannach's desperate devils.

Because it was a home, a fortress, and a livelihood —the only way to make a living that this culture knew. If you destroyed enough rafts, there would not be enough fish-catching or fish-storing capacity to keep the folk alive. It was as simple as that.

"We'll sink you!" screamed T'heonax. He stood up, beating his wings, crest aquiver, tail held like an iron bar. "We'll drown every last whelp of you!"

"Possible so," said van Rijn. "This is supposed to scare us? If we give up now, we are done for anyhow. So we take you along to hell with us, to shine our shoes and fetch us cool drinks, *nie?*"

Delp said, with trouble in his gaze: "We did not come to Achan for love of destruction, but because hunger drove us. It was you who denied us the right to take fish which you yourselves never caught. Oh, yes, we did take some of your land too, but the water we must have. We can *not* give that up."

Van Rijn shrugged. "There are other seas. Maybe we let you haul a few more nets of fish before you go."

A captain of the Fleet said slowly: "My lord Delp has voiced the crux of the matter. It hints at a solution. After all, the Sea of Achan has little or no value to you Lannach'honai. We did, of course, wish to garrison your coasts, and occupy certain islands which are sources of timber and flint and the like. And naturally, we wanted a port of our own in Sagna Bay, for emergencies and repairs. These are questions of defense and self-sufficiency, not of immediate survival like the water. So perhaps—"

"*No!*" cried T'heonax.

It was almost a scream. It shocked them into silence. The admiral crouched panting for a moment, then snarled at Tolk: "Tell your leader . . . I, the final authority . . . I refuse. I say we can crush your joke of a navy with small loss to ourselves. We have no reason to yield anything to you. We may allow you to keep the uplands of Lannach. That is the greatest concession you can hope for."

"Impossible!" spat the Herald. Then he rattled the translation off for Trolwen, who arched his back and bit the air.

"The mountains will not support us," explained Tolk more calmly. "We have already eaten them bare—that's no secret. We must have the lowlands. And we are certainly not going to let you hold any land whatsoever, to base an attack on us in a later year."

"If you think you can wipe us off the sea now, without a loss that will cripple you also, you may try," added Wace.

"I say we can!" stormed T'heonax. "And will!"

"My lord—" Delp hesitated. His eyes closed for a second. Then he said quite dispassionately: "My lord admiral, a finish fight now would likely be the end of our nation. Such few rafts as survived would be the prey of the first barbarian islanders that chanced along."

"And a retreat into The Ocean would *certainly* doom us," said T'heonax. His forefinger stabbed. "Unless you can conjure the trech and the fruitweed out of Achan and into the broad waters."

"That is true, of course, my lord," said Delp.

He turned and sought Trolwen's eyes. They regarded each other steadily, with respect.

"Herald," said Delp, "tell your chief this. We are not going to leave the Sea of Achan. We cannot. If you insist that we do so, we'll fight you and hope you can be destroyed without too much loss to ourselves. We have no choice in that matter.

"But I think maybe we can give up any thought of occupying either Lannach or Holmenach. You can keep all the solid land. We can barter our fish, salt, sea harvest, handicrafts, for your meat, stone, wood, cloth, and oil. It would in time become profitable for both of us."

"And incidental," said van Rijn, "you might think of this bit too. If Drak'ho has no land, and Lannach has no

ships, it will be sort of a little hard for one to make war
on another, *nie?* After a few years, trading and getting
rich off each other, you get so mutual dependent war is
just impossible. So if you agree like now, soon your troubles are over, and then comes Nicholas van Rijn with
Earth trade goods for all, like Father Christmas my
prices are so reasonable. What?"

"Be still!" shrieked T'heonax.

He grabbed the chief of his guards by a wing and
pointed at Delp. "Arrest that traitor!"

"My lord—" Delp backed away. The guard hesitated.
Delp's warriors closed in about their captain, menac-
ingly. From the listening lower decks there came a groan.

"The Lodestar hear me," stammered Delp, "I only
suggested . . . I know the admiral has the final say—"

"And my say is, 'No,'" declared T'heonax, tacitly dropping the matter of arrest. "As admiral and Oracle, I forbid it. There is no possible agreement between the Fleet
and these . . . these vile . . . filthy, dirty, animal—" He
dribbled at the lips. His hands curved into claws, poised
above his head.

A rustle and murmur went through the ranked Drak'-
honai. The captains lay like winged leopards, still cloaked
with dignity, but there was terror in their eyes. The Lannachska, ignorant of words but sensitive to tones,
crowded together and gripped their weapons more
tightly.

Tolk translated fast, in a low voice. When he had finished, Trolwen sighed.

"I hate to admit it," he said, "but if you turn that
marswa's words around, they are true. Do you really,
seriously think two races as different as ours could live
side by side? It would be too tempting to break the

pledges. They could ravage our land while we were gone on migration, take all our towns again . . . or we could come north once more with barbarian allies, bought with the promise of Drak'ho plunder—We'd be back at each other's throats, one way or another, in five years. Best to have it out now. Let the gods decide who's right and who's too depraved to live."

Almost wearily, he bunched his muscles, to go down fighting if T'heonax ended the armistice this moment.

Van Rijn lifted his hands and his voice. It went like a bass drum, the length and breadth and depth of the castle raft. And nocked arrows were slowly put back into their quivers.

"Hold still! Wait just a bloody minute, by damn. I am not through talking yet."

He nodded curtly at Delp. "You have some sense, you. Maybe we can find a few others with brains not so much like a spoonful of moldy tea sold by my competitors. I am going to say something now. I will use Drak'ho language. Tolk, you make a running translation. This no one on the planet has heard before. I tell you Drak'ho and Lannacha are *not* alien! They are the same identical stupid race!"

Wace sucked in his breath. "What?" he whispered in Anglic. "But the breeding cycles—"

"Kill me that fat worm!" shouted T'heonax.

Van Rijn waved an impatient hand at him. "Be quiet, you. I make the talkings. So! Sit down, both you nations, and listen to Nicholas van Rijn!"

❋ **XX** ❋

The evolution of intelligent life on Diomedes is still largely conjectural; there has been no time to hunt fossils. But on the basis of existing biology and general principles, it is possible to reason out the course of millennial events.

Once upon a time in the planet's tropics there was a small continent or large island, thickly forested. The equatorial regions never know the long days and nights of high latitudes: at equinox the sun is up for six hours to cross the sky and set for another six; at solstice there is a twilight, the sun just above or below the horizon. By Diomedean standards these are ideal conditions which will support abundant life. Among the species at this past epoch was a small, bright-eyed arboreal carnivore. Like Earth's flying squirrel, it had developed a membrane on which to glide from branch to branch.

But a low-density planet has a queasy structure. Continents rise and sink with indecent speed, a mere few hundreds of thousands of years. Ocean and air currents are correspondingly deflected; and, because of the great axial tilt and the larger fluid masses involved, Diomedean currents bear considerably more heat or cold than do Earth's. Thus, even at the equator, there were radical climatic shifts.

A period of drought shriveled the ancient forests into scattered woods separated by great dry pampas. The flying pseudo-squirrel developed true wings to go from copse to copse. But being an adaptable beast, it began also to prey on the new grass-eating animals which herded over the plains. To cope with the big ungulates, it grew in size. But then, needing more food to fuel the larger body, it was forced into a variety of environments, seashore, mountains, swamps—yet by virtue of mobility remained interbred rather than splitting into new species. A single individual might thus face many types of country in one lifetime, which put a premium on intelligence.

At this stage, for some unknown reason, the species—or a part of it, the part destined to become important—was forced out of the homeland. Possibly diastrophism broke the original continent into small islands which would not support so large an animal population; or the drying-out may have progressed still further. Whatever the cause, families and flocks drifted slowly northward and southward through hundreds of generations.

There they found new territories, excellent hunting—but a winter which they could not survive. When the long darkness came, they must perforce return to the tropics to wait for spring. It was not the inborn, automatic reaction of Terrestrial migratory birds. This animal was already too clever to be an instinct machine; its habits were *learned*. The brutal natural selection of the annual flights stimulated this intelligence yet more.

Now the price of intelligence is a very long childhood in proportion to the total lifespan. Since there is no action-pattern built into the thinker's genes, each generation must learn everything afresh, which takes time. Therefore, no species can become intelligent unless it or its environment first produces some mechanism for keeping the parents together, so that they may protect the young during the extended period of helpless infancy and ignorant childhood. Mother love is not enough; Mother will have enough to do, tending the suicidally inquisitive cubs, without having to do all the food-hunting and guarding as well. Father must help out. But what will keep Father around, once his sexual urge has been satisfied?

Instinct can do it. Some birds, for example, employ both parents to rear the young. But elaborate instinctive compulsions are incompatible with intelligence. Father has to have a good selfish reason to stay, if Father has brains enough to *be* selfish.

In the case of man, the mechanism is simple: permanent sexuality. The human is never satisfied at any time of year. From this fact we derive the family, and hence the possibility of prolonged immaturity, and hence our cerebral cortex.

In the case of the Diomedean, there was migration. Each flock had a long and dangerous way to travel every year. It was best to go in company, under some form of organization. At journey's end in the tropics, there was the abandon of the mating season—but soon the unavoidable trip back home, for the equatorial islands would not support many visitors for very long.

Out of this primitive annual grouping—since it was not blindly instinctive, but the fruit of experience in a gifted animal—there grew loose permanent associations. Defensive bands became co-operative bands. Already the exigencies of travel had caused male and female to specialize their body types, one for fighting, one for burden-bearing. It was, therefore, advantageous that the sexes maintain their partnership the whole year around.

The animal of permanent family—on Diomedes, as a rule, a rather large family, an entire matrilineal clan—with the long gestation, the long cubhood, the constant change and challenge of environment, the competition for mates each midwinter with alien bands having alien ways: this animal had every evolutionary reason to start thinking. Out of such a matrix grew language, tools, fire, organized nations, and those vague unattainable yearnings we call "culture."

Now while the Diomedean had no irrevocable pattern of inborn behavior, he did tend everywhere to follow certain modes of life. They were the easiest. Analogously, humankind is not required by instinct to formalize and regulate its matings as marriage, but human societies have almost invariably done so. It is more comfortable for all concerned. And so the Diomedean migrated south to breed.

But he did not have to!

When breeding cycles exist, they are controlled by some simple foolproof mechanism. Thus, for many birds on Earth it is the increasing length of the day in spring-time which causes mating: the optical stimulus triggers hormonal processes which reactivate the dormant gonads. On Diomedes, this wouldn't work; the light cycle varies too much with latitude. But once the proto-intelligent Diomedean had gotten into migratory habits—and therefore must breed only at a certain time of the year, if the young were to survive—evolution took the obvious course of making that migration itself the governor.

Ordinarily a hunter, with occasional meals of nuts or fruit or wild grain, the Diomedean exercised in spurts. Migration called for prolonged effort; it must have taken hundreds or thousands of generations to develop the flying muscles alone, time enough to develop other adap-tations as well. So this effort stimulated certain glands, which operated through a complex hormonal system to waken the gonads. (An exception was the lactating female, whose mammaries secreted an inhibiting agent.)

During the great flight, the sex hormone concentration built up—there was no time or energy to spare for its dissipation. Once in the tropics, rested and fed, the Diomedean made up for lost opportunities. He made up so thoroughly that the return trip had no significant effect on his exhausted glands.

Now and then in the homeland, fleetingly, after some unusual exertion, one might feel stirrings toward the opposite sex. One suppressed that, as rigorously as the human suppresses impulses to incest, and for an even more practical reason: a cub born out of season meant death on migration for itself as well as its mother. Not that the average Diomedean realized this overtly; he just accepted the taboo, founded religions and ethical systems and neuroses on it. However, doubtless the vague, lingering year-round attractiveness of the other sex had been an unconscious reason for the initial development of septs and flocks.

When the migratory Diomedean encountered a tribe which did not observe his most basic moral law, he knew physical horror.

Drak'ho's Fleet was one of several which have now been discovered by traders. They may all have originated as groups living near the equator and thus not burdened by the need to travel; but this is still guesswork. The clear fact is that they began to live more off the sea than the land. Through many centuries they elaborated the physical apparatus of ships and tackle, until it had become their entire livelihood.

It gave more security than hunting. It gave a home which could be dwelt in continuously. It gave the possibility of constructing and using elaborate devices, accumulating large libraries, sitting and thinking or debating a problem—in short, the freedom to encumber oneself with a true civilization, which no migrator had except to the most limited degree. On the bad side, it meant grindingly hard labor and aristocratic domination.

This work kept the deckhand sexually stimulated; but warm shelters and stored sea food had made his birthtime independent of the season. Thus the sailor nations grew into a very humanlike pattern of marriage and child-raising: there was even a concept of romantic love.

The migrators, who thought him depraved, the sailor considered swinish. Indeed, neither culture could imagine how the other might even be of the same species.

And how shall one trust the absolute alien?

⚙ XXI ⚙

"It is these ideological pfuities that make the real nasty wars," said van Rijn. "But now I have taken off the ideology and we can sensible and friendly settle down to swindling each other, *nie?*"

He had not, of course, explained his hypothesis in such detail. Lannach's philosophers had some vague idea of evolution, but were weak on astronomy; Drak'ho science was almost the reverse. Van Rijn had contented himself with very simple, repetitive words, sketching what must be the only reasonable explanation of the well-known reproductive differences.

He rubbed his hands and chortled into a tautening silence. "So! I have not made it all sweetness. Even I cannot do that overnights. For long times to come yet, you each think the others go about this in disgusting style. You make filthy jokes about each other . . . I know some good ones you can adapt. But you know, at least, that you are of the same race. Any of you could have been a solid member of the other nation, *nie?* Maybe, come changing times, you start switching around your ways to live. Why not experiment a little, ha? No, no, I see you can not like that idea yet, I say no more."

He folded his arms and waited, bulky, shaggy, ragged, and caked with the grime of weeks. On creaking planks, under a red sun and a low sea wind, the scores of winged warriors and captains shuddered in the face of the unimagined.

Delp said at last, so slow and heavy it did not really break that drumhead silence: "Yes. This makes sense. I believe it."

After another minute, bowing his head toward stone-rigid T'heonax: "My lord, this does change the situation. I think—it will not be as much as we hoped for, but better than I feared—We can make terms, they to have all the land and we to have the Sea of Achan. Now that I know they are not . . . devils . . . animals—Well, the normal guarantees, oaths and exchange of hostages and so on—should make the treaty firm enough."

Tolk had been whispering in Trolwen's ear. Lannach's commander nodded. "That is much my own thought," he said.

"Can we persuade the Council and the clans, Flock-chief?" muttered Tolk.

"Herald, if we bring back an honorable peace, the Council will vote our ghosts godhood after we die."

Tolk's gaze shifted back to T'heonax, lying without movement among his courtiers. And the grizzled fur lifted along the Herald's back.

"Let us first return to the Council alive, Flockchief," he said.

T'heonax rose. His wings beat the air, cracking noises like an ax going through bone. His muzzle wrinkled into a lion mask, long teeth gleamed wetly forth, and he roared:

"No! I've heard enough! This farce is at an end!"

Trolwen and the Lannacha escort did not need an interpreter. They clapped hands to weapons and fell into a defensive circle. Their jaws clashed shut automatically, biting the wind.

"My lord!" Delp sprang fully erect.

"Be still!" screeched T'heonax. "You've said far too much." His head swung from side to side. "Captains of the Fleet, you have heard how Delp hyr Orikan advocates making peace with creatures lower than the beasts. Remember it!"

"But my lord—" An older officer stood up, hands aloft in protest. "My lord admiral, we've just had it shown to us, they aren't beasts . . . it's only a different—"

"Assuming the Eart'ho spoke truth, which is by no means sure, what of it?" T'heonax fleered at van Rijn. "It only makes the matter worse. We know beasts can't help themselves but these Lannach'honai are dirty by choice. And you would let them live? You would . . . would *trade* with them . . . enter their towns . . . let your young be seduced into their—No!"

The captains looked at each other. It was like an audible groan. Only Delp seemed to have the courage to speak again.

"I humbly beg the admiral to recall, we've no real choice. If we fight them to a finish, it may be our own finish too."

"Ridiculous!" snorted T'heonax. "Either you are afraid or they've bribed you."

Tolk had been translating *sotto voce* for Trolwen. Now, sickly, Wace heard the commander's grim reply to his Herald: "If he takes that attitude, a treaty is out of the question. Even if he made it, he'd sacrifice his hostages to us—not to speak of ours to him—just to renew the war whenever he felt ready. Let's get back before I myself violate the truce!"

And there, thought Wace, *is the end of the world. I will die under flung stones, and Sandra will die in Glacier Land. Well . . . we tried.*

He braced himself. The admiral might not let this embassy depart.

Delp was looking around from face to face. "Captains of the Fleet," he cried, "I ask your opinion . . . I implore you, persuade my lord admiral that—"

"The next treasonable word uttered by anyone will cost him his wings," shouted T'heonax. "Or do you question my authority?"

It was a bold move, thought Wace in a distant part of his thuttering brain—to stake all he had on that one challenge. But of course, T'heonax was going to get away with it; no one in this caste-ridden society would deny his absolute power, not even Delp the bold. Reluctant they might be, but the captains would obey.

The silence grew shattering.

Nicholas van Rijn broke it with a long, juicy Bronx cheer.

The whole assembly started. T'heonax leaped backward and for a moment he was like a bat-winged tomcat.

"What was that?" he blazed.

"Are you deaf?" answered van Rijn mildly. "I said—" He repeated, with tremolo.

"What do you mean?"

"It is an Earth term," said van Rijn. "As near as I can render it, let me see . . . well, it means you are a—" The rest was the most imaginative obscenity Wace had heard in his life.

The captains gasped. Some drew their weapons. The Drak'ho guards on the upper decks gripped bows and spears. "Kill him!" screamed T'heonax.

"No!" Van Rijn's bass exploded on their ears. The sheer volume of it paralyzed them. "I am an embassy, by damn! You hurt an embassy and the Lodestar will sink you in hell's boiling seas!"

It checked them. T'heonax did not repeat his order; the guards jerked back toward stillness; the officers remained poised, outraged past words.

"I have somethings to say you," van Rijn continued, only twice as loud as a large foghorn. "I speak to all the Fleet, and ask you yourselves, why this little pip squeaker does so stupid. He makes you carry on a war where both sides lose—he makes you risk your lives, your wives and cubs, maybe the Fleet's own surviving—why? Because he is afraid. He knows, a few years cheek by jowl next to the Lannach'honai, and even more so trading with my company at my fantastic low prices, things begin to change. You get more into thinking by your own selves. You taste freedom. Bit by bit, his power slides from him. And he is too much a coward to live on his own selfs. *Nie,* he has got to have guards and slaves and all of you to make bossing over, so he proves to himself he is not just a little jellypot but a real true Leader. Rather he will have the Fleet ruined, even die himself, than lose this propup, him!"

T'heonax said, shaking: "Get off my raft before I forget there is an armistice."

"Oh, I go, I go," said van Rijn. He advanced toward the admiral. His tread reverberated in the deck. "I go back and make war again if you insist. But only one small question I ask first." He stopped before the royal presence and prodded the royal nose with a hairy forefinger. "Why you make so much fuss about Lannacha home lifes? Could be maybe down underneath you hanker to try it yourself?"

He turned his back, then, and bowed.

Wace did not see just what happened. There were guards and captains between. He heard a screech, a bellow from van Rijn, and then a hurricane of wings was before him.

Something—He threw himself into the press of bodies. A tail crashed against his ribs. He hardly felt it; his fist jolted, merely to get a warrior out of the way and see—

Nicholas van Rijn stood with both hands in the air as a score of spears menaced him. "The admiral bit me!" he wailed. "I am here like an embassy, and the pig bites me! What kind of relations between countries is that, when heads of state bite foreign ambassadors, ha? Does an Earth president bite diplomats? This is uncivilized!"

T'heonax backed off, spitting, scrubbing the blood from his jaws. "Get out," he said in a strangled voice. "Go at once."

Van Rijn nodded. "Come, friends," he said. "We find us places with better manners."

"Freeman . . . Freeman, where did he—" Wace crowded close.

"Never mind where," said van Rijn huffily.

Trolwen and Tolk joined them. The Lannacha escort fell into step behind. They walked at a measured pace across the deck, away from the confusion of Drak'honai under the castle wall.

"You might have known it," said Wace. He felt exhausted, drained of everything except a weak anger at his chief's unbelievable folly. "This race is carnivorous. Haven't you seen them snap when they get angry? It's . . . a reflex—You might have known!"

"Well," said van Rijn in a most virtuous tone, holding both hands to his injury, "he did not *have* to bite. I am not responsible for his lack of control or any consequences of it, me. All good lawyer saints witness I am not."

"But the ruckus—we could all have been killed!"

Van Rijn didn't bother to argue about that.

Delp met them at the rail. His crest drooped. "I am sorry it must end thus," he said. "We could have been friends."

"Perhaps it does not end just so soon," said van Rijn.

"What do you mean?" Tired eyes regarded him without hope.

"Maybe you see pretty quick. Delp"—van Rijn laid a paternal hand on the Drak'ho's shoulder—"you are a good young chap. I could use a one like you, as a part-time agent for some tradings in these parts. On fat commissions, natural. But for now, remember you are the one they all like and respect. If anything happens to the admiral, there will be panic and uncertainty . . . they will turn to you for advice. If you act fast at such a moment, you can be admiral yourself! Then maybe we do business, ha?"

He left Delp gaping and swung himself with apish speed down into the canoe. "Now, boys," he said, "row like hell."

They were almost back to their own fleet when Wace saw clotted wings whirl up from the royal raft. He

gulped. "Has the attack . . . has it begun already?" He
cursed himself that his voice should be an idiotic squeak.

"Well, I am glad we are not close to them." Van Rijn,
standing up as he had done the whole trip, nodded complacently. "But I think not this is the war. I think they
are just disturbed. Soon Delp will take charge and calms
them down."

"But—*Delp?*"

Van Rijn shrugged. "If Diomedean proteins is deadly
to us," he said, "ours should not be so good for them,
ha? And our late friend T'heonax took a big mouthful of
me. It all goes to show, these foul tempers only lead to
trouble. Best you follow my example. When I am
attacked, I turn the other cheek."

❈ XXII ❈

Thursday Landing had little in the way of hospital facilities: an autodiagnostician, a few surgical and therapeu-
tical robots, the standard drugs, and the post
xenobiologist to double as medical officer. But a six
weeks' fast did not have serious consequences, if you
were strong to begin with and had been waited on hand,
foot, wing, and tail by two anxious nations, on a planet
none of whose diseases could affect you. Treatment progressed rapidly with the help of bioaccelerine, from
intravenous glucose to thick rare steaks. By the sixth
Diomedean day, Wace had put on a noticeable amount
of flesh and was weakly but fumingly aprowl in his room.

"Smoke, sir?" asked young Benegal. He had been out
on trading circuit when the rescue party arrived; only
now was he getting the full account. He offered cigarettes with a most respectful air.

Wace halted, the bathrobe swirling about his knees. He reached, hesitated, then grinned and said: "In all that time without tobacco, I seem to've lost the addiction. Question is, should I go to the trouble and expense of building it up again?"

"Well, no, sir—"

"Hey! Gimme that!" Wace sat down on his bed and took a cautious puff. "I certainly am going to pick up all my vices where I left off, and doubtless add some new ones."

"You, uh, you were going to tell me, sir . . . how the station here was informed—"

"Oh, yes. That. It was childishly simple. I figured it out in ten minutes, once we got a breathing spell. Send a fair-sized Diomedean party with a written message, plus of course one of Tolk's professional interpreters to help them inquire their way on this side of The Ocean. Devise a big life raft, just a framework of light poles which could be dovetailed together. Each Diomedean carried a single piece; they assembled it in the air and rested on it whenever necessary. Also fished from it: a number of Fleet experts went along to take charge of that angle. There was enough rain for them to catch in small buckets to drink—I knew there would be, since the Drak'honai stay at sea for indefinite periods, and also this is such a rainy planet anyhow.

"Incidentally, for reasons which are now obvious to you, the party had to include some Lannacha females. Which means that the messengers of both nationalities have had to give up some hoary prejudices. In the long run, that's going to change their history more than whatever impression we Terrestrials might have made, by such stunts as flying them home across The Ocean in a single day. From now on, willy-nilly, the beings who went on that trip will be a subversive element in both cultures; they'll be the seedbed of Diomedean internationalism. But that's for the League to gloat about, not me."

Wace shrugged. "Having seen them off," he finished, "we could only crawl into bed and wait. After the first few days, it wasn't so bad. Appetite disappears."

He stubbed out the cigarette with a grimace. It was making him dizzy.

"When do I get to see the others?" he demanded. "I'm strong enough now to feel bored. I want company, dammit."

"As a matter of fact, sir," said Benegal, "I believe Freeman van Rijn said something about"—a thunderous "*Skulls and smallpox!*" bounced in the corridor outside—"visiting you today."

"Run along then," said Wace sardonically. "You're too young to hear this. We blood brothers, who have defied death together, we sworn comrades, and so on and so forth, are about to have a reunion."

He got to his feet as the boy slipped out the back door. Van Rijn rolled in the front entrance.

His Jovian girth was shrunken flat, he had only one chin, and he leaned on a gold-headed cane. But his hair was curled into oily black ringlets, his mustaches and goatee waxed to needle points, his lace-trimmed shirt and cloth-of-gold vest were already smeared with snuff, his legs were hairy tree trunks beneath a batik sarong, he wore a diamond mine on each hand and a silver chain about his neck which could have anchored a battleship. He waved a ripe Trichinopoly cigar above a four-decker sandwich and roared:

"So you are walking again. Good fellow! The only way you get well is not sip dishwater soup and take it easily, like that upgebungled horse doctor has the nerve to tell me to do." He purpled with indignation. "Does one thought get through that sand in his synapses, what it is costing me every hour I wait here? What a killing I can make if I get home among those underhand competition jackals before the news reaches them Nicholas van Rijn is alive after all? I have just been out beating the station engineer over his thick flat mushroom he uses for a head, telling him if my spaceship is not ready to leave tomorrow noon I will hitch him to it and say giddap. So you will come back to Earth with us your own selfs, *nie*?"

Wace had no immediate reply. Sandra had followed the merchant in.

She was driving a wheelchair, and looked so white and thin that his heart cracked over. Her hair was a pale frosty cloud on the pillow, it seemed as if it would be cold to touch. But her eyes lived, immense, the infinite warm green of Earth's gentlest seas; and she smiled at him.

"My lady—" he whispered.

"Oh, she comes too," said van Rijn, selecting an apple from the fruit basket at Wace's bedside. "We all continue our interrupted trip, maybe with not so much fun and games aboard—" He drooped one little obsidian eye at her, lasciviously. "Those we save for later on Earth when we are back to normal, ha?"

"If my lady has the strength to travel—" stumbled Wace. He sat down, his knees would bear him no longer.

"Oh, yes," she murmured. "It is only a matter of following the diet as written for me and getting much rest."

"Worst thing you can do, by damn," grumbled van Rijn, finishing the apple and picking up an orange.

"It isn't suitable," protested Wace. "We lost so many servants when the skycruiser ditched. She'd only have—"

"A single maid to attend me?" Sandra's laugh was ghostly, but it held genuine amusement. "After now I am to forget what we did and endured, and be so correct and formal with you, Eric? That would be most silly, when we have climbed the ridge over Salmenbrok together, not?"

Wace's pulse clamored. Van Rijn, strewing orange peel on the floor, said: "Out of hard lucks, the good Lord can pull much money if He chooses. I cannot know every man in the company, so promising youngsters like you do go sometimes to waste on little outposts like here. Now I will take you home to Earth and find a proper paying job for you."

If *she* could remember one chilled morning beneath Mount Oborch, thought Wace, he, for the sake of his manhood, could remember less pleasant things, and name them in plain words. It was time.

He was still too weak to rise—he shook a little—but he caught van Rijn's gaze and said in a voice hard with anger:

"That's the easiest way to get back your self-esteem, of course. Buy it! Bribe me with a sinecure to forget how Sandra sat with a paintbrush in a coalsack of a room, till she fainted from exhaustion, and how she gave us her last food . . . how I myself worked my brain and my heart out, to pull us all back from that jailhouse country and win a war to boot—No, don't interrupt. I know you had some part in it. You fought during that naval engagement: because you had no choice, no place to hide. You found a nice nasty way to dispose of an inconvenient obstacle to the peace negotiations. You have a talent for that sort of thing. And you made some suggestions.

"But what did it amount to? It amounted to your saying to me: 'Do this! Build that!' And I had to do it, with nonhuman helpers and stone-age tools, I had to design it, even! Any fool could once have said, 'Take me to the Moon.' It took brains to figure out how!

"Your role, your 'leadership,' amounted to strolling around, gambling and chattering, playing cheap politics, eating like a hippopotamus while Sandra lay starving on Dawrnach—and claiming all the credit! And now I'm supposed to go to Earth, sit down in a gilded pigpen of an office, spend the rest of my life thumb-twiddling . . . and keep quiet when you brag. Isn't that right? You take your sinecure—"

Wace saw Sandra's eyes on him, grave, oddly compassionate, and jerked to a halt.

"I quit," he ended.

Van Rijn had swallowed the orange and returned to his sandwich during Wace's speech. Now he burped, licked his fingers, took a fresh puff of his cigar, and rumbled quite mildly:

"If you think I give away sinecures, you are being too optimist. I am offering you a job with importance for no reason except I think you can do it better than some knucklebone heads on Earth. I will pay you what the job is worth. And by damn, you will work your promontory off."

Wace gulped after air.

"Go ahead and insult me, public if you wish," said van Rijn. "Just not on company time. Now I go find me who it was put the bomb in that cruiser and take care of him. Also maybe the cook will fix me a little Italian hero sandwich. Death and dynamite, they want to starve me to bones here, them!"

He waved a shaggy paw and departed like an amiable earthquake.

Sandra wheeled over and laid a hand on Wace's. It was a cool touch, light as a leaf falling in a northern October, but it burned him. As if from far off, he heard her:

"I awaited this to come, Eric. It is best you understand now. I, who was born to govern . . . my whole life has been a long governing, not? . . . I know what I speak of. There are the fake leaders, the balloons, with talent only to get in people's way. Yes. But he is not one of them. Without him, you and I would sleep dead beneath Achan."

"But—"

"You complain he made you do the hard things that used your talent, not his? Of course he did. It is not the leader's job to do everything himself. It is his job to order, persuade, wheedle, bully, bribe—just that, to make people do what must be done, whether or not they think it is possible.

"You say, he spent time loafing around talking, making jokes and a false front to impress the natives? Of course! Somebody had to. We were monsters, strangers, beggars as well. Could you or I have started as a deformed beggar and ended as all but king?

"You say he bribed—with goods from crooked dice—and blustered, lied, cheated, politicked, killed both open and sly? Yes. I do not say it was right. I do not say he did not enjoy himself, either. But can you name another way to have gotten our lives back? Or even to make peace for those poor warring devils?"

"Well . . . well—" The man looked away, out the window to the stark landscape. It would be good to dwell inside Earth's narrower horizon.

"Well, maybe," he said at last, grudging each word. "I . . . I suppose I was too hasty. Still—we played our parts too, you know. Without us, he—"

"I think, without us, he would have found some other way to come home," she interrupted. "But we without him, no."

He jerked his head back. Her face was burning a deeper red than the ember sunlight outside could tinge it.

He thought, with sudden weariness: *After all, she is a woman, and women live more for the next generation than men can. Most especially she does, for the life of a planet may rest on her child, and she is an aristocrat in the old pure meaning of the word. He who fathers the next Duke of Hermes may be aging, fat, and uncouth; callous and conscienceless; unable to see her as anything but a boisterous episode. It doesn't matter, if the woman and the aristocrat see him as a man.*

Well-a-day, I have much to thank them both for.

"I—" Sandra looked confused, almost trapped. Her look held an inarticulate pleading. "I think I had best go and let you rest." After a moment of his silence: "He is not yet so strong as he claims. I may be needed."

"No," said Wace with an enormous tenderness. "The need is all yours. Good-by, my lady."

AFTERWORD

Thinking about this early novel after a lapse of years, I believe I can see what its wellsprings are. They include the old pulp conventions of storytelling and a desire to change or, at any rate, spoof these. Falstaff, Long John Silver, and other amiable literary rogues, as well as a few real figures from the Renaissance; L. Sprague de Camp's unique combination of humor and adventure; above all, Hal Clement's marvelously detailed and believable fictional worlds. I do not say that *The Man Who Counts* matches any of its inspirers. Certainly I would write a bit differently today. Yet it does represent my first serious venture into planet-building and the first full-scale appearance of Nicholas van Rijn. Thus I remain fond of it.

After being serialized in *Astounding* (today's *Analog*) it had a paperback edition. The latter was badly copy-edited and saddled with the ludicrous title of *War of the*

Wing-Men. I am happy that now, at last, the proper text and name can be restored.

Planet-building is one of the joyous arts, if you have that sort of mind. The object is to construct a strange world which is at the same time wholly consistent, not only with itself but with what science knows of such matters. Any extra-scientific assumptions you make for story purposes—e.g., faster-than-light travel—should not be necessary to the world itself. So, taking a star of a given mass, you calculate how luminous it must be, how long the year is of a planet in a given orbit around it, how much irradiation that planet gets, and several more things. (Of course, I simplify here, since you ought also to take account of the star's age, its chemical composition, etc.) These results will be basically influential on surface features of the planet, the kind of life it bears, evolution of that life, and so on endlessly. There is no rigid determinism: at any given stage, many different possibilities open up. However, those which you choose will in their turn become significant parameters at the next stage . . . until at last, perhaps, you get down to the odor of a flower and what it means to an alien individual.

Because science will never know everything, you are allowed reasonable guesses where calculation breaks down. Nonetheless—quite apart from flaws which sharp-eyed readers may discover in your facts or logic—you can be pretty sure that eventually science *will* make discoveries which cast doubt, to say the very least, on various of your assumptions. History will have moved on, too, in directions you had not foreseen for your imaginary future. You are invited to play what Clement calls "the game" with this unrevised text of mine.

I was saved from making one grievous error, by my wife. Looking over my proposed life cycle of the Diomedeans, she exclaimed, "Hey, wait, you have the females flying thousands of miles each year while they're the equivalent of seven months pregnant. It can't be done. I know." I deferred to the voice of experience, and redesigned. As I have remarked elsewhere, planet-building ought to be good therapy for the kind of mental patient who believes he's God.

Despite the hazards, I've come back to it again and again, always hoping that readers will share some of the pleasure therein.

—Poul Anderson, 1978

INTRODUCTION

⚙ ESAU ⚙

The following tale is here because it shows a little more of the philosophy and practice which once animated the Polesotechnic League. Grip well: already these were becoming somewhat archaic, if not obsolete. Nevertheless, the person concerned appears to have soared high for long years afterward. Children of his moved to Avalon with Falkayn. This story was written in her later years by one of them, Judith, drawing upon her father's reminiscences when she was young and on a good knowledge of conditions as they had been in his own youth. It appeared in a periodical of the time called *Morgana*.

—Hloch of the Stormgate Choth
The Earth Book of Stormgate

ESAU

The cab obtained clearance from certain machines and landed on the roof of the Winged Cross. Emil Dalmady paid and stepped out. When it took off, he felt suddenly very alone. The garden was fragrant around him in a warm deep-blue summer's dusk; at this height, the sounds of Chicago Integrate were a murmur as of a distant ocean; the other towers and the skyways between them were an elven forest through which flitted will-o'-the-wisp aircars and beneath which—as if Earth had gone transparent—a fantastic galaxy of many-colored lights was blinking awake farther than eye could reach. But the penthouse bulking ahead might have been a hill where a grizzly bear had its den.

The man squared his shoulders. *Haul in,* he told himself. *He won't eat you.* Anger lifted afresh. *I might just eat him.* He strode forward: a stocky, muscular figure in a blue zipskin, features broad, high of cheekbones, snubnosed, eyes green and slightly tilted, hair reddish black.

But despite stiffened will, the fact remained that he had not expected a personal interview with any merchant prince of the Polesotechnic League, and in one of the latter's own homes. When a live butler had admitted him, and he had crossed an improbably long stretch of trollcat rug to the VieWall end of a luxury-cluttered living room, and was confronting Nicholas van Rijn, his throat tightened and his palms grew wet.

"Good evening," the host rumbled. "Welcome." His corpulent corpus did not rise from the lounger. Dalmady didn't mind. Not only bulk but height would have dwarfed him. Van Rijn waved a hand at a facing seat; the other gripped a liter tankard of beer. "Sit. Relax. You look quivery like a blanc-mange before a firing squad. What you drink, smoke, chew, sniff, or elsewise make amusements with?"

Dalmady lowered himself to an edge. Van Rijn's great hook-beaked, multichinned, mustached and goateed visage, framed in black shoulder-length ringlets, crinkled with a grin. Beneath the sloping brow, small jet eyes glittered at the newcomer. "Relax," he urged again. "Give the form-fitting a chance. Not so fun-making an embrace like a pretty girl, but less extracting, ha? I think maybe a little glass Genever and bitters over dry ice is a tranquilizator for you." He clapped.

"Sir," Dalmady said, harshly in his tension, "I don't want to seem ungracious, but—"

"But you came to Earth breathing flame and brim-rocks, and went through six echelons of the toughest no-saying secretaries and officers what the Solar Spice and Liquors Company has got, like a bulldozer chasing a cowdozer, demanding to see whoever the crockhead was what fired you after what you done yonderways. Nobody had a chance to explain. Trouble was, they assumptioned you knew things what they take for granted. So natural, what they said sounded to you like a flushoff and you hurricaned your way from them to somebody else."

Van Rijn offered a cigar out of a gold humidor whose workmanship Dalmady couldn't identify except that it was nonhuman. The young man shook his head. The merchant selected one himself, bit off the end and spat that expertly into a receptor, and inhaled the tobacco to ignition. "Well," he continued, "somebody would have got through into you at last, only then I learned about you and ordered this meeting. I would have wanted to talk at you anyhows. Now I shall clarify everything like Hindu butter."

His geniality was well nigh as overwhelming as his wrath would have been, assuming the legends about him were true. *And he could be setting me up for a thunderbolt*, Dalmady thought, and clung to his indignation as he answered:

"Sir, if your outfit is dissatisfied with my conduct on Suleiman, it might at least have told me why, rather than sending a curt message that I was being replaced and should report to HQ. Unless you can prove to me that I bungled, I will not accept demotion. It's a question of personal honor more than professional standing. They think that way where I come from. I'll quit. And . . . there are plenty of other companies in the League that will be glad to hire me."

"True, true, in spite of every candle I burn to St. Dismas." Van Rijn sighed through his cigar, engulfing Dalmady in smoke. "Always they try to pirate my executives what have not yet sworn fealty, like the thieves they are. And I, poor old lonely fat man, trying to run this enterprise personal what stretches across so many whole worlds, even with modern computer technology I get melted down from overwork, and too few men for helpers what is not total gruntbrains, and some of them got to be occupied just luring good executives away from elsewhere." He took a noisy gulp of beer. "Well."

"I suppose you've read my report, sir," was Dalmady's gambit.

"Today. So much information flowing from across the light-years, how can this weary old noggle hold it without data flowing back out like ear wax? Let me review to make sure I got it tesseract. Which means—ho, ho!—straight in four dimensions."

Van Rijn wallowed deeper into his lounger, bridged hairy fingers, and closed his eyes. The butler appeared with a coldly steaming and hissing goblet. *If this is his idea of a small drink*—! Dalmady thought. Grimly, he forced himself to sit at ease and sip.

"Now." The cigar waggled in time to the words. "This star what its discoverer called Osman is out past Antares, on the far edge of present-day regular-basis League activities. One planet is inhabited, called by humans Suleiman. Subjovian; life based on hydrogen, ammonia, methane; primitive natives, but friendly. Turned out, on the biggest continent grows a plant we call . . . um-m-m . . . bluejack, what the natives use for a spice and tonic. Analysis showed a complicated blend of chemicals, answering sort of to hormonal stuffs for us, with synergistic effects. No good to oxygen breathers, but maybe we can sell to hydrogen breathers elsewhere.

"Well, we found very few markets, at least what had anythings to offer we wanted. You need a special biochemistry for bluejack to be beneficent. So synthesis would cost us more, counting investment and freight charges from chemical-lab centers, than direct harvesting by natives on Suleiman, paid for in trade goods. Given that, we could show a wee profit. Quite teensy—whole operation is near-as-damn marginal—but as long as things stayed peaceful, well, why not turn a few honest credits?

"And things was peaceful, too, for years. Natives cooperated fine, bringing in bluejack to warehouses. Outshipping was one of those milk runs where we don't knot up capital in our own vessels, we contract with a freighter line to make regular calls. Oh, *ja,* contretemps kept on countertiming—bad seasons, bandits raiding caravans, kings getting too greedy about taxes—usual stuffing, what any competent factor should could handle on the spot, so no reports about it ever come to pester me.

"And then—Ahmed, more beer!—real trouble. Best market for bluejack is on a planet we call Babur. Its star, Mogul, lies in the same general region, about thirty light-years from Osman. Its top country been dealing with Technic civilization off and on for decades. Trying to modernize, they was mainly interested in robotics for some reason; but at last they did pile together enough outplanet exchange for they could commission a few hyperdrive ships built and crews trained. So now the Solar Commonwealth and other powers got to treat them with a little more respect; blast cannon and nuclear missiles sure improve manners, by damn! They is still small tomatoes, but ambitious. And to them, with the big domestic demand, bluejack is not an incidental thing."

Van Rijn leaned forward, wrinkling the embroidered robe that circled his paunch. "You wonder why I tell you what you know, ha?" he said. "When I need direct reports on a situation, especial from a world as scarcely known as Suleiman, I can't study each report from decades. Data retrieval got to make me an abstract. I check with you now, who was spotted there, whether the machine give me all what is significant to our talking. Has I been correct so far?"

"Yes," Dalmady said. "But—"

Yvonne Vaillancourt looked up from a console as the factor passed the open door of her collation lab. "What's wrong, Emil?" she asked. "I heard you clattering the whole way down the hall."

Dalmady stopped for a look. Clothing was usually at a minimum in the Earth-conditioned compound, but, while he had grown familiar with the skins of its inhabitants, he never tired of hers. Perhaps, he had thought, her blonde shapeliness impressed him the more because he had been born and raised on Altai. The colonists of that chill planet went heavily dressed of necessity. The same need to survive forced austere habits on them; and, isolated in a largely unexplored frontier section, they received scant news about developments in the core civilization.

When you were half a dozen humans on a world whose very air was death to you—when you didn't even have visitors of your own species, because the ship that regularly called belonged to a Cynthian carrier—you had no choice but to live in free and easy style. Dalmady had had that explained to him while he was being trained for this post, and recognized it and went along with it. But he wondered if he would ever become accustomed to the *casualness* of the sophisticates whom he bossed.

"I don't know," he answered the girl. "The Thalassocrat wants me at the palace."

"Why, he knows perfectly well how to make a visi call."

"Yes, but a nomad's brought word of something nasty in the Uplands, and won't come near the set. Afraid it'll imprison his soul, I imagine."

"M-rn-m, I think not. We're still trying to chart the basic Suleimanite psychology, you know, with only inadequate data from three or four cultures to go on . . . but they don't seem to have animistic tendencies like man's. Ceremony, yes, in abundance, but nothing we can properly identify as magic or religion."

Dalmady barked a nervous laugh. "Sometimes I think my whole staff considers our commerce an infernal nuisance that keeps getting in the way of their precious science."

"Sometimes you'd be right," Yvonne purred. "What'd hold us here except the chance to do research?"

"And how long would your research last if the company closed down this base?" he flared. "Which it will if we start losing money. My job's to see that we don't. I could use cooperation."

She slipped from her stool, came to him, and kissed him lightly. Her hair smelled like remembered steppe grass warmed by an orange sun, rippling under the rings of Altai. "Don't we help?" she murmured. "I'm sorry, dear."

He bit his lip and stared past her, down the length of gaudy murals whose painting had beguiled much idle time over the years. "No, I'm sorry," he said with the stiff honesty of his folk. "Of course you're all loyal and—It's me. Here I am, the youngest among you, a half-barbarian herdboy, supposed to make a go of things . . . in one of the easiest, most routinized outposts in this sector . . . and after a bare fifteen months—"

If I fail, he thought, *well, I can return home, no doubt, and dismiss the sacrifices my parents made to send me to managerial school offplanet, scorn the luck that Solar Spice and Liquors had an opening here and no more experienced employee to fill it, forget every dream about walking in times to come on new and unknown worlds that really call forth every resource a man has to give. Oh, yes, failure isn't fatal, except in subtler ways than I have words for.*

"You fret too much." Yvonne patted his cheek. "Probably this is just another tempest in a chickenhouse. You'll bribe somebody, or arm somebody, or whatever's needful, and that will once again be that."

"I hope so. But the Thalassocrat acted—well, not being committed to xenological scholarly precision, I'd say he acted worried too." Dalmady stood a few seconds longer, scowling, before: "All right, I'd better be on my way." He gave her a hug. "Thanks, Yvonne."

She watched him till he was out of sight, then returned to her work. Officially she was the trade post's secretary-treasurer, but such duties seldom came to her except when a freighter had landed. Otherwise she used the computers to try to find patterns in what fragments of knowledge her colleagues could wrest from a world—an entire, infinitely varied world—and hoped that a few scientists elsewhere might eventually scan a report on Suleiman (one among thousands of planets) and be interested.

Airsuit donned, Dalmady left the compound by its main personnel lock. Wanting time to compose himself, he went afoot through the city to the palace.

If they were city and palace.

He didn't know. Books, tapes, lectures, and neuroinductors had crammed him with information about this part of this continent; but those were the everyday facts and skills needed to manage operations. Long talks with his subordinates here had added a little insight, but only a little. Direct experience with the autochthons was occasionally enlightening, but just as apt to be confusing. No wonder that, once a satisfactory arrangement was made with Coast and Upland tribes (?), his predecessors had not attempted expansion or improvement. When you don't understand a machine but it seems to be running reasonably smoothly, you don't tinker much.

Outside the compound's forcefield, local gravity dragged at him with forty percent greater pull than Earth's. Though his suit was light and his muscles hard, the air recycler necessarily included the extra mass of a unit for dealing with the hydrogen that seeped through any material. Soon he was sweating. Nevertheless it was as if the chill struck past all thermostatic coils, into his heavy bones.

High overhead stood Osman, a furious white spark, twice as luminous as Sol but, at its distance, casting a bare sixteenth of what Earth gets. Clouds, tinged red by organic compounds, drifted on slow winds through a murky sky where one of the three moons was dimly visible. That atmosphere bore thrice a terrestrial standard pressure. It was mostly hydrogen and helium, with vapors of methane and ammonia and traces of other gas. Greenhouse effect did not extend to unfreezing water.

Indeed, the planetary core was overlaid by a shell of ice, mixed with rock, penetrated by tilted metal-poor strata. The land glittered amidst its grayness and scrunched beneath Dalmady's boots. It sloped down to a dark, choppy sea of liquid ammonia whose horizon was too remote—given a 17,000–kilometer radius—for him to make out through the red-misted air.

Ice also were the buildings that rose blocky around him. They shimmered glasslike where doorways or obscure carved symbols did not break their smoothness. There were no streets in the usual sense, but aerial observation had disclosed an elaborate pattern in the layout of structures, about which the dwellers could not or would not speak. Wind moved ponderously between them. The air turned its sound, every sound, shrill.

Traffic surged. It was mainly pedestrian, natives on their business, carrying the oddly shaped tools and containers of a fireless neolithic nonhuman culture. A few wagons lumbered in with produce from the hinterland; their draught animals suggested miniature dinosaurs modeled by someone who had heard vague rumors of such creatures. A related, more slender species was ridden. Coracles bobbed across the sea; you might as well say the crews were fishing, though a true fish could live here unprotected no longer than a man.

Nothing reached Dalmady's earphones except the wind, the distant wave-rumble, the clop of feet and creak of wagons. Suleimanites did not talk casually. They did communicate, however, and without pause: by gesture, by ripple across erectile fur, by delicate exchanges between scent glands. They avoided coming near the human, but simply because his suit was hot to their touch. He gave and received many signals of greeting. After two years—twenty-five of Earth's—Coast and Uplands alike were becoming dependent on metal and plastic and energy-cell trade goods. Local labor had been eagerly available to help build a spaceport on the mesa overlooking town, and still did most of the work. That saved installing automatic machinery—one reason for the modest profit earned by this station.

Dalmady leaned into his uphill walk. After ten minutes he was at the palace.

The half-score natives posted outside the big, turreted building were not guards. While wars and robberies occurred on Suleiman, the slaying of a "king" seemed to be literally unthinkable. (An effect of pheromones? In every community the xenologists had observed thus far, the leader ate special foods which his followers insisted would poison anyone else; and maybe the followers were right.) The drums, plumed canes, and less identifiable gear which these beings carried were for ceremonial use.

Dalmady controlled his impatience and watched with a trace of pleasure the ritual of opening doors and conducting him to the royal presence. The Suleimanites were a graceful and handsome species. They were plantigrade bipeds, rather like men although the body was thicker and the average only came to his shoulder. The hands each bore two fingers between two thumbs, and were supplemented by a prehensile tail. The head was round, with a parrotlike beak, tympani for hearing, one large golden-hued eye in the middle and two smaller, less developed ones for binocular and peripheral vision. Clothing was generally confined to a kind of sporran, elaborately patterned with symbols, to leave glands and mahogany fur available for signals. The fact that Suleimanite languages had so large a nonvocal component handicapped human efforts at understanding as much as anything else did.

The Thalassocrat addressed Dalmady by voice alone, in the blue-glimmering ice cavern of his audience room. Earphones reduced the upper frequencies to some the man could hear. Nonetheless, that squeak and gibber always rather spoiled the otherwise impressive effect of flower crown and carven staff. So did the dwarfs, hunch-backs, and cripples who squatted on rugs, and skin-draped benches. It was not known why household servants were always recruited among the handicapped. Suleimanites had tried to explain when asked, but their meaning never came through.

"Fortune, power, and wisdom to you, Factor." They didn't use personal names on this world, and seemed unable to grasp the idea of an identification which was not a scent-symbol.

"May they continue to abide with you, Thalassocrat." The vocalizer on his back transformed Dalmady's version of local speech into sounds that his lips could not bring forth.

"We have here a Master of caravaneers," the monarch said.

Dalmady went through polite ritual with the Uplander, who was tall and rangy for a Suleimanite, armed with a stoneheaded tomahawk and a trade rifle designed for his planet, his barbarianism showing in gaudy jewels and bracelets. They were okay, however, those hill-country nomads. Once a bargain had been struck, they held to it with more literal-mindedness than humans could have managed.

"And what is the trouble for which I am summoned, Master? Has your caravan met bandits on its way to the Coast? I will be glad to equip a force for their suppression."

Not being used to talking with men, the chief went into full Suleimanite language—his own dialect, at that—and became incomprehensible. One of the midgets stumped forward. Dalmady recognized him. A bright mind dwelt in that poor little body, drank deep of whatever knowledge about the universe was offered, and in return had frequently helped with counsel or knowledge. "Let me ask him out, Factor and Thalassocrat," he suggested.

"If you will, Advisor," his overlord agreed.

"I will be in your debt, Translator," Dalmady said, with his best imitation of the prancing thanks-gesture.

Beneath the courtesies, his mind whirred and he found himself holding his breath while he waited. Surely the news couldn't be really catastrophic!

He reviewed the facts, as if hoping for some hitherto unnoticed salvation in them. With little axial tilt, Suleiman lacked seasons. Bluejack needed the cool, dry climate of the Uplands, but there it grew the year around. Primitive natives, hunters and gatherers, picked it in the course of their wanderings. Every several months, terrestrial, such a tribe would make rendezvous with one of the more advanced nomadic herding communities, who bartered for the parched leaves and fruits. A caravan would then form and make the long trip to this city, where Solar's folk would acquire the bales in exchange for Technic merchandise. You could count on a load arriving about twice a month. Four times in an Earthside year, the Cynthian vessel took away the contents of Solar's warehouse . . . and left a far more precious cargo of letters, tapes, journals, books, news from the stars that were so rarely seen in these gloomy heavens.

It wasn't the most efficient system imaginable, but it was the cheapest, once you calculated what the cost would be—in capital investment and civilized-labor salaries—of starting plantations. And costs must be kept low or the enterprise would change from a minor asset to a liability, which would soon be liquidated. As matters were, Suleiman was a typical outpost of its kind: to the scientists, a fascinating study and a chance to win reputation in their fields; to the factors, a comparatively easy job, a first step on a ladder at the top of which waited the big, glamorous, gorgeously paid managerial assignments.

Or thus it had been until now.

The Translator turned to Dalmady. "The Master says this," he piped. "Lately in the Uplands have come what he calls—no, I do not believe that can be said in words alone—It is clear to me, they are machines that move about harvesting the bluejack."

"What?" The man realized he had exclaimed in Anglic. Through suddenly loud pulses, he heard the Translator go on:

"The wild folk were terrified and fled those parts. The machines came and took what they had stored against their next rendezvous. That angered this Master's nomads, who deal there. They rode to protest. From afar they saw a vessel, like the great flying vessel that lands here, and a structure a-building. Those who oversaw that work were . . . low, with many legs and claws for hands . . . long noses. . . . A gathering robot came and shot lightning past the nomads. They saw they too must flee, lest its warning shot become deadly. The Master himself took a string of remounts and posted hither as swiftly as might be. In words, I cannot say more of what he has to tell."

Dalmady gasped into the frigid blueness that enclosed him. His mouth felt dry, his knees weak, his stomach in upheaval. "Baburites," he mumbled. "Got to be. But why're they doing this to us?"

Brush, herbage, leaves on the infrequent trees, were many shades of black. Here and there a patch of red or brown or blue flowering relieved it, or an ammonia river cataracting down the hills. Further off, a range of ice mountains flashed blindingly; Suleiman's twelve-hour day was drawing to a close, and Osman's rays struck level through a break in roiling ruddy cloud cover. Elsewhere a storm lifted like a dark wall on which lightning scribbled. The dense air brought its thunder-noise to Dalmady as a high drumroll. He paid scant attention. The gusts that hooted around his car, the air pockets into which it lurched, made piloting a fulltime job. A cybernated vehicle would have been too expensive for this niggardly rewarding planet.

"There!" cried the Master. He squatted with the Translator in an after compartment, which was left under native conditions and possessed an observation dome. In deference to his superstitions, or whatever they were, only the audio part of the intercom was turned on.

"Indeed," the Translator said more calmly. "I descry it now. Somewhat to our right, Factor—in a valley by a lake—do you see?"

"A moment." Dalmady locked the altitude controls. The car would bounce around till his teeth rattled, but the grav field wouldn't let it crash. He leaned forward in his harness, tried to ignore the brutal pull on him, and adjusted the scanner screen. His race had not evolved to see at those wavelengths which penetrated this atmosphere best; and the distance was considerable, as distances tend to be on a subjovian.

Converting light frequencies, amplifying, magnifying, the screen flung a picture at him. Tall above shrubs and turbulent ammonia stood a spaceship. He identified it as a Holbert-X freighter, a type commonly sold to hydrogen breathers. There had doubtless been some modifications to suit its particular home world, but he saw none except a gun turret and a couple of missile tube housings.

A prefabricated steel and ferrocrete building was being assembled nearby. The construction robots must be working fast, without pause; the cube was already more than half-finished. Dalmady glimpsed flares of energy torches, like tiny blue novas. He couldn't make out individual shapes, and didn't want to risk coming near enough.

"You see?" he asked the image of Peter Thorson, and transmitted the picture to another screen.

Back at the base, his engineer's massive head nodded. Behind could be seen the four remaining humans. They looked as strained and anxious as Dalmady felt, Yvonne perhaps more so.

"Yeh. Not much we can do about it," Thorson declared. "They pack bigger weapons than us. And see, in the corners of the barn, those bays? That's for blast cannon, I swear. Add a heavy-duty forcefield generator for passive defense, and it's a nut we can't hope to crack."

"The home office—"

"Yeh, they *might* elect to resent the invasion and dispatch a regular warcraft or three. But I don't believe it. Wouldn't pay, in economic terms. And it'd make every kind of hooraw, because remember, SSL hasn't got any legal monopoly here." Thorson shrugged. "My guess is, Old Nick'll simply close down on Suleiman, probably wangling a deal with the Baburites that'll cut his losses and figuring to diddle them good at a later date." He was a veteran mercantile professional, accustomed to occasional setbacks, indifferent to the scientific puzzles around him.

Yvonne, who was not, cried softly, "Oh, no! We can't! The insights we're gaining—"

And Dalmady, who could not afford a defeat this early in his career, clenched one fist and snapped, "We can at least talk to those bastards, can't we? I'll try to raise them. Stand by." He switched the outercom to a universal band and set the Come In going. The last thing he had seen from the compound was her stricken eyes.

The Translator inquired from aft: "Do you know who the strangers are and what they intend, Factor?"

"I have no doubt they come from Babur, as we call it," the man replied absently. "That is a world"—the more enlightened Coast dwellers had acquired some knowledge of astronomy—"akin to yours. It is larger and warmer, with heavier air. Its folk could not endure this one for long without becoming sick. But they can move about unarmored for a while. They buy most of our blue-jack. Evidently they have decided to go to the source."

"But why, Factor?"

"For profit, I suppose, Translator." *Maybe just in their nonhuman cost accounting. That's a giant investment they're making in a medicinal product. But they don't operate under capitalism, under anything that human history ever saw, or so I've heard. Therefore they may consider it an investment in . . . empire? No doubt they can expand their foothold here, once we're out of the way—*

The screen came to life.

The being that peered from it stood about waist-high to a man in its erect torso. The rest of the body stretched behind in a vaguely caterpillar shape, on eight stumpy legs. Along that glabrous form was a row of opercula protecting tracheae which, in a dense hydrogen atmosphere, aerated the organism quite efficiently. Two arms ended in claws reminiscent of a lobster's; from the wrists below sprouted short, tough finger-tendrils. The head was dominated by a spongy snout. A Baburite had no mouth. It—individuals changed sex from time to time—chewed food with the claws and put it in a digestive pouch to be dissolved before the snout sucked it up. The eyes were four, and tiny. Speech was by diaphragms on either side of the skull, hearing and smell were associated with the tracheae. The skin was banded orange, blue, white, and black. Most of it was hidden by a gauzy robe.

The creature would have been an absurdity, a biological impossibility, on an Earth-type world. In its own ship, in strong gravity and thick cold air and murk through which shadowy forms moved, it had dignity and power.

It thrummed noises which a vocalizer rendered into fairly good League Latin: "We expected you. Do not approach closer."

Dalmady moistened his lips. He felt cruelly young and helpless. "G-g-greeting. I am the factor."

The Baburite made no comment.

After a while, Dalmady plowed on: "We have been told that you . . . well, you are seizing the bluejack territory. I cannot believe that is correct."

"It is not, precisely," said the flat mechanical tone. "For the nonce, the natives may use these lands as heretofore, except that they will not find much bluejack to harvest. Our robots are too effective. Observe."

The screen flashed over to a view of a squat, cylindrical machine. Propelled by a simple grav drive, it floated several centimeters off the ground. Its eight arms terminated in sensors, pluckers, trimmers, brush cutters. On its back was welded a large basket. On its top was a maser transceiver and a swivel-mounted blaster.

"It runs off accumulators," the unseen Baburite stated. "These need only be recharged once in thirty-odd hours, at the fusion generator we are installing, unless a special energy expenditure occurs . . . like a battle, for instance. High-hovering relay units keep the robots in constant touch with each other and with a central computer, currently in the ship, later to be in the blockhouse. It controls them all simultaneously, greatly reducing the cost per unit." With no trace of sardonicism: "You will understand that such a beamcasting system cannot feasibly be jammed. The computer will be provided with missiles as well as guns and defensive fields. It is programmed to strike back at any attempt to hamper its operations."

The robot's image disappeared, the being's returned. Dalmady felt faint. "But that would . . . would be . . . an act of war!" he stuttered.

"No. It would be self-protection, legitimate under the rules of the Polesotechnic League. You may credit us with the intelligence to investigate the social as well as physical state of things before we acted and, indeed, to become an associate member of the League. No one will suffer except your company. That will not displease its competitors. They have assured our representatives that they can muster enough Council votes to prevent sanctions. It is not as if the loss were very great. Let us recommend to you personally that you seek employment elsewhere."

Uh-huh . . . after I dropped a planet . . . I might maybe get a job cleaning latrines someplace, went through the back of Dalmady's head. "No," he protested, "what about the autochthons? They're hurting already."

"When the land has been cleared, bluejack plantations will be established," the Baburite said. "Doubtless work can be found for some of the displaced savages, if they are sufficiently docile. Doubtless other resources, ignored by you oxygen breathers, await exploitation. We may in the end breed colonists adapted to Suleiman. But that will be of no concern to the League. We have investigated the practical effect of its prohibition on imperialism by members. Where no one else is interested in a case, a treaty with a native government is considered sufficient, and native governments with helpful attitudes are not hard to set up. Suleiman is such a case. A written-off operation that was never much more than marginal, out on an extreme frontier, is not worth the League's worrying about."

"The principle—"

"True. We would not provoke war, nor even our own expulsion and a boycott. However, recall that you are not being ordered off this planet. You have simply met a superior competitor, superior by virtue of living closer to the scene, being better suited to the environment, and far more interested in succeeding here. We have the same right to launch ventures as you."

"What do you mean, 'we'?" Dalmady whispered. "Who are you? What are you? A private company, or—"

"Nominally, we are so organized, though like many other League associates we make no secret of this being *pro forma*," the Baburite told him. "Actually, the terms on which our society must deal with the Technic aggregate have little relevance to the terms of its interior structure. Considering the differences—sociological, psychological, biological—between us and you and your close allies, our desire to be free of your civilization poses no real threat to the latter and hence will never provoke any real reaction. At the same time, we will never win the freedom of the stars without the resources of modern technology.

"To industrialize with minimum delay, we must obtain the initial capacity through purchases from the Technic worlds. This requires Technic currency. Thus, while we spend what appears to be a disproportionate amount of effort and goods on this bluejack project, it will result in saving outplanet exchange for more important things.

"We tell you what we tell you in order to make clear, not only our harmlessness to the League as a whole, but our determination. We trust you have taped this discussion. It may prevent your employer from wasting our time and energy in counteracting any foredoomed attempts by him to recoup. While you remain on Suleiman, observe well. When you go back, report faithfully."

The screen blanked. Dalmady tried for minutes to make the connection again, but got no answer.

Thirty days later, which would have been fifteen of Earth's, a conference met in the compound. Around a table, in a room hazed and acrid with smoke, sat the humans. In a full-size screen were the images of the Thalassocrat and the Translator, a three-dimensional realism that seemed to breathe out the cold of the ice chamber where they crouched.

Dalmady ran a hand through his hair. "I'll summarize," he told them wearily. The Translator's fur began to move, his voice to make low whistles, as he rendered from the Anglic for his king. "The reports of our native scouts were waiting for me, recorded by Yvonne, when I returned from my own latest flit a couple of hours ago. Every datum confirms every other.

"We'd hoped, you recall, that the computer would be inadequate to cope with us, once the Baburite ship had left."

"Why should the live crew depart?" Sanjuro Naka-mura asked.

"That's obvious," Thorson said. "They may not run their domestic economy the way we run ours, but that doesn't exempt them from the laws of economics. A planet like Babur—actually, a single dominant country on it, or whatever they have—still backward, still poor, has limits on what it can afford. They may enjoy shorter lines of communication than we do, but we, at home, enjoy a lot more productivity. At their present stage, they can't spend what it takes to create and maintain a permanent, live-staffed base like ours. Suleiman isn't too healthy for them, either, you know, and they lack even our small background of accumulated experience. So they've got to automate at first, and just send somebody once in a while to check up and collect the harvest."

"Besides," Alice Bergen pointed out, "the nomads are sworn to us. They wouldn't make a deal with another party. Not that the Baburites could use them profitably anyway. We're sitting in the only suitable depot area, the only one whose people have a culture that makes it easy to train them in service jobs for us. So the Baburites have to operate right on the spot where the bluejack grows. The nomads resent having their caravan trade ended, and would stage guerrilla attacks on live workers."

"Whew!" Nakamura said, with an attempted grin. "I assure you, my question was only rhetorical. I simply wanted to point out that the opposition would not have left everything in charge of a computer if they weren't confident the setup would function, including holding us at bay. I begin to see why their planners concentrated on developing robotics at the beginning of modernization. No doubt they intend to use machines in quite a few larcenous little undertakings."

"Have you found out yet how many robots there are?" Isabel da Fonseca asked.

"We estimate a hundred," Dalmady told her, "though we can't get an accurate count. They operate fast, you see, covering a huge territory—in fact, the entire territory where bluejack grows thickly enough to be worth gathering—and they're identical in appearance except for the relay hoverers."

"That must be some computer, to juggle so many at once, over such varying conditions," Alice remarked. Cybernetics was not her field.

Yvonne shook her head; the gold tresses swirled. "Nothing extraordinary. We have long-range telephotos, taken during its installation. It's a standard multichannel design, only the electronics modified for ambient conditions. Rudimentary awareness: more isn't required, and would be uneconomic to provide, when its task is basically simple."

"Can't we outwit it, then?" Alice asked.

Dalmady grimaced. "What do you think my native helpers and I have been trying to do thereabouts, this past week? It's open country; the relayers detect you coming a huge ways off, and the computer dispatches robots. Not many are needed. If you come too close to the blockhouse, they fire warning blasts. That's terrified the natives. Few of them will approach anywhere near, and in fact the savages are starting to evacuate, which'll present us with a nice bunch of hungry refugees. Not that I blame them. A low-temperature organism cooks

easier than you or me. I did push ahead, and was fired on
for real. I ran away before my armor should be pierced."

"What about airborne attack?" Isabel wondered.

Thorson snorted. "In three rattly cars, with handguns?
Those robots fly too, remember. Besides, the centrum
has forcefields, blast cannon, missiles. A naval vessel
would have trouble reducing it."

"Furthermore," interjected the Thalassocrat, "I am
told of a threat to destroy this town by airborne weapons,
should a serious assault be made on yonder place. That
cannot be risked. Sooner would I order you to depart
for aye, and strike what bargain I was able with your
enemies."

He can make that stick, Dalmady thought, *by the simple process of telling our native workers to quit.*

Not that that would necessarily make any difference.
He recalled the last statement of a nomad Master, as the
retreat from a reconnaissance took place, Suleimanites
on their animals, man on a gravscooter. "We have abided
by our alliance with you, but you not by yours with us.
Your predecessors swore we should have protection from
skyborne invaders. If you fail to drive off these, how shall
we trust you?" Dalmady had pleaded for time and had
grudgingly been granted it, since the caravaneers did
value their trade with him. *But if we don't solve this
problem soon, I doubt the system can ever be renewed.*

"We shall not imperil you," he promised the Thalassocrat.

"How real is the threat?" Nakamura asked. "The
League wouldn't take kindly to slaughter of harmless
autochthons."

"But the League would not necessarily do more than
complain," Thorson said, "especially if the Baburites

argue that we forced them into it. They're banking on its indifference, and I suspect their judgment is shrewd."

"Right or wrong," Alice said, "their assessment of the psychopolitics will condition what they themselves do. And what assessment have they made? What do we know about their ways of thinking?"

"More than you might suppose," Yvonne replied. "After all, they've been in contact for generations, and you don't negotiate commercial agreements without having done some studies in depth first. The reason you've not seen much of me, these past days, is that I've buried myself in our files. We possess, right here, a bucketful of information about Babur."

Dalmady straightened in his chair. His pulse picked up the least bit. It was no surprise that a large and varied xenological library existed in this insignificant outback base. Microtapes were cheaply reproduced, and you never knew who might chance by or what might happen, so you were routinely supplied with references for your entire sector. "What do we have?" he barked.

Yvonne smiled wryly. "Nothing spectacular, I'm afraid. The usual: three or four of the principal languages, sketches of history and important contemporary cultures, state-of-technology analyses, statistics on stuff like population and productivity—besides the planetology, biology, psychoprofiling, et cetera. I tried and tried to find a weak point, but couldn't. Oh, I can show that this operation must be straining their resources, and will have to be abandoned if it doesn't quickly pay off. But that's been just as true of us."

Thorson fumed on his pipe. "If we could fix a gadget—We have a reasonably well-equipped workshop. That's where I've been sweating, myself."

"What had you in mind?" Dalmady inquired. The dullness of the engineer's voice was echoed in his own.

"Well, at first I wondered about a robot to go out and hunt theirs down. I could build one, a single one, more heavily armed and armored." Thorson's hand flopped empty, palm up, on the table. "But the computer has a hundred; and it's more sophisticated by orders of magnitude than any brain I could cobble together from spare cybernetic parts; and as the Thalassocrat says, we can't risk a missile dropped on our spaceport in retaliation, because it'd take out most of the city.

"Afterward I thought about jamming, or about somehow lousing the computer itself, but that's totally hopeless. It'd never let you get near."

He sighed. "My friends, let's admit that we've had the course, and plan how to leave with minimum loss."

The Thalassocrat stayed imperturbable, as became a monarch. But the Translator's main eye filmed over, his tiny body shrank into itself, and he cried: "We had hoped—one year our descendants, learning from you, joining you among the uncounted suns—Is there instead to be endless rule by aliens?"

Dalmady and Yvonne exchanged looks. Their hands clasped. He believed the same thought must be twisting in her: *We, being of the League, cannot pretend to altruism. But we are not monsters either. Some cold accountant in an office on Earth may order our departure. But can we who have been here, who like these people and were trusted by them, can we abandon them and continue to live with ourselves? Would we not forever feel that any blessings given us were stolen?*

And the old, old legend crashed into his awareness.

He sat for a minute or two, unconscious of the talk that growled and groaned around him. Yvonne first noticed the blankness in his gaze. "Emil," she murmured, "are you well?"

Dalmady sprang to his feet with a whoop.

"What in space?" Nakamura said.

The Factor controlled himself. He trembled, and small chills ran back and forth along his nerves; but his words came steady. "I have an idea."

Above the robes that billowed around him in the wind, the Translator carried an inconspicuous miniature audiovisual two-way. Dalmady in the car which he had landed behind a hill some distance off, Thorson in the car which hovered to relay, Yvonne and Alice and Isabel and Nakamura and the Thalassocrat in the city, observed a bobbing, swaying landscape on their tuned-in screens. Black leaves streamed, long and ragged, on bushes whose twigs clicked an answer to the whining air; boulders and ice chunks hunched among them; an ammonia fall boomed on the right, casting spray across the field of view. The men in the cars could likewise feel the planet's traction and the shudder of hulls under that slow, thick wind.

"I still think we should've waited for outside help," Thorson declared on a separate screen. "That rig's a godawful lash-up."

"And I still say," Dalmady retorted, "your job's made you needlessly fussy in this particular case. Besides, the natives couldn't've been stalled much longer." *Furthermore, if we can rout the Baburites with nothing but what was on hand, that ought to shine in my record. I'd like to think that's less important to me, but I can't deny it's real.*

One way or another, the decision had to be mine. I am the Factor.

Its a lonesome feeling. I wish Yvonne were here beside me.

"Quiet," he ordered. "Something's about to happen."

The Translator had crossed a ridge and was gravscooting down the opposite slope. He required no help at that; a few days of instruction had made him a very fair driver, even in costume. He was entering the robot-held area, and already a skyborne unit slanted to intercept him. In the keen Osmanlight, against ocherous clouds, it gleamed like fire.

Dalmady crouched in his seat. He was airsuited. If his friend got into trouble, he'd slap down his faceplate, open the cockpit, and swoop to an attempted rescue. A blaster lay knobby in his lap. The thought he might come too late made a taste of sickness in his mouth.

The robot paused at hover, arms extended, weapon pointed. The Translator continued to glide at a steady rate. When near collision, the two-way spoke for him: "Stand aside. We are instituting a change of program."

Spoke, to the listening computer, in the principal language of Babur.

Yvonne had worked out the plausible phrases, and spent patient hours with vocalizer and recorder until they seemed right. Engineer Thorson, xenologists Nakamura and Alice Bergen, artistically inclined biologist Isabel da Fonseca, Dalmady himself and several Suleimanite advisors who had spied on the Baburites, had created the disguise. Largely muffled in cloth, it didn't have to be too elaborate—a torso shaven and painted; a simple mechanical caterpillar body behind, steered by the hidden tail, automatically pacing its six legs with the wearer's two; a flexible mask with piezoelectric controls guided by the facial muscles beneath; claws and tendrils built over the natural arms, fake feet over the pair of real ones.

A human or an ordinary Suleimanite could not successfully have worn such an outfit. If nothing else, they were too big. But presumably it had not occurred to the Baburites to allow for midgets existing on this planet. The disguise was far from perfect; but presumably the computer was not programmed to check for any such contingency; furthermore, an intelligent, well-rehearsed actor, adapting his role moment by moment as no robot ever can, creates a gestalt transcending any minor errors of detail.

And . . . logically, the computer *must* be programmed to allow Baburites into its presence, to service it and collect the bluejack stored nearby.

Nonetheless, Dalmady's jaws ached from the tension on them.

The robot shifted out of the viewfield. In the receiving screens, ground continued to glide away underneath the scooter.

Dalmady switched off audio transmission from base. Though none save Yvonne, alone in a special room, was now sending to the Translator, and she via a bone conduction receiver—still, the cheers that had filled the car struck him as premature.

But the kilometers passed and passed. And the blockhouse hove in view, dark, cubical, bristling with sensors and antennae, cornered with the sinister shapes of gun emplacements and missile silos. No forcefield went up. Yvonne said through the Translator's unit: "Open; do not close again until told," and the idiot-savant computer directed a massive gate to swing wide.

What happened beyond was likewise Yvonne's job. She scanned through the portal by the two-way, summoned what she had learned of Baburite automation technology, and directed the Translator. Afterward she said it hadn't been difficult except for poor visibility; the builders had used standard layouts and programming languages. But to the Factor it was an hour of sweating, cursing, pushing fingers and belly muscles against each other, staring and staring at the image of enigmatic units which loomed between blank walls, under bluish light that was at once harsh and wan.

When the Translator emerged and the gate closed behind him, Dalmady almost collapsed.

Afterward, though—well, League people were pretty good at throwing a celebration!

"Yes," Dalmady said. "But—"

"Butter me no buts," van Rijn said. "Fact is, you reset that expensive computer so it should make those expensive robots stand idle. Why not leastwise use them for Solar?"

"That would have ruined relations with the natives, sir. Primitives don't take blandly to the notion of technological unemployment. So scientific studies would have become impossible. How then would you attract personnel?"

"What personnel would we need?"

"Some on the spot, constantly. Otherwise the Baburites, close as they are, could come back and, for example, organize and arm justly disgruntled Suleimanites against us. Robots or no, we'd soon find the bluejack costing us more than it earned us. . . . Besides, machines wear out and it costs to replace them. Live native help will reproduce for nothing."

"Well, you got that much sense, anyhows," van Rijn rumbled. "But why did you tell the computer it and its robots should attack *any* kind of machine, like a car or spacecraft, what comes near, and anybody of any shape what tells it to let him in? Supposing situations change, our people can't do nothings with it now neither."

"I told you, they don't need to," Dalmady rasped. "We get along—not dazzlingly, but we get along, we show a profit—with our traditional arrangements. As long as we maintain those, we exclude the Baburites from them. If we ourselves had access to the computer, we'd have to mount an expensive guard over it. Otherwise the Baburites could probably pull a similar trick on us, right? As is, the system interdicts any attempt to modernize operations in the bluejack area. Which is to say, it protects our monopoly—free—and will protect it for years to come."

He started to rise. "Sir," he continued bitterly, "the whole thing strikes me as involving the most elementary economic calculations. Maybe you have something subtler in mind, but if you do—"

"Whoa!" van Rijn boomed. "Squat yourself. Reel in some more of your drink, boy, and listen at me. Old and fat I am, but lungs and tongue I got. Also in working order is two other organs, one what don't concern you but one which is my brain, and my brain wants I should get information from you and stuff it."

Dalmady found he had obeyed.

"You need to see past a narrow specialism," van Rijn said. "Sometimes a man is too stupid good at his one job. He booms it, no matter the consequentials to everything else, and makes trouble for the whole organization he is supposed to serve. Like, you considered how Babur would react?"

"Of course. Freelady Vaillancourt—" *When will I be with her again?*—"and Drs. Bergen and Nakamura in particular, did an exhaustive analysis of materials on hand. As a result, we gave the computer an additional directive: that it warn any approaching vehicle before opening fire. The conversation I had later, with the spaceship captain or whatever he was, bore out our prediction."

(A quivering snout. A bleak gleam in four minikin eyes. But the voice, strained through a machine, emotionless: "Under the rules your civilization has devised, you have not given us cause for war; and the League always responds to what it considers unprovoked attack. Accordingly, we shall not bombard.")

"No doubt they feel their equivalent of fury," Dalmady said. "But what can they do? They're realists. Unless they think of some new stunt, they'll write Suleiman off and try elsewhere."

"And they buy our bluejack yet?"

"Yes."

"We should maybe lift the price, like teaching them a lesson they shouldn't make fumblydiddles with us?"

"You can do that, if you want to make them decide they'd rather synthesize the stuff. My report recommends against it."

This time Dalmady did rise. "Sir," he declared in anger, "I may be a yokel, my professional training may have been in a jerkwater college, but I'm not a congenital idiot who's mislaid his pills and I do take my pride seriously. I made the best decision I was able on Suleiman. You haven't tried to show me where I went wrong, you've simply had me dismissed from my post, and tonight you drone about issues that anybody would understand who's graduated from diapers. Let's not waste more of our time. Good evening."

Van Rijn avalanched upward to his own feet. "Ho, ho!" he bawled. "Spirit, too! I like, I like!"

Dumbfounded, Dalmady could only gape.

Van Rijn clapped him on the shoulder, nearly felling him. "Boy," the merchant said, "I didn't mean to rub your nose in nothings except sweet violets. I did have to know, did you stumble onto your answer, which is beautiful, or can you think original? Because you take my saying, maybe everybody understands like you what is not wearing diapers no more; but if that is true, why, ninety-nine point nine nine percent of every sophont race is wearing diapers, at least on their brains, and it leaks out of their mouths. I find you is in the oh point oh one percent, and I want you. Hoo-ha, how I want you!"

He thrust the gin-filled goblet back into Dalmady's hand. His tankard clanked against it. "Drink!"

Dalmady took a sip. Van Rijn began to prowl.

"You is from a frontier planet and so is naive," the merchant said, "but that can be outlived like pimples. See, when my underlings at HQ learned you had pulled our nuts from the fire on Suleiman, they sent you a standard message, not realizing an Altaian like you would not know that in such cases the proceeding is SOP," which he pronounced "sop." He waved a gorilla arm, splashing beer on the floor. "Like I say, we had to check if you was lucky only. If so, we would promote you to be manager someplace better and forget about you. But if you was, actual, extra smart and tough, we don't want you for a manager. You is too rare and precious for that. Would be like using a Hokusai print in a catbox."

Dalmady raised goblet to mouth, unsteadily. "What do you mean?" he croaked.

"Entrepreneur! You will keep title of factor, because we can't make jealousies, but what you do is what the old Americans would have called a horse of a different dollar.

"Look." Van Rijn reclaimed his cigar from the disposal rim, took a puff, and made forensic gestures with it and tankard alike while he continued his earthquake pacing. "Suleiman was supposed to be a nice routine post, but you told me how little we know on it and how sudden the devil himself came to lunch. Well, what about the real new, real hairy—and real fortune-making—places? Ha?

"You don't want a manager for them, not till they been whipped into shape. A good manager is a very high-powered man, and we need a lot of him. But in his bottom, he is a routineer; his aim is to make things go smooth. No, for the wild places you need an innovator in charge, a man what likes to take risks, a heterodoxy if she is female—somebody what can meet wholly new problems in unholy new ways—you see?

"Only such is rare, I tell you. They command high prices: high as they can earn for themselves. Natural, I want them earning for me too. So I don't put that kind of factor on salary and dangle a promotion ladder in front of him. No, the entrepreneur kind, first I get his John Bullcock on a ten-year oath of fealty. Next I turn him loose with a stake and my backup, to do what he wants, on straight commission of ninety percent.

"Too bad nobody typed you before you went in managerial school. Now you must have a while in an entrepreneurial school I got tucked away where nobody notices. Not dull for you; I hear they throw fine orgies; but mainly I think you will enjoy your classes, if you don't mind working till brain-sweat runs out your nose. Afterward you go get rich, if you survive, and have a big ball of fun even if you don't. Hokay?"

Dalmady thought for an instant of Yvonne; and then he thought, *What the deuce, if nothing better develops, in a few years I can set any hiring policies I feel like;* and: "Hokay!" he exclaimed, and tossed off his drink in a single gulp.

INTRODUCTION

❈ HIDING PLACE ❈

"The world's great age begins anew . . . "

As it has before, and will again. The comings and goings of man have their seasons.

They are no more mysterious than the annual cycle of the planet, and no less. Because today we are sailing out among the stars, we are more akin to Europeans overrunning America or Greeks colonizing the Mediterranean littoral than to our ancestors of only a few generations ago. We, too, are discoverers, pioneers, traders, missionaries, composers of epic and saga. Our people have grown bolder than their fathers, ambitious, individualistic; on the darker side, greed, callousness, disregard for the morrow, violence, often outright banditry have returned. Such is the nature of societies possessed of, and by, a frontier.

Yet no springtime is identical with the last. Technic civilization is not Classical or Western; and as it spreads ever more thinly across ever less imaginable reaches of space—as its outposts and its heartland learn, for good or ill, that which ever larger numbers of nonhuman peoples have to teach: it is changing in ways unpredictable. Already we live in a world that no Earthbound man could really have comprehended.

He might, for instance, have seen an analogy between the Polesotechnic League and the mercantile guilds of medieval Europe. But on closer examination he would find that here is something new, descended indeed from concepts of the Terrestrial past but with mutation and miscegenation in its bloodlines.

We cannot foretell what will come of it. We do not know where we are going. Nor do most of us care. For us it is enough that we are on our way.

—Le Matelot

HIDING PLACE

Captain Bahadur Torrance received the news as befitted a Lodgemaster in the Federated Brotherhood of Spacemen. He heard it out, interrupting only with a few knowledgeable questions. At the end, he said calmly, "Well done, Freeman Yamamura. Please keep this to yourself till further notice. I'll think about what's to be done. Carry on." But when the engineer officer had left the cabin—the news had not been the sort you tell on the intercom—he poured himself a triple whiskey, sat down, and stared emptily at the viewscreen.

He had traveled far, seen much, and been well rewarded. However, promotion being swift in his difficult line of work, he was still too young not to feel cold at hearing his death sentence.

The screen showed such a multitude of stars, hard and winter-brilliant, that only an astronaut could recognize individuals. Torrance sought past the Milky Way until he identified Polaris. Then Valhalla would lie so-and-so many degrees away, in *that* direction. Not that he could see a type-G sun at this distance, without optical instruments more powerful than any aboard the *Hebe G.B.* But he found a certain comfort in knowing his eyes were sighted toward the nearest League base (houses, ships, humans, nestled in a green valley on Freya) in this almost uncharted section of our galactic arm. Especially when he didn't expect to land there, ever again.

The ship hummed around him, pulsing in and out of four-space with a quasi-speed that left light far behind and yet was still too slow to save him.

Well . . . it became the captain to think first of the others. Torrance sighed and stood up. He spent a moment checking his appearance; morale was important, never more so than now. Rather than the usual gray coverall of shipboard, he preferred full uniform: blue tunic, white cape and culottes, gold braid. As a citizen of Ramanujan planet, he kept a turban on his dark aquiline head, pinned with the Ship-and-Sunburst of the Polesotechnic League.

He went down a passageway to the owner's suite. The steward was just leaving, a tray in his hand. Torrance signaled the door to remain open, clicked his heels and bowed. "I pray pardon for the interruption, sir," he said. "May I speak privately with you? Urgent."

Nicholas van Rijn hoisted the two-liter tankard which had been brought him. His several chins quivered under the stiff goatee; the noise of his gulping filled the room, from the desk littered with papers to the Huy Brasealian jewel-tapestry hung on the opposite bulkhead. Something by Mozart lilted out of a taper. Blond, big-eyed, and thoroughly three-dimensional, Jeri Kofoed curled on a couch, within easy reach of him where he sprawled in his lounger. Torrance, who was married but had been away from home for some time, forced his gaze back to the merchant.

"Ahhh!" Van Rijn banged the empty mug down on a table and wiped foam from his mustaches. "Pox and pestilence, but the first beer of the day is good! Something with it is so quite cool and—um—by damn, what word do I want?" He thumped his sloping forehead with one hairy fist. "I get more absent in the mind every week. Ah, Torrance, when you are too a poor old lonely fat man with all powers failing him, you will look back and remember me and wish you was more good to me. But then is too late." He sighed like a minor tornado and scratched the pelt on his chest. In the near tropic temperature at which he insisted on maintaining his quarters, he need wrap only a sarong about his huge body. "Well, what begobbled stupiding is it I must be dragged from my-all-too-much work to fix up for you, ha?"

His tone was genial. He had, in fact, been in a good mood ever since they escaped the Adderkops. (Who wouldn't be? For a mere space yacht, even an armed one with ultrapowered engines, to get away from three cruisers, was more than an accomplishment; it was very nearly a miracle. Van Rijn still kept four grateful candles burning before his Martian sandroot statuette of St. Dismas.) True, he sometimes threw crockery at the steward when a drink arrived later than he wished, and he fired everybody aboard ship at least once a day. But that was normal.

Jeri Kofoed arched her brows. "Your first beer, Nicky?" she murmured. "Now really! Two hours ago—"

"Ja, but that was before midnight time. If not Greenwich midnight, then surely on some planet somewhere, *nie?* So is a new day." Van Rijn took his churchwarden off the table and began stuffing it. "Well, sit down, Captain Torrance, make yourself to be comfortable and lend me your lighter. You look like a dynamited custard, boy. All you youngsters got no stamina. When I was a working spaceman, by Judas, we made solve all our own problems. These days, death and damnation, you come ask me how to wipe your noses! Nobody has any guts but me." He slapped his barrel belly. "So what is be-jingle-bang gone wrong now?"

Torrance wet his lips. "I'd rather speak to you alone, sir."

He saw the color leave Jeri's face. She was no coward. Frontier planets, even the pleasant ones like Freya, didn't breed that sort. She had come along on what she knew would be a hazardous trip because a chance like this—to get an in with the merchant prince of the Solar Spice & Liquors Company, which was one of the major forces within the whole Polesotechnic League—was too good for an opportunistic girl to refuse. She had kept her nerve during the fight and the subsequent escape, though death came very close. But they were still far from her planet, among unknown stars, with the enemy hunting them.

"So go in the bedroom," Van Rijn ordered her.

"Please," she whispered. "I'd be happier hearing the truth."

The small black eyes, set close to Van Rijn's hook nose, flared. "Foulness and fulminate!" he bellowed. "What is this poppies with cocking? When I say frog, by billy damn, you jump!"

She sprang to her feet, mutinous. Without rising, he slapped her on the appropriate spot. It sounded like a pistol going off. She gasped, choked back an indignant screech, and stamped into the inner suite. Van Rijn rang for the steward.

"More beer this calls for," he said to Torrence. "Well, don't stand there making bug's eyes! I got no time for fumblydiddles, even if you overpaid loafer do. I got to make revises of all price schedules on pepper and nutmeg for Freya before we get there. Satan and stenches! At least ten percent more that idiot of a factor could charge them, and not reduce volume of sales. I swear it! All good saints, hear me and help a poor old man saddled with oatmeal-brained squatpots for workers!"

Torrance curbed his temper with an effort. "Very well, sir. I just had a report from Yamamura. You know we took a near miss during the fight, which hulled us at the engine room. The converter didn't seem damaged, but after patching the hole, the gang's been checking to make sure. And it turns out that about half the circuitry for the infrashield generator was fused. We can't replace more than a fraction of it. If we continue to run at full quasi-speed, we'll burn out the whole converter in another fifty hours."

"Ah, s-s-so." Van Rijn grew serious. The snap of the lighter, as he touched it to his pipe, came startlingly loud. "No chance of stopping altogether to make fixings? Once out of hyperdrive, we would be much too small a thing for the bestinkered Adderkops to find. Hey?"

"No, sir. I said we haven't enough replacement parts. This is a yacht, not a warship."

"Hokay, we must continue in hyperdrive. How slow must we go, to make sure we come within calling distance of Freya before our engine burns out?"

"One-tenth of top speed. It'd take us six months."

"No, my captain friend, not so long. We never reach Valhalla star at all. The Adderkops find us first."

"I suppose so. We haven't got six months' stores aboard anyway." Torrance stared at the deck. "What occurs to me is, well, we could reach one of the nearby stars. There just barely might be a planet with an industrial civilization, whose people could eventually be taught to make the circuits we need. A habitable planet, at least—maybe . . ."

"*Nie!*" Van Rijn shook his head till the greasy black ringlets swirled about his shoulders. "All us men and one woman, for life on some garbagey rock where they have not even wine grapes? I'll take an Adderkop shell and go out like a gentleman, by damn!" The steward appeared. "Where you been snoozing? Beer, with God's curses on you! I need to make thinks! How you expect I can think with a mouth like a desert in midsummer?"

Torrance chose his words carefully. Van Rijn would have to be reminded that the captain, in space, was the final boss. And yet the old devil must not be antagonized, for he had a record of squirming between the horns of dilemmas. "I'm open to suggestions, sir, but I can't take the responsibility of courting enemy attack."

Van Rijn rose and lumbered about the cabin, fuming obscenities and volcanic blue clouds. As he passed the shelf where St. Dismas stood, he pinched the candles out in a marked manner. That seemed to trigger something in him. He turned about and said, "Ha! Industrial civilizations, *ja*, maybe so. Not only the pest-begotten Adderkops ply this region of space. Gives some chance perhaps we can come in detection range of an un-beat-up ship, *nie?* You go get Yamamura to jack up our detector sensitivities till we can feel a gnat twiddle its wings back in my Djakarta office on Earth, so lazy the cleaners are. Then we go off this direct course and run a standard naval search pattern at reduced speed."

"And if we find a ship? Could belong to the enemy, you know."

"That chance we take."

"In all events, sir, we'll lose time. The pursuit will gain on us while we follow a search-helix. Especially if we spend days persuading some nonhuman crew who've never heard of the human race, that we have to be taken to Valhalla immediately if not sooner."

"We burn that bridge when we come to it. You have might be a more hopeful scheme?"

"Well . . . " Torrance pondered a while, blackly.

The steward came in with a fresh tankard. Van Rijn snatched it.

"I think you're right, sir," said Torrance. "I'll go and—"

"Virginal!" bellowed Van Rijn.

Torrance jumped. "What?"

"Virginal! That's the word I was looking for. The first beer of the day, you idiot!"

The cabin door chimed. Torrance groaned. He'd been hoping for some sleep, at least, after more hours on deck than he cared to number. But when the ship prowled through darkness, seeking another ship which might or might not be out there, and the hunters drew closer . . . "Come in."

Jeri Kofoed entered. Torrance gaped, sprang to his feet, and bowed. "Freelady! What—what—what a surprise! Is there anything I can do?"

"Please." She laid a hand on his. Her gown was of shimmerite and shameless in cut, because Van Rijn hadn't provided any other sort, but the look she gave Torrance had nothing to do with that. "I had to come, Lodgemaster. If you've any pity at all, you'll listen to me."

He waved her to a chair, offered cigarettes, and struck one for himself. The smoke, drawn deep into his lungs, calmed him a little. He sat down on the opposite side of the table. "If I can be of help to you, Freelady Kofoed, you know I'm happy to oblige. Uh . . . Freeman Van Rijn . . ."

"He's asleep. Not that he has any claims on me. I haven't signed a contract or any such thing." Her irritation gave way to a wry smile. "Oh, admitted, we're all his inferiors, in fact as well as in status. I'm not contravening his wishes, not really. It's just that he won't answer my questions, and if I don't find out what's going on I'll have to start screaming."

Torrance weighed a number of factors. A private explanation, in more detail than the crew had required, might indeed be best for her. "As you wish, Freelady," he said, and related what had happened to the converter. "We can't fix it ourselves," he concluded. "If we continued traveling at high quasi-speed, we'd burn it out before we arrived; and then, without power, we'd soon die. If we proceed slowly enough to preserve it, we'd need half a year to reach Valhalla, which is more time than we have supplies for. Though the Adderkops would doubtless track us down within a week or two."

She shivered. "Why? I don't understand." She stared at her glowing cigarette end for a moment, until a degree of composure returned, and with it a touch of humor. "I may pass for a fast, sophisticated girl on Freya, Captain. But you know even better than I, Freya is a jerkwater planet on the very fringe of human civilization. We've hardly any spatial traffic, except the League merchant ships, and they never stay long in port. I really know nothing about military or political technology. No one told me this was anything more important than a scouting mission, because I never thought to inquire. Why should the Adderkops be so anxious to catch us?"

Torrance considered the total picture before framing a reply. As a spaceman of the League, he must make an effort before he could appreciate how little the enemy actually meant to colonists who seldom left their home world. The name "Adderkop" was Freyan, a term of scorn for outlaws who'd been booted off the planet a century ago. Since then, however, the Freyans had had no direct contact with them. Somewhere in the unexplored deeps beyond Valhalla, the fugitives had settled on some unknown planet. Over the generations, their numbers grew, and so did the numbers of their warships. But Freya was still too strong for them to raid, and had no extraplanetary enterprises of her own to be harried. Why should Freya care?

Torrance decided to explain systematically, even if he must repeat the obvious. "Well," he said, "the Adderkops aren't stupid. They keep somewhat in touch with events, and know the Polesotechnic League wants to expand its operations into this region. They don't like that. It'd mean the end of their attacks on planets which can't fight back, their squeezing of tribute and their overpriced trade. Not that the League is composed of saints; we don't tolerate that sort of thing, but merely because free-booting cuts into the profits of our member companies. So the Adderkops undertook, not to fight a full-dress war against us, but to harass our outposts till we gave it up as a bad job. They have the advantage of knowing their own sector of space, which we hardly do at all. And we were, indeed, at the point of writing this whole region off and trying someplace else. Freeman Van Rijn wanted to make one last attempt. The opposition to doing so was so great that he had to come here and lead the expedition himself.

"I suppose you know what he did. Used an unholy skill at bribery and bluff, at extracting what little information the prisoners we'd taken possessed, at fitting odd facts together. He got a clue to a hitherto untried segment. We flitted there, picked up a neutrino trail, and followed it to a human-colonized planet. As you know, it's almost certainly their own home world.

"If we bring back that information, there'll be no more trouble with the Adderkops. Not after the League sends in a few Star class battleships and threatens to bombard their planet. They realize as much. We were spotted; several warcraft jumped us; we were lucky enough to get away. Their ships are obsolete, and so far we've shown them a clean pair of heels. But I hardly think they've quit hunting for us. They'll send their entire fleet cruising in search. Hyperdrive vibrations transmit instantaneously, and can be detected up to about one light-year distance. So if any Adderkop picks up our 'wake' and homes in on it—with us crippled—that's the end."

She drew hard on her cigarette, but remained otherwise calm. "What are your plans?"

"A countermove. Instead of trying to make Freya—uh—I mean, we're proceeding in a search-helix at medium speed, straining our own detectors. If we discover another ship, we'll use the last gasp of our engine to close in. If it's an Adderkop vessel, well, perhaps we can seize it or something; we do have a couple of light guns in our turrets. It may be a nonhuman craft, though. Our intelligence reports, interrogation of prisoners, evaluation of explorers' observations, and so on, all indicate that three or four different species in this region possess the hyperdrive. The Adderkops themselves aren't certain about all of them. Space is so damned *huge*."

"If it does turn out to be nonhuman?"

"Then we'll do what seems indicated."

"I see." Her bright head nodded. She sat for a while, unspeaking, before she dazzled him with a smile. "Thanks, Captain. You don't know how much you've helped me."

Torrance suppressed a foolish grin. "A pleasure, Freelady."

"I'm coming to Earth with you. Did you know that? Freeman Van Rijn has promised me a very good job."

He always does, thought Torrance.

Jeri leaned closer. "I hope we'll have a chance on the Earthward trip to get better acquainted, Captain. Or even right now."

The alarm bell chose that moment to ring.

The *Hebe G.B.* was a yacht, not a buccaneer frigate. When Nicholas van Rijn was aboard, though, the distinction sometimes got a little blurred. So she had more legs than most ships, detectors of uncommon sensitivity, and a crew experienced in the tactics of overhauling.

She was able to get a bearing on the hyperemission of the other craft long before her own vibrations were observed. Pacing the unseen one, she established the set course it was following, then poured on all available juice to intercept. If the stranger had maintained quasi-velocity, there would have been contact in three or four hours. Instead, its wake indicated a sheering off, an attempt to flee. The *Hebe G.B.* changed course, too, and continued gaining on her slower quarry.

"They're afraid of us," decided Torrance. "And they're not running back toward the Adderkop sun. Which two facts indicate they're not Adderkops themselves, but do have reason to be scared of strangers." He nodded, rather grimly, for during the preliminary investigations he had inspected a few backward planets which the bandit nation had visited.

Seeing that the pursuer kept shortening her distance, the pursued turned off their hyperdrive. Reverting to intrinsic sublight velocity, converter throttled down to minimal output, their ship became an infinitesimal speck in an effectively infinite space. The maneuver often works; after casting about futilely for a while, the enemy gives up and goes home. The *Hebe G.B.*, though, was prepared. The known superlight vector, together with the instant of cutoff, gave her computers a rough idea of where the prey was. She continued to that volume of space and then hopped about in a well-designed search pattern, reverting to normal state at intervals to sample the neutrino haze which any nuclear engine emits. Those nuclear engines known as stars provided most; but by statistical analysis, the computers presently isolated one feeble nearby source. The yacht went thither . . . and wan against the glittering sky, the other ship appeared in her screens.

It was several times her size, a cylinder with bluntly rounded nose and massive drive cones, numerous housings for auxiliary boats, a single gun turret. The principles of physics dictate that the general conformation of all ships intended for a given purpose shall be roughly the same. But any spaceman could see that this one had never been built by members of Technic civilization.

Fire blazed. Even with the automatic stopping-down of his viewscreen, Torrance was momentarily blinded. Instruments told him that the stranger had fired a fusion shell which his own robogunners had intercepted with a missile. The attack had been miserably slow and feeble. This was not a warcraft in any sense; it was no more a match for the *Hebe G.B.* than the yacht was for one of the Adderkops chasing her.

"Hokay, now we got that foolishness out of the way and we can talk business," said Van Rijn. "Get them on the telecom and develop a common language. Fast! Then explain we mean no harm but want just a lift to Valhalla." He hesitated before adding, with a distinct wince, "We can pay well."

"Might prove difficult, sir," said Torrance. "Our ship is identifiably human-built, but chances are that the only humans they've ever met are Adderkops."

"Well, so if it makes needful, we can board them and force them to transport us, *nie?* Hurry up, for Satan's sake! If we wait too long here, like bebobbled snoozers, we'll get caught."

Torrance was about to point out they were safe enough. The Adderkops were far behind the swifter Terrestrial ship. They could have no idea that her hyperdrive was now cut off; when they began to suspect it, they could have no measurable probability of finding her. Then he remembered that the case was not so simple. If the parleying with these strangers took unduly long—more than a week, at best—Adderkop squadrons would have penetrated this general region and gone beyond. They would probably remain on picket for months: which the humans could not do for lack of food. When a hyperdrive did start up, they'd detect it and run down this awkward merchantman with ease. The only hope was to hitch a ride to Valhalla soon, using the head start already gained to offset the disadvantage of reduced speed.

"We're trying all bands, sir," he said. "No response so far." He frowned worriedly. "I don't understand. They must know we've got them cold, and they must have picked up our calls and realize we want to talk. Why don't they respond? Wouldn't cost them anything."

"Maybe they abandoned ship," suggested the communications officer. "They might have hyperdriven lifeboats."

"No." Torrance shook his head. "We'd have spotted that. . . . Keep trying, Freeman Betancourt. If we haven't gotten an answer in an hour, we'll lay alongside and board."

The receiver screens remained blank. But at the end of the grace period, when Torrance was issuing space armor, Yamamura reported something new. Neutrino output had increased from a source near the stern of the alien. Some process involving moderate amounts of energy was being carried out.

Torrance clamped down his helmet. "We'll have a look at that."

He posted a skeleton crew—Van Rijn himself, loudly protesting, took over the bridge—and led his boarding party to the main air lock. Smooth as a gliding shark (the old swine was a blue-ribbon spaceman after all, the captain realized in some astonishment), the *Hebe G.B.* clamped on a tractor beam and hauled herself toward the bigger vessel.

It disappeared. Recoil sent the yacht staggering.

"Beelzebub and botulism!" snarled Van Rijn. "He went back into hyper, ha? We see about that!" The ulcerated converter shrieked as he called upon it, but the engines were given power. On a lung and a half, the Terrestrial ship again overtook the foreigner. Van Rijn phased in so casually that Torrance almost forgot this was a job considered difficult by master pilots. He evaded a frantic pressor beam and tied his yacht to the larger hull with unshearable bands of force. He cut off his hyperdrive again, for the converter couldn't take much more. Being within the force-field of the alien, the *Hebe G.B.* was carried along, though the "drag" of extra mass reduced quasi-speed considerably. If he had hoped the grappled vessel would quit and revert to normal state, he was disappointed. The linked hulls continued plunging faster than light, toward an unnamed constellation.

Torrance bit back an oath, summoned his men, and went outside.

He had never forced entry on a hostile craft before, but assumed it wasn't much different from burning his way into a derelict. Having chosen his spot, he set up a balloon tent to conserve air; no use killing the alien crew. The torches of his men spewed flame; blue actinic sparks fountained backward and danced through zero gravity. Meanwhile the rest of the squad stood by with blasters and grenades.

Beyond, the curves of the two hulls dropped off to infinity. Without compensating electronic viewscreens, the sky was weirdly distorted by aberration and Doppler effect, as if the men were already dead and beating through the other existence toward Judgment. Torrance held his mind firmly to practical worries. Once inboard, the nonhumans made prisoner, how was he to communicate? Especially if he first had to gun down several of them . . .

The outer shell was peeled back. He studied the inner structure of the plate with fascination. He'd never seen anything like it before. Surely this race had developed space travel quite independently of mankind. Though their engineering must obey the same natural laws, it was radically different in detail. What was that tough but corky substance lining the inner shell? And was the circuitry embedded in it, for he didn't see any elsewhere?

The last defense gave way. Torrance swallowed hard and shot a flashbeam into the interior. Darkness and vacuum met him. When he entered the hull, he floated, weightless; artificial gravity had been turned off. The crew was hiding someplace and . . .

And . . .

Torrance returned to the yacht in an hour. When he came on the bridge, he found Van Rijn seated by Jeri. The girl started to speak, took a closer look at the captain's face, and clamped her teeth together.

"Well?" snapped the merchant peevishly.

Torrance cleared his throat. His voice sounded unfamiliar and faraway to him. "I think you'd better come have a look, sir."

"You found the crew, wherever the sputtering hell they holed up? What are they like? What kind of ship is this we've gotten us, ha?"

Torrance chose to answer the last question first. "It seems to be an interstellar animal collector's transport vessel. The main hold is full of cages—environmentally controlled compartments, I should say—with the damnedest assortment of creatures I've ever seen outside Luna City Zoo."

"So what the pox is that to me? Where is the collector himself, and his fig-plucking friends?"

"Well, sir." Torrance gulped. "We're pretty sure by now, they're hiding from us. Among all the other animals."

A tube was run between the yacht's main lock and the entry cut into the other ship. Through this, air was pumped and electric lines were strung, to illuminate the prize. By some fancy juggling with the gravitic generator of the *Hebe G.B.*, Yamamura supplied about one-fourth Earth-weight to the foreigner, though he couldn't get the direction uniform and its decks felt canted in wildly varying degrees.

Even under such conditions, Van Rijn walked ponderously. He stood with a salami in one hand and a raw onion in the other, glaring around the captured bridge. It could only be that, though it was in the bows rather than the waist. The viewscreens were still in operation: smaller than human eyes found comfortable, but revealing the same pattern of stars, surely by the same kind of optical compensators. A control console made a semicircle at the forward bulkhead, too big for a solitary human to operate. Yet presumably the designer had only had one pilot in mind, for a single seat had been placed in the middle of the arc.

Had been. A short metal post rose from the deck. Similar structures stood at other points, and boltholes showed where chairs were once fastened to them. But the seats had been removed.

"Pilot sat there at the center, I'd guess, when they weren't simply running on automatic," Torrance hazarded. "Navigator and communications officer . . . here and here? I'm not sure. Anyhow, they probably didn't use a copilot, but that chair bollard at the after end of the room suggests that an extra officer sat in reserve, ready to take over."

Van Rijn munched his onion and tugged his goatee. "Pestish big, this panel," he said. "Must be a race of bloody-be-damned octopussies, ha? Look how complicated."

He waved the salami around the half circle. The console, which seemed to be of some fluorocarbon polymer, held very few switches or buttons, but scores of flat luminous plates, each about twenty centimeters square. Some of them were depressed. Evidently these were the controls. Cautious experiment had shown that a stiff push was needed to budge them. The experiment had ended then and there, for the ship's cargo lock had opened and a good deal of air was lost before Torrance slapped the plate he had been testing hard enough to make the hull reseal itself. One should not tinker with the atomic-powered unknown; most especially not in galactic space.

"They must be strong like horses, to steer by this system without getting exhausted," went on Van Rijn. "The size of everything tells likewise, *nie?*"

"Well, not exactly, sir," said Torrance. "The viewscreens seem made for dwarfs. The meters even more so." He pointed to a bank of instruments, no larger than buttons, on each of which a single number glowed. (Or letter, or ideogram, or what? They looked vaguely Old Chinese.) Occasionally a symbol changed value. "A human couldn't use these long without severe eyestrain. Of course, having eyes better adapted to close work than ours doesn't prove they are not giants. Certainly that switch couldn't be reached from here without long arms, and it seems meant for big hands." By standing on tiptoe, he touched it himself: an outsize double-pole affair set overhead, just above the pilot's hypothetical seat.

The switch fell open.

A roar came from aft. Torrance lurched backward under a sudden force. He caught at a shelf on the after bulkhead to steady himself. Its thin metal buckled as he clutched. "Devilfish and dunderheads!" cried Van Rijn. Bracing his columnar legs, he reached up and shoved the switch back into position. The noise ended. Normality returned. Torrance hastened to the bridge doorway, a tall arch, and shouted down the corridor beyond: "It's okay! Don't worry! We've got it under control!"

"What the blue blinking blazes happened?" demanded Van Rijn, in somewhat more high-powered words.

Torrance mastered a slight case of the shakes. "Emergency switch, I'd say." His tone wavered. "Turns on the gravitic field full speed ahead, not wasting any force on acceleration compensators. Of course, we being in hyperdrive, it wasn't very effective. Only gave us a—uh—less than one G push, intrinsic. In normal state we'd have accelerated several Gs, at least. It's for quick getaways and . . . and . . ."

"And you, with brains like fermented gravy and bananas for fingers, went ahead and yanked it open!"

Torrance felt himself redden. "How was I to know, sir? I must've applied less than half a kilo of force. Emergency switches aren't hair-triggered, after all! Considering how much it takes to move one of those control plates, who'd have thought the switch would respond to so little?"

Van Rijn took a closer look. "I see now there is a hook to secure it by," he said. "Must be they use that when the ship's on a high-gravity planet." He peered down a hole near the center of the panel, about one centimeter in diameter and fifteen deep. At the bottom a small key projected. "This must be another special control, ha? Safer than that switch. You would need thin-nosed pliers to make a turning of it." He scratched his pomaded curls. "But then why is not the pliers hanging handy? I don't see even a hook or bracket or drawer for them."

"I don't care," said Torrance. "When the whole interior's been stripped—There's nothing but a slagheap in the engine room, I tell you, fused metal, carbonized plastic . . . bedding, furniture, anything they thought might give us a clue to their identity, all melted down in a jury-rigged cauldron. They used their own converter to supply heat. That was the cause of the neutrino flux Yamamura observed. They must have worked like demons."

"But they did not destroy all needful tools and machines, surely? Simpler then they should blow up their whole ship, and us with it. I was sweating like a hog, me, for fear they would do that. Not so good a way for a poor sinful old man to end his days, blown into radioactive stinks three hundred light-years from the vineyards of Earth."

"N-n-no. As far as we can tell from a cursory examination, they didn't sabotage anything absolutely vital. We can't be sure, of course. Yamamura's gang would need weeks just to get a general idea of how this ship is put together, let alone the practical details of operating it. But I agree, the crew isn't bent on suicide. They've got us more neatly trapped than they know, even. Bound helplessly through space—toward their home star, maybe—in any event, almost at right angles to the course we want."

Torrance led the way out. "Suppose we go have a more thorough look at the zoo, sir," he went on. "Yamamura talked about setting up some equipment . . . to help us tell the crew from the animals!"

The main hold comprised almost half the volume of the great ship. A corridor below, a catwalk above, ran through a double row of two-decker cubicles. These numbered ninety-six, and were identical. Each was about five meters on a side, with adjustable fluorescent plates in the ceiling and a springy, presumably inert plastic on the floor. Shelves and parallel bars ran along the side walls, for the benefit of animals that liked jumping or climbing. The rear wall was connected to well-shielded machines; Yamamura didn't dare tamper with these, but said they obviously regulated atmosphere, temperature, gravity, sanitation, and other environmental factors within each "cage." The front wall, facing on corridor and catwalk, was transparent. It held a stout air lock, almost as high as the cubicle itself, motorized but controlled by simple wheels inside and out. Only a few compartments were empty.

The humans had not strung fluoros in this hold, for it wasn't necessary. Torrance and Van Rijn walked through shadows, among monsters; the simulated light of a dozen different suns streamed around them: red, orange, yellow, greenish, and harsh electric blue.

A thing like a giant shark, save that tendrils fluttered about its head, swam in a water-filled cubicle among fronded seaweeds. Next to it was a cageful of tiny flying reptiles, their scales aglitter in prismatic hues, weaving and dodging through the air. On the opposite side, four mammals crouched among yellow mists: beautiful creatures, the size of a bear, vividly tiger-striped, walking mostly on all fours but occasionally standing up; then you noticed the retractable claws between stubby fingers, and the carnivore jaws on the massive heads. Farther on the humans passed half a dozen sleek red beasts like six-legged otters, frolicking in a tank of water provided for them. The environmental machines must have decided this was their feeding time, for a hopper spewed chunks of proteinaceous material into a trough and the animals lolloped over to rip it with their fangs.

"Automatic feeding," Torrance observed. "I think probably the food is synthesized on the spot, according to the specifications of each individual species as determined by biochemical methods. For the crew, also. At least, we haven't found anything like a galley."

Van Rijn shuddered. "Nothing but synthetics? Not even a little glass Genever before dinner?" He brightened. "Ha, maybe here we find a good new market. And until they learn the situation, we can charge them triple prices."

"First," clipped Torrance, "we've got to find them."

Yamamura stood near the middle of the hold, focusing a set of instruments on a certain cage. Jeri stood by, handing him what he asked for, plugging and unplugging at a small power-pack. Van Rijn hove into view. "What goes on, anyhows?" he asked.

The chief engineer turned a patient brown face to him. "I've got the rest of the crew examining the ship in detail, sir," he said. "I'll join them as soon as I've gotten Freelady Kofoed trained at this particular job. She can handle the routine of it while the rest of us use our special skills to . . . " His words trailed off. He grinned ruefully. "To poke and prod gizmos we can't possibly understand in less than a month of work, with our limited research tools."

"A month we have not got," said Van Rijn. "You are here checking conditions inside each individual cage?"

"Yes, sir. They're metered, of course, but we can't read the meters, so we have to do the job ourselves. I've haywired this stuff together, to give an approximate value of gravity, atmospheric pressure and composition, temperature, illumination spectrum, and so forth. It's slow work, mostly because of all the arithmetic needed to turn the dial readings into such data. Luckily, we don't have to test every cubicle, or even most of them."

"No," said Van Rijn. "Even to a union organizer, obvious this ship was never made by fishes or birds. In fact, some kind of hands is always necessary."

"Or tentacles." Yamamura nodded at the compartment before him. The light within was dim red. Several black creatures could be seen walking restlessly about. They had stumpy-legged quadrupedal bodies, from which torsos rose, centaur-fashion, toward heads armored in some bony material. Below the faceless heads were six thick, ropy arms, set in triplets. Two of these ended in three boneless but probably strong fingers.

"I suspect these are our coy friends," said Yamamura. "If so, we'll have a deuce of a time. They breathe hydrogen under high pressure and triple gravity, at a temperature of seventy below."

"Are they the only ones who like that kind of weather?" asked Torrance.

Yamamura gave him a sharp look. "I see what you're getting at, skipper. No, they aren't. In the course of putting this apparatus together and testing it, I've already found three other cubicles where conditions are similar. And in those, the animals are obviously just animals: snakes and so on, which couldn't possibly have built this ship."

"But then these octopus-horses can't be the crew, can they?" asked Jeri timidly. "I mean, if the crew were collecting animals from other planets, they wouldn't take home animals along, would they?"

"They might," said Van Rijn. "We have a cat and a couple parrots aboard the *Hebe G.B., nie?* Or, there are many planets with very similar conditions of the hydrogen sort, just like Earth and Freya are much-alike oxygen planets. So that proves nothings." He turned toward Yamamura, rather like a rotating globe himself. "But see here, even if the crew did pump out all the air before we boarded, why not check their reserve tanks? If we find air stored away just like these diddlers here are breathing . . ."

"I thought of that," said Yamamura. "In fact, it was almost the first thing I told the men to look for. They've located nothing. I don't think they'll have any success, either. Because what they did find was an adjustable catalytic manifold. At least, it looks as if it should be, though we'd need days to find out for certain. Anyhow, my guess is that it renews exhausted air and acts as a chemosynthesizer to replace losses from a charge of simple inorganic compounds. The crew probably bled all the ship's air into space before we boarded. When we go away, if we do, they'll open the door of their particular cage a crack, so its air can trickle out. The environmental adjuster will automatically force the chemosynthesizer to replace this. Eventually the ship'll be full of enough of their kind of air for them to venture forth and adjust things more precisely." He shrugged. "That's assuming they even need to. Perhaps Earth-type conditions suit them perfectly well."

"Uh, yes," said Torrance. "Suppose we look around some more, and line up the possibly intelligent species."

Van Rijn trundled along with him. "What sort intelligence they got, these bespattered aliens?" he grumbled.
"Why try this stupid masquerade in the first places?"

"It's not too stupid to have worked so far," said Torrance dryly. "We're being carried along on a ship we
don't know how to stop. They must hope we'll either
give up and depart, or else that we'll remain baffled until
the ship enters their home region. At which time, quite
probably a naval vessel—or whatever they've got—will
detect us, close in, and board us to check up on what's
happened."

He paused before a compartment. "I wonder . . ."

The quadruped within was the size of an elephant,
though with a more slender build indicating a lower gravity than Earth's. Its skin was green and faintly scaled, a
ruff of hair along the back. The eyes with which it looked
out were alert and enigmatic. It had an elephant-like
trunk, terminating in a ring of pseudodactyls which must
be as strong and sensitive as human fingers.

"How much could a one-armed race accomplish?"
mused Torrance. "About as much as we, I imagine, if
not quite as easily. And sheer strength would compensate. That trunk could bend an iron bar."

Van Rijn grunted and went past a cubicle of feathered
ungulates. He stopped before the next one. "Now here
are some beasts might do," he said. "We had one like
them on Earth once. What they called it? Quintilla? No,
gorilla. Or chimpanzee, better, of gorilla size."

Torrance felt his heart thud. Two adjoining sections
each held four animals of a kind which looked extremely
hopeful. They were bipedal, short-legged and long-
armed. Standing two meters tall, with a three-meter arm
span, one of them could certainly operate that control

console alone. The wrists, thick as a man's thighs, ended in proportionate hands, four-digited including a true thumb. The three-toed feet were specialized for walking, like man's feet. Their bodies were covered with brown fleece. Their heads were comparatively small, rising almost to a point, with massive snouts and beady eyes under cavernous brow ridges. As they wandered aimlessly about, Torrance saw that they were divided among males and females. On the sides of each neck he noticed two lumens closed by sphincters. The light upon them was the familiar yellowish-white of a Sol-type star.

He forced himself to say, "I'm not sure. Those huge jaws must demand corresponding maxillary muscles, attaching to a ridge on top of the skull. Which'd restrict the cranial capacity."

"Suppose they got brains in their bellies," said Van Rijn.

"Well, some people do," murmured Torrance. As the merchant choked, he added in haste, "No, actually, sir, that's hardly believable. Neural paths would get too long, and so forth. Every animal I know of, if it has a central nervous system at all, keeps the brain close to the principal sense organs: which are usually located in the head. To be sure, a relatively small brain, within limits, doesn't mean these creatures are not intelligent. Their neurones might well be more efficient than ours."

"Humph and hassenpfeffer!" said Van Rijn. "Might, might, might!" As they continued among strange shapes: "We can't go too much by atmosphere or light, either. If hiding, the crew could vary conditions quite a bit from their norm without hurting themselves. Gravity, too, by twenty or thirty percent."

"I hope they breathe oxygen, though—Hoy!" Torrance stopped. After a moment, he realized what was so eerie about the several forms under the orange glow. They were chitinous-armored, not much bigger than a squarish military helmet and about the same shape. Four stumpy legs projected from beneath to carry them awkwardly about on taloned feet; also a pair of short tentacles ending in a bush of cilia. There was nothing special about them, as extra-Terrestrial animals go, except the two eyes which gazed from beneath each helmet: as large and somehow human as—well—the eyes of an octopus.

"Turtles," snorted Van Rijn. "Armadillos at most."

"There can't be any harm in letting Jer—Miss Kofoed check their environment too," said Torrance.

"It can waste time."

"I wonder what they eat. I don't see any mouths."

"Those tentacles look like capillary suckers, I bet they are parasites, or overgrown leeches, or something else like one of my competitors. Come along."

"What do we do after we've established which species could possibly be the crew?" asked Torrance. "Try to communicate with each in turn?"

"Not much use, that. They hide because they don't want to communicate. Unless we can prove to them we are not Adderkops. . . . But hard to see how."

"Wait! Why'd they conceal themselves at all, if they've had contact with the Adderkops? It wouldn't work."

"I think I tell you that, by damn," said Van Rijn. "To give them a name, let us call this unknown race the Eksers. So. The Eksers been traveling space for some time, but space is so big they never bumped into humans. Then the Adderkop nation arises, in this sector where humans never was before. The Eksers hear about this awful new species which has gotten into space also. They land on primitive planets where Adderkops have made 'raids, talk to natives, maybe plant automatic cameras where they think raids will soon come, maybe spy on Adderkop camps from afar or capture a lone Adderkop ship. So they know what humans look like, but not much else. They do not want humans to know about them, so they shun contact; they are not looking for trouble. Not before they are all prepared to fight a war, at least. Hell's sputtering griddles! Torrance, we have *got* to establish our bona fides with this crew, so they take us to Freya and afterward go tell their leaders all humans are not so bad as the slime-begotten Adderkops. Otherwise, maybe we wake up one day with some planets attacked by Eksers, and before the fighting ends, we have spent billions of credits!" He shook his fists in the air and bellowed like a wounded bull. "It is our duty to prevent this!"

"Our first duty is to get home alive, I'd say," Torrance answered curtly. "I have a wife and kids."

"Then stop throwing sheepish eyes at Jeri Kofoed. I saw her first."

The search turned up one more possibility. Four organisms the length of a man and the build of thick-legged caterpillars dwelt under greenish light. Their bodies were dark blue, spotted with silver. A torso akin to that of the tentacled centauroids, but stockier, carried two true arms. The hands lacked thumbs, but six fingers arranged around a three-quarter circle could accomplish much the same things. Not that adequate hands prove effective intelligence; on Earth, not only simians but a number of reptiles and amphibia boast as much, even if man has the best, and man's apish ancestors were as well-equipped in this respect as we are today. However, the round flat-faced heads of these beings, the large bright eyes beneath feathery antennae of obscure function, the small jaws and delicate lips, all looked promising.

Promising of what? thought Torrance.

Three Earth-days later, he hurried down a central corridor toward the Ekser engine room.

The passage was a great hemicylinder lined with the same rubbery gray plastic as the cages, so that footfalls were silent and spoken words weirdly unresonant. But a deeper vibration went through it, the almost subliminal drone of the hyper-engine, driving the ship into darkness toward an unknown star, and announcing their presence to any hunter straying within a light-year of them. The fluoros strung by the humans were far apart, so that one passed through bands of humming shadow. Doorless rooms opened off the hallway. Some were still full of supplies, and however peculiar the shape of tools and containers might be, however unguessable their purpose, this was a reassurance that one still lived, was not yet a ghost aboard the Flying Dutchman. Other cabins, however, had been inhabited. And their bareness made Torrance's skin crawl.

Nowhere did a personal trace remain. Books, both folio and micro, survived, but in the finely printed symbology of a foreign planet. Empty places on the shelves suggested that all illustrated volumes had been sacrificed. Certainly one could see where pictures stuck on the walls had been ripped down. In the big private cabins, in the still larger one which might have been a saloon, as well as in the engine room and workshop and bridge, only the bollards to which furniture had been bolted were left. Long low niches and small cubbyholes were built into the cabin bulkheads, but when all bedding had been thrown into a white-hot cauldron, how could one guess which were the bunks . . . if either kind were? Clothing, ornaments, cooking and eating utensils, everything was destroyed. One room must have been a lavatory, but all the facilities had been ripped out. Another might have been used for scientific studies, presumably of captured animals, but was so gutted that no human was certain.

By God, you've got to admire them, Torrance thought. Captured by beings whom they had every reason to think of as conscienceless monsters, the aliens had not taken the easy way out, the atomic explosion that would annihilate both crews. They might have, except for the chance of this being a zoo ship. But given a hope of survival, they snatched it, with an imaginative daring few humans could have matched. Now they sat in plain view, waiting for the monsters to depart—without wrecking their ship in mere spitefulness—or for a naval vessel of their own to rescue them. They had no means of knowing their captors were not Adderkops, or that this sector would soon be filled with Adderkop squadrons; the bandits rarely ventured even this close to Valhalla. Within the limits of available information, the aliens were acting with complete logic. But the nerve it took!

I wish we could identify them and make friends, thought Torrance. The Eksers would be damned good friends for Earth to have. Or Ramanujan, or Freya, or the entire Polesotechnic League.—With a lopsided grin: I'll bet they'd be nowhere near as easy to swindle as Old Nick thinks. They might well swindle him. That I'd love to see!

My reason is more personal, though, he thought with a return of bleakness. If we don't clear up this misunderstanding soon, neither they nor we will be around. I mean soon. If we have another three or four days of grace, we're lucky.

The passage opened on a well, with ramps curving down either side to a pair of automatic doors. One door led to the engine room, Torrance knew. Behind it, a nuclear converter powered the ship's electrical system, gravitic cones, and hyperdrive; the principles on which this was done were familiar to him, but the actual machines were enigmas cased in metal and in foreign symbols. He took the other door, which opened on a workshop. A good deal of the equipment here was identifiable, however distorted to his eyes: lathe, drill press, oscilloscope, crystal tester. Much else was mystery. Yamamura sat at an improvised workbench, fitting together a piece of electronic apparatus. Several other devices, haywired on breadboards, stood close by. His face was shockingly haggard, and his hands trembled. He'd been working this whole time, with stimpills to keep him awake.

As Torrance approached, the engineer was talking with Betancourt, the communications man. The entire crew of the *Hebe G.B.* were under Yamamura's direction, in a frantic attempt to outflank the Eksers by learning on their own how to operate this ship.

"I've identified the basic electrical arrangement, sir," Betancourt was saying. "They don't tap the converter directly, like us; so evidently they haven't developed our stepdown methods. Instead, they use a heat exchanger to run an extremely large generator—yeah, the same thing you guessed was an armature-type dynamo—and draw A.C. for the ship off that. Where D.C. is needed, the A.C. passes through a set of rectifier plates which, by looking at 'em, I'm sure must be copper oxide. They're bare, behind a safety screen, though so much current goes through that they're too hot to look at close up. It all seems kind of primitive to me."

"Or else merely different," sighed Yamamura. "We use a light-element-fusion converter, one of whose advantages is that it can develop electric current directly. They may have perfected a power plant which utilizes moderately heavy elements with small positive packing fractions. I remember that was tried on Earth a long while ago, and given up as impractical. But maybe the Eksers are better engineers than us. Such a system would have the advantage of needing less refinement of fuel—which'd be a real advantage to a ship knocking about among unexplored planets. Maybe enough to justify that clumsy heat exchanger and rectifier system. We simply don't know."

He stared head-shakingly at the wires he was soldering. "We don't know a damn thing," he said. Seeing Torrance: "Well, carry on, Freeman Betancourt. And remember, *festina lente.*"

"For fear of wrecking the ship?" asked the captain.

Yamamura nodded. "The Eksers would've known a small craft like ours couldn't generate a big enough hyperforce field to tug their own ship home," he replied. "So they'll have made sure no prize crew could make off with it. Some of the stuff may be booby-trapped to wreck itself if it isn't handled just so; and how'd we ever make repairs? Hence we're proceeding with the utmost caution. So cautiously that we haven't a prayer of figuring out the controls before the Adderkops find us."

"It keeps the crew busy, though."

"Which is useful. Uh-huh. Well, sir, I've about got my basic apparatus set up. Everything seems to test okay.

Now let me know which animal you want to investigate
first." As Torrance hesitated, the engineer explained: "I
have to adapt the equipment for the creature in question,
you see. Especially if it's a hydrogen breather."

Torrance shook his head. "Oxygen. In fact, they live
under conditions so much like ours that we can walk
right into their cages. The gorilloids. That's what Jeri and
I have named them. Those woolly, two-meter-tall bipeds
with the ape faces."

Yamamura made an ape face of his own. "Brutes that
powerful? Have they shown any sign of intelligence?"

"No. But then, would you expect the Eksers to do so?
Jeri Kofoed and I have been parading in front of the
cages of all the possible species, making signs, drawing
pictures, everything we could think of, trying to get the
message across that we are not Adderkops and the genuine article is chasing us. No luck, of course. All the animals did give us an interested regard except the
gorilloids . . . which may or may not prove anything."

"What animals, now? I've been so blinking busy—"

"Well, we call 'em the tiger apes, the tentacle centaurs,
the elephantoid, the helmet beasts, and the caterpiggles.
That's stretching things, I know; the tiger apes and the
helmet beasts are highly improbable, to say the least,
and the elephantoid isn't much more convincing. The
gorilloids have the right size and the most efficient-look-
ing hands, and they're oxygen breathers as I said, so we
may as well take them first. Next in order of likelihood,
I'd guess, are the caterpiggles and the tentacle centaurs.
But the caterpiggles, though oxygen breathers, are from
a high-gravity planet; their air pressure would give us
narcosis in no time. The tentacle centaurs breathe hydrogen. In either case, we'd have to work in space armor."

"The gorilloids will be quite bad enough, thank you kindly!"

Torrance looked at the workbench. "What exactly do you plan to do?" he asked. "I've been too busy with my own end of this affair to learn any details of yours."

"I've adapted some things from the medical kit," said Yamamura. "A sort of ophthalmoscope, for example; because the ship's instruments use color codes and finely printed symbols, so that the Eksers are bound to have eyes at least as good as ours. Then this here's a nervous-impulse tracer. It detects synaptic flows and casts a three-dimensional image into yonder crystal box, so we can see the whole nervous system functioning as a set of luminous traces. By correlating this with gross anatomy, we can roughly identify the sympathetic and parasympathetic systems—or their equivalents—I hope. And the brain. And, what's really to the point, the degree of brain activity more or less independent of the other nerve paths. That is, whether the animal is thinking."

He shrugged. "It tests out fine on me. Whether it'll work on a nonhuman, especially in a different sort of atmosphere, I do not know. I'm sure it'll develop bugs."

"'We can but try,'" quoted Torrance wearily.

"I suppose Old Nick is sitting and thinking," said Yamamura in an edged voice. "I haven't seen him for quite some time."

"He's not been helping Jeri and me either," said Torrance. "Told us our attempt to communicate was futile until we could prove to the Eksers that we knew who they were. And even after that, he said, the only communication at first will be by gestures made with a pistol."

"He's probably right."

"He's not right! Logically, perhaps, but not psychologically. Or morally. He sits in his suite with a case of brandy and a box of cigars. The cook, who could be down here helping you, is kept aboard the yacht to fix him his damned gourmet meals. You'd think he didn't care if we're blown out of the sky!"

He remembered his oath of fealty, his official position, and so on and so on. They seemed nonsensical enough, here on the edge of extinction. But habit was strong. He swallowed and said harshly, "Sorry. Please ignore what I said. When you're ready, Freeman Yamamura, we'll test the gorilloids."

Six men and Jeri stood by in the passage with drawn blasters. Torrance hoped fervently they wouldn't have to shoot. He hoped even more that, if they did have to, he'd still be alive.

He gestured to the four crewmen at his back. "Okay, boys." He wet his lips. His heart thuttered. Being a captain and a Lodgemaster was very fine until moments like this came, when you must make a return for all your special privileges.

He spun the outside control wheel. The air-lock motor hummed and opened the doors. He stepped through, into a cage of gorilloids.

Pressure differentials weren't enough to worry about, but after all this time at one-fourth G, to enter a field only ten percent less than Earth's was like a blow. He lurched, almost fell, gasped in an air warm and thick and full of unnamed stenches. Sagging back against the wall, he stared across the floor at the four bipeds. Their brown fleecy bodies loomed unfairly tall, up and up to the coarse faces. Eyes overshadowed by brows glared at him. He clapped a hand on his stun pistol. He didn't want to shoot it, either. No telling what supersonics might do to a nonhuman nervous system; and if these were in truth the crewfolk, the worst thing he could do was inflict serious injury on one of them. But he wasn't used to being small and frail. The knurled handgrip was a comfort.

A male growled, deep in his chest, and advanced a step. His pointed head thrust forward, the sphincters in his neck opened and shut like sucking mouths; his jaws gaped to show the white teeth.

Torrance backed toward a corner. "I'll try to attract that one in the lead away from the others," he called softly. "Then get him."

"Aye." A spacehand, a stocky slant-eyed nomad from Altai, uncoiled a lariat. Behind him, the other three spread a net woven for this purpose.

The gorilloid paused. A female hooted. The male seemed to draw resolution from her. He waved the others back with a strangely human-like gesture and stalked toward Torrance.

The captain drew his stunner, pointed it shakily, resheathed it, and held out both hands. "Friend," he croaked.

His hope that the masquerade might be dropped became suddenly ridiculous. He sprang back toward the air lock. The gorilloid snarled and snatched at him. Torrance wasn't fast enough. The hand ripped his shirt open and left a bloody trail on his breast. He went to hands and knees, stabbed with pain. The Altaian's lasso whirled and snaked forth. Caught around the ankles, the gorilloid crashed. His weight shook the cubicle.

"*Get him! Watch out for his arms! Here—*"

Torrance staggered back to his feet. Beyond the melee, where four men strove to wind a roaring, struggling monster in a net, he saw the other three creatures.

They were crowded into the opposite corner, howling in basso. The compartment was like the inside of a drum.

"Get him out," choked Torrance. "Before the others charge."

He aimed his stunner again. If intelligent, they'd know this was a weapon. They might attack anyway. . . . Deftly, the man from Altai roped an arm, snubbed his lariat around the gargantuan torso, and made it fast by a slip knot. The net came into position. Helpless in cords of wire-strong fiber, the gorilloid was dragged to the entrance. Another male advanced, step by jerky step. Torrance stood his ground. The animal ululation and human shouting surfed about him, within him. His wound throbbed. He saw with unnatural clarity: the muzzle full of teeth that could snap his head off, the little dull eyes turned red with fury, the hands so much like his own but black-skinned, four-fingered, and enormous. . . .

"All clear, skipper!"

The gorilloid lunged. Torrance scrambled through the airlock chamber. The giant followed. Torrance braced himself in the corridor and aimed his stun pistol. The gorilloid halted, shivered, looked around in something resembling bewilderment, and retreated. Torrance closed the air lock.

Then he sat down and trembled.

Jeri bent over him. "Are you all right?" she breathed. "Oh! You've been hurt!"

"Nothing much," he mumbled. "Gimme a cigarette."

She took one from her belt pouch and said with a crispness he admired, "I suppose it is just a bruise and a deep scratch. But we'd better check it, anyway, and sterilize. Might be infected."

He nodded but remained where he was until he had finished the cigarette. Further down the corridor, Yamamura's men got their captive secured to a steel framework. Unharmed but helpless, the brute yelped and tried to bite as the engineer approached with his equipment. Returning him to the cubicle afterward was likely to be almost as tough as getting him out.

Torrance rose. Through the transparent wall, he saw a female gorilloid viciously pulling something to shreds, and realized he had lost his turban when he was knocked over. He sighed. "Nothing much we can do till Yamamura gives us a verdict," he said. "Come on, let's go rest a while."

"Sick bay first," said Jeri firmly. She took his arm. They went to the entry hole, through the tube, and into the steady half-weight of the *Hebe G.B.* which Van Rijn preferred. Little was said while Jeri got Torrance's shirt off, swabbed the wound with universal disinfectant, which stung like hell, and bandaged it. Afterward he suggested a drink.

They entered the saloon. To their surprise, and to Torrance's displeasure, Van Rijn was there. He sat at the inlaid mahogany table, dressed in snuff-stained lace and his usual sarong, a bottle in one hand and a Trichinopoly cigar in the other. A litter of papers lay before him.

"Ah, so," he said, glancing up. "What gives?"

"They're testing a gorilloid now." Torrance flung himself into a chair. Since the steward had been drafted for the capture party, Jeri went after drinks. Her voiced floated back, defiant:

"Captain Torrance was almost killed in the process. Couldn't you at least come watch, Nick?"

"What use I should watch, like some tourist with haddock eyes?" scoffed the merchant. "I make no skeletons about it, I am too old and fat to help chase large economy-size apes. Nor am I so technical I can twiddle knobs for Yamamura." He took a puff of his cigar and added complacently, "Besides, that is not my job. I am no kind of specialist, I have no fine university degrees, I learned in the school of hard knockers. But what I learned is how to make men do things for me, and then how to make something profitable from all their doings."

Torrance breathed out, long and slow. With the tension eased, he was beginning to feel immensely tired. "What're you checking over?" he asked.

"Reports of engineer studies on the Ekser ship," said Van Rijn. "I told everybody should take full notes on what they observed. Somewhere in those notes is maybe a clue we can use. If the gorilloids are not the Eksers, I mean. The gorilloids are possible, and I see no way to eliminate them except by Yamamura's checkers."

Torrance rubbed his eyes. "They're not entirely plausible," he said. "Most of the stuff we've found seems meant for big hands. But some of the tools, especially, are so small that—Oh, well, I suppose a nonhuman might be as puzzled by an assortment of our own tools. Does it really make sense that the same race would use sledge hammers and etching needles?"

Jeri came back with two stiff Scotch-and-sodas. His gaze followed her. In a tight blouse and half knee-length skirt, she was worth following. She sat down next to him rather than to Van Rijn, whose jet eyes narrowed.

However, the older man spoke mildly. "I would like if you should list for me, here and now, the other possibilities, with your reasons for thinking of them. I have seen them too, natural, but my own ideas are not all clear yet and maybe something that occurs to you would joggle my head."

Torrance nodded. One might as well talk shop, even though he'd been over this ground a dozen times before with Jeri and Yamamura.

"Well," he said, "the tentacle centaurs appear very likely. You know the ones I mean. They live under red light and about half again Earth's gravity. A dim sun and a low temperature must make it possible for their planet to retain hydrogen, because that's what they breathe, hydrogen and argon. You know how they look: bodies sort of like rhinoceri, torsos with bone-plated heads and fingered tentacles. Like the gorilloids, they're big enough to pilot this ship easily.

"All the others are oxygen breathers. The ones we call caterpiggles—the long, many-legged, blue-and-silver ones, with the peculiar hands and the particularly intelligent-looking faces—they're from an oddball world. It must be big. They're under three Gs in their cage, which can't be a red herring for this length of time. Body fluid adjustment would go out of kilter, if they're used to much lower weight. Even so, their planet has oxygen and nitrogen rather than hydrogen, under a dozen Earth-atmospheres' pressure. The temperature is rather high, fifty degrees. I imagine their world, though of nearly Jovian mass, is so close to its sun that the hydrogen was boiled off, leaving a clear field for evolution similar to Earth's.

"The elephantoid comes from a planet with only about half our gravity. He's the single big fellow with a trunk ending in fingers. He gets by in air too thin for us, which indicates the gravity in his cubicle isn't faked either."

Torrance took a long drink. "The rest all live under pretty terrestroid conditions," he resumed. "For that reason, I wish they were more probable. But actually, except the gorilloids, they seem like long shots. The helmet beasts—"

"What's that?" asked Van Rijn.

"Oh, you remember," said Jeri. "Those eight or nine things like humpbacked turtles, not much bigger than your head. They crawl around on clawed feet, waving little tentacles that end in filaments. They blot up food through those: soupy stuff the machines dump into their trough. They haven't anything like effective hands—the tentacles could only do a few very simple things—but we gave them some time because they do seem to have better developed eyes than parasites usually do."

"Parasites don't evolve intelligence," said Van Rijn. "They got better ways to make a living, by damn. Better make sure the helmet beasts really are parasites—in their home environments—and got no hands tucked under those shells—before you quite write them off. Who else you got?"

"The tiger apes," said Torrance. "Those striped carnivores built something like bears. They spend most of their time on all fours, but they do stand up and walk on their hind legs sometimes, and they do have hands. Clumsy, thumbless ones, with retractable claws, but on all their limbs. Are four hands without thumbs as good as two with? I don't know. I'm too tired to think."

"And that's all, ha?" Van Rijn tilted the bottle to his lips. After a prolonged gurgling he set it down, belched, and blew smoke through his majestic nose. "Who's to try next, if the gorilloids flunk?"

"It better be the caterpiggles, in spite of the air pressure," said Jeri. "Then . . . oh . . . the tentacle centaurs, I suppose. Then maybe the—"

"Horse maneuvers!" Van Rijn's fist struck the table. The bottle and glasses jumped. "How long it takes to catch and check each one? Hours, *nie?* And in between times, takes many more hours to adjust the apparatus and chase out all the hiccups it develops under a new set of conditions. Also, Yamamura will collapse if he can't sleep soon, and who else we got can do this? All the whiles, the forstunken Adderkops get closer. We have not got time for that method! If the gorilloids don't pan out, then only logic will help us. We must deduce from the facts we have, who the Eksers are."

"Go ahead." Torrance drained his glass. "I'm going to take a nap."

Van Rijn purpled. "That's right!" he huffed. "Be like everybody elses. Loaf and play, dance and sing, enjoy yourselfs the liver-long day. Because you always got poor old Nicholas van Rijn there, to heap the work and worry on his back. Oh, dear St. Dismas, why can't you at least make some *one* other person in this whole universe do something useful?"

. . . Torrance was awakened by Yamamura. The gorilloids were not the Eksers. They were color blind and incapable of focusing on the ship's instruments; their brains were small, with nearly the whole mass devoted to purely animal functions. He estimated their intelligence as equal to a dog's.

The captain stood on the bridge of the yacht, because it was a familiar place, and tried to accustom himself to being doomed.

Space had never seemed so beautiful as now. He was not well acquainted with the local constellations, but his trained gaze identified Perseus, Auriga, Taurus, not much distorted since they lay in the direction of Earth. (And of Ramanujan, where gilt towers rose out of mists to catch the first sunlight, blinding against blue Mount

Gandhi.) A few individuals could also be picked out, ruby Betelgeuse, amber Spica, the pilot stars by which he had steered through his whole working life. Otherwise, the sky was aswarm with small frosty fires, across blackness unclouded and endless. The Milky Way girdled it with cool silver, a nebula glowed faint and green, another galaxy spiraled on the mysterious edge of visibility. He thought less about the planets he had trod, even his own, than about this faring between them which was soon to terminate. For end it would, in a burst of violence too swift to be felt. Better go out thus cleanly when the Adderkops came, than into their dungeons.

He stubbed out his cigarette. Returning, his hand caressed the dear shapes of controls. He knew each switch and knob as well as he knew his own fingers. This ship was his; in a way, himself. Not like that other, whose senseless control board needed a giant and a dwarf, whose emergency switch fell under a mere slap if it wasn't hooked in place, whose—

A light footfall brought him twisting around. Irrationally, so strained was he, his heart flew up within him. When he saw it was Jeri, he eased his muscles, but the pulse continued quick in his blood.

She advanced slowly. The overhead light gleamed on her yellow hair and in the blue of her eyes. But she avoided his glance, and her mouth was not quite steady.

"What brings you here?" he asked. His tone fell even more soft than he had intended.

"Oh . . . the same as you." She stared out the viewscreen. During the time since they captured the alien ship, or it captured them, a red star off the port bow had visibly grown. Now it burned baleful as they passed, a light-year distant. She grimaced and turned her back to it. "Yamamura is readjusting the test apparatus," she said thinly. "No one else knows enough about it to help him, but he has the shakes so bad from exhaustion he can scarcely do the job himself. Old Nick just sits in his suite, smoking and drinking. He's gone through that one bottle already, and started another. I couldn't breathe in there any longer, it was so smoky. And he won't say a word. Except to himself, in Malay or something. I couldn't stand it."

"We may as well wait," said Torrance. "We've done everything we can, till it's time to check a caterpiggle. We'll have to do that spacesuited, in their own cage, and hope they don't all attack us."

She slumped. "Why bother?" she said. "I know the situation as well as you. Even if the caterpiggles are the Eksers, under those conditions we'll need a couple of days to prove it. I doubt if we have that much time left. If we start toward Valhalla two days from now, I'll bet we're detected and run down before we get there. Certainly, if the caterpiggles are only animals too, we'll never get time to test a third species. Why bother?"

"We've nothing else to do," said Torrance.

"Yes, we do. Not this ugly, futile squirming about, like cornered rats. Why can't we accept that we're going to die, and use the time to . . . to be human again?"

Startled, he looked back from the sky to her. "What do you mean?"

Her lashes fluttered downward. "I suppose that would depend on what we each prefer. Maybe you'd want to, well, get your thoughts in order or something."

"How about you?" he asked through his heartbeat.

"I'm not a thinker." She smiled forlornly. "I'm afraid I'm just a shallow sort of person. I'd like to enjoy life while I have it." She half turned from him. "But I can't find anyone I'd like to enjoy it with."

He, or his hands, grabbed her bare shoulders and spun her around to face him. She felt silken under his palms. "Are you sure you can't?" he said roughly. She closed her eyes and stood with face tilted upward, lips half parted. He kissed her. After a second she responded.

After a minute, Nicholas van Rijn appeared in the doorway.

He stood an instant, pipe in hand, gun belted to his waist, before he flung the churchwarden shattering to the deck. "So!" he bellowed.

"Oh!" wailed Jeri.

She disengaged herself. A tide of rage mounted in Torrance. He knotted his fists and started toward Van Rijn.

"So!" repeated the merchant. The bulkheads seemed to quiver with his voice. "By louse-bitten damn, this is a fine thing for me to come on. Satan's tail in a mousetrap! I sit hour by hour sweating my brain to the bone for the sake of your worthless life, and all whiles you, you illegitimate spawn of a snake with dandruff and a cheese mite, here you are making up to my own secretary hired with my own hard-earned money! Gargoyles and *Götter-dämmerung*! Down on your knees and beg my pardon, or I mash you up and sell you for dogfood!"

Torrance stopped, a few centimeters from Van Rijn. He was slightly taller than the merchant, if less bulky, and at least thirty years younger. "Get out," he said in a strangled voice.

Van Rijn turned puce and gobbled at him.

"Get out," repeated Torrance. "I'm still the captain of this ship. I'll do what I damned well please, without interference from any loud-mouthed parasite. Get off the bridge, or I'll toss you out on your fat bottom!"

The color faded in Van Rijn's cheeks. He stood motionless for whole seconds. "Well, by damn," he whispered at last. "By damn and death, cubical. He has got the nerve to talk back."

His left fist came about in a roundhouse swing. Torrance blocked it, though the force nearly threw him off his feet. His own left smacked the merchant's stomach, sank a short way into fat, encountered the muscles, and rebounded bruised. Then Van Rijn's right fist clopped. The cosmos exploded around Torrance. He flew up in the air, went over backward, and lay where he fell.

When awareness returned, Van Rijn was cradling his head and offering brandy which a tearful Jeri had fetched. "Here, boy. Go slow there. A little nip of this, ha? That goes good. There, now, you only lost one tooth and we get that fixed at Freya. You can even put it on expense account. There, that makes you feel more happy, *nie?* Now, girl, Jarry, Jelly, whatever your name is, give me that stimpill. Down the hatchworks, boy. And then, upsy-rosy, onto your feet. You should not miss the fun."

One-handed, Van Rijn heaved Torrance erect. The captain leaned a while on the merchant, until the stimpill removed aches and dizziness. Then, huskily through swollen lips, he asked, "What's going on? What d' you mean?"

"Why, I know who the Eksers are. I came to get you, and we fetch them from their cage." Van Rijn nudged Torrance with a great splay thumb and whispered almost as softly as a hurricane, "Don't tell anyone or I have too many fights, but I like a brass-bound nerve like you got. When we get home, I think you transfer off this yacht to command of a trading squadron. How you like that, ha? But come, we still got a damn plenty of work to do."

Torrance followed him in a daze: through the small ship and the tube, into the alien, down a corridor and a ramp to the zoological hold. Van Rijn gestured at the spacemen posted on guard lest the Eksers make a sally. They drew their guns and joined him, their weary slouch jerking to alertness when he stopped before an air lock.

"*Those?*" sputtered Torrance. "But—I thought—"

"You thought what they hoped you would think," said Van Rijn grandly. "The scheme was good. Might have worked, not counting the Addkerkops, except that Nicholas van Rijn was here. Now, then. We go in and take them all out, making a good show of our weapons. I hope we need not get too tough with them. I expect not, when we explain by drawings how we understand all their secret. Then they should take us to Valhalla, as we can show by those pretty astronautical diagrams Captain Torrance has already prepared. They will cooperate under threats, as prisoners, at first. But on the voyage, we can use the standard means to establish alimentary communications . . . no, terror and taxes, I mean rudimentary . . . anyhows, we get the idea across that all humans are not Adderkops and we want to be friends and sell them things. Hokay? We go!"

He marched through the air lock, scooped up a helmet beast, and bore it kicking out of its cage.

Torrance didn't have time for anything en route except his work. First the entry hole in the prize must be sealed, while supplies and equipment were carried over from the *Hebe G.B.* Then the yacht must be cast loose under her own hyperdrive; in the few hours before her converter quite burned out, she might draw an Adderkop in chase. Then the journey commenced, and though the Eksers laid a course as directed, they must be constantly watched lest they try some suicidal stunt. Every spare moment must be devoted to the urgent business of achieving a simple common language with them. Torrance must also supervise his crew, calm their fears, and maintain a detector-watch for enemy vessels. If any had been detected, the humans would have gone off hyperdrive and hoped they could lie low. None were, but the strain was considerable.

Occasionally he slept.

Thus he got no chance to talk to Van Rijn at length. He assumed the merchant had had a lucky hunch, and let it go at that.

Until Valhalla was a tiny yellow disc, outshining all other stars; a League patrol ship closed on them; and, explanations being made, it gave them escort as they moved at sublight speed toward Freya.

The patrol captain intimated he'd like to come aboard. Torrance stalled him. "When we're in orbit, Freeman Agilik, I'll be delighted. But right now, things are pretty disorganized. You can understand that, I'm sure."

He switched off the alien telecom he had now learned to operate. "I'd better go below and clean up," he said. "Haven't had a bath since we abandoned the yacht. Carry on, Freeman Lafarge." He hesitated. "And—uh—Freeman Jukh-Barklakh."

Jukh grunted something. The gorilloid was too busy to talk, squatting where a pilot seat should have been, his big hands slapping control plates as he edged the ship into a hyperbolic path. Barklakh, the helmet beast on his shoulders, who had no vocal cords of his own, waved a tentacle before he dipped it into the protective shaftlet to turn a delicate adjustment key. The other tentacle remained buried on its side of the gorilloid's massive neck, drawing nourishment from the bloodstream, receiving sensory impulses, and emitting the motor-nerve commands of a skilled space pilot.

At first the arrangement had looked vampirish to Torrance. But though the ancestors of the helmet beasts might once have been parasites on the ancestors of the gorilloids, they were so no longer. They were symbionts. They supplied the effective eyes and intellect, while the big animals supplied strength and hands. Neither species was good for much without the other; in combination, they were something rather special. Once he got used to the idea, Torrance found the sight of a helmet beast using its claws to climb up a gorilloid no more unpleasant than a man in a historical stereopic mounting a horse. And once the helmet beasts were used to the idea that not all humans were enemies, they showed a positive affection for them.

Doubtless they're thinking what lovely new specimens we can sell them for their zoo, reflected Torrance. He slapped Barklakh on the shell, patted Jukh's fur, and left the bridge.

A sponge bath of sorts and fresh garments took the edge off his weariness. He thought he'd better warn Van Rijn, and knocked at the cabin which the merchant had curtained off as his own.

"Come in," boomed the bass voice. Torrance entered a cubicle blue with smoke. Van Rijn sat on an empty brandy case, one hand holding a cigar, the other holding Jeri, who was snuggled on his lap.

"Well, sit down, sit down," he roared cordially. "You find a bottle somewhere in all those dirty clothes in the corner."

"I stopped by to tell you, sir, we'll have to receive the captain of our escort when we're in orbit around Freya, which'll be soon. Professional courtesy, you know. He's naturally anxious to meet the Eks—uh—the Togru-Kon-Tanakh."

"Hokay, pipe him aboard, lad." Van Rijn scowled. "Only make him bring his own bottle, and not take too long. I want to land, me, I'm sick of space. I think I'll run barefoot over the soft cool acres and acres of Freya, by damn!"

"Maybe you'd like to change clothes?" hinted Torrance.

"Ooh!" squeaked Jeri, and ran off to the cabin she sometimes occupied. Van Rijn leaned back against the wall, hitched up his sarong and crossed his shaggy legs as he said: "If that captain comes to meet the Eksers, so let him meet the Eksers. I stay comfortable like I am. And I will not entertain him with how I figured out who they were. That I keep exclusive, for sale to what news syndicate bids highest. Understand?"

His eyes grew unsettlingly sharp. Torrance gulped. "Yes, sir."

"Good. Now do sit down, boy. Help me put my story in order. I have not your fine education, I was a poor lonely hardworking old man from I was twelve, so I would need some help making my words as elegant as my logic."

"Logic?" echoed Torrance, puzzled. He tilted the bottle, chiefly because the tobacco haze in here made his eyes smart. "I thought you guessed—"

"What? You know me so little as that? No, no, by damn. Nicholas van Rijn never guesses. I *knew*." He reached for the bottle, took a hefty swig, and added magnanimously, "That is, after Yamamura found the gorilloids alone could not be the peoples we wanted. Then I sat down and uncluttered my brains and thought it all over.

"See, it was simple eliminations. The elephantoid was out right away. Only one of him. Maybe, in emergency, one could pilot this ship through space—but not land it, and pick up wild animals, and care for them, and all else. Also, if somethings go wrong, he is helpless."

Torrance nodded. "I did consider it from the spaceman's angle," he said. "I was inclined to rule out the elephantoid on that ground. But I admit I didn't see the animal-collecting aspect made it altogether impossible that this could be a one-being expedition."

"He was pretty too big anyhow," said Van Rijn. "As for the tiger apes, like you, I never took them serious. Maybe their ancestors was smaller and more biped, but this species is reverting to quadruped again. Animals do not specialize in being everything. Not brains and size and carnivore teeth and cat claws, all to once.

"The caterpiggles looked hokay till I remembered that time you accidental turned on the bestonkered emergency acceleration switch. Unless hooked in place, what such a switch would not be except in special cases, it fell rather easy. So easy that its own weight would make it drop open under three Earth gravities. Or at least there would always be serious danger of this. Also, that shelf you bumped into, they wouldn't build shelves so light on high-gravity planets."

He puffed his cigar back to furnace heat. "Well, so might be the tentacle centaurs," he continued. "Which was bad for us, because hydrogen and oxygen explode.

I checked hard through the reports on the ship, hoping I could find something that would eliminate them. And by damn, I did. For this I will give St. Dismas an altar cloth, not too expensive. You see, the Eksers is kind enough to use copper oxide rectifiers, exposed to the air. Copper oxide and hydrogen, at a not very high temperature such as would soon develop from strong electricking, they make water and pure copper. Poof, no more rectifier. So therefore ergo, this ship was not designed for hydrogen breathers." He grinned. "You has had so much high scientific education you forgot your freshlyman chemistry."

Torrance snapped his fingers and swore at himself.

"By eliminating, we had the helmet beasts," said Van Rijn. "Only they could not possible be the builders. True, they could handle certain tools and controls, like that buried key; but never all of it. And they are so slow and small. How could they ever stayed alive long enough to invent spaceships? Also, animals that little don't got room for real brains. And neither armored animals nor parasites ever get much. Nor do they get good eyes. And yet the helmet beasts seemed to have very good eyes, as near as we could tell. They looked like human eyes, anyhows.

"I remembered there was both big and little cubbyholes in these cabins. Maybe bunks for two kinds of sleeper? And I thought, is the human brain a turtle just because it is armored in bone? A parasite just because it lives off blood from other places? Well, maybe some people I could name but won't, like Juan Harleman of the Venusian Tea & Coffee Growers, Inc., has parasite turtles for brains. But not me. So there I was. Q.," said Van Rijn smugly, "E.D."

Hoarse from talking, he picked up the bottle. Torrance sat a few minutes more, but as the other seemed disinclined to conversation, he got up to go.

Jeri met him in the doorway. In a slit and topless blue gown which fitted like a coat of lacquer, she was a fourth-order stun-blast. Torrance stopped in his tracks. Her gaze slid slowly across him, as if reluctant to depart.

"Mutant sea-otter coats," murmured Van Rijn dreamily. "Martian firegems. An apartment in the Stellar Towers."

She scampered to him and ran her fingers through his hair. "Are you comfortable, Nicky, darling?" she purred. "Can't I do something for you?"

Van Rijn winked at Torrance. "Your technique, that time on the bridge, I watched and it was lousy," he said to the captain. "Also, you are not old and fat and lonesome; you have a happy family for yourself."

"Uh—yes," said Torrance. "I do." He let the curtain drop and returned to the bridge.

CHRONOLOGY OF TECHNIC CIVILIZATION

◎ COMPILED BY SANDRA MIESEL ◎

The Technic Civilization series sweeps across five millennia and hundreds of light-years of space to chronicle three cycles of history shaping both human and non-human life in our corner of the universe. It begins in the twenty-first century, with recovery from a violent period of global unrest known as the Chaos. New space technologies ease Earth's demand for resources and energy permitting exploration of the Solar system.

ca. 2055   "The Saturn Game" (*Analog Science Fiction*, hereafter *ASF*, February, 1981)

22nd C   The discovery of hyperdrive makes interstellar travel feasible early in the twenty-second century. The Breakup sends humans off to colonize the stars, often to preserve cultural identity or to try a social experiment. A loose government called the Solar Commonwealth is established. Hermes is colonized.

2150   "Wings of Victory" (*ASF*, April, 1972) The Grand Survey from Earth discovers alien races on Yithri, Merseia, and many other planets.

23rd C   The Polesetechnic League is founded as a mutual protection association of space-faring merchants. Colonization of Aeneas and Altai.

24th C   "The Problem of Pain" (*Fantasy and Science Fiction*, February, 1973)

2376   Nicholas van Rijn born poor on Earth Colonization of Vixen.

2400   Council of Hiawatha, a futile attempt to reform the League. Colonization of Dennitza.

2406   David Falkayn born noble on Hermes, a breakaway human grand duchy.

2416   "Margin of Profit" (*ASF*, September, 1956) [van Rijn] "How to Be Ethnic in One Easy Lesson" (in *Future Quest*, ed. Roger Elwood, Avon Books, 1974)

❧ ❧ ❧

2423   "The Three-Cornered Wheel" (*ASF*, April, 1966) [Falkayn]

❀ ❀ ❀

stories overlap

2420s "A Sun Invisible" (*ASF*, April, 1966)
[Falkayn]

"The Season of Forgiveness" (*Boy's Life*,
December, 1973) [set on same planet as
"The Three-Cornered Wheel"]

The Man Who Counts (Ace Books, 1978 as
War of the Wing-Men, Ace Books, 1958
from "The Man Who Counts," *ASF*,
February-April,1958) [van Rijn]

"Esau" (as "Birthright," *ASF* February,
1970) [van Rijn]

"Hiding Place" (*ASF*, March, 1961) [van
Rijn]

❀ ❀ ❀

stories overlap

2430s "Territory" (*ASF*, June, 1963) [van Rijn]

"The Trouble Twisters" (as "Trader Team,"
ASF, July-August, 1971) [Falkayn]

"Day of Burning" (as "Supernova," *ASF*
January, 1967) [Falkayn]
Falkayn saves civilization on Merseia,
mankind's future foe.

"The Master Key" (*ASF* August, 1971)
[van Rijn]

Satan's World (Doubleday, 1969 from *ASF*,
May-August, 1968) [van Rijn and Falkayn]

"A Little Knowledge" *(ASF*, August, 1971)

The League has become a set of ruthless cartels.

❀ ❀ ❀

2446 "Lodestar" (in *Astounding: The John W. Campbell Memorial Anthology.* ed. Harry Harrison. Random House, 1973) [van Rijn and Falkayn]

Rivalries and greed are tearing the League apart. Falkayn marries van Rijn's favorite granddaughter.

2456 *Mirkheim.* (Putnam Books, 1977) [van Rijn and Falkayn]

The Babur War involving Hermes gravely wounds the League. Dark days loom.

late 25th C Falkayn founds a joint human-Ythrian colony on Avalon ruled by the Domain of Ythri. [same planet—renamed—as "The Problem of Pain."]

26th C "Wingless" (as "Wingless on Avalon," *Boy's Life*, July, 1973) [Falkayn's grandson] "Rescue on Avalon" (in *Children of Infinity.* ed. Roger Elwood. Franklin Watts, 1973) Colonization of Nyanza.

2550 Dissolution of the Polesotechnic League.

27th C The Time of Troubles brings down the Commonwealth. Earth is sacked twice and left prey to barbarian slave raiders.

ca. 2700   "The Star Plunderer" (*Planet Stories*, hereafter *PS*, September, 1952)
Manuel Argos proclaims the Terran Empire with citizenship open to all intelligent species. The Principate phase of the Imperium ultimately brings peace to 100,000 inhabited worlds within a sphere of stars 400 light-years in diameter.

28th C   Colonization of Unan Besar.
"Sargasso of Lost Starships" (*PS*, January, 1952)
The Empire annexes old colony on Ansa by force.

29th C   *The People of the Wind* (New American Library from *ASF*, February-April, 1973)
The Empire's war on another civilized imperium starts its slide towards decadence. A descendant of Falkayn and an ancestor of Flandry cross paths.

30th C   The Covenant of Alfazar, an attempt at détente between Terra and Merseia, fails to achieve peace.

3000   Dominic Flandry born on Earth, illegitimate son of an opera diva and an aristocratic space captain.

3019   *Ensign Flandry* (Chilton, 1966 from shorter version in *Amazing*, hereafter *AMZ*, October, 1966) Flandry's first collision with the Merseians.

3021   *A Circus of Hells* (New American Library,
              1970. incorporates "the White King's War,"
              Galaxy, hereafter *Gal*, October, 1969.
              Flandry is a Lieutenant (j.g.).

3022   Degenerate Emperor Josip succeeds weak
              old Emperor Georgios.

3025   *The Rebel Worlds* (New American Library,
              1969)
              A military revolt on the frontier world of
              Aeneas almost starts an age of Barracks
              Emperors. Flandry is a Lt. Commander,
              then promoted to Commander.

3027   "Outpost of Empire" (*Gal*, December,
              1967) [not Flandry]
              The misgoverned Empire continues fraying
              at its borders.

3028   *The Day of Their Return* (New American
              Library, 1973) [Aycharaych but not
              Flandry]
              Aftermath of the rebellion on Aeneas.

3032   "Tiger by the Tail" (*PS*, January, 1951)
              [Flandry]
              Flandry is a Captain and averts a
              barbarian invasion.

3033   "Honorable Enemies" (*Future Combined
              with Science Fiction Stories*,
              May, 1951) [Flandry]
              Captain Flandry's first brush with enemy
              agent Aycharaych

3035   "The Game of Glory" (*Venture*, March,
              1958) [Flandry]
              Set on Nyanza, Flandry has been knighted.

3037   "A Message in Secret" (as *Mayday Orbit*, Ace Books, 1961 from shorter version, "A Message in Secret," *Fantastic*, December, 1959) [Flandry]
Set on Altai.

3038   "The Plague of Masters" (as *Earthman, Go Home!*, Ace Books, 1961 from "A Plague of Masters," *Fantastic*, December, 1960–January, 1961.) [Flandry]
Set on Unan Besar.

3040   "Hunters of the Sky Cave" (as *We Claim These Stars!*, Ace Books, 1959 from shorter version, "A Handful of Stars, *AMZ*, June, 1959) [Flandry and Aycharaych]
Set on Vixen.

3041   Interregnum: Josip dies. After three years of civil war, Hans Molitor will rule as sole emperor.

3042   "The Warriors from Nowhere" (as "The Ambassadors of Flesh," *PS*, Summer, 1954.) Snapshot of disorders in the war-torn Empire.

3047   *A Knight of Ghosts and Shadows* (New American Library, 1975 from *Gal* September/October-November/December, 1974) [Flandry]
Set on Dennitza, Flandry meets his illegitimate son and has a final tragic confrontation with Aycharaych.

3054   Emperor Hans dies and is succeeded by his sons, first Dietrich, then Gerhart.

3061   *A Stone in Heaven* (Ace Books, 1979)
                  [Flandry]
                  Admiral Flandry pairs off with the daughter
                  of his first mentor from *Ensign Flandry*.

3064   *The Game of Empire* (Baen Books, 1985)
                  [Flandry]
                  Flandry is a Fleet Admiral, meets his
                  illegitimate daughter Diana.

early 4th
millennium The Terran Empire becomes more rigid
                  and tyrannical in its Dominate phase. The
                  Empire and Merseia wear each other out.

mid 4th
millennium The Long Night follows the Fall of the
                  Terran Empire.War, piracy, economic
                  collapse, and isolation devastate countless
                  worlds.

3600   "A Tragedy of Errors" (*Gal*, February,
                  1968)
                  Further fragmentation among surviving
                  human worlds.

3900   "The Night Face" (Ace Books, 1978. as *Let
                  the Spacemen Beware!*, Ace Books, 1963
                  from shorter version "A Twelvemonth and
                  a Day," *Fantastic Universe*, January, 1960)
                  Biological and psychological divergence
                  among Surviving humans.

4000   "The Sharing of Flesh" (*Gal*, December,
                  1968)
                  Human explorers heal genetic defects and
                  uplift savagery.

7100   "Starfog" (*ASF*, August. 1967)
                 Revived civilization is expanding. A New
                 Vixen man from the libertarian
                 Commonalty meets descendants of the
                 rebels from Aeneas.

Although Technic Civilization is extinct, another—and perhaps better—turn on the Wheel of Time has begun for our galaxy. The Commonalty must inevitably decline just as the League and Empire did before it. But the Wheel will go on turning as long as there are thinking minds to wonder at the stars.

❂ ❂ ❂

Poul Anderson was consulted about this chart
but any errors are my own.

The Following is an excerpt from:

YOUNG FLANDRY

POUL ANDERSON

Available from Baen Books
January 2010
trade paperback

Ensign Dominic Flandry, Imperial Naval Flight Corps, did not know whether he was alive through luck or management. At the age of nineteen, with the encoding molecules hardly settled down on your commission, it was natural to think the latter. But had a single one of the factors he had used to save himself been absent—He didn't care to dwell on that.

Besides, his troubles were far from over. As a merchant ship belonging to the Sisterhood of Kursoviki, the *Archer* had been given a radio by the helpful Terrans. But it was crapout; some thimblewit had exercised some Iron Age notion of maintenance. Dragoika had agreed to put back for her home. But with a foul wind, they'd be days at sea in this damned wallowing bathtub before they were even likely to speak a boat with a transmitter in working order. That wasn't fatal per se. Flandry could shovel local rations through the chowlock of his helmet; Starkadian biochemistry was sufficiently like Terran that most foods wouldn't poison him, and he carried vitamin supplements. The taste, though, my God, the taste!

Most ominous was the fact that he *had* been shot down, and at no large distance from here. Perhaps the Seatrolls, and Merseians, would let this Tigery craft alone. If they weren't yet ready to show their hand, they probably would. However, his misfortune indicated their preparations were more or less complete. When he chanced to pass above their latest kettle of mischief, they'd felt so confident they opened fire.

"And then the Outside Folk attacked you?" Ferok prodded. His voice came as a purr through whistle of wind, rush and smack of waves, creak of rigging, all intensified and distorted by the thick air.

"Yes," Flandry said. He groped for words. They'd given him an electronic cram in the language and customs of Kursovikian civilization while the transport bore him from Terra. But some things are hard to explain in pre-industrial terms. "A type of vessel which can both submerge and fly rose from the water. Its radio shout drowned my call and its firebeams wrecked my craft before mine could pierce its thicker armor. I barely escaped my hull as it sank, and kept submerged until the enemy went away. Then I flew off in search of help. The small engine which lifted me was nigh exhausted when I came upon your ship."

Truly his gravity impeller wouldn't lug him much further until the capacitors were recharged. He didn't plan to use it again. What power remained in the pack on his shoulders must be saved to operate the pump and reduction valve in the vitryl globe which sealed off his head. A man couldn't breathe Starkadian sea-level air and survive. Such an oxygen concentration would burn out his lungs faster than nitrogen narcosis and carbon dioxide acidosis could kill him.

He remembered how Lieutenant Danielson had gigged him for leaving off the helmet. "Ensign, I don't give a ball of fertilizer how uncomfortable the thing is, when you might be enjoying your nice Terra-conditioned cockpit. Nor do I weep at the invasion of privacy involved in taping your every action in flight. The purpose is to make sure that pups like you, who know so much more than a thousand years of astronautics could possibly teach them, obey regulations. The next offense will earn you thirty seconds of nerve-lash. Dismissed."

So you saved my life, Flandry grumbled. *You're still a snot-nosed bastard.*

Nobody was to blame for his absent blaster. It was torn from the holster in those wild seconds of scrambling clear. He had kept the regulation knife and pouchful of oddments. He had boots and gray coverall, sadly stained and in no case to be compared with the glamorous dress uniform. And that was just about the lot.

Ferok lowered the plumy thermosensor tendrils above his eyes: a frown. "If the vaz-Siravo search what's left of your flier, down below, and don't find your body, they may guess what you did and come looking for you," he said.

"Yes," Flandry agreed, "they may."

He braced himself against pitch and roll and looked outward—tall, the lankiness of adolescence still with him—brown hair, gray eyes, a rather long and regular face which Saxo had burned dark. Before him danced and shimmered a greenish ocean, sun-flecks and white-caps on waves that marched faster, in Starkadian gravity, than on Terra. The sky was pale blue. Clouds banked gigantic on the horizon, but in a dense atmosphere they did not portend storm. A winged thing cruised, a sea animal broached and dove again. At its distance, Saxo was only a third as broad as Sol is to Terra and gave half the illumination. The adaptable human vision perceived this as normal, but the sun was merciless white, so brilliant that one dared not look anywhere near. The short day stood at late afternoon, and the temperature, never very high in these middle northern latitudes, was dropping. Flandry shivered.

Ferok made a contrast to him. The land Starkadian, Tigery, Toborko, or whatever you wanted to call him, was built not unlike a short man with disproportionately long legs. His hands were four-fingered, his feet large and clawed, he flaunted a stubby tail. The head was less anthropoid, round, with flat face tapering to a narrow chin. The eyes were big, slanted, scarlet in the iris, beneath his fronded tendrils. The nose, what there was of it, had a single slit nostril. The mouth was wide and carnivore-toothed. The ears were likewise big, outer edges elaborated till they almost resembled bat wings. Sleek fur covered his skin, black-striped orange that shaded into white at the throat.

He wore only a beaded pouch, kept from flapping by thigh straps, and a curved sword scabbarded across his back. By profession he was the boatswain, a high rank for a male on a Kursovikian ship; as such, he was no doubt among Dragoika's lovers. By nature he was impetuous, quarrelsome, and dog-loyal to his allegiances. Flandry liked him.

Ferok lifted a telescope and swept it around an arc. That was a native invention. Kursoviki was the center of the planet's most advanced land culture. "No sign of anything yet," he said. "Do you think yon Outsider flyboat may attack us?"

"I doubt that," Flandry said. "Most likely it was simply on hand because of having brought some Merseian advisors, and shot at me because I might be carrying instruments which would give me a clue as to what's going on down below. It's probably returned to Kimraig by now." He hesitated before continuing: "The Merseians, like us, seldom take a direct role in any action, and then nearly always just as individual officers, not representatives of their people. Neither of us wishes to provoke a response in kind."

"Afraid?" Lips curled back from fangs.

"On your account," Flandry said, somewhat honestly. "You have no dream of what our weapons can do to a world."

"World . . . hunh, the thought's hard to seize. Well, let the Sisterhood try. I'm happy to be a plain male."

Flandry turned and looked across the deck. The *Archer* was a big ship by Starkadian measure, perhaps five hundred tons, broad in the beam, high in the stern, a carven post at the prow as emblem of her tutelary spirit. A deckhouse stood amidships, holding galley, smithy, carpenter shop, and armory. Everything was gaudily painted. Three masts carried yellow square sails aloft, fore-and-aft beneath; at the moment she was tacking on the latter and a genoa. The crew were about their duties on deck and in the rigging. They numbered thirty male hands and half a dozen female officers. The ship had been carrying timber and spices from Ujanka port down the Chain archipelago.

"What armament have we?" he asked.

"Our Terran deck gun," Ferok told him. "Five of your rifles. We were offered more, but Dragoika said they'd be no use till we had more people skilled with them.

Otherwise, swords, pikes, crossbows, knives, belaying pins, teeth, and nails." He gestured at the mesh which passed from side to side of the hull, under the keel. "If that twitches much, could mean a Siravo trying to put a hole in our bottom. Then we dive after him. You'd be best for that, with your gear."

Flandry winced. His helmet was adjustable for underwater; on Starkad, the concentration of dissolved oxygen was almost as high as in Terra's air. But he didn't fancy a scrap with a being evolved for such an environment.

"Why are you here, yourself?" Ferok asked conversationally. "Pleasure or plunder?"

"Neither. I was sent." Flandry didn't add that the Navy reckoned it might as well use Starkad to give certain promising young officers some experience. "Promising" made him sound too immature. At once he realized he'd actually sounded unaggressive and prevaricated in haste: "Of course, with the chance of getting into a fight, I would have asked to go anyway."

"They tell me your females obey males. True?"

"Well, sometimes." The second mate passed by and Flandry's gaze followed her. She had curves, a tawny mane rippling down her back, breasts standing fuller and firmer than any girl could have managed without technological assistance, and a nearly humanoid nose. Her clothing consisted of some gold bracelets. But her differences from the Terran went deeper than looks. She didn't lactate; those nipples fed blood directly to her infants. And hers was the more imaginative, more cerebral sex, not subordinated in any culture, dominant in the islands around Kursoviki. He wondered if that might trace back to something as simple as the female body holding more blood and more capacity to regenerate it.

"But who, then, keeps order in your home country?" Ferok wondered. "Why haven't you killed each other off?"

"Um-m-m, hard to explain," Flandry said. "Let me first see if I understand your ways, to compare mine. For instance, you owe nothing to the place where you live, right? I mean, no town or island or whatever is ruled, as a ship is . . . right? Instead—at any rate in this part of the world—the females are organized into associations like the Sisterhood, whose members may live anywhere, which even have their special languages. They own all important property and make all important decisions through those associations. Thus disputes among males have little effect on them. Am I right?'

"I suppose so. You might have put it more politely."

"Apology-of-courage is offered. I am a stranger. Now among my people—"

A shout fell from the crow's nest. Ferok whirled and pointed his telescope. The crew sprang to the starboard rail, clustered in the shrouds, and yelled.

Dragoika bounded from the captain's cabin under the poop. She held a four-pronged fish spear in one hand, a small painted drum beneath her arm. Up the ladder she went, to stand by the quartermistress at the wheel and look for herself. Then, coolly, she tapped her drum on one side, plucked the steel strings across the recessed head on the other. Twang and thump carried across noise like a bugle call. *All hands to arms and battle stations!*

"The vaz-Siravo!" Ferok shouted above clamor. "They're on us!" He made for the deckhouse. Restored to discipline, the crew were lining up for helmets, shields, byrnies, and weapons.

Flandry strained his eyes into the glare off the water. A score or so blue dorsal fins clove it, converging on the ship. And suddenly, a hundred meters to starboard, a submarine rose.

A little, crude thing, doubtless home-built to a Merseian design—for if you want to engineer a planet-wide war among primitives, you should teach them what they can make and do for themselves. The hull was greased leather stretched across a framework of some undersea equivalent of wood. Harness trailed downward to the four fish which pulled it; he could barely discern them as huge shadows under the surface. The deck lay awash. But an outsize catapult projected therefrom. Several dolphin-like bodies with transparent globes on their heads and powerpacks on their backs crouched alongside. They rose onto flukes and flippers; their arms reached to swing the machine around.

"Dommaneek!" Dragoika screeched. "Dommaneek Falandaree! Can you man ours?"

"Aye, aye!" The Terran ran prow-ward. Planks rolled and thudded beneath his feet.

On the forward deck, the two females whose duty it was were trying to unlimber the gun. They worked slowly, getting in each other's way, spitting curses. There hadn't yet been time to drill many competent shots, even with a weapon as simple as this, a rifle throwing 38 mm. chemical shells. Before they got the range, that catapult might—

"Gangway!" Flandry shoved the nearest aside. She snarled and swatted at him with long red nails. Dragoika's drum rippled an order. Both females fell back from him.

He opened the breech, grabbed a shell from the ammo box, and dogged it in. The enemy catapult thumped. A packet arced high, down again, made a near miss and burst into flame which spread crimson and smoky across the waves. Some version of Greek fire—undersea oil wells—Flandry put his eye to the range finder. He was too excited to be scared. But he must lay the gun manually. A hydraulic system would have been too liable to breakdown. In spite of good balance and self-lubricating bearings, the barrel swung with nightmare slowness. The Seatrolls were rewinding their catapult . . . before Andromeda, they were fast! *They* must use hydraulics.

Dragoika spoke to the quartermistress. She put the wheel hard over. Booms swung over the deck. The jib flapped thunderous until crewmales reset the sheets. The *Archer* came about. Flandry struggled to compensate. He barely remembered to keep one foot on the brake, lest his gun travel too far. *Bet those she-cats would've forgotten*. The enemy missile didn't make the vessel's superstructure as intended. But it struck the hull amidships. Under this oxygen pressure, fire billowed heavenward.

Flandry pulled the lanyard. His gun roared and kicked. A geyser fountained, mingled with splinters. One draught fish leaped, threshed, and died. The rest already floated bellies up. "Got him!" Flandry whooped.

Dragoika plucked a command. Most of the crew put aside their weapons and joined a firefighting party. There was a hand pump at either rail, buckets with ropes bent to them, sails to drag from the deckhouse and wet and lower.

Ferok, or someone, yelled through voices, wind, waves, brawling, and smoke of the flames. The Seatrolls were coming over the opposite rail.

They must have climbed the nets. (*Better invent a different warning gadget*, raced through Flandry's mind.)

They wore the Merseian equipment which had enabled their kind to carry the war ashore elsewhere on Starkad. Waterfilled helmets covered the blunt heads, black absorbent skinsuits kept everything else moist. Pumps cycled atmospheric oxygen, running off powerpacks. The same capacitors energized their legs. Those were clumsy. The bodies must be harnessed into a supporting framework, the two flippers and the fluked tail control four mechanical limbs with prehensile feet. But they lurched across the deck, huge, powerful, their hands holding spears and axes and a couple of waterproof machine pistols. Ten of them were now aboard . . . and how many sailors could be spared from the fire?

A rifle bullet wailed. A Seatroll sprayed lead in return. Tigeries crumpled. Their blood was human color.

Flandry rammed home another shell and lobbed it into the sea some distance off. "Why?" screamed a gunner.

"May have been more coming," he said. "I hope hydrostatic shock got 'em." He didn't notice he used Anglic.

Dragoika cast her fish spear. One pistol wielder went down, the prongs in him. He scrabbled at the shaft. Rifles barked, crossbows snapped, driving his mate to shelter between the deckhouse and a lifeboat. Then combat ramped, leaping Tigeries, lumbering Seatrolls, sword against ax, pike against spear, clash, clatter, grunt, shriek, chaos run loose. Several firefighters went for their weapons. Dragoika drummed them back to work. The Seatrolls made for them, to cut them down and let the ship burn. The armed Tigeries tried to defend them. The enemy pistoleer kept the Kursovikian rifle shooters pinned down behind masts and bollards—neutralized. The battle had no more shape than that.

A bullet splintered the planks a meter from Flandry. For a moment, panic locked him where he stood. What to do, what to do? He couldn't die. He mustn't. He was Dominic, himself, with a lifetime yet to live. Outnumbered though they were, the Seatrolls need but wreak havoc till the fire got beyond control and he was done. *Mother! Help me!*

For no sound reason, he remembered Lieutenant Danielson. Rage blossomed in him. He bounded down the ladder and across the main deck. A Seatroll chopped at him. He swerved and continued.

Dragoika's door stood under the poop. He slid the panel aside and plunged into her cabin. It was appointed in barbaric luxury. Sunlight sickled through an oval port, across the bulkhead as the ship rolled, touching bronze candlesticks, woven tapestry, a primitive sextant, charts and navigation tables inscribed on parchment. He snatched what he had left here to satisfy her curiosity, his impeller, buckled the unit on his back with frantic fingers and hook in his capacitors. Now, that sword, which she hadn't taken time to don. He re-emerged, flicked controls, and rose.

Over the deckhouse! The Seatroll with the machine pistol lay next it, a hard target for a rifle, himself commanding stem and stern. Flandry drew blade. The being heard the slight noise and tried awkwardly to look up. Flandry struck. He missed the hand but knocked the gun loose. It flipped over the side.

He whirred aft, smiting from above. "I've got him!" he shouted. "I've got him! Come out and do some real shooting!"

The fight was soon finished. He used a little more energy to help spread the wet sail which smothered the fire.

After dark, Egrima and Buruz again ruled heaven. They cast shivering glades across the waters. Few stars shone through, but one didn't miss them with so much other beauty. The ship plowed northward in an enormous murmurous hush.

Dragoika stood with Flandry by the totem at the prow. She had offered thanks. Kursovikian religion was a paganism more inchoate than any recorded from ancient Terra—the Tigery mind was less interested than the human in finding ultimate causes—but ritual was important. Now the crew had returned to watch or to sleep and they two were alone. Her fur was sparked with silver, her eyes pools of light.

"Our thanks belong more to you," she said softly. "I am high in the Sisterhood. They will be told, and remember."

"Oh, well." Flandry shuffled his feet and blushed.

"But have you not endangered yourself? You explained what scant strength is left in those boxes which keep you alive. And then you spent it to fly about."

"Uh, my pump can be operated manually if need be."

"I shall appoint a detail to do so."

"No need. You see, now I can use the Siravo powerpacks. I have tools in my pouch for adapting them."

"Good." She looked awhile into the shadows and luminance which barred the deck. "That one whose pistol you removed—" Her tone was wistful.

"No, ma'am," Flandry said firmly. "You cannot have him. He's the only survivor of the lot. We'll keep him alive and unhurt."

"I simply thought of questioning him about their plans. I know a little of their language. We've gained it from prisoners or parleys through the ages. He wouldn't be too damaged, I think."

"My superiors can do a better job in Highport."

Dragoika sighed. "As you will." She leaned against him, "I've met vaz-Terran before, but you are the first I have really known well." Her tail wagged. "I like you."

Flandry gulped. "I . . . I like you too."

"You fight like a male and think like a female. That's something new. Even in the far southern islands—" She laid an arm around his waist. Her fur was warm and silken where it touched his skin. Somebody had told him once that could you breathe their air undiluted, the Tigeries would smell like new-mown hay. "I'll have joy of your company."

"Um-m-m . . . uh." *What can I say?*

"Pity you must wear that helmet," Dragoika said. "I'd like to taste your lips. But otherwise we're not made so differently, our two kinds. Will you come to my cabin?"

For an instant that whirled, Flandry was tempted. He had everything he could do to answer. It wasn't based on past lectures about taking care not to offend native mores, nor on principle, nor, most certainly, on fastidiousness. If anything, her otherness made her the more piquant. But he couldn't really predict what she might do in a close relationship, and—

"I'm deeply sorry," he said. "I'd love to, but I'm under a—" what was the word?—"a geas."

She was neither offended nor much surprised. She had seen a lot of different cultures. "Pity," she said. "Well, you know where the forecastle is. Goodnight." She padded aft. En route, she stopped to collect Ferok.

—and besides, those fangs were awfully intimidating.

DID YOU KNOW YOU CAN DO ALL THESE THINGS AT THE
BAEN BOOKS WEBSITE ?

‡ Read free sample chapters of books   [SCHEDULE]

‡ See what new books are upcoming   [SCHEDULE]

‡ Read entire Baen Books for free   [FREE LIBRARY]

‡ Check out your favorite author's titles   [CATALOG]

‡ Catch up on the latest Baen news & author events
   [NEWS] or [EVENTS]

‡ Buy any Baen book   [SCHEDULE] or [CATALOG]

‡ Read interviews with authors and artists   [INTERVIEWS]

‡ Buy almost any Baen book as an e-book individually
or an entire month at a time   [WEBSCRIPTIONS]

‡ Find a list of titles suitable for young adults
   [YOUNG ADULT LISTS]

‡ Communicate with some of the coolest fans in science
fiction & some of the best minds on the planet
   [BAEN'S BAR]

GO TO
WWW.BAEN.COM